PRAISE FOR THE ACK-ACK MACAQUE TRILOGY

'A mind-expanding cyber-thriller.'
The Guardian

'More fun than a barrel of steampunk monkeys.'
Milwaukee Journal

'As much utterly irresponsible fun as you could hope to have with a monkey without having to explain yourself to the police.'
SF Reviews

'Fizzes with wild ideas... A ripping yarn about murder, mayhem and monkeys.'
Philip Reeve, author of *Mortal Engines*

'An action-adventure plot that pulls you right along...
Everybody loves the monkey.'
Steampunk Magazine

'A highly enjoyable romp with page-turning action.'
Interzone Magazine

'The much-anticipated "monkeypunk" novel.'
SFX Magazine

'Hit after hit after hit, until the reader is left breathless, reeling slightly and in severe need of a banana daiquiri. 10/10'
Fantasy Faction

'Ridiculously readable, thoroughly entertaining,
and packed full of ideas.'
SFFWorld

'A rollicking, madcap sci-fi adventure story, it's a thoughtful novel and it's got a monkey with a gun. What's not to love?'
Cult Den

'Without a doubt, one of the best reads
I've enjoyed in a long, long time.'
SpecFiction

'Shows just what is possible by combining new ideas and creating a
unique world... Gareth L. Powell will be an author to look out for.'
Fantasy Book Review

'Powerful, intelligent, filled with ideas, clever touches
and brilliant characters.'
Morpheus Tales

'I can't recommend this highly enough.
I didn't just like this, I loved it.'
The Eloquent Page

'An entertaining read, one that is engaging, effectively written,
and just damned good fun.'
Parallaxed Journal

'Make sure you don't miss these amazing books.'
The Book Plank

'The most fun I've had with a novel in quite a long time
and you need to read it too, trust me.'
Dave Hutchinson, author of *Europe in Autumn*

'Great fun.'
Adam Roberts, author of *Jack Glass*

'Ack-Ack is an inspired creation, a monkey with attitude, issues and a
hole where his heart should be... riotous fun.'
The Guardian

'Bigger, badder and with more explosions... Like a movie franchise, the
first book sets up the world and the tone and the second raises the stakes
and cranks up the action.'
Pornokitsch

ACK-ACK MACAQUE

MACAQUE

THE COMPLETE TRILOGY

ACK-ACK MACAQUE • HIVE MONKEY • MACAQUE ATTACK

Ominubus first published 2017 by Solaris
an imprint of Rebellion Publishing Ltd,
Riverside House, Osney Mead,
Oxford, OX2 0ES, UK

www.solarisbooks.com

ISBN 978-1-78108-605-6

Cover by Jake Murray

10 9 8 7 6 5 4 3 2 1

A CIP catalogue record for this book is available from the
British Library.

Designed & typeset by Rebellion Publishing

Printed in Denmark

For my family

In September 1956, France found herself facing economic difficulties at home and an escalating crisis in Suez. In desperation, the French Prime Minister came to London with an audacious proposition for Sir Anthony Eden: a political and economic union between the United Kingdom and France, with Her Majesty Queen Elizabeth II as the new head of the French state.

Although Eden greeted the idea with scepticism, a resounding Anglo-French victory against Egypt persuaded his successor to accept and, despite disapproving noises from both Washington and Moscow, Harold Macmillan and Charles de Gaulle eventually signed the Declaration of Union on 29th November 1959, thereby laying the foundations for a wider European commonwealth.

And now, one hundred years have passed...

ACK-ACK MACAQUE

PART ONE

DIGITAL GHOSTS

Des hommes raisonnables? Des hommes
détenteurs de la sagesse? Des hommes inspirés
par l'esprit?… Non, ce n'est pas possible.

Pierre Boulle, *La Planète des Singes*

BREAKING NEWS

From *The European Standard*, online edition:

King Injured In Grenade Attack
Assailant Targets Royal Motorcade

PARIS, 11 JULY 2058 – The King and the Duchess of Brittany have been injured by an explosion on the streets of Paris.

An air ambulance flew His Majesty King William V, ruler of the United Kingdom of Great Britain, France, Ireland and Norway, and Head of the United European Commonwealth, to a private hospital last night, where surgeons battled for three hours to save his life.

The royal couple were on their way to a formal reception at the Champs-Elysées Plaza Hotel, where they were due to announce plans for next year's Unification Day celebrations, which will mark the centenary of the merger between France and Great Britain.

Eyewitness reports say that shots were fired as the royal motorcade turned onto the Champs-Elysées and a missile, possibly a rocket-propelled grenade, struck the royal limousine.

Following the explosion, police shot dead an unidentified assailant, who died at the scene.

The King and the Duchess were cut from the wreckage by emergency services and rushed to hospital by helicopter. In a statement issued this morning, Buckingham Palace confirmed that the King suffered a critical head injury, but is now resting comfortably after surgery to relieve pressure on his brain. It is not known if the King's soul-catcher suffered any damage.

Her Grace Alyssa Célestine, the Duchess of Brittany, received treatment for minor injuries, and reportedly spent the night by her husband's bedside.

This latest tragedy comes only a year after the King's son was involved in a helicopter crash while serving in the South Atlantic. The prince survived his ordeal, but seven of his colleagues were not so fortunate.

Since news of the Paris attack broke, the Palace has been inundated with messages of sympathy and concern.

As speculation rises, no republican terror group has yet claimed responsibility and official sources have so far declined to comment.

The investigation continues.

Read more | Like | Comment | Share

Related Stories

World leaders express shock at Paris attack

PM blames dissident republican terror groups

Next year's centenary celebrations to be postponed?

Hong Kong sovereignty negotiations "in trouble"

TuringSoft: Céleste Tech fails in hostile takeover bid for rival computer company

Nuclear tensions on Indo-Chinese border?

Countdown to launch of first privately funded "light sail" probe

Global population hits 8.5 billion

CHAPTER ONE
VICTORIA AT PADDINGTON

THE MOMENT VICTORIA Valois stepped down from the Heathrow train, she saw the detective waiting for her at the ticket barrier. He was there to escort her to her dead husband's apartment. Slowly, she walked towards him. Fresh off the train, after her flight from Paris, she still wore the thick army surplus coat and heavy boots she'd pulled on that morning. As she walked, she could feel the retractable quarterstaff in her coat pocket bump against her thigh. She sniffed the air. Under different circumstances, it might have been nice to have been back in London. Paddington's concourse smelled the way she remembered, of engine grease and fast food. Trains pulled in and out. Metal luggage trolleys rattled. Pigeons flapped under the glazed, wrought-iron roof.

She stopped in front of the barrier.

"I'm Valois."

"Welcome to London, Miss Valois. I'm Detective Constable Simon Malhotra. We spoke on the phone." He glanced behind her. "Do you need any help with your bags?"

Victoria shook her head.

"I haven't brought any. I'm hoping this won't take long."

"Ah, of course."

Outside the station, the pavements were slick with rain. He led her to his car and opened the passenger door.

"Shall we go straight there, or do you need to freshen up first?"

Victoria ducked into the proffered seat. The car was an old Citroën, its interior warm with the autumnal odours of cold coffee, damp clothes and cheap pine air freshener. A half-eaten croissant lay on the grimy dashboard, wrapped in a napkin. She wrinkled her nose.

"Let's just get this over with, shall we?"

Malhotra closed the door and hurried around to the driver's side.

"Okay." He settled behind the wheel and loosened his tie. He pressed the ignition and Victoria heard the electric engine spin up, whining into life. The wipers clunked back and forth. The indicator light ticked, and Malhotra eased the car out into the late morning traffic.

Victoria let her head fall back against the headrest. As the skyliner ground its way across the Channel, she hadn't bothered trying to sleep. The bunk in her cabin had remained undisturbed. She'd spent most of the night in a chair by the porthole, using her jacket as a blanket, watching the rain clump and slither on the glass, smudging the lights of the other gondolas; asking herself the same question, over and over again: *How could Paul possibly be dead?*

Malhotra took them out onto Edgware Road, then south past Marble Arch, and onto Park Lane. The road and sky were as grey and wet as each other.

"So." He glanced across at her as they passed the gaunt trees and black railings of Hyde Park. "Is this your first time in London?"

Victoria didn't bother turning her head.

"I worked for three years as the London correspondent for *Le Monde*," she said. "I met my husband here. He worked for Céleste Technologies. We moved to Paris when they offered him a position there."

Malhotra sucked his teeth. He seemed embarrassed to have brought up the subject.

"Your husband. Yes, of course."

They came to Hyde Park Corner and the Wellington Arch, with its statue of a black iron chariot. Suddenly, they were in five lanes of traffic. Rain fell in front of bright red brake lights. Black hackney cabs jostled for position. Absently, Victoria touched her fingers to the side of her head, and felt her nails scrape the thick ridge of scar tissue concealed behind the curtain of her hair.

"We separated a few months ago. He moved back here."

"But you're from Paris?"

"Originally, *oui, c'est ça.*"

"And now you live on a skyliner? That must be exciting!"

She shrugged at his enthusiasm. A double-decker bus drew alongside, windows steamed.

"It's okay." She watched the rain coat the brick and stone of London: capital city of the United European Commonwealth, site of the European Parliament, and seat of His Majesty King William V. She hadn't been back here in over a year.

Oh, Paul.

She took a long breath.

"Can you tell me something, Detective Malhotra?"

The young man spared her another glance.

"Sure, if I can."

"How did he die?"

Ahead, a traffic light turned red. Malhotra downshifted the gears and brought the car to a standstill.

"He was murdered."

Victoria squeezed her fists together in her lap.

"I know that. I just don't know *how* he died."

The light flickered to amber, then green. Malhotra let out the clutch and the Citroën's electric motor pulled them forward. He took a right onto Brompton Road, and then a left onto Sloane Street. Victoria's neural software tracked their progress via an online map. In her mind's eye, a blinking red arrow marked her current position, the streets laid out in tangles around it. If she wanted to, she could zoom right in to pavement level, or right out until the world seemed the size of a football held at arm's length. She would never be lost. As long as she had a wireless connection, she would always know exactly where she was.

"Are you sure you want to know?" Malhotra's tone suggested he was trying to protect her. Victoria rubbed her eyes with forefinger and thumb, dispelling the map display. To hear the grisly details of her husband's murder was pretty much the last thing she wanted right now. Yet that old journalistic instinct itched at her and wouldn't let go. She had to know the full story, whatever the cost.

"Someone should know what happened to him," she said reasonably. "Someone who loved him."

The detective puffed air through his cheeks.

"All right, then. If you're sure." He gave her a sideways glance. "But not here. I'll go through it all with you when we get to the flat, okay?"

They passed over Vauxhall Bridge and into Battersea. Paul's apartment lay on the second floor of a building by the river, opposite a Renault car dealership. Malhotra parked on the dealership's forecourt. As today was a Sunday, the business was closed.

"Come on," he said. He led her across the road to the front of the apartment block, with its beige brickwork and chipped black iron railings. The rain dampened her hair, and she could feel her heart fluttering in her chest.

Although the cool, detached part of her brain — the part she didn't really think of as *her* — told her Paul was dead, the news still hadn't really sunk in at a gut level. She hadn't assimilated it properly. Even now, as they climbed the steps to his apartment, she half-expected to find him inside when she opened the door. He'd be standing there in his kitchen, wearing one of his ridiculous Hawaiian shirts, laughing at her for being so gullible.

He couldn't be dead. He couldn't leave her feeling this empty and desolate. He just couldn't.

She fingered the retractable quarterstaff in her pocket, and thought back to the moment she'd first been given the news.

SHE'D BEEN ON top of the skyliner when one of the Commodore's stewards came to find her. She'd been working through her morning routine on the main helipad, practicing her stick fighting technique. The dawn breeze chilled her sweat. The retractable carbon fibre staff whirled in her hand, its weight solid and reassuring.

Left shoulder.

Right shoulder.

Block.

Parry.

Her technique mixed traditional European stick fighting with moves stolen from the Japanese disciplines of jōdō and bōjutsu. She was recording the session on her neural prosthesis and live streaming it to a laboratory near Paris, where the surgeons who'd rebuilt her could use the data to monitor the continuing integration of the natural and artificial components in her brain.

Beneath her bare feet, the skyliner *Tereshkova* ground its way across France, its nuclear-powered propellers labouring against a stiff westerly. Almost a kilometre in length, the giant airship consisted of five rigid, cigar-shaped hulls bound side-by-side in a raft formation. The two outermost hulls sported engine nacelles and large rudder fins. The three inner hulls glittered with promenade decks, satellite dishes and helipads.

That morning, Victoria had the largest pad to herself, atop the skyliner's central hull. All was silent, save for the flap of the wind and the hum of the engines. Far ahead, an ice-cream tower of cumulus caught the sun as it stretched twelve thousand feet into the sky above Paris. Her calves ached. She'd been practising hard for an hour. Her feet were sore from slapping and twisting on the hard rubber surface. Her shoulder muscles burned with the effort of swinging her staff. Still she kept practising, pushing herself to exhaustion. The sweat flew from her with every move. The staff felt like an extension of her will. Yet, even as she threw herself into the physicality of the dance, an internal stillness remained: a part of her mind unaffected by adrenalin and fatigue.

Following her accident, surgeons had been forced to install artificial neurons, replacing large sections of her damaged brain with pliable, gel-based processors. Although the surgery had saved her life, it had left her unable to read or write. Where once she'd spent her days dashing off articles and blog posts, her brain now refused to parse written text. When she looked at a newspaper headline or SincPad screen, all she saw were squiggles, and the only way she could decode them was via a text-recognition app loaded into the gelware. The app stimulated the speech centres of her brain, so that her lips moved as she read, and she gleaned the meaning of the words as she heard herself speak them. The process was slow and often frustrating, and the app prone to mistakes.

Her hands squeezed the staff as she tried to channel her frustration into the fight.

Left shin.

Right shin.

Step back.

Pivot.

She slid forward on the balls of her feet, reached up and brought the end of the staff smacking down onto the head of her imaginary opponent.

"Hai!"

She let the swing's momentum drop her to her knees. Sweat dripped from her forehead onto the black rubber of the helipad. Her chest heaved. She might be half machine, but the alternative was worse; and every breath a victory of sorts.

After a few lungfuls, she looked up, and saw one of the skyliner's white-jacketed stewards standing nervously at the top of the stairwell. She straightened up and walked over to where she'd left her towel.

"Yes?"

The steward cleared his throat. "The Commodore sends his compliments, ma'am. He would like you to join him at your earliest convenience. It seems there is a message for you, from London."

Victoria rubbed her face, and then draped the towel over her shoulder. She retracted the staff to a twelfth of its length, and slipped it into her pocket.

"Do I have time to shower and change?"

The steward glanced at her, taking in her damp hair, her stained black vest and sweat pants.

"That may be advisable, ma'am."

And so, ten minutes later, scrubbed and combed, Victoria knocked at the door of the Commodore's cabin, down in the main gondola, just behind the bridge. She had pulled on a pair of black jeans and a crew neck sweater. Her hair was clean but tied back, revealing the thick scar on her right temple.

"Come in, Victoria, come in." The Commodore rose from behind a large aluminium desk. He wore a white military dress jacket, open at the neck, and a cutlass dangled from his belt.

Victoria's legs were stiff from the workout. The Commodore invited her to take a seat. From his desk, he pulled a bottle of Russian vodka and two glasses. He filled them both, and slid one across to her.

"Drink this," he said. He had white hair and black eyebrows, and ivory-yellow teeth that seemed too large for his mouth. Although he insisted on speaking Russian to his crew, he always spoke English for her; partly because he had a soft spot for her, and partly because he knew from experience that her grasp of the Russian language extended only as far as the phrase '*Ya ne govoryu po russki*', which she was pretty sure meant, 'I don't speak Russian'.

She touched the glass with one finger, turning it slightly, but didn't pick it up.

Most of the back wall of the cabin was taken up by a large picture window. Through it, she could see one of the engine nacelles on the skyliner's outermost starboard hull. She could feel the faint vibration of the airship's engines through the metal deck.

"What's going on?" she asked.

The Commodore picked an imaginary speck of lint from the knee of his cavalry trousers.

"There is a call for you, from England." He picked the phone handset from his desk and passed it to her. "But I am very much afraid it is bad news."

AT THE TOP of the stairs, Detective Constable Malhotra pushed a key into the lock of the apartment door, turned it, and let the door swing open. The lights were off in the hallway. He gestured for her to go in first.

"Try not to touch anything that's marked." He checked his watch impatiently. He obviously had places he'd rather be.

Victoria ignored him. She hesitated on the threshold. As a former reporter, this wasn't the first murder scene she'd had cause to visit; but it was the first in which she'd had such a personal stake. She knew that as soon as she set foot in the flat, she'd have to start accepting the truth, and admit to herself that she really had lost Paul forever.

All these months, a part of her had clung to a slender thread of hope, praying that one day, somewhere down the line, they'd be reconciled, their differences forgotten. But now, that hope was about to be cut forever. She felt a brief urge to turn and run, leaving the entire situation unresolved; but when she closed her eyes, the feeling passed. She hadn't come all this way just to linger on the doormat with the pizza flyers and free newspapers. As Paul's only next of kin, it was up to her accept and mourn his loss; to go through his stuff, and sort out the paperwork.

Heart thudding, she stepped inside. Her boot heels clicked on the parquet floor. Ahead, a narrow galley kitchen lay at the end of the short hallway. On her right, an open door led into a lounge. Dirty footprints showed where the police and coroners had been about their business. The air held lingering traces of sweat and cheap aftershave; and, beneath those, something organic, like the smell of a butcher's shop on a hot day.

With her hand over her mouth and nose, she took a few paces into the room. Bloodstains darkened the wooden floor and papered walls, each accompanied by a handwritten label. Some drops had splattered the glass, and these had been circled and numbered in marker pen ink. Beyond the window, the Thames curled its way through the heart of the city, its surface the sullen hue of day-old coffee, chopped into ripples by the wind.

She pulled her eyes away from the stains. Paul's medical qualifications hung framed on the wall above the fireplace. Beneath them, a flat screen TV lay face down and smashed on the floor, having obviously been knocked over during a scuffle. The police had covered the sofa with a plastic sheet. Before it, a dozen old virtual reality games consoles lay heaped in various stages of disassembly on a low pine coffee table. Her gaze lingered over the accompanying screwdrivers, lumps of solder and twisted scraps of wire as she remembered Paul tinkering with them, six months ago, before their separation. He'd had a thing for retro machines and, after hours in the operating theatre, he found the intricate work of restoring them calmed him.

Her eyes were drawn back to the dried blood by the window. She swallowed. At her sides, her knuckles were white.

Malhotra said, "Are you okay?"

She turned to him. They were eye-to-eye, almost touching. She could smell the fusty bonfire reek of cigarettes on his breath and clothes. She took him by the lapels of his stupid coat.

"Tell me how he died."

The detective looked down at her hands.

"I told you, he was murdered."

"By who?"

Malhotra took her by the wrists and gently pulled her hands free. He stepped back, out of reach.

"We don't know."

Victoria leaned forward. "There's something you're not telling me, isn't there?"

Malhotra wouldn't look at her. He scratched his cheek.

"I don't know if I should—"

"Just tell me."

He took a deep breath. "Okay. Your husband. You knew he was bisexual, right?"

Victoria let her arms fall to her sides.

"Yes." Of *course* she did. She'd always known he swung both ways. For a brief moment, they'd been in love. Then after the accident, for some reason, he'd stopped swinging her way.

She touched the scar tissue at the side of her head.

"Well," Malhotra continued, straightening his collar, "we think he might have been killed by someone he met. Someone he brought back here for, you know..."

"For sex?"

He glanced back down the hall, towards the front door.

"Um, yeah."

"Not an intruder?"

"There's no sign of forced entry, so we're assuming he knew his attacker."

Victoria turned back into the room. She could feel the two halves of her mind butting up against each other: one in a turmoil of grief and jealousy, the other calmly weighing the facts. Her gaze fell on the stained floor.

"What about his soul-catcher?"

The detective rubbed the back of his neck, beneath his collar.

"I'm afraid whoever attacked him took it with them. Ripped it right out, in fact."

Victoria swallowed back her revulsion. Soul-catchers were cranially-implanted webs, similar to her own implants but much smaller and less invasive. They didn't penetrate the brain as hers did; they were simply used to record the wearer's neural activity so that, after death, they could generate a crude, temporary simulation of that individual's personality, allowing them to say their goodbyes and tie up their affairs. In order to remove his soul-catcher, Paul's assailant would have needed to crack open his skull—a procedure usually only carried out as part of an autopsy.

Malhotra reached into his coat and pulled out a brown envelope, from which he extracted a photograph. He handed it to her, unable to meet her eyes.

"This is how we found him."

The photograph had been taken in this room, from almost the exact spot where Victoria now stood. The victim lay in a pool of thick, fresh blood, his head smashed open like an egg, and his skull disturbingly empty. She made a face and looked away.

"Yes, that's him."

"Are you sure?"

She closed her eyes.

"I'm sure." Despite the bruising, and the hair matted to his face, there could be no doubt. The facial recognition software in her neural prosthesis confirmed it.

"I'm afraid it gets worse," Malhotra said. He tapped the picture with his finger, drawing her attention back to the wet cavity revealed by the smashed skull. "His head's empty." The detective took the photo from her and slipped it back into its envelope. "Whoever it was, they took his brain."

Victoria felt the room lurch around her. "What do you mean, they *took* it?"

"They removed his brain and took it with them." Malhotra swallowed. "We've found no trace of it."

Giddiness came in a sudden wave. She put a hand to her forehead. Not knowing what else to do, she retreated inside herself, allowing her more rational, artificial side to momentarily take charge. She heard herself say, "I guess that explains all the blood." Then, disgusted with herself, she walked over to the window and looked out at the river. The tide was low. Gulls fussed and squabbled on the mud. Barges pushed their way up and down stream. To one side, she could see the four white chimneys of Battersea Power Station; to the other, just visible above the trees and other buildings lining the river, the topmost spires of the Palace of Westminster and the Parliament of the United European Commonwealth.

How many times had Paul stood here, looking out at this view? Had it been the last thing he'd ever seen? Had he known his killer? A tear slid down her cheek. She brushed it away with the back of her hand. Without a recording from his soul-catcher, she'd never hear his voice again, never see his face...

When she turned back into the room, she found Malhotra still standing in the doorway, looking uncomfortable. He obviously didn't know what to say.

"Do you have anything to go on?" she asked him.

He hunched his shoulders. "Whoever this was, they came prepared. There's a hundred different DNA samples in this room alone. The killer must have swept up hair and skin cells from the back seat of a bus or Tube train, and emptied them here to cover his tracks."

"You say 'his'?"

Malhotra shrugged. He didn't care. "As I said, we're working on the assumption that the assailant was male, and most likely a sexual partner."

"But you're guessing?"

Malhotra took his hands out of his pockets. "Unless we find his soul-catcher, I'm very much afraid we're grasping at straws." He gestured at the electronics spread on the table. "We've taken his laptop and we're examining it for clues, but so far we've got nothing."

Victoria opened her mouth, and then closed it again. A thought flashed into her head. She felt herself go cold and prickly. She had remembered what it was that Paul had been doing with the VR games consoles. The memory had been dredged, bright and shiny, from the gel lattice of her brain. Very slowly, she turned on her heel and stepped over to the cluttered coffee table.

"Could you give me a minute, please detective?"

"Are you all right?"

She waved him away. "I'll be okay. It's just all been a bit of a shock. I need some time to process. A few minutes alone."

She heard him sigh.

"I'll be in the car. Gather what you need, then come on down when you're ready. Don't be too long."

She listened to his footsteps as he walked to the door and went down the stairs to the street. When she was certain he'd gone, she started rooting through the components on the table, looking for a particular unit.

"Oh, please let it be here," she muttered. Her fingers scrabbled through piles of old circuit boards and other electronic debris, until finally closing with relief on the object she sought. She pulled it free from the mess: an old Sony games console with a battered casing and broken controller. Paul had unobtrusively inserted the black lens of an infrared port into the console's rear panel, next to its power cable. The console wouldn't run games any more, but Paul had used his experience in memory retrieval to modify it for a different, highly illegal, purpose. Victoria turned it over and over in her hands. The tears were running freely now. Inside this scuffed and scratched shell lay her one and only hope of ever seeing him again.

She hardly dared breathe.

One of the side-effects of having half her brain rebuilt was that she had a near-perfect memory. It could be both a blessing and a curse, but right now she was grateful for it. Concentrating, she recalled Paul standing in their Paris apartment, about eight months previously. He'd been wearing cargo pants and a rock band t-shirt; a new gold stud in his right ear, and a pen stuck behind his left.

"You mustn't tell anyone about this," he'd said. And then he'd shown her what he'd hidden in the guts of this old console, tucked away in a pair of fat, newly-installed memory chips.

Guided by the recollection of his hands, her fingers slid over the plastic casing. She found the glassy infrared port on the back panel, and pulled back her hair. The ridge of scarring on her right temple enclosed a row of input jacks: USB, drug feed, and infrared. They were tiny windows into her skull, put there by the technicians when they rebuilt her; windows designed to help them monitor the experimental technology they'd crammed into her head, but also windows which, months after the surgery, she'd learned to exploit for her own ends.

She plugged the old console into the wall, and flipped the power switch to the 'on' position. The console quivered in her hands like a frightened animal, and a green LED came to life. Hands shaking, she raised the box to her temple and, reaching deep within her own mind, activated her own infrared port. Something clicked. Something connected. The box in her hands purred, downloading data directly from its memory store to the gelware in her head. When it had finished, she dropped the box onto the plastic-wrapped sofa and keyed up the mental commands she needed in order to run the saved file. She blinked once, twice. A cobweb dragged itself across her eyeball.

And Paul appeared.

CHAPTER TWO
HOLES IN THE MOON

THE SPITFIRE'S COCKPIT stank of aviation fuel and monkey shit. The long-tailed macaque at the controls had to use all the strength in his hairy arms to keep the wings level. He'd taken a pasting from a pair of Messerschmitts over the Normandy coast. Dirty black smoke streamed back from the engine, almost blinding him, and one of his ailerons had come loose, forcing him to lean hard on the opposite rudder pedal in order to keep the nose up.

To the RAF, the monkey's codename was Ack-Ack Macaque. He'd had another name once, back in the mists of his pre-sentience, but now he couldn't remember what it might have been. Nor did he care. Behind him, his assailants lay smashed and tangled in the smoking, splintered wreckage of their aircraft. Behind them, the Allies were caught in a long and bloody battle to reclaim Europe from the Nazi hordes. Steam-driven British tanks ground towards Paris like tracked battleships, their multiple turrets duelling with the fearsome heat rays of the insect-like German tripods which bestrode the French countryside, laying waste to every town and village in their path.

Ahead, through the gun sights and bullet-proof glass of the windshield, the monkey could see the gleam of England's chalky cliffs. Below his wings, the hard, ceramic-blue waters of the English Channel.

Almost home.

He saw pill boxes and machine gun nests on the beach at the foot of the cliff. Lines of white surf broke against the sand, and the cliff towered above him: an immovable wall of white rock, at least three hundred feet in height. He glanced down at his dashboard and tapped the altimeter. The dial wasn't working. He let out an animal screech. His leathery hands hauled back on the stick. The engine spluttered, threatening to stall. The propeller hacked at the sky.

Come on, come on!

The nose rose with aching slowness. For a second, he wasn't sure if he would make it. For an agonising second, the plane seemed to hang in the air—

Then the cliff's grassy lip dropped away beneath his wings, and he saw the Kent countryside spread before him like a chequered blanket. He took his right hand off the stick, and scratched at the patch covering his left eye socket.

"Crap."

That had been *way* too close.

A couple of miles inland, through the engine smoke, he caught sight of the aerodrome, and his heart surged.

"Ack-Ack Macaque to Home Tower. Ack-Ack Macaque to Home Tower. I'm coming in hot. Better have the fire crews standing by. Over."

He let the nose drop again, trading his hard-won altitude for a little additional speed, until his wheels almost brushed the tops of the hedgerows lining the fields.

"Roger that, Ack-Ack Macaque. Standing by. Good luck and we'll see you on the ground."

He cleared the first hedge, scattering a herd of dairy cows; and then the second. A skeletal tree snatched at the tip of his starboard wing. The aerodrome's perimeter fence appeared. He pulled back just enough to clear it, and the airfield yawned open like the arms of an anxious parent, ready to catch him.

The Spitfire's wheels squeaked as they hit the concrete. The stick juddered in his hand.

Somehow, he kept the nose straight.

THE DYING SPIT finally bumped to a halt at the far end of the field and the engine burst into flames. By the time the fire crews reached it, the plane wasn't worth saving. Ammunition popped and sputtered in the flames. Paint blistered.

They found Ack-Ack Macaque sitting on the grass at the edge of the runway, with his flying goggles loose around his neck.

"I need a drink," he said, so they gave him a ride back to the Officers' Mess.

The Mess was housed in a canvas marquee at the end of a row of semi-cylindrical steel Nissen huts. When he pushed through the khaki flap that served as its door, the crowd inside fell silent. People stopped talking and playing cards. Everyone turned to look at him: a monkey in a greasy flight suit, with a leather patch over one eye and a chromium-plated revolver on each hip. Pipe smoke curled above their heads. Their faces were amused and curious, and he didn't recognise any of them. They were all new recruits. They had moustaches and slicked-back hair, and they wore brand new flying jackets over crisp RAF uniforms. Ignoring them, he loped over to a corner table and climbed onto a chair. After a moment, the Mess Officer shuffled over.

"Tea or coffee, squire?"

Ack-Ack Macaque fixed the man with his one good eye and spoke around the remains of the cigar still clamped between his yellowed teeth.

"Bring me a daiquiri." He undid his belt and slapped his holsters onto the table. "And see if you can scare up a banana or two, will you?"

"Right-o, sir. You sit tight, I'll be right back."

As the N.C.O. scurried away, Ack-Ack Macaque unzipped his flight jacket. Around him, heads turned away and discussions resumed. In the corner of the tent, someone started bashing out a Glen Miller tune on the old upright piano.

Ack-Ack Macaque settled back in his chair and closed his eye. The cigar had helped clear the reek of aviation fuel from his nostrils, and now all he wanted was a rest. He used a dirty fingernail to worry a strand of loose tobacco from his oversized incisors, and yawned. He couldn't remember the last time he'd slept. He seemed to have been awake forever, flying one sortie after another in an endless string of confused dogfights, fuelled only by nicotine and sheer bloody-mindedness.

Of course, it didn't help that the front line kept shifting, and nobody knew for sure where anything was. Planes defected from one side to the other, and then back again, on an almost daily basis. People who were your most trusted comrades on one mission might become your deadliest opponents on the next, and vice versa. He glared around the Mess, wondering which of these young upstarts would be the first to betray him.

He used to find it easier. In the early days, he'd capered around like one of those cartoon characters from those shorts they sometimes screened in the ready room. A smile and a cheeky quip, and somehow the war hadn't seemed so bad. But then his quips had dried as the death toll rose. The shrinks called it 'battle fatigue'. He'd seen it happen before, to other pilots. They lived too long, lost too many comrades, and withdrew into themselves. They stopped taking care of themselves and then, one day, they stopped caring altogether. They took crazy chances; pushed their luck out beyond the ragged limit; and died.

Was that what he was doing? He'd gone up against that pair of 'schmitts this morning, even though they'd had the height advantage. He should have turned and fled. If one of his squad had been so reckless, he'd have boxed their ears. He'd been fortunate to make it home in one piece, and he knew it.

Was he pushing his luck? With a sigh, he dropped the soggy butt of his cigar and ground it with his boot.

"What's up, skipper?" The Scottish accent belonged to Mindy Morris, a new recruit to the squadron. "I heard you took a bit of a battering out there."

He opened his baleful eye. They were always new recruits, all these kids. Yet Mindy was one of the youngest he'd seen. She couldn't have been much over fourteen years old.

"Stop smiling," he said. "If you bare your teeth at me like that, I'm liable to rip your face off."

The girl's eyes whitened.

"Sorry, I didn't mean—"

"Don't take it personally." He kicked a chair out for her. "It's a primate thing. Now, sit down."

The Mess Officer brought over a daiquiri in a cocktail glass, which he placed on the table.

"Will that be all, squire?"

Ack-Ack Macaque scowled at him. "What, no bananas?"

"I'm afraid not, sir. There's a war on, you know. Can I get you something else instead?"

Ack-Ack Macaque picked up the cocktail glass in his hairy hand and tipped the contents into his mouth. He smacked his lips.

"Bring me rum." He turned back to Mindy Morris, where she sat perched on the edge of her chair.

"You might want to watch it with the eye contact, too," he warned her. "If I get drunk, I might take a stare as a challenge."

The girl dropped her gaze to her hands, which were knotted in her lap.

"Sorry, sir."

The Mess Officer returned with a bottle of rum, which he set down without a word.

Ack-Ack Macaque said, "Now, do you want a drink, kid?"

Mindy gave a shake of her head. She had green eyes and very short ginger hair. No make-up. Ack-Ack Macaque picked up the bottle and pulled out the cork with his teeth. He spat it onto the floor.

"Well," he said, "if you don't want a drink, what *do* you want?"

The girl squirmed in her chair. Her cheeks were flushed.

"I know you lost a wingman yesterday." She hesitated, trying to gauge his reaction. "And I hoped…"

Ack-Ack Macaque sloshed rum into his glass. The neck of the bottle clinked against the rim. He was aware that the pilots on the surrounding tables were eavesdropping on the conversation, even as they pretended not to.

"You hoped I'd let you fly with me?"

Mindy swallowed hard.

"Yes, sir."

"How old are you?"

"Sixteen, sir."

Ack-Ack Macaque gave her a sceptical look. She flushed a deeper shade of crimson. "All right, all right. I'm fifteen. But I know how to fly a kite, and I know when to follow orders, and when to keep my mouth shut."

Ack-Ack Macaque scratched at a sudden itch. He hoped he hadn't picked up fleas again.

"Where are you from, Morris?"

"Glasgow, sir."

"Have you ever killed anyone?"

The girl frowned.

"I don't understand."

Ack-Ack Macaque picked a crumb of bread from the hairs on his chest, and popped it into his mouth.

"Have you ever been in a dogfight?"

The girl leaned forward excitedly. "No, but I've racked up hundreds of hours of flight experience on simula—" She stopped herself. "On training aircraft. I've racked up hundreds of hours on training aircraft."

Ack-Ack Macaque sipped his drink. He looked at the freckles on Mindy's nose. Something about her youth made him feel very old and very tired.

"I don't need someone who's just going to get themselves, or me, killed."

"Oh, I won't, sir. I promise you that." She looked up at him with eyes the colour of a summer meadow. "Please sir. This means a lot to me."

Ack-Ack Macaque sighed. She wasn't the first rookie pilot to want to fly with him. After all, he was the most famous pilot in the European theatre. The kids treated him like a grizzled old gunslinger: someone against whom to measure their own skills and nerve. Over the past few months, many had tried to keep up with him, and many had died as a result. He couldn't remember all their names. They came, flew with him for a while, and then died. Some got sloppy, others over-confident, and some were just plain unlucky. But they all died eventually, leaving no more impression on the world than if they'd never existed in the first place. All trace of them vanished. Nobody grieved for them, and he seemed to be the only one able to remember that they'd ever been there at all.

He looked around at the young, fresh faces sat at the other tables. They could be called to fight at a moment's notice. Many of them would die in the hours and days ahead; yet few seemed the slightest bit perturbed. They behaved as if they were on holiday: laughing, joking and flirting. Over drinks, they casually compared the number of kills they'd made as if discussing the scores of an elaborate cricket match. How could they be so blasé in the face of almost certain death? How could life mean so little to them? For all the impression they made on the world, they may as well have been shadows.

He put down his glass and reached again for the bottle. As he poured, he looked at Mindy.

"Do you ever feel like you're the only real person here, and everyone else is just pretending?"

The room fell silent. The music stopped. Mindy sat back in her chair. Her eyes leapt left and right, as if unsure what to do. Nobody else moved. Nobody breathed.

Ack-Ack Macaque looked around at their frozen faces.

"What's the matter?" He lowered the bottle to the table. "What did I say?"

Then, growing closer, he heard the bass thrum of enemy aircraft engines. An airman burst into the tent, half into his flight jacket.

"Ninjas! A whole squadron of them!"

Chairs scraped on the wooden floor. Their faces expressing both relief and excitement, the crowd rushed for the door, pulling on gloves and flight helmets as they went.

Left at his table, Ack-Ack Macaque took a final swill from the bottle. The rum was as sweet and dark as coffee. Rivulets ran into the fur beneath his chin. He clamped a fresh cigar in place and gathered his holsters from the table. Through the open door, he could see the boomerang silhouettes of German flying wings lumbering across the airfield, spilling black-clad paratroopers. Chutes blossomed at the far end of the aerodrome, as a squad of ninjas tried to attack the tower, brandishing swords and submachine guns. A second wave fell towards the aeroplane hangars, armed with flame throwers and throwing stars.

Mindy was waiting for him at the door.

"Come on, Morris," he said around the cigar. "It's that time again."

"And what time would that be, skipper?"

Ack-Ack Macaque drew his guns: two silver Colts big enough to shoot holes in the moon. Holding them, he felt his energy returning. A grin peeled his lips from his clenched yellow teeth.

"Time to blow shit up."

CHAPTER THREE
BATSHIT CHATROOMS OF DOGGERLAND

11.30PM IN PARIS. On the steps of the Turkish Embassy, His Royal Highness Prince Merovech, the Prince of Wales, shook hands with the Turkish Ambassador and thanked him for a wonderful evening. Then, after dutifully waving for the paparazzi, he slid into the comfort of a waiting limousine.

As the car pulled away from the kerb, he let his shoulders sag, and his smile sank back beneath the aching muscles of his face. With one hand, he undid his bow tie, and the top two buttons of his crisp white shirt. With the other, he took a bottle of cold imported lager from the mini fridge behind the driver's seat and popped the cap. Then, cradling the bottle in his lap, he let his head rest against the cool black of the tinted window. Beyond the bulletproof, rain-streaked glass, trees lined the side of the road, and reflected streetlamps glimmered off the waters of the Seine. On the opposite bank, the Eiffel Tower reared above the trees, lit by spotlights, with both the Union Flag and the French Tricolour hanging sodden from its mast.

The flags reminded Merovech of a line from his great-grandmother's famous Unification speech, where she'd spoken about the way Dover and Calais had once been joined by a chalk ridge called Doggerland; and how the Seine, the Thames and the Rhine had all been tributaries flowing into a mighty river delta, the remains of which now lay submerged beneath the English Channel.

"Our two great countries have always been linked beneath the surface," she'd said, before going on to announce plans for the construction of a tunnel to reunite the two countries—a project which wouldn't be completed until nearly fifteen years later, in 1971.

She had made that speech almost one hundred years ago, and yet every school child knew it by heart. The political merger of Britain and France had been a key turning point in European history: a cause for optimism and hope on a continent still nursing the hangover from two devastating World Wars.

Merovech took a sip from the beer bottle. Good news for Europe, yes; but not so good for him. With the hundredth anniversary of Anglo-French unification only days away, his life had become a stultifying round of yawn-worthy cocktail parties, receptions and ceremonies. He ate, slept and moved to a strict itinerary, with hardly a moment for himself. At heart, he'd always been grateful for the privileges which came with his royal title, but recently, he'd found it hard not to resent the accompanying responsibilities: the boredom and wasted time.

Some people said he hadn't been the same since that helicopter crash in the Falklands. Perhaps they were right?

His trousers squeaked as he shifted position on the soft leather seat.

His SincPhone rang. He pulled it from the inside pocket of his tux and groaned.

"Hello, mother."

From the phone's tiny screen, Duchess Alyssa's face glared out at him. She wore a plain navy-blue business suit with a string of pearls, and a slash of red lipstick.

"Don't you 'mother' me. What's this I hear about you missing the press conference this afternoon?"

In the darkness, Merovech shrugged.

"The Prime Minister was the one giving the speech. I didn't have anything to say. They just wanted me there to make up the numbers."

"Nevertheless, you were supposed to be there. A prince has certain obligations, Merovech. Like it or not, while your father remains in a coma, you are his representative and heir, and it's time you started to act like it."

"I had studying to do."

"Nonsense. I expect you were out chasing that little purple-haired floozy again, weren't you?"

Merovech bridled, but held his tongue. The truth was, he had been studying but, from long experience, knew he wouldn't get anywhere by arguing. Once his mother had her mind made up about something, there was little he could do to change it.

"Look, I really don't have time for youthful rebellion right now. There's too much to do. Honestly, Merovech, you're going to be twenty years old in a few months. When are you going to start facing up to your responsibilities?"

Merovech lowered his eyes, trying to look contrite.

"Sorry mother," he mumbled.

The Duchess glared at him.

"Whatever. I'm not prepared to discuss this any further over an unsecured line. I trust you were polite to the Turkish ambassador?"

"He's invited me to play golf with him next week."

"Very well." She brought the phone close to her face, so that she seemed to loom out at him in the darkness of the limo. "Now get home, and get to bed. We'll finish this talk in the morning."

She hung up. Merovech held the phone for a few moments and sighed. Then he folded it up, dropped it onto the seat beside him, and went back to watching the streetlights of Paris drift past the smoky window.

Paris and London were very similar cities. They had the same stores, the same billboards. The same weather. The kids even used the same bilingual slang, or "Franglais" as they called it. Yet despite these superficial similarities, and despite having been born and raised in London, something about the neoclassical streets of the French capital—something he couldn't quite put his finger on—made him regard the city as his home.

When the phone beeped again, he winced, expecting another reprimand, but found instead a text message from Julie. For the past three weeks, they'd been seeing each other in secret. The message invited him to meet her in a café on the South Bank, at midnight. He read it twice, and smiled to himself as he slipped the phone back into his pocket.

Perhaps tonight wouldn't be a complete waste, after all.

HE REACHED THE café half an hour later, wearing an old red hoodie and a pair of battered blue jeans. He had the brim of a baseball cap pulled low over his forehead, shading his eyes. He'd read somewhere that ninety per cent of facial recognition depended on the hair and eyes, and he hoped that by keeping the brim of his cap low, he'd remain anonymous. So far, no-one on the rain-soaked streets had paid him the slightest attention, and he wanted it to stay that way.

The café stood, shouldered between two taller buildings, on a narrow street south of the river, across the water from the flying buttresses and gothic exuberance of Notre Dame, and a few doors down from the famous 'Singe-Vert' nightclub, where the Beatles had cut their teeth in the early 1960s, playing a formative two year residency before returning to England to record their first single.

Inside, the place was quiet, even for a rainy November Sunday in Paris. He shook out his umbrella. The dinner crowd had gone and only the solitary drinkers remained. A radio behind the counter played spacey Parisian electronica: low, dirty beats and breathy female vocals. The whole place smelled of coffee and red wine. Steam from the silver espresso machine fogged the mirror behind the counter. A sign on the café's glass door advertised free

WiFi. A small TV at the end of the counter showed a news channel. The sound was off and the screen too far away for him to read the headline ticker. All he could see were the pictures: troops from China, India and Pakistan facing each other across the windswept borders of Kashmir. Another murder victim in London. UN helicopters plucking survivors from the floods in Thailand.

The café's proprietor was a bored-looking woman in her late fifties, with thick, dark eyebrows and a mole on her cheek. If she recognised him as he came in, she gave no sign.

The walls of the café were covered in framed photographs of old-fashioned Zeppelins from the 1930s, and the newer, much larger, modern skyliners.

Working together in the decades following their unification, and partly in response to pressure from the Americans, who were less than thrilled by the alliance, Anglo-French engineers built a new generation of lighter-than-air behemoths. Merovech glanced at the pictures as he crossed the floor. In the last decades of the twentieth century, skyliner production had kept alive the British and French shipyards, rescuing them from a post-war drop in demand. And during the economic turbulence of the 'seventies and 'eighties, when the tantrums of the OPEC nations forced the Western world to take a long, hard look at its dependence on oil, the skyliners had really come into their own, offering cheap and relatively carbon-neutral transportation. Now, with their impellers driven by nuclear-electric engines originally designed for use in orbital satellites, the big old ships still plied the world's trade routes, unfettered by the market peaks and troughs that had so bedevilled the traditional airlines.

Julie was sat at the table farthest from the door, against the back wall. She looked up from her coffee as he approached.

"Did you get away okay?"

Julie Girard was a native Parisian and a fellow politics and philosophy student at the Pantheon-Sorbonne University. She had purple hair. She wore jeans and a sweater under her anorak. He wanted to kiss her. Instead, he slipped into the opposite chair and said, "I went out through a service entrance."

"They will be angry."

He gave a shrug. "What can they do? They can't keep me locked away forever."

Julie glanced around the café. Her shoulder bag hung from the back of her chair. As she moved her head, he caught the glint of silver music beads in her ears.

"But is it safe for you to be out like this, on your own?" She looked worried. "I did not think. I should not have asked you—"

A candle burned on the table, little more than a stub jammed into the neck of a wax-streaked wine bottle. He reached around it and took her hand.

"I'm not on my own. I have you."

She raised an eyebrow. "And what good am I going to be if someone comes at you with a gun?"

He squeezed her fingers. They were cool and dry. His were wet and cold from the rain.

"No-one's going to come at me with a gun."

"You don't know that. Look at what happened to your father."

His jaw tensed. He let go of her hand, and sat back in his chair.

"I can't live in fear of terrorists, Julie. If I do, they've already won."

She ran her index fingernail around her coffee cup's rim.

"I'm sorry," she said. "I just had to see you. It's been nearly a week."

So far, the majority of their relationship had taken place online using anonymous, pay-as-you-go smart phones, skipping from one fake social media profile to another in a series of snatched conversations and cryptic status updates. Physical meetings had been rare.

She brushed a purple strand of hair behind her ear, revealing a yellowing bruise at the side of her eye.

"What happened to your face?"

She put a hand up to touch it, and he saw her wince.

"Nothing."

"It doesn't look like nothing."

Julie flicked her hair forward, covering the wound in a spray of purple strands.

"It is just a bruise."

"Was it your father? Did he hit you again? Because if he did—"

"Leave it, Merovech."

"But, Julie, I can—"

"I said, leave it." She sat back with a huff. Merovech took a deep breath, trying to quell his own anger. This wasn't the first time he'd seen her sporting a bruise on her arm or face.

"You just say the word and I'll have him taken—"

Julie glared at him.

"I do *not* want to talk about it," she snapped. "Not tonight, not ever."

Merovech swallowed back his irritation. "Then what do you want to do?"

She held his gaze for a few seconds, as if trying to decide something. Then she leant down and delved into her shoulder bag. When she popped back up, she held a SincPad.

SincPads were all but ubiquitous. They'd been invented at the turn of the century, as the Commonwealth government pumped investment into the silicon fens of Cambridgeshire, supporting a burgeoning IT industry buoyed up by the work of such pioneers as Alan Turing, Clive Sinclair, and Tim Berners-Lee. And now, like skyliners, they came in all shapes and sizes, from palm-sized smart phones to giant, interactive wall displays. Everybody had one, in some shape or form. They were everywhere. The one Julie held had roughly the same dimensions as a refill pad of A4 paper, and she'd decorated its casing with stickers from a dozen political and environmental causes, all of which were now frayed and peeling. She tapped the screen to bring up a video player, and then placed the pad on the table between them.

"You will not believe this," she said.

Merovech leaned forward on his elbows. The picture showed a monkey in a leather jacket, squatting on a chair. The creature had a patch over its left eye, a silver pistol on each hip, and thick fleece-lined boots at the ends of its hairy legs. It was in discussion with a young, redheaded girl in a blue uniform. Tinkly piano played in the background.

Julie froze the playback. She pointed at the monkey.

"Do you know who this is?"

Merovech shook his head. The animal looked like something from a Manga cartoon.

Julie leaned close.

"His name is Ack-Ack Macaque. He is a character in an immersive MMORPG."

"A what?"

"A Massive Multi-player Online Role-Playing Game." She frowned. "You have really never heard of him?"

Merovech shrugged. He didn't play war games. They brought back too many memories.

"Should I have done?"

"Frankly, yes. The game is owned by Céleste Technologies. Does that ring any bells?"

"My mother's company?"

"*Mais oui.*" Julie gave a slow nod, as if talking to an idiot. "They have been running the game for about a year now. I cannot believe you have not heard of it."

Merovech crossed his arms.

"If you remember, I spent most of last year in the Falkland Islands, doing my national service. We didn't have much time for games."

Julie bit her lip. "The crash. Oh, Merovech, I forgot. I am so sorry."

He closed his eyes and, for a moment, found himself back in the blackness of the sinking chopper, scrabbling at his harness, reliving the underwater cries and struggles of his comrades, the creak of metal, and the heart-stopping cold of the seawater pouring through the open hatch. He shivered. Seven men had been dragged to a freezing death at the bottom of the South Atlantic. He'd been lucky to get out at all. He would have drowned had some unknown hands not pushed him through the hatch, against the flow of the incoming sea.

"And besides," he said to change the subject, "the Duchess and I don't talk as often as you might think." In fact, he had as little personal contact as possible with his mother. They didn't get along at all. He lived in a secure penthouse a short walk from the university, and only travelled to the Élysée Palace for official functions.

Julie reached over and brushed his fingers with her own.

"I am sorry, I did not—"

He brushed a palm across the table's sticky surface.

"It doesn't matter. Now, you were about to tell me about this monkey?"

She sat back and licked her lower lip.

"The game is set in a fictionalised World War Two." Her voice was low and urgent. "Players get points by completing missions, shooting down opponents, and so on. They use the points to upgrade their planes and buy better weapons. In between missions, they hang out and socialise." With a purple fingernail, she tapped the picture of the monkey. "This is the main guy. Players can fly with him and fight for the Allies or, if they are really good, switch sides and try to take him down. But here is the twist: in this game, you only get one life. If you get shot down and your parachute does not work, you are dead. You cannot log back in for another try."

"That sounds a bit rough."

"It makes the game more realistic. The players have something to lose. They have to decide how much safety they give up in return for glory."

"And the monkey, what happens to him?"

Julie turned her palms upward.

"Nobody knows. He has never lost a fight. The game is set up that way. He is nearly impossible to kill."

Merovech sat back in his chair and yawned.

"Is this going somewhere?" He felt uncomfortable with his back to the door. He glanced over his shoulder. The windows were orange from the streetlights. Pedestrians splashed past. The rain looked as if it might turn into sleet.

Julie tapped the screen again, to get his attention.

"I want to show you this," she said.

He looked down at the monkey beneath her finger.

"And what *is* this?"

Julie's fingertips circled the monkey's face. "In my philosophy class, we have been looking at the rights of artificial intelligences, and we suspect Ack-Ack Macaque falls into that category."

"The game?"

"The monkey. The character."

"Are you sure?"

Julie reached over and squeezed his hand.

"The company made kind of a big deal about it. It is part of the challenge of the game, setting human players up against a sophisticated AI, with a one-shot chance of beating it."

Merovech looked at his watch. He'd already heard Julie's rants about the evils of enslaving sentient beings, no matter their origin, and he'd been hoping for something more romantic. He knew they didn't have much time. He could already imagine the panic amongst the SO1 agents charged with his protection. The last time he'd done this, they'd had half the city's police out looking for him, and his mother had been livid.

"So what?" He let his impatience show. "It's not like it's really alive or anything, is it?"

Julie let go of his hand. She arched her eyebrows, refusing to be drawn.

"Just watch this."

She hit the play button. The monkey stroked its chin in a gesture that would have looked thoughtful on a human. It swilled the rum around in its glass, drained it and reached for the bottle.

"Do you ever feel like you're the only real person here," it asked, "and everyone else is just pretending?"

The picture jumped and he saw the same scene from another viewpoint. Then another, and another.

Julie said, "Nearly every player in the bar recorded that scene. The videos are all up on the Web. The chat rooms are going batshit."

The film came to an end, frozen on a picture of the monkey's face.

Julie said, "Do you see what this means?"

Merovech didn't.

She bent forward excitedly. Her hands fluttered over the table like startled grouse.

"It means the damn thing is starting to question its own existence!"

Several heads turned in their direction. Merovech put a hand on her arm. "Shhh."

"But—"

"We're trying not to attract attention, remember?"

Julie shook him off.

"Merovech, listen to me. I have some friends coming. They will be here in a few minutes."

Merovech sat up, alarmed. His eyes automatically scanned the place for a back way out—an old habit, drummed into him by years of security briefings.

"What friends?"

"Other students from my course. They have seen this footage, and they are as concerned about it as I am."

Merovech felt his cheeks burning. *Oh God, please don't let any of them be paps.*

"We are going to do something about the monkey," Julie said. She reached over and placed both of her hands on top of his. "And we need your help."

Ten minutes later, Merovech found himself in the back of a black Volkswagen van, heading out of the city. The streetlamps threw moving shadows through the driver's window. Two students occupied the front seats. The back of the van was windowless and bare. Merovech sat on the floor with his back against the wall. For the first time in his life, he felt out of his depth. He didn't know how far he could trust these people. From the little he'd gleaned from Julie, they were obviously highly politicised. What if they were republican sympathisers? What if they tried to kidnap him for ransom? He had no back-up, no security.

Julie huddled beside him, her arm hooked in his. He was only here because of her. He didn't want her running off and getting into trouble; and he hoped he could talk her out of whatever it was she had planned.

A young man sat opposite them, with dark eyes and a stripe of beard that looked as if it had been drawn on with eyeliner.

"This is Frank," Julie said. "He is in charge."

Frank wore an army surplus jacket, skinny black jeans and American baseball boots. A large pendant hung from his neck. The fingers on his right hand were stained yellow. He said, "*Tu es sûr qu'on peut lui faire confiance?*"

Julie put a protective hand on Merovech's shoulder.

"Of course we can trust him. He can get us in there. He knows the layout."

Frank narrowed his eyes. He switched to English.

"Is this true?"

Merovech returned his stare. The enclosed gloom and metal walls of the van were making him uncomfortable.

"I haven't agreed to anything."

"*Merde.*" Frank bit his lip and looked away.

"What's the matter?" Julie asked.

"What's the *matter*?" Frank flung a hand at Merovech. "We are sitting in a stolen van, on the way to committing an illegal act, and you bring along the heir to the British *throne*! I mean, *putain de merde*!" He fumbled in his pocket and pulled out a pack of cheap cigarettes. He extracted one but, as he went to light it, Merovech leaned over and put a hand on his arm.

"She didn't bring me. I brought myself."

Frank gave him an incredulous squint.

"And do you know what we are going to do tonight, 'your highness'?"

Merovech straightened.

"Why don't you tell me?"

Frank shook him off. He lit the cigarette.

"We believe your mother's company has an AI imprisoned on its game servers."

"So what?"

Frank exhaled grey smoke into the cramped space. "We are going to break in and free it."

In the rattling semi-darkness, Merovech looked at Julie. The shadow of her hair hid part of her face. Her eyes were fixed on him.

"You haven't got a hope," he said. "The Céleste campus has too much security. You won't get five metres before the security systems pick you off."

Frank coughed on his cigarette. "Oh, you think so?"

Merovech gave him a level stare.

"I know so."

Frank's upper lip twitched.

"Well, we are going, *rosbif*, whether you like it or not."

The van pulled off the main road, onto a pockmarked concrete service road running parallel with a high chain link fence. From his pocket, Frank pulled an elastic ski mask.

"And if you are going to be coming with us, you will have to be putting this on."

CHAPTER FOUR
THE SMILING MAN

FROM WHERE VICTORIA stood, Paul's image appeared to be standing in the centre of the room. He'd been thirty-two years old when he died—a man of medium height and slim build, with peroxide white hair and tattoos on his forearms. He wore a gold ear stud, a pair of rimless rectangular glasses, and a yellow and green Hawaiian shirt beneath a white doctor's coat.

Of course, he wasn't really there at all. The picture, drawn from the file she'd downloaded from the games console, was being projected into the visual centres of her brain via augmented reality routines built into her neural gelware.

As she watched, he looked around, and wiped a hand across his face.

"Erm...?"

Victoria's heart clenched in her chest. She had an overwhelming urge to take him in her arms.

"Hello, Paul."

"Vicky?" His gaze flicked past her, unseeing. "What's going on? Where are you? Why can't I see anything?"

His image had a translucent, nebulous quality.

"Relax," she told him.

He knuckled his eyes. "But I'm blind!"

"No, you're not. In fact, you're not really Paul at all."

Slowly, he lowered his hands. His brows creased.

"Oh no," he said. "I'm a back-up, aren't I?"

"I'm afraid so."

"But if I'm the back-up, that means I'm dead, doesn't it?"

"Yes."

He frowned. "Then why can't I remember it? The last thing I remember is—"

"You're the second back-up. The illegal one, from the console. I'm running you as an app on my neural gelware."

He did a double-take.

"You can do that?"

"Yes."

"Where are we?"

"I'm standing in your flat." Pushing her fists into the pockets of her army coat, she turned and walked toward the window. Paul's image moved with her, maintaining its apparent position relative to her field of view.

"But if I'm the second back-up, what happened to the first? Do the police have it?"

"I'm afraid not. Look, there's no easy way to say this, so I'm just going to come right out with it, okay?"

He passed a hand across his brow.

"Okay."

Victoria swallowed hard. She let her forehead rest against the window. The glass was cold.

"You were murdered. Here in your flat. And whoever did it took your brain, soul-catcher and all."

Paul's hands leapt to the back of his neck. He huffed air through his cheeks.

"Jesus Christ."

"Quite."

Victoria touched her hair, which was still damp from the rain. Paul's fists were clenched and his eyes were wide and desperate. He looked on the verge of freaking out.

"I'm going to give you read-only access to my sensory feed," she said to distract him. "I'll get an imaging program to use my eyes and ears to construct a picture of the outside world for you."

She took a deep breath. When it came to tinkering with her own neural software, the technicians at Céleste Technologies were understandably discouraging. Getting them to give her the required passwords had taken a lot of persuasion. Now, all she had to do was concentrate on a specific phrase.

"*Licorne, archipel, Mardi*," she whispered in French. Then, in English: "Unicorn, archipelago, Tuesday."

In her mind's eye, menus blossomed like flowers. She shivered. In command mode, her thoughts had a crisp clarity. She felt like a murky ocean fish pulled up gasping into the bright sunlight.

Working as swiftly as she could, she made the necessary adjustments, and dropped back into the familiar waters of her organic neurons.

Before her, Paul blinked.

"Hey, I can see!" He turned his head back and forth, frowning. "Why can't I look around?"

"You're seeing though my eyes," she told him. "You see whatever I see." She panned her gaze across the river, and the buildings on the far shore. Then, without wanting to, she glanced down at rust-coloured smears on the wooden floor. Her vision swam with tears.

"I'm sorry," she said.

"Why, what's—"

"I'm just sorry, okay?"

She turned and walked back towards the door. She wanted to leave. She stopped halfway.

"Remember when we met, three years ago?" He had been a memory retrieval expert for Céleste Technologies, working to extract memories from damaged soul-catchers. This was in London, before the company moved him to Paris. She'd interviewed him for a story, and somehow they'd clicked. They'd fallen in love. Or at least, she'd thought they had.

Life, it seemed, was seldom as simple.

First came the helicopter accident, then six months of tests and recuperation; and finally, last Christmas, their separation.

Since the breakup of their marriage she'd been living on board the *Tereshkova*, an elderly skyliner under the command of her godfather, an eccentric Russian billionaire with a penchant for cavalry uniforms and fine vodka. At the moment, the *Tereshkova* loomed over Heathrow, taking on cargo and passengers for the long trans-Atlantic haul to Mexico and the Southern United States. When she was done here, she'd rejoin it.

Until then...

"You looked after me," she said. "After the accident. You got me into the Céleste programme. Now it's my turn to do the same for you."

Paul looked down at himself. He ran his hands over his shirt.

"But I... I'm dead."

Victoria ran her tongue over her dry lips. "Maybe I can't save you. But I can find out who did this. I can do that, at least."

"But, what about me?"

Victoria felt the tears rise again. She sniffed them back.

"I'll keep your file in storage, so I can reboot you if I have any questions. Until then, I guess this is goodbye." She opened a mental menu, ready to terminate the simulation.

"No!"

She paused, irritated by the interruption. She didn't want this to be any harder than it was already.

"What?"

"Please don't switch me off." He sounded like a little boy. "I know I'm just a recording. I know that. But I'm all that's left. If you switch me off, I'll be gone. Just gone."

Victoria rubbed her face with both hands. "So, what am I supposed to do with you? Leave you running in my head?"

Paul gave a cautious thumbs-up.

"Please?"

Victoria heard the downstairs front door slam. She said, "But how long will you last?" Back-ups lacked a missing ingredient, everybody knew that. They could only persist for so long before their thoughts became muddled and their awareness died.

Paul stuck out his chin.

"Long enough. Come on, Vicky. You're not the only one in need of answers."

He had that pleading look.

"Okay." Her voice was gruff. "I'll think about it."

Something crashed on the stairs.

Paul cocked his head. "What was that?"

"I don't know."

Victoria walked to the front door and looked out, into the stairwell. Detective Constable Malhotra lay sprawled at the foot of the stairs. His throat had been cut. A man stood over him. Tall and skeletally thin, he had a long black coat and a gleaming bald pate. Bloody fingers gripped a matt black knife. Slickness glistened on the blade. He looked up at her with eyes as dead as a snake's.

"Ah, Victoria," he said. His features were twisted in a permanent thin-lipped smile. He stepped over Malhotra and put a foot on the first step. "I've been waiting for you..." He reached out long fingers and curled them around the banister rail.

"Run," Paul said in her head. "Get out of here."

She took a step back. She couldn't run: he blocked her only exit; she had nowhere to go. Instead, her hand flew to the pocket of her coat and came up holding the retractable staff.

"Stay back." She gave a flick of her wrist and the staff sprang out to its full length. The man's smile didn't falter.

"I've been waiting for you, Victoria. I knew you'd come." He came up the stairs towards her, scraping the tip of his black knife against the wall. The scratching noise set her nerves on edge. She stepped back into the flat and took up a defensive stance in the hallway. There was no point locking the door when she knew he would be able to open it with a kick. Her only hope was to fight. Her perception of time slowed as the adrenalin in her blood triggered the fight-or-flight protocols in her gelware. She felt her muscles tense as targets and escape routes were evaluated. Felt her fingers tighten on the carbon fibre staff.

And still he came, smiling all the way.

"Who are you?"

The man didn't answer. He didn't even pause in the doorway. With a flap of his black coat, he sprang at her. Warning icons flashed in her mind. She swung. He feinted to the side. The tip missed his head and hit the wall, jarring her. She pulled back for another swing, but he moved too fast. A bony arm flicked out like the head of a striking viper. A hand closed around her neck. She felt herself slammed backwards, into the unyielding hardwood of the kitchen door. The air huffed out of her. The staff clattered to the floor.

She couldn't breathe.

She kicked her feet but his arms were too long: she couldn't get her knee up to his groin. Darkness hustled the edges of her vision. Paul's image grew faint. She thrashed but the fingers wrapped her throat like steel cables.

No, not like this!

Without releasing his grip, the smiling man turned her sideways, pressing her cheek against the smooth paintwork of the kitchen door. Her lungs burned. Her throat muscles scrabbled desperately for breath that wouldn't come.

Please...

Sensing her pain, the gelware came online, interpreting her suffocation as evidence of major physical trauma. Adrenalin poured into her system, but it was already too late.

As she tipped forwards into a spreading black pool of unconsciousness, the last thing she felt was the blade of his knife carving into the flesh at the back of her neck.

CHAPTER FIVE
CLIMBING TREES AND KILLING NAZIS

A COUPLE OF hours after the ninja attack at the aerodrome, Ack-Ack Macaque took to the skies again, this time at the controls of a twin-engine de Havilland troop carrier, with Mindy Morris, the new Scottish recruit, perched in the co-pilot's chair. Both wore combat fatigues and camouflage paint. Behind them, fifteen paratroopers sat strapped into webbing in the plane's main cabin.

Night fell as they crossed the Channel. He kept the plane low, to avoid enemy radar, and skimmed across the Normandy coast at treetop height. Their objective lay ahead, in the wooded grounds of the picturesque Chateau du Molay, where intelligence reports indicated that the German army were building launch facilities for their V2 rockets.

As they approached the Chateau's estate, Ack-Ack Macaque unfastened his straps and pulled his aviator goggles down over his eyes.

"We're nearly over the target," he said to Mindy. "Haul ass as soon as we're clear. They'll scramble everything they have to intercept you, so get low and stay fast."

Morris flipped a salute. He returned it with a hairy hand, then moved through the connecting door, into the rear compartment.

The paratroopers sat in two ranks, facing each other down the length of the plane. As one, their heads snapped in his direction. He pulled a cigar from the pocket of his flying jacket and lit up.

"Okay, dumbasses, listen here." He had to shout over the noise of the de Havilland's engines. "We're a minute from the target. Get yourselves unstrapped and line up at the hatch. I go first. The rest of you follow at two second intervals."

He scampered along the gangway to the hatch. The troops had submachine guns strapped across their chests. He had his revolvers, and a shoulder bag filled with grenades. He hooked the static line from his parachute to the rail above. When he jumped, it would pull open his 'chute as he left the plane.

"Get ready," he said.

The lights went out, and he popped the hatch.

"Geronimo!"

The air roared around him, snatching at his clothes. His cigar burned like an angry red star. He felt the snap and jolt of the 'chute opening. Then trees rushed up at him out of the darkness. He crashed through their upper branches, arms thrown up to shield his face. For a few seconds, his world became a storm of splintering twigs. Then his harness snagged on something, jerking him so hard his teeth snapped together, biting through the end of his cigar.

When his vision cleared, he found himself swinging above a darkened forest floor. The soles of his boots dangled twenty feet above the shadowed moss and leaves. He had no idea where the rest of his squad had come down. Leaves rustled in the midnight breeze. He kicked his boots off and let them fall away. He cut his way out of his harness and slithered up the canvas straps into the branches above, bayonet clamped in his teeth. If he knew anything—aside from aerial combat—it was climbing trees.

Climbing trees and killing Nazis.

German ninjas were good. They could move through a forest almost soundlessly, cross a field of wet grass without bending a single blade. But however hard they tried, they couldn't hide their smell. Even if they bathed for a week, he'd still pick up the tang of their soap. Hanging from a branch by his feet and tail, Ack-Ack Macaque lay in wait, a chrome-plated revolver in each hand.

Darkness above, darkness below. Nothing but the sound of his own rasping breath. No smells but those of dark soil and fallen leaves.

He stayed motionless for several minutes, until he was quite sure he was alone. Then he holstered the revolvers and pulled himself up into the forest canopy.

MOVING THROUGH THE branches, it took him only a few minutes to reach the edge of the woods. Beyond, the Chateau stood unlit in the moonlight, its windows shuttered and curtains drawn. Guards patrolled in the gravel drive in front of the building, where half a dozen black-painted V2 rockets rested on parked mobile launch trailers, and a tripod fighting machine towered over everything else.

The fighting machines were the latest in a long line of diabolical Nazi inventions. They stood twenty metres in height, balanced on three sturdy legs, and bestrode the countryside like giant insects, belching clouds of diesel smoke and dispensing fire and death from the artillery mounted on their thick, armoured bodies.

Ack-Ack Macaque checked the luminous hands of his wristwatch. If his squad had survived the jump, they'd be lurking in the trees nearby, awaiting his signal. Their mission was simple: destroy as much equipment as possible, and recover codebooks and operating instructions for the rockets.

Ack-Ack Macaque dropped from branch to branch, until his bare feet hit the mossy ground beneath the tree. He pulled his revolvers from their holsters and let out a screech.

In answer, the tree line lit up with small arms fire. The German guards scattered. Some shot back. He heard the *pap pap pap* of their bullets punching through the undergrowth.

"Okay," he muttered, "let's get this over with."

On all fours, he scurried in the direction of the Chateau, running directly beneath the towering tripod. Shots whined past him like angry bees. The grass felt cool beneath his palms.

At the front door, he dropped into a shoulder roll and came up with a grenade in either hand. He tossed both at the nearest V2 trailer and, while they were still in the air, whipped out his revolvers and plugged the four guards nearest to him.

A throwing star hissed past his face. He turned. Black-clad ninjas ran at him. Five or six of them, with blood-red swastikas sewn on their chests. Teeth bared, he started shooting, knowing they'd be on him before he got them all.

But then the ground bucked. A flash. A roaring blast. White heat hit him, and slammed him against the wall of the chateau.

ACK-ACK MACAQUE lay in the rubble for what seemed like a very long time. His ears rang. Everything smelled of brick dust and plaster, and scorched monkey hair. From where he lay, he could see that part of the chateau's façade had collapsed, spilling stone and broken glass onto the gravel driveway. A fire raged on one of the upper floors.

He got to his feet, miraculously unhurt, and brushed dust from his singed fur. Ten metres away, a smoking crater marked the spot where the V2 had detonated on its trailer. The other trailers had been damaged in the blast. Two had tipped over. One was on fire. The tripod fighting machine lay on its side, its body smashed amongst the trees, one insectile leg sticking upward at an awkward angle.

Ack-Ack Macaque looked around for the ninjas who'd been about to attack him. They lay twisted and dead in the wreckage of the chateau's front wall, their limbs as bent and broken as twigs, their internal organs pulverised by the blast wave from the exploding rocket.

"This isn't right," he said. He patted his chest and stomach. Not a scratch on him. No internal pain. He caught sight of something silver: his guns. He picked them up and looked around. Over the noise in his ears, he heard the sounds of fighting in the trees. The battle had moved into the forest.

"Not right at all." He frowned at the bomb crater. The blast had been enough to demolish the solid stone frontage of the old chateau, but somehow he'd emerged unscathed.

"There's no way in hell I could have survived that." The ninjas had been squashed like bugs. How had he escaped? It didn't seem fair. Why was he always the last one standing? His mind filled with images of burning planes. Over the past few months, he'd seen so many young pilots crash to their deaths; yet here he was again, with hardly a scratch on him.

Fatigue rinsed away the last of his strength. Everything seemed pointless and hollow, and all he wanted was to rest.

He had two bullets left in each revolver. Legs unsteady and ears still ringing from the explosion, he began to walk in the direction of the gunfire. As he did so, he saw a group of German guards emerge from the trees.

"Hey!" he hollered. "Over here!"

They turned towards him and opened fire. He didn't even try to dodge. He was too tired. He kept walking as their shots peppered the ground around his feet, kicking up mud and gravel. He heard bullets whine past, inches from his face; he felt the wind of their passing, yet nothing hit him. The Germans emptied their weapons, and then lowered them. They didn't seem to know what to do. Some of them started to reload.

Ack-Ack Macaque's fists were clenched around the butts of his Colts. His lips were drawn back to show his fangs.

"Is that it?" he demanded. His tail thrashed back and forth. "Is that the best you've got?"

The Germans began to back away. Ack-Ack Macaque screeched at them. His heart rattled in his chest. All the exhaustion and fear bubbled up inside him, like water boiling in a pan. He hadn't slept in such a long, long time.

"Come on! Why won't you kill me too? Look at me, I'm standing right here!" He was almost upon them now, yet none of them raised a weapon. Even the ones who'd reloaded seemed nonplussed and unsure what to do. He hissed at them. He beat his chest with his forearms, challenging them. Two of them turned and fled. The rest stood there wide-eyed, guns drooping.

He wanted to fling his own shit at them. Rub it in their gormless faces.

"Why's it always me?" He sprang at the nearest, and they crashed back together, into the grass. The man struggled, but Ack-Ack Macaque shook him by the lapels of his tunic.

"Why won't you kill me?" he screeched, canines centimetres from the man's face. "*Why can't I die?*"

TECHSNARK
BLOGGING WITH ATTITUDE

Everybody Loves The Monkey

Posted: 24/11/2059 – 5:00pm GMT

| Share |

With dozens of major new titles released every month, the game world thrives on novelty. How then, given that it's been a full twelve months since the launch of Céleste's flagship product *Ack-Ack Macaque*, can the title still be the number one most popular game on the immersive entertainment market? I mean, that's not how it works, right?

Wrong.

The reasons for *Ack-Ack Macaque*'s phenomenal success are fourfold:

First off, they've managed to keep interest high by strictly limiting the number of players allowed in-game at any one time. New players can't join until old ones are killed off or quit. With only 10,000 places up for grabs, and an estimated world gaming population of around 30 million, this lends the game a certain exclusivity.

Secondly, the whole one-life deal means players see the game as the ultimate test of their abilities. In the world of *Ack-Ack Macaque*, just like in real life, there are no second chances, and the challenge is to survive as long as possible. Players who don't take the game seriously get wasted early, and they don't get to come back. Once you're out of the game, you're out for good. Those who've put a lot of time and effort into developing their characters have a vested interest in keeping them alive.

Thirdly, the whole social media side of the game makes it more than just a shoot-em-up. In between missions, players get to hang out together. They can talk to their friends, trade planes and equipment, and form alliances. There's even an online dating agency operating entirely within the game's virtual world.

And lastly, there's the immersive experience itself, which is still light years ahead of its nearest rivals. The world of *Ack-Ack Macaque* has been so faithfully rendered that it's sometimes hard to distinguish it from reality. It's like being transported to another planet. The sun feels warm on your face and the food tastes the way food should. When you touch the other players, they feel solid and human. A punch feels like a punch, a kiss feels like a kiss. And a bullet to the chest feels like a bullet to the chest.

Put these things together, and it's not hard to see why the game's become such a monster. For a few hundred bucks, you can buy yourself a whole new life.

And let's not forget the appeal of the iconic monkey himself. I really have to take my hat off to Céleste for creating such a believable character. Truly a masterpiece of artificial intelligence and CGI animation, he neither acts nor talks like a computer. In fact, you could almost believe he was a real monkey.

A year after he first appeared on our gaming screens, you can now see his face everywhere, from lunch boxes, screensavers and t-shirts to plush toys and action figures. His trademark screech became last year's highest-selling ringtone, and millions of viewers continue to re-watch his most famous exploits on YouTube. Last Halloween, half the kids in my neighbourhood were dressed as him.

And therein lies the appeal of this game. Simply put, everybody loves the monkey. Long may he continue to fly.

Ack-Ack Macaque is available on SincPad, TuringBox, and Playcube 180. A PC version is also in development.

Read more | Like | Comment | Share

CHAPTER SIX
ARMED AND HUMOURLESS

MEROVECH, JULIE AND Frank climbed down from the back of the van. They were parked on a service road in an industrial park north of Paris, on the edge of the Céleste Technologies campus. Squalls of rain blew across the sculptured lawns. Merovech lifted the bottom of his ski mask and filled his lungs with wet night air. He could feel the coldness of it in his chest, and it felt good after the suffocating fug of the smoke-filled van. The driver and his companion were already at work on the security fence with an oxyacetylene cutting torch. The blue flame roared. Hot metal hissed when the rain touched it.

Merovech blinked away afterimages. He looked around.

"Is that a camera?" He pointed to a black globe atop a metal pole a few metres along the fence.

Frank flicked a dismissive hand.

"*C'est cassé.*"

"How do you know?"

Frank opened his coat to reveal the butt of an airgun tucked into his belt. "Because we broke it."

The cutting torch flicked off, and a circle of security fence fell inward, onto the lawn. The two men with the torch stepped back, allowing Frank to duck through the hole.

"*Allez!*"

Bent double, pendant swinging, Frank ran across the lawn, towards an ornamental hedge. Julie ducked towards the fence, ready to follow, but Merovech caught her arm.

"Are you sure you want to do this?"

Behind her ski mask, her pupils were dilated.

"We must."

She slipped through the fence, and was gone.

Merovech looked back, down the empty road, in the direction of the city. He could leave now. He could walk away, use his phone to summon his bodyguards, and be back in his rooms at the University, warm and safe, within the hour.

But what would happen to Julie?

He knew the Céleste labs well. At his mother's insistence, he'd endured exhaustive and uncomfortable health checks at the facility each and every month for the past ten years. He'd had gene tweaks to edit out some of his family's less desirable traits; corneal grafts to improve his eyesight; and a whole barrage of hormones, vitamins and other supplements designed to boost his mental and physical wellbeing. As a result, he knew the layout of the building by heart, and he also knew how tight the security was. Frank and Julie didn't have a hope. Without him, they couldn't achieve their objective, and would both likely end up in jail, if they didn't first attract the lethal ire of the armed and humourless security bots.

Although he couldn't give a toss about Frank, he didn't want to see Julie throwing her life away over some obscure philosophical point. They might have only known each other for a few short weeks, but he liked her.

He realised the driver and his mate were looking at him impatiently. The driver jerked a thumb at the hole.

"*Et toi?*"

Merovech bristled. He wasn't used to be being spoken to so impolitely. He reached up and peeled off his mask.

"Get stuffed."

He ducked through the hole. He smelled wet earth. The rain pricked his cheeks. The wind ruffled his hair, but it was nothing compared to the squalling gales of the Falklands.

Okay, he thought, enough messing around. *Time to step in.*

If he wanted to annoy the Duchess and keep Julie out of harm's way, he'd have to take charge. Standing tall, he strode over to the hedge where Frank and Julie sheltered.

"Get up," he said.

They looked up at him.

Julie said, "Your mask—"

"It doesn't matter." He turned to Frank. "If we're going to do this, let's do it properly. No more crawling around in the mud."

Frank climbed to his feet. He wiped the dirt from his hands with a lip curl of disgust.

"What did you have in mind, *Anglais?*"

The rain ran its cold fingertips down Merovech's face.

"I can get you inside, but you'll have to follow me and do exactly as I say."

* * *

THE LABORATORY BUILDING'S main entrance was quiet. The lights were on, but that was only because they were always on. No people were around. A single security bot sat before the smoked glass doors. Shaped like a fat tyre lying on its side, its upper surfaces bristled with an array of lethal and non-lethal weaponry. A single turbofan filled the hole in the centre of its body. Direction and orientation were controlled by smaller fans spaced around its circumference. Right now, it idled a metre or so above the path's slick flagstones; but Merovech knew it could move with astonishing speed if provoked.

As he marched towards it—with Julie and Frank hurrying to keep up with him—the bot's fan whispered into a higher gear. Several gun barrels swivelled in his direction, and a red laser stabbed out once, twice, and thrice. Their retinas had been scanned.

"Welcome, Prince Merovech." The bot's voice was an uneven jumble of pre-recorded syllables sequenced together to make words. The machine had neither intelligence or self-awareness, its behaviour simply the result of algorithms and pre-programmed responses.

"Good evening." Merovech was conscious that every word and gesture he made would be recorded. "My friends here don't have security clearance, but I am taking them into the building. Is that okay?"

The bot's weaponry twitched uncertainly. The fan noise increased in pitch. The machine seemed to be having difficulty.

"Weapon detected." The main cannon turned toward Frank. Range finders clicked. A red dot appeared on his chest.

Frank's coat fell open, revealing the airgun tucked into his belt. Three more red dots appeared, and he let out a whimper.

Merovech suppressed a smile. He glanced at Julie.

Do something, she mouthed.

He sighed. As tempting as it would be to let the security bot shred Frank, he couldn't let it happen. Not in front of Julie. Using a tone of voice learned on the parade ground, he barked: "Override code, alpha two niner Buckingham."

For a second, nothing happened. Frank looked on the verge of wetting himself. Then the bot's motor whined away to silence and its gun barrels drooped.

"Proceed," it said.

Frank let out a held breath.

"*Putain.*"

Merovech turned away. Julie was looking at him open-mouthed. The rain had plastered her hair to the sides of her face.

"What was that?" she asked. "What did you just *do?*"

Merovech ignored her. Instead of replying, he led them through the smoked glass doors into the main foyer area. They had to jog to keep up with him. During the day, the foyer would be a bustle of activity, but right now the reception desks were deserted and the corridors were silent, save for the distant hum of an automated vacuum cleaner, off somewhere cleaning an office.

Merovech strode straight over to the elevators. Usually, for his health checks, he rode up to the private ward on the seventh floor—the same ward to which his father had been brought last year following the terrorist attack on the Champs-Elysées. Right now, though, he was going to take them to the computer labs on the fifth. If they were going to find an enslaved AI anywhere, he was sure they'd find it there. They loaded in and he thumbed the button. The walls of the elevator were mirrored. In the harsh blue light from the overhead strips, Julie and Frank's reflections were pale, grubby and scared.

"Okay," Merovech said. "I've brought you inside. What happens next?"

From his pocket, Frank pulled a gelware memory stick. His hands were still shaking.

"We locate the AI and download it onto this. Then we take it somewhere where it'll be safe from exploitation."

"And where's that?"

"A server farm." He looked Merovech nervously up and down. "Probably best you do not know exactly where."

The overhead light caught his pendant. A glint of glass. Merovech frowned. He reached out and took hold of it.

"What's this?"

Frank tried to pull away but a sharp tug stopped him.

"Leave it alone."

Another jerk and the chain snapped. Merovech held the pendant in his palm, where it nestled black and smooth, like a pebble, with an inlaid pinprick lens.

"A life-logger? You brought a life-logger on an illegal break-in?"

Frank pulled himself up defiantly.

"We are striking a blow for freedom. We have a duty to record—"

"What about her?" Merovech jabbed a thumb at Julie. "Did you think about her at all?"

Frank shrugged.

"We had masks..."

Merovech wanted to hit him. Instead, he looked down at the object in his hand. A life-logger recorded its wearer's GPS coordinates, body temperature and heart rate, as well as everything it saw through its little camera and heard via its microphone.

"Is this live now or record only?"

Frank rubbed his lower lip with the back of his hand.

"Live. Ten minute delay."

That meant the pictures from the device were being automatically uploaded to the Internet. Merovech swore under his breath.

"How do you turn it off?"

"You cannot. Now please be careful with it. Those things are expensive."

The elevator doors pinged open and they stepped out into a corridor. Merovech dropped the pendant onto the floor and ground it under the sole of his shoe. After a couple of twists, he felt the plastic casing crack and splinter.

"Hey!" Frank's face flushed. "You owe me for that."

Merovech pushed him up against the wall, and pulled the airgun from his belt. Then he stepped back and tossed it into a waste paper bin. He pointed back into the elevator.

"I saved your life down there. Do you understand that? I saved your life. I think that makes us even, don't you?"

He took a deep, calming breath. Then he checked his watch.

"Okay, we've got ten minutes. Whatever you're going to do, you'd better do it fast."

Frank looked surprised.

"You're still helping us? But why?"

Merovech shrugged.

"My reasons are my own, and none of your business. I'll help you get into the server room, and I'll guide you back to the fence afterwards." He looked at Julie. "After that, you're on your own."

THEY LEFT JULIE in the first office they came to. She slipped behind the desk and began tapping at the computer keyboard.

"Go ahead," she said. "I'll see what I can do from here."

Wordlessly, Merovech and Frank continued along the corridor, past other empty offices and storerooms, until they came to a glass door decorated with the Ack-Ack Macaque game logo: a stylised art deco rendition of the monkey's face, eye patch and all, assembled from blue geometric triangles.

Frank said, "I guess this must be the place."

Merovech checked his watch. Even without the life-logger, his deactivation of the sentry bot would have been flagged somewhere. A response team was almost certainly on its way. The only question was whether he could get Julie clear of the building before the heat came down. He wasn't worried for himself. After all, he was nineteen years old, and next in line to the throne. The worst he could expect was a bollocking from his mother.

"Let's make this quick." He pushed through the door and found himself standing in a white-floored laboratory that smelled of sweat, shit and strong disinfectant.

Frank flapped a hand in front of his nose.

"Phew!"

A couch stood in the centre of the room, surrounded by medical apparatus: monitors, drips, and the like. A figure lay recumbent, with its back to them.

Frank said, "What the hell is this? It smells like a zoo in here. Where are the servers?"

Merovech took a step forward. He looked at the arm lolling over the side of the couch: thin and long, and covered in chestnut hair. He walked around to the front. The prone figure had broad shoulders, long arms and short legs. Wires from various machines had been plugged into jacks set into the hair on top of its bulging scalp. Several drips had been set up around the figure, and tubes of clear liquid ran from bags into intravenous ports on its arms. Half a dozen electrodes and other sensor patches were stuck at various points on its shaggy torso, and a leather eye patch covered its left eye.

Merovech looked up at Frank, who had his arms folded across his chest as if cold.

"I think we've found your monkey."

Frank took a step closer, eyes wide and nervous. He curled his lip.

"What the hell is this?"

Merovech looked down at the creature where it lolled against the straps holding it in place. Its good eye was closed, and a silver line of drool hung from the corner of its mouth. He pointed to the cables protruding from jacks in the creature's skull.

"This thing must be wired straight into the game."

Frank gave him a blank look. Merovech picked a syringe from a kidney dish on a side table. He thought of his own experiences in the clinic on the seventh floor, and the stultifying ambassadorial reception he'd attended earlier that evening. He sympathised with the creature. He knew what it was to be held in place, trapped by forces you were powerless to resist, and compelled to play a part chosen for you by somebody else.

He bent close. The animal smelled sourly of sweat, stale piss and dirty hair. The bulges beneath the skin of its skull were most likely gelware processors.

"They've taken a monkey and made it intelligent by adding extra brainpower." He looked up as Julie pushed through the door, a sheaf of computer printout in her hand. "The question is, what are we going to do about it?"

Frank threw up his hands.

"'Do about it?' We do nothing, of course! I did not come here for a monkey!"

Merovech shot him a glare.

"I wasn't talking to you." Slowly, he reached out and brushed the animal's fur. He'd been expecting the hairs to be coarse, but they were much softer than he'd imagined.

"You came here wanting to free a thinking being," he said to Julie. "Well, I think I've you found one."

BREAKING NEWS

From *The New York Times*, online edition:

Beijing Sends Tough Message as Hong Kong Military Exercise Provokes Hostility

23 NOVEMBER, 2059 – As talks to decide the future sovereignty of Hong Kong flounder, Beijing demands an end to Franco-British naval exercises in the South China Sea.

Hong Kong has been under the control of the United Kingdom since it was ceded to the British at the end of the First Opium War in 1841. Since then, it has become one of the world's most important centres of trade.

Talks to return the area to Chinese control began in 1995 but were abandoned in 1997 when an agreement could not be reached.

This latest round of talks began following the Chinese invasion of Taiwan in 2045, and has been seen by most commentators as a last ditch attempt by both London and Beijing to resolve the situation without conflict.

Now that the talks have apparently failed, tensions in the area are at breaking point.

This morning, the Chinese government condemned an ongoing exercise by the combined Franco-British navy as "naked provocation."

So far, there has been no official response from London, but it is believed that the Prime Minister has cut short his visit to Berlin, and will address the House of Commons later this evening.

As the crisis mounts, China is rumoured to be planning its own exercise in the area on Monday.

Read more | Like | Comment | Share

Related Stories

Indian and Pakistani troops clash in disputed border region

Chinese taikonauts complete successful Moon orbit

Where's the monkey? Online gamers complain

Dutch neurologist reported missing

Mexico in "secret talks" to join United States?

Céleste Tech readies "light sail" probe for flight to Mars

New find brings total number of potentially habitable exoplanets to 7

Police play down talk of brain-stealing serial killer after another body discovered in London

CHAPTER SEVEN
STARS LIKE GLITTER

THE HELICOPTER'S ENGINE failed on a routine ship-to-ship transfer. Strapped into a chair beside the Prince, Victoria felt her stomach lurch as the cabin seemed to surge upwards.

She was the only journalist on the flight, and she'd fought hard to be there, to get exclusive coverage of the final days of Merovech's year-long National Service. Now, warning lights flashed and sirens wailed. The cabin tipped sideways and down, and her stomach flipped again. Beside her, the Prince pressed his face to the window.

"We're still over the water." He sounded more startled than scared.

She grabbed his sleeve.

"What do we do?"

He gave her a blank look. He was only eighteen years old, and plainly as scared as she was.

The pilot called: "Crash positions! Brace! Brace!" Then the water came up and slapped them. The impact threw Victoria against her straps so hard she bit her tongue. She heard shouts and screams, and the freight-train roar of seawater gushing into the cabin.

They were sinking.

Her nostrils filled with the smell of brine, and she recalled the safety briefings she'd endured, knowing that even if she managed to escape the stricken craft, she'd be unlikely to survive for more than a few minutes in the freezing waters of the South Atlantic. In a panic, she scrabbled at her harness.

Beside her, the Prince unclipped himself and leant over to help. He pulled her out of her seat. Then other hands grabbed him and bundled him away, towards the open hatch.

The cabin heaved again, caught on the swell. The walls creaked. Victoria lost her footing and fell across the aisle. The fall seemed to take forever. She saw dark water sloshing through the cabin and, in a single instant of freezing clarity, knew her time had come.

And then, pressing up at the window, she saw a face! A mean face with a cruel smile and the flat dead eyes of a shark. The Smiling Man had found her! He'd killed Detective Malhotra, and now he'd come for her. Here, in the South Atlantic, a year ago.

Time unfroze. Limp as a ragdoll, she plunged toward the windows on the opposite wall. Her head smacked the jagged edge of an open equipment locker and—

VICTORIA COUGHED HERSELF awake, spluttering up from the depths of a cold, dark sea. Her lips were dry and cracked, and her tongue lay in her mouth like an old leather bookmark. The air lay heavy with disinfectant and air freshener. Hospital smells.

Non, c'est pas vrai, pas encore. Not again.

She'd been dreaming about the helicopter crash: her brush with death in the South Atlantic, over a year ago. Either the head injury or the hypothermia would have killed her, had the copter not come down within metres of the aircraft carrier that it had been heading for.

And the Smiling Man. Oh God, the Smiling Man. How had he wormed his way into her dream? And what had he done to her? She remembered his footsteps on the wooden stairs. The scrape of the knife along the wall. Malhotra. All that blood...

Somebody cleared their throat.

"Victoria?"

She opened her eyes and stiffened. A figure stood at the foot of her bed, hands folded, hair white and brows black. Gold braid festooned a long tunic.

"Commodore?"

"I am here, my dear." He moved closer and took her hand, his fingers rough to the touch, but nevertheless warm and comforting. "How are you feeling?"

She tried to sit up and winced in pain.

"What happened to me?"

"You were attacked." Still holding her hand, the Commodore perched a hip on the edge of the bed. With his free hand, he adjusted the cutlass hanging from his belt. "But you're back on the *Tereshkova* now. You're safe."

"Attacked?" With her free hand, she reached back and found a thick wad of bandage, and stubble where she'd expected hair.

"Yes. Your implants sent an emergency signal to Céleste. I am listed as your next of kin, so they called me. They told me you were dead, but I sent a chopper anyway. I thought it would be quicker than an ambulance, and it was. We got to you in less than ten minutes."

He rose and walked over to the window. From where she lay, Victoria could see dark clouds edged with embers of sunset. She moved her hand forward, over her shaven scalp.

"My hair?" She was afraid to ask. She could feel the memory of the attack in her neural processor, waiting to be accessed, but couldn't bring herself to open it. The flashes that leaked through were bad enough; she didn't need to relive the whole thing in high definition.

The Commodore cleared his throat.

"They took your soul-catcher. We had to operate quickly to stem the bleeding." He gestured at his own thinning white hair. "We didn't have time to spare, so we just shaved it all off, I'm afraid. The surgeon patched you up as best he could, but you're going to be weak for a while." He lowered his hand. "And you're going to have to wear a collar to support your head, until the muscles heal. That means plenty of rest, and no stick fighting."

Victoria touched the bandage at the back of her head.

"Why aren't I dead?"

The old man smoothed his moustache with finger and thumb, moved his weight from one polished boot to the other.

"Whoever did this, they must have been in a hurry. They went for the catcher and tore it out by the root. They left you for dead." His fists clenched and unclenched. She could see he was upset. If her soul-catcher had been attached to living, organic tissue, its removal would have been fatal. The haemorrhages alone would have killed her. For the second time in a year, it seemed her life had been saved by the gelware in her cranium.

"How bad is it?"

The Commodore shook his head regretfully.

"He punched a hole in the base of your skull with a knife. Luckily for you, it's slightly off-centre, just behind and below your left ear, so your spinal column's intact. The surgeon replaced the missing bone fragments and stapled the wound. It should heal, eventually."

Victoria's lips were dry. She ran her tongue over them.

"This isn't the first time I've had my head cut open."

The Commodore checked his wristwatch, a large antique timepiece covered in studs and dials. Standing by the window, with his white hair and crisply ironed uniform, the old rogue still cut quite a dash. For the umpteenth time, she tried to guess his age, and failed, settling for somewhere between sixty and seventy years old.

Although he was her godfather, she knew little of him, aside from the fact that in his time he'd been both a Russian air force officer and a cosmonaut, and that he'd been asked to be her godfather because he'd once saved her mother from a charging rhinoceros. There were many rumours about him—that he used to work for the KGB; that he'd won the *Tereshkova* in a card game in St. Petersburg—but few hard facts.

"The police want a statement, when you're ready."

"The police?"

He made shushing motions with his hands.

"There's no hurry. They can wait." The skyliner was autonomous under international law, and the Metropolitan Police had no jurisdiction.

Victoria closed her eyes. She didn't have the energy to keep them open. She thought of the poor, dead detective in the stairwell, and the room seemed to spin around her.

"I don't feel so good."

The Commodore pulled the sheet up to her chin.

"Try to rest. The anaesthetic will make you groggy. You have been slipping in and out for half an hour or so. We have already had this conversation twice."

She smiled despite herself.

"What do the police think happened?"

She heard the Commodore shuffle his boots on the deck.

"They think the detective's killer took your soul-catcher in order to cover his tracks."

Victoria twitched her head. The movement brought a fresh flare of pain.

"No, that's not what happened." The drugs were pulling at her again. Her arms and legs felt heavy, as if weighed down by sodden clothes, and she felt herself slipping back beneath the waves, sucked down by the groaning silhouette of the sinking chopper.

The Commodore gave her a gentle pat on the shoulder.

"Shhh." His voice seemed to come from a great distance. "Rest now. Tell me all about it when you are feeling stronger."

VICTORIA SLEPT FOR a time. She didn't know how long. When she woke again, the lights in the sickbay were low. Outside, the sky had darkened and the clouds cleared. She could see a few stars and, on the underside of the skyliner's hull, the warm red smoulder of a navigation light.

She tried to assess her internal damage. According to the clock readout in the corner of her vision, two days had passed since the attack. She hadn't felt it. Her biological clock had been disrupted by anaesthetic and shock. In addition to the pain at the back of her head, her throat felt bruised and swollen, and there were tender spots on her back and chest.

She found it galling to be back in a hospital bed, and humiliating to have been taken down so easily, especially after all her quarterstaff training. The hallway had been too narrow for her to swing her stick properly, and the Smiling Man had possessed a strength that belied his thin frame.

But it wasn't his strength or his speed that bothered her most. The thought making her skin crawl was that he'd known her *name*. This hadn't been a random attack; he'd known who she was, and he'd been there specifically to kill her.

But why?

She didn't know him. As far as she knew, she'd never seen him before. The only thought she had that made any sense was that the attack was linked to Paul's murder. But how?

Thinking of Paul, she screwed her eyes tight and pictured her internal file index. Had he survived? She scanned down the list of folders until she found the one she'd created to house his digital back-up. With relief, she saw that it was intact, and still active.

Thank God.

Holding her breath, she accessed the icon, and Paul's image swam into view before her, Hawaiian shirt, white coat and all. From this angle, he seemed to be pasted onto the sickbay's ceiling, from which vantage he scowled down at her.

"Where the hell have you been?"

"Excuse me?"

He hugged himself, hands on bare elbows, and she saw the fear underlying his anger.

"I thought you were dead." He put his head on one side and looked around, absently fingering his beard. "Why are we in hospital? What happened?"

Victoria clenched her fists, resisting the urge to touch her scalp.

"I lost my soul-catcher."

"Shit." He put a comforting hand out to her, then seemed to realise what he was doing, and dropped it. "Where are we?"

"Back on the skyliner."

"Are you going to be okay?"

"I don't know." She tried to shift position in the bed. The sheets were lank and coarse around her. "I think so. Probably."

Paul rubbed his chin.

"When that smiling guy burst in, I thought we were toast."

Victoria didn't reply. She'd been terrified. Even now, she shied away from the memory. Of course, she'd been beaten up before, in pursuit of stories. It was a professional hazard of journalism. But this time it was different. Nobody had ever tried to kill her before. Things had never been that personal.

True, she'd almost died when that Navy helicopter fell into the Atlantic; but that had been a malfunction, an accident. It was quite another thing to feel a man's hands around your windpipe, deliberately choking the life out of you; to have a knife driven into the skin at the back of your neck.

And yet...

Her investigative instincts clamoured for attention. There was a bigger story here, she could feel it.

Paul frowned at her expression.

"What is it?"

With her head still resting on her pillow, Victoria laced her fingers together and looked up at the ceiling.

"Paul, I need to ask you about your sex life."

"My *what?*"

"Your sex life. The police think you may have known your killer."

"And just because I'm bi, that means it has to be someone I'm sleeping with?"

"Were you bringing men back to the flat?"

"No."

"But since the separation—"

"No."

"You mean you've never—"

"No!"

A silence grew between them. Finally, Victoria said, "You were looking through my eyes when I got attacked. Did you get a good look at the man who did it? Did you recognise him?"

Paul gave his head an angry shake.

"Not my type, sweetheart." He wagged a finger at her. "But I'll tell you this for nothing. Whoever he is, he's got your soul."

CHAPTER EIGHT
CAFFEINE

PRINCE MEROVECH, HEIR to the British throne, sat hunched on bare floorboards in the downstairs back room of a farmhouse somewhere south of Louviers, out where the fields were endlessly flat and the roads ran straight for miles on end; where metal water towers bestrode the landscape like Martian war machines, and bare trees stood in lines against the horizon. He still wore the same jeans, trainers and faded red hoodie that he'd worn to meet Julie in the café, although now his trainers and the cuffs of his jeans were spattered with mud, and the hoodie held the lingering whiff of Frank's cigarettes. His elbows were resting on his knees and he held the baseball cap in his hands, turning it absently, worrying the rim with his fingers. A manila folder lay on the floor beside him.

The room was bare, its only concession to furniture being an old mattress, which the monkey lay on, curled in the folds of an unzipped sleeping bag. From where he sat by the door, Merovech watched the animal twitch and moan in its sleep.

The farmhouse belonged to Julie's uncle, but he was away, and not expected back until the day after next.

The printed documents in the manila folder were the ones Julie had printed from the Céleste servers. Merovech hadn't read them yet. He'd been awake for close to twenty-four hours, and now he had a headache, and all he wanted was to rest. He leaned his head back against the whitewashed plaster wall and closed his eyes. Through the closed door, he could hear Julie and Frank arguing in the kitchen. They were both speaking English, which he suspected was for his benefit. They wanted to be overheard.

Frank said, "This is stupid. It's just an animal. It needs a vet."

Julie spluttered indignantly.

"So, now I am stupid, am I?"

"Well, if you are so clever, can you tell me what the hell we are going to do with it? We do not even know what it eats. Or if it is dangerous."

"The poor thing has been drugged. It needs our help."

"Bullshit. This isn't about the monkey. I know you, Julie. This is all about you getting cosy with *le petit prince anglais*."

Merovech heard wooden chair legs scrape on flagstones kitchen floor.

"You leave him out of it."

Frank laughed. "You're the one who invited him."

Julie's hand slapped the tabletop.

"We would never have got in and out of that place without him."

Frank laughed. "Yeah, and a fat lot of good it has done us. Look around you. We're fugitives. *Des fugitifs avec ce crétin de singe.*"

"You are so full of shit, Frank. All that *merde* you've been feeding me."

"I meant what I said."

"No, you did not! It was all talk. We finally find an artificial intelligence, and you want nothing to do with it."

"That thing is not an AI."

"Of course it is. Just because it is not built of chips and wire, that does not mean—"

"*Je m'en fous.*"

"Frank!"

"Fuck off."

A glass smashed.

"*Fif!*"

"*Salope!*"

Frank stormed out. Merovech heard the front door slam behind him.

When I get out of here, he thought, *I'm going to have him thrown into jail.* The thought brought the barest flicker of a smile. He took a deep breath in through his nose and exhaled slowly, trying to relax. He needed to sleep. He knew his security people would be going berserk but, right now, he was too tired to care. He lay down on the hard floor and pulled the hoodie up to cover his head. He would have a nap, then decide what to do about Julie and the monkey.

He had just closed his eyes when he heard Julie's footsteps clumping in his direction, and the back room door swung open on irritable hinges.

"How's our patient?"

Merovech sighed. He looked up at her, then across at the monkey.

"He's resting."

"You heard the argument?"

"I couldn't really miss it."

Julie fiddled with the door handle. "I am sorry. Frank can be a little highly-strung."

"Frank's a pillock."

She smiled.

"Would you like some coffee?"

Merovech hauled himself stiffly to his feet, resigning himself to wakefulness.

"Yes, please. That would be nice."

As he moved toward the door, Julie bent and retrieved the manila folder he'd left on the floor.

"Have you read this yet?"

"No."

She frowned, and pushed it into his hands.

"Then I really think you should."

She dragged him into the kitchen and made him sit him at the table. Heat came from logs crackling in the fireplace. Utensils hung from nails in the blackened wooden mantel. Julie busied herself filling a pan with water while he slid the A4 sheets of paper from the folder.

"What's this all about?"

She hooked the pan over the fire, and spooned instant coffee granules into a tin mug. The spoon clanked on the rim.

"Just read it."

Merovech scanned the dense blocks of text. The air had the sweet, sticky tang of burning pine. His eyes watered with exhaustion.

"Have you read it?"

Sap popped in the fire. Julie laid the spoon on the counter. She leaned on her elbows, as if for support. Even rumpled and tired, she looked beautiful.

"*Oui.*"

"Then why don't you give me the gist?"

She picked at the corner of a fingernail. Beyond the half-open shutters of the window, a wet dawn had begun to break.

"I cannot, I am sorry." Her eyes glittered.

Concerned, Merovech leaned forward.

"What's the matter? What is it?" He reached for her hand, but she stepped back.

"This will not be easy to hear," she said. "And I should not be the one to tell you."

"Tell me what?"

"About your mother."

"My mother?" Merovech pushed himself up, out of the chair. Water bubbled in the pan over the fireplace. "*What* about my mother?"

Julie swallowed, looking petrified.

"I did a search on the Céleste severs. I was looking for information on their AI projects. And I found you."

"Me?"

She looked at the floor.

"The files were encrypted, but easy to access from within the system."

"And what did they say?"

She sniffed.

"You are not what you think you are, Merovech. You are not even—" She turned away.

"Not even what?"

She stifled a sob.

"I am sorry, I cannot do this." She ran to the wall and flung aside a curtain, revealing a sagging wooden staircase. Merovech listened to her footsteps thump up it and onto the first floor landing. He heard a door slam.

Alone, he looked around. Steam rose from the boiling pan of water. Rain spots dappled the window. He still held the papers in his hand. He dropped them onto the table as if they might bite him, and rubbed his forehead with thumb and index finger.

He'd been in and out of the Céleste facility for years. Of course they had a file on him; that was no surprise. But why had it upset Julie so badly? For a moment, he entertained the idea of a fatal disease. Could his last batch of tests have turned up a tumour, or other anomaly, which the doctors had somehow neglected to mention?

His eyes fell on the tin mug into which Julie had spooned the coffee granules. Longing for a drink, he crossed to the fireplace and tried to lift the pan of boiling water.

"Ow! Damn!"

The pan hit the floor with a metallic crash. Water burst over the flagstones. Merovech sucked his fingers and cursed his stupidity. Wrapped up in thought, it hadn't occurred to him to use the cloth that hung beside the grate.

After a moment, he pulled his fingers from his lips and blew on them. They were red and stinging, but not seriously hurt. Ruefully, he reached for the cloth. The pan had landed on its side, and a little water remained: perhaps enough for half a cup. He picked it up and poured it into the mug of granules that Julie had left. The fridge was empty of cream, so he gave the coffee a perfunctory stir, rattling the spoon against the mug's tin sides, and was about to lift it to his lips when he became aware of another presence in the room. He turned his head to the back room door and stiffened.

"Who are you?" Ack-Ack Macaque stood in the doorway, scratching his balls. His solitary eye looked yellow and bloodshot, and his fur had bald patches where the electrodes had been removed. He smacked his lips together and sniffed the air. "Is that coffee?"

Merovech looked down at the half-empty mug in his hand.

"Um, yes."

He hadn't expected the monkey to speak. But of course it could. He'd heard it talking in the clip of the game he'd been shown in the café.

The animal shuffled over and snaked the cup from him. He huffed the steam into his cavernous nostrils, and sighed; then tipped the rim to his lips with a noisy slurp.

"Ah, that's the stuff." He drew the back of his hand across his mouth and ran a pink, human-looking tongue over his pointed white incisors. Then he fixed Merovech with his one good eye.

"Now," he said gruffly, "who the hell are you, where the fuck are we, and how did I get here?"

CHAPTER NINE
IMAGINARY FLOOR

FROM THE WINDOW of her cabin on the *Tereshkova*, seven hundred feet above the rain-drenched asphalt of Heathrow's main cargo terminal, Victoria Valois watched a sullen dawn break over West London. She had wrapped herself in her thick army surplus coat, and pushed her feet into her sturdiest pair of boots. She wore a turtle neck sweater to hide the tight, elasticised collar the ship's surgeon had given her to support and protect the damaged muscles in the back of her neck; and a black, Russian style hat to hide her shorn and stapled scalp.

"I want it back," she said.

Behind her, the Commodore cleared his throat.

"I still do not think this course of action is wise."

"Fuck wise," she snapped. "You've seen the news reports the same as I have. Three more killings in the last two days. All with knives, and all targeting the victim's brain and soul-catcher. And I've got the inside scoop. I know what the killer looks like."

"But the police—"

Victoria turned to face him. The cabin felt crowded with the two of them in it. It was an economical space, with bunks built into the wall, a small metal sink and a fold-down writing table. Victoria slept on the upper bunk and used the lower one for storage.

"Whoever that *bâtard* is, he's got my soul. Paul's too. Lord knows what he's doing with them." As a journalist, she'd heard rumours of secret military interrogation programs for the souls of captured soldiers; she'd spoken to gang members who dealt in illegally obtained back-ups, selling them on abroad as virtual slaves, put to work in electronic brothels or gold farms, or made to fight in gladiatorial arenas.

The Commodore raised his palm.

"Yes. I know." A shadow crossed his face. "Believe me, I know. All I'm saying is that I do not think it safe for you to attend the funeral. Whoever this killer is, he will be annoyed you survived, and he will not want you to identify him."

Victoria gave her head a small shake, and winced and the pain.

"It's Paul's funeral," she said. "I'm not going to miss it for anything."

In the corner of her eye, Paul's image waved a virtual hand.

"What do you want?"

He put his hands together, fingertips touching his bristly chin.

"First of all, thanks. For saying you'll go the funeral. I mean, I've got no one else. Literally. So, I appreciate it." He shuffled his baseball boots on an imaginary floor. "But secondly, I agree with the Commodore. You can't go, it's way too dangerous."

Victoria's arms were across her chest.

"It's not your decision."

"But it is my funeral."

"So?"

He cast around, avoiding her gaze. "So, I can un-invite you if I want to."

Victoria laughed despite herself.

"Shut up," she said, as kindly as she could.

The Commodore's bushy white brows frowned at her.

"To whom exactly are you talking?"

"No-one." With a mental command, she silenced Paul and pushed his image to the far edge of her visual field.

"I'm going to the funeral," she said as firmly as she could, addressing both the old man and the digital ghost, "and that's all there is to it."

She saw Paul throw his hands up in disgust. In the real world, the Commodore wrapped his gnarled fingers around the pommel of the cutlass at his waist.

"Well, at least take one of my stewards. You need an armed bodyguard."

"No. Thank you, but no. I appreciate the offer, but I don't want to scare him off. I want to draw him out."

She reached down and pulled an old Tupperware sandwich box from the bags and suitcases piled on the lower bunk. Inside, wrapped in an oily hand towel, lay a replacement for the retractable carbon fibre quarterstaff she'd lost at Paul's apartment. She took it out and held it before him, weighing it in the palm of her hand.

"Besides, I'll have this."

The Commodore huffed.

"You are in no condition to fight, young lady. And besides, you had one of those before, and it didn't do you much good."

Victoria felt her cheeks redden. Her fingers tightened around the metal shaft.

"Next time will be different."

* * *

AN HOUR LATER, despite the protestations of both the Commodore and the *Tereshkova*'s chief surgeon, Victoria took a helicopter from the pad atop the skyliner's central hull. The helicopter's pilot wore mirrored aviator shades and chewed gum. He took her to Battersea Park, bringing the chopper down to kiss the grass for only as long as it took her to clamber down from the cockpit. Then, as soon as she was clear, he was off again and up, peeling away across the Thames.

Victoria smoothed down the rumples in her coat. Warm sun touched her face. The air on her skin felt just crisp enough to be refreshing, and so clear it seemed to chime like a bell. Quite a contrast from the rain she remembered from her last visit. Her breath came in little drifts of vapour. She walked towards the edge of the park, hands in pockets. Despite her bravado, her neck hurt a lot more than she had been prepared to admit. The stitches were tight and sore, and the staples hurt like needles driven into her flesh.

It's my choice, she thought. Two serious head wounds in two years. I can feel like a victim, or I can feel like a survivor. It's up to me.

She took a taxi across Battersea Bridge into Chelsea, and west along the river, past the rows of houseboats moored beneath the embankment wall. Holding her head as still as possible, she watched as they drove through the brown brick terraces of Chelsea, with their black iron railings and plastic For Sale signs, to the Exhibition Centre at Earl's Court, where the driver turned right and pulled over at the kerb. The ride had only taken a few minutes. Victoria paid and climbed stiffly out, onto the pavement in front of the gates of Brompton Cemetery.

As she entered the graveyard, an Airbus whined overhead on its way to Heathrow. The trees were black and bare. She walked along the central driveway. Beneath her coat, the retracted quarterstaff swung against her thigh. The graves, their stones the colour of weathered bone, ranged from simple, overgrown headstones to sprawling mausoleums, their inscriptions too smudged by lichen and neglect for her text-recognition software to decode.

"I don't see any fresh burials," she said. "The place looks full. How come you get to be buried here?"

In the corner of her vision, Paul blinked. She knew he could see the path and the surrounding stones through her eyes, and she felt an unexpected prickle of sympathy, supposing that it couldn't be an easy thing to attend your own funeral.

"My grandparents were sort of rich," he said. "We have a family plot. As I'm the only surviving heir, I guess I get to be buried in it."

Ahead, towards the rear of the cemetery, they found a loose knot of people standing around a casket. Maybe half a dozen in all, including the priest.

"We're late," Paul said.

Victoria stopped walking. She recognised two of the people as distant, estranged relatives of Paul: distant cousins she hadn't seen since the wedding. They frowned at her, clearly less than thrilled by her presence.

She ignored them, fixing her attention on the coffin. She tried to imagine Paul's body lying inside that plain wooden box—not the phantom in her eye, but the real Paul, the one she'd loved so hard, and then lost.

"Are you okay?" Paul asked.

She shook her head. How could she be, with her husband lying hollow-skulled beneath that lid? However convincing the simulation in her head might be, the real man had gone. Her eyes stung like paper cuts. She opened and closed her fists, fighting down an urge to tear open the box and beg him to wake up.

After what seemed an eternity, the priest closed his little black book, and the small congregation watched in silence as the pallbearers lowered the coffin into the earth.

The priest threw a handful of soil onto the lid.

"Ashes to ashes, dust to dust." He made the sign of the cross.

The mourners turned away and began to break into groups. They rubbed their hands together. Their breath steamed. Someone made a joke.

Victoria stood silently, looking at the grave, hating them all.

"I'm sorry," Paul said.

She wiped her eyes with gloved fingers.

"What for?"

"For your loss."

A train clattered past, wheels screeching as it pulled into the Tube station at West Brompton. Further to the north, a triple-hulled skyliner chugged over Earl's Court, the winter sun glinting off its brass fittings and carbon fibre bodywork.

"It's your loss, too."

"I know."

Paul fell silent. Victoria looked down at her hands. She didn't know what else to do or say. When she finally looked up, she saw a woman staring at her from the far side of the hole in the ground. The woman was somewhere in her late forties. She wore a long, elegant coat with fur around the collar and cuffs, and a small pillbox hat with a wisp of black veil. As she walked around the lip of the grave, the shins of her leather boots kicked the hem of her coat.

"Do you know her?"

Paul glanced up from his reverie.

"It's Lois."

"Who's Lois?"

"We worked together in Paris. I wonder what she's doing here?"

"I think we're about to find out."

The woman approached, and stopped a few paces away.

"Victoria?"

"Yes?"

The woman seemed relieved. She stepped forward and offered a gloved hand.

"My name's Lois Lapointe. I worked with your late husband. I'm so sorry about what happened."

"Thank you."

Another train whined into the station. Victoria heard the bong of a platform announcement.

"Do you mind if I walk out with you?"

"Not at all." Victoria turned and began strolling back towards the gate. Lois Lapointe fell into step beside her.

"I recognised you from a picture Paul kept on his desk," she said.

"Have you come all the way from Paris?"

"I have." Lois put a gloved hand on Victoria's sleeve. "There is something I must tell you. Something very important." She gestured to a wooden bench at the side of the gravel path. "Can we sit?"

Victoria hesitated.

"Can't we talk somewhere warmer? I could buy you a coffee?"

The grip on her sleeve tightened.

"Please," Lois urged. "I don't have much time. I know why your husband was murdered." She glanced nervously at the surrounding stones. "And I think I might be next."

CHAPTER TEN
SPACE SHUTTLE STACK

MEROVECH READ TO the end of the last printed page. Then slowly, he placed it face-down on the table with the others.

"Bad news?"

Ack-Ack Macaque sat opposite, on an old wooden chair, wrapped in a ratty towelling dressing gown that Merovech had found for him.

"My whole life is a lie."

The monkey stuck its bottom jaw forward.

"You too, huh?"

Merovech scowled. "I'm serious."

"So am I." Ack-Ack Macaque reached under the gown's hem and caught hold of his tail. He started to groom the hair at its tip.

"It's not easy for me, you know. One moment I'm fighting the Second World War, the next I'm somewhere in France and you tell me it's 2059."

Merovech tapped the papers on the table in front of him.

"You don't understand."

"That's for shit-damn sure!"

"No. My mother. She's been lying to me. All this time, all these years."

Ack-Ack Macaque stopped grooming his tail.

"You want to trade problems? I'll trade. Believe me, I'll trade."

Merovech put a hand to his head. His world felt ready to crash around him in ruins.

"Please. Just give me a minute. I need to think."

The monkey glared at him.

"Well, when you're all done 'thinking', perhaps you could explain to me how I got here?"

"We rescued you."

"Rescued?"

Merovech scratched his cheek, annoyed at the distraction. "You were in a laboratory. We broke in and got you out."

"A Nazi laboratory?"

"What? No. No, you have to forget all that. The Nazis and the war, none of that really happened. It was all a game, all make believe."

"A *game*?"

"A computer game. You know what a computer is, right?"

"Like an adding machine?"

"Yes, exactly. Like an extremely complex adding machine. You were plugged into one, and it created this whole game world around you."

Ack-Ack Macaque stuck a finger into his right nostril. He had a root around, then pulled the finger out and examined the end thoughtfully.

"Why would they do that?"

"As I said, it was a game. People played against you."

"So, I was like a puppet?"

Merovech shrugged.

"Yeah, I guess you could look at it that way."

The monkey was silent for a little while. Then he said, "Suppose all that's true. Just tell me one thing."

"What?"

"Whose ass do I have to kick?"

"What do you mean?"

"I mean, who do I have to kill for putting me in that game? All this time, I thought it was real. All those deaths... Just tell me. Was it you?"

Merovech held up his hands.

"No. We're the ones who got you out, remember? We rescued you."

"Rescued me from who?"

"From Céleste."

"Who the fuck is Céleste when she's at home?"

Merovech turned over the stack of papers before him. He tapped the company logo at the top of the first page.

"Céleste Technologies. They're a corporation. A multi-national group of companies."

"And you rescued me from them?"

"Yes, sort of."

"What do you mean, sort of?"

"Well." Merovech scratched his cheek again. He needed a shave. "The thing is, it's my mother's company."

"Your mother's?" Ack-Ack Macaque sat back with a scowl.

"If it's any consolation, she's been lying to me as well."

"You poor baby."

"I'm serious. All my life, she's been using me. Not telling me the truth."

"So you rescued me to piss her off?"

"Something like that."

Merovech rolled his eyes at the absurdity of it all. Here he was trying to pour his heart out to a monkey, but the monkey had troubles of its own. Suddenly, he felt very young, and very alone.

They were silent for a few minutes, both lost in their own woes. Then Ack-Ack Macaque bent forward across the table. "You know what we need, Merovech?"

Merovech gave up. He shrugged.

"What?"

A hairy palm slapped the wood hard enough to raise dust.

"Booze! And lots of it!"

With a maniacal laugh, the monkey sprang from his chair and began rooting through the kitchen cabinets, chattering to himself. Tins fell and rolled across the flagstones. Crockery clacked; cutlery clashed.

Merovech heard Julie's bare feet on the wooden stairs, and turned as she pulled aside the curtain. Wrapped in a grey towel, she looked pale and skinny, with her eyeliner smudged and her hair flattened on one side, where she'd been lying on it.

"'*Allo*," she said.

Merovech felt his heart quicken. Most of the girls he met in the course of his duties were prim and elegant, with perfect complexions and finishing school manners. They liked riding horses. They wore diamond necklaces and expensive designer gowns, and their smiles lit up the pages of society magazines.

Julie was different. Born and raised in the suburbs of Paris, the only thing she rode was the Metro. She had none of the poise and daintiness of the girls he was used to; but even rumpled and hollow-eyed, she made him feel warm and breathless.

His first instinct was to reach for her, but something stopped him. He looked at his hands. What if he touched her and she flinched away? Now that she knew the truth about him, how could he expect her feelings not to have changed? He turned to the embers smouldering in the hearth.

"I read the file."

She frowned. "Are you all right?"

"I don't know."

She took a couple of steps in his direction, then stopped, unsure. She gave the monkey a wary look.

"What is it doing?"

"Looking for a drink."

Merovech clenched his fists and thought of his apartment in Paris: the pristine tiled kitchen; the wardrobe of designer clothes; and the shelves and shelves of books about the city, its culture and history. He longed to be back there, in his sanctuary. He wanted to close the door and shut out the world, lose himself in one of the slender novels by Hemingway or Fitzgerald. His bedroom window had a view up Montmartre to the white spires of the Sacré Cœur. At dawn on a crisp autumn morning, the basilica's calcite stone seemed to glow impossibly white and, with its trio of bullet-shaped domes, and a lingering mist at its base, the whole structure would remind him of a space shuttle stack, primed and ready to hurl itself like a fist at the morning sky.

He hugged himself, trying to soak up warmth from the fire. How had everything gone so wrong, so fast? Right now, he knew his security team would be ransacking his apartment for clues to his whereabouts. And after last night's break-in, they'd also be looking for Frank and Julie.

"Damn." He put his fist to his lips. "Where's Frank?"

Julie took a step back. Her gaze flickered to the front door, then away.

"He is gone."

"Is he coming back?"

"I do not think so." She ran angry fingers through tangled purple hair. "Why do you ask?"

Merovech strode to the window. He could see the lane leading across the fields to the main road. No sign of Frank.

"The police will be looking for him. And not just the police, the secret service too. If they find him, they'll find us."

Julie bit her lip.

"Frank would never rat us out."

Merovech walked over and took her by the shoulders.

"I was a Marine," he said. "I'm trained to withstand interrogation. And do you know what they taught me? Everybody cracks, sooner or later. Everybody."

Julie squirmed in his grip.

"They would not torture him."

He let her go. "Of course they would. They've lost the heir to the throne, for Christ's sake. That's an embarrassment they'll do whatever it takes to rectify."

Julie rubbed her shoulders, where his hands had squeezed her flesh.

"Then why not hand yourself in? What can they do to you? They cannot send you to jail."

Merovech glanced down at the papers on the worn wooden table.

"I think they've done enough to me already." He picked up the file and the loose pages, and dropped them into the grate, where he watched them crisp and shrivel.

"Then what are you going to do?"

Without taking his eyes from the fire, he leaned an arm on the chimney breast.

"I don't know."

On the other side of the kitchen, a plate smashed on the stone floor. White chips skittered across the flagstones. Ack-Ack Macaque crawled out from the bottom of a pine dresser and pulled himself upright.

"You need answers, son."

At the sound of his voice, Julie jerked in surprise. The monkey ignored her. He regarded Merovech with one-eyed dispassion, expression unreadable.

"I don't know about you, but I've had enough of being someone else's puppet. Someone's been messing with both of us, and I say we get out of here, and go pound the shit out of them."

Merovech bridled.

"You're talking about my mother?"

Ack-Ack Macaque bent his hairy hand into the shape of a gun, and drew an imaginary bead on Merovech's forehead.

"Bingo."

"You think we should confront her?"

The monkey sprang onto the table.

"You know her better than I do. What do *you* think?"

Slowly, Merovech wiped his hand across his mouth.

"No," he said at length, "I've got a better idea. Those papers mention Doctor Nguyen. I remember him. He's a gelware specialist. He probably worked on both of us. He lives down in Chartres. That's not too far from here. We should go and see him, and see what he knows."

Ack-Ack Macaque bunched his fists. His knuckles were like rows of walnuts.

"Yeah, let's do that. Let's go find the fucker, and *make* him talk."

CHAPTER ELEVEN
FUZZY BOUNDARY

A BRIGHT NOVEMBER afternoon in a London cemetery. Wet leaves littered the neatly-clipped lawns. Victoria Valois and Lois Lapointe sat together on a cold wooden bench. Sparrows danced on the gravel path at their feet, hoping for breadcrumbs. Around them, the dirty white gravestones seemed to leech all the heat from the air. Even the constant background sounds of the city seemed muted.

Victoria sat patiently, wrapped in her long military coat, as the other woman composed herself.

"As I said before, I used to work with your husband at the Céleste laboratories. We were on Doctor Nyguyen's team." She paused. The gloved fingers of her right hand worried the fur cuff of her left sleeve. Victoria watched her without speaking. As a journalist, she'd found that one of the best ways to get someone to talk was simply to sit still and say nothing. They spoke to fill the silence, and you could often learn more from listening than from asking any number of questions.

"We were working on memory retrieval," Lois said. "Soul-catchers. Other gelware projects." She stopped picking at her cuff and glanced at Victoria. "I was there the night they brought you in, after the helicopter crash."

Victoria didn't really remember anything after the helicopter ditched in the South Atlantic. Thrown off her feet as the stricken craft rolled on the swell, she'd smashed her skull into the sharp edge of an open storage locker, and hadn't been expected to survive. She'd been stabilised by the surgeons on the aircraft carrier and flown back to France, but the prognosis hadn't been good. She hadn't been expected to regain consciousness, and wouldn't have done had Céleste not performed the experimental procedure that saved her life.

Since then, she'd spent the past twelve months recovering from the crash, adjusting, and learning to use and integrate the new areas of her brain. At first, nothing had smelled right. She got words muddled up and had trouble remembering people's names. But these were expected side-effects from the trauma and surgery, and her underlying personality seemed unaltered, as far as she or anyone else could tell.

No, she couldn't blame the accident for her separation from Paul. She couldn't really blame Paul either. They'd mistaken friendship for love and married in haste. The cracks had been there long before she left Paris for the Falkland Islands.

Now, sitting in the cemetery, her skull healing once again, she probed the insides of her mind, trying to locate the fuzzy boundary between the organic and the artificial.

"You were the first human we operated on. We'd never replaced large sections of a human brain. Soul-catchers, yes. But full-scale replacement of entire lobes, no. Before you, we'd been confined to rats and monkeys." Lois looked up at the clear, blue sky. "At least, that's the official story."

Victoria frowned.

"There was someone else?" She felt herself stiffen, scenting a story. "I thought I was the first."

"You were the first *official* subject. But there was someone before you."

"Paul never said anything."

Lois gave a bitter smile. "He wouldn't have. None of us would. We were sworn to silence."

"So, who was it?"

Lois sat forward. She rubbed her arms against the cold.

"The Prince."

"Prince *Merovech*?"

"Yes. We'd been working on him for five years. Adding extra processors as he matured. Taking—" She broke off with a shudder. "When you came in, we used you as a guinea pig. We had some final techniques to test, before…"

"What techniques?"

Lois shook her head, unable to continue. Victoria gave her a tissue, then got to her feet and took a couple of steps away from the bench, scuffing her boots on the gravel path. Another plane banked overhead. A single-hulled cargo Zeppelin chugged north over Kensington, adverts shining on its flanks.

"Is she telling the truth?"

Paul took off his glasses. He wiped them on his shirt, then slid them back onto his nose. It was a habitual gesture. From her perspective, he seemed to be floating in the air above the gravestones at the edge of the path, a digital shade with his trainers ten centimetres above the cold grass.

"Yes," he admitted. He scratched his chin. "It's all true."

"But all this time. Even in the hospital, you said nothing."

"I couldn't tell anyone." He paused. "Are you angry?"

"Angry?" Victoria shoved her fists into the pockets of her coat.

Idiot.

"I'll deal with you later."

She turned on her heel, to face Lois Lapointe, who looked at her curiously, the traces of concern flickering around the corners of her eyes.

"Who are you talking to?"

"Never mind. It doesn't matter. What I want to know is why you're here, now, telling me all this?"

The other woman stopped hugging herself. She raised her chin.

"Because I think they're going to kill me. Just like they killed your husband, and every other member of Nguyen's team."

"Who's going to kill you?"

Lois glanced from left to right. She lowered her voice.

"Céleste."

"Because of what you did to Merovech?"

"No, because of what we did to the King."

A tall man stepped through the stone gate at the entrance to the cemetery. He wore a black coat and a matching wide-brimmed fedora, and carried lilies in the crook of his arm, the ends of their stems wrapped in newspaper. He had his head down, and Victoria couldn't see his face. Her heart tapped in her chest. Had her plan worked? Was this the man who'd attacked her? Had she drawn him out?

She swallowed, feeling suddenly vulnerable. At Paul's flat, the Smiling Man had moved with startling speed and terrifying ruthlessness. She reached into her pocket and touched the mobile phone that the Commodore had pushed into her hands as she left his cabin.

"I'll have an armed guard standing by," he'd promised. "If you get into trouble, you call me. Punch the first number on the speed dial and we'll be with you in minutes."

She thumbed the keyboard, sending the signal. Better to do so now, while she still could.

I'm being paranoid, she thought, *but am I being paranoid enough?*

Triggered by her elevated pulse rate, the gelware in her head displayed a list of options, ranging from mild sedation to immediate flight. She cancelled it all with a blink, and took a deep breath. "Come on," she said to Lois. "Let's walk."

They set off across the grass, between the monuments. Victoria held Lois by the elbow, almost pushing her along.

"Tell me about the King," she said.

Lois looked around with wide eyes. "What is it? Who are we running from?"

Victoria jerked her arm, encouraging her to keep walking. A quick glance over her shoulder revealed the skinny black figure still pacing in their direction.

"Never mind. Keep talking. You say they're going to kill you. I need to know why."

Lois stumbled, her feet unsteady in her high-heeled boots.

"They brought the King to us, after the rocket attack in Paris." She was panting with fear and exertion. "He'd been injured and we were told to retrieve his soul-catcher."

Victoria's free hand rose to the plastic collar at her throat. She looked back. The man still followed, pigeons flapping around his feet, long strides eating up the distance between them.

"Go on," she said.

Lois slowed. "We didn't need to do it."

Victoria pulled her forwards, between a pair of matched mausoleums.

"What do you mean?"

"He wasn't that badly injured. He had some cuts and bruises. There was blood, but—"

They came out into a double row of gravestones, and onto another gravel path. Other people were around. An old man on a bench. A young woman with a pushchair.

"You took it out anyway?"

Lois let her head drop.

"We did as we were told."

In the corner of Victoria's eye, Paul's image folded itself into a crouch. His arms were over his head, as if trying to block out the world.

Lois Lapointe began to cry.

"Who told you to do it?"

Lois sniffled. "The order came from the top."

Victoria looked back. The man was now only a couple of dozen paces behind them, and still advancing. As she watched, he raised his head, and she saw the dead eyes and thin smile.

As she met his gaze, the lilies fell from his grip. One-by-one, they dropped onto the lawn, revealing in their place the squat black barrels of a sawn-off shotgun.

Victoria's neural prostheses tagged the weapon as a threat and fired her adrenal glands up to maximum production. Time seemed to slow. The noise of the traffic on Brompton Road became a drawn-out growl. Her heart tripped like a hammer in her chest. She became aware of the cold air on her cheeks, the roughness of her clothes against her skin, and the throbbing wound at the back of her neck. Her calves tensed. Her fingers curled.

"Miss Valois, how disappointing to see you alive." In the sunlight, the Smiling Man's skin looked like parchment stretched across the frame of his face. "And Miss Lapointe. So nice to finally meet you in person."

To Victoria's heightened awareness, the pigeons flapping up from the man's feet moved as if pulling themselves through resin. She gave Lois a shove, sending them both in opposite directions, and reached into her coat for her quarterstaff.

The gun fired. She saw smoke bloom from the left barrel, aimed at the spot where she'd just been standing. Her neural settings were running way beyond the safety limits proscribed by Céleste's technicians. She'd hacked her own head, and they'd have a fit when they saw the readouts. She dipped her shoulder, tucked in her chin, and fell into a roll, coming up with the staff held in front of her. A flick of the wrist, and it leapt out to its full length.

Okay, she thought, *this time I'm ready for you.*

The Smiling Man's eyes swivelled in her direction, white with surprise. She saw his arm twitch and, with glacial slowness, the gun turned towards her. She leapt across the gravel path. Two quick, crouching steps. The second barrel fired, the shot ripping through the air above her head. Her staff whirled. She knocked the shotgun aside and drove the tip into his chest. He fell back and Victoria dropped with him, using her weight to accelerate his fall. As he hit the ground, she drove her knee into his stomach, trying to crush the breath from him. A knife appeared in his right hand. In slow motion, she saw it spring into his palm from the sleeve of his coat. He swiped it at her midriff but she leant back and, as the black blade crawled past her stomach, reached out with both hands and broke his wrist. He cried out, and she rose to her feet, standing astride him, the end of the quarterstaff poised to deliver a killing blow to his still-smiling face. Her heart flailed against her ribs. She could feel the blood pulse in her temples and neck.

"Don't you move," she said. "Don't you fucking move."

CHAPTER TWELVE
HILLS LIKE WHALE BACKS

JULIE'S UNCLE KEPT an elderly Citroën HY in a barn behind the house. The keys were on a nail by the barn door. At dusk, Julie took them and passed them to Merovech.

"You'll have to drive," she said.

The van had corrugated steel sides and a protruding snout. The seats were worn and the cab smelled of petrol. In the back, hessian sacks covered the floor.

The Citroën HY had been the workhorse of the United Kingdoms for over a century, used by couriers, builders and every farm and small business that needed to shift materials from one place to another. Produced in huge numbers between the end of the war and the start of the nineteen-nineties, they'd seen off the challenge of the American Ford Transit to become a symbol of European enterprise. Even now, half a century on, you still found them all across France, Belgium, Norway and the Netherlands. They had acquired a retro chic. They were old but reliable and, in a rural setting like this, utterly unremarkable. Merovech took the wheel and coaxed the engine into life.

"Come on," he said.

Julie climbed in beside him, and the monkey slithered over the seat, into the back. They'd found him some clothes in the upstairs wardrobe: a pair of blue denim jeans, which he wore turned up at the ankles, and an old raincoat. With the hood up, he could almost pass for a human teenager. At a distance. To a blind man with no sense of smell.

In his hands, the monkey held Julie's SincPad. The blue screen illuminated his leathery face. Julie had shown him how to access the Internet, and now he pawed the keypad, finding out as much as he could about the fictional game world Céleste had built around him.

Merovech released the brake and eased the van forward, towards the main road. The track was rough, with deep ruts. Every time they hit a pothole, the monkey swore.

After a minute or two, they reached the road. A string of orange lights stretched away in either direction. Merovech crunched the three-speed gearbox. He pressed the accelerator and hauled left on the wheel. The van wallowed out onto the tarmac. On both sides, beyond the puddles of light cast by the streetlights, the ploughed fields of the French countryside seemed as smooth and level as a dark sea, distant hills looming like whale backs against the horizon.

Julie touched her forehead to the glass.

"I wonder if the police have found Frank yet?"

Merovech shrugged. He didn't care about Frank. He had the hood of his top pulled forward and the brim of his baseball cap yanked down almost to the bridge of his nose, shadowing his face. He kept his eyes focused on the little cone of light thrown by the van's headlamps, while a single question whirled around inside his head.

Who am I?

He'd been born in London and educated at a number of specially selected schools, including Eton. His life had been classrooms and dormitories until the age of eighteen, when he'd left school to complete a year's tour in the Royal Marines, before starting his degree in Politics at the Sorbonne University. He'd been the dutiful Prince, and his life had been mapped for him, his every move governed by the dictates of tradition and protocol.

Well, he thought, *to hell with that.*

He gunned the engine. The rules had changed. If the documents Julie had given him were correct, he wasn't a prince at all. The blood burning in his veins and arteries wasn't royal; it wasn't anything. He'd been decanted from a test tube at the Céleste facility, and implanted into his mother's womb: not his father's son at all, but a forgery with no real claim to the throne.

He gave a small, bitter laugh. Loss of power also meant loss of obligation and responsibility. If Doctor Nguyen confirmed the veracity of those documents then, for the first time in his life, Merovech would be out from under. No more stifling receptions; no more public appearances. He would be free. Whatever he did next would be his decision, and his alone.

His eye caught the teardrop gleam of a star in the sky, and the smile died on his lips, swept away by the sudden memory of standing with his father at an open palace door, looking out across the gardens. How old had he been then? Three or four years old, maybe? He remembered the gentle smell of lavender, and the way his father's hand wrapped his.

Looking out at the night, he'd asked what the stars were made of, and his father had smiled down at him.

"Big fires in the sky, a long, long way away."

Merovech's young eyes had widened. He'd known what fires were, and he loved the smell of the gardeners' bonfires. Only stars didn't crackle the way twigs and leaves crackled. And when he took a long breath in through his nose, he couldn't smell their smoke; only his father's cologne and the earthy scents of the sleeping garden.

That had been one of his earliest memories. Thinking about it now, his throat went tight. His eyes swam and his nose prickled, and a ragged, anguished sigh pushed its way from his lips.

Julie looked at him, startled.

"What is it?"

"I've lost my father."

"He is dead?"

"No." He didn't know how to explain the upwelling of grief and loneliness that burned inside him; he simply didn't have the words.

I've lost everything, he thought. Everything that matters. If his father had never really been his father, then none of those memories mattered. They had all been lies.

He swallowed hard, fighting back tears like a little boy abandoned at boarding school: upset, betrayed—angry with his parents, yet desperate for them.

Julie put her hand on his shoulder.

"What can I do?"

He shook his head. What could anyone do? His life had been snatched away.

"Get off." He twitched his shoulder, and Julie pulled her hand back.

"I am sorry, I—"

"Why are you still here?" he asked. "You shouldn't be here. You should have left."

"What are you talking about?"

"Everyone's looking for me. The police, the secret service. If you stay with me, you're going to be in trouble."

"And you want to know why I haven't cut and run?"

"Yes." Everybody else had left him, why not her?

Julie ran a hand through her purple hair. She turned her face to look out the window. Orange lights slid across her cheek.

"I'm surprised you have to ask." She pulled a cigarette from her pocket and lit up. The lighter flared yellow in her cupped hands.

Merovech wrinkled his nose.

"I thought you'd quit?"

Julie blew smoke at the glass. She put her feet up on the dashboard.

"You are not my father." She took another tight drag, pinching the cigarette between finger and thumb. The tip flared orange. He saw it reflected on the windscreen.

They passed through a village. He caught a glimpse of stone houses and a mediaeval church spire. A cafe's yellow lights. The illuminated green cross of a pharmacy. Then they were out among the fields again, the old van's left front wheel hugging the road's central white lines.

He sniffed wetly.

Funny, he thought. Even after a hundred years of unification, the French still drove on the right and the English still drove on the left.

Some things would never change.

He looked across at Julie. Her elbows were resting on her knees. She stared forward, over the points of her boot toes, and wouldn't meet his eye.

He'd watched her earlier, as they prepared to leave the house. She'd been fixing her lipstick in the kitchen, leaning across the sink to the mirror, one foot slightly raised; holding back her hair, twisting her face to the light. She'd seemed so alien, and yet so familiar, and he'd wanted to hold her, to feel the warmth of her curves against him; to trace each dip and shadow of her clothing; to smell her hair and skin, and taste her blueberry-painted lips.

As he watched her now, she scratched her lower lip with a purple thumbnail.

"*Tu es complètement débile.*"

"But—"

"Oh, shut up. You know why I am here, okay? We both know. Do I have to spell it out?"

The road unwound before them. The silence stretched. Merovech didn't know what to say, so he concentrated on nursing the rattling old van, coaxing as much speed as he could from the aged engine.

Minutes passed. Julie finished her cigarette and popped it out of the window. In the rear view mirror, Merovech saw a burst of red sparks as it hit the tarmac.

"I am not some floozy, okay? Despite what Frank thinks, I am not here for the money or the fame, or any of that shit. I am not doing this because of who you are, okay? I am doing it because of who *you* are." She twisted her forefinger in her hair. "Do you understand what I am saying?"

Merovech felt his cheeks redden in the darkness. He opened his mouth to say something foolish but, before he could, a wild monkey screech came from the interior of the van. His foot hit the brake and the tyres squealed. They slithered to a stop.

"Turn on the radio!"

"What?"

Ack-Ack Macaque leapt from the darkness in the back of the van, SincPad in one hand, the other pointed at the dial on the dash.

"Turn it on!"

Julie reached out and pressed a button. Music tumbled into the cab.

"Find the BBC."

She clicked a couple of presets. On the third, they heard the measured tones of a newsreader.

"...*resting comfortably. The Prince collapsed following a reception at the Turkish embassy last night. In a statement, the Palace attributes his collapse to exhaustion brought about by worry for his ailing father, who remains in a critical condition a year after being attacked by Republican terrorists on the Champs-Elysées.*

"*The statement also denounces as a hoax Internet footage apparently showing the Prince involved in a raid on a research laboratory.*

"*The footage, taken using a life-logger pendant, claimed to show the Prince helping members of an extremist digital rights group gain access to the laboratories. However, all trace of the footage has been removed from the group's website, and nobody from the organisation has been available for comment.*

"*In other news, tensions continue to grow in the South China Sea as Royal Navy warships—*"

Julie turned it off. She opened her mouth to speak, but the monkey got there first.

"Okay, my boy. Time to talk." Hard primate fingers dug into Merovech's shoulder. He tried to shake them off.

"What do you mean?"

The pressure increased.

"You heard the man. They have Prince Merovech safely in hospital." Merovech felt fetid breath hot against his neck and ear. "And if that's true, then I've got to ask: who the hell are you?"

CHAPTER THIRTEEN
CASSIUS BERG

THE *TERESHKOVA'S* BRIG comprised a small cell with a bunk, a porthole the size of a grapefruit, and a door made of thick, soundproof glass. The Smiling Man paced back and forth. His coat, hat and shoes had been confiscated, leaving him in an open-necked shirt and a pair of Levis jeans, both black. Without the hat, Victoria saw that he was balder than her. His head perched on the end of a scrawny neck, giving him the appearance of a caged vulture.

With her arms wrapped tightly across the butterflies in her chest, Victoria watched him move back and forth, his weight always on the balls of his feet as if waiting for a chance to pounce; his smile still in place, his eyes devoid of expression.

Beside her, the Commodore said, "He won't talk. He won't even tell us his name."

"No clues at all?"

Victoria ached all over. Hacking the safety restrictions in her gelware had been a dangerous thing to do. Her muscles hurt from being asked to move so quickly, and with such force.

The Commodore smoothed his white moustache with a gnarled forefinger.

"No. Only one. A tattoo on his wrist. A Greek letter."

"Which one?"

"Omega."

"Any idea what it means?"

The old man shook his head. "It could be anything." He looked across at her. "Or nothing. Are you sure you are up to this?"

Victoria brushed a strand of artificial hair from her eyes. The wig he had given her itched, but it covered the mess at the back of her head. The staples were tiny hard rivets in a mass of bruised flesh. The hair would grow back around them, but she'd be left with a grisly scar. Another disfiguring memento to match the one on her temple, from the helicopter crash.

"I'll be fine."

"All right, then." He reached out and tapped a six-digit code into the numerical keypad beside the glass door. Bolts slid back into the frame with a series of soft clunks, and the door hinged open.

The Smiling Man stopped pacing. He stepped back against the porthole and watched as they entered.

Victoria's stomach threatened to curdle with something that was neither anger nor fear, but comprised of both. The gelware took notice of her increased breathing and heart rate and she felt her head go deliciously light as it pumped a mild sedative into her bloodstream, calming her. Her arms unfolded and she stood, fists clenched and ready at her sides.

Across the cell, the Smiling Man regarded her, his gaze as blank as a statue.

"Victoria Valois, you are irritatingly hard to kill."

Victoria swallowed down the last of her nerves. This was the first time she'd been able to study his thin face properly, and she could see that the skin had been pulled up and back across his skull, which had in turn pulled the corners of his mouth into the semblance of an unwavering grin. He couldn't stop smiling, even if he wanted to.

Bad face lift, she thought. But the amusement died before it reached her lips.

"I'm very happy to disappoint you," she said, flexing her fingers. "Now, how about you tell me who you are, and why you're trying to kill me?"

The man looked from Victoria to the Commodore.

"I really think you should let me go."

The Commodore raised an unkempt eyebrow. "Oh you do, do you?"

"I have powerful friends."

The old man scowled. "Are you trying to threaten me, *dolbayed?*"

"I am."

The Commodore's hand went to the pommel of his cutlass.

"Be careful, comrade. You are not in England anymore. On this ship, I make the rules."

They held each other's gaze for a few seconds, then the Smiling Man let out a snort and turned away.

"My name is Cassius Trenton Berg." He waved a hand airily. "Not that the information will do you any good. You will find no record of me in any data bank, anywhere in the world. I simply tell you because, when my friends come and burn your little airship out from under you, I want you to remember that I warned you. And as you die, I want my name to be the last one on your miserable lips."

The Commodore's fingers curled around the hilt of his sword.

"*Blyadski koze!*" His knuckles were white. "Nobody threatens my ship."

Berg's smile stayed fixed.

"I am not threatening, Commodore, I am simply stating a fact. If you do not release me, straight away, your ship will be destroyed."

Victoria put a restraining hand on the Commodore's arm.

"You're not going anywhere until you tell me why you tried to kill me. Why you killed Paul, and Malhotra."

Berg raised an eyebrow.

"Malhotra?"

"The detective."

"Ah." Berg flicked his hand again. "He wasn't important. He just happened to be in my way."

"And how about Paul? We know he was on the team at Céleste with Lois Lapointe. We know about the King." She looked for a reaction. "That's it, isn't it? Céleste stole the King's soul-catcher, and now you're covering it up. You're killing them off one-by-one. But who are you working for? Céleste? Someone else?"

Berg wagged a long finger.

"Be careful, Victoria."

"Careful?" She snatched the wig from her head. "Or what? You already tried to kill me. How much worse could it possibly get?"

Berg considered her bristled head without comment, then turned away.

"You have absolutely no idea."

The Commodore swore in Russian.

"Then why don't you enlighten us, comrade?"

Berg crossed his arms.

"You'll get nothing from me."

Victoria glared at him. She thought of him swooping at her in the hallway of Paul's apartment, black coat billowing. The feel of his knife at the back of her head. The sound of his shotgun in the frosty graveyard. And she longed to wipe the smirk from his face.

Then she remembered the crime scene photograph Malhotra had shown her, and something clenched inside her, like a fist.

"Get some handcuffs, Commodore," she said. "I have an idea."

THE *TERESHKOVA'S* CENTRAL cargo hold occupied a cavernous space aft of the main gondola, within the curve of the main hull's outer shell. Each of the skyliner's hulls held identical holds. The lower part of a helium bag formed a convex ceiling. The floor curved up at the edges, narrowing as it rose towards the rear, where a pair of clamshell doors gave access to a crane assembly mounted on the outer skin, used for raising and lowering shipping containers between hold and ground.

Victoria blew into her hands. The cargo hold wasn't insulated. The air felt colder in here than it had elsewhere, and she was glad of her thick coat.

"So," she said. "Are you going to talk?"

Her prisoner gave a haughty sniff. She'd bound his wrists with a plastic cable tie. His shoulders were hunched against the cold and, standing on the metal deck, he kept shifting from one shoeless foot to another.

They were alone. The Commodore had been called to the bridge, to oversee the *Tereshkova*'s scheduled departure from Heathrow.

"You killed my husband." The words were tight in her throat. The Smiling Man gave a shrug.

"I've killed a lot of people."

From Victoria's viewpoint, Paul's digital ghost seemed to hover at Berg's shoulder, giving the illusion that the victim and his murderer were standing side-by-side.

"Ugly bleeder, ain't he?"

She suppressed a smile at the churlishness in Paul's voice, although she had to concede that he did have a point. Berg's attenuated limbs and tapering face had a reptilian, almost birdlike cast, as if he'd been put together using the fossilised bones of an excavated, predatory dinosaur.

"He certainly is."

Cassius Berg glanced at her.

"I beg your pardon?"

Victoria ran a gloved hand over the bristles of her shaven head. Without her long hair to cover it, the ridge of scar tissue at her temple, and the various cranial jacks implanted along its length, stood out. Touching it made her feel ugly and lopsided.

"I wasn't talking to you."

In her head, she heard Paul say, "What's the matter with the skin of his face?"

"I'm not sure." She took a step closer to the Smiling Man, and examined the papery vellum stretched across his cheeks. "A stroke or surgery, perhaps. Maybe a graft of some sort?"

"You mean he's wearing someone else's face?"

"It's possible." She stepped back again, out of reach. "Disgusting, but possible."

For the first time, she saw signs of agitation on her prisoner's face. A muscle twitched beneath his left eye. A crease appeared in the skin between his brows.

"Who are you talking to?"

"My husband."

Berg's head twitched. "That's impossible. Your husband's dead."

"So you *do* remember killing him?"

Berg drew himself up to his full height. "I remember killing him *and* tearing out his brain, soul-catcher and all." He sounded angry. Victoria pressed her lips together, swallowing back her distaste.

"Then how come," she tapped the side of her head, "he's in here, speaking to me, right now?"

The furrow between Berg's eyebrows grew deeper. Suspicious eyes searched her face.

"What you have to decide," Victoria continued, "is whether I'm concussed and delusional, or whether I really do have an angry murder victim in my head, telling me what to do." She pulled the quarterstaff from her pocket. "Either way, you're in a whole lot of trouble."

The Smiling Man drew back.

"You can't hurt me."

Victoria flicked the staff out to its full extent.

"Are you sure?"

She took a step closer. In her eye, Paul chewed the knuckle of his left index finger, his face a picture of grim expectation.

"Where do you want me to hit him first?" she asked.

Berg took another step back and stopped. The cargo doors were behind him. He had nowhere left to go.

The door controls hung on the wall to Victoria's right. Green button to open, red to shut. Holding the staff in one hand, she reached out.

"Last chance," she said. Her finger pressed the green button. The cargo doors gave a metallic groan and peeled apart, opening like the petals of a flower.

Berg stood silhouetted against the light. The *Tereshkova*'s engines were pushing it up and away from Heathrow's cargo terminal. They were already at what must have been a thousand feet. Victoria saw hotels and roads sliding beneath them. Tiny cars.

"Now talk," she called, raising her voice above the rush of the wind.

Berg looked down at the landscape passing below.

"I'm backed-up," he said, with only the slightest trace of hesitation. "If I fall, my friends will find me. I *will* live again."

Victoria brought the staff to bear, ready to give him a shove.

"Are you willing to bet your life on that? We're a long way up, and I'm not sure your soul-catcher will survive an impact from this height." She gave a theatrical shrug. "But if you're so sure, you might as well jump, because unless you tell me what I want to know, it's your only way out."

She felt her heart banging in her chest. The words coming from her lips felt strange, as if they belonged to somebody a lot tougher than she was, and she drew strength from them. Berg's heels were now inches from the edge of the deck, and she felt electrified. All it would take to kill him would be one strike from the end of her staff. One little push.

Their eyes met, and held.

Berg seemed to be trying to read her face, searching for any hint of a bluff. She glared at him, determined not to blink or look away.

Finally, after what seemed a small, eye-watering eternity, she saw something break in his posture. He looked back at the airport falling astern, and his shoulders fell. His chest seemed to sag in on itself.

"Okay," he said. "Okay. I'll talk."

CHAPTER FOURTEEN
BLOWING SMOKE RINGS AT THE STARS

DOCTOR NGUYEN LIVED in a detached house on the outskirts of Chartres, a cathedral town ninety kilometres south-west of Paris. Merovech parked the boxy old Citroën van on the opposite side of the street. He killed the ignition and the engine rattled away to silence.

"This is it."

According to the clock on the dashboard, the time was eleven-thirty. The road was quiet. The cheery yellow glows in the windows of the whitewashed neighbouring houses spoke of home and hearth and family; but the lights were off in Nguyen's place.

Merovech turned in his seat.

"Perhaps you should stay here," he said.

From the back of the van, Ack-Ack Macaque regarded him with a baleful eye.

"That suits me fine."

Merovech faced Julie.

"Are you coming?"

"Do you want me to?"

He looked across at the darkened house. The upstairs shutters were open but the curtains were drawn. No sign of life at all.

"I don't know. Perhaps you'd better wait here." He got out, breath steaming in the night air. Stars poked through clouds stained orange with reflected town light and, a few houses down, a dog barked in a yard.

"I won't be long," he said. He hurried across to the far kerb and up the short path to Nguyen's front door, where he paused.

In his memory, Doctor Nguyen was a short, stern man in black hospital scrubs, with a stethoscope forever slung around his neck. If the documents he'd read were to be believed, Nguyen and his team had *done* things to him. Surgical things.

He felt his heart quicken. All those times he'd been given anaesthetic for routine operations—tonsils, appendix, wisdom teeth—they'd taken the opportunity to stuff more and more gelware into his head.

He raised his fist to pound the door. He didn't care if Nguyen was asleep, he wanted answers. He wanted to haul the old buzzard out of bed and confront him; let him know how *betrayed* he felt. But, even as he pulled back his hand, he noticed that the door was ajar: resting against its frame, but not completely closed. The catch had not engaged. He could open it with a push.

"I wouldn't do that if I were you."

The voice came from the side of the house. Merovech took a step back, fists raised.

"Who's there?"

"A friend."

A young girl stepped from behind the whitewashed wall of the house. She wore a fur-lined jacket several sizes too large for her skinny frame, a leather flying cap, and a pair of aviator goggles, which she'd pushed up onto her forehead.

"Prince Merovech, I presume?" Her accent was Scottish, which seemed incongruous here, in the sleeping suburbs of a small French town. "Is the monkey with you?"

"I'm here to see Doctor Nguyen."

The girl gave a little shake of her head. She looked somehow familiar. "Nguyen's dead. Murdered. I found him this morning, and I've been waiting for you ever since."

"Who are you?"

The girl stepped back.

"I'm here to help." She retrieved a sizeable holdall from behind the wall. "Now please, if you have the monkey, I need to see him."

Merovech shrugged. He led her back across the road to the van and opened the back doors. Inside, Ack-Ack Macaque crouched against the back of the driver's seat, fangs bared as if expecting trouble. When he saw the girl, he jerked upright and blinked his solitary eye.

"Morris?"

She touched two fingers to her brow in salute.

"What-ho, skipper."

MEROVECH DROVE UNTIL he found a place where they could pull onto the verge in the shadow of some trees. Beyond the trees, ploughed fields stretched away to the horizon. He got out and walked a few metres down the road, his hands deep in the pockets of his red hoodie. Julie called after him but he ignored her. He needed a few moments to calm the turmoil in his head.

Forty-eight hours ago, his life had made sense. Now, almost nothing did. And he couldn't go back. There was no reset button. He felt much as he had after the helicopter crash—dazed and numb, with this horrible, sick feeling that something huge and irreversible had happened to him. Something no amount of privilege or royalty could ever undo.

He looked up at the stars, trying to connect the dots, trying to find meaning in their random scatter. The air smelled of ploughed earth and damp, wet leaves.

When he turned to look back at the van, he saw Julie's silhouette stood by the passenger door, arms folded, watching him.

Had it really been only three weeks since their first meeting, in Paris?

He'd been on his way back from a Norwegian bar in the business district, where he'd been enjoying an evening of akevitt and pickled herring with some of his classmates. He'd been there at the invitation of the proprietor, an ambitious young Norwegian politico. Norway had been part of the burgeoning United Kingdom since 1959, and its assimilation had encouraged the other Scandinavian nations to signup to the newly-formed European Commonwealth—the first step in a process that led eventually to the 1982 Gothenburg Treaty, and the implementation of the United European Commonwealth's single market.

Merovech and his friends had all been half-drunk on the akevitt, and reeked of fish and onions. For fun, they'd dared themselves to take the Metro home from the restaurant. It was their idea of an adventure. Luckily, the train wasn't crowded, and they found plenty of room to sit.

Obviously, Merovech's presence caused something of a stir among the other passengers. Phone cameras clicked and whirred, but his bodyguard, Izolda, kept anyone from bothering him directly. She was a former Olympic wrestler, and had the kind of stare that could stop grown men in their tracks.

A purple-haired girl occupied the seat across the aisle, and Merovech thought he recognised her. Was she a fellow student? He was sure he'd seen her around the campus, but each time he tried to catch her eye, she looked away.

She's gorgeous, he thought. *But not in an obvious way.* There was nothing self-conscious or artificial about her. She wasn't dressed to impress anyone.

He watched her all the way to his stop.

When they pulled in and the doors opened, Izolda hustled him out onto the platform.

He glanced back at the girl, trying to fix her face in his memory, wanting to remember her in the morning. As he did so, she pressed her hand up against the window. She'd scrawled her mobile phone number across her palm in purple lipstick.

"Call me," she mouthed.

The train started to move. He whipped out his SincPhone and, walking to keep pace with the window, punched her number into the keypad with his thumb. If he'd been thinking clearly, he would have used his phone to take a photo of the number. As it was, he got the last digit just as he reached the end of the platform.

The train pulled away from him, pushing itself into the tunnel, faster and faster. The wind of it ruffled his hair. He lifted the phone to his ear. She let it ring twice before she answered.

"Do you want to get a coffee?" she said.

WHEN MEROVECH GOT back to the van, the other three were standing in the pool of light cast by its headlamps. Morris had her holdall open and was rummaging through the contents. Ack-Ack Macaque now wore her fleece-lined jacket and aviator goggles, and puffed away on a huge cigar. The smoke smelled sticky and rank in the clear night air. As Merovech approached, they stopped talking and turned to him.

"Are you okay?" Julie looked concerned. Merovech walked over and gave her a hug. She was soft and reassuring in his arms, and he clung to her the way that in the South Atlantic, he'd clung to the ropes of the life raft.

"Thank you."

For a moment, she seemed nonplussed. Then she put a hand to the back of his neck.

"*De rien.*"

He pulled back, holding her at arm's length.

"I mean it. I'm sorry about what I said before. I know why you're here. And believe me, I'm glad you are."

He took her hand, and turned to face Morris and the scowling monkey.

"Okay," he said to the girl, "let's start with you."

Mindy stopped rooting around in her holdall and rose to her feet. She wore a green v-neck sweater and skinny black jeans. Having given the oversized flying jacket to Ack-Ack Macaque, she seemed somehow smaller.

"I was just explaining to your friend that my real name's not Morris, your royal highness. In real life, people call me K8." She held out a hand. Merovech didn't take it.

"Kate?"

"No, kay-eight. Letter kay followed by numeral eight."

"Really?"

"It's a gamer thing."

"So, why introduce yourself as Mindy Morris?"

The girl looked at him, then glanced at Julie.

"He doesn't know who you are," Julie explained quietly. "He doesn't play the game."

Merovech looked between them.

"Ah!" He clicked his fingers. "*That's* where I've seen you. You were in the clip, with *him*." He pointed at Ack-Ack Macaque, who was now leaning against the van's radiator, blowing smoke rings at the stars.

"That's right." K8 took her hand back and self-consciously used it to smooth down the front of her sweater. "I'm a professional game player."

"But 'Morris'?"

"I never use my real name. I play characters. Céleste Tech hired me to keep an eye on the big guy here."

Merovech smiled despite himself.

"You're his handler?"

Ack-Ack Macaque bristled.

"She's my wingman." He tapped ash from the end of his cigar. "Or rather, she was. In the game."

"The programmers at Céleste were worried that he'd started to think about things too deeply. Started to question the world around him. The last time that happened, they had to get a whole new monkey."

"Wait, he's not the first Ack-Ack Macaque?"

K8 shook her head.

"Apparently, there have been five to date." She glanced apologetically at Ack-Ack Macaque. "I didn't find this out until after they hired me, but as each one went off the rails, they simply loaded the root personality into a new monkey, and the audience was none the wiser. They accepted it as an upgrade. Nobody outside Céleste knew it was a real monkey. They all thought it was an AI."

"So, why bother hiring you?" Julie asked.

K8 grinned.

"I'm cheaper than a new monkey."

Beyond the trees, Merovech saw the lights of a skyliner heading for the passenger terminal at Toussus-le-Noble Airport. Against the night sky, its gondola portholes shone like the windows of a floating village: warm and unreachably far away.

"How did you find us?"

The grin slid from the girl's face.

"I heard about the raid. They called me and told me not to bother coming in to work. I thought at first it might be animal rights activists, but when I heard the rumour on the Internet that you were involved, your royal highness, I knew the two of you'd show up at Nguyen's place sooner or later."

"And you found him dead?"

"Yes. I saw him through the window. The top of his head was missing." She rubbed her lips with the back of her hand.

"And you didn't call the police?"

"I didn't want to frighten you off."

Still leaning against the Citroën's grille, Ack-Ack Macaque rolled his cigar between finger and thumb. From where Merovech stood, he was a long-armed silhouette between the glare of the headlamps to either side.

"What happened to them?"

Merovech squinted against the light.

"Pardon?"

Ack-Ack Macaque pushed himself upright and took a step towards K8. His voice was low, barely a growl.

"The other four. The ones before me. What happened to them?"

K8 put her hands in her pockets. She took them out again. She didn't seem to know what to do with them.

"They're dead, skipper."

"All four of them?"

"They were put down."

Beside him, Merovech heard Julie Girard suck air through her teeth.

"*Mais c'est du meutre ça!*"

Ack-Ack Macaque glared at her.

"Murder? You can say that again, sweetheart." With a flick of his hairy wrist, he sent the cigar flipping out onto the tarmac of the empty road. "The question is, what are we going to do about it?"

Merovech met his stare.

"What did you have in mind?"

Ack-Ack Macaque clawed at his hips, fingers curling around non-existent pistols.

"Kicking in doors, blowing up shit. The usual. Why, do you have a better idea?"

Merovech rubbed an itch on the tip of his nose.

"They've screwed us both over," he said. "I'm just not sure the 'all guns blazing' approach is the best one, strategically speaking."

"Fuck strategy." Ack-Ack Macaque drew himself up to his full height. "Those motherfuckers at Céleste have killed me four times already, and enough is e-fucking-*nough*."

K8 stepped up to Merovech. Her head came up to his collarbone.

"You don't know the half of it," she said. "Don't forget, I worked with Nguyen. I saw stuff. I know about you." She tapped her temple. "I know all about the gelware they pumped into your head."

Merovech looked down at her.

"I've read Nguyen's notes," he said stiffly. "I know I'm a clone."

K8 gave a snort. "You're a lot more than that, your highness. There's more gelware in your head than anything else. You and the skipper here, you're two of a kind." She crossed her arms, looking up at him like the precocious kid she was. "The thing is, I'll bet you haven't figured out why the Duchess had you grown in the first place?"

Merovech restrained an impulse to seize her by the lapels.

"If you know something, tell me."

The girl held his gaze for a couple of seconds, as if searching his eyes for something. Then she turned on her heel and began to pace back and forth in the light, talking as she went.

"Okay, here it is. I told you, I'm a professional game player. Some people would call that a fancy name for a hacker. And in my case, they'd be right." She walked back to her holdall, where it lay on the grass. The van lights caught the steam of her breath in the cold night air.

"I was thirteen years old when I cracked the firewall at Céleste Tech. Six months later, they offered me a job, and I've been working for them ever since.

"When they called me in to look after the monkey, I got suspicious. I knew it wasn't a real AI. So, I did some digging. I found Nguyen's notes. He ran both projects, and he kept pretty detailed records." She knelt and pulled a SincPad from the bag. "Here, I downloaded it all onto this. If you want to go public, this is all the evidence you'll need."

She handed Merovech the pad and stepped back, to the edge of the circle of light.

"Nguyen and your mother. They've been working on this for a long time."

"On what?"

"Artificial brains in organic bodies. Brains into which they can download stored personalities. The skipper here, he was a prototype. A proof of concept. You, though." She raised her palms to Merovech. "You're the real prize."

CHAPTER FIFTEEN
COMMAND MODE

VICTORIA VALOIS KEPT the end of her quarterstaff trained on the Smiling Man as he stood, hands bound before him, in front of the gaping doors of the *Tereshkova*'s cargo hold.

They were powering west, above Slough and Windsor. She could see the reservoirs at Colnbrook and Wraysbury; the grey ribbon of the M25; and the Georgian splendour of Windsor Castle, with its large central tower.

"Okay," she said. "Tell me about that tattoo on your wrist."

He looked down at his hands. One of his wrists was swollen, where she'd tried to break it in the graveyard.

"It's Omega," he said. "The last letter of the Greek alphabet."

"I know that. But what does it *mean?*"

His eyes came up to meet hers.

"It's the symbol of my order. We are the Undying. We believe in an end to things, a benevolent Eschaton at the end of the universe. An Omega Point."

Victoria tightened her grip on the staff.

"What's that got to do with Paul? With Lois and the King?" She *had* to know the full story.

Berg glanced over his shoulder at the town below. He was just inside the threshold of the open doors. Beyond, the deck's lip extended another half a metre into the sky. When the doors closed, it would form a narrow ledge.

"Nguyen and his team were expendable. They knew too much of our plans."

In Victoria's head, Paul scratched his peroxide hair and said, "He's talking about the night they brought the King in. The night of the assassination attempt."

"What happened that night? Lois started to tell me, but we were interrupted."

Thinking she was talking to him, Berg opened his mouth. She silenced him with a raised hand. She wanted to hear what Paul had to say.

"We were called into the Céleste facility. It was late. The King and the Duchess were there. We were told to remove the King's soul-catcher."

"Even though his injuries weren't serious enough to warrant surgery?" Paul shuffled his trainers.

"Nguyen told us it was necessary."

"And you never spoke of it?"

"I couldn't. We were told it was a national security matter. We had to sign all sorts of forms."

Victoria considered this for a moment. Then she turned her attention back to Berg.

"And I suppose *you're* tidying up the loose ends from that night?"

"Amongst other things."

"So, tell me. Who gave the order to remove the King's soul-catcher?"

Berg rolled his head from side to side, like a vulture trying to swallow a chunk of flesh.

"Oh, come on, Victoria. Isn't it obvious?"

She narrowed her eyes. "You tell me. What would anyone have to gain by removing it?"

The Smiling Man turned and used his bound hands to gesture at the battleship silhouette of Windsor Castle.

"Control of the throne."

Victoria frowned.

"No, that's ridiculous. The Duchess—"

Berg let out a sound that could have been a chuckle.

"Yes, the Duchess. Of course, the Duchess. *Her* company. *Her* husband. *Her* technology."

"So, the assassination attempt?"

"All part of her plan, I'm afraid. The King is indisposed, so the Duchess becomes Regent until Prince Merovech finishes his studies, at which point he assumes the throne."

"So, Merovech's part of this?"

"Yes, although he doesn't know it yet." Berg took a deep breath, as if preparing to unburden himself. The temperature in the hold had dropped considerably, and she could see him shivering.

"When Merovech takes the throne, he will be working for us. His first act as monarch will be to dissolve the civilian government and impose martial law. He will have the backing of the armed forces. We've spent years getting our people into key positions. When the takeover happens, it will be swift and decisive."

Victoria adjusted her grip on the quarterstaff. Every instinct in her body screamed at her to slam the tip into his moronic smirk.

"How do we stop him?"

Berg raised his chin, looking down his nose at her.

"I don't think you can. The plan's already underway. When the Mars probe's ready for launch, the Duchess will announce that she's resigning the Regency, and Merovech will ascend." He raised his hands, asking for the plastic binding to be removed. "Everything will be in place. The new order will rise."

Victoria closed her eyes. She moved her consciousness away from the emotions swamping the organic side of her brain. There would be time for panic later. Right now, she had to keep going. She couldn't afford to crumple. With her mind in command mode, she opened her eyes, her thoughts as cold and clear as the sky outside.

"You killed my husband," she stated. "And you tried to kill me."

Berg jerked, startled by the sudden calm in her voice, the sudden change in focus. His wrists chafed against the plastic cable tie, trying to pull free.

"Now, look—"

"Be quiet." She took a step forward, swinging the quarterstaff, marvelling at the mathematical beauty of its arcs, the perfect unity of its form and function.

"But you don't understand. I'm one of the Undying. I'm one of the survivors. I *will* make it to the life everlasting."

Victoria threw the staff up with one hand and caught it with the other. She reviewed her memories of Paul, from their first kiss to their wedding night. Whatever his faults, whatever he'd done, he hadn't deserved to die such a horrible death.

"How many people have you killed?"

The Smiling Man took a step back, beyond the track of the doors, onto the very lip of the deck. He couldn't retreat any further, yet Victoria still saw defiance in his eyes. He stood straight and tall, like a dinosaur stretching on its hind legs.

"Twenty-four," he said.

Victoria took another pace towards him, staff held like a javelin. The gelware threw targeting graphics across her sight.

"And how many of their brains did you take?"

His eyes were on the staff now. He looked less certain of himself.

"Nineteen. But they will live again. They're on the Mars probe. All the dead. All their soul-catchers. Even yours."

"Mine?"

"All of them."

"But why?"

"So they can live again, and take their places in the new global order."

Victoria felt something sour rise in her throat. One of her hands gripped the staff, ready to strike if he tried to move. The other reached for the door controls. She pressed the red button with the heel of her hand, and the doors shuddered. With a piercing squeal, they began to close.

Afraid of being shut out on the ledge, Berg tried to step to safety, but a swipe from the staff kept him where he was.

"Hey! You can't do this!" With his wrists bound in front of him, he found it hard to keep his balance. "Let me in."

Victoria kept the staff poised.

"This is for my husband," she said. Their eyes met. Berg's were white all the way around. Without emotion, she watched him teeter. The wind snatched at his clothing. She saw one of his heels slip. For an instant, his entire weight rested on the toes of one foot. A cry escaped his smiling lips.

And he was gone.

Victoria ran forward, and caught a final glimpse of him: a black stick figure cart-wheeling down through the bright afternoon air, legs flailing. She saw office blocks; an industrial estate. And then, with an echoing clang, the doors shut, closing out everything but the cold.

BREAKING NEWS

From *Le Journal de Nouvelle Science*, online edition:

Mars Probe "Days From Launch"

26 NOVEMBER 2059 – Inside sources at Céleste Tech have indicated that their long-heralded interplanetary "light sail" probe may be just days from launch.

Designed by engineers at the Céleste Technologies facility near Paris, the probe, dubbed 'New Dawn', will slingshot around the sun before unfurling a large "sail" to catch the solar wind and ride it to Mars.

If the launch is successful, the probe should reach Mars some time in 2061.

The project, which has been shrouded in secrecy, recently caused controversy when rumours started to circulate that its payload would include so-called "terraforming packages".

The packages are believed to contain specially-tailored microbial life forms, including algae and extremophile bacteria, designed to absorb carbon dioxide from the Martian atmosphere and replace it with oxygen.

Such packages would be a theoretical first step in any effort to turn the Red Planet into a second Earth, but campaigners are opposed to what they see as the wanton contamination of an unspoilt wilderness, about which we still know comparatively little.

Although officials remain tight-lipped about a definite date for the launch, inside sources say they expect it to coincide with celebrations to mark the hundredth anniversary of the founding of the European Commonwealth.

Read more | Like | Comment | Share

Related Stories

Record levels of seawater acidity blamed for failing fish stocks

As new pills go on the market, we ask: should you erase bad memories, even if you can?

Hackers retaliate after police raid

Doubts surround centennial celebrations as Prince Merovech still "recovering in seclusion"

Skyliner *Grace Marguerite* celebrates sixty years of continuous international flight

Céleste Games unveils "new and improved" Ack-Ack Macaque character

Salvage teams race to save Venetian treasures

Chinese taikonauts begin return journey to Earth

Fans in Iowa mark centenary of Buddy Holly plane crash

CHAPTER SIXTEEN
CLOCKWORK NINJAS

THEY DROVE FOR the coast, Merovech at the wheel and Julie at his side. He needed to confront his mother, but wanted to do it on his terms, not hers; which meant finding his own way across the Channel.

Beside him, Julie seemed pensive. She kept chewing her bottom lip and wringing her hands in her lap. She hadn't spoken in half an hour.

In the back of the van, K8 huddled with Ack-Ack Macaque over a SincPad screen. She'd been gently connecting wires from the jacks in his head to a router plugged into the pad. This was her idea of fighting back.

"The best way to hurt Céleste and draw a lot of attention is to take down the game," she said. "And the best way to do that is to find the new monkey and kick its ass."

Ack-Ack Macaque picked at his teeth.

"Find the big guy and take him out. Gotcha."

K8 tapped a command into the pad, linking his artificially uplifted brain directly into the online game.

"Yeah, standard primate power play. Do you think you can handle it?"

"Do monkeys shit in the woods?"

His yellow eye flickered shut. K8 slid the final jack into place, covered his head with the leather skull cap, and rocked back. She met Merovech's glance in the rear view mirror.

"He's in."

"Do you think this will work?"

K8 gave the monkey's hand an affectionate pat.

"Aye, probably. If he can get in there and cause enough trouble to get noticed, then we can blow this thing sky high." She shuffled forward and leaned between the front seats. "According to *Techsnark*, the game has ten thousand registered user accounts, and many more watching the action on YouTube. That's a massive, ready-made audience, right there."

They were on a back road, somewhere in Brittany, and it was now well after midnight. From the passenger seat, Julie said, "Won't they just block him?"

"I don't know if they can. He's hardwired into the game. He's part of it. And besides, they might not even notice him. Not for a while, anyway. If they think digital rights activists snatched him, the last thing they'll be expecting is for him to hook back in." K8 looked between Merovech and Julie, and frowned. "How are you two holding up?"

Merovech stifled a yawn. For the past hour, he'd been watching the road's central white line spool through the headlamps' arc, his fingers squeezing the wheel as his mind struggled to parse the evening's revelations.

He thought back to his time in the South Atlantic, before the helicopter crash.

"When in doubt," his old commanding officer had been fond of saying, "make a plan and stick to it. Chunk everything down into small, achievable objectives."

Rather than try to plan how he was going to get across the Channel, travel to Cornwall, and confront his mother without running afoul of either customs officials or her personal security team, he was focusing instead on reaching the coast. He knew that the parents of an old school friend had a yacht at Saint-Malo, and he hoped he'd be able to persuade them to take him across. In the meantime, he had the morale of his troops to consider.

"I could do with a break," he said. "And a coffee."

Beside him, Julie stretched like a waking cat.

"Coffee sounds good."

Ack-Ack Macaque stood blinking in the sudden light. He'd asked K8 to spawn him on the edge of one of the British airfields, at dawn, and the transition from the gloom and discomfort of the rattling old van to the warm sun and summer smells of the English countryside had been almost instantaneous. He took a deep breath in through his flattened nose. From his point of view, he was now standing in a meadow adjacent to the airfield's perimeter fence. Buttercups waved in a light breeze. Bees droned. He drank it all in. Then, as if remembering something, his hands dropped to his hips, and his fingers closed eagerly on the holstered butts of his giant Colts.

"Hello, old friends."

The guns were familiar and reassuring and, for a moment, everything seemed to be back the way it had been. But he knew in his heart that it wasn't. Now he'd discovered the truth about himself, the rules had changed. He no longer cared who won the war. He could see the game world for the sham it had always been, and he was here to tear it down. He'd broken out of his prison, and now he'd returned to wreak bloody vengeance on his former jailers. This wasn't a homecoming, it was a farewell tour.

A bazooka lay in the grass at his feet, like a long section of drainpipe. Beside it, a box of shells and a dozen grenades. K8 had hacked his profile to include the extra items. He wasn't sure what 'hacking' meant, but he appreciated her efforts. For what he had in mind, he'd need all the firepower he could get his hands on.

He pulled a cigar from the inside pocket of his flight jacket and lit up, thinking what a shame it was that K8 couldn't be there herself, in her guise as Mindy Morris. He'd grown used to having her as his co-pilot, and it seemed wrong for her to miss out on all the fun.

He heard a deep growling thrum from the south-east: a wave of boomerang-shaped flying wings powering in across the rolling fields, their triple propellers shimmering in the morning light. There were maybe a dozen in all, hurried along by six or seven darting, shark-like Messerschmitts.

Behind him, on the aerodrome, he heard the scramble bell ring. Another ninja parachute raid, as predictable as clockwork.

As the planes approached, he stood his ground, watching the funny-looking craft loom larger and larger in the morning sky. When the first parachute canopies blossomed, he drew the Colts and grinned around his cigar. This was going to be a riot.

He put bullets through the two lowest paratroopers. The others jerked around in their harnesses, searching the ground for the source of the shots. He heard them calling to each other in a panicky mixture of German and Japanese. Then they were down, rolling in the grass, their shrouds settling around them in clouds of gently falling silk.

Swords sang from their scabbards. Japanese steel flashed in the English summertime. Colts firing and fangs bared, Ack-Ack Macaque leapt to meet them.

CHAPTER SEVENTEEN
EXPIRED LEASE

VICTORIA VALOIS SAT on a bar stool, in a lounge on one of the skyliner's starboard gondolas. She was watching the spirits quiver in the bottles hanging behind the bar. They were rippling in time to the almost subliminal vibrations of the *Tereshkova*'s engines.

The lounge had been decorated in a 1930s 'Golden Era of Travel' style, with art deco fixtures, ceiling fans, and plenty of prominent rivets on the bulkheads. A painting hung over the cash register, portraying the Commodore as a young man, in a white dress uniform with a bright scarlet sash.

A row of large circular portholes filled much of the starboard wall. Perched on her stool at the counter, Victoria had her back to them. She didn't feel much like looking out, or down.

The bar counter itself had a thin copper top which had, over the years, acquired a patina of dents and nicks as unique as a fingerprint. The steward wore white gloves and served the drinks on small cork coasters.

Victoria was on her third gin and tonic. Her flaxen wig lay scrunched on the bar before her. Right now, she didn't care what she looked like, and her scarred, shaven head kept the other passengers from trying to engage her in conversation. She couldn't read the labels on the bottles behind the bar because she'd disabled the text recognition on her visual feed. She didn't want it whispering brand names in her mind every time she glanced at the shelves.

"Two years ago, I was happy," she said. She could see Paul in the corner of her eye: a peroxide ghost in a white coat and loud shirt, sitting with its head in its hands.

"Two years ago, I had a job. I had a husband. I had my own hair and I could *write*." Faces turned in her direction. She ignored them. "Now what have I got?"

She picked up her glass. Bubbles clung to the underside of the lime slice floating at the top. What had she got? She'd let the lease expire on the Parisian apartment she'd shared with Paul. Now all she had was a crumpled wig; the clothes she stood up in; the loan of a small cabin on the *Tereshkova*; and Paul.

"Hey," she said. "I'm talking to you."

Paul raised his eyes to her. He hadn't spoken since the Smiling Man fell from the lip of the cargo hold.

"I know, I'm choosing not to listen."

Victoria swilled the drink around in her glass.

"Oh, really?"

"Yeah." He clambered to his feet. "Because some of us have real problems, what with being dead and everything."

She slammed the glass down on its coaster.

"That's hardly my fault, is it? If you'd come clean in the first place, if you'd told someone about that night with the King, maybe all of this could have been avoided. Maybe you'd still be—"

She stopped herself, and let out a long, tired breath. Paul scowled.

"Hey, I'm the one who got his brains scooped out."

"Yeah, and I just killed a man. Because of you. So shut the fuck up, okay?"

She drained the gin and tonic, and pushed the glass across the counter.

"Another one," she said.

The steward came over.

"Madam, I have to ask you to keep your voice—"

"Just fill it up."

In her eye, she saw Paul shaking his head.

"I'd never have thought you were capable of something like that."

"Well then, I guess we really didn't know each other as well as we thought."

The steward placed a glass of gin and a small bottle of tonic on the bar, and turned away without a word. He knew she was the Commodore's goddaughter. If she wanted to sit at the bar and talk to herself, it was no business of his.

Victoria emptied the tonic into the glass until the bubbles ran over the rim and down, into a fizzing puddle on the copper counter.

"Besides, he deserved it, and I will not let you make me feel guilty."

Paul put his arms out.

"I'm not trying to. I know you, Vicky. I know you're guilty enough already. I can hear it in your voice."

"Get lost."

She picked up the wet glass and took a mouthful. The tonic fizzled on her tongue. The ice cubes dabbed her upper lip.

Cassius Berg had been a hired assassin. He'd murdered Paul, and all those others. He was a killer and, given the slightest chance, he would have killed her as well. He'd already tried to once, and only failed by the slimmest of margins. Why should she feel guilty for his death? Her actions had been entirely logical.

In her eye, Paul had his arms crossed, each fist clenched in the opposite armpit.

"You really want me to 'get lost'?"

"Right now? Yes."

He dropped his arms. "Well, if that's how you feel, maybe you should turn me off?"

"What?"

"You heard me." He turned away from her, shoulders hunched.

Victoria opened her mouth to snap back at him, but the words wouldn't come. Anger turned to sadness. She put her elbows on the bar and rubbed her temples.

"Ah, *merde*."

All of a sudden, all she wanted was to make her way back down the narrow gangway to her little cupboard of a cabin, to close the door and shut out the world. Instead, she took a swallow from her glass, wiped her lips on the back of her hand, and drew herself up in her seat.

"I'm sorry," she said. Paul's white-clad shoulders twitched. He looked around.

"Are you serious? In all the years I've known you, you've never once said—"

"It's an apology, Paul. Take it or leave it." She drained the glass and pushed it across the counter for a refill.

Still sitting, Paul twisted around to face her. From her point of view, he seemed to be cross-legged on the shelf behind the bar, his back against the row of optics hanging from the wall.

"Okay." He scratched his beard. "Okay, I'm sorry too. I didn't mean to be an asshole about it. I'm just kind of shocked, you know?"

The steward came forward and refilled Victoria's glass. This time, he poured the tonic himself, avoiding spillages.

"You're shocked? Imagine how I feel." She turned in her seat to find the lounge behind her empty, the other passengers having decided to take their evenings elsewhere. Paul's image moved with her, so that he now seemed to float above the tables. Beyond the portholes, she caught sight of blue sky and white cloud.

"I did it for you, you know." She reached back and grabbed her newly-filled glass. "Because of what he did to you."

Paul gave a slow nod.

"I know. It's just I can't get over how you can think you know someone, even be married to them, and still they surprise you."

Victoria found herself shaking her head. She leaned back, her elbows against the cold metal of the bar.

"You don't need to tell me. I thought we were in love, remember?"

Paul squirmed. "We were. At least, I loved you. I still do. It's just—"

"Yeah?"

"Yeah." He bit his lower lip. "We had some good times, though, didn't we?"

"Yes, yes we did." Victoria sipped her drink. "And for what it's worth, I still love you, too. I'd be dead if it hadn't been for you. If you hadn't got me onto that Céleste programme after the crash…"

Paul waved a modest hand. "What else was I going to do? Besides, Nguyen thought you'd make an ideal test subject."

"Oh he did, did he?"

"Of course. It was a chance for him to try out some of the techniques we were going to use on the Prince. And, because you were travelling with Merovech when the crash happened, it was excellent publicity."

"And you just let them do it?"

A pained expression crossed his face.

"I couldn't let you die."

"So, you really did care?" In darker moments, she'd wondered why he'd tried so hard to save her life, only to separate from her six months later.

Paul pulled off his glasses and wiped them on the hem of his white coat.

"Of course I did. Our sexualities may not have been compatible, but I loved you as much as I've ever loved anyone. You were my wife, and it would have killed me to let you die without exploring every option, even if it meant turning you over to Nguyen."

Victoria looked down at her drink. "So," she said. "What now? You saved my life; I avenged your death. I guess that makes us even."

"I guess so." Paul slipped the spectacles back onto his nose. "There's just one thing."

"What?"

"I really don't want to go."

Victoria felt herself sag. She put a hand to her head.

"Oh, Paul."

He leant towards her. "Seriously. I know we agreed that you'd keep me running until you solved my murder. And, well, we've done that. But still, I don't want to be turned off. Not now, not yet."

Victoria slid down from the stool and walked over to the portholes on the starboard wall. She bent slightly, one arm on the wall for support, and looked out at the countryside passing below. She saw fields and hedges laid out like a patchwork picnic blanket. Roads like seams.

Paul was quiet for a long time. Then he asked:

"Do you believe in God, Vicky? I mean, really?"

Her lips pursed. Her fingernails tippy-tapped the metal wall. She hadn't really thought about it in years.

"I guess there might be a higher power, somewhere out there. But if there is, it's going to be stranger than anything we can imagine." She took a sip from her glass. "Why do you ask?"

"Because I don't believe in anything. I don't think there's anything waiting for us when we die. This is it. This is all we get, and it's not enough."

Below, the serried ranks of a conifer plantation. Wide, straight firebreaks like grassy highways. A stream glinting like a vein of bronze.

"You know what happens to back-ups," Victoria said quietly. "You better than anyone."

Paul raised his index finger.

"There was that old guy in Edinburgh. You interviewed him for your paper. He lasted six months."

The *Tereshkova* passed into cloud.

"But he still fell apart, in the end."

"We all fall apart in the end."

Victoria straightened up and turned back to the empty lounge.

"Then what do you suggest? I can't have you in my head for the next six months. We'll drive each other nuts."

"You could transfer my file into a different processor. Another gelware brain. Then all we'd have to do is find a way to grow a body to put it in."

Victoria gaped.

"You're crazy."

Paul held up his hand, fending off her accusation.

"No, I'm sure it can be done."

Victoria moved back to the bar. The steward regarded her with palpable weariness, but she didn't care. She'd had enough for one night.

"Really? And what makes you think it's even possible?"

Paul reached up and scratched his ear.

"Because that's what we were working on at Céleste."

CHAPTER EIGHTEEN
LA MANCHE

THEY REACHED THE outskirts of Saint-Malo a little after dawn. Merovech's friend's parents had an apartment in one of the new, upscale arcologies overlooking the sea, far along the coast from the walls of the old, partially-flooded port city; and out of sight of the container ships anchored at the mouth of the Rance River.

There were around thirty ships in all, all retrofitted to provide emergency housing for ecological refugees from the low lying countries further up the coast. Anchored in the shelter of the estuary, they formed a floating shantytown for those displaced by rising sea levels and seasonal floods. Some of the ships were lashed together, linked by gangways and laundry lines; while others stood alone, each a separate neighbourhood in its own right, with its own customs and hierarchies.

Geoffrey Renfrew hadn't really been a friend, of course; he'd just been someone who'd hung around on the edge of Merovech's social circle at school, trying to ingratiate himself. Merovech remembered him as a pale, greasy boy with watery eyes and a laugh that sounded like a cat sneezing.

He parked the old Citroën van on a concrete service road leading to the arcology. Weeds poked through cracks in the road, but the buildings themselves looked immaculate.

Built like a vast step pyramid, with terrace gardens along each step, and a vast light well running down the centre, the arcology was a self-contained, secure community. Fortified against crime, social unrest and terrorist attack, it provided an expensive, aspirational refuge for the upper middle class. Wind turbines turned their carbon fibre blades on either side of the building's private marina.

"There's no way we're going to get in there," K8 said. "Those places have everything: electric fences, face and gait recognition, biometric scanners, the works."

Merovech pulled out his SincPhone.

"I'll call them. They can meet us somewhere and take us to the yacht."

K8 looked him up and down.

"What are we going to do about the skipper here? I'm assuming the harbour will have some sort of security. Even if it's just CCTV, they're going to spot a monkey, no matter what we dress him in."

Merovech smiled. On the way here, they'd passed a pet supply store in an out-of-town retail development, and it had given him an idea.

"You leave that to me," he said.

THREE HOURS LATER, Merovech, Julie and K8 were ensconced in the cramped but comfortable galley of Geoffrey's parents' yacht: a thirty-foot catamaran by the name of *Peggy Sue*.

Geoffrey's parents were pleased to see him, and anxious to be hospitable; but they couldn't hide their puzzlement at the suddenness and secrecy of his arrival. They seated their guests around a small plastic table and poured them drinks.

Geoffrey's father, Jerry, was a former meat magnate from Cambridgeshire. He wore blue denim jeans and a bootlace tie with a silver steer's head. He'd made his fortune selling vat-grown beef, cloned from the finest available livestock, to restaurants and fast food chains. A pioneer in his field, his most controversial scheme involved a range of hamburgers that he claimed contained meat cloned directly from the skin cells of pop stars and celebrities. Fans could now eat their heroes, he said. The resulting media frenzy made him rich—but when the patties in the buns turned out to be ordinary pork instead of vat-grown human flesh, he'd been forced to take early retirement.

Standing by the yacht's hatch with a mug of coffee in his hand, he had a wide smile and easygoing manner, which instantly put them all at their ease.

Geoffrey's mother, Patricia, turned out to be fond of a glass of Chardonnay and, after half an hour, had begun to slur her words. She wore a tight dress, pearls, and pink polyurethane heels that matched her nails and lipstick.

She adored Julie's purple hair.

"Of course we'll take you across to England, your royal highness." She patted Merovech on the knee. "Anything for a friend of Geoffrey's."

"Thank you." Merovech gave his sincerest, paparazzi-friendly smile. "I really am grateful."

Mrs Renfrew eyed his tatty jeans and old red hoodie.

"But can't you tell us what all this is about? Are you in some kind of trouble? They're saying on the news that you had a collapse."

"Now Patricia," Jerry warned. "Don't pry,"

Merovech let his smile broaden.

"That's quite all right, Mister Renfrew." He slid his arm around Julie's shoulders. "The truth is, we're eloping. The stuff on TV's just a cover story. We're trying to get to Gretna Green without the news channels getting wind of it. Do you think you can help us?"

Mrs Renfrew clapped a hand to her mouth.

"A wedding? Oh, my lord!" She fanned herself with both hands.

Julie leaned forward conspiratorially, touching the older woman's wrist.

"It's a secret, Mrs Renfrew. You must *promise* not to tell. At least, for now. Afterwards, if you want to, you can tell all your friends how you helped us elope."

Patricia Renfrew's eyes were wide and glittering with the prospect of a royal wedding.

"Can we trust you?" Merovech asked.

"Of course, my loves, of course. We'll do anything we can, won't we Jerry?"

"Yes, dear." Mister Renfrew thumbed tobacco into a well-worn pipe. "We'll cast off at high tide. Should have you across in a couple of hours, eh? Where do you want to go, Southampton or Portsmouth?"

"Either, as long as we can avoid any official entanglements."

Jerry smiled a slow and easy smile.

"You just leave that to me, my boy. Now, the three of you had better stay down here until we're clear of land. We don't want anyone catching sight of you before we're even underway, now do we?"

He stepped through the hatch and climbed up the wooden steps to the deck. Patricia tottered after him, wineglass in hand.

"Make yourselves at home," she called from the hatchway. "Are you sure your doggie will be all right in there?"

Merovech glanced at the pet carrier, which was an enclosed plastic basket made to transport Alsatians and Great Danes. It was the largest he'd been able to find at the out-of-town pet store and, with K8's help, he'd been able to stuff Ack-Ack Macaque into it.

"He'll be fine."

"What kind of dog is he?"

"A big one."

Patricia frowned. She took a couple of clacking steps back into the cabin, towards the box.

"Look," said Julie, trying to distract her, "I'll level with you, okay? We stole the dog."

Patricia Renfrew's plucked and painted brows drew closer together, like indignant caterpillars.

"You *stole* it?"

"From a laboratory." Julie's voice dropped to a whisper. "You wouldn't believe the experiments they were doing to the poor creature. Shampoo in the eyes. Electrodes on the head. By the end, they had him on forty cigarettes a day."

Patricia's eyes narrowed. She took another sip of chardonnay, and then looked from Julie to the pet carrier. She burst into peals of cackling laughter.

"Oh, that's priceless!" she gasped, slapping Julie on the shoulder. "You really had me going there, for a second."

WHEN THEY WERE a mile out into the Channel, Jerry judged it safe for them to come up on deck. Merovech followed K8 and Julie up the wooden stairs from the galley, and the three of them emerged blinking in the afternoon sunlight, clutching at rails to support themselves as the boat rocked.

Jerry stood at the wheel. "If you have a moment, your highness, I'd like to show you something."

He crouched down and opened a metal locker, to reveal a pair of matt-black automatic pistols.

"One for me and one for the wife," he said proudly. "We picked them up last year, when we were sailing around the Gold Coast, in case we got hit by pirates." He took hold of the catamaran's wheel. "And besides, if it all kicks off with China, it won't hurt to have some additional protection, eh?"

Merovech looked up at the flapping sails.

"I've been out of touch for a couple of days. How's it going in China?"

Jerry looked solemn. For the first time since meeting Merovech and his friends, the sparkle seemed to have gone from his eyes.

"Not well at all, I'm afraid."

"Hong Kong?"

"And Indian troops pressuring the western borders." Jerry leant his forearms on the wheel, staring ahead, over the bows, pipe clenched in his teeth. "The whole area's one big flashpoint."

Merovech huffed air through his cheeks. He still held a commission in the Royal Navy, and his time in the South Atlantic had given him a keen sense of what it meant to be part of the crew of a warship, thousands of miles from home and family. If it came to war, it would be the men and women with whom he'd served who'd bear the brunt.

"Let's hope it won't come to that."

Jerry raised his eyebrows. "Amen to that."

They stood in pensive silence for a couple of minutes, enjoying the way the twin hulls cut through the grey waters.

Finally, Jerry said, "Do you think it will go nuclear?"

Merovech looked out to sea, at the container ships looming towards them, each as big as a small town, boxed-up and set adrift.

"I hope not."

Julie stood near the stern, gazing back at the shore. Jerry nodded towards her.

"I thought you might know something. Maybe they'd warned you it might happen, and that's why you were running away to get married, before it did."

Merovech smiled. "No, that's not the reason."

Jerry seemed relieved, although still not entirely convinced. They were riding a stiff south-westerly blowing up from the Bay of Biscay, and Merovech filled his lungs. He could feel the sea air clear the fatigue and cobwebs from his mind. He'd spent far too long cramped up in that van, driving at night. Being out here in the sunlight, surrounded by the ocean, the blustery wind chipping sprays of white from the wave crests, felt like being reborn.

"What happens to you," Jerry asked, "if the balloon does go up?"

Merovech didn't want to think about it. As heir to the throne, he knew he'd be protected. He'd been briefed by his security people. By the time the sirens sounded, he'd be safe and secure, half a mile underground.

"It won't come to that."

Jerry raised an eyebrow.

"I hope you're right, my boy. I really do." He straightened and fastened his grip on the catamaran's helm. "Still, I can't help wondering if we would be in this situation if the whole Unification thing had never happened."

Looking down at the water grazing the hull, Merovech frowned.

"What do you mean?"

Behind him, Jerry gave a grunt.

"Just that if the UK hadn't expanded so quickly, and if we hadn't had France on our side, maybe we wouldn't have clung so hard to Hong Kong in the first place? Perhaps we've been a little overconfident?"

Merovech shrugged. He didn't have any answers. Julie came to the rail. She tucked a straggle of fluttering hair behind her ear and looked up at him.

"How are you doing?" he asked her.

She turned to glance back at the receding shore. Gulls flapped in their wake.

"I don't know. I guess when this is all over, I am going to be in trouble, aren't I? I don't even have a passport with me." She shivered. "My father will be *furieux*."

Merovech put his arm around her.

"Don't you worry about your father. You're going to be okay." He gave her a squeeze. "I'm going to look after you."

She leant into his embrace, snuggling up against him for warmth.

"Well," she mused, "if I am going to run off with anyone, I suppose I could not do much better than the heir to the throne, now could I?"

Merovech smiled into the wind. They were crossing the world's busiest shipping lanes—a major artery of global commerce—and he could see six or seven large vessels at various distances, including container ships, car transporters, and oil tankers. No ferries, though. Few passengers crossed the Channel by boat these days. Most chose the high-speed rail link through the Channel Tunnel. The rest took berths on skyliners.

Merovech scanned the horizon ahead, searching for a particular cigar-shaped silhouette.

"Don't worry," he said. He looked back at Jerry, but the older man seemed absorbed with his compass and SatNav. "I've got a plan."

Julie turned to him.

"You do?"

Merovech gave her a smile.

"I think so."

He would have said more, but a scream cut the air. Patricia clacked up from the galley, heels wobbling, empty wineglass in hand. She glared at Julie, chest heaving.

"You!"

"What's the matter, Mrs Renfrew?"

The older woman's eyes were narrow slits.

"Don't you 'Mrs Renfrew' me, young lady." Her hand swung around to point back down the steps. "Your so-called 'dog' just told me to go and fuck myself!"

CHAPTER NINETEEN
SLOTTING INTO PLACE

In the six months that Victoria had been aboard the *Tereshkova*, she'd only once had occasion to visit the old airship's bridge, at the front of the main gondola. Normally, the room was out of bounds to all but the crew, and protected by armed guards but, a few days after she'd arrived on board and thrown herself on her godfather's hospitality, he'd invited her to take the tour.

"And this is where the magic happens," he'd said, ushering her inside with a flourish.

But when she'd stepped through the hatch, Victoria had been surprised: the room seemed far too small, considering the size of the five-hulled airship that it controlled: barely large enough for three workstations, one each for the navigator, helmsman and commanding officer. The front wall was mostly glass: a grid of rectangular windows that curved down into the floor, offering a panoramic view of the sky and ground ahead. The window frames were titanium, decorated with brass flourishes.

The Commodore had tapped his workstation's screen, bringing up a schematic of the airship.

"We control the whole thing from here. Airspeed, pitch and altitude. We can even operate each engine individually, for really complex manoeuvres."

Uninterested in the computer, Victoria had looked around in disappointment.

"No big steering wheel?"

The Commodore had a braying laugh.

"Goodness no, child. What do you think this is, the *Graf Zeppelin*?"

"I thought that was the effect you were going for."

The Commodore stopped laughing.

"She may look old, but the old girl has life in her yet." His moustache drooped. "More perhaps than I."

"Don't say that."

"I speak only the truth. I am an old man. When I am gone, she will still be here." His eyes regarded her from half-closed lids. "And *someone* will need to fly her."

*   *   *

SHE THOUGHT OF that visit now, as she made her way forward, along the gangway to the Commodore's cabin, which sat directly behind the bridge. It was less utilitarian and considerably more spacious than the control room, with a case of books, a couple of potted plants, and a thick Persian rug. She knocked on the door and let herself in.

Her godfather sat behind his wide aluminium desk, the top buttons of his dress tunic undone. He'd left his cutlass in an elephant's foot umbrella stand by the window.

"Come in and have a seat." He reached into his desk drawer and she heard the clink of glass. "Would you like a drink?"

Victoria declined. She still had all that gin in her system.

"You wanted to see me?"

The old man swept his hand across the desk, activating the SincPad display built into its top.

"I have had one of my people finding out all they can about the Undying. I thought I would summarise it for you, rather than forward it. I know you have trouble reading."

"Oh."

He looked up. "Is there a problem?"

Victoria felt her cheeks colour.

"I assumed you'd called me here to talk about what happened to Cassius Berg."

"What is there to say?"

Victoria got to her feet. "I killed him."

"He fell."

"Only because I closed the doors." She could barely bring herself to look her godfather in the eye.

The Commodore sighed. He clasped his gnarly hands on the desktop and regarded her from under his shaggy brows.

"And what do you want me to do, my dear? Arrest you? Throw you in the brig?"

"I killed him."

The Commodore leaned back.

"Yes, you did. And that's something you're going to have to work out how to live with. But for what it's worth, I think you did the right thing. He was a murdering psychopath. A rabid dog. You did the world a favour by putting him to sleep. And after what he did to you, I would have thrown that *govniuk* off this ship myself." He reached back into the desk drawer and pulled out the bottle of vodka that he kept there.

"Truth be told, I have been impressed by the way you are handling yourself over the past few days. What would you say to a permanent job on my security team?"

"Security?"

"Yes. An airship this size, we get all sorts. Terrorists. Smugglers. Spies. You would be surprised."

Victoria bit her lip. This wasn't the direction she'd expected this meeting to take; yet she found herself tempted and strangely flattered by the old man's offer.

"And I would live here, on the *Tereshkova*, permanently?"

The Commodore threw his arms wide in a gesture of welcome.

"You would be one of my crew."

She'd been aboard the airship for nearly six months now, since the breakup of her marriage, when she'd walked out on Paul with nowhere else to go. And now, thinking about it, she realised that the creaking bulkheads and narrow gangways of the gondolas felt more like home than any place she could think of, London and Paris included.

"Thank you," she said, truly grateful. The Commodore smiled his toothy smile. He twisted the cap off the bottle.

"Are you sure you don't want one?"

"Quite sure."

"Good, because you stink of gin. Now, sit down, be quiet and listen to what I have found." He poured himself a drink, then reactivated the desktop, pulling up a text file.

"According to this, the Undying are a relatively new cult. At least, it is only recently that they have become widely known. There is some evidence that they have been working in secret for some time." He brushed the screen again, bringing up another document, this one containing false colour Hubble photos of gas clouds and galaxies. "They preach a doctrine of transhumanism and digital immortality, and they have some powerful supporters."

He made a circle on the table with his finger, spinning one of the displayed documents to face her. She peered at it, seeing only black marks on a white page.

So far, Paul had been silently watching the meeting through her eyes, and now he spoke.

"It's a list of names," he said. "Celebrities, politicians, business people.

Half the board of directors at Céleste—"

"Céleste *again?*" Victoria got to her feet and began to pace, ticking off points on her fingers as she spoke.

"Paul and Lois both worked for Céleste, under a man named Nguyen. Cassius Berg killed Paul and tried to kill Lois. But Berg was one of the Undying, which means he had links to the Board of Directors at Céleste."

The Commodore frowned. "Céleste are killing their own people?"

"Last year, according to both Paul and Lois, Doctor Nguyen performed an unnecessary removal of the King's soul-catcher."

The old man stroked his moustache. "And the King's been in a coma ever since."

Victoria stopped moving. She found herself looking at an old framed photograph of the Commodore as a youth, clad in the orange pressure suit of a Russian cosmonaut, helmet tucked proudly under his arm.

"You put it all together, and it seems the management at Céleste used Berg to try to silence everyone on Nguyen's team."

The Commodore reached for his vodka glass.

"A cover-up, you mean? But what exactly are they covering, and where do you fit in?"

Victoria pursed her lips.

"I'm not sure. Nguyen operated on me as well, around the same time. Perhaps that has something to do with it?"

In her head, Paul said, "Or maybe they figured that once they'd killed me, it would be a good idea to whack my nosy, former journalist ex-wife, before she started digging around?"

Victoria shrugged.

"Whatever. The thing is, Berg implied that the assassination attempt and the removal of the King's soul-catcher were both part of a conspiracy to seize the throne, and that Duchess Célestine was behind it."

The Commodore tapped the smooth surface of his desk.

"Her name *is* on this list, as a member of the Undying."

Victoria felt the pieces slotting into place, the way they used to do when she'd been closing in on a really good story.

"She owns Céleste. It's her company. She's the founder and CEO. And since that night, she's also been acting as Regent."

"*Okhuyet!*" The Commodore drained his glass. He turned in his chair, to look out of the window at the English countryside passing beneath the *Tereshkova*. They were running along the south coast, heading for the Atlantic and labouring against a brisk south-westerly.

Victoria began to walk back and forth again, across the thick Persian rug, her heavy boots leaving criss-cross grip patterns.

"So the Duchess deposed her own husband and took his place. But to what ends? When Merovech finishes his studies, he'll be ready to assume the throne and she'll be out on her ear."

"Unless he's part of the plot," The Commodore said. "From what you've told me, Berg implied as much, and the Duchess *is* his mother, after all."

Victoria tapped her fingertips against her chin. She had a glimmering, but that wasn't it.

"But then why go to all this trouble?" she asked. "The King was never in the best of health. The throne would have been Merovech's in a few years, anyway."

The old man studied her.

"You sound as if you have a theory."

She leant her knuckles on the desk.

"Paul says the team at Céleste were working on a way to transfer stored personalities into living bodies, and when they rebuilt my brain, they were using me as a guinea pig for some of their techniques." She saw Paul nodding his spiky, platinum head in agreement. "And Lois Lapointe mentioned something about the Prince receiving additional gelware implants. What if those two things are somehow connected?" She straightened up again. Her mouth had gone dry. "What if Merovech takes the throne, but isn't Merovech inside? What if they're planning to load a different personality into him?"

The Commodore rolled the empty vodka glass between his palms.

"Whose personality?"

Victoria tapped her chin again. The gin had worn off and her head buzzed.

"I don't know. Maybe a high-ranking member of the Undying?"

The old man huffed air through his cheeks.

"That's quite a theory."

Victoria banged her hand on the desk. "It's more than that, Commodore. If I'm right, it's a bloody coup d'état!"

CHAPTER TWENTY
NEUTRAL TERRITORY

ACK-ACK MACAQUE appeared in the catamaran's hatchway, wearing the leather jacket and flying goggles K8 had given him. He scratched his chest, and put an arm out to steady himself. He glared around at the grey waters of the English Channel, and his tail twitched.

"I hate boats."

His words seemed to break a spell. Mrs Renfrew screamed again, clearly distraught at the sight of a talking monkey. At the same time, her husband—galvanised by her terror—dropped to his knees and pulled open the metal locker containing the automatic pistols. He came up brandishing one.

"Get back!"

Ack-Ack Macaque blinked at him in puzzlement.

"What's your problem?"

The gun shook. Merovech stepped over and put his hand on the older man's forearm.

"Give me the gun, Jerry."

Mister Renfrew struggled.

"But, but—"

His knuckles were white. Merovech took hold of the pistol's barrel, and twisted both weapon and wrist. Something snapped. Mister Renfrew gave a cry of pain and indignation, and released the gun.

"What are you doing?" Mrs Renfrew didn't know whether to look at her husband or the monkey.

Julie bent and scooped the second gun from the locker. She passed it to Merovech.

"Okay," he said. "Let's get these two below."

Mr Renfrew had dropped to his knees in the cockpit, cheeks ashen, arms and shoulders curled around the pain of a broken wrist. Merovech tossed one of the guns to Ack-Ack Macaque, and used his free hand to haul the man to his feet.

"Come on," he said.

He could feel his heart beating in his chest. After days of running and hiding, it felt good to be doing something positive: to be taking charge of the situation, as he'd been trained to do.

He shepherded the old couple down into the interior of the yacht, and into one of the cabins.

"I'm sorry about this," he said as he closed the wooden door. "But I'm afraid there's more going on here than you realise."

He tucked the gun into the back of his jeans and clumped back up on deck. The wind ran its fingers through his hair.

"Okay," he rubbed his hands. "K8, get down there and make sure they don't escape. And while you're there, I want you to get on the radio and hail a skyliner. She's called the *Tereshkova*, and if she's running to schedule, she should be somewhere hereabouts."

He turned to Julie.

"Skyliners are neutral territory. If I can get you and K8 on board, you'll be safe from arrest. You'll have time to figure out what you want to do next."

Julie looked back at the French coast, which was now little more than a strip of green on the horizon.

"But, my father—" She reached up to touch the fading bruise on her cheek.

"Forget him," Merovech said. "He can't touch you here. You'll be safe."

"What about me?" Ack-Ack Macaque had his back to the rail. He was passing the gun Merovech had given him from leathery hand to leathery hand, testing its weight and balance.

"That's up to you," Merovech said. "How did you get on in the game?"

The monkey shrugged.

"I killed a few people. Nobody important. I didn't have time for much else."

"Would you like to go back in?"

Ack-Ack Macaque opened his mouth and picked at a yellow canine.

"I'm going to wreck it," he said. "Those motherfuckers at Céleste have it coming."

Merovech nodded.

"Okay, get below and have K8 hook you back in. We'll leave you in there until you've done what you need to do."

"And then what?"

Merovech reached back and took hold of the gun in his waistband. He pulled it out and checked the magazine.

"We've been running too long, and I've had enough. When you've finished killing the new monkey in the game, you and I are going to start fighting back, for real."

PART TWO

THE DEAD AND THE UNDYING

Yet you, my creator, detest and spurn me, thy creature, to whom thou art bound by ties only dissoluble by the annihilation of one of us.

Mary Shelley, *Frankenstein*

CHAPTER TWENTY-ONE
CHIMPANZEES DON'T HAVE TAILS

THE CHOPPER WAS an amphibious model, with large floats instead of landing skis. By the time it reached the *Tereshkova*'s helipad, Victoria and the Commodore were there, waiting to greet it.

The Commodore wore his full dress uniform: a white jacket with plenty of gold braid, cavalry trousers, and a pair of knee-length riding boots. Although Victoria still wore her thick green greatcoat, beneath it, she'd changed into a clean pair of black jeans and a black roll-neck top, to conceal the freshly reapplied dressings at the back of her neck. She'd given up with the wig the Commodore had given her, and settled instead on a plain fleece hat.

As the helicopter's hatch opened, the Commodore clicked his heels together and bowed at the waist.

"Welcome, your highness."

Prince Merovech stepped down onto the rubberised surface of the pad and saluted.

"Permission to come aboard, Commodore?"

In the jeans and hoodie that he wore, he looked much like any other teenage boy from the streets of Paris or London. He was only nineteen years old yet, Victoria knew, he was a teenager already acquainted with the harsh realities of both public life and military combat. A boy who'd had to grow up fast, and take on more than many adults ever did.

"A pleasure to see you again, Miss Valois." He had to shout over the engine noise.

"Your highness."

Behind Merovech, a girl with purple hair. Behind her, a redheaded, boyish-looking kid in a green sweater.

And behind them all came the monkey.

Victoria took a moment to take him in. He stood much taller than she would have expected, yet not quite upright, and he was chewing the soggy end of an unlit cigar. A leather patch covered one of his eyes, while the other glared about him, sizing everything up as a possible threat. He looked powerful and dangerous, as much animal as man.

And who the hell, she thought, gave him a gun?

She tailed along as the Commodore led the party down, through the stairwells and gangways in the body of the airship, to the comfort of the main gondola's dining room.

"Come," he said. "Be seated. Make yourselves at home."

Like the lounge bar, the dining room had been done out in homage to the pioneers of airship travel, from the spotless white tablecloths to the polished wooden fixtures and the patterned wallpaper on the bulkheads. The windows were wide and gave the room a light, airy feel, making it seem a lot bigger than it actually was. Between the windows, the Commodore had placed framed photographs of Russian heroes, including Yuri Gagarin, and the woman after whom he'd named the airship itself, Valentina Tereshkova, the first female astronaut.

The Prince and his entourage settled themselves around the largest table, and refreshments were served: tea for the Prince, coffee for Julie Girard, cola for the kid known as K8, and a daiquiri for the monkey. Victoria ordered a soda water. The gin had left her dehydrated and headachy, and she needed something to freshen her up.

When they'd all been served, and the formalities taken care of, the Commodore put his hands on the table.

"We were surprised to receive your radio message, your highness. We were given to understand that you were indisposed."

Merovech considered this.

"I thank you for your hospitality, Commodore. All I can say is that rumours of my ill health have been greatly exaggerated."

"And your simian friend?"

"A long story, I'm afraid. The truth of it is, we're in a spot of bother, and could really use your help."

Victoria leant forward in her chair.

"We know about the Undying and their plan to seize the throne," she said. "And we know you're involved."

Merovech's eyes narrowed.

"'Seize the throne'?"

Victoria slipped off her hat, revealing the jacks studding the scar on her temple. "You and I were in the hospital at the same time, Merovech. They took out the damaged parts of my brain and pumped my head full of gelware. And they did the same to you. Only the bits they took out of your head weren't damaged at all."

The Prince regarded her for a long, thoughtful moment.

"And do you know why they did that?"

Victoria swallowed. This was it. Time to put all the pieces together and make some wild accusations.

"The Undying have infiltrated Céleste. They're using you as a pawn. The minute you take the throne, they'll pump another personality into your head."

Merovech glanced at Julie Girard, then back at Victoria.

"What makes you say that?"

Victoria felt her cheeks flush. "They sent an assassin to kill every member of Doctor Nguyen's team. We stopped him and he—" She took a deep breath. "He talked."

They were all looking at her now.

Merovech said, "Nguyen's dead. We went to his house."

"So, you knew about this?"

The Prince shook his head.

"We were starting to piece it together. K8 used to work for Céleste, and she hacked their internal server. Then, when we broke into the corporate building, Julie found Nguyen's notes."

The Commodore raised his eyebrows.

"You broke in?"

Julie smiled. "Yes, and we got a lot more than we bargained for."

Victoria recognised the girl's accent. She said, "*Tu es de Paris?*"

"*Oui. Je suis étudiante à la Sorbonne. Et vous?*"

"*J'ai vécu un moment à Paris. Maintenant j'habite ici.*" She looked back to Merovech and switched to English. "So, you're on the run, are you?"

The Prince didn't even blink.

"We are. At least, for the moment. That's why we're here." He turned to the Commodore. "Would it be possible for us to claim asylum on your vessel, sir?"

The old man smoothed his white moustache with thumb and index finger, considering his answer. When he finally spoke, he said, "I suppose that could be arranged."

Merovech smiled. Julie and K8 looked relieved.

"Thank you."

The Commodore held up a hand.

"Just be good enough to answer me one question." He levelled a finger at Ack-Ack Macaque, who was at that moment in the process of cleaning his ear with his little finger. "What is the deal with the chimpanzee?"

Ack-Ack Macaque bristled. His solitary eye glared at the Commodore.

"Have you seen my tail, man? Chimpanzees don't have tails."

The Commodore bowed his head.

"Forgive me, I meant no offence. But my question remains. Who are you, and where did you come from? To whom do you belong?"

Ack-Ack Macaque picked up his daiquiri glass and began to lick the sugar from the rim.

"I'm my own monkey," he said between slurps, "and I don't belong to anyone, not anymore."

"We rescued him from the Céleste laboratories," Merovech explained. "As far as I'm concerned, he's his own person. But there's a lot of proprietary tech crammed into his head, and I'm sure Céleste will be keen to get it back."

The Commodore sighed.

"So, you bring me a fugitive prince, a teenage computer hacker, a burglar, and a stolen monkey?"

Merovech clapped his hands together and rubbed them.

"I'm afraid that's about the size of it." He turned his attention to Victoria.

"So, what else did your assassin have to say?"

CHAPTER TWENTY-TWO
IRRESISTIBLE FORCE

ONE OF THE *Tereshkova*'s stewards showed K8 and Ack-Ack Macaque to a crew cabin in the farthest port gondola, away from the areas permitted for use by ordinary passengers.

The room was small and cramped, lit by a lamp fixed to the wall. His nostrils twitched at the pervasive stench of unwashed sheets and Russian cologne. A pair of cabin beds stood to either side of the narrow space that ran the length of the room from door to porthole. Beneath the porthole, a nightstand, and a couple of chairs. The washroom was down the hall.

"Are you ready to get back in there?" K8 asked, sitting cross-legged on the bed. She had the SincPad and connective leads in her lap. Even to Ack-Ack Macaque, who wasn't very good at reading human expressions, she looked tired.

She's just a kid, he thought. But she was his kid. He had no idea where she came from, but she was the closest thing he had to a friend right now. She'd been a member of his squadron, and as such, he'd do everything in his power to look after and protect her. Over the years, he'd lost so many kids. He'd seen them shot out of the sky by flak, gunned down by enemy pilots, and skewered by black-clad ninjas. He'd watched their planes spiral into hillsides, trailing smoke and flames, and it had eaten away at him. Survivor's guilt, they called it. Yet, out here in the real world, none of those deaths counted. They hadn't really happened at all. They'd all been a part of the game. The characters may have died, but the players were still alive. They were still at their consoles and SincPads, still living and breathing, even if they couldn't get back into the game. After months of guilt and grief, the knowledge felt like a weight taken from his shoulders.

He leant against the back of the closed cabin door and lit a cigar. K8 wrinkled her nose.

"Are you allowed to smoke in here?"

"I don't give a crap." He spoke through teeth clenched on the cigar's butt. "I've got bigger things to worry about right now. Like, who I am, and *what* I am."

K8 fiddled with one of the connective wires in her lap, straightening out its kinks and tangles.

"Maybe I can help you fill in some of the blanks."

"More hacking?"

A mischievous grin. "Hardly. I worked there, remember? I got trained. They wanted me to know how important you were. They even gave me a *brochure*."

Ack-Ack Macaque took the cigar from his mouth. He raised his muzzle and huffed a trio of expanding smoke rings at the low metal ceiling.

"So, what did it say in this brochure? What am I, a kids' toy?"

K8 laughed brightly. The lamplight caught the short copper curls of her hair.

"You're a weapons system, Skipper. A prototype. The game's just a fortunate spin-off, a bit of extra cash. The real money's in intelligent guidance systems. Drones, missiles. Even space probes. They didn't want to go to all the trouble of developing genuine AI, so they thought they'd do the next best thing, and start bootstrapping primates."

She leaned forward and lowered her voice almost to a whisper. "But here's the thing nobody else knows, the bit I *did* get from hacking the server. That probe they're sending to Mars, it isn't full of terraforming bacteria. No, that's just a cover story. A diversion. Really, it's full of souls."

Ack-Ack Macaque moved the cigar from one side of his mouth to the other. "Souls?"

"Recorded personalities." She tapped the back of her neck, at the base of her skull. "Thousands of them, harvested from the dead and dying."

"To what end?"

"To download, once they get there. Don't forget these guys are pretty heavily into the whole transhumanism trip. The probe's the size of a London bus. There's machinery in there. It's going to build android bodies for the Undying faithful—bodies that don't need to breathe or eat or sleep. And then, they'll have the whole of Mars to themselves. By the time the Americans or Chinese get around to sending a manned mission, they'll find an established colony of robot cultists already in place."

Ack-Ack Macaque considered this. He hadn't understood everything she'd said, but he thought he'd gleaned the gist. Or some of it, at least.

"You say thousands. Is the cult really that big?"

K8's expression darkened.

"The faithful probably number a couple of hundred. The rest have been harvested from hospitals and morgues. A ready-made slave army."

Ack-Ack Macaque tapped ash onto the deck.

"Robots, Morris? Really?"

"Yes, Skipper. They already had a prototype. They built it using what they learned working on Victoria Valois. They stretched some skin over its face and uploaded a personality into it. Called it Berg."

"What happened to it?"

K8 shrugged. She had no idea. Instead, she held up one of the connective leads by its copper jack.

"Are you ready to get in there and cause some trouble?"

Ack-Ack Macaque held his cigar at arm's length, considering. Then he dropped it to the deck and ground it out with the toe of his boot.

"Yeah." He hopped up onto the bed beside her and rolled onto his back. "If it's the best way to hurt Céleste, then hook me in."

K8 shuffled close to his head as he made himself comfortable.

"I've been fiddling with the parameters," she said. "I think I've rigged it so you'll have unlimited ammo. Cool, huh?"

Ack-Ack Macaque grinned, exposing his incisors.

"Can you make it so I can't die?"

K8 tipped her head on one side.

"I think you're almost immortal already. After all, why name the game after you if you can get killed off easily? There'd be no challenge."

Ack-Ack Macaque wriggled on the blanket, adjusting his position. K8 removed the goggles from the top of his head, and smoothed down the chestnut-coloured hair on his scalp.

"Maybe that's what happened with the other four monkeys," he said. "Maybe they got killed and had to be replaced?"

K8 shook her head.

"You don't die if you get wasted in the game. Not in the real world. You just get disconnected."

"So, the new version of me...?"

"He's just an uplifted monkey, same as you are, jacked into the game. He's probably in the same lab, in the same couch where they had you."

"But is he indestructible too?"

"Not entirely. Neither of you is. You're both just very, very hard to kill." She plugged the leads into the sockets on the edge of the SincPad. "So, I guess we're about to answer that age-old question."

"What question?"

She bent over him, sliding the other end of the cables, one by one, into the corresponding ports on the top of his head.

"The question of what happens when an irresistible force meets an immovable object."

EVERYTHING WENT BLANK. Then, half a second later, Ack-Ack Macaque found himself standing once more in the perpetual summer of a fictional 1944. This time, K8 had dropped him closer to the main action, behind a hangar on his old airbase.

Everything was exactly as he remembered it, from the acrid tang of engine grease to the feel of the warm tarmac beneath his bare feet. He drew his Colts. Nobody in sight. The main action was taking place at the end of the row of hangars, in the Officers' Mess. He could hear somebody hammering out a tune on the piano. Glasses clinking. Voices raised in laughter.

This had been his life for as long as he could remember. This field, that tent. Those planes on the runway. He felt his lips pull back from his teeth, exposing his canines.

Okay motherfuckers, he thought. *Time for a dose of reality.*

Keeping low, he loped from hangar to hangar, working his way towards the sounds of merriment. Was his replacement inside the tent? Some of the planes seemed to be missing from the runway. Perhaps he was, perhaps he wasn't. Ack-Ack Macaque paused at the corner of the final hangar, and tightened his grip on the Colts.

There was only one way to find out.

He licked his teeth, checking them for sharpness. Then, still hunched as low as possible, he scampered around to the front of the tent. When he got there, he straightened up as far as he could and, holding his gigantic silver revolvers high, kicked open the door.

Instantly, the piano music stopped. All the heads turned in his direction.

Same old crowd, he thought. Young, talkative and cavalier. His thumbs drew back the hammers on the Colts.

"Where's the monkey?" he snapped. They looked at him in puzzlement. Nobody spoke. From the corner of the tent, the cockney Mess Officer bustled towards him, all white jacket, slicked back hair and pencil moustache.

"Afternoon, squire. What can I get you? The usual, is it?"

Ack-Ack Macaque looked him up and down. The wide-boy patter never changed. The man was an obvious construct, part of the program. How come he'd never noticed before?

He pressed the barrel of one of the Colts to the Mess Officer's forehead, and pulled the trigger. The gun went off with a satisfyingly deafening bang, and red mist blew from the back of the man's head. But he didn't fall down. He stood there, holding his silver tray, looking stupid.

"Evenin' squire." His jaw flapped, caught in a loop. "Evenin' squire. Evenin' squire. Evenin' squire…"

Ack-Ack Macaque kicked him aside. The kids on the nearest tables were starting to get to their feet, their mouths half open in alarm, their eyes wide with surprise. He shot them all, one at a time. *Blam! Blam! Blam!* Heads and arms flopped. Men and women screamed. Blood flew everywhere, but he knew it meant nothing. None of these deaths were real, they were just a means to an end: a way of attracting the big guy's attention.

He reached out a hairy arm and grabbed an airman by the lapels.

"Where is he?" he snarled. The kid was seventeen or eighteen, with the first wispy suggestions of a goatee beard.

"I don't understand."

"The other monkey. Where is he?"

The kid's eyes rolled in his head.

"What other monkey?"

Ack-Ack Macaque leaned in close, bringing his teeth right up to the kid's cheek.

"There's another version of me. A new one. He's not here right now. *Where is he?*"

The kid wriggled in his grip.

"Took off about an hour ago, heading for the *Brunel*. But I thought that was you. What is this? What's happening?"

Ack-Ack Macaque released him, letting him drop to the rough wooden boards of the tent's floor.

"Things have changed," he said. "There's a new monkey in town. Tell your friends."

He turned on his heel and stalked out onto the runway. A few of the mechanics were loitering, disturbed by the sound of gunfire but unsure how to react. He plugged them all. What did it matter? None of them were really here.

He swarmed up the side of the nearest Spitfire. It wasn't his plane, but it would do. The seat would have been narrow for a man, but gave him plenty of room. He settled into position on the parachute pack and closed the pilot's door. Then he pulled closed and latched the canopy hood. He wound the rudder to full right, to counter the plane's torque, and pressed the starter buttons. The fuel pressure light came on and the engine coughed. The four-bladed prop spun into life, and the aircraft strained forward against its brakes.

Ack-Ack Macaque's large nostrils quivered with the smell of aviation fuel and hot metal. He saw survivors stumbling from the Officers' Mess, and pointed upward with his index finger.

"I'm going up," he called. "Get out of the way."

They looked at him with pale incomprehension, milling around in front of the plane. Frustrated, he switched to his middle finger. "Oh, up yours."

He took hold of the throttle and the plane leapt forward, scattering the onlookers like chickens. Laughing, and still waving his one-fingered salute, Ack-Ack Macaque taxied to the end of the runway. He hadn't bothered plugging his headset into the radio, so he couldn't hear the protestations of the tower. Instead, he fixed his eyes on the horizon and let out a piercing, fang-filled jungle screech.

This was it. This was him, where he'd always been. Where he'd always belonged: behind the joystick of a Spitfire, ready to take on the world.

And boy, was the world in trouble.

HALF AN HOUR later, high in the clear skies above Northern France, Ack-Ack Macaque gripped the stick of his Spitfire as the plane vibrated around him. Ahead, enemy fighters danced like gnats in his crosshairs, harrying a much larger, far more ponderous vessel.

Flagship of the Allies' aerial fleet, the aircraft carrier *Brunel* dominated the sky. With dimensions similar to one of its seagoing counterparts, it was easily the largest vessel in the European theatre. On its back, serried ranks of Nissen huts housed an entire squadron of single-seater Hurricane fighter-bombers. The planes were launched and recovered via a metal runway slung between the two over-sized, armoured airships that formed the bulk of the carrier's mass. The propellers of fifty Rolls Royce engines powered the beast, and gun emplacements bristled along its flanks and undercarriage.

Half a dozen German fighters were currently attempting to mount an attack on the carrier, but were being held at bay by three of the *Brunel*'s Hurricanes, and a solitary Spitfire.

Ack-Ack Macaque leant on the throttle, urging his plane higher. The air in the cockpit turned bitterly cold. His breath came in puffs of vapour, but he didn't care. It wasn't real cold, was it? Just an illusion, like everything else. He kept his attention on the dogfight unfolding before him, squinting to pick his adversary from the wheeling wings and chattering cannons of the British planes.

He saw a Messerschmitt fall from the fray, trailing smoke and flames, an aileron flapping loose. Above it, the Spitfire wheeled. Compared to the functional lines of its prey, it was as sleek as a hawk; and where its RAF roundels should have been, it sported a grinning, painted monkey's face.

"There you are." He pulled on the stick to give chase, ignoring the other planes. Coming up from beneath the fight, he hadn't yet been spotted by the other pilots. For now, he had the element of surprise.

Okay, he thought, let's hope the world's watching. He mashed the trigger button with his leathery thumb, and felt the rattle of the wing-mounted cannons. His shots caught his target across the underside of its fuselage, midway between the wings and rudder. He caught a glimpse as he hurtled past vertically, propeller clawing the thin air, and his plane threatened to stall. He pulled back, flipping the bird over onto its back. The yellow nose of a Messerschmitt lunged at him, but he rolled away from its attack, snarling.

"I should have dealt with them first," he muttered. "Too late now."

He looked around for the other Spitfire, and was alarmed to see it looping around behind him. Its guns blazed and he felt the bullets rip into his wings. Swearing silently, he kicked the rudder pedal and hauled the stick back to his hip, tipping the horizon over in a vertiginous rolling turn.

More impacts, like rocks on a tin roof. The seat convulsed beneath him. He pulled harder. German planes whirled across his view, zooming and banking, thrown into disarray, and he kept his thumb on the trigger, hoping to clear a few from the sky.

With merciless savagery, he threw his Spitfire from side to side, feinting one way and then another. Two more bursts hit him, but then he went left as his pursuer went right. Both planes screamed around in a banking turn that brought them face-to-face.

Ack-Ack Macaque fired, and saw the cannons on his counterpart's wings do likewise. The two planes were shredding each other. Bullets slammed into the cockpit around him. The propeller splintered. Invisible hammer blows shattered the windshield. But still he kept firing. Only when collision seemed unavoidable did he knock the stick sideways.

The air roared through his fur. He pulled his goggles down over his eyes and tried to turn for another attack. The engine spluttered ominously, releasing gouts of black smoke. Hot oil peppered his fur. The prop had been partially shattered and the stick felt sloppy in his hands.

Panicked and vulnerable, he scanned the skies for the other planes, only to see the German Messerschmitts circling at a distance, watching the duel in apparent confusion. For a few moments, he couldn't place the other Spitfire. Then it appeared from behind the great sausage shape of the *Brunel*'s starboard gasbag, trailing smoke. As he watched, the pilot brought its nose up just enough to make the lip of the metal runway, and the plane hit the deck like a pancake, slithering on its belly, skidding around and around until—like an injured wasp blundering into a spider's web—it was caught by the crash netting at the runway's far end.

Trying to get a better view, Ack-Ack Macaque pressed his face to the jagged remnants of his cockpit's canopy. For a moment, he dared to hope he'd been victorious. Then he saw a long-armed figure clambering from the wreck, and his lips peeled back in a snarl.

"You don't get away that easily, monkey boy!"

With its prop splintered, the stricken Spit juddered violently. The engine, freed from the drag of the blades, threatened to shake itself, and the plane, apart. Ack-Ack Macaque fought to keep the wings level as he tried to reach the runway of the carrier *Brunel*, suspended between the twin dirigibles which bore its weight, an off-centre control tower midway down its length like the funnel of a ship. He side-slipped, bringing the plane's nose into line with the crash netting at the runway's end, where his opponent's plane lay on its belly, smoke billowing from its shot-up engine.

K8 thought he was practically indestructible, and he hoped she was right, because this wasn't going to be the daintiest landing he'd ever made. The *Brunel* loomed larger and larger in his crosshairs, filling his forward view. He could see deck hands sprinting for cover. Pale faces at the windows of the control tower. At the last moment, he pulled his knees up to his chest and braced his feet against the dashboard. A wild scream filled his throat, and the Spitfire's prop buried itself in the metal deck at upwards of sixty miles per hour.

CHAPTER TWENTY-THREE
WINGSUIT

MEROVECH AND JULIE found themselves alone in one of the first class cabins, behind the dining room in the main gondola. They perched opposite each other, he on the edge of the bed, she on a chair by the nightstand.

The walls of the cabin were currently a blank, gunmetal grey, but the SincPad screens covering them offered a variety of augmented reality options, from the lush greens and plunging cliffs of Big Sur to the lone and level sands of the Egyptian desert, and he watched Julie's purple fingernail flick through the menu. As she scrolled, she said,

"I am sorry I got you into this."

Merovech leaned forward.

"You didn't get me into it. I was in it already, I just didn't know."

"But if I had not taken you on that raid—"

"You did me a favour. I had to find out sometime. If I hadn't gone along with you, I might never have known the truth. I might have gone back into that clinic one day and come back out as somebody else. In fact, I'm pretty sure you've saved my life."

"You say that, and yet you want to risk it all by going back there and confronting her?"

"I have to. Whatever else she is, she's still my mother."

The walls were still grey, like the inside of a battleship. Merovech felt a chill pass through him.

"But my father. He's not really my father at all."

"I am sorry. I know you loved him."

"I can hardly believe it." He shook his head, trying to clear it.

"I *am* sorry."

"But how could he not have known?"

"Why should he have done? Your mother simply lied to him. With Nguyen's help, she could have faked the pregnancy easily enough."

Merovech closed his eyes. His mother and father had always been distant figures, more so than the parents of most of the boys at his boarding school, and even as a young child, he'd come to understand that they were people to be visited rather than lived with. He'd left his nursery at four years old, and had never gone back. The school had been his home. And when he'd left there at eighteen, he'd gone straight into the army for a year's national service; and then on to university in Paris. School holidays aside, he hadn't lived under the same roof as his mother in over fifteen years.

He knelt before Julie.

"Okay, she grew me and lied to me and filled my head with gelware." He put his hands on her knees. "But what does that make *me*, Jules? What am I? Am I even human?"

Her eyes glittered. She reached a hand to cup his chin.

"Oh, Merovech. You are whoever you want to be. You are not to blame for any of this." She put a hand up to touch the fading bruise at the side of her eye. "Whatever our parents have done to us, it is not our fault. We did not ask for any of it. We have to think of ourselves now. We have to salvage whatever we can."

"No." Merovech climbed to his feet. "If I have to live with what she's done to me, the only way I can do so is by understanding *why* she did it."

"But you do not have to confront her. You could send her a message. Make a phone call."

"No. I want to hear her say it in person. I want to look into her eyes."

"But, the danger—"

He crossed his arms.

"Life's short, Jules. All we can do is make the best of it. I learned that lesson in the Falklands."

Julie wiped her face with the sleeve of her cardigan.

"Why don't you just stay here? The *Tereshkova* is going all the way to Mexico. We could go together, leave all this behind."

Merovech sighed.

"I've got one of the planet's most recognisable faces. Wherever I go, there'll always be somebody trying to dig up a story or take a picture. I can't run from this. And besides, I need to know why she's done what she's done."

Julie pushed up the sleeves of her grey wool cardigan, and then pulled them back down again.

"Please, Merovech."

He reached down and picked her hand from her lap. "I need to do this, Jules. I need answers. And the only way I'll get them is by facing up to her."

Julie's fingers pulled at his.

"Or you could just, you know, stay here, with me."

"I can't."

"But why not? If we go to South America, we can find a little place and start again, somewhere away from your mother. It will just be the two of us. No parents at all."

Merovech pursed his lips, enticing visions of white sand, grass huts and palm trees momentarily flickering, and then dying, behind his eyes.

"My mother owns one of the biggest technology companies on the planet. She's one of the world's richest women, and she has at her disposal the combined resources of the British and French secret services. Do you seriously think there's *anywhere* in this world she couldn't find us?" He pointed to his face. "And as I said, it's not like I can easily hide, is it?"

Julie pouted. She tapped the touch screen menu, and the grey walls flickered away, replaced by a view across Hong Kong harbour, taken from the hundredth floor of a hotel at dawn, with low red mist over the water and the skyscrapers shining like bronze spears. She looked at the view for a long time and then said:

"So, how are you planning to do it?"

At first, Merovech assumed the wall image to be a still photograph. The city and its surroundings seemed motionless, like a held breath at sunrise. Then his eye caught a small boat cutting through the water.

"I'm not sure. I need time to think."

He pulled off his hoodie. He'd been wearing the t-shirt beneath for three days now, and it stank. The Commodore's staff had left clean towels on the bed, and white robes hanging on a hook on the back of the cabin door. He picked up a towel.

"I'm going to take a shower." He reached for the door handle but, as he did so, a knock came from the other side. He pulled it aside to find Victoria Valois standing in the gangway with a large kit bag slung over her shoulder. She'd shed the heavy coat she'd been wearing when they met earlier, and was clad from toe to chin in black. She'd replaced her fleece hat with a long silk headscarf.

"We need to talk."

VICTORIA LED HIM up the metal steps and along the wire-supported walkways of the airship's interior, back up to the helipad at the top of the vessel. As he climbed out onto the springy black surface, the wind snatched at him like a thousand frozen fingers, and he rubbed his arms, wishing for his discarded hoodie.

"What can I do for you, Miss Valois?"

She gave a flick of her hand. "Please, call me Victoria." She walked to the rail at the forward edge and looked out, across the bows. The silk scarf streamed back from her head like a mare's mane.

"As we were in the hospital together," she said. "I just wanted to ask: now you know about Céleste, and what they did to you while you were in there, what are you planning to do about it?"

Beyond the curve of the airship's bow, Merovech could see the coast of Hampshire, with its submerged beaches and flooded harbours. He took a long breath in through his nose.

"I'm going to find a way to confront my mother. After that, I'm not sure."

"Would you like some help?"

He slid his fingers into the pockets of his jeans.

"No, thank you. This is about me. It's my problem, and it's up to me to fix it."

She turned to him, scarf whipping.

"What if it can't be fixed? This affects us both, Merovech. My husband worked for your mother's company, and they killed him for it. If there's a reckoning to be had, I want to be in on the action." She leant her hip on the rail and crossed her arms. "You're a smart kid, and you've done well to get this far. But what are you going to do, arrest her?"

Merovech shrugged. The thought had crossed his mind.

Victoria clicked her tongue.

"Forget it. She's surrounded by her own security people. Berg said she had members of the army supporting her. You wouldn't last five minutes. Remember, she tried to kill your father, and she's planning to kill you. Your personality, at least. If you try to tackle her alone, you'll be giving her exactly what she wants."

Merovech shivered. The cold air seemed to slice right through him.

"We're going to expose her," he said. "We're going to make the whole plot public. That's why we've hooked the monkey back into the game. We're going to use it to get the word out. These plots rely on power and secrecy. Once enough people know, we'll have the weight of numbers on our side. She can't run from the Internet."

Victoria let the kit bag slip from her shoulder, onto the deck. She said, "That won't be enough, I'm afraid. Not without concrete proof."

"Then what do you suggest?"

"Tomorrow's Unification Day. From what I can gather from the news channels, the Duchess will be celebrating it onboard her liner, the *Maraldi*, where she'll be supervising the launch of the Martian probe. The invited guests will include most of the people on the Commodore's list of the Undying. The King will be there too, moved by private ambulance, and, if what Berg implied is true, I don't give much for his chances of surviving the night."

At the mention of his father, Merovech let out a long breath.

"But why? She's been with him since the assassination attempt. Why hasn't she killed him already?"

"The timing has to be right. The death of a king isn't something you can easily cover up. She has to be sure her plan will work."

"But if I'm not there, she can't go ahead, can she?"

"Of course she can. She'll be worried about you going public, so she'll have to act now, and act fast. But my guess is that she'll stick to her original plan as far as possible. She'll declare you king, but tell everyone you're suffering from nervous exhaustion, or something like that. That way, when you do eventually surface, no-one's going to believe what you're saying, and she'll have an excuse to get you into the Céleste facility."

"So, we confront her there, in front of the television cameras?"

"Absolutely not. You stay here, your highness. We need you alive. If the King dies, you're the only one with a credible claim to the throne, and the gelware in your head's the only real evidence we have."

"So, what do you suggest?"

"I'll go in."

"By yourself?"

"I'll take the monkey. From what I hear, he's an expert at breaking into places and causing havoc."

"But how will you get in? That place will be locked down tight. You'd never get near it."

Victoria smiled. She crouched beside the kit bag and pulled out a suit made of black material. She shook it out and it flapped in the wind.

"Have you ever seen one of these before?" The suit had parachute-like flaps of material between the legs and under the arms. "It's called a 'wingsuit'. It's an extreme sport thing." She began folding it back up, wrapping it up in her arms. "We'll be at our closest approach to the ship tomorrow, around 6pm. This time of year, it will be dark. We can jump from here and glide in, silent and undetected."

"Then what?"

"I'm a journalist. I'll infiltrate the offices, look for as much proof as possible." She smiled. "And if all else fails, I'll let the monkey loose."

Merovech waved his hands.

"No, it's too dangerous. I can't let you do it."

Victoria's lips whitened. "I don't need your permission, Merovech. This is personal, for me and Paul. The only reason I'm talking to you at all is because we'll need your support if everything turns to shit." She stuffed the wingsuit back into its bag and pulled the heavy zipper closed. Then she stood, wiped her hands together, and put them on her hips.

"Find a camera when your father dies," she said. "Video, webcam, whatever, and make a speech. Claim the throne, expose your mother, and upload the files from K8's SincPad to the news channels. It's the only way to stop her."

Merovech swallowed something hot and sour.

"But I'm not the King's son. I'm not really in line."

Victoria stopped in her tracks. She looked him up and down, and her lips kinked in a half-smile.

"Well, you won't be the first bastard to seize power. But if I were you, I'd probably think twice before mentioning that on air, okay?"

THE COMMODORE INVITED her to join him on the *Tereshkova*'s bridge as he turned the old airship to the south-west, driving its five linked hulls into the teeth of the prevailing wind.

Honoured to be allowed back into this most inner of sanctums, Victoria leant up against the curved array of rectangular windows that formed the room's front wall. The grid of glass wrapped around to the sides, and swept down into the floor, providing maximum visibility for the three crew stations. Leaning up against its outward curve felt like leaning over the abyss; like flying. As the bows nosed around, she watched the beaches of Dorset's Jurassic Coast slide away to her right and, for the first time in days, felt her spirits rise, if only momentarily. Far to the left, the edge of Europe presented as a dark blue line against the horizon; and, straight ahead, she could see the hazy indigo waters of the Bay of Biscay.

On the bridge behind her, the pilot's and navigator's workstations were unoccupied and empty, and the Commodore had full control of the vessel.

The elderly Russian's skin seemed greyer than usual. His face held the washed-out sepia look of a photograph bleached by sunlight. The brass buttons of his jacket were unfastened, the sides held together only by the red sash that looped over his left shoulder and dropped to the empty scabbard on his right hip. Having instructed the flight computer to make the necessary course adjustments, the gnarled fingers of his hand lay on the keyboard of the SincPad set into the arm of his command couch. The other gripped the knee of his cavalry trousers.

"The sooner we are out over the Atlantic and away from Commonwealth airspace, the happier I will be." He gave her a look from beneath his brows. "You do realise that we are all fugitives now, don't you?"

Victoria pushed away from the concave glass wall. She said, "We're not the ones plotting a coup."

"Nevertheless, we are the ones harbouring an absconded prince, and a stolen monkey."

"They can't touch us here, though, can they?"

The old man looked grave.

"Ordinarily, no. Skyliners are neutral territory. But there has never been a situation quite like this one before. A claim for sanctuary from an ordinary criminal is one thing. A lost heir to the throne? That is something else again. Who knows what they might do to get him back? What they might be capable of?"

Victoria pushed her hands into the pockets of her long coat.

"What can they do?"

"Berg said they would burn this ship from under us."

"Berg was a lunatic."

"He was also a dangerous man, Victoria, and I would not disregard any of his threats." The Commodore drummed his immaculately neat fingernails on the touchpad's glass. "As a matter of fact, that is one of the reasons I invited you here. I wanted to talk. Have you given any more thought to my offer?"

"To join your crew?"

"Yes. You have a knack for sniffing out trouble, and you have shown you can handle yourself. I could use a person with your talents."

"I'm flattered."

"Do not be. I simply state the facts. Up here, we have the freedom of the skies. But we are also a target for hijackers, smugglers and terrorists. I need you, Victoria. I need your nose for trouble."

Sunlight shimmered on the sea.

She said, "This thing with Paul—"

The old man raised a hand.

"You have to finish it. I understand matters of honour. But what will you do afterwards? Where else will you go?"

Hands still in her pockets, Victoria stepped away from the front wall.

"I hadn't given it much thought."

"Perhaps you should." He accessed one of the softscreens on the cabin wall and tapped up a headline from the BBC. "Especially as the police now think that you killed Constable Malhotra."

"Me?"

"Yes. I know it is bullshit, you know it is bullshit. But once the press got hold of it..." He waved exasperated hands at the black and white CCTV image of her that accompanied the story. "If you were a member of my crew, I could at least protect you."

Victoria's fingers brushed the padded headrest at the back of the empty pilot's couch. The air on the bridge seemed cooler than elsewhere on the ship. The rear bulkhead bore a plaque, listing the *Tereshkova*'s place of construction as the Filton Aeroplane Works in Bristol, England; its date of completion as June 15, 1980; and its original name as the *Great Western*.

Seventy-nine years old, she thought with a tiny shake of her head. These grand old ships. Their designers had been in love with romantic twentieth century notions of sea travel, from a time when transatlantic liners such as the *Mauretania* were a byword for luxury and speed. Now, those passengers rich and impatient enough to pay the carbon tax could opt to fly the supersonic airliners, while the rest still cruised the skies in the cramped elegance of a skyliner's cabin.

Looking back, she realised that the past six months she'd spent aboard the *Tereshkova* had been among the most settled she could remember. After university, her life had been one long whirl, constantly moving from job to job, from assignment to assignment. Paul had offered her a fleeting taste of stability, and she'd loved him for it; but their relationship had foundered on the rocks of his sexuality, and now he was dead, if not-quite gone, and nowhere else felt much like home anymore.

Her hand went out to touch the metal wall, its surface clogged beneath thickly accumulated layers of paint and memory. She thought of the changes it had been through, the people and places it had seen, and she felt a prickle of kinship. Like the *Tereshkova*, she'd travelled the world and, despite being battered and patched, clung to her identity. She'd done her time and plied her course, and here she still was, still toiling onwards when so many others had fallen by the wayside. A lifetime of constant travel. Every day different, every day the same. Nothing to hold either of them anywhere. No baggage, no regrets. Just the wide open sky and the shimmering horizon.

"Okay, I'll do it. I'll take the job." In her pocket, the knuckles of her hand brushed the haft of the retracted quarterstaff. "But first, I need you to do something for me."

CHAPTER TWENTY-FOUR
HEROICS OF YOUTH

ACK-ACK MACAQUE LAY in a foetal position amidst the scrambled, burning fragments of his shattered plane, and laughed. He wrapped his arms around his knees and rocked back and forth. Fires smouldered around him. Thick, greasy roils of smoke filled the sky above him like greedy fingerprint smudges on a blue vase. And he was alive! He'd slammed his delicate, beautiful fighter into an iron deck at sixty miles an hour and survived with only a few cuts and scratches and some singed fur. He was alive, and as indestructible as a god. The laugh gurgled in his throat.

"You were right, K8. You were right." His goggles were missing a lens. He pushed them up onto the top of his head. All those missions, all those desperate fights and daring escapes—he could have walked though them all with his head held high, and still prevailed.

He sat up, dislodging a shower of broken glass from his flight jacket. The air stank of spilled aviation fuel. His adversary's plane lay enmeshed in crash netting at the far end of the runway, some hundred metres from where he sat, in the shadow of the conning tower. Brushing himself down, he climbed to his feet, reached into his jacket for a cigar, and lit it.

Here was where it would happen. He would kill or be killed and, if K8 was right, the world would know.

With the cigar clamped securely in place, he shuffled towards the other wreck, leathery fingers curling and uncurling above the holsters strapped to his thighs, ready to draw at the slightest provocation. He bore no malice to his replacement. The monkey didn't know it was being used any more than he had. It would unquestioningly accept the world it found around itself as real, and play along accordingly. If anything, he pitied it.

The remaining Messerschmitts circled overhead like vultures, sensing death on the wind. Other planes had joined them, but none were fighting. They were waiting to see what he would do. He gave them the finger.

"Enjoy the show, creeps." Although they didn't know it yet, they'd had all the entertainment they were going to get from him. The game was over.

This was the end. *Götterdämmerung*. The end of the war, and the end of this world.

Ahead, a figure ducked under the wing of the Spit caught in the nets. When it stood upright, he saw it had short, bowed legs and long, dangling arms. The jacket it wore was identical to his, but the creature had no eye patch, and looked younger than he did, with fewer wrinkles around its eyes and snout. A silk scarf fluttered at its neck. It carried a bazooka at its hip, and spare shells dangled from its waist.

"Who are you supposed to be?" The creature's voice lacked the gravel of cigars and rum, and Ack-Ack Macaque felt the hackles prickle between his shoulder blades. His thumbs hooked over the tops of his holsters.

"Be careful who you're staring at, boy."

The bazooka shifted. Lips slid back from sharp, pointed teeth.

"Or what?"

Ack-Ack Macaque rolled his cigar from one side of his mouth to the other. The younger monkey's eyes and stance betrayed the cheap heroics of youth, as yet unscathed by the endless, grinding procession of dogfights and lost comrades. He hadn't yet had time to become bitter, to start questioning his place in the war and the world.

"Because I'm you, you idiot. At least, an older, less sanitised version of you."

"What are you talking about?"

Ack-Ack Macaque drummed his fingers against the butts of his Colts.

"What's your name?"

"Ack—"

"Yeah, mine too. What's your real name? Can you remember?"

The younger monkey let its mouth open and shut. Its tail twitched like a snake caught under a car tyre.

"They used to—"

"Yes?"

"Teiko. They used to call me Teiko."

"Well, look around you, Teiko. The sky, the clouds. None of this is real."

The younger monkey's eyes didn't move. The insolence of his stare bordered on direct physical challenge, and it was all Ack-Ack Macaque could do not to scream and leap in response.

The bazooka barrel wavered.

"It seems real enough to me," Teiko said. "Now, talk. Tell me who you really are."

"I am telling you, you're just not listening." Ack-Ack Macaque pulled himself up to his full height. "I used to be a character in a video game. Then I got out, into the real world, and they replaced me with you. You're me, but with all the rough edges sanded off. You're the reboot. You're younger and you don't smoke. I bet you don't even drink, do you?"

The other primate's lips slid back from its teeth.

"I have no idea what you're talking about. Just tell me whose side you're on. Ours," his eyes flicked up at the circling Messerschmitts, "or theirs."

Ack-Ack Macaque took the cigar from his mouth and said, "There are no sides anymore. That's what I'm saying. All this, everything you see and feel and touch. All this is a game, an illusion, and you're not really here. You're lying on a couch in a laboratory with wires sticking into your brain."

Teiko made an agitated, chattering noise.

"You don't believe me? Then ask yourself why those German planes aren't attacking. Ask yourself how I crashed my Spitfire into the deck and climbed out unhurt."

"Shut up!" The bazooka barrel began to shake.

"It's not luck that's kept you alive, Teiko, it's the game. You're hard to kill because you're the main character. You're the one on the box. The one with your face on mugs and t-shirts and who-knows-what other crap."

"I said, *shut up.*"

Ack-Ack Macaque screwed the cigar back into place. His hands dropped to his thighs, and he closed his fingers around the handles of his revolvers. All he had to do was draw and fire.

"Why don't you try to make me?"

"I'll kill you."

"No, you won't."

The younger monkey raised the bazooka to shoulder height, ready to fire.

"Do you want to make a bet?"

Ack-Ack Macaque grinned around the soggy end of his cigar.

"Do you want to suck my balls?"

They held each other's stare, their fangs bared in challenge. The moment stretched. The very air between them seemed to shimmer.

Come on, you bastard. Come on.

Ack-Ack Macaque saw his opponent's eyes start to water. Leathery fingers squeezed the bazooka's trigger. Smoke and flames blew from both ends, and Ack-Ack Macaque pitched himself sideways, as out flew a shell the size of a small freight train. He shoulder-rolled across the deck, and came up with the Colts gripped in his hands, his trigger fingers squeezing for all they were worth. Bullets spinged and spanged from the wrecked Spit's bodywork. Teiko dropped the bazooka and lunged. Ack-Ack Macaque tried to plug him, but the guns seemed to twist away, the game unwilling to allow a fatal shot.

They crashed together and rolled, scratching, gouging and biting; trying to rip out each other's throats. Teeth snapped, and Ack-Ack Macaque felt hot breath against the side of his face. He let the guns fall away and reached for the blade in his boot. If bullets wouldn't work, he'd have to do it the traditional way, with an old school monkey knife fight.

AMSTERDAM, FEBRUARY 2054. A shabby and poorly-lit warehouse by the waterfront. Stacked crates contain smuggled Armenian cigarettes, repurposed Japanese laptops and knock-off German porn. Dormant fork-lifts block the aisles like sleeping sentry robots. The air smells of blood, sawdust and monkey shit. In the centre of the room, lights hanging from the ceiling illuminate a makeshift ring: a circle of hay bales, and the crowd around it. Bets are taken, fistfuls of money are exchanged.

Ack-Ack Macaque stands panting in the ring, a cutthroat razor clasped in his hand. His forearm has been stained red and sticky to the elbow. He's bleeding from a dozen cuts, but he doesn't care. This is all he knows. The ring is his world, the fight his life.

At his feet, a flea-bitten chimp lies quivering. Thick ropes of blood pump from its slashed throat. Floating specks of sawdust spin and clump in the spreading puddle. The crowd are shouting. Some are incensed, others aroused. He doesn't know the chimp's name; and after four straight fights, he's not entirely sure of his own. It certainly isn't Ack-Ack Macaque. That name comes later, far from here, in a laboratory outside Paris. Right now, his nostrils quiver with the stench of sweat and pheromones. His arms shake with fatigue.

He looks down at his former opponent, in time to see the chimp rattle its last. The poor creature stops struggling. Its body goes slack and its bowels let go, adding to the stink and mess on the concrete floor.

Somewhere in the crowd, a woman watches. She works on behalf of an agency, which works in turn for Céleste. She's been looking to procure a monkey with character and fighting spirit, and now she's smiling. He's won four straight fights. There are scars all over his body, and a filthy, yellowing bandage covering the gouged ruins of his suppurating left eye: he couldn't be more perfect. Without taking her eyes from him, she reaches into her elegant Parisian shoulder bag to retrieve a white, platinum-sheathed

SincPhone. Her fingernails speed-dial a number, and she puts the phone to her ear.

Meanwhile, unaware of her scrutiny, Ack-Ack Macaque folds away his razor and shambles over to his owner and screeches at him. His owner is a skinny Malaysian with bad teeth and dark sweat patches beneath the arms of his linen jacket. In response to his inarticulate screeches, the man hands him his reward: a lit cigarette. The bitterness of the smoke clears the lingering stench of the dead chimp's dung. The nicotine makes his head swim. He chatters happily to himself, perching on the edge of a wooden pallet in order to savour every breath.

He hardly notices when the smartly-dressed woman steps from the crowd with a fistful of money, and makes his owner the kind of offer it would be extremely foolhardy to refuse.

TEIKO SQUIRMED BENEATH him, but Ack-Ack Macaque had the weight of experience. They were perilously close to the edge of the deck, but he didn't care. He knew he couldn't die, not really. This was all illusion: he had nothing to lose. Using all his strength, he pulled his rival towards the abyss.

"Stop struggling," he growled. The younger monkey didn't listen. He let out a howl and tried to sink his teeth into Ack-Ack Macaque's arm. Ack-Ack Macaque slapped him. "Shut up. I have something to say."

He pushed away and rose to his feet. Teiko blinked up at him, wary as any cornered animal.

"We both have to die," Ack-Ack Macaque told him. "We have to show them that this is all bullshit. This is all fake. The kids playing this game think you're some kind of high tech computer intelligence, but you're just a monkey with a computerised brain, same as I am." He turned and walked a few steps back towards the conning tower. He raised his arms to the circling planes above and raised his voice. "The people at Céleste are lying to you! They've lied to us all! They're planning to take over—"

Pain lanced his thigh, sharp and unexpected. He squealed and fell, and Teiko was on him, the blade of his knife now sticky with Ack-Ack Macaque's blood. Ack-Ack Macaque raised his arm to block a second slash, and cried out again as he felt steel bite though his sleeve, into skin and muscle.

Damn it, he thought, *I wasn't finished!*

He reached around and grabbed the younger monkey by the back of his leather jacket. With all his strength he heaved upwards, lifting his opponent just enough to give him room to twist his hips sideways, throwing Teiko off balance.

They rolled over together, gripping each other's stabbing arms. Deadlocked.

"Let go, you moron."

Teiko's teeth snapped at his face.

"I'll kill you!"

"No, you fucking won't." Ack-Ack Macaque tried to wrench his arm free from the younger monkey's grip. "I always win. That's all there is to it."

Teiko laughed, fierce and mad. "Look at your arm, grandpa. You're bleeding."

The sudden pang of doubt was as intense as the pain from his stab wounds. In all his years, Ack-Ack Macaque had never been injured like this. He'd survived dozens of plane crashes with only cuts and bruises; legions of German ninjas had yet to lay a blade on him; and yet this young upstart had already stuck him twice, once through the leg and once through the arm. For the first time in his life, he felt truly unsure. He had no idea what would happen next. He'd assumed this would be a simple monkey smack-down. A bit of a scuffle between near-immortals. But now, locked in Teiko's fighting embrace, he understood that—in the game at least—he was caught in a fight to the death. When it was done, he might wake up on the *Tereshkova* with K8; but in the meantime, he'd feel every stab, every slash and bite. He'd become used to the painless violence of the game; but this was Amsterdam all over again. If Teiko got the better of him, it would *really* hurt.

Well, he thought, *fuck that*.

They might share an implanted core personality, but Teiko was younger, and therefore less experienced. He was so busy trying to get his knife into Ack-Ack Macaque's neck that he'd left his face exposed. Their noses were practically touching, close enough that Ack-Ack Macaque could smell the sickening sweetness of his breath.

A quick butt to the face. Teiko yelped, rolling away. His hands flew to his crushed nose, and Ack-Ack Macaque pounced. Straddling the younger monkey, he used both hands to drive the blade of his knife straight through Teiko's throat. The blade slid through flesh and gristle until it hit the spinal column. Teiko's legs thrashed. Ack-Ack leaned his full weight on the pommel of the knife. He felt the vertebrae part, and the tip punch through, into the metal of the *Brunel*'s flight deck. Teiko let out a wheezing, bubbling moan, and shook spastically.

And then he was still, and it was all over.

Ack-Ack Macaque clambered to his feet. The high altitude wind blowing across the carrier seemed to freeze the very marrow of his bones, and a strange, desolate sadness welled up from the core of his belly.

Teiko was dead. He'd just killed the closest thing in the world that he had to a brother. And damn Céleste for making him do it. Damn them for making him *at all!*

Looking over the edge of the carrier's deck, he spat into the void.

"The people at Céleste are in bed with the cult of the Undying," he said, voice gruff and flat. K8 had told him that in the past, thousands of people had watched recordings of his adventures in the game. He hoped someone was recording this right now. "They're behind the attack on the King. They're trying to use Merovech to plunge Europe into martial law. Don't trust them! Don't let them—"

The world convulsed. The sky flickered like the eyelids of a dying ape, and everything went white.

ACK-ACK MACAQUE BLINKED. Blinded by the flash, he rubbed his walnut-like knuckles into his eyes. When he lowered them, he found himself back in the cramped passenger cabin, on board the *Tereshkova*, with K8.

He was out of the game. Back in the real world—whatever that meant.

He smacked his lips. His arm and leg were uninjured, and free of stab wounds.

"What happened?"

K8 reached over and began to remove the wires from his head.

"Céleste panicked," she told him. "They shut down the game servers."

BREAKING NEWS

From *The London & Paris Times*, online edition:

Party Like It's 2059

28 NOVEMBER 2059 – Tomorrow, the peoples of Great Britain, France and Norway will celebrate 100 years of political and cultural togetherness.

Celebrations start at dawn, with a druidic ceremony at Stonehenge, and the lighting of a string of hilltop beacons, from the Falkland Islands in the south, to the ancient town of Hammerfest in Norway.

The day will climax with a concert in Hyde Park and simultaneous firework displays in London, Edinburgh, Paris, Cardiff, Belfast and Oslo.

The celebrations come almost exactly a year after the attempted assassination of King William V, and police in all cities will be on high alert, determined to prevent further atrocities. Roadblocks have been set up in a number of major cities, and key members of known regionalist and republican protest groups have been pre-emptively detained.

Although still in a coma, the King is expected to symbolically participate in the celebrations. An air ambulance will move him to the luxury liner *Maraldi*, owned by his wife, Her Grace, Alyssa Célestine, Duchess of Brittany. The liner will be anchored in the English Channel, midway between Britain and France. Once on board, his majesty will be present to 'witness' a celebratory fireworks display and, via satellite from the mid-Atlantic, the launch of the UK's first Martian probe.

Read more | Like | Comment | Share

Related Stories

Tensions rise as Chinese warships capture the crew of a British patrol boat

Weather conditions "ideal" for launch of Martian probe

Centenary concert will "reflect a century of musical cross-pollination"

Millions of users left angry as Céleste Tech pulls plug on smash-hit game

Stock market falls amid fears of Chinese export ban

"Nuclear doomsday clock" moved one minute closer to midnight

Police use water cannons to break up anti-war demos in Paris

90 years of the Internet: the anniversary of the first ARPANET link

Fears for future of Nanda Devi Biosphere Reserve as troops clash in fresh fighting along disputed border

Cease and desist: Céleste Tech lawyers threaten legal reprisals against fans posting online Macaque videos

Prank blamed for monkey outburst

CHAPTER TWENTY-FIVE
REPLICANT ZOMBIE

VICTORIA STOOD AT the head of the dining table in the *Tereshkova*'s main lounge, her hands resting on the curved steel back of a chair.

"So, we're in agreement?"

Merovech and Julie sat to her right; the Commodore and K8 to her left. The monkey perched at the far end, chomping on an unlit cigar.

Merovech's fingers traced circles on the polished wood.

"And you're sure she's planning a coup?"

"As sure as we are about anything right now."

"Then you have my vote. She needs to be stopped."

Julie Girard put her hand on his arm.

"Are you sure? Even after everything we have seen, she is still your mother."

Merovech covered her hand with his. He raised his eyes to Victoria.

"You have to prevent her from killing my father."

"We'll do our best."

On the other side of the table, the Commodore harrumphed.

"I still don't like it. It all seems far too dangerous. Why do you have to go down there, onto her ship? Why can't you stay up here and let the Prince broadcast to the nation?"

Victoria shook her head.

"Because I don't think it would work. We've been through this. K8 and our monkey friend have put the word out to the gaming community. Hopefully that will build. But the Duchess has already put out a story that Merovech's had some kind of nervous breakdown. If he starts posting videos on the web, it will be easy for the media to dismiss them as paranoid fantasies." She let go of the chair and straightened her back. "The macaque videos are going viral. If we're going to capitalise on the publicity, the only way will be to do something direct, and public."

The old man fingered his moustache.

"I'm still not clear what you plan to do if, and I mean if, you get aboard."

"I'm a journalist. If there's a shred of proof on that tub, I'll find it. And then we'll confront her."

"In front of the television cameras?"

"Ideally, yes."

"And what if the TV cameras ignore you? This woman, she has great influence, yes?"

Victoria smiled. She inclined her head to the far end of the table, where Ack-Ack Macaque sat with his feet up, a fingernail worrying at something caught between his front teeth.

"Trust me, *nobody's* going to ignore him."

The Commodore crossed his arms. Gold braid glimmered at his wrists.

"Bah. I still do not like it. But, as always, you have my support."

"Thank you. Merovech, are you ready to speak to the nation when the time comes?"

"K8's patched us into a satellite feed. As soon as we get your signal, we can start broadcasting."

"Do you know what you're going to say?"

"No, but I'm sure it will come to me."

Victoria rubbed her hands together. In the corner of her eye, she could see Paul's image.

"How about you?" she asked.

He scratched his ear.

"You know me, Vicky. In for a penny, in for a pound."

"Okay, then."

She looked at the faces around the table.

"Make no mistake, if we fail at this, we'll be tried as traitors. That means lengthy jail sentences, or worse."

Merovech untangled himself from Julie and rose to his feet.

"Thank you," he said, holding out his hand for her to shake. Victoria shook her head instead.

"Don't thank me yet. I told you, I'm not a royalist. I'm not doing this for you. I'm doing it for Paul."

"I understand. But, thank you anyway."

At the other end of the table, Ack-Ack Macaque pulled the wet, flattened cigar butt from his yellow teeth.

"Yap, yap, yap. So we've all got a stake in this. That's why we're here. Can we get on and do something now? 'Cos personally speaking, I'm pissed off and I want to break stuff and hurt people."

Victoria smiled, lips tight and thin. With her brain locked into planning mode, her thoughts rang with the crisp, bell-like clarity of spring morning.

She clapped her hands.

"*Ecoutez-moi bien*. Okay, we've got a few hours. Merovech, you carry on jotting down ideas for your speech. *Julie, tu l'aides*. And you, monkey man, you're with me."

Ack-Ack Macaque took his feet off the table.

"Where are we going?"

"To the armoury."

THE COMMODORE LED them aft, past the kitchens and staff quarters, to the armoury, located adjacent to the brig, as far from the passenger cabins and public areas as possible.

The door opened to a sixteen digit pass code typed into a keypad set into the bulkhead. The lock clunked, and the steel door swung aside.

Inside, the armoury was about the size of a cheap hotel bathroom. Weaponry lined the walls: police shotguns; long-range sniper rifles; handheld rail guns; a box of grenades. Even a pair of classic Kalashnikovs. The old man gestured like a conjuror.

"Is there anything here that will be of use to you?"

Looking around at the racks, Ack-Ack Macaque widened his one good eye. He rubbed his leathery hands together and his tongue lolled out in a toothy grin.

"How about, all of it?"

He pulled a chrome-plated revolver from one rack and a grenade launcher from another, and turned to Victoria with one in each hand.

"What do you think?"

Victoria looked him up and down, taking in not only the weapons but also his jacket, half-eaten cigar and leather skull cap. A few days ago, she'd have balked at the idea of a talking monkey—especially one with a gun in each hand. Now, when she looked at the macaque, she saw something of herself in it. Neither of them would be alive were it not for the invasive experiments of Doctor Nguyen. And now, together, they were going to get their revenge.

"You'll do."

LATER, BACK IN her cabin, she stood in front of the mirror with her head bare. Her wig and hat lay on the bottom bunk, with the boxes and strewn clothes that made up the entirety of her earthly possessions. The mirror had a simple pine frame, and had been fixed to the wall by two screws. In its reflective surface, the face she saw squinting back at her was that of her younger self, as she'd looked a year ago, recovering from the surgery that had saved her life. Since then, she'd grown used to having hair again, and having lost it for a second time, her head seemed disproportionately small. The scar ridge stood out from her temple, the exposed metal jacks shining like rivets. Her fingers brushed them, one at a time.

What was she? Without the surgery, she would have died. But the surgery had removed over half her brain, so in some senses, perhaps she *had* died. She couldn't survive now without the gelware, there wasn't enough of her left. Over sixty per cent of her brain had been replaced. Was the remainder enough to claim continuity? Could she still say she was the person she'd once been, or had she become a reanimated ghost, a replicant zombie with delusions of humanity? Certainly, the things she'd done over the past two days would have petrified and repulsed her former self.

Had she really killed a man? In the emotionally-detached serenity of command mode, the action of closing the doors on Berg had seemed logical, perhaps even easy. And even now, she was still half sure it had been the right thing to do.

She glared at her reflection. He'd had it coming. What did she have to feel guilty about? The Smiling Man had tried to kill her twice, and he'd killed her stupid husband. She hadn't asked for any of it. Berg had come barging into her life, just as she'd been starting to piece it back together, and wrecked it all over again. He'd deserved everything he'd gotten, and his employers, Céleste Industries and the Cult of the Undying, deserved a whole lot more. She touched the side of her head again. They'd turned her into this ugly cyborg creature. And not only her, but also Prince Merovech and Ack-Ack Macaque. In their laboratories, Nguyen and his team had built three deeply traumatised and dysfunctional creatures, convinced each of them that it was real, and then launched them, one-by-one, out into the world.

Her lips hardened into a thin line. Well, to hell with them all. Had they learned nothing from *Frankenstein*? She picked an automatic pistol from the pile of weaponry on the top bunk and checked the magazine. The firearm felt heavy and cold in her hand.

The creatures were coming home.

CHAPTER TWENTY-SIX
SLAVE ARMY

K8 CAME TO Merovech's cabin. She had her arms crossed and a scowl on her freckled face.

"We've lost access to the Internet, so there's not much I can do. Now that Ack-Ack Macaque's been thrown out of the game, I feel like a spare part."

From the bunk, Julie gave a tired smile. "Tell me about it. Merovech has gone to the library to work on his speech, and I am sitting here going crazy."

"Aye, you and me both, then, is it?"

"It seems that way."

K8 put her hands on her hips.

"Hey, I hear tell that you hacked your way into the Céleste servers, too. You must be kind of handy with a computer, eh?"

Julie laughed. She'd thought she had some skills but, compared to this freckled Scottish kid, she was really just an amateur.

"Still," K8 continued, "there's some pretty scary shit in those files, yeah?"

Julie swung her legs off the bunk. "I did not see much. As soon as I found the documents on Merovech, I hit print and went to find him."

"Ah, you were lucky." K8 scratched her short, carroty hair. "I had a good root around and I found all kinds of things. Plans for stuff straight out of your worst nightmares."

"Like what?"

"Compulsory back-ups. Soul-catchers fitted to everyone, by force if necessary."

Julie made a face.

"I would not want one."

"You wouldn't have any choice. If Célestine takes the throne, she'll order laws to make it a criminal offence not to have a catcher implanted. It's basic Undying philosophy: back everything up so nothing gets lost. They have plans for a storage facility in a bunker beneath their laboratories in Paris. If war breaks out with China, they want to have saved as many backed-up personalities as possible before the bombs start falling."

Julie stood. She rubbed her arms as if cold.

"It all sounds ghastly."

"That isn't the worst of it."

"No?"

"From what I read in those files, I think the Undying are trying to deliberately provoke the Chinese. I think they want a war."

"*Putain-de-merde!* Why would anyone want to start a nuclear war?" Julie's mind flashed to the horror stories her grandfather had told her. He'd grown up in the 1980s, as Soviet Russia squared off against the European Commonwealth, and his teenage memories were filled with the anxiety of seemingly inevitable apocalypse, when the best a young man could hope for was to be incinerated in the first few seconds of an exchange, rather than surviving to face a lingering death from sickness or starvation. She shivered. Surely the governments of the world had learned from the Cold War, and the insanity of Mutually Assured Destruction? "I thought they wanted Mars. So why would they kill everyone on Earth?"

K8 bit her lip.

"Well, what if they're planning to do the same on Earth as they are on Mars?"

"Which is?"

"Download all the backed-up minds into android bodies, like Berg's, and take over."

"That is crazy!"

"Is it? Androids don't worry about radiation or lack of food. With China and Europe flattened, there'd be no-one to stop them rebuilding and taking over. The Duchess would have the world at her feet, and a perfect slave army do to her bidding." She stopped talking. Julie looked at her with her mouth hanging open.

"That is horrible." Framed by her purple hair, her face seemed paler than usual.

"Are you okay?" K8 asked.

Julie swallowed.

"I really need a cigarette." She puffed air from her cheeks. "Do you have any?"

"I don't smoke."

"I did not think so." She pulled herself upright. "Okay. First things first. We must tell Merovech, and the others. We must get them all to read those files of yours. They all need to know the stakes for which we are playing."

"Do they?" K8 shuffled her feet. "Because it seems to me they're under enough pressure. Victoria and the monkey, they're both pretty strung out right now. I don't know if they could cope."

"So what? We say nothing?"

K8 thought about it. "I suppose we could tell Merovech, if you wanted to. He should know, I guess. We could let him make the decision."

"He is in the library."

"So you said."

Julie straightened her t-shirt and hitched up her jeans.

"Then let us go and see him." She moved to step past K8, but as she reached for the cabin's door, an alarm sounded. Both girls jumped.

"*Putain!*" Julie swore. "What now?"

CHAPTER TWENTY-SEVEN
INCANDESCENT JUNGLE FURY

THE THREE HELICOPTERS came from the north-east in the late afternoon. Standing on the *Tereshkova*'s bridge, Victoria watched their progress on one of the wall-mounted display screens.

"Do you think they'll try shooting at us?"

In his chair, the Commodore shook his silver head. The top buttons of his tunic were undone.

"No. If they really wanted to kill us, they would have sent jets. It would be faster. My guess is, this is a boarding party. They want the young prince intact, yes?"

"What can we do?"

"Very little. Our radio transmissions are being blocked, so we can't tell anyone or call for help. We could alter course, but they are smaller and more manoeuvrable."

"You have anti-piracy weapons."

"Yes. But to use them would be a declaration of war. Better, I think, to let *them* make the first move."

TEN MINUTES LATER, as the swollen orange sun dipped low in the afternoon sky, Victoria stood at the edge of the landing pad atop the *Tereshkova*'s central hull, her quarterstaff extended to its full length, and her pistol pushed into the pocket of her army coat. The wind chilled her naked scalp. Behind her stood a shifting mob of the airship's stewards, flak jackets and helmets strapped over their white tunic uniforms, each of them self-consciously cradling a rail gun or pistol from the armoury. Beside her, the Commodore stood, the white tails of his dress uniform fluttering, the gnarled fingers of his right hand resting on the pommel of his cutlass.

Together, they watched the helicopters crest the edge of the gas bag, circling in like piranhas, their flanks painted with the eye-twisting black and white stripes of dazzle camouflage—geometric patterns designed to conceal their exact shape and size. Through their open sides, Victoria saw machine gun-toting, black-clad troops ready to deploy the moment the wheels hit the deck.

In the corner of her eye, Paul's image twitched.

"I don't like the look of this," he said.

Victoria took a firmer grip on the staff.

"Shut up," she told him.

He gave her an offended look.

"Don't forget whose neural-ware I'm running on. If you get killed, that's me dead too."

"And there I was thinking you were concerned for my wellbeing."

"I am! Of course I am. But we're in this together now. If you get killed, we both die."

The lead 'copter came in low, presenting its belly as it dropped. Victoria leaned into the downdraught.

"You're already dead. Now, get out of my head and keep quiet. I need to concentrate."

She raised the staff into a defensive position and ran through a mental litany of her opponents' most vulnerable points: ankles, knees, throats and wrists. A quarterstaff wouldn't be much use in a firefight, but at close quarters, it could be deadly. And in the meantime, she had the pistol. As the helicopter kissed the pad, she reached into her pocket and, heart beating in her chest, closed her fist around the gun's cold butt. Whatever else she'd been, she'd never been a soldier. Even in the Falklands, she'd only ever reported from the sidelines of the fighting.

This close, the helicopter's engines were deafening. Black figures spilled from its hatches, taking up positions on either side, wearing thick flak jackets, gas masks and combat helmets.

An officer stepped forward with a salute.

"Commodore, I am Captain Summers of His Majesty's Special Air Service, and you are hereby required to hand over the Prince of Wales, His Royal Highness, Prince Merovech." The gas mask's eyes were convex blisters of glass. They turned in her direction. "And the fugitive and murder suspect, Victoria Valois. Failure to comply with either request will result in the use of deadly force."

The Commodore's medals jangled as he drew himself up. Beneath his bushy brows, his eyes glowered like coals.

"I have to inform *you*, Captain, that you are in breach of international law, specifically those treaties concerning the independence and autonomy of individual skyliners. Any attempt to use force against a passenger or member of my crew will be considered an act of piracy, and responded to accordingly."

The other two helicopters circled at a safe distance, rotors chopping the sky, out of range of small arms fire, but close enough for the snipers on board to draw a bead on anyone who tried to draw a weapon.

The butterflies churning in Victoria's stomach threatened to force their way up through her chest and throat, and out into the open air. Sensing her agitation, the gelware tried to push even more adrenalin into her bloodstream, and she had to concentrate hard in order to stop her arms from shaking. Against the metal of the staff, her palms were slick.

The Captain and the Commodore glared at each other: a heavily armoured, bug-eyed shock trooper trying to stare down an old fashioned man of honour carrying only a sword.

"I'm sorry, Commodore, but this really is your last chance. I have been authorised to take whatever steps are necessary to recover the Prince."

"The Prince has requested asylum aboard this vessel and, as such, I am legally obligated, by the terms of the applicable treaties, to protect him."

The wind blew colder. The troopers around the helicopter were as immobile as statues, their black, snub-nosed submachine guns trained on the Commodore's crew.

"My orders are quite specific, Commodore."

"As is my resolve, *Captain*. Now, I am asking you politely to please leave my vessel."

Captain Summers lowered his mask.

"You can't hope to prevail. Your crew will be slaughtered. Please, Commodore, stand down and let me do my job."

The Commodore frowned. He looked from the soldiers to his own men, then up at the twin helicopters circling the pad; and, for the first time, Victoria saw a shiver of doubt in his eyes. He turned to her.

"Perhaps you should go below?"

She shook her head. She'd be damned if she'd let him fight her battles.

"I'm not going anywhere."

Summers cleared his throat.

"Time's up, Commodore. Please, stand aside." He raised his pistol. Behind him, his troopers tensed into firing positions, the barrels of their weapons covering everyone on the pad.

Victoria tasted sick at the back of her throat, and swallowed it back. The Commodore's men were hopelessly outgunned. The fight would last seconds, and there would be few, if any, survivors. Her fingers squeezed the stock of the pistol in her pocket, but she didn't dare draw it. To do so would call down the ire of the snipers circling above.

This was going to be a bloodbath.

Summers said, "I'm going to count to three."

As the sun moved ever lower, the sky behind him had taken on a purple aspect.

"One."

Victoria transferred her weight from one boot to the other. If she overclocked herself again, could she draw her pistol fast enough to make a difference? Paul's image cowered in the corner of her eye, nervously chewing the fingers of one hand.

"Two."

She felt the wind against her exposed scalp. Even this far up, it smelled of the sea.

"Thr—"

"Halt!"

The voice was Merovech's. He climbed from a hatchway at the edge of the pad and strode forward, between the two opposing forces.

"Tell your men to stand down, Captain."

Summers lowered his gun and threw the prince a stiff salute.

"I'm afraid I can't do that, sir. My orders are detailed and specific, and—"

"Do you know who I am?"

"Yes sir, of course, sir. But my orders are to get you on that chopper. Right away, sir."

Merovech thrust his chin forward. "And if I refuse?"

Summers raised his pistol again.

"Then I'm afraid I'll have to insist, sir."

Victoria saw Merovech blink in surprise, eyes trying to focus on the end of the gun barrel. For a split second, Summers seemed to be about to pull the trigger.

And then everything changed.

Gunshots rang out. One of the orbiting helicopters dropped away, bullet holes stitched across its windshield, the pilots slumped forward against their controls. Victoria threw herself forward onto the pad's yielding rubber surface. She heard cries, and saw members of the Commodore's crew scattering, running for cover. But the troopers weren't firing at them; they had other things to worry about. In amongst them, cutting through their ranks, came a blur of incandescent jungle fury.

Frustrated by its inability to dampen the adrenalin in her system, the gelware kicked her into command mode. In slow motion, she saw a hairy arm swat a trooper aside, breaking his neck and twisting his gas mask askew. One of his comrades took a bullet through the lower jaw, spraying bone shards and gristle into the faces of his companions. And at the heart of it all, Ack-Ack Macaque whirled, meat cleaver in one hand, huge silver revolver in the other. Used to fighting superhuman German ninjas, the monkey seemed to be making short work of the lumbering British commandoes. In front of her, she saw Summers turn, ready to fire at the creature, and brought her quarterstaff scything around at ankle height. The blow jarred her shoulder. The SAS Captain yelled and fell, hands wrapped around his right ankle. Victoria raised herself to her knees and pulled the pistol from her pocket.

"Stay there," she ordered.

The burning helicopter had disappeared, leaving only a dirty trail of black smoke against the sunset to show where it had spiralled out of sight. The second moved erratically, more concerned about avoiding incoming fire than harassing the people on the *Tereshkova*'s pad. She looked around for the Commodore. The old man seemed to have fallen awkwardly. He was using the cutlass as a stick to pull himself upright. She watched as he clambered painfully to his feet and brushed down the front of his white tunic. Then, with obvious effort, he limped to where Summers lay wrapped around his pain, and brandished the tip of his sword in the younger man's face.

"Call off your men."

Merovech came up beside him.

"That's an order, *Captain*."

Summers looked from one to the other, lips tight against clenched teeth. For a moment, his eyes burned with defiance. Then, as his men let forth fresh screams, Victoria saw acceptance of the situation steal over him. He raised a gauntleted hand to his throat mike.

"All units, stand down." He spoke the words as if they were rotten to the taste. "Now call off the monkey."

The Commodore sheathed his cutlass. He put a hand on Merovech's shoulder for support.

"Can you, my boy?"

Merovech pulled a SincPhone from his pocket.

"K8? We're all done here. Can you put the big fella back on his leash?"

If a reply came, Victoria didn't hear it. A loud bang came from below, and the skyliner shuddered like a truck on a cattle grid. She staggered, but managed to keep her footing.

"The engines!" cried the Commodore. "We've been hit!"

Thrown off-balance, he clung to Merovech as the deck began to tip.

CHAPTER TWENTY-EIGHT
DIRTY BOMB

FROM THE TERESHKOVA'S bridge, the situation became distressingly clear. Through the great curving forward window, Victoria saw smoke billowing from one of the starboard engine nacelles. The blades of the impeller had been blown back and twisted so that, in the last orange rays of the setting sun, they resembled the curled legs of a dead spider. Above the nacelle's smouldering remains, the fabric of the hull had been gouged and torn by shrapnel. Ribbons of material flapped free.

At their respective workstations, the Commodore and the pilot fought to maintain control, throttling the port engines back to compensate for the sudden lack of starboard thrust.

"We're losing pressure in hulls four and five," the pilot said, reading data from his screen. Already, as the damaged hulls bled away their buoyancy, the Tereshkova had begun to wallow to the side.

In his chair, the Commodore scowled.

"Well, if we are going down, we are not going down without a fight. Increase power to the port engines, and give me full rudder."

"Aye, sir." The pilot was a gangly Muscovite with thick glasses and a spreading paunch: more of a computer programmer than a pilot in the old and accepted sense of the word. "But what about the passengers? If we ditch in the water…"

"Get our helicopters in the air. I want all non-essential personnel off the ship. And get a team over to the damaged sections, see if there is anything we can salvage."

"Aye, sir."

"And tell them to take Geiger counters, for heaven's sake. That was a nuclear engine, and I do not want anybody to take stupid chances if there's been a containment breach."

He turned his attention to Victoria.

"I do not suppose there is any point in ordering you to leave?"

She shook her head.

"I'm a member of your crew now, remember? Besides, I don't have anywhere else to go." She glanced back to the window, and the engine belching smoke and, possibly, radioactive fallout.

"Was it a missile?"

The old man shook his white-haired head. "A missile could not have penetrated our defences without detection. This must have been a bomb. Deliberate sabotage."

"Was it the commandoes?" She found that hard to believe. Who would purposefully detonate a nuclear engine? She knew the units used on the skyliners were designed to survive crashes intact, and so she wasn't worried about a nuclear explosion; but if the bomb had torn a hole in the engine's fuel containment, the effect would be similar to the detonation of a terrorist "dirty" bomb, spreading airborne radioactive contamination across a wide area, blown on the wind.

The Commodore pursed his lips and brushed his moustache with a crooked fingertip. "They never got further than the landing pad. This must have been someone else. I don't know who but, right now, I have more important matters of concern, such as keeping us airborne." His fingers danced across the pad before him, making adjustments to the Tereshkova's trim and pitch.

"Any casualties?" she asked.

The pilot looked up. "Mostly minor injuries at this point, but we still have two passengers unaccounted for. At least our transmissions are being jammed no longer. If we go down, we can call for help."

"Anything I can do?"

The Commodore waved her away. "We do not need you here. We can manage. It will be dark soon. Go find Merovech and the monkey. Follow the plan." He tapped in a command and snarled something in Russian.

Victoria hesitated. This could be the last time they spoke face-to-face. She felt she should say something, but nothing came. Events were spiralling too quickly.

"Go," he said. And so, she went.

With a hollowness inside her, she left the bridge and made her way aft, to the main lounge, where Merovech and his entourage were holed up, recovering from the confrontation on the helipad. K8 was busily applying bandages to Ack-Ack Macaque's cuts and scrapes, while the monkey chewed at another cigar. Blood stained the white fleece cuffs of his flight jacket.

Julie Girard sat on a chair, her leg propped up and bandaged. She looked pale and scared. In the confusion of the skirmish, she'd been hit in the thigh by a rail gun's steel needle. Merovech sat beside her, holding her hand. When he saw Victoria, he stood.

"What's happening?"

Victoria ran a hand back over the fuzz on her scalp.

"We're evacuating the passengers. What's happening up top?"

Merovech's dirty fingernails rasped at the stubble on his cheek. "The soldiers wanted to leave. They were worried about radiation."

"You let them go?"

"I saw no reason to keep them."

K8 looked up. "Is there anything I can do to help?"

Victoria shrugged. "That depends whether or not you know anything about skyliner systems."

The girl smiled.

"Do you remember the *Nova Scotia*, two years ago? Somebody hacked her flight computer remotely, and had her flying in circles around the Empire State building for two days before they managed to fix it."

"Let me guess, that someone was you?"

"Bingo."

"Go on, then. The rest of you, grab whatever you need and get to one of the choppers."

"No." Merovech's voice was quiet but firm. "I'm staying here. We have to do what we planned. For my father's sake, we have to go through with it."

"What about Julie?"

Julie Girard tried to sit up straight. An empty packet of painkillers fell from her lap. "If Merovech is staying, I am staying too."

"Are you sure? You're already hurt, and it might not be safe."

"I do not care." She looked up at the young prince and reached for his hand. "As long as we are together, that is all that matters."

The bulkheads creaked.

Merovech's eyes lingered on her bandage. When he looked up again, Victoria could see the wetness glittering in his eyes.

"I'm so sorry," he said.

Julie tried to shush him.

"It is not your fault, my love."

"Yes it is. My mother's responsible for this. For all of it." He turned to Victoria. "This has gone on long enough. She has to be exposed, whatever it takes."

The emotion in his voice stilled the room. Nobody wanted to speak. They all looked at each other. Finally, Victoria said, "Okay, whatever you say.

In that case, we do what we said before. Merovech, you take Julie. Make her comfortable and record your message. Have it ready to broadcast as soon as we have the media's attention." She turned to the door. "Monsieur Macaque, it's time for you and I to suit up."

THE WINGSUITS WERE one-piece black garments of lightweight material, with inflatable flaps between the legs and under the arms, and a parachute on the back. Paul claimed to have once dated an extreme sports enthusiast, and said he knew the basics, and Victoria had seen plenty of online videos, and had a fair idea of how they worked. She had also taken a lengthy course in skydiving as part of her preparation for her visit to the South Atlantic—training which had proved useless when her aircraft ditched in the ocean, a few hundred metres from its carrier.

"Okay," Paul said in her head, "You have to remember to keep your arms and legs tensed. It's like freefall, but you control the glide using your body. If you get into difficulty, open your 'chute."

They couldn't carry much equipment, but had a number of weapons—including her quarterstaff—strapped to their backs, on either side of their parachute packs.

"I'll cope." She turned to the monkey beside her. "How are you doing?"

Ack-Ack Macaque had his aviator goggles pulled down over his eyes. Beneath the wingsuit, he wore his fur-lined leather jacket, and he'd shunned a helmet in favour of the leather skullcap K8 had given him.

"Everyone needs to know who he is," K8 had explained when Victoria protested. "He needs to look the way he does in the game, so they recognise him at a glance. Otherwise, he's just a crazy monkey running loose."

Now, standing at the passenger hatchway, just aft of the lounge in the main gondola, Ack-Ack Macaque looked serious and professional.

"Don't worry about me."

He had sticking plasters on his cheeks and across the bridge of his nose, but the injuries didn't seem to bother him. Or maybe they did, and Victoria couldn't read his body language. Sometimes, she thought, you could almost forget what he was; but, every now and then, he did or said something that threw you, reminding you that deep down, he really was a wild animal with a head full of artificial brains, and not a human being at all.

Although, she thought, *who am I to talk?*

She used her neural software to access an online map, showing the relative positions of the *Tereshkova* and Duchess Célestine's liner, the *Maraldi*.

"Right," Paul said. "If you get this right, you can expect to get a glide ratio of two point five to one. That means you'll travel two and a half metres forward for every metre you drop. We're currently around eight thousand feet above the Channel, which means you can probably expect to get just shy of two and a half kilometres out of these things. How far is it to the liner?"

"Seven kilometres."

"Ah."

"If the *Tereshkova* gets any closer, the RAF will shoot it down."

"Then what are you expecting to do? You can't swim four and a half kilometres!"

Victoria smiled. "We won't have to. There's a two-masted yacht *en route* to the *Maraldi* from Southampton. It passed underneath us a few minutes ago. We should be able to make it aboard without too much trouble."

Paul raised his eyebrows.

"God, Vicky. You're so fearless now, I can't believe it. You've really changed."

"I've always been this way." Her grin was fierce. "You just chose not to notice."

The hatch had a glass window set into it, but all she could see was her own reflection. Outside, the sky had grown dark.

The shoulder pocket of her suit held a SincPhone. She unravelled the hands-free earpiece and fitted it to the side of her head. The microphone dangled just below her chin.

"How are we doing, Commodore?"

On the other end of the line, the old man sounded grim and tired, his voice seemingly hacked out of ancient Russian stone.

"We are still here, Victoria. For now, that is victory enough."

The old airship gave a low, metallic groan of complaint, like an old-fashioned tramp steamer caught in a heavy sea. With the two starboard hulls losing gas, the other three were having to take the strain of their increasing weight.

"Good luck," she said. It didn't seem like an adequate farewell, but she couldn't think of anything else to say. They were all heading into harm's way, and who knew what might happen?

She cut the connection and turned to Ack-Ack Macaque.

"Are you ready?"

He gave her a wide, toothy grin. "As ready as I'll ever be, considering I don't usually fly without a plane."

Victoria took hold of the wheel that opened the hatch, and began to turn it. As she did so, she remembered the gut-roiling terror that had seized her former self before each parachute jump. That terror was missing now. Yes, she was nervous, but that timid, earlier version of her was dead and gone. Vicky the journalist had been killed in action in the South Atlantic, and now only Victoria the cyborg remained.

The lock disengaged and the hatch swung inwards. Beyond, the night was black.

"Okay," she said, summoning all her courage, "follow me."

She pulled her goggles down over her eyes. Then, gripping the sides of the hatchway frame, she launched herself out, headfirst into the night. In her mind, Paul cried out in fear. The wind snatched at the fabric of her suit, and she fell.

CHAPTER TWENTY-NINE
ALL SET FOR THE LIFE ETERNAL

MEROVECH HALF-CARRIED JULIE to the *Tereshkova*'s infirmary, where he helped her onto one of the bunks and cut the denim from her wounded leg. The room was small and economical, with sterile white surfaces and ranks of sliding drawers packed with pills, dressings and surgical implements. Two bunks occupied the centre of the room, for emergency cases. Normally, the medical officer treated passengers in their own cabins, but he himself had been wounded in the fighting, with two gunshot wounds to the groin, and had therefore been airlifted away with the other non-essential personnel, leaving the sickbay unmanned. Luckily, as a soldier, Merovech had been trained to give first aid.

"It's just a gash." He used a wad of cotton wool to sponge the blood. "A nasty one, though."

Each time he touched her, Julie sucked air through her teeth.

"It hurts."

"I'm sorry."

She summoned a strained smile. "Why are you apologising? It is not your fault."

The rail gun needle had scraped her thigh at a shallow angle, ripping out a furrow six inches in length and half an inch wide: painful, but thankfully not deep enough to cause any real, lasting damage. Merovech did his best to clean it up, and then applied a thick pad and bandages.

"You probably need stitches in that. Perhaps when this is all over—"

Strands of purple hair swayed as Julie shook her head.

"I will be okay, I think."

"If you don't get it stitched, you'll have a scar."

She shrugged. "Then I will have a scar. And a story to tell."

She watched him rinse his hands in the steel washbasin, then shake them, and wipe them dry against the back pockets of his jeans.

"It will not put you off?"

He turned to her. "Excuse me?"

"The scar." She pointed to the fresh bandages. "It won't put you off me?"

Merovech's lips twitched: the closest he felt he could get to a proper smile right now. He stepped over to the bed and took her hand in his.

"No," he said, "it won't."

"Good. Because we make a good team, you and I, *n'est-ce pas?*"

"*Oui, c'est vrai.*" He circled her knuckles with his thumb.

"Then, what is the matter?" she asked. "I can see you're troubled."

Merovech sighed.

"Those soldiers in the helicopter. They were only doing their job."

Her hand tightened in his.

"They were trying to take you away."

"They were just following orders. And we killed them. They were British soldiers, and I stood by and watched them die."

"What else could we have done?"

He let go of her hand and pushed his fists into his eyes.

"I was a British soldier. I wore the same uniform. I flew in the same choppers, handled the same weapons and ate the same food." He lowered his hands and looked at her. "Now, what does that make me?"

Julie touched his knee with her fingers.

"This is not your fault, Merovech. Really not. You did not ask to be put in this position."

"Maybe I should have gone with them?"

Julie's eyes widened. "No! We need you. *I* need you."

"But the cost..."

"Forget the cost, Merovech. Do you understand that? Forget. The. Cost."

He pulled back.

"But—"

"No buts!" Julie reached for him. "*Je t'aime*, Merovech, you know that. But there is more at stake here than you realise. Your mother has to be stopped, and you are the only one who can, whatever it takes."

"If she wants the throne—"

"The throne is not what she is after. K8 read her private files. She wants the whole world."

"What?"

"K8 found the evidence. We were waiting for the right time to tell you. This stand-off with China, it is part of your mother's plan. She is deliberately provoking them."

"Why would she do that?"

"When the Céleste probe gets to Mars, the Undying plan to download themselves into robot bodies and terraform the planet."

"Yes, but—"

"Mars has no magnetic field. The surface gets a lot of radiation, and the robots are built to withstand it."

A cold hand closed around Merovech's heart.

"And so if China attacks—"

"World War Three. Everybody gets blown back to the Stone Age, and the Undying get two planets instead of one."

"Jesus Christ. Is that even possible?"

Julie lay back on the pillow, her hair fanning out around her head.

"*Je ne sais pas*. But K8 thinks so, from what she saw when hacking the files."

The walls of the airship groaned, and the deck shuddered, tipping another degree or two to starboard.

"If anyone is going to stop her, Merovech, it has to be you."

Merovech flexed his fists.

"What can I do?"

Julie hitched herself up onto her elbows.

"The people need a leader they can trust."

Merovech looked up at the low ceiling, which had been painted white, rivets and all.

"Then they'll have to elect one. I'll expose my mother, and I'll take the throne. I'll do what needs to be done, for my country." His hands clenched, fingers digging into palms, knuckles white. "But afterwards, when the dust's settled, I'm going to abdicate."

Julie put a hand to her mouth.

"Are you serious?"

Merovech perched on the bed beside her.

"Deadly serious. I've been thinking about this a lot, ever since the crash. And I've not been happy for a while."

Julie opened and closed her mouth, digesting his words. Then she said, "Is that what you really want?"

"It is." He smiled at her. "I can't bear the formality. All those endless receptions. And besides, the succession isn't mine, remember? It turns out I'm no more entitled to it than my mother. And with all this illegal gelware in my head, I may not even be fit to rule at all. As soon as things get back to normal, I'll call a referendum and let the people decide."

Someone rapped on the sickbay door. Merovech turned to find the Commodore leaning against the frame.

"Excuse the interruption." The old man's jacket had been left undone, and his sash had gone missing. Beneath his moustache and bushy white brows, his face seemed pale and strained. "But I thought you should know, we caught the saboteur."

"Where was he?"

"My men found him hiding in the starboard cargo bay. Now we have the *kozyol* in the lounge." He turned, holding his injured hip with one hand, and gestured Merovech to follow. "Come, he wishes to speak with you."

"Why me?"

"I do not know. But he refuses to talk to anybody else."

THE COMMODORE'S CREWMEN had strapped the saboteur to a chair in the centre of the main lounge. He was a young man around Merovech's age. Plastic packing strips bound his left wrist and right ankle to the chair. He wore a creased white shirt and thin black tie. In his right hand, he cupped a smouldering cigarette.

He looked up as Merovech approached.

"Hey, your highness." Diamonds of sweat shone on his brow. His hair and shirt looked damp.

"You wanted to see me?"

"I sure did." The man's face cracked into a white-toothed grin. "I got a message for you, man."

Merovech crossed his arms, making no effort to conceal his impatience. "What is it?"

The man wagged his cigarette. "Hey, not so fast. Why the rush? Don't you want to know who I am first?"

Merovech tapped a toe against the deck. "To be honest, I couldn't give a damn."

The young man's grin broadened. "Well, my name's Linton. Linton Martin, and I sure am pleased to meet you." He stuck the cigarette in the corner of his mouth and held out his hand. Merovech ignored it.

"I suppose you're working for my mother, too?"

Smoke curled from Linton's mouth. A bead of sweat rolled down his face.

"You know it, baby." He took another big hit from the cigarette, tipped his head back, and blew smoke at the ceiling.

The Commodore stepped forward, favouring his bad hip. One of his polished boots dragged against the deck.

"He came on board at Heathrow, as a legitimate passenger." The old man spoke through clenched teeth, his voice dripping with a mixture of pain and disgust. "A last minute booking."

Merovech didn't take his eyes from the prisoner. "He must be one of the 'friends' that Berg warned us about."

With a low metallic groan, the deck tipped further. Merovech adjusted his footing.

"It's getting worse."

The Commodore scowled. "Perhaps you should reconsider your decision to stay?"

Merovech gave a firm shake of his head.

"No, I'm going to see this through. If I run now, I'll be running for the rest of my life. This is my best and only chance to end this, here and now."

In the chair, Linton chuckled, clearly enjoying himself. The Commodore glared at him.

"Let me know when you are finished with this *kozyol*," he said to Merovech.

"What are you going to do with him?"

The Commodore's lip curled, revealing teeth the colour of old ivory. "Lock him in the brig. If we crash into the sea, he crashes with us."

Linton chortled again. His left foot tapped against the floor. The fingers of both hands twitched.

"That is *so* not going to happen."

"Why do you say that?" Merovech lowered himself onto one knee, bringing their faces level. "You don't think we'll crash?"

Linton bobbed his head, as if in time to music.

"No, man. I don't think you'll get me to the brig."

"Why not?"

"Because I'll be dead before you get me there." He sucked the last of the cigarette and dropped the butt to the deck, where he ground it out with the point of his shoe.

Merovech felt a frisson of unease.

"Another bomb?"

Linton stopped jiggling. His blue eyes seemed to sparkle.

"Suicide pills." He cackled. "How fucking cool is *that*?"

"You've taken them?"

"Yeah, baby. And the clock's ticking."

Merovech shook his head in disbelief.

"Don't you care?"

Linton wiped his forehead on the sleeve of his shirt. Then he reached into his shirt pocket and pulled out a soft pack of American cigarettes. Only two remained. He extracted one with his teeth and let the pack fall to the floor.

"It doesn't bother me. I'm backed-up, baby. All set for the life eternal."

Merovech stood, and brushed off the knee of his jeans.

"Do you really believe that?"

"Sure thing."

Merovech felt his cheeks flush. He wanted to strangle this infuriating kid.

"That won't be *you*," he said. "Just a copy. Don't you get it? You'll be dead."

"I'll live again, baby."

"No, you won't, not really." Merovech sighed, fatigue and pity leeching the anger from him. "Just because, somewhere, a robot remembers you, it doesn't mean that you, the real you, won't be dead."

Linton gave a dismissive flick of his fingers.

"You believe what you want to believe, man. But time's running out, and I've got a message I need to pass on before I check out of *this* body, and into the *next*."

Merovech rocked back on his heels.

"Come on then, spill it. What's the message, and who's it from? My mother?"

Linton grinned around his unlit cigarette.

"It's from Doctor Nguyen."

"Nguyen's dead."

"No, he ain't." The kid's breathing became laboured. The sweat continued to roll off him. "Of course he ain't. And he says to tell you, he'll see you and your friends real soon."

As he finished speaking, the colour drained from his face. He gave a grunt of pain and bent forward, as if punched in the gut. With a shaking hand, he took the cigarette from his mouth and spat blood and phlegm onto the deck. Then he sat back upright, wiped the drool from his lip, and looked around at the armed guards lining the walls of the lounge. Sweat poured down his face.

"Okay." He waggled the cigarette defiantly. "Which one of you motherfuckers has a light?"

CHAPTER THIRTY
ZERO

SPREAD-EAGLED IN THE roaring darkness, Victoria fell towards the sea. She could feel the wind ripping at the flaps of material beneath her arms and between her legs. Air filled her cheeks, snatching away her breath, and buffeting her chest like the mane of a bucking horse.

The monkey was somewhere behind her, lost in the night. Far to her right, the orange lights of Torquay and Salcombe; to her left, Cherbourg and Guernsey; and ahead, on the wine-dark sea, the red and green running lights of the yacht ferrying guests and provisions to the *Maraldi*.

The darkness made it hard to visually judge height and distance, but readouts chattered in her head as her gelware interfaced with real-time GPS positioning systems, counting down to the moment she'd have to open her 'chute. But with the yacht moving away from her at a fair clip, the only question on her mind was whether or not she'd have the height and speed to catch it before it moved out of range, and she found herself stuck in the cold waters of the Channel, miles from land.

Her chest muscles ached with the effort of keeping her arms rigid, but she knew the slightest twitch could alter her direction or angle of descent, so she kept them as steady as she could. She'd minimised Paul's image, but could still see a thumbnail of him in her peripheral vision, both hands wrapped across his mouth as he watched the fall through her eyes. She tried to ignore him. If she screwed this up, she'd screw it up for both of them, and that would be that. But right now, she didn't need additional pressure; she had enough to worry about.

Her goggles pushed against her face. She didn't have a lot of altitude left. She'd have to pull her ripcord in the next thirty seconds.

The boat loomed larger and larger beneath her, a ghostly feathered wake churning from its stern.

Twenty seconds. The countdown spiralled. She could smell the brine.

"Pull the cord!" Paul yelled.

Fifteen.

Come on, come on.

With five seconds to spare, she zipped over the vessel, high above its twin masts. The yacht's windows were lit. People were partying.

Zero. She yanked the release, and the black silk canopy billowed from her backpack. The wind caught it and jerked her back, hard enough to snap her teeth shut. Bruised and winded, she dangled like a rag doll, legs and arms swinging loose.

"Get out of the harness *before* you hit the water," Paul warned. "You don't want to get tangled in the lines."

For a second, she thought she caught sight of the second black 'chute: a movement against the stars. Then the sea seemed to rush at her, much too fast. She unclipped the front of her harness. Before she could shrug it off, her boots hit the swell and she plunged into water so cold she thought it would stop her heart.

The speed of her descent carried her down in a maelstrom of bubbles. Frantically, she thrashed her arms free from the harness and, lungs bursting, kicked upwards.

The surface seemed further than she'd expected. When her head broke through, her face hit the sodden underside of the parachute, which lay draped on the ocean like a woefully inadequate pool cover. She flailed at it.

"Find a seam," Paul called as her fingers scrabbled for purchase on the sodden material. "Find a seam and follow it to the front of the 'chute. Don't go sideways or you'll get caught in the lines at either end."

Sensing her panic, the gelware switched her into command mode. She felt time slow and stretch, and her fear evaporated. She was still trapped, but now it was simply a problem to be overcome rather than a cause for alarm.

Using her teeth, she pulled off a glove and ran her freezing fingers across the underside of the parachute until she found a row of stitching. Then, in accordance with Paul's suggestion, she kicked her feet, following it. Moments later, she ducked under the edge of the material, and out into open air.

For a few breaths, she was content to bob with the rise and fall of the water. Then, she turned to face the approaching yacht.

It came at her like a knife through the waves, its sails cupping the wind. She struck out sideways, her movements hampered by her waterlogged clothes, her booted feet kicking ineffectually.

After a few moments of struggle, the boat caught up with her. The wave of froth at its bow shouldered her aside. The yacht was a dignified old wooden vessel, with two masts and a row of portholes just above the waterline. As it slid past, she lunged with all her strength. Cold fingers caught the rim of the nearest porthole, and the boat dragged her along with it, spray smashing up against her arms and chest.

So far, so good. Now all she had to do was find a way to clamber up onto the deck, preferably without detection. She heaved, dragging herself forward by her fingertips. The sea sucked at the flap of material between her legs, reluctant to release her. She could barely feel her hands, and her strength had begun to ebb, dissipating into the water with the last of her body heat. One final pull. Her vision went red. Her pulse throbbed at her temples.

"Come on!" Paul urged. She strained until she felt the muscles in her arms would snap, but still the edge of the deck remained frustratingly beyond her reach.

She fell back, clinging to the porthole's rim, defeat washing through her. The sea clawed at her legs with a thousand fingers, and she knew she couldn't hold on.

"I can't do it," she cried.

In her eye, Paul had both hands on the top of his head, fingers digging into his peroxide hair.

"You can't give up now."

"It's not. About. Giving. Up." Each word was an effort, shouted into a wall of stinging, salty spray. "It's about. Not. Being able. To. Fucking. Reach."

Her fingers were beginning to work loose, losing purchase on the wet steel frame. Her forearms were solid ropes of pain.

"Hold on, Vicky."

"I can't!"

To let go would be to drown. She wouldn't have the strength to keep herself afloat against the weight of her sodden flight suit. It would be a suffocating and unpleasant way to die, but at least it would be relatively quick, and the gelware would be there to ease her through it on a wave of painkillers. And as for Paul, she could turn him off at any time. Perhaps that would be the kindest thing: to grant him instant, unknowing oblivion, and spare him her final moments.

Teeth clenched, she brought up the mental menu options to end his simulation.

"Sorry, Paul." She'd execute the command as her fingers slipped from the porthole rim. Already, her left hand had worked almost completely loose, and now clung on by fingertips alone. When it slipped, the jerk would be enough to pull her right hand free as well.

"No," Paul cried, "wait!"

"Can't."

She could hear music from the party inside the ship: teeny-boppers cooing Franglais slang over a bubblegum Euro-trance beat. Millimetre by millimetre, her fingertips scraped toward the rim. These were the final seconds of both their lives.

"I'm sorry."

The water pulled at her thighs. She closed her eyes and prepared for death.

BUT DEATH DIDN'T come.

Instead, a strong leathery hand caught her by her flight suit's collar, and hauled her up, over the rail.

She lay coughing and shivering on the yacht's wooden deck. Ack-Ack Macaque sat on his heels beside her. He'd unzipped his wingsuit and now wore only his skullcap and leather jacket. A bullet belt circled his narrow hips, loaded with shells; his goggles were loose around his neck and, in his hand, he held the chrome-plated revolver he'd taken from the *Tereshkova*'s armoury. Tail twitching, he regarded her with his single, yellow eye.

"I've never jumped out of a plane before," he said. "In real life, I mean. Kind of fun."

Victoria levered herself into a sitting position and looked around. The deck seemed deserted. Music came from an open hatchway amidships, louder here than it had been from her earlier perch.

"Where—" She coughed. "Where are the crew?" They were passing through one of the busiest shipping lanes in the world, yet the deck was dark and deserted.

The monkey gave a nod of his head, back towards the stern.

"There's two in the wheelhouse."

"Have they seen us?"

"I don't think so. They're watching TV. The boat seems to be driving itself."

Victoria pulled down the zip of her wingsuit and kicked it off. She retrieved her quarterstaff from its strap on the back of the suit, and kicked the rest under the rail, into the sea. Her feet were still numb from the water. Watching her, Ack-Ack Macaque scratched at the fur on his cheek.

"You're dry," she realised. Then, "How did you get aboard?"

He looked up at the masts stretching into the sky above them.

"I saw you ditch in the sea, but the boat was getting away from me. It was all I could do to catch it. I pulled my 'chute at the last second, and came down as close as I could to the mast. Then I simply unclipped my harness and dropped onto the yardarm."

"That sounds dangerous."

Ack-Ack Macaque gave a small shrug. "No worse than jumping from one tree into another. The 'chute blew away, and I climbed down the rigging."

Victoria glanced at Paul. His translucent image seemed to hang in the air above the rail. He had his fingers laced behind his head and his eyes screwed shut, so she quietly minimised his image without speaking. After all he'd been through over the past few days, she figured the poor guy deserved a little private time in which to freak out.

The wind blew across the deck and straight through her wet clothes. Her hands shook. To still them, she gripped the carbon fibre shaft of her quarterstaff.

"Okay," she said through chattering teeth, "we need to make our way to the hold and lie low until we reach the *Maraldi*."

Ack-Ack Macaque waggled his revolver towards the bows. "The hatch is that way. If we stay low, they won't see us."

He started to move, but Victoria caught his arm. She would have liked nothing more than to get below decks, out of the cold evening air; yet something held her back: some instinct scratching at the inside of her skull, warning of danger.

"This isn't right."

Ack-Ack Macaque crouched beside her, his eye scanning the deck for threats.
"How so?"

"There should be more security. I expected at least three or four people on deck, keeping watch. I thought we'd have to sneak on board."

"We *are* sneaking on board."

"Yes, but I wasn't expecting it to be this easy. Look, they don't even have security cameras."

The monkey turned to fix her with his sallow stare.

"So, maybe we got lucky?"

A soft whine came from somewhere astern, rising in pitch.

"I don't think so."

Victoria sprang to her feet and ran, her wet feet pushing against the slick planking on the deck. How could she have been so stupid? Of *course* they'd have security bots.

She heard other turbines spin up, and risked a glance over her shoulder in time to see three fat, tyre-shaped sentinels rise from behind the wheelhouse, red and green targeting lasers glittering from their rims.

The cargo hatch lay ahead of her, but she knew she'd never reach it in time; and even if she did, they'd know where to find her. Her only escape would be to throw herself over the rail. But would that really be an escape? The bots could fly over water as easily as they could fly over land, and they were quite capable of picking her off when she came up for air. And anyway, having escaped drowning once, she wasn't in any hurry to get back in the water.

Shots came from behind her as the monkey emptied his revolver at their pursuers. She turned, having nowhere else to go, and saw one of the bots spiralling drunkenly, its manoeuvring fans splintered and smoking from multiple bullet hits.

As it fell, the other two bots let rip. Gun barrels flashed. Ack-Ack Macaque staggered under a hail of impacts, and went down with a screech. The silver revolver flew from his fingers.

Horrified, Victoria dropped the quarterstaff and stepped back, hands in the air, ready to surrender.

For half a second, she considered trying to overclock her neural processes, but knew she didn't have time to lay in the necessary commands; and even if she did, she seriously doubted she'd be able to move fast enough to dodge the bots' fire.

Instead, she stood there, dripping wet and shivering as lasers caressed the material of her shirt. Water slapped and gurgled against the hull. Her lips held the tang of sea salt and, far beyond the rail, the orange town lights of England shimmered on the water.

Range finders whirred. She closed her eyes.

And the first shot punched her in the chest.

TECHSNARK
BLOGGING WITH ATTITUDE

Ack-Ack Macaque Still Offline

Posted: 28/11/2059 – 9:00pm GMT

| Share |

Three hours after the unexplained crash of Céleste Tech's online flagship, rumours are starting to surface, with gamers reporting an epic battle between the old and new versions of the well-loved title character.

Early reports speak of YouTube clips showing two monkeys fighting on top of a flying aircraft carrier. But if those clips ever existed, they've since been purged.

That hasn't stopped the rumour mill, and fan sites across the web from going crazy with speculation. The apparent 'death' of the title character at the hands of its earlier self has been seen in some quarters as proof that somebody, somewhere has finally 'won' the game.

Ack-Ack Macaque is famous for offering its players only one shot at an in-game 'life' and, it seems, that policy extends to the title character itself. The question is, with one monkey dead and the other missing, what happens next?

The only thing we can be certain of is that the game remains offline, and players still can't log on.

In the wake of the crash, several hacker groups have claimed responsibility for the appearance of the second monkey, but Céleste's PR department remains resolutely tight-lipped about the entire affair, issuing only a short statement to the effect than normal service will be resumed as soon as possible.

With every offline hour costing Céleste a fortune in subscriptions and advertising revenue, we can only hope they mean what they say.

Publicity stunt, hack attack or FUBAR? Only time will tell.

Read more | Like | Comment | Share

CHAPTER THIRTY-ONE
NGUYEN

ACK-ACK MACAQUE woke on a hard tile floor, and groaned. His tongue felt like a dry old rag; his hands and feet had been lashed with twine, and his chest felt like a pincushion. He couldn't sit up, but he could turn his head.

The room upon whose floor he lay seemed to be some sort of storage locker or changing room. Six neoprene wetsuits dangled from a rack of pegs above a utilitarian wooden bench. Rope-handled plastic bins sat at either end of the bench, diving masks piled in one, flippers in the other. Against the opposite wall, a wire rack held twelve oxygen cylinders. The room had only one door: of polished wood, with a small porthole set into it. From beyond it, he could hear music, raised voices, and the clink of glasses.

Still on the yacht, then.

Victoria lay unconscious on the tiles beside him, an inch-long tranquiliser dart sticking from the right side of her chest, just below the collarbone. He worked his dry lips.

"Victoria?"

The effort of speaking triggered a glowering pain behind his eye, as hot and fragile as any hangover. In frustration, he gave his wrists a twist, testing his restraints. The rope felt shiny and uncomfortable, like nylon.

When I get out of here, he thought, *somebody is really going to get* bitten.

Another twist, and he felt the glossy cord scrape into his flesh. The fibres creaked, but he didn't have the strength to try again. The sedatives in his system had him pinned beneath the weight of a bone-deep, soul-crushing fatigue, and he longed for the simple comforts and cold certainties of the Officers' Mess. Illusion it may have been, but life had been so much easier when all he'd had to worry about was the war. No crazy bald chicks or runaway princes, just one clear mission objective after another. And before the war, woozy, pre-conscious memories of rum-fuelled Amsterdam bar fights, of a life unburdened by self-analysis or self-awareness, where all that concerned him was the knife in his opponent's hand.

He closed his eye and pressed his head back against the cold tile. The pressure seemed to soothe the pounding ache. Then, over the distant sounds of merriment, he heard footsteps in the hall outside.

Oh, what now?

The door pushed open and a man entered. He was tall and thin, and dressed in evening wear. In his hand, he held a patent leather case.

"Ah, you're awake. Good. I thought you might be." He sat on the bench and placed the case flat on the wood beside him.

Ack-Ack Macaque blinked up at him. "Who are you?"

The man looked down at himself and smiled. His black hair had been gelled back and parted, his eyes held the barest suggestion of epicanthic folds, and his shiny skin glowed with the sepia tones of an old Victorian photograph.

"Forgive me. The last time we met, you were on an operating table and I—" He smoothed a hand down the lapel of his dinner jacket. "I had a different face."

"Doctor Nguyen?"

The man tipped his head in a polite bow. "The same."

"The man who—"

"The man who made you, yes. And your little friend there."

Using his elbows to push himself up, Ack-Ack Macaque struggled into a sitting position. "But you're dead."

Nguyen popped the clasps of his leather briefcase.

"Not dead, my simian friend. Simply upgraded into a better body." He raised the lid of the case, revealing row upon row of gleaming surgical instruments.

"Now," he said, "I must give you another shot of tranquiliser. Enough to hold you until we reach the *Maraldi,* and its excellently well-equipped infirmary."

Ack-Ack Macaque snarled. This was the man who'd turned him from knife-wielding primate to plane-flying freak; the man who'd pumped his skull full of plastic brain cells and burdened him with an intelligence he'd neither desired nor sought. Fighting the heaviness in his bones, he flexed his shoulders and pulled. The rope bit through his skin and he roared, but he kept pulling. At the same time, he swung his legs around and got himself into a kneeling position. The nylon rope stretched. He could feel the damp fibres pulling against each other. From the bottom of his jungle soul, he squeezed every last scrap of wild strength. His wrists flared with agony. And then the rope snapped, and he was free, his fingers clawing for the face of his creator.

Nguyen didn't flinch. Instead, he looked Ack-Ack Macaque in the eye. "*Masaru!*"

The strength fled from Ack-Ack Macaque's arms. His lunge became a collapse, and he fell sprawling at his tormentor's feet, limbs twitching.

Nguyen laughed harshly.

"I built you, stupid monkey. Did you not think I might have included a safe word in your programming?"

He rummaged in his case and pulled out a hypodermic needle and a small glass bottle of tranquiliser.

Ack-Ack Macaque flopped like a fish on the floor. All he wanted was to rip out this man's throat with his teeth, but his arms and legs were numb and useless. Eventually, he stopped thrashing and lay panting with his nose against the tiles.

"Why?" he asked.

Nguyen looked down at him in surprise. "Why did I make you?" The man pushed the needle through the rubber membrane at the neck of the bottle, into the colourless liquid within.

"You and your predecessors were prototypes. First attempts. We had planned to raise an army of uplifted monkeys." He stared wistfully into the middle distance. "But, as it turns out, humans are easier to control." He pulled back the plunger and filled the syringe. "Luckily, we found another use for you. A profitable use."

"The game?"

"Indeed. Our programmers needed an artificial intelligence at the heart of their game, so we gave them one." He smiled. "Although not perhaps the one they were expecting."

Ack-Ack Macaque coughed. The tiles smelled of seawater and bleach.

"And Victoria?"

"A happy accident. She was dying, so we had nothing to lose. We used her as a test bed. We could try things, new techniques that we hadn't dared try on the Prince."

"And now you're an android?"

"Yes." Nguyen drew himself up, looking down appreciatively at his new body. "One of the first. Soon, there will be thousands. When the bombs start falling and the people come to the shelters we've set up, we'll begin the process of transforming them. They will enter frail and scared, and leave as virtual supermen, with the world in flames at their feet."

Ack-Ack Macaque shook his head, nose rubbing against the cold floor.

"You're insane."

"Is it insane to want to rebuild the world, to put right the mistakes of history and eradicate disease and suffering?"

Ack-Ack Macaque turned his head and hawked phlegm.

"The way you're doing it, yes."

Nguyen placed the glass vial back into his case.

"These are the goals I have worked for all my life. Humanity can, and will, be improved."

"Whether it wants to be or not?"

Nguyen came and stood beside Ack-Ack Macaque, shoes inches from his face. He looked down.

"What it wants doesn't matter. Left alone, the human race will kill itself. It has already wrecked the environment which sustains it. Without our help, how much longer do you think it will survive? Strong leaders are needed. We will found a new society, based on science and reason, and we will save humanity from itself."

"But first you've got to kill everyone, right? In order to save them?"

"Enough!" Abruptly, Nguyen crouched, and caught Ack-Ack Macaque by the scruff of his neck, android fingers firm and strong. "Why am I arguing with you, anyway? You're nothing but an animal."

"At least I've still got my own junk. I'm not some metal eunuch."

The needle pricked his skin, sliding into the side of his neck. He tried to twist away, but couldn't break Nguyen's iron grip.

"Don't struggle."

Nguyen depressed the plunger, pushing icy liquid into Ack-Ack Macaque's veins. Then the grip loosened, and Nguyen climbed to his feet.

Ack-Ack Macaque looked up at him, heart hammering.

"There's just one thing I don't get."

"And what's that?"

"Merovech. If you're all turning yourself into cyborgs, why do you still need Merovech?"

The doctor returned the needle to his case.

"When we first planned all of this, the Duchess was to transfer her consciousness into Merovech's body. She was to become a strong new leader, and found a new royal dynasty, moving from host to host down the generations, immortal and all-powerful." His voice seemed to waver, echoing in Ack-Ack Macaque's ears as the drugs bit chunks from his awareness.

"Since these new android bodies came on stream, all that seems rather redundant," Nguyen continued. "Still, we need him as a figurehead. The

Duchess is a powerful woman, but even she can't order the prime minister to declare war. If we are to see our plan through, we need to load Her Grace's personality into Merovech when he becomes King."

Shadows blotted the corners of Ack-Ack Macaque's sight. He tried to say something, but couldn't. His thoughts became light and airy, as if someone had thrown open a window in the stuffiness of his mind. The tiles no longer felt uncomfortable beneath him. He pictured clouds and Spitfires, and the warehouses of the Amsterdam waterfront. He wondered how long it would take to—

CHAPTER THIRTY-TWO
ARTIFICIAL THUNDER

LINTON MARTIN DIED in the chair in the centre of the *Tereshkova*'s main lounge, wracked by cramps. Whatever he'd swallowed took a long time to kill him, and he sweated his way through another cigarette before the end finally came.

When it was close, with his teeth clenched against the pain, rivulets of perspiration running down his face, and the muscles in his neck standing out like steel hawsers, he fixed Merovech with a wild glare and hissed, "I *will* live again."

Then the half-smoked dog-end of his final cigarette fell from his fingers. His left leg shot out straight and his hands clawed the air. An agonising convulsion shook him, juddering every muscle, curling his arms against his chest. For a second he stayed rigid, vibrating with pain. And then he buckled. His limbs went slack and he fell to one side. The chair fell with him. His skull hit the deck with a solid clunk, and he lay there in a tangle, eyes bulging and tongue lolling wetly from his lips.

Merovech turned away. He'd seen men die before, but that didn't make it any easier to watch. He stood with the Commodore as the stewards rolled Linton onto a canvas stretcher.

"Throw him out," the Commodore growled, his damaged hip braced against the tilt of the deck. "We need to lose as much weight as we can."

"Not so fast." Merovech put a hand on the sleeve of the old man's tunic. The Commodore scowled, clearly annoyed at having his orders questioned in front of his crew.

"You want to keep him?"

"Of course not. But if we get through this, we're going to need all the evidence we can find."

The Commodore huffed, clearly unconvinced. But he turned back to his men, who were hesitating in the doorway, and said, "Take him to the galley and put him in one of the freezers. Throw the food out if you have to. It is not like we will be needing it."

Then he began to limp towards the bridge, dragging his bad leg behind him.

Merovech followed. As in the lounge, the floor in the connecting corridor leant at an alarming fifteen degrees to starboard, making the slippery metal deck treacherous.

"How much more can she take?"

Bracing himself against the walls of the corridor, the Commodore didn't look around. "We are still losing gas. The bags are compartmentalised. If only two or three compartments are damaged, we will be fine. If more, then we have real trouble."

"We'll still have enough to stay airborne, though?"

"Perhaps." A shrug. "Who knows?"

They passed the galley. Steel pots swung from ceiling hooks. Shards of smashed crockery covered the floor.

"What are we going to do?"

The Commodore stopped moving. "I won't abandon her." His gnarled hand gave the bulkhead an affectionate pat. "I am too old to mourn again. If she goes down, I go with her."

And then he was off, using his hands to steady himself. They came to the bridge, where the pilot and navigator fought to keep the massive craft on an even keel. The Commodore barked something in his native tongue, and the pilot snarled back; a string of guttural curses.

"We cannot stay up much longer," the Commodore translated.

"But we're not crashing?"

"No. Not yet. Although the strain on the hulls is great, and we should land if we can."

From the other workstation, the navigation officer threw a brisk salute, and spoke at length, with many accompanying hand gestures. The Commodore scowled, then shambled over to peer at the man's screen. From the inside pocket of his tunic, he produced a pair of reading glasses, which he balanced on the bridge of his nose as he scanned the data. He gave a grunt; and then he straightened up and turned to Merovech.

"We have two RAF fighter jets circling us in the darkness. They say they are reluctant to fire while you remain aboard, but neither will they let us deviate from our present course."

Merovech frowned. "They actually *want* us to reach the *Maraldi?*"

The Commodore slipped the spectacles back into his pocket, as deftly as any conjuror, and smoothed down the tips of his moustache.

"It seems you have a appointment to keep."

*   *   *

Returning to the sickbay, Merovech found Julie Girard looking strained. The painkillers weren't doing enough to dull the stinging needle wound in her thigh. But when she saw him, her brow furrowed not in pain, but concern.

"Are you okay?" she asked. "You look very pale."

Merovech came over and sat beside her. He took her hand.

"I'm scared, Jules. I'm angry and I'm scared."

"What can I do?"

Merovech took a long, ragged breath. "Nothing. That's the trouble. I've got the speech ready to go, but my father's down there, and he could be dying, and all we can do is wait. It makes me feel so bloody helpless."

He turned his head to the porthole. The sky was dark, but he sensed the jets all the same: out there in the blackness, circling like sharks.

"When I found out what had been done to me, what my own mother had done to me, I wanted to confront her. I was furious and hurt and all those other things."

Julie touched his hand. "You had every right to be."

"I know. But now it's all unravelled. We're fighting for our lives, and I don't know what to do. There's too much at stake and I can't see a way out. She's got the Air Force and the Navy, and what have we got?"

The walls gave a metallic shudder. Julie's fingers moved up to his cheek. She brushed at his hair, tidying it.

"We have got a monkey."

Merovech smiled in spite of himself.

"I love you."

Julie's hand dropped into her lap. "Do not say that unless you mean it."

"I do. In fact, if we get out of this alive—"

"Do not say it."

Merovech cleared his throat. The words were boiling up inside him. "If we make it through this in one piece, I want you to marry me."

Julie blinked at him, stunned.

"Are you serious?" She slammed her palms onto the blanket. "Are you *really* serious?"

Merovech pulled back.

"But, I thought—"

"We could both be killed in a few hours. Personally, I will be amazed if I am not dead or in jail by the morning. How can you be thinking about marriage at a time like this?"

"What better time is there?"

Julie scraped her lower lip with a purple thumbnail. "What about my father?"

"He can't stop us."

She shook her head. "You do not know him. You do not know what he can be like."

Merovech huffed air through his cheeks. He thought he had a pretty good idea of exactly what the old bastard could be like.

"Forget about him."

In a tight, irritated gesture, Julie wiped her hair back with the fingertips of one hand. "That might be easy for you to say. I cannot forget about him, Merovech, he is my *father*."

Where she'd pulled the purple strands back, he caught sight of the faded shadow on her cheek: the yellowed remains of the bruise that had so angered him in the café.

"Well," he snapped, "he doesn't deserve to be."

"*What?*"

"You heard me. You can keep denying it, but we both know what he is, and what he's done to you."

She waved a hand in front of her face, trying to ward off his words.

"No! *Non!*"

Far beyond the gondola's walls, Merovech heard the distant roar of the circling planes: a rumble in the dark, like artificial thunder.

"I can keep you safe," he said.

"Safe?" Julie looked around the listing cabin. "You call *this* 'safe'?"

"You know what I mean."

She shook her head, eyes flashing, and he drew back, expecting her to shout. She didn't. Instead, she dropped her chin to her chest and took a series of deep, calming breaths. When she finally looked up and spoke, it was with a firmness that surprised him.

"I know you think you are doing the right thing, but you are going about it all wrong. I love you, Merovech, I really do. I would not be here if I did not. But that does not mean I need you to *rescue* me. I don't need a big handsome prince to come riding in and fight all my battles for me."

"I didn't—"

She put a finger to his lips. "I am not a princess, I am tougher than that, and I solve my problems myself, in my own way and in my own time. And if you really, truly want to be with me, then that is something you will have to learn to accept, okay?"

She pulled her finger back.

"And yes, Merovech."

Merovech blinked foolishly, his composure in tatters. "Yes what?"

Julie smiled, and spoke slowly, as if addressing an idiot.

"Yes, if we make it through this alive, I will marry you."

CHAPTER THIRTY-THREE
PERSONAL FRANKENSTEIN

"AH, YOU'RE AWAKE," the man said. "Welcome back."

Victoria blinked up at him from the bed.

"Who are you?" She tried to move, but her arms and legs wouldn't respond. She smelled antiseptic and cold steel. The ceiling was low, white and curved. "What's happening, where are we?"

"You are on board the *Maraldi*, in the infirmary. You have been unconscious for some time."

Victoria's vision swam. She creased her eyes, trying to focus.

"And you are?"

"Come, come, Victoria. Surely someone with your background can figure that one out?"

Victoria ran her tongue over her lower lip. She'd never seen this man before, but there was something familiar about the condescension in his tone. She took a guess.

"Doctor Nguyen?"

The man gave a small smile. "Very good."

"Why can't I move?"

"When I installed your gel-based processors, I also installed an override command. A simple word that renders you immobile."

"Why would you do that?"

He moved over to the sink and turned on the taps. "I was designing the perfect slave army," he said over his shoulder. "I wanted to make sure they couldn't revolt."

As he washed and dried his hands, Victoria ran over what she knew about him.

Doctor Kenta Nguyen had been born in Osaka in the late nineteen eighties, and was now over seventy years old. He was a graduate of the Human Genome Project and, until leaving Japan to take up a research position with Céleste, he had been one of the leading innovators in the ongoing Japanese biotech revolution. She remembered him as a small, cantankerous man in a tweed suit. Now, he stood tall and limber in a dinner jacket and bow tie. He looked around thirty years old, and in amazing physical shape.

"You're an android," she said with a hammer-blow of realisation, "just like Berg."

Nguyen shook water from his hands and turned back to her.

"Ah, poor Berg. He was one of our earliest successes, and quite unhinged. I was terribly sad to lose him."

"He was a murdering psychopath."

Nguyen gave a small, pitying shake of his head.

"He was a loyal soldier." He reached for a packet of surgical gloves, and extracted two. "And all his so-called 'victims' *will* live again."

Victoria let herself sneer.

"Bullshit."

"Really, Miss Valois? Look at me." He flattened a palm against his chest. "I left my body in Paris, and yet here I am, as alive as you."

"I don't call that life."

Nguyen sighed like a disappointed schoolmaster.

"And what about you, Victoria? May I remind you that the brain in your head is more than fifty per cent synthetic. And yet you claim to be alive, do you not?"

"That's different."

"Is it?" He examined his hand. "I'll grant you that these bodies are far from perfect. I'm still having trouble integrating some of the finer senses, for example. But they will suffice, for now. Bodies like this will keep us all alive when the bombs fall, and we can improve them later. After all, we will have hundreds, maybe thousands, of years."

"Speak for yourself."

Nguyen gave a small, tight smile.

"I haven't introduced you to my assistant, have I?"

He clapped his hands twice, and a girl tottered into the room on six-inch heels. She looked to be somewhere in her early twenties. She wore a white lab coat over a tight cocktail dress. Long, blonde hair fell around her shoulders, curling down to an ample cleavage. In her hands, she held a silver tray of surgical implements.

"Victoria," Nguyen said with a flourish, "meet Vic."

Victoria frowned. Beneath the girl's make-up and fake tan, the skin held the stiff, waxy sheen that identified her as another of Nguyen's androids.

"What is this?"

Nguyen smiled. "This is you. This is what I did when Berg brought me your soul-catcher." He reached out and curled his fingers in the girl's hair. "I call her 'Vic'."

Watching him, Victoria felt her skin prickle. Bats flapped their wings in her chest cavity.

"Three days ago," Nguyen said, "I took your back-up and I loaded it into this body. This is you, Victoria. Your memories, your personality, your 'soul'."

The girl stood, inert as a waxwork, her blue eyes fixed on the middle distance.

Victoria's mouth was dry.

"I don't believe you. I would never have let you do that. I would have fought—"

Nguyen waved her to silence.

"Oh, I am more than aware of that." He untangled his fingers from the girl's hair. "And believe me, until I installed the behavioural safeguards, this one fought like the devil herself. Now, though, she is incapable of violence." He reached out and cupped one of the girl's heavy breasts in his palm. "But why worry about violence when she and I have so many better things we could be doing? Isn't that right, Vic?"

The girl blinked. She looked down at the hand holding her breast.

"Yes, Doctor Nguyen."

He smiled. "You see, Miss Valois, even you can be tamed."

Immobile on the bed, Victoria felt her cheeks burn.

"You sack of shit."

Nguyen gave a disapproving click of his tongue.

"Such language." He let go of the girl and pulled the surgical gloves on over his artificial fingers: first one hand, and then the other. "You have to see the big picture, Miss Valois. These bodies, these hands, are simply tools. With them, we will save the world."

"By destroying it?"

Nguyen shook his head. "I am a doctor. My job is to make people better. To make the human race *better*." He snapped the elastic cuff of the last glove into place, and selected a shiny silver scalpel from the tray in his assistant's hands. As he picked it up, the blade caught the light: cold, and thinner than paper.

"You've caused us considerable trouble," he said. "We should have had Merovech by now. Without him, the Duchess cannot order a strike against the Chinese. She does not have the authority."

"Too bad."

Nguyen's lips thinned. "No matter. He will be here soon enough. The RAF are bringing him to us." He looked at his watch. "And as soon as the Mars probe's safely away, he'll order the launch of a cruise missile at Shenzhen City. The war will start on schedule."

He took up position at the head of the bed. "We've been preparing for this for years. With the industrial resources of Céleste at our disposal, we've constructed legions of android bodies, and converted as many of our followers as we can." He showed her the scalpel. "And now, I'm afraid, it's your turn."

Victoria's vision swam. Her pulse hammered in her throat until she could hardly draw breath.

"What are you doing?"

Nguyen leant over the bed. She felt his palm enfolding the back of her head in much the same way he'd just enfolded the blonde girl's breast.

"Now," he said, "Let's get that gelware out of there, and into a new body."

"No!"

"Hush now."

He held her firmly, his weight pressing down on her, and she felt a sickening prick as the scalpel punctured the skin at the crown of her head. She wanted to kick and flail, but her limbs wouldn't respond.

The blonde girl watched her. Their eyes met.

"Vic, help me!"

The girl looked to Nguyen, and back, but otherwise remained motionless.

The blade moved, slicing obscenely downwards, and Victoria screamed as she felt the skin of her scalp part. The tip scraped bone and Nguyen straightened his back. His gloved hands were red with her blood.

"I'm going to need the saw," he said, and stepped into the adjoining room.

Victoria felt tears rolling down her face, to join the hot blood soaking into the sheet beneath her head. Too many men had had their fingers in her cranium. Why couldn't they leave her alone?

Why couldn't they just let her die?

Hopelessly, she blinked up his window and enabled the sound.

"Paul?" she said.

His eyes were wide and his knuckles were red where he'd been chewing on them.

"I'm here, Vicky. I'm here."

"What should I do?"

"I don't know." He sounded almost hysterical.

"I'm out of options, Paul."

He screwed up his eyes in thought. His fingers tugged at his beard.

"Try talking to the robot?"

"Vic? She can't help."

"We haven't *got* anything else."

Victoria took a breath. The android still watched her, its face devoid of expression.

"Okay," she said, and raised her voice. "Please, help me, Vic."

The android tilted her head. From the adjoining room, Victoria could hear Nguyen moving equipment.

"Please?"

Without a word, Vic stepped up to the bed, and Victoria's heart jumped as she took one of the scalpels from her tray.

"What are you doing?"

Vic put her finger to her luscious red lips. Then she placed the scalpel in Victoria's numb hand, and wrapped the unresponsive fingers around it.

"Wait," she whispered, and then stepped back to her former place.

Nguyen appeared in the doorway, carrying an electric saw. His eyes narrowed, and he looked from Victoria to the android.

"You can ask her all you like, but she won't help you. She can't. She's programmed to obey me, and me alone."

He carried the saw over to the work surface and plugged it into a wall socket. He revved it a couple of times and then, seemingly satisfied, he turned back to the bed.

"I'm afraid this will hurt," he said. "But don't worry, the hurt won't last. And when you awake, you'll be just like her."

He flicked the switch and the blade whined. As he moved to bring it down on Victoria's head, the blonde spoke. With a Japanese curse of irritation, Nguyen flicked the saw off again.

"What did you say?"

Vic turned and set her tray down on the side. When she turned back, her expression had hardened.

"I said, 'Osaka'."

Victoria felt her limbs twitch. Nguyen frowned in puzzlement. Then his eyes opened wide as he realised what was happening.

"No, don't say—!"

Freed from her restriction, Victoria stabbed upward with all her strength. The scalpel caught the doctor under his chin and punched up, through the roof of his mouth, into the base of his brain. He staggered back with a roar, and Victoria rolled off the opposite side of the bed. Her arms and legs were a flaming agony of needles and pins, but at least they were working again.

She crawled to the feet of the blonde girl, and pulled herself up on the material of her white coat.

"Thanks," she gasped.

Nguyen leant on the bed, the scalpel's handle still protruding from beneath his chin. Fat blue gobs of fluid dripped from the wound.

Vic watched him dispassionately. "He shouldn't have let me into his files," she said. "I found all the command words. Now quickly, repeat this after me. Tango. Honshu. Hellas. Basin."

Nguyen turned his head in their direction, fury burning in his eyes. His thumb activated the saw in his hand. Victoria ran her tongue over her dry lips.

"Tango. Honshu. Hellas. Basin."

The android smiled. "Thank you."

"Those were your command words?"

"Oh yes."

"What are you going to do?"

"What do you think?" She reached into the pocket of her lab coat and pulled out Victoria's quarterstaff.

"Where did you get that?"

"He gave it to me as a souvenir. He thought it was funny." She shook it out to its full length. "Now, get down."

She pushed past Victoria and lunged across the room. The staff's tip caught Nguyen in the chest, pushing him off-balance, but he responded with a swipe from the whirring saw. The girl parried, and brought the other end of the stick around to connect with the side of his head. Nguyen staggered and went down on one knee.

With her back to the wall, Victoria recognised the moves Vic used: they were the same ones she'd been practising herself, over and over again, for the past six months. She felt her fingers grip, and her arms twitch in sympathy with every thrust and parry.

For a moment, Nguyen seemed to gain the upper hand. He caught hold of the girl's sleeve and delivered a couple of resounding whacks to the side of her head. Victoria looked around for a weapon with which to help, but all she could see was the steel tray. She clicked herself into command mode and dialled everything up to eleven: heart rate, adrenalin, metabolism, the works. Then, with every ounce of her amplified strength, she took the tray and swung the narrow edge of it at the back of Nguyen's neck. The hacking blow jarred her arm, but she felt something crack. The doctor's head lolled forward. His grip on his opponent loosened, and Vic skipped back, out of reach. She raised the quarterstaff to her shoulder and smacked it end-first into Nguyen's face. The blow sent him reeling against the bed. A second snapped his head back; and a third severed whatever was left in his neck, tearing his head from its mount.

The head hit the deck with a solid clump, and rolled in a small half-circle before settling. Victoria and Vic stared at it. Then Vic walked over and kicked it full in the face, slamming it against the wall, leaving a dent. Then she kicked it again, and again. On the fourth kick, Victoria reached out and took her arm.

"I think he's dead." The head had split, revealing a mass of wiring, circuitry, and oozing gel; and beneath all that, something greasy, pale and organic. Vic stood stiffly, glaring down at the mess she'd made.

"You don't know what he did. What he made me do. What it was like."

Victoria gave Vic's shoulder a squeeze, and mentally issued the instructions to drop herself out of command mode.

"It's okay now. It's over."

Vic gave a snort. She retracted the quarterstaff and dropped it onto the bed. "It's not over. It'll never be 'over'. Just look at the state of me." She took hold of her over-sized breasts. "Look at these stupid things. If he wasn't already dead, I'd tear them off and choke him with them."

"He is dead," Victoria said. Vic ignored her.

"When I was you, I didn't know whether I was properly human. Think how I feel now."

"You are still me."

"No, you don't believe that any more than I do. I'm the back-up, same as Paul. Just a ghost in a machine."

Victoria wanted to comfort her, but didn't know how. How were you supposed to hug an android?

"I remember being you," Vic said, "but I also have new memories, memories I don't want to have to live with."

"You could help me," Victoria suggested, trying to massage some feeling back into her forearms. "We could put an end to all this, forever."

Still looking down at the glistening, oozing remains of Nguyen's shattered skull, Vic shook her head.

"No." She sat on the edge of the hospital bed. "No, I don't think so."

"You know what's at stake?"

A shrug. "Some of it."

"Don't you care?"

Vic turned to her, eyes narrowed to slits. "Don't you dare, okay? Don't you dare. You do *not* get to lecture me."

"I'm sorry, I—"

"I didn't know you'd survived. I thought you'd died in Paul's flat. I thought I was all that was left. And that bastard wrapped me in this stupid body and raped me, over and over again." Fingers spread wide, she ground the heels of her palms into her forehead, just above her right eye, in a gesture Victoria recognised as one of her own.

"I'm just the back-up," Vic said. "I'm not the real Victoria Valois, you are. And I can't take it anymore." She looked down at her synthetic body with a lip-curl of disgust. "Honestly, I don't want to live this way."

Victoria clenched her fists. The pins and needles were wearing off.

"What are you saying?"

"Oh come on, you know exactly what I'm saying."

Victoria stopped rubbing her arms and hugged herself. She could tell the girl was hurting, and hurting badly. All her doubts had fled. Despite what she'd said to Nguyen and Berg, she now knew beyond all question that a back-up's pain could be every bit as raw and deep as a human's.

"Please," she said. "Please help us."

"No." Vic gave an emphatic shake of her blonde head. "I've killed our personal Frankenstein, the rest's up to you. All I need you to do is deactivate me."

Victoria glanced down at the head lying smashed on the deck at their feet.

"I'm not sure I can."

Vic turned to her. She reached out to touch the stubble on Victoria's scalp, then drew back her hand.

"All you have to do is repeat a few words."

"Another deactivation code?"

"*Oui.*"

The two women held each other's gaze for several seconds. Victoria felt as if she should have something profound and comforting to say, but nothing came to mind. She just sat there, trying not to cry. Eventually, Vic took her hand and gave it a gentle squeeze, rubbing the knuckles with her thumb in the same way her mother—*their* mother—used to do.

"Okay?"

"Okay."

"We'd better make this quick. You need to get out of here before someone finds you."

"Don't worry about that."

"Nevertheless." Vic sat up a little straighter. "I'm ready. I don't want to think about it any longer."

Victoria felt a tear welling. She switched her focus away from the emotion, into the comforting detachment of the gelware, and wiped her eye with a forefinger.

"All right," she said.

Vic smiled, but there was pain behind it.

"Repeat after me. Corduroy. Home. Champagne. Cherry blossom."

Victoria pulled breath through her teeth.

"Corduroy. Home." She gripped Vic's hand in both of hers. The walls of the infirmary seemed to fall away into non-existence.

"Champagne." The world collapsed around them and, in that single moment, nothing else mattered. They were alone with their humanity.

Vic whispered, "Take care of Paul."

Victoria nodded. Vic's irises were discs of pure cobalt. Perfect black singularities burned at their centres, behind which dwelt a creature who shared her memories, a creature who, up until a few days ago, had been her. She'd come here to get her soul back, and here it was. She had so much she wanted to say, so much she felt she could learn. And yet her lips moved seemingly of their own volition, wanting nothing more than to end this poor girl's suffering.

"Cherry blossom."

CHAPTER THIRTY-FOUR
HARD REBOOT

ACK-ACK MACAQUE woke face-down in a cupboard, head pounding. Moving carefully, he flexed his arms and legs. They seemed to be working again, although they felt bruised, as if he'd been roughly manhandled. But at least he was no longer paralysed. Whatever Nguyen had done to him, unconsciousness seemed to have sorted it out, resetting his system to its default state. Was that what K8 meant when she talked of a hard reboot? Simply turning the system 'off and on again'? If it worked for her SincPad, why shouldn't it work for his gelware?

He pushed himself up into a sitting position.

Where the fuck am I this time?

The cupboard was cramped and smelled musty, lit only by light leaking around the closed door. The floorboards at its base were rough, untreated wood, and he shared them with mops, buckets, and a selection of cleaning products, which added their own sharp ammonia tang to the air.

He felt around the door, leathery fingers brushing the wooden frame. The door had no handle on the inside, but it seemed to open outwards, and he thought he could probably open it with a kick.

But what was out there? He guessed they were on the *Maraldi*, the Duchess's floating super-liner. Nguyen had given him that much. But what if Nguyen was out there, waiting for him? The man could cripple him with a single word.

Ack-Ack Macaque pulled one of the mops from its bucket. He took hold of the damp, stringy head and snapped it off, leaving a jagged wooden spike. If Nguyen tried to speak, he'd ram this makeshift spear down the bastard's throat, and keep pushing until it came out of his ass.

With one hand on the wall, he pulled himself upright. The drugs were still loose in his system, but he had a weapon now, and that made him feel a whole lot better. He was back in control, back in the kind of situation he could understand: outnumbered and outgunned, but armed and ready to break a few heads.

He gave the door an experimental push, and felt the resistance of a catch.

Still, it didn't feel too solid. He braced himself against the rear wall of the cupboard, and kicked. The door cracked. It moved in its frame, but the catch held. Spear at the ready, he gave it another whack, and it sprang open.

White light streamed in, bringing with it a wave of antiseptic hospital smells. The room beyond the cupboard was obviously some sort of sickbay. Victoria Valois sat in the centre, cradling the head and stroking the hair of a tall, blonde girl. She looked up without surprise, her eyes red-rimmed and haunted.

"She's dead."

Ack-Ack Macaque stepped through the doorway and waddled up to the bed. He gave the girl a sniff. Her eyes were open, but un-reactive.

"Who was she?"

Victoria gave the golden hair a final smooth, then laid the head on the mussed sheets of the bed. She kissed her fingers, and pressed them to the girl's cheek. Then, with one hand on the bed rail for support, she levered herself into a standing position.

"She was me."

A headless corpse lay on the floor between the bed and the door.

"And that was?"

"Nguyen. He's dead, too."

Ack-Ack Macaque looked at the crushed remains of the man's head.

"No shit." Victoria turned away, and Ack-Ack Macaque's nose wrinkled as he saw the gaping flaps of skin on the back of her head. The flesh from the crown to the back of her neck had been cut to the bone. Dark, glistening blood slathered her collar and soaked the back of her shirt. "I can see that. But how about you?"

She turned back to him.

"I'm okay. I think I've lost some blood."

"Sit back down. We need to get you patched up."

She waved him away. "I'll be fine."

"No, you won't."

He pushed her gently back, into a sitting position on the edge of the bed, then rifled the drawers for dressings and surgical tape.

"You need stitches," he said.

Victoria put a hand to the back of her head. Her fingers came away bloody, and she looked at them curiously.

"You might be right." Her voice was flat. She was either in shock, or locked into command mode.

Ack-Ack Macaque found some thread, a bottle of anaesthetic, and a pack of syringes. He held them up to show her, and she frowned.

"Have you ever done this before?"

He remembered sewing up the wounded thigh of his co-pilot, after the man had been hit by shrapnel over Dunkirk—but that had been in the game, not reality, and things had been simpler back then.

"Sort of." He shuffled around behind the bed and laid his haul out on the sheet behind her. Then he fetched the sharpened mop handle, and handed it to her.

"This'll take a few minutes," he said. "If anyone comes in, stick them with that."

He bit open the pack of syringes and filled one from the anaesthetic bottle. He had no idea what a standard dose might be, so he took a guess, filling the syringe a quarter full. If it wasn't enough, he figured he could always add more later. The last thing he wanted to do now was knock her out cold.

His hands were shaking, and he didn't know whether it was because of the drugs in his system, or apprehension at what he was about to do.

Come on, he thought. *Pull yourself together. It's a flesh wound, not brain surgery.*

But the wound, made with precision and a sharp blade, stirred memories in him—memories of warehouse fights and knife cuts on his forearms; of his arm jarring as his blade scraped an opponent's ribcage, parting fur and sinew from bone; and the intolerable stinging of his torn left eye as its gloopy fluid caked the fur of his cheek and chin. He shivered.

A long time ago, a long way away.

He'd been a different monkey then. Now, he was something else. Something older and wiser.

Gritting his teeth, he placed one hand over Victoria's left ear to steady himself, and used the other to bring the needle close to the lip of the slash. Beneath the welling blood, he caught the ceramic whiteness of living bone.

"Hold still," he muttered gruffly, swallowing down his distaste. "Because, from experience, I think this is probably gonna hurt."

TEN MINUTES LATER, they were done. He snapped the thread and threw the needle over his shoulder. The stitches were clumsy and rough, but they would hold. He applied a thick wad of gauze and taped it into place, and then stepped back.

"How's that feel?"

Victoria reached around so that her fingertips brushed the bandage.

"I can't feel a thing. Just some tightness, maybe."

"Good." He walked around the bed to face her. "Because it's going to sting like fuck when that anaesthetic wears off. Now, do me a favour, and open the porthole."

He took the spear from her hands, turned it point-down, and stabbed it into Nguyen's severed head. The point squelched through the wet brain tissues like a fork through pâté. When he felt it hit the floor, he bent at the knees and raised the head from the ground. Holding it aloft on the end of his spear, he carried it over to where Victoria had un-dogged the circular window. The head was a little too large to fit through the gap, so he jammed it into the frame and used the stick to ram it through. On the third shove, it popped out and disappeared, leaving only a scraped clump of blood and hair on the window hinge.

He threw the stick out after it, and turned to Victoria.

"I just want to be sure."

He looked at the blonde girl on the bed, her dead eyes still staring sightlessly into space. "What about her?"

Victoria stepped between them. "You leave her alone."

"I wasn't suggesting—"

"I don't care. Just leave her alone."

He held up his palms in a placatory gesture. "Fine. I was only going to ask what you wanted to do with her. I wasn't going to shove her out the window."

He went back to the drawers lining the walls, looking for knives and scalpels—anything he could use as a weapon. An open doorway led into an adjoining room, filled with medical equipment: monitors, respirators, things whose function he couldn't even begin to guess. And there, resting on top of Doctor Nguyen's briefcase, he recognised the gun he'd brought with him from the *Tereshkova*. He let out a screech of triumph and scooped it up. He'd emptied it against the sentry robots on the yacht, but still had plenty more bullets on his leather belt. He pulled out six and pushed them into place.

When he'd finished reloading, he walked back into the main infirmary. Victoria was waiting for him, wearing the white coat she'd stripped from the dead girl on the bed. She'd also retrieved her quarterstaff, and now held it at her side, ready for use. Her eyes were clear and hard.

"All right, monkey man, we've got business to finish." She tapped her chest with her free thumb. "I'm going in search of Célestine's cabin. Do you know what you have to do?"

Ack-Ack Macaque grinned, exposing his teeth.

"Same as I always do, right?" He snapped the reloaded Colt back together and spun the barrel. "Blow shit up, and hurt people."

CHAPTER THIRTY-FIVE
GENERAL SNEAKINESS

VICTORIA LEFT THE monkey in the corridor outside the infirmary. They went in opposite directions: him aft, towards the sounds of merriment and partying; her deeper into the luxury suites towards the bow. As she walked, she slipped the retracted quarterstaff into the front pocket of her borrowed white coat. Then she reached beneath the coat and pulled the SincPhone from her jacket's shoulder pocket. Although it was supposedly watertight, a few drops of seawater had worked their way into the casing behind the touch screen, and the inside of the glass had turned misty with condensation. She tapped at the speed dial that would connect her with the *Tereshkova*'s bridge, and held her breath. Could the elderly airship still be airborne? She very much hoped so, because without Merovech's speech, this whole exercise might still count for nothing.

"*Slushayu?*"

"Commodore. It's Victoria. I'm on the *Maraldi*. How are things at your end?"

The old man took his face away from the microphone and yelled something at one of his crew in Russian. When he came back on the line, he sounded tired.

"We are still losing gas, but we will be with you shortly."

"You're coming here? They're letting you through?"

"I'm afraid they are insisting upon it. You see, they are very keen to get their hands on our young guest."

"What are you going to do?"

"Our orders are to put down on the water a few hundred metres from the *Maraldi*. Boats will take us aboard before the *Tereshkova* deflates and sinks."

"Are you going to do it?" With Merovech and the Commodore detained, what chance would she and the monkey have?

"I have no other choice." The old man's voice dropped. "Although, I strongly suspect the Prince will be the only one of us to make it to the liner alive."

"You think they'll leave you to sink?"

"If we are lucky. That way some of us stand a chance. But I do not think they will do so, and there are warships in these waters."

"Can't you call for help? What about the other skyliners?"

"This is not their fight. And what can they do, anyway, save threaten to boycott London and Paris?"

"You need to get a message to Merovech. Tell him to get in touch with the British fleet off Hong Kong. I don't care how he does it, but get them to turn around. The Undying are deliberately trying to provoke war with China." The Duchess might not be able to order an attack herself, but Berg had told her that the Undying had allies in the armed forces and, with tensions in the region at breaking point, a single shot might be enough to trigger a catastrophe.

In the background of the call, she heard voices and the grinding sound of stressed metal. The Commodore swore. "I will tell him. Until then, we await your signal."

The line went dead. Victoria slipped the phone back into her jacket. With the Unification Day celebrations in full swing, the lower decks were quiet. She passed a couple of dazed-looking revellers, but they were more intent on finding their way back to their room than questioning her, and spared her only a cursory glance.

What was it about white coats? To wrap yourself in one was to cloak yourself in an aura of authority. People no longer saw your face, only the coat, and assumed you were supposed to be there, that you knew what you were doing, and were best left alone to do it. Whatever it was, donning one had been a smart move, and Victoria was cheered to see her old journalistic instincts for infiltration and general sneakiness were still as alive and alert as ever. After all, this wasn't the first time she'd crept into an office suite searching for evidence to back up a story. Although, she reminded herself, it was the first time she'd done so on a boat, with the digital ghost of her dead husband haunting her peripheral vision and the threat of imminent nuclear war hanging over everything like an oncoming tempest.

Célestine and her cohorts must be planning to ride out the first strikes here, she thought, in the middle of the Bay of Biscay, far enough from any major targets to avoid immediate blast effects, and secure in the knowledge that the new synthetic bodies they had waiting for them would protect them from the radiation and subsequent fallout.

Well, screw them. She wasn't going down without a fight. This world might be doomed but, until she saw the first mushroom clouds, she wouldn't quit trying to save it.

She came to a smoked glass door leading to a foyer, off which she saw a series of breakout rooms, each with its own boardroom-style table and wall-mounted rank of SincPad flatscreens. At the far end of the foyer, she could see a wooden door with a brass plaque bearing the name Duchess Alyssa Célestine, and the legend: Chief Executive Officer, Céleste Group LLC.

Paul spoke in her mind.

"Security cameras," he said.

Victoria's gaze flickered to the corner of the room's ceiling, where a marble-sized black globe nestled like a spider.

"There's not much I can do about that." She checked the time. Less than an hour remained until the scheduled launch of the Mars rocket. Up in the main ballroom, the party would be in full swing. "Maybe no-one's watching?"

"And what if they are?"

"We'll have to risk it."

Trying to look confident, she pushed her way through the glass doors, into the foyer area. Inside, the air felt drier, and held the rubbery aftertaste of freshly-laid carpet. With luck, any security personnel not enjoying the festivities would be preoccupied searching for threats coming from outside the vessel, rather than from within. Even so, she could feel her heart knocking in her chest.

She marched across to the office at the far end of the foyer and opened the door. The lights were on inside, but the room was deserted, and smaller than she'd been expecting, with much of the space being taken up by a solid wooden desk.

"Clock's ticking," Paul said. Victoria ignored him. As planned, she stepped around behind the desk and activated its touch screen. A security screen shimmered into being, with boxes for username and password. She pulled out her SincPhone and dialled K8.

"Are you ready to do your stuff?"

"Oh yeah."

"Right, I'm connecting you." Victoria took a USB cable from her other jacket pocket and connected the phone to a port on the desk, giving K8 access to the processors within. Then, as she waited for K8 to hack her way back into the Céleste servers, she took another cable from her pocket and inserted the end into one of the sockets on her temple. With the jack in place and the cable dangling like a loose braid, she picked up the phone and held it to her ear.

"How are we doing?"

"Almost there."

Victoria heard keystrokes. Then the screen on the desk in front of her cleared to reveal a file directory.

"Gotcha," K8 muttered.

A cursor appeared on the screen in front of Victoria, scrolling down the menu. She watched it click down a couple of levels, opening sub-directories, until it found the group of files it wanted.

"Okay," K8 said. "That's what we need. Over to you."

"Thanks. Be seeing you." Victoria broke the connection and disconnected the phone, replacing its cable with the one attached to her head. She visualised her internal menu. With the hardwire connection in place, it was the work of moments to copy the files K8 had selected from the desk to the gelware in her skull. They were far too large to have been sent over a mobile connection, and this seemed the next best option: once they were in her head, nobody could take them from her by force, short of drilling their way in and physically removing the gel.

Transfer complete, she pulled the cable from her head, spooled it, and put it back in her jacket. Job done. Now, all she had to do was save a king, expose a coup, and possibly prevent a nuclear war.

"How do you think the monkey's getting on?" Paul asked.

Victoria shrugged. "I haven't heard any gunfire."

"Is that a good sign or not?"

"Who knows?"

She crept to the door and slipped back out of the office, into the foyer area with the smoked glass doors. Half a dozen glass-walled breakout rooms led off this reception area, three on either side. Apart from the middle one on the right, they all had their blinds and doors partly open. That one had all its blinds firmly closed, screening it from the area where Victoria stood, and the breakout rooms on either side.

She stopped walking.

Paul said, "Come on. What are you waiting for?"

"There's something in there."

"In where?"

"That room. Look at the blinds. There's something in there. I'm going to take a look."

Paul scratched dubiously at the pale bristles of his goatee. "I don't think—"

"The one thing I know how to do is smell out a story. And trust me, this room stinks."

She stepped over and opened the door. The lights inside were off, but she could make out a hospital gurney standing between the central conference table and one of the glass walls. A figure lay on it, but in the gloom, she couldn't see its face. Holding her breath, she felt along the wall beside the door until her fingers found the light switch.

"We should go," Paul said, whispering even though nobody but her could possibly have heard him.

"No."

She flicked the switch and the strip lights on the ceiling flickered into life. Now she could see that the figure on the gurney was male; but his features were so sallow and sunken that it took her a few seconds before the memories clicked into place and she recognised him.

In her head, she heard Paul gasp.

"That's—"

"Yes."

An IV drip stood beside the gurney. She pushed it aside and touched her fingers to the man's forehead. The skin felt loose and cold. His eyes were closed, and he wasn't breathing.

"But, that's the King!"

"No," she said. "That *was* the King."

"What do you mean?"

She stepped back and yanked the phone from her pocket.

"He's dead."

CHAPTER THIRTY-SIX
I'M NOT A ROYALIST

DESPONDENT, MEROVECH WALKED back to his cabin. He found Julie still on the bed, where he'd left her, back against the wall and legs stretched out in front of her.

"Any luck?" she asked.

"No reply." He flopped down on the bed beside her. In accordance with Victoria's message, he'd been trying to radio the British fleet in the waters around Hong Kong. "We tried everything, but if they're listening, they haven't responded."

Julie bit her lip. "But if they launch a missile, that's it, is it not? Game over."

Merovech rubbed his eyes. "The navigator recorded my message and he's broadcasting it on a continuous loop. I don't know what else to do."

They were silent for a few moments, each lost in their own thoughts. Then Julie pulled her good knee up to her chin and hugged it.

"*Je veux appeller mon père.*"

"What?"

"I want to call my father."

Merovech sat up. "Yes, but now? I don't have a phone."

"I have my SincPad in my bag. I can make a video call with it. Can you get it for me?"

"Are you sure?"

Julie turned a baleful eye on him. "Of course I am sure! Look around you, Merovech. The world's about to end. When else am I going to call him?"

Merovech sighed, and slid off the bed. He scooped Julie's bag from the floor and passed it to her.

"What are you going to say?"

She didn't look up. She unzipped the bag and pulled out the electronic tablet.

"I do not know yet."

"Are you going to tell him about us?"

"Merovech, please!" She pressed the power button and the screen came alive with the TuringSoft logo. "I said, I do not know. Now sit down quietly, or go for a walk. I do not want you interrupting."

"But, Jules—"

"No." She glared at him. "This might be the last time I ever speak to him. So can you *please* just sit down and shut up?"

She tapped the screen to bring up a dial pad, and then used it to enter a thirteen-digit phone number. Arms folded, Merovech watched her.

The pad gave three long, single-tone rings, and a male voice answered.

"*'Allo?*"

"Papa?"

"Julie? Is that you? Where are you?" Julie's father was a slightly-built man in his early fifties. From where Merovech stood, his image appeared upside down: horn-rimmed glasses; dark, receding hair; and a thin, nervous moustache. From what could be seen in the backdrop of the picture, he seemed to be in a study lined with books. The titles were in English and French.

"*Papa, écoute! Je suis sûr.* I am safe. I am on a skyliner with Merovech."

"*Le prince anglais?* Why are you with him? The television says he is in hospital."

Julie glanced up at Merovech.

"I am going to marry him."

Her father leaned in towards the camera. "Bullshit!"

"*Non papa, c'est vrai.*" Julie ran an agitated hand through her purple hair. "Merovech. I am calling because I thought you should know. I do not need your blessing."

Her father rocked back. With one hand, he adjusted his glasses.

"*Je veux vous rentrer maintenant.*"

Julie's teeth scraped her bottom lip.

"No. I will never come back."

"You will do as I say!"

"No. I am not a child any more. You cannot intimidate me any more."

"Intimidate you?" The man shook the phone he was holding.

"*Oui.* But now, you know what? It doesn't matter anymore."

The man on the screen sneered.

"*Vous êtes très courageux sur le téléphone.* We will see if you are so brave when we meet face-to-face."

"That is never going to happen."

"And why is that? Because you have your prince to protect you?"

"No!" Julie brought the pad right up to her face. Her knuckles were white on its rim. "Because if you ever come near me again, I will fucking kill you!"

"Julie!"

"*Je suis libre!* I am free. I do not know how long it will last, but I am *never* coming back to you. *Comprend?*"

"Hey!"

"Burn in hell."

She tossed the pad aside. Taken by surprise, Merovech lunged for it, but he wasn't quick enough, and the device shattered against the riveted seam of the cabin's metal wall. The casing came apart and glass chips skittered across the floor.

TWO MINUTES LATER, K8 burst into the cabin, a SincPhone held in her outstretched hand.

"Here," she said, thrusting it at him.

Merovech backed away. He'd been trained never to speak on an unguarded line, especially if he didn't know the other caller. It was a royal thing. "Who is it?"

"Just take it." She pushed the phone into his hands, and stepped back, eyes wide like a frightened child.

Watching her, Merovech raised the phone to his ear.

"Hello?"

"Merovech?" The line was scratchy. "It's Victoria. I've found your father."

"Is he—?"

"*Non.* I'm afraid not. We were too late. I am so sorry."

The cabin seemed to swirl around him. He put out a hand to steady himself.

"Okay," he said. "Thank you. Thank you for telling me." He passed the phone back to K8 and turned to Julie. He could hear the blood roaring in his ears, and his head felt light, as if he might faint. The memories of his childhood spilled through his mind like photographs tipped from an upturned shoebox.

From the bed, Julie asked, "Are you all right?"

He shook his head, feeling like a lost child.

"Not really, no."

"Your father?"

"He's dead." The words sounded hollow and lifeless, incapable of carrying the freight of grief and meaning they represented.

"Oh. *Je suis désolée.*" Her face crumpled. She tried to shuffle forward without bending her bandaged leg. "I am so sorry."

"That's what Victoria said."

"What are you going to do?"

Merovech shrugged. Had no idea. He seemed incapable of thought.

"What can I do?"

"Well." Julie sniffed. She took a long, shuddering breath and then sat up straight, pushing her shoulders back. Her eyes were red and tear-smudged. "You are King now."

Anger stirred. "We both know that's bullshit."

"Yes." Julie leant forward, reaching for his hand. "We know that. But we do not have to *tell* anybody. Not just yet. For now, you should be King. Our countries need you. This is what you have spent your whole life training for."

Merovech put a hand to his brow. He'd been expecting this for a year, ever since the grenade attack in Paris; but now it was here, he didn't know how to react. His hands trembled. Something bubbled in his throat, but he didn't know whether it was a laugh or a sob.

"You're in shock," Julie said. "We both are. Sit down."

Merovech shook his head. "No. I can't do this." He looked around. He wanted to get out. He needed to be alone.

"You have to."

"I can't, I'm not ready."

"You have always known this might happen. This is what you were born for."

"But, I'm not even—"

"Hey!" The voice was K8's. Standing in the doorway, she fixed Merovech with a glare, and waved an accusing finger at him. "It doesn't matter what you want, sunshine. Heaven knows, I'm not a royalist. But right now, you have to step up, 'cos you're the only one of us that can."

"She is right," Julie chipped in. "When this is over, you can do whatever you like. Until then, we need you." She threw her hands in the air. "Hell, the entire *world* needs you."

"Uh-huh," K8 agreed. "There's a war coming, and you're the only one with a chance of stopping it."

The deck juddered beneath their feet, and tipped another three or four degrees to starboard. K8 put out a hand to steady herself on the doorframe. Somewhere aft, they heard something crack and snap.

Merovech closed his eyes. He couldn't be king because he wasn't of the royal bloodline; because of his mother and what she'd done to him.

"She grew me in a test tube," he said. "She grew me and passed me off as my father's son. And then she subjected me to all those tests. All those endless tests." He balled his fists. He'd been raised a prince but really, he was no better off than the monkey. They'd both been living in fantasy worlds.

Well, screw that.

Screw them all.

Too many people had died. Now the game was over, because he had decided it was over. If he had to take the crown, even for a few hours, it would be worth it to bring his mother, and her whole rank conspiracy, down. K8 was right: he had a war to stop and a coup to expose. Inside, he felt cold and dangerous, like the cutting edge of a knife. Every gram of resentment and frustration, every moment of fear or doubt, every scrap of anger: they were all funnelled into this single moment; all wadded together in his chest, and compressed until they shone with the hardness of diamond.

This must be what it feels like to be a king, he thought. And in that instant, knew exactly what he had to do.

He opened his eyes. K8 took one look at his face and shrank back into the corridor.

"Where are you going?" Julie called after him. In the doorway, he turned to her.

"The bridge," he said, as the walls groaned again. "I've got a speech to make."

BREAKING NEWS
From *The European Standard*, online edition:

ARMAGEDDON:
Could 'back door' leave us defenceless?

29TH NOVEMBER 2059 – As the Chinese and British navies rattle their sabres in the waters of the South China Sea, rumours abound of a hitherto-unsuspected 'back door' in many of the silicon chips which are used to run everything from missile defence systems to public transport networks and nuclear power plants—chips which were manufactured in China, the world's largest exporter of cheaply-produced electrical components.

If true, these rumours raise the terrifying possibility that any war between our two countries would end in humiliating defeat, with the Chinese military able to remotely subvert and disable every piece of hardware with a connection to the Internet, thereby paralysing our business, military and critical infrastructure systems ahead of any attack, whether by nuclear or conventional weapons.

Speaking at a hastily-convened press conference in Cheltenham, an unnamed GCHQ spokesman described the situation as "our worst nightmare".

Read more | Like | Comment | Share

Related Stories

World stock markets crash

UN Security Council in emergency session

Hollywood stars pay for access to luxury underground shelters

"Nuclear Doomsday Clock" reaches one second to midnight

Thirteen killed in post office shoot-out

Oxygen signatures in atmosphere of extrasolar planet may indicate presence of life

Unification Day celebrations marred by anti-war riots in Glasgow, Manchester, and Marseille. Troops deployed

New government website tells householders how to 'Protect and Survive'

UK couple feared missing after yacht found adrift off Isle of Wight

CHAPTER THIRTY-SEVEN
HYSTERICAL STRENGTH

THE UNIFICATION DAY celebrations were being held on the liner's upper deck, from where the assembled glitterati would watch the Mars probe's ascent on a giant plasma screen. The upper deck was a well sunk into the top of the ship. Cabins, balconies and terraces surrounded it on all sides, providing shelter from the wind. A running track followed its outer edge, and a landscaped swimming pool took up much of its centre.

Looking down from one of the balconies at the rear of the arena-shaped space, Victoria Valois guessed that maybe a thousand people were milling in knots around the pool. The women wore evening dresses, the men black tie. Beneath the plasma screen—which currently showed a live BBC feed—a stage had been erected, on which a band played a medley of classic songs from the past hundred years, from the raw rock and roll of the Beatles' early Parisian-influenced recordings, to the rave-punk beats of the latest cross-channel download sensation. Armed guards prowled the roofs of the surrounding cabins, but they were mainly looking outwards, at the ocean, rather than in at the milling crowd. Camera crews covered the stage from every angle, waiting for the big moment, when the Duchess would speak to the nation.

Victoria shrugged off the magic white coat, trusting her black jacket and trousers to keep her concealed in the shadows of the darkened balcony. In her hand, she gripped the retracted quarterstaff. Squinting, she scanned the deserted terraces surrounding the main arena, but couldn't see anything monkey-shaped. She'd been expecting to find him at the centre of a brawl. Where was he?

The band came to the end of its set and shuffled off the stage. Victoria checked the time: only a few minutes until the launch—from a converted oil platform in the Bay of Biscay—of the rocket carrying the Mars probe. And, after that, who could tell? Had Merovech managed to get a message to the fleet in Hong Kong? Could war be averted? She felt a shiver run down the nape of her neck. For all she knew, the nukes were already in the air.

She put a hand to the bandage at the back of her head. The anaesthetic the monkey had given her seemed to be holding the pain at bay for the moment, but she knew it wouldn't last forever, and the collar she wore to support her head chafed the skin beneath the hinge of her jaw. She should be in a hospital bed, she thought, rather than skulking around darkened balconies. And if she lived through the next few minutes, a hospital bed was exactly where she hoped she'd end up—although, she told herself, she'd rather die than become one of Nguyen's androids.

Below, the crowd had begun to press expectantly forward towards the stage. In her head, she heard Paul mutter something.

"What did you say?"

He looked up, startled by her voice.

"I said, you should have left the big stick at home and packed a sniper rifle instead." He held his hand up, and squinted along the length of his index finger, drawing a bead on an imaginary target.

Irritated, Victoria squeezed the quarterstaff.

"Perhaps you should have suggested that when we were planning this?"

Paul laughed. "This is planned?" He dropped his hand and shook his head. "And yeah, I might have said something, but you kept me on mute most of the time."

"Can you blame me?"

His pale eyebrows shot up. "And what's that supposed to mean."

Victoria's voice was a murderous whisper. "It means, now is hardly the time to be bitching and moaning about what we do or do not have. Now, either say something constructive, or *tais-toi*."

She needed to be closer to the stage. Directly beneath her balcony, a raised first-floor terrace ran all the way around the edge of the arena. If she could get down to that, she could hopefully work her way around to the stage without being seen by the crowds on the arena's floor. She glanced over her shoulder, at the glass doors from which she'd emerged. If she went back inside, she was more likely to bump into a security patrol, and she didn't fancy getting lost in the *Maraldi*'s warren-like maze of corridors and stairwells.

Moving as stealthily as possible, she stepped over to the balcony's side rail and swung her legs over. For a moment, she dangled by her hands, and then dropped. The fall took longer than she'd expected, and she hit the deck harder than she would have liked; but her parachute training kicked in and she rolled with the impact.

She ended up lying on her front beside a potted palm tree, at the end of a row of white plastic sun loungers. Keeping as still as possible, she lifted her head, braced for the sounds of discovery and alarm. But none came. Of the guards she could see on the rim of the arena, none seemed to be looking in her direction. Bars and cafés ringed the terrace, but they were all in darkness, shutters pulled and glass doors closed. The waist-high rail at the edge of the terrace hid her from the eyes of the crowd around the pool below.

In her head, Paul swore. His hand clutched the chest of his Hawaiian shirt.

"Jesus Christ! You could have warned me you were going to do that."

"Sorry."

Below, the crowd applauded. Using her hands, she pushed herself up into a kneeling position, and risked a peep over the rail. On the plasma screen, the BBC had switched to a live feed from the launch site. The rocket was a silver needle poking skyward from the clunky industrial frame of the repurposed oil rig, its flanks picked out from the surrounding darkness by the glare of powerful spotlights. Vapour streamed from its skin, catching the light.

In front of the screen, another spotlight picked out the figure of a woman, and Victoria felt herself tense. There she was: Her Grace Alyssa Célestine, the Duchess of Brittany; CEO of Céleste Group; and mother to Merovech, the Prince of Wales.

As she approached the podium, the crowd subsided. A new window appeared, superimposed over part of the picture on the plasma screen, showing a close-up of her face and shoulders. She held herself regally, chin up and shoulders back. Her necklace and tiara sparkled. Her greying hair had tiny roses woven into it that matched her lipstick, and her teeth were dazzling white. Her eyes, narrow and grey, surveyed the crowd.

Duchess Alyssa had been a successful businesswoman before meeting and marrying William in 2039; and she'd kept her independence, playing an active boardroom role in all her companies, in addition to her royal duties.

"My friends and honoured guests," she began, her words echoing from speakers placed all around the arena. "It is with the greatest regret that I have to announce that the journey from England has proven too great a strain for my husband, and that he sadly passed away a few minutes ago." She lowered her head. The crowd stood stunned. Victoria heard gasps. After maybe thirty seconds, Duchess Alyssa raised her head again, and her eyes bored into the camera.

"Just before he died, he asked me to convey the following message—"

At that moment, rough hands seized Victoria's ankles and pulled hard. She found herself sliding backwards across the polished floor of the terrace, into the shade of an empty café. She tried to struggle, but the hands grabbed her shoulder and thigh, and flipped her over, onto her back.

Ack-Ack Macaque stood over her, regarding her with his one good eye, his pistol pointing at the bridge of her nose.

"Oh," he said, raising the weapon. "It's you."

Victoria looked up at him in disbelief.

"What the hell are you playing at? You almost gave me a heart attack!"

The monkey grinned.

"Sorry, I had to be sure. From behind, you humans all look alike."

Victoria elbowed herself up into a sitting position, and Ack-Ack Macaque crouched beside her.

"I've been working my way around this level," he said. "So far, I've run into three armed guards." He drew a finger across his throat.

Duchess Alyssa's voice continued from the podium. Victoria said, "We should be down there. We need to get to the stage."

"No worries." Ack-Ack Macaque holstered his gun and drew a wicked-looking hunting knife. Victoria felt her eyes widen. Lord only knew where he'd got it, but she was prepared to bet its former owner wouldn't be needing it back any time soon. He sprang to his feet, and reached down to pull her upright.

"Enough sneaking around," he said. "Let's try a good, old-fashioned frontal assault. I'll clear a path, you get to the microphone."

Victoria glanced up at the armed guards: tiny silhouettes against the night sky.

"What about them?"

"They won't fire into the crowd."

"Are you sure about that?"

"Hell, no." That goofy grin again. He led her over to the edge of the terrace.

"It's too far for you to jump," he said. "I'll hold the rail and lower you."

"Can you do that?"

"I'm stronger than I look."

On the plasma screen behind the stage, the launch countdown had reached t-minus five minutes. In the upper right-hand corner of the screen, large white digits ticked off the remaining seconds.

They might as well be counting down to the end of the world, Victoria thought. She looked at Paul's ghost, projected over her field of vision, and sighed.

"If we've got to go, I guess we may as well go out fighting."

Before Paul could answer, Ack-Ack Macaque clapped Victoria on the shoulder.

"That's the spirit!" He slithered over the rail and dangled by one hand. He raised the other to her. "Now you. Come on!"

Victoria hooked a leg over the precipice. The floor looked very distant. She guessed five or six metres. In her eye, she saw Paul cover his face with his hands.

Where's your sarcasm now?

She let herself hang. Ack-Ack Macaque took her hand in his and lowered her. His grip felt like a wire trap. His body stank like a zoo. He lowered her and adjusted his hold. And before she knew it, her boots dangled above the arena floor, her hand gripped in the prehensile toes of his feet.

"Ready?"

She licked her lips. Now or never.

"Ready."

The toes uncurled and she fell. She tried to roll as she hit the floor but, this time, she smacked her knee against the deck.

Swearing, she rolled over and scrambled painfully to her feet, trying to put as little weight on the throbbing joint as possible.

Ack-Ack Macaque landed beside her, lithe and nimble, hunting knife at the ready.

"Okay, lady," he said. "I'll see you at the stage."

And with that, he was off, bounding towards the crowd. She flicked her quarterstaff to its full extent and followed, hobbling as best she could.

Ahead, the monkey crashed through the hindmost ranks of the audience. His knife flashed. His arms and legs became a windmill of savage blows. Taken by surprise, men and women screamed. Some crashed into the pool; others were felled where they stood. Panic spread like a bow wave before him, as the rows nearer the front turned to find the source of the disturbance bearing down upon them, yellow eye glaring, fangs gnashing. And on he ploughed, hardly breaking stride, as they scrambled to get out of his way.

She tried to keep pace. At first, the crowd were mostly too busy fleeing to pay her much attention; but that didn't last. As they picked themselves up from the monkey's assault, they turned on her, their eyes and mouths wide with murderous anger.

A young man in a white tux tried to rush her, and she fought him back. But by then, she was surrounded. She held the staff in front of her, circling warily.

"Stay back," she warned.

On the stage, Duchess Alyssa had become aware of the commotion. Her speech faltered. And, at that moment, the BBC coverage behind her changed abruptly. The floodlit silver rocket vanished, and Merovech's face appeared. He was seated in the Commodore's chair on the bridge of the *Tereshkova*. A 'breaking news' banner scrolled beneath him.

"That's enough!" he shouted, his voice ringing from the speakers around the arena. He drew himself up in the chair and glared into the camera lens. "My name's Merovech, Prince of Wales. I am the rightful heir to the throne, and I hereby claim what is mine."

Duchess Alyssa's crimson lips drew back from her perfect teeth in a snarl of rage.

"No!" She turned to the side of the stage making 'cutting' motions with her hands.

Merovech ignored her. "I have been the victim of a dark conspiracy, an attempted coup. But despite that, I am here to take up my father's crown." He leant forward, towards the camera, his projected face glowering down at the crowd. "And my first act as your new king is to order the immediate withdrawal of our ships in the South China Sea, and the arrest of my mother, the Duchess of Brittany."

The crowd erupted. Some were horrified, others applauded. Their voices filled the arena. The men surrounding Victoria looked at each other. And then one of them tried to grab her. She stepped back and brought the tip of the staff smacking up into his left temple, dropping him where he stood. But by doing so, she'd put herself in reach of the man behind her. His hands clawed at her shoulders. She tried to twist away, but the other two caught hold of the ends of her staff and yanked it from her fingers.

She heard gunfire, and renewed screams, but couldn't see where they came from, or who was shooting. Her world collapsed into a blur of thrashing arms and legs. She felt herself punched and kicked. The gelware did its best to smother the pain of each blow. She lashed out and felt her knuckles crunch into meat and bone, but too many people were on her now, and she was suffocating beneath their weight. It was like trying to fight the incoming tide. She couldn't breathe. She tried to kick, but her legs were pinned.

Okay, she thought. *Time to get drastic.*

Retreating back inside herself, she kicked her consciousness up into command mode and dialled all the settings as high as she could. Time stretched. The pummelling of fists and bodies slowed to an insistent jostling.

She opened her eyes, and felt her heart buck in her ribcage as her adrenal glands came online, flooding her bloodstream with hysterical strength.

At least two hands held her right arm. She tugged it free and punched upward, towards the stars. Her knuckles clipped one man's face, and buried themselves in the gut of another. She pulled back and struck again. And again. Voices cried in pain and indignation. Some of the weight pinning her eased. She squirmed a leg free and let fly a kick that lifted one of her attackers off the ground, sending him rolling and tumbling into the swimming pool. A sideways jab with her left elbow broke somebody's nose. And then the survivors were scrambling to get away from her, leaving only the unconscious and unmoving to weigh her down. She struggled free and scrambled to her feet. At least one of her ribs was cracked. Her nose bled and her knuckles were a ragged mess, but she didn't care. Terror and regret were safely confined to the biological section of her brain, their voices muffled like those of noisy neighbours, and quite separate from the rest of her thoughts. Locked into the artificial clarity of her operating system, all she felt was fierce exhilaration. Nuclear fire might pour from the heavens at any moment but, until it did, she wasn't going to surrender to anybody. She'd been hurt enough. She'd been drugged, attacked and operated upon, and now it was her turn to fight back. At least thirty guys ringed her now. She didn't stand a chance, and knew it; yet, somehow, it hardly mattered. She flexed her shoulders. The faces surrounding her betrayed fear and anger. Somewhere near the stage, Ack-Ack Macaque fought a similar battle of his own, against equally insurmountable odds.

As she glanced in that direction, she saw the plasma screen cut to static. A pulled plug or an electromagnetic pulse? Were the bombs falling on London already?

The Duchess stood in front of the screen, caught in the glare of the world's media. She pointed a long finger into the crowd, shouting instructions no-one could hear.

Victoria looked back to the men around her. They were edging forward. She recognised a few from her days as a journalist: a scattering of minor politicians, a few media types, one or two millionaires. Some of them clutched broken chair legs; others held champagne bottles as improvised clubs. She turned around slowly, staring them each in the eye. Then she hawked, and spat bloody phlegm at their feet.

One of the men stepped forward. He was a good head and shoulders taller than her, and built like the proverbial brick shithouse. The arms of his tuxedo bulged with muscle. He had the shaven head and swollen neck of a professional boxer, and each and every one of his fingers sported a thick gold ring.

Here we go, she thought.

But then, before he could get close enough to strike, the sky flashed, and heads turned. The light came from the west. Instinctively, Victoria flinched away, waiting for the heat and fire of a nuclear blast. But the shockwave never came, and when she raised her head again, she saw a spear of light rising into the night sky.

The rocket had launched.

All those stolen souls were on their way to Mars, and she could do nothing to stop them. Was there a copy of her aboard, or had Vic been the only one?

She didn't have much time to consider the question, as no-neck turned his attention back to her, his lip curled in a sneer. Behind him, the rest of the mob flexed. His contempt of her made them brave. They were getting ready to rush her again and, this time, she wouldn't be able to fight them all off.

This was it.

"Goodbye, Paul."

She took up a defiant stance, bloodied knuckles raised and ready.

And something huge blocked out the stars.

The big guy didn't see it: he had his back to it. He swung at her with a paw like a bag of pig's trotters, and she ducked to the side. But by now, the others had seen what was coming, and they had started to run.

Victoria laughed at them. Where could they go? The *Tereshkova* was longer and wider than the *Maraldi*, and it was diving right at them. There could be no escape.

She stood and watched the crippled airship grow larger and larger, filling the oval of sky described by the rim of the arena. And then, just as she judged it was about to hit, she turned and threw herself full-length into the swimming pool.

CHAPTER THIRTY-EIGHT
MONKEY-EX-MACHINA

THE CRASH WENT on and on. Coming in at a relatively shallow angle, the *Tereshkova* pancaked onto the liner like a whale throwing itself onto a rock. The belly of the gondola scraped the upper surfaces of the ship, snapping off radar and communication antennae. The tops of the funnels crumpled, and the *Maraldi* heaved sideways, pushed almost completely over, before righting itself as the *Tereshkova*'s five sterns dropped into the sea and the noses came up, relieving some of the pressure on the liner's superstructure.

Glass and debris rained into the arena. The water in the swimming pool sloshed back and forth, and Victoria had to fight to stay afloat. Struggling against the weight of her sodden clothes, she pushed through a floating morass of dead bodies and broken patio furniture. She reached the edge of the pool and hauled herself out. Water ran from her, and she collapsed onto the deck.

Overhead, the five hulls of the *Tereshkova* formed a roof to the arena. The hatches of the main gondola were flung open, and ropes thrown out. Then, before anyone on the *Maraldi* had time to react, white-jacketed stewards were sliding down, rifles and submachine guns from the Commodore's armoury slung over their crisply-ironed shoulders.

Victoria lay on the deck, bleeding from a dozen separate wounds, and laughed.

"You mad old goat," she said. "You crazy, stubborn, brilliant man."

And then, he was there in person, coming down one of the ropes, hand-over-hand. She recognised his white hair and red sash, and the cutlass dangling from his belt. And there, behind him, was Merovech: the new king himself, sliding into battle with the troops.

In her eye, she saw Paul hovering over her, looking concerned.

"Vicky? Are you okay?"

She laughed again. "I'm fine. I'm going to hurt like hell tomorrow; but right now, I feel brilliant."

"That's the drugs talking."

"Damn straight."

She used her sleeve to wipe blood and snot from her nose, then sat up and pulled herself stiffly to her feet. The Commodore's boots had touched down on the deck a short distance away, and she limped over to greet him.

The old man had his cutlass drawn, and was using it to direct his stewards, while barking orders in Russian. His yellow teeth gnashed beneath the white forest of his moustache.

"Be careful." She squinted at the sword. "Or you'll have somebody's eye out with that."

He turned to her. Despite the white hair and injured hip, he looked twenty years younger, and his eyes held a wild glint. He gripped her shoulder with his free hand. "Good to see you, girl."

Her soaked clothes were dripping onto the deck. She looked at the stage. "Where's Célestine?"

"The Duchess?" The Commodore scowled. From his belt, he pulled an automatic pistol. "Take this," he said.

Victoria palmed the gun. It was heavier than she'd been expecting: a solid chunk of metal in her hand.

"Over there." The Commodore waved the tip of his sword at the other side of the pool, where Merovech stalked in the direction of the stage, still clad in his ratty jeans and red hoodie, a black Uzi machine pistol clasped in his hands. "Follow him."

With a piratical grin, he turned back to his men, who were fanning out across the arena, and waved his cutlass above his head.

"Keep going!" he bellowed. "Get to the bridge! Take that, and we take the ship!"

Victoria watched him go, dragging his bad leg behind him. Then she turned and made her way around the pool to intercept Merovech. He was moving at a trot, but slowed when he saw her coming.

"My mother?"

"She was on the stage. I didn't see which way she went."

"That's okay. I know this ship. I know where she'll be heading. Come on."

With his hood thrown back and chin jutting forward, he strode to the rear of the arena, and Victoria did all she could to keep up. She'd never seen him look so determined or move with such a sense of unstoppable purpose. The raw cadet she'd once sat beside on a South Atlantic helicopter had gone, leaving a soldier in his place.

He led her along corridors and down several stairwells, always moving towards the stern.

"There's a dock at the back of the ship. She'll be trying to reach one of the speedboats." He spared a glance for her injuries, looking at her cuts and scrapes, and the way she favoured her injured knee. "You don't have to come. You can stay here if you need to."

"No." Victoria's voice was firm. "I want to see this through to the end."

Merovech looked as if he understood. "You still need to get the full story, don't you?"

She gripped the pistol in her hand.

"There's more to it than that."

She followed him down another flight of stairs and out onto an open section of deck, running alongside a row of passenger cabins. The sea air felt cool and soothing on her skin, and she filled her lungs, relishing the dank overtones of salt and iodine.

They heard feet slapping on the deck behind them and turned. Ack-Ack Macaque joined them. He had been running. His eye patch had been ripped off. Clumps of fur were missing from around his face, and one of the sleeves of his leather flight jacket hung loose, where it had split along a seam.

He stopped and pulled a cigar from the jacket's inner lining.

"Are you going after the Duchess?" Merovech gave a nod. The monkey jammed the cigar between his teeth and spoke around it. "Swell. I guess I'll tag along with you, then."

He pulled a cheap plastic lighter from his other pocket, and sucked the cigar into life, huffing out clouds of pungent blue smoke in the process.

Merovech looked from him to Victoria.

"Follow me," he said.

THEY CAUGHT UP with Duchess Alyssa at the top of the dock, on a gangway overlooking the water. Her progress had been hampered by her gown, and by the high heels that dangled from one hand. In her other hand, she carried a fire axe, which she must have torn from a corridor wall during her flight from the stage.

The dock behind and below her was an open area at the *Maraldi*'s stern, with berths for pleasure craft. At either end of the gangway on which she stood, stairs led down on to pontoons, to which the smaller vessels were moored.

Standing with her back to the rail, the Duchess dropped her shoes and took hold of the axe in both hands, ready to swing at the first person to step within reach.

"Don't come any closer," she warned.

Merovech levelled his Uzi at her.

"Put the axe down, mother."

Duchess Alyssa laughed and tossed her hair. Her voice held a hysterical edge.

"Or what? Are you going to shoot me? Are you going to shoot your own mother?"

Merovech's lip curled. "You're not my mother."

"Yes I am!" She let go of the axe with one hand and thumped her chest. "We're the same flesh and blood. You came from me. I carried you in my womb. I gave birth to you."

"But you were still going to kill him," Victoria snapped.

Duchess Alyssa turned to her, lip curled.

"Oh, the reporter. How many times have we tried to kill you now?"

"Too many."

She turned her attention to Ack-Ack Macaque. "And the monkey! How glorious. All my little birdies home at once."

She took a fresh grip on the axe handle.

"Now," she said. "Which of you wants it first?"

Merovech held his Uzi in both hands. His knuckles were white.

"You killed my father," he said.

Duchess Alyssa gave a snort.

"He wasn't your father."

"You let me think he was!"

"So what? Are you going to arrest me? You're not really the King, you know. Or has my baby gotten all ambitious, all of a sudden?"

Merovech adjusted his stance. "What you tried to do to me was monstrous. You would have killed me, erased my mind. But if my life has to be a lie, at least I can make it a lie of my choosing. And if I want to be king, I will be King." He took a step towards her. "You might think I'm nothing more than a clone, mother. But I'm *your* clone. Do you expect me to be any less determined than you?"

Duchess Alyssa moved the axe from one shoulder to the other, like a batsman warming up at the crease, ready to deliver a devastating backhand swipe.

"All right," she said. "Let me tell you how this is going to work. I have somewhere I need to be. You three are each going to take one step back and stay where you are until I reach the steps at the end of this gangway. I'm going to take one of the smaller boats." She tapped a bare foot against the metal deck. "You can keep this one, for all the good it will do you."

Victoria looked to Merovech. The young man didn't move. Slowly, he raised the machine pistol so that the barrel pointed directly at his mother's face.

"No," he said. "Let me tell *you* how this works. You're going to drop that axe and put your hands on your head. Then I'm going to march you back upstairs, and you can confess everything in front of the cameras, on live TV."

The Duchess gave a pitying shake of her head. "You can't stop me, Merovech. Look at you. All three of you. I've never seen such a sorry mess."

"It's over, mother."

Duchess Célestine tossed her hair. "I'm afraid it's very far from over. In fact, it's just getting started. There's a war coming, Merovech, and after that, things are going to be very different. The world will be a much better place."

"A radioactive wasteland."

The Duchess laughed scornfully. "A clean slate. Can't you see that, Merovech? Can't you imagine a world without sickness and death? A world where we can strive for the stars, unfettered by bureaucracy and corruption, unencumbered by the weak and ignorant? A world where everybody works together, and everybody knows their place?"

Ack-Ack Macaque gave a snarl.

"You sound a lot like the people I used to fight."

Célestine glowered down her nose. "And what would you know?"

Half crouched and ready to spring, the monkey let his lips draw back from his fangs.

"I know a fascist when I see one."

The Duchess smiled.

"Call it what you like, you can't stop me. None of you can. You can't even kill me. There's a copy of my mind on its way to Mars as we speak, and a new body waiting for me ashore. Nguyen will—"

"Nguyen's dead," Victoria said. "I killed him."

"You?" For the first time, the older woman seemed genuinely taken aback.

Merovech took another step towards her.

"Put the axe down, mother."

The Duchess backed up against the rail. Her nostrils quivered.

"No!" She glared around at the three of them. For a moment, Victoria thought she would let fly with the axe; but instead, evidently seeing no way out, the woman's left hand dropped to the decorative handbag slung over her right shoulder, and emerged with her fingers clutching the knobbed fruit shape of a shiny black hand grenade. She hooked a thumb through the pull-ring. "Now please, all of you put your weapons down and step away."

Merovech lowered his gun.

"You wouldn't."

Duchess Célestine's eyes were narrow slits. "What have I got to lose? I may fall here, but I will rise again. As the Empress of two worlds."

She raised the grenade and used her teeth to pull the pin from its mount.

With a cry, Merovech lunged forward, but she brought the axe around in a one-handed sweep that caught him on the left shoulder, sending him staggering sideways. The Uzi clattered from his grip.

"Idiot boy!"

Her cry galvanised Victoria. Without stopping to think, she squeezed the trigger of the pistol the Commodore had given her. It bucked in her hands. A loud bang, and the recoil almost shattered her wrists. Duchess Alyssa gave a grunt and looked down. The bullet had drilled a smoking hole through the fabric of her gown. The axe fell from her hand, and she tottered, still clutching the grenade. In Victoria's mind, Paul yelled at her to get down, but she knew she didn't have time to get away. The gangway offered nowhere to hide. The explosion would kill them all.

But then, from beside her: a streak of fur. Ack-Ack Macaque sprang forward in a flying crouch. He wrapped his long arms around the Duchess's legs and heaved upward. She screamed, and he screeched, and together they tipped over the edge of the gangway, thirty feet above the floating dock beneath.

Victoria threw herself down beside Merovech, who moaned and clutched his shoulder, thick red blood slathering his fingers. Below, the grenade exploded in mid air. The gangway convulsed beneath her, smacking against her hard enough to drive the wind from her body. She tasted blood. The roar of the blast rattled the enclosed dock, battering her senses.

And then, there was nothing but the sound of fire alarms and the smell of burning.

She lay still for a long time, hardly daring to believe she was still alive.

The monkey had saved them. But at what cost?

She turned her aching head to the edge of the walkway, and her eyes caught sight of something brown wrapped around the chrome rail. She got to her feet, every inch of her body complaining bitterly, and struggled over to it.

Hanging by his tail, Ack-Ack Macaque dangled above the smoking black remains of a splintered, burning pontoon, his crumpled cigar still wedged between his teeth. Thirty feet below, gown shredded by the explosion, the Duchess lay face-down in the water.

"You're alive!"

He glared up at her with his one good eye. With his cuts and scrapes, he looked like something from a taxidermist's nightmare.

"Yeah. So, quit gawping and help me up."

She reached for his outstretched hand.

"I thought, for a moment, that you were—"

"Me too." He rolled the end of the cigar around in his mouth. "But, you know, once you've fallen out of a few trees, it turns out you get to be pretty good at catching yourself."

With her thighs braced against the rail, she gave a heave. She helped Ack-Ack Macaque onto the gangway, and they both flopped down onto their knees, panting. From her jacket pocket, her phone rang. On the fourth ring, she pulled it out and answered it. The call was from Julie.

"Is Merovech there? Is he all right?"

Victoria glanced at the boy lying a few feet from her, still clutching his shoulder.

"He will be. What's going on? Have we captured the ship?"

"Yes, but—" Julie's voice faltered. Victoria could hear her breath rasping on the other end of the line. "I have some bad news."

Victoria felt cold inside.

"What is it?"

"It's the Commodore." Julie's voice dropped to a hoarse whisper. "He's dead."

CHAPTER THIRTY-NINE
ALL THE MYRIAD COUNTRIES STRETCHED BENEATH

As DAWN BROKE over the Channel, clear and cold, Victoria stood on the rubberised helipad atop the *Tereshkova*'s central hull, looking out over the sea. There would be no stick fighting practice this morning: she had her right arm in a sling and, beneath the loose woollen jersey she now wore, extensive bandaging to hold her ribs in place.

In her left hand, she gripped the Commodore's bloodstained tunic. One of the stewards had given it to her, along with an envelope addressed to her in the old man's handwriting.

Injured as he was, the Commodore had finally been killed while capturing the *Maraldi*'s bridge: shot through the heart at point blank range, by a man already skewered on the tip of his cutlass.

Her godfather's body now lay beneath a sheet in the *Tereshkova*'s infirmary, awaiting burial at sea.

She draped the jacket over the rail, and reread the letter.

My dearest Victoria, it began. *I have no children of my own, and no wife. Therefore, in the event of my death, it is my fondest wish that you become sole beneficiary of my estate—including ownership of the* Tereshkova. *My lawyers will be in touch to discuss the details. In the meantime, please take care of the old girl.*

The end of the letter contained all the command codes and bank account numbers she would need to operate the old airship, and was signed with an ornate, and unreadable, flourish.

The paper flapped in the breeze. She folded it in half, and slipped it into the back pocket of her jeans. Then she reached out and touched the medals pinned to the breast of the stained tunic.

"Goodbye, old friend."

Overnight, the airship had been partially patched. Another skyliner had arrived, and had donated part of its helium reserves to re-inflate a few of the *Tereshkova*'s newly-repaired gas bags. The sabotaged engine had been examined and declared safe, the bomb having failed to crack the reactor housing. And now, the skyliner loomed over the water, still listing slightly to starboard but otherwise buoyant, a couple of hundred metres from the damaged liner.

Looking across at the dazzling white ziggurat-like terraces of the *Maraldi*, Victoria saw where the upper stories had borne the brunt of the *Tereshkova*'s impact: smashed windows; snapped aerials; a broken funnel. The liner wouldn't be going anywhere under her own steam for a while, and would be towed back to Portsmouth as soon as a hastily-despatched aircraft carrier arrived to take her passengers aboard.

Victoria planned to limp the *Tereshkova* back to Heathrow for repairs.

The wind blew in from the south-west, fresh with the promise of a new morning. Behind her, the sun climbed higher in the eastern sky, throwing her shadow across the fabric of the hull.

"It looks as if it's going to be a nice day," she said.

Floating in the air before her, Paul's image smiled.

"You know," he said, "for a while back there, I didn't think we were going to make it."

Victoria wriggled her fingers. Her arm felt stiff in its sling.

"Me neither." But when the Commodore's men had found her sitting on the gangway, watching the monkey trying to stem Merovech's axe wound with rolled up folds of his own clothing, they'd brought the news she hadn't dared hope for: that the British fleet had turned around, and was sailing for home with no shots fired. The holocaust for which she'd been bracing herself had been averted. At least, for today.

Now, standing on the helipad, she felt desolate and desiccated, as if every drop of fear and despair had been wrung from her.

"So," Paul asked, scratching his bearded chin. "What now?"

Victoria turned and peered into the east, using her hand to shade her eyes from the sun's orange glare.

"I don't know. If the repairs hold long enough to reach Heathrow, I might stay here, on the *Tereshkova*." She patted the pocket containing the Commodore's letter. "It is mine now, after all."

Paul shuffled his trainers on an invisible floor. "I meant, what now for you and me? Where do we go from here?"

"I guess that depends on how long you last before you start to fragment. The longest I ever heard of a back-up being run was six months."

He looked sheepish. "Do you think you could put up with me for that long?"

Victoria pursed her lips.

"Perhaps." She wouldn't admit it, but she'd started to get used to having him around, and she didn't like the idea of losing him. Too much had been lost already, and she didn't want to go back to being lonely and alone.

"If we do this," she said, "we're going to have to come up with a few ground rules. I like your company, but I need my privacy, if you know what I'm saying?"

Paul held up his hands. "Oh, absolutely. Anything you want." He grinned. "And who knows what will happen in six months? If I'm lucky, I might get an android body, after all. Then you'll never get rid of me."

Victoria pantomimed a shudder.

"What a horrible thought."

She started hobbling back towards the hatchway. As she drew close, it opened, and Merovech appeared, with Julie in tow, her weight braced against a crutch.

The young King looked tired. He also had his arm in a sling, and an extensively bandaged shoulder; but he'd taken the time to shave and change. She looked down at the red military jacket he wore.

"It's one of the Commodore's," he said. "Julie didn't think you'd mind."

Victoria smiled. "It suits you."

Merovech stuck his lip out, clearly unconvinced.

"You have to address the nation," Julie told him. "If you are going to be the King, you need to look the part."

He took her hand in his. For a moment, they looked into each other's eyes. Then Merovech turned back to Victoria.

"And how are you?"

Victoria blew air through her cheeks. "Oh, you know. Look like shit, feel like shit."

He grinned.

"Well, you'll be pleased to know that we have all the members of the Undying cult detained. At least, the ones who were on the *Maraldi* last night. As for the rest, we have their names from my mother's files, and the police can deal with them."

Victoria looked around. "Where's the monkey?"

Julie cleared her throat.

"He is down in the lounge, eating bananas and drinking daiquiris with the press. They cannot get enough of him and, frankly, I think he likes the attention. He is already talking about suing Céleste for the copyright to his image."

"I hope he's got a good lawyer."

Merovech shook his head. "He won't need one. With my mother dead, her share of the company passes to me. And it's a controlling interest, so I can do whatever I like."

"Well, you are the King."

His young face darkened, like a cloud passing across the sun.

"For now, anyway." He took her hand. "Thank you, Victoria. You've done so much, I can't begin to—"

"Ah, *c'est rien.*"

"No, I'm serious. If there's anything I can do, just say the word. How about a knighthood? A stately home? Something like that?"

Victoria laughed, and gently extricated her fingers from his grip.

"I don't think so." She turned to look back along the length of the hull, towards the airship's tail. "I have a place here now."

At that moment, Ack-Ack Macaque stuck his dishevelled head through the stairwell hatch. His fur looked patchy and ragged; he had a few new scars around his muzzle; and safety pins held the sleeve of his jacket in place. K8 had fashioned him a new eye patch from gauze, and he'd bummed half a dozen cigars from the assembled reporters.

"Hey," he said. "What are you all doing up here? You're missing all the fun."

Victoria held up her hand, warding him away.

"We've all had more than enough 'fun' for one day, thank you."

"Then what'cha doing?"

"We're getting ready to leave."

The monkey pulled himself up onto the helipad and lit a cigar. K8 followed him out, blinking in the sunlight.

"In that case," he said, "we're coming with you."

"What about the cameras?" Victoria asked. "What about your fans?"

Ack-Ack Macaque stuck his bottom lip out. "I'm not cut out for stardom. I'm a pilot." He blew smoke at the clear dawn sky. "And, with the old man gone, and his pilot injured, I'm guessing you could do with someone to fly this tub for you? Am I right?"

"Can you fly an airship?"

Ack-Ack Macaque cracked his knuckles.

"I can fly anything." His face dropped into a simian scowl. "I've got a hell of a lot I need to figure out. This will keep me out of trouble while I decide what I'm going to do with the rest of my life. And besides, there's a whole world out there that I never knew existed. I'd like to see some of it."

"And K8?"

"Well, we'll need a navigator, won't we?" Ack-Ack Macaque scratched his cheek. "From what I can see, most of this ship's run by computer, and she can do anything with them." He grinned proudly. "The girl's a goddamn genius."

Victoria's hand fell to her side.

"Okay then, it's settled. Welcome to the crew, Monsieur Macaque. And you, K8. We set sail in an hour."

The monkey touched leathery fingers to his brow in salute.

"Much obliged, skip. What's our heading?"

"First London, for repairs. After that, we'll play it by ear."

Merovech laced his fingers in Julie's, and looked at the three of them. "Where do you think you'll go?"

Ack-Ack Macaque scratched his belly. Even battered and scorched, he looked ready for another adventure, and Victoria knew for certain that, with him at the wheel, life on board the *Tereshkova* would never be dull.

She watched as he turned and grinned into the wind, his yellow eye scanning the far horizon, taking in the cloud-flecked cobalt dome of the sky, and all the myriad countries stretched beneath.

He took a pull on his cigar.

"Everywhere," he said.

HIVE
MONKEY

PART ONE

BOMBS AND BULLETS

We have met the enemy and he is us.

Walt Kelly, *Pogo*

CHAPTER ONE
DAZZLE CAMOUFLAGE

IT STARTED WITH a gunshot.

Wrapped in a woollen coat and scarf, his greying hair blown unkempt and wild, William Cole leant against the painted railings at the end of the harbour wall. He looked out over the Severn Estuary. High above the water, against a pale November sky, an airship forged upriver. From where he stood, he could hear the bass thrum of the fifteen nuclear-electric engines that powered its vast, five-hulled bulk, and see the low afternoon sunlight flash against the spinning blades of its impellers, turning them to coin-like discs of bronze.

Unusually, the skyliner's owners had chosen to paint the cigar-shaped hulls with jagged black and white lines. The lines looked unsightly, but William knew the patterns were designed to disguise the airship's exact shape and heading, hindering attacks from ground-based weapons. Allied warships used the same trick, known as 'dazzle camouflage', in World War Two, to confuse German U-boats. The crazy stripes hurt his tired eyes, but he could still read the airship's name, stencilled on its prow in blocky red letters: *Tereshkova*. Named after the cosmonaut, he supposed. Valentina Tereshkova had been the first woman in space, launched into the void two years after Gagarin's pioneering flight. Now though, almost a century later, and long after the collapse of the Soviet Union, how many people remembered her? Humans were still footling around in low Earth orbit, in tin can space stations. The glittering future she represented hadn't come to pass. Some promising early steps had been made, such as the space probe that was even now carrying the uploaded minds of hundreds of individuals to Mars, but no flesh-and-blood astronauts had been as far as the Moon in over eighty years. The dreams of the twentieth century were long dead, and space had become little more than a curiosity: a relic of the Cold War, an industrial park on the outskirts of global politics.

He ground his clenched hands into his coat pockets, shivering against the cold.

"Where are you going today, Valentina? And where have you been?" Skyliners like her hardly ever stopped moving, and they never touched down. They spent their lives aloft, being serviced by smaller, more agile craft. This one had probably just crossed the Atlantic from America, en route to London and Europe. Each of its five cigar-shaped hulls had one large gondola slung beneath it, and two or three smaller ones dotted along its length. Yellow lights burned in their windows and portholes. "And why the crazy paint job?"

William closed his eyes. Five years ago, at the age of thirty-nine, he'd crossed the Atlantic himself, on a similar vessel. He'd packed his laptop and manuscripts, and bought a one-way ticket to the European Commonwealth. He'd come to make his fortune as a writer, and marry the love of his life. Her name had been Marie, and she'd been a reviewer for *The Guardian*. They first met at a book launch in Greenwich Village and dated for a while. It hadn't worked out, but a decade after they split up she came to New York for a conference. They had dinner together and got talking about old times. By that point, they were both divorced and single. She hadn't read any of his books, and he hadn't seen any of her columns; but somehow, buzzed on wine and, in her case, jetlag, they hit it off again. When she went back to England, he followed and, six months later, they were married, at a small registry office in Kensington, with a reception paid for by his publisher.

Ah, Marie.

Marie with the auburn hair and easy smile, snatched away so soon. Had she really been dead two years now? Had a whole *twenty-four months* really passed? He'd crossed an ocean for her, given up his life in America, his friends and family, his ex-wife, only to let her slip away from him, across another ocean, into that undiscovered country from whose bourn no traveller returns.

With his hands gripping the railings, he looked down to the tidal mud at the foot of the harbour wall. He hadn't slept in four days. Below him, the low tide had fallen back to reveal the rounded teeth of a collapsed jetty, its splintered planks protruding from the rippled mudflats like the fossilised remnants of some prehistoric lake village. Gulls bobbed on the sluggish swell; scraps of black seaweed lay strewn and tangled at the high water mark; and a late afternoon breeze ran a comb through the wiry grass. The pain of Marie's loss, so abrupt and unfair, had terrified him. He couldn't face up to it. Not knowing what else to do, and fearing he wasn't strong enough to bear the grief, he'd taken all his hurt and packed it down inside, where he thought it couldn't harm him. He couldn't cope with it, so he buried it. He put it off. Over the following months, he wrapped his grief in protective layers of drug and alcohol abuse. Now, when he tried to remember her, he had difficulty picturing her face with any clarity, or remembering her smell, or the sound of her voice. He'd tried so hard to block out the pain that now he could hardly recall anything about her, and his attempts to spare himself the weight of her loss had only brought him closer to losing her.

The wind blew through him, leaving him empty. For a long time, he simply stood and stared at the water.

Then his SincPhone rang. On the fourth ring, he answered it.

"Hello?"

"Will, it's Max. How are you doing? I'm not interrupting anything, am I?"

"Not really."

William looked back to the black and white airship, and the rippling reflection it cast over the muddy waters of the Severn. He felt set adrift, alone, and left behind. Now Marie was dead, there was nothing permanent in his life. Perhaps, if she'd lived, they might have had a family, maybe put down roots somewhere; but no. Home for him had been a succession of rented rooms, usually above shops of one sort or another; the walls an endless parade of peeling, painted magnolia; the utilitarian furniture pocked with the dents of a thousand small impacts, and pitted with the tiny smallpox circles of ancient cigarette burns.

"Great. Because we need to talk."

William moved the phone from one ear to the other. Max was just about the last person he wanted to hear from.

"This is about the Mendelblatt book, isn't it?" Lincoln Mendelblatt, the Jewish private eye, had been the hero of three of his previous novels.

"I've had Stella on the phone again this afternoon," Max said. "She's very unhappy. You're almost a month overdue."

William groaned inwardly. "Tell her it's coming."

"I did, and I think she bought it, for now. But listen, Will, I need those pages. And I need them, like, yesterday."

A pair of gulls scuffled on the mud, their cries sharp and desolate.

"It's nearly finished," William lied. "I'm on the last chapter."

"Really? You're that close?"

"Sure. Look, it's Friday afternoon. Give me the weekend, and I'll get something over to you by the beginning of next week. Maybe Wednesday."

"You promise?"

"I promise."

There was a silence on the other end. Then, "You sound terrible, Will. Are you using again?"

The sun went behind a cloud.

"No." William sniffed and wiped his nose on the back of his hand. It was a nervous reflex. "Not at all. Not for ages. I'm just a bit groggy today. A cold, that's all."

He heard Max sigh. "Just make sure that first draft hits my inbox by Wednesday morning, or we're going to have words, you understand? Harsh words. You're in the last chance saloon, buddy, and it's high time to shit, or get off the—"

William opened his hand, and let the phone fall. It tumbled end-over-end and hit the water. A small splash, some ripples, and it was gone.

"Goodbye, Max." *Whisper your clichés to the drowned sailors and scuttling crabs at the bottom of the sea.*

William turned up the collar of his coat. The wool felt scratchy against his beard. Hands in pockets, he walked back, past the lock gates, and along the apartment-lined edge of the marina, heading home to where his laptop waited, the cursor blinking hopelessly on the first blank white page of his unwritten book.

Portishead was a coastal dormitory town in South West England, twenty minutes drive from the city of Bristol. It had a high street, shops, and a drive-through McDonald's. The town's marina had once been an industrial dockyard serving a coal-fired power station. Now, only the stone quay remained. The rest had been transformed in the early decades of the century. The bustling railway sidings had given way to cafés and a leisure centre, the cranes to waterfront apartments and a primary school. The dock itself had been retrofitted as a marina and, instead of the rusty cargo ships of old, now housed a flotilla of private yachts and pleasure boats. The rigging on their masts rattled in the wind; little turbine blades spun on their cabin roofs; and Union Jacks and French Tricolours flapped from their sterns.

William walked to the end of the quayside and out onto the road. Yellow leaves swirled from the trees and skittered around his feet. His latest apartment, which felt dank, lifeless and suffocating even on the sunniest of days, lay on the other side of the road, in a block overlooking a supermarket car park. In the summer, with the windows open, all he could hear was the rattle and crash of shopping trolleys and the slam of car doors.

Standing at the kerb, trying to summon the energy to cross the road and climb the stairs, he saw one of his neighbours emerge from the building. She was on her way to work, car keys in one hand and briefcase in the other, a triangle of toast clamped between her teeth. He didn't know her name, but gathered she was a nurse, working shifts at one of the local hospitals. They'd passed in the corridor a couple of times, but only ever exchanged superficial pleasantries.

Maybe I should go into town, he thought. *I could call in on Sparky, and pick up a couple of wraps to see me through the weekend.* Sparky was his dealer, and William had been buying cheap amphetamines, or 'cooking speed', from him for over a year now. For a moment he wondered if a few hits of the powder would get him going, fire up the old synapses and get the words crackling out onto the page.

He slipped a hand into his trouser pocket and pulled out his door key.

No, he told himself. *Sparky's the last person you need to be around. You've spent the last four days wired out of your damn mind, and you've produced nothing, not one word. The sooner you straighten up and start writing, the sooner you'll have something to give to Max. And if you don't get started soon, you'll have to pay back the advance. And you can't, because you've spent it already. You've frittered it away on takeaways and whiskey, and drugs and cigarettes.*

His neighbour crossed the street, and smiled around the toast as she passed him. The sun emerged again, and he blinked up at it, shading his sleep-deprived eyes from its golden light.

AND THAT'S WHEN the first shot rang out.

He heard a noise like a car backfiring, and something smacked into the wall of the leisure centre. At first, he didn't know what had happened—a spark of metal on brick, a puff of dust. Stupidly, he thought somebody had thrown a stone. Then he saw the car parked against the opposite kerb. The driver's window was down, and an inhuman face snarled at him from beneath a white fedora. He saw an ape-like creature with a wide mouth and a bulbous nose, and a gun held in its fist. Half man and half beast, it looked like some sort of caveman, and he frowned at it, sure his eyes deceived him. Then the gun barrel puffed, and a bullet whined past his face. Instinctively, he cowered back, covering his chest and stomach with his hands. His body felt huge, exposed and vulnerable. He turned his shoulder away from the car. Every muscle cringed in anticipation, braced for the impact of the next shot.

But the next shot never came. Instead, the car exploded.

For an instant, William's world turned to light and noise. He felt the heat of the blast on his hands and face. His ears popped as he was thrown off his feet.

He hit the ground hard enough to drive all the breath from his body, and lay gasping, looking up at the trees. Leaves whirled down around him like snow. Car alarms shrilled. The air stank of the napalm tang of burning petrol. Across the street, the force of the explosion had shattered all the windows on the front of the apartment block. Pedestrians shouted and screamed. The girl with the briefcase crouched next to him. Her hair was a mess, and her jacket was ripped. She had a gash across one cheek like a ragged fingernail scratch. She asked him something, but he couldn't hear what she said. His ears were still recovering.

"Are you okay?" she repeated.

He swallowed. His throat and mouth were dry. "I don't know." His hands and face stung where shrapnel had nicked and scratched them. He eased an inch-long splinter of glass from the back of his hand, and let it fall onto the pavement.

"That man in the car." She spoke fast, gabbling with shock. "He had a gun. He was shooting at you."

William closed his eyes.

"Yes."

"But why? Why was he doing that?"

He tried to move, and winced at the pain in his back. He'd played football in high school, back in Ohio, and knew what it felt like to be flattened by a quarterback twice his size.

"I don't know. Is he—?"

She glanced at the tangled wreck.

"How did you do that?"

"Do what?"

"How did you make his car blow up like that?"

"Me?" William felt the world roll giddily around his head. His brain hadn't caught up yet, hadn't fully processed what had happened. He elbowed himself up into a sitting position. "I didn't do anything. How could I?"

The girl turned wide eyes to the black, greasy smoke belching up from the car's gutted shell.

"Well, *somebody* certainly did."

"It wasn't me."

Something popped in the wreckage, and they both flinched.

"Come on," his neighbour said. "I think we'd better move."

CHAPTER TWO
CITY LIGHTS

"WHO ARE YOU calling foul-mouthed, you twat?"

The tabloid journalist took a step back, brandishing his press ID like a shield. They were in the *Tereshkova*'s main passenger lounge, aft of the airship's bridge.

"N-not me," he stammered. "*I* know what you're like."

Ack-Ack Macaque's leather flight jacket creaked as he pushed up from his barstool.

"Then what are you saying?" The monkey rubbed the patch covering the socket that had once housed his left eye. He'd done a handful of interviews over the past twelve months, and hadn't enjoyed any of them. And now here was this clown, bothering him when he was trying to enjoy a quiet cigar.

"You're a national hero in the Commonwealth," the man said. The name 'Nick Dean' was printed beneath his photo. "But some parts of the British Press have criticised you as a poor role model for children."

Ack-Ack Macaque stood up straight. "Fuck them." He slapped the counter. "I stopped a nuclear war, what more do they want?"

Dean pocketed his card. A tiny camera drone hovered above his right shoulder like a tame dragonfly. "They say you drink, swear and smoke too much, and you play with guns."

"I don't play with guns."

"Yes, you do. You're fiddling with one right now."

Ack-Ack Macaque snatched his fingers away from his holster, and coughed.

"What can I say? When you've got a massive pair of Colts strapped to your hips, every problem coming your way looks like something that needs the shit shooting out of it."

"And that's why you were thrown out of the Plaza Hotel in New York, wasn't it?"

He bristled. "I wasn't thrown out. They simply asked me to leave."

"The neighbours complained about the smell. And the ricochets."

Ack-Ack Macaque grinned, exposing his yellow canines. "Hey, that wasn't my fault. The clock radio startled me."

"And so you blew it to bits?"

"When I left, they were still picking bits of plastic from the walls and ceiling."

Dean leant forward. "The *New York Times* said that if Nobel Prizes were given out for smoking cigars and wrecking stuff, you'd be top of the list."

"I suppose." Ack-Ack Macaque looked around the lounge. They were alone apart from the barman and a guy in a white suit. "Now, how about you fuck off and leave me in peace?"

Ignoring him, Dean pulled out an electronic notepad and moved his finger down to the next question on his list.

"We're currently approaching an airfield on the outskirts of Bristol," he read aloud. "This is the first time you've returned to the UK since last winter, when you helped overthrow the previous political regime. What have you being doing with yourself since then?"

Ack-Ack Macaque tapped his knuckles against the bar. "Lying on tropical beaches," he muttered. "Drinking cocktails, and taking pot shots at jet skis."

Dean frowned at him. He wanted a proper interview. "What have you *really* been doing?"

Ack-Ack Macaque took a deep breath, and made an effort not to plant a fist in the guy's stupid face. *May as well get this over with,* he thought. *Then maybe the bastards will leave me alone.*

"Well," he said, trying to force some enthusiasm into his tone, "I've been working as a pilot."

"Here on the *Tereshkova?*"

"Yes, here on the *Tereshkova.* We've been all over the North Atlantic. Middle America and the Caribbean; the East Coast of the United States; Newfoundland, and the North Polar Ocean."

Dean's finger tapped the notebook's screen. "The events of last year thrust you into the limelight. You went from being a cult figure in a computer game to being a real life celebrity. Everybody wanted to interview you. There was even talk of a TV series. Why'd you turn your back on all of that?"

"I'm not cut out for fame."

"You'd rather be a humble pilot?"

Ack-Ack Macaque caught hold of his tail and began grooming it, picking bits of fluff and lint from the hairs at the end. At a table across the room, the guy in the white suit sipped his coffee and pretended not to listen.

"For now. While I figure out what I'm going to do with my life."

"Any ideas?"

"None so far." He stopped cleaning his tail. "Moving from the game world to the real one takes some adjustment, you know." Learning that he'd been raised to sentience in order to play the central figure in a computer game had been something of a shock, especially when he found himself pulled from the make-believe online world and thrust head-first into a plot to assassinate the King of England. "And it doesn't help that I'm the only one of my kind."

"There were others like you, at the lab?"

"There was one." He scowled down at his fingernails, remembering a desperate scuffle on the deck of a flying aircraft carrier, and the obscene feel of his knife cutting into another monkey's throat. "Look," he said, "can we talk about something else? It's Friday night. I should be out drinking and puking."

Dean ran his finger down the list. "Okay, just a few more questions. You started life as a normal macaque. Then Céleste Technologies filled your head with gelware processors and upgraded you to self-awareness."

"I thought we were supposed to be changing the subject?"

"I'm getting there, okay? As my readers will know, they had you plugged into an online WWII role-playing game, didn't they?"

Ack-Ack felt his lips peel back. As the main character in the game, he'd been practically invincible. But he hadn't known that, and he hadn't known it was a game. As far as he'd been concerned, every day had been a fight for survival.

Since the events of last year, and the collapse of the *Ack-Ack Macaque* MMORPG, when he went from being one of the world's most iconic video game characters to its most famous living, breathing monkey, several new games had arisen to fill the niche left by its demise. *Captain Capuchin; Marmoset Madness; Heavy Metal Howler*—according to K8, none of them were as realistic or convincing as his game had been, because their main characters were animated using standard computer simulated AI, instead of the artificially-uplifted brains of actual flesh and blood animals. In fact, the whole uplifting process had been made illegal. There were no other walking, talking animals left in the world; he was the only one, and now always would be.

"I don't want to talk about this." He pulled out a cigar, bit the tip off, and lit up. Dean sighed.

"You're not making this easy," he said.

Ack-Ack Macaque shrugged. Smoke curled between his teeth.

"Hey, it's not my fault. This is my evening off, my chance to pull a Bueller. Spend all night drinking rum in the bath, that sort of thing. I didn't ask to be pestered."

Dean rolled his eyes. The camera drone hung in the air, a few centimetres from his ear. Its tiny fans made a gentle hissing noise.

"Don't you want to tell your story?"

Ack-Ack Macaque huffed again. He pinched the cigar between his forefinger and thumb, and puffed a smoke ring at the ceiling.

"No. Now, I've asked you to fuck off once." He fixed the man with his one good eye. "Do I have to ask you again?"

Dean picked up his notebook and pushed it into the pocket of his coat. The tips of his ears were bright scarlet.

"There's a story here, and one way or another, I'm not leaving until I get it."

Ack-Ack Macaque blew a second, smaller smoke ring.

"Suit yourself." His hand snaked out and plucked the camera drone from the air. In one fluid movement, he brought it slamming down against the edge of the bar. Its plastic casing shattered, and the little fan motors died.

"Hey!" Dean took a step forward. "Do you know how much those things cost?"

Ack-Ack Macaque grabbed him by the lapels and pulled him close enough that their faces almost touched.

"Do I look as if I give a shit?"

Dean flinched as spittle sprayed his face. He swallowed, and turned away from the smell of the cigar.

"You idiot," he said. "You stupid, bloody idiot."

Ack-Ack Macaque released him, and turned for the door.

Behind him, Dean said, "You'll be hearing from my solicitor. That's assault, matey. Assault and criminal damage." His voice rose, buoyed up by righteous fury. "You'll pay for this. I'll crucify you in print, you just see if I don't."

Ack-Ack Macaque closed his eye.

"Get lost," he said, voice low and dangerous.

Dean ignored him.

"I've got witnesses, haven't I?" He pointed to the guy in the white suit. "You just wait until you see tomorrow's headlines, pal. You just wait."

For a second, Ack-Ack Macaque considered turning around and punching the guy's Adam's apple out through the back of his neck. He imagined the crunch of knuckles hitting larynx, and ground his teeth. So tempting…

In the end, though, he had to content himself with walking away. He couldn't assault passengers, however annoying they might be. He couldn't even hurl his own shit at them. He'd had that drummed into him time and time again, and was in no mood for another lecture. Instead, he stepped out into the corridor and let the door swing shut behind him.

Fists clenched and cigar clamped in his teeth, he stalked to the dining room, where he found the evening buffet still in full swing, and the airship's owner drinking her first Martini of the night.

Victoria Valois had left her blonde wig in her cabin. Some days, she just didn't care what she looked like. Looking at her now, the smooth lines of her bald scalp were misshapen by a thick ridge of scar tissue bulging from her right temple, into which had been inlaid various input jacks, USB ports, and infrared sensors. The victim of a severe head trauma a few years back, half her brain had been replaced with experimental gelware processors, making her as much of an artificial creature as he was.

"Hey, boss." His voice was gruff. "How are we doing?"

She looked up from her glass. Her eyes were the same pale colour as the dawn sky. She wore a black t-shirt and blue jeans, and had a white military dress tunic draped over her shoulders. Her fighting stick lay on the table before her: a twelve-inch cylinder of metal that would, at a shake, spring out to almost six feet in length.

"We're about ten minutes from the airport, still running on autopilot." She picked the cocktail stick from the glass, and waved an impaled olive in his direction. "Do you want to bring us in, or are you still on leave?"

The tunic she wore came from the wardrobe of the *Tereshkova*'s former owner, the Commodore. An eccentric Russian millionaire with a proud military history, the Commodore had been killed in action while boarding the royal yacht during last November's shenanigans, and had bequeathed his elderly skyliner to Victoria, his goddaughter and only living relative.

"I might as well." Ack-Ack Macaque scowled around his cigar. "The evening's pretty much ruined now, anyway."

"How so?"

"That journalist who came on board in New York."

"Has he been pestering you?"

"Yeah."

"Have you hurt him?"

Ack-Ack Macaque shook his head. "He's fine. I just told him to sling his hook."

Victoria raised an eyebrow.

"Is that all?"

"Well, I may have squashed his bug."

She rolled her eyes.

"How commendably restrained of you." She dropped the cocktail stick back into her glass.

Ack-Ack Macaque grinned.

"Well," he said, "I'd better get to work." He threw her a floppy-armed salute and loped through the lounge, pausing only to snake an unguarded cheese and pickle sandwich from the buffet.

By the time he reached the bridge at the front of the gondola, brushing crumbs from the hairs on his chin and chest, the landing field had come into sight. Not that they would be landing, of course. Through the curved glass windscreen that comprised the entire front wall of the gondola, he could see helicopters and smaller blimps awaiting their arrival, ready to lift cargo and passengers to the helipads fixed onto the upper surfaces of the *Tereshkova*'s five hull sections.

He reached the pilot's station and settled himself behind the instrument console, in the familiar scuffed and worn leather chair. The controls of the *Tereshkova*, like those of all modern aircraft, were computerised. There was no joystick like there had been in his Spitfire, and no old-fashioned nautical steering wheel like there had been in the early Zeppelins—only a glass SincPad screen that displayed an array of virtual instruments and readouts. He could adjust the craft's heading and pitch by running his leathery fingertips over illuminated symbols, and control the vessel's speed and height using animated slide bars. It looked deceptively simple—so simple, in fact, that a child could grasp it—but he knew from experience that there was a lot more to piloting something this large. It wasn't as easy as it looked. For a start, the big, old airship would only turn sluggishly, and you had to finely balance the thrust to compensate for crosswinds and turbulence. If you wanted to bring it to a dead stop, you had to start slowing five miles in advance. Right now, as they approached the airfield's perimeter, they were crawling forward at walking pace. Each of the airship's engine nacelles could be controlled individually. Some were providing forward momentum, others reverse thrust, while the rest were pushing edge-on to the prevailing south-westerly, holding the big craft steady against the wind.

Looking forward through the big, curved windshield, Ack-Ack Macaque saw the city lights of Bristol laid out beyond the runways and hangars like sequins on a black cushion: the white and red streams of cars and buses;

the twisted spider's webs of orange streetlamps; and the harsh daylight glow of a stadium's floods. The sight filled him with excitement. Nick Dean could go hang. Somewhere down there would be music and drinking, in a place with low lights and shadowy booths, where he could get comfortably shitfaced without attracting a large crowd. After a seventy-two hour crossing from New York, he intended to party: to get drunk with strangers, and see where the night took him.

Not that it would be enough, of course. It was never enough. Whatever he did, he couldn't scratch the itch that niggled him. He couldn't find anything to match the heady excitement of life in the game world, with the heightened reality of its constant action, and everything painted for him in the simple brushstrokes of a childhood summer's afternoon. The memory of it haunted him like an addiction, and sometimes it was all he could do to blot it out with drink.

He sighed.

Later, he'd take the new Spitfire out for a few hours, he decided. Nothing blew away the cobwebs of a hard night like the high, thin clarity of the dawn. For him, flying was the only thing in this world even close to the exhilaration of the game.

The Spit was an original, one of a number built during the Second World War, but then packed in crates as the War drew to a close, and buried by British forces in Burma. Since their excavation in the early 2020s, more than thirty had been reassembled and refurbished. His had been one of the first out of the ground, and had been lovingly restored to full flightworthiness. Victoria had bought it for him as a present. It was her way of saying thank you and, since inheriting the Commodore's billions, she could easily afford it.

Currently, he had the Spit housed in a hangar at the stern of the *Tereshkova*'s outermost starboard hull, along with the airship's complement of passenger helicopters. A four-hundred-metre-long runway ran diagonally across the top of the five hulls, to the opposite edge of the airship. It was just long enough for him to take off and land, providing the wind was blowing in the right direction and the *Tereshkova* wasn't moving too quickly.

Yes, a flight would be good. He'd enjoy getting up into the clouds: just him at the controls of the Spit, just the way it had been in the seemingly endless virtual summer of 1944, when all he'd had to worry about was the next dogfight.

Simian fingers tapping on the glass control screens, he brought the old airship into position above the airport's main apron, and eased back on the forward thrust, slowing it to a halt so that its shadow hung over the waiting choppers, blotting out half the sky like the footprint of an alien mothership. He puffed on his cigar, and rubbed his hands together. The city lay before him like an untended buffet table, ripe for plundering, and alive with tantalising possibilities.

Oh yes, tonight was going to be a good night. He could feel it in his bones.

CHAPTER THREE
BETTER ANGELS

"PLEASE, CAPTAIN." THE American threw his arms wide. "I'm desperate."

Victoria Valois considered him. Lack of sleep had left his eyes rheumy and red; the pores on his nose were enlarged; and his hair and beard were uncombed and wild, as if he'd dragged himself backwards through a hedge—an impression reinforced by the myriad nicks and scratches on his cheeks and forehead.

"I don't doubt it."

His name was William Cole. Apparently, he'd come aboard with the first of the passengers, and had immediately asked to see her, to request sanctuary. They were in her cabin now, behind the *Tereshkova*'s bridge, and she was sitting at her desk, in front of the large picture window that comprised most of the back wall. The office, like the skyliner itself, had once belonged to the Commodore, and there were still traces of him everywhere. She had hardly changed a thing. The books on the bookshelves were his, as was the ancient Persian rug covering the steel deck, and the cutlass sticking at an angle from the tasteless old elephant-foot umbrella stand.

She sat back.

"Pourquoi?"

"Because somebody's trying to kill me."

Victoria made a steeple of her fingers. "So you said, but why have you come here? Why have you come to me?"

Cole leant forward. Beneath the scratches, his face looked puffy and soft. She had him pegged for an alcoholic, or maybe a junkie.

"Firstly, because you're the only skyliner in town right now." He counted off the reasons on his fingers. "And secondly, because you've got a reputation for pretty tight security. Nobody can get on board without being scanned for weapons."

Victoria picked up one of the fountain pens that lay on the desk jotter. The brain surgery she'd undergone had left her unable to read or write, and so the pen was useless to her; but she still liked to fiddle with it while she talked, like an ex-smoker sucking on a plastic straw. "Who are you, Mister Cole?"

"I'm a writer."

"Oh?" She raised an eyebrow. "What sort of a writer?" She herself had been a journalist, back before the head wound that left her incapable of parsing written text.

Cole looked down at his hands. "I'm a novelist."

Victoria frowned.

"Who'd want to kill a novelist?" She drummed the end of the pen against the blotter. "Aside from another novelist, I mean. What sort of stuff do you write?"

"Science fiction."

"Ah, I see." She sat back in her chair. "Well, of course, I don't really read that stuff myself." She rubbed her nose with a forefinger. "But my husband does."

"Your husband?" It was Cole's turn to frown. "Forgive me, ma'am, but on the flight up here, I checked your public profile. It said your husband was dead."

Victoria narrowed her eyes. Even after a year of unwanted fame, she couldn't get used to the idea that strangers could be familiar with details of her personal life.

"Yes, he is." She put the pen on the desk. "But he still has his uses." She raised her gaze to the security camera above the door. "Paul? I assume you're listening?"

"Oh, yes." The voice came from an intercom speaker bolted to the metal ceiling. Paul had been murdered a year ago, for his unwitting part in the conspiracy to bring about Armageddon; but Victoria had managed to rescue a back-up copy of his personality. At first, she'd stored it in her own head, running it on the neural gelware prosthesis that filled half her skull; but that hadn't been a very satisfactory arrangement for either of them. She needed her privacy, and he needed something to occupy him. And so, a couple of months ago, with K8's help, she had uploaded his electronic essence to the *Tereshkova*'s main processors, where there was enough computing power to sustain him almost indefinitely. The process had been difficult and risky. They couldn't turn him off without resetting him to his initial state, which would have meant losing all the memories he'd accumulated since being reactivated. So they'd been forced to set up a seamless fibre optic link between Victoria's cranial processors and the computers in the *Tereshkova*, and then transfer him along it. Back-ups were notoriously delicate, prone to falling apart at the slightest disruption, but somehow they'd done it. He had the chance to survive a little longer. And their relationship, which had once been torrid, then awkward, seemed now to have settled into a deep, caring friendship. The love was still there. Love, for them, had never been a problem. They'd stayed close all through their disastrous marriage and subsequent separation; it was only his sexuality that drove them apart. He'd stopped finding her desirable, and it had broken both their hearts.

Now, a thirty-centimetre-tall image of him shimmered into existence before her, projected from a hologram generator built into the surface of the desk. He appeared to be in his late twenties, with spiky, peroxide blonde hair, and a blue and turquoise Hawaiian shirt worn over combat trousers. He'd been dead for a year, and they'd never been closer. Freed from the needs and desires of the flesh, he'd simply stopped caring about sex. That side of things had ceased to matter. What counted now, for both of them, was that the love remained. And love was what it was all about. They were both lonely, damaged creatures, but together, they had found some measure of companionship and contentment.

Her eyes flicked to a piece of paper stuck to the wall beside the desk. Paul had found a quote from an old short story, and printed it out for her. It said: '*Throughout history, love served a serious evolutionary purpose. It compelled us to look after those around us, and to allow them to look after us. This was the root of community, and the groups which survived and prospered were those with the most love.*' And that, for her, more or less summed it up.

She bent her face down to Paul's level and poked a thumb in Cole's direction.

"Have you ever heard of this guy?"

Paul's sprite turned to face the man in the chair. His fingers scratched at the pale stubble on his chin.

"William Cole? Hell, *yes*." He held his hands out. "Mister Cole, it's an honour to meet you. I've read all your Mendelblatt books."

Cole raised an eyebrow. The hologram couldn't really see him. His attentiveness was a carefully constructed illusion. Paul's actual 'eyes' were the security cameras set into the corners of the office ceiling.

"All *three* of them?"

"Absolutely. Jesus." The little figure rubbed his forehead with the back of his hand. He shuffled his trainers. "*Better Angels* is one of my top ten favourite books of all time. Seriously, I must have read it a dozen times over, at least."

Victoria flicked a finger through the projected image to get his attention. "Can you think of any reason why anybody would want to kill him?"

Paul put a hand to his garishly attired chest, fingers splayed. "Absolutely not. The man's a genius." He gave Cole a shy glance. "Like Dick, Ballard and Chandler, all rolled into one. Really, I mean. Wow."

Victoria sighed. "Please excuse my husband's nerdgasm, Mister Cole. What you have to understand is that, however free and bohemian we may seem to you, the truth of the matter is that, on a skyliner, everything is determined by weight and cost. We can only afford to feed so many mouths, and we only have room for a fixed number of passengers, and a fixed number of crew. If I were to grant you sanctuary aboard this vessel, you would either have to pay your way, or work your passage."

The American wiped his lower lip on the back of his hand. "I understand."

"Well, which is it to be?"

Cole patted his trouser pockets. "Being temporarily devoid of funds, I will have to opt for the latter." He smiled ruefully. "Tell me what I can do."

Victoria shook her head. It didn't work like that. "No, *you* tell *me* what you can do, and then *I'll* decide how best to use you."

Cole spread his hands. "I don't have a lot of skills. Beyond writing, obviously."

"Can you cook?"

"A little."

Victoria picked up the pen and tapped it against the edge of her desk. "The chef needs a new helper. The last one jumped ship earlier tonight. He got a better offer, apparently. Can you scrub pans and wash dishes?"

"If that's what it takes."

"That is exactly what it takes, Mister Cole." She rose, and extended her hand. "Welcome aboard. If you wait in the passenger lounge, I'll have one of my stewards show you to your quarters." They shook, and the author turned to leave. As he opened the door, she spoke again. "Oh, and Mister Cole?"

"Yes?"

"If it turns out you've done anything despicable to warrant this murder attempt, I'll throw you off this ship myself. Do I make myself clear?"

"Perfectly clear, Captain. And thanks."

TEN MINUTES LATER, William Cole found himself alone in a narrow cabin in the central gondola. In contrast to the passenger cabins, which were comparatively spacious, the crew cabins were narrow and utilitarian, with barely enough room to stand beside the bunk bed that took up the majority of the available space. There was no window, and nowhere to sit. The room smelled of garlic, farts and old cologne. Moving carefully in the confined space, William changed into a pair of pyjama trousers and an old t-shirt. The covers on the top bunk were mussed and grubby, so he climbed into the unused lower bed and closed his eyes.

He could hear his pulse thumping in his ears. The three hours since the explosion had been a frantic rout. Still groggy from the blast, he hadn't bothered waiting for the police to arrive. Instead, he was up and moving as soon as he felt able to stand. During last year's nuclear standoff with China, he'd developed an emergency plan in case the missiles flew, and now, he was following it. He wasn't going to hang around and wait for a second gunman to come looking for him.

Shaking off the protests of his neighbour, he crossed the road, taking care to give the burning car a wide berth, and picked his way into his apartment. The bomb blast had strewn fragments of glass across the front room, and they crunched beneath his shoes as he gathered up his passport and bank cards and stuffed them into his pockets. His hands were shaking. This wasn't drug paranoia: somebody really *was* trying to kill him.

He had a rucksack ready packed, containing everything he needed, from first aid supplies to powdered food and iodine tablets. It was his 'bug-out' bag, and it was stashed beneath his bed, where he could find it in the dark. All through the international crisis, he'd felt better knowing it was there. He knelt down and pulled it out by its canvas straps. He grabbed the electronic notebook containing the handwritten first chapters of the book he was working on, stuck it in a side pocket, and added a couple of spare batteries. Then he was out of the door and clattering down the concrete steps to the block's basement garage. He owned an old Renault with ninety-four thousand miles on the clock. It took him as far as the skyliner passenger terminal at Filton, where he abandoned it in the long-stay car park without a backward glance.

This was his plan: get airborne, and ride out the crisis. If somebody wanted him dead, he wasn't going to stick around long enough for them to take another pop. Better to get airborne and keep moving while he figured out his next move.

The gunman—if indeed the ape-like thing in the car had been a man—had been killed, but that didn't mean the danger had passed. The creature had been a pawn, and his death simply a way to protect the person, or persons, that had hired him. William knew enough to understand that the first rule of covering up an assassination was to kill the assassin. It had just been luck that the bomb had blown prematurely. Once whoever was behind the attack discovered their man had failed, they'd send somebody else, sure as eggs were eggs. The only thing that puzzled him was who 'they' might be. As far as he knew, he had no enemies. An obsessive fan would have acted alone and, as far as he knew, he hadn't said or written anything to anger extremist groups of any persuasion. He simply didn't have that many readers.

After all, he thought as he lay on the bunk in the *Tereshkova's* cabin, *who pays attention to science fiction writers, anyway? We're the motley fools of literature. We caper and dance on the page, and nobody takes us seriously—certainly not seriously enough to send assassins.*

The mattress felt firm beneath him, and the sheets had the reassuring hotel roughness of cotton that had been washed and boiled a thousand times. Four days of amphetamine-charged wakefulness pressed down on his eyes; they felt like two peeled onions stuffed into the crevices of his face. He needed to sleep, to recharge his mental and physical batteries, yet he felt his heart jump at every unfamiliar creak and bang. The *Tereshkova* had her own soundtrack: a constant accompaniment made up of the hum of the engines and the purr of the air-conditioning units; the buffeting of the wind; the clank and gurgle of the water pipes; and the knock and slam of cabin doors up and down the corridor. He could even hear snatches of dance music from the passenger lounge.

He kicked off his shoes and turned on his side. Fleeing here had been instinct: simple self-preservation. Now, he had to work out his next move. According to her schedule, the *Tereshkova* was bound for Mumbai, by way of Paris, Prague, Istanbul, Cairo, and Dubai. If he kept his head down and his nose clean, he could ride her all the way to India, and after that, who knew? Perhaps he'd find passage to Hong Kong and Tokyo, and then across the Pacific to San Francisco, and the whole North American continent.

Or, he realised, he could alight at any one of those stops, and claim sanctuary on another skyliner, headed somewhere else. With a bit of planning and forethought, he could switch from one ship to another, criss-crossing the globe until his trail became too tangled to trace. He had his passport, and he had his notebook. He could work on his novel during his off-duty hours, without Max or Stella breathing down his neck. Or he could tear it all up and write something else. The Lincoln Mendelblatt books had made his name and attracted him a readership, but he was sick of the character.

The Jewish private eye stories were set in a fictional world in which the UK and France had never merged, and England now stood on the edge of a federal Europe; a world of financial chaos and Middle Eastern oil wars, in which Westminster's loyalties leaned closer to Washington than Paris.

Stupid.

During the nuclear crisis, he'd had an epiphany; a moment of clarity in which he'd realised he didn't want to go to his grave remembered only for a series of trashy sci-fi detective novels. That realisation was, he admitted to himself, the real reason he was a month overdue on the latest instalment. He'd lost all enthusiasm for the setting. In the grip of real world events, his invented globe seemed paltry and irrelevant. Now, he wanted to be remembered for something nobler and more worthy. He had higher aspirations—aspirations that had become buried under the accumulated silt of convenience and expediency. He was tired of being passed over for awards and accolades, and tired of people's eyes glazing over when he told them what he wrote. He wanted to go mainstream and write serious literature. He wanted to write a book so searing and heartfelt that, one day, a girl in a library somewhere would read it and it would make her cry, and fall in love with him. If he had to depart this life, why not take a stab at literary immortality? Why not leave his mark on the world, once and for all?

He owed it to himself. Five years ago, when he'd hopped that first skyliner from Dayton to Liverpool, and then caught a freezing train south to Bristol, his plan had been to set up home with Marie and write the Great Transatlantic Novel. He'd been an overweight middle-aged man in love, but what great plans he'd harboured, what ambitions!

Lying on his back, staring up at the underside of the chef's bunk, he felt something harden inside him. He owed it to himself, and he owed it to Marie. She'd died believing he could do it, believing he could reach for the rarefied literary heights and escape the sweaty backstreets of pulp. When he'd started out, he'd been young and callow, with nothing original to say about the human condition. He'd been bored and lazy, and suffering through the slow motion car crash that had been his first marriage. No wonder he'd taken to writing escapism. Now, though, he was older, and could draw on the bitterness of two years of grief, disillusionment and drug addiction; and he had the rest of his life to gather more new experiences.

Exhaustion weighed on his bones like a heavy quilt, and yet, lying there, he felt the first tickle of optimism. Maybe this disruption was what he'd needed all along? Instead of moping around the flat, blitzing his grief with chemicals, he should have been out in the world, getting a change of scenery and dirtying his hands with some honest toil. Sweat would help him now more than speed ever could. Here on the *Tereshkova*, he'd labour as a kitchen hand during the days and write in the evenings, with no distractions, drugs or deadlines. He felt a moment's shame that it had taken a car bomb to shake him out of his rut, but now it had, he knew he'd been given a chance to make a new start, a clean start. All he had to do was seize it.

He scratched his nose. Hadn't Kerouac sailed out as a ship's cook during the Second World War? Maybe you couldn't write convincingly about life unless you were out there living it, shoulder-to-shoulder with everyone else—up to your elbows in the world, scraping your knuckles against its rough edges.

Lying there in the darkness, he curled his fingers into tight fists. For the first time in months, he felt alive. He didn't know who had tried to kill him, or why, but that didn't matter right now. What mattered more than anything else was that he suddenly had a reason to go on; he could see a path in front of him, and knew how to walk it. After years of doubt and misery, he could finally see how to become the writer he wanted to be.

His eyes were raw and dry. Closing them, he surrendered to his accumulated fatigue and, wrapped in an itchy blanket, on an airship bound for foreign parts, fell asleep dreaming of the places he'd see and the books he'd write.

HE WAS WOKEN by the squeak of the cabin door's hinges. The room was still dark, and he had no idea how much time had passed. The door had been opened a crack. A dim light pushed its way in from the corridor, and he rubbed his eyes. William tensed. With his mouth dry and heart hammering, he lay as still as he could. Through half-closed eyelids, he saw a shadow slip into the room. Hardly daring to breathe, he wished for a weapon. He heard the rustle of cloth, the soft tread of a shoe against the metal deck.

"William?" The voice was male, and American. "Are you there?" The figure crouched beside the bunk, and shone a torch at him. It wore robes, like a monk's habit. A cowl shadowed its face. Gulping down breaths, William shrank back into the corner, shielding the glare with a hand held in front of his eyes.

"Who are you, what do you want?"

The figure didn't answer. Instead, it reached up and lowered the hood, revealing its face, and William gaped as he found himself staring into features that were almost an exact reflection of his own.

"I know this is an awful shock," his double said, "but please try to relax."
He spoke through a clenched jaw. Sweat shone on his brow and upper lip.
"My name's Bill," he said. The words sounded forced. "I know you'll have
a lot of questions, and I promise I'll try to answer them. But right now, you
need to loosen your fists and listen." He let the robe fall open, revealing
a black shirt and tie. The shirt had a hole in it. The material was sodden
around it, and stuck to his skin. He coughed wetly.

"Is that blood?" The realisation seemed to jolt William out of his
paralysis. He opened his mouth to cry for help, but Bill pulled a gun from
the folds of his sleeves.

"I wouldn't do that, if I were you."

William looked into the black, unblinking eye of the barrel.

"Who are you?"

For long seconds, the gun remained unwavering. Then, with another
cough, the man turned his hand sideways, and offered William the pistol's
grip.

"I told you," he wheezed. "My name's Bill." He coughed again. "I'm
here to save your life."

CHAPTER FOUR
THE GESTALT

WITH THE *TERESHKOVA* stationary above the airfield, and passengers already disembarking, Ack-Ack Macaque switched on the autopilot to keep the vessel in place against the jostling coastal wind, and then knuckle-walked aft from the bridge.

"It's fuck-this-shit o'clock," he told the Russian navigator. Time to kick back with a couple of cold lagers, and maybe a rum daiquiri or two. Then later, catch a ride down to the airfield with one of the passenger 'copters, and hit a few bars. In New York, K8 had found him a fedora and raincoat and, as long as he wore the collar turned up, and the hat pulled low enough to shade his face, he hoped he wouldn't attract too much in the way of unwelcome attention.

Intent on his plans, he shuffled past Victoria's office. As he did so, the door opened and she beckoned to him.

"I've got someone in here who's extremely keen to meet you," she said. She still wore the military tunic but, since he'd last seen her, she'd replaced her wig: a platinum blonde bob which covered the jacks implanted into her temple, and the extensive scarring at the back of her head. Ack-Ack Macaque could smell the Martini on her breath. He looked past her to the figure standing by her desk. It was the same man who'd been in the bar when he'd had his skirmish with the reporter, Nick Dean.

"Who's that?"

"Mister Reynolds is here as a representative of the Gestalt."

Ack-Ack Macaque eyed the man up and down. "I should have guessed that." Like all members of the cult, Reynolds wore an immaculately white three-piece suit, with matching white shoes and a white tie, and his face held the same distracted, beatific calm they all radiated. "The question is: what does he want?"

Victoria's smile thinned. "Well, why don't you come in and *ask him*?"

She stood aside, and turned to her visitor.

"Mister Reynolds, please allow me to introduce our pilot. You'll have to excuse his manners, but he's only barely housetrained."

Ack-Ack Macaque glared at her. Reynolds bowed in greeting.

"Mister Macaque. May we say that this is indeed a pleasure?"

Ack-Ack Macaque scratched the chestnut-coloured hairs on his chest. "For you, maybe. But I've got places to be, and havoc to wreak."

The man's smile remained unwavering. "Of course, of course. We understand, and we are sorry for the intrusion."

Ack-Ack Macaque shivered. He'd run into a few of these Gestalt types in the States, and it creeped him out when they referred to themselves in the plural.

Part religion, part social experiment, the Gestalt used wireless technology to link its members' soul-catchers, networking them together in a web of shared thoughts and blurred identities.

"I met some of you weirdos in New York." Ack-Ack Macaque dug into the pocket of his aviator jacket, searching for a cigar. "I didn't know you'd spread to the UK already."

The man's dreamlike smile clicked up a notch. "We can assure you, we get everywhere." He held out a hand, and Ack-Ack Macaque made a face. He didn't want to shake. He didn't even want to be in the same room.

"So," he said, "what do you want with me?"

"We saw your unfortunate altercation earlier, and we thought maybe we could offer you our help?"

"Help? What sort of help?"

"We have a proposal."

"I'm not the marrying type."

The man's smile tightened. "Please, hear us out. We have been following your case with great interest. A humble monkey raised to sentience? What insights you must have, what unique perspectives."

Ack-Ack Macaque rolled his eye. He didn't like where this was going. He pulled the cigar from his pocket, bit the end off, and spat it into Victoria's wicker wastepaper basket.

"Look, don't get any funny ideas. I'm not going to join your little club, okay?" The idea made him queasy. He'd had enough scientists and engineers crawling around in his skull. He didn't need any more.

"But you would be so welcome." Reynolds rocked back and forth on his heels. "We have smoothed things over with Mister Dean, and reimbursed him for the cost of his camera."

"I didn't ask you to do that."

"It is our pleasure. Our Leader is so very keen to make your acquaintance."

"You guys have a leader?" Ack-Ack Macaque cocked an eyebrow. "I thought you guys were like some vast hive."

"Every hive has a queen." Reynolds licked the tip of his thumb, and used it to smooth his eyebrows. Two quick flicks. "Or, in our case, a king."

"And who is this king?" In his peripheral vision, Ack-Ack Macaque sensed Victoria tensing, bursting with unvoiced questions. He tried to ignore her.

"To find that out," Reynolds said smoothly, "you'll first have to agree to meet him."

"Sorry, but that's not going to happen."

"Are you quite sure?"

"Sure as shit."

"Please, Mister Macaque. Will you at least consider it? Your brain is mostly composed of gelware, so you wouldn't need additional implantation; at least, not much. The process of integration could be achieved in minutes, and quite painlessly. And I think it would be of great benefit to you."

"No, absolutely not." Ack-Ack Macaque rolled the cigar between finger and thumb, listening to the tobacco leaves crackle. Reynolds took a step closer.

"Welcoming you into the Gestalt would immeasurably enrich our whole." His breath stank of coffee and mints. Ack-Ack Macaque curled his lip, exposing an incisor.

"If you don't get out of my face right now," he growled, "I'll enrich *your* hole with the toe of my boot."

Reynolds ignored the threat. He reached out his arms as if asking for a hug.

"You wouldn't have to be alone."

Alone.

The word rang in the air like the toll of a funeral bell. Cold fingers gripped Ack-Ack Macaque's stomach, and squeezed. He felt his arms and legs shake. Then, without consciously willing it, he stepped forward and slapped Reynolds hard across the face. The man staggered back against the desk.

"Shut your mouth."

He pulled back his long arm for another strike, but Victoria stepped in front of him. She had her fighting stick in her hand, but hadn't yet flicked it out to its full length. He glared at her, his single eye wide and wild, but she didn't flinch. She didn't submit. Instead, she met his gaze and held it. In another monkey, this would have been tantamount to a direct physical challenge, and Ack-Ack Macaque had to fight down an instinctual surge of aggression. If he got hold of her, he could snap her like a twig. But Victoria was his friend, and saviour: he owed her everything. He might be the alpha male on this tub, but she was definitely the alpha female, and he knew she wouldn't tolerate any of his shit. She had no patience for insurrection or threats. The last person to raise a hand against her had been dropped from the *Tereshkova*'s cargo hatch, several thousand feet above Windsor Castle. He eyed the fighting stick in her hand, and let out a long, shuddering breath.

"Yes, boss." He dropped his chin. His palm stung where it had struck Reynolds' cheek.

"Thank you." Victoria gave him a final glare, and then turned to Reynolds, who leant drunkenly against the desk, his fingers dabbing at a split and bloodied lip.

"I am so sorry, Mister Reynolds." She took his elbow and helped him upright. "But I believe you've been given your answer. Now, do you require medical attention?"

Reynolds shot Ack-Ack Macaque a sideways glance.

"We are sorry you feel that way, Mister Macaque." His voice was quiet, the earlier self-assurance muted. "For what it's worth, we were only trying to help you."

Ack-Ack Macaque shrugged his leather-clad shoulders. He didn't need any help. He tossed the cigar into his mouth, and caught it in his teeth.

Victoria hustled Reynolds towards the cabin door. Looking back, she pointed a bony finger at Ack-Ack Macaque.

"You, stay here."

Ack-Ack Macaque harrumphed. He folded his arms and sat on the edge of the metal desk.

"I'm not going anywhere, boss."

He watched her escort the white-suited man to the corridor. Reynolds had a hand to his bruised face. He was lucky not to have a broken jaw.

It would have served him right, Ack-Ack Macaque thought.

He fished around for his lighter. When he looked back up, Reynolds was watching him, ignoring whatever apologies Victoria was making.

"You will come to us and let us help you eventually, you know." Not even the cut lip could disguise the certainty in the man's voice. "After all, where else can you go? Where else can someone like you ever truly belong?"

WHEN VICTORIA CAME back, her cheeks were flushed and her lips almost white.

"*Putain de merde*," she said. "What was that all about?"

Ack-Ack Macaque's jacket creaked as he shrugged a shoulder.

"You're lucky I didn't shoot him."

Victoria looked him up and down, nostrils flared. "If you had, you'd be in the brig right now, and we wouldn't be having this conversation."

Ack-Ack Macaque flicked his lighter into life. It was a Zippo with a brushed aluminium case, and he was rather fond of it, even though it stank of petrol fumes.

"I can't help it," he grumbled. "Those Gestalt bastards make my pelt crawl." He thumbed the wheel to ignite the wick, and then used the flame to light the cigar. As he puffed it into life, he heard the air-conditioning fans whisper into action.

Victoria wrinkled her nose and flapped a hand in front of her face. "Mine too. But I can't have you slapping passengers around, especially in my office. Are we clear?"

He tapped a pair of fingers to his forehead in salute. "Clear as crystal, boss."

She narrowed her eyes. "You haven't been on the espresso again, have you? Because we all know what happened last time."

Ack-Ack Macaque waggled his head.

"No, boss."

Victoria drew herself up. Then she let out a long, cleansing breath, and threw her blonde wig onto the desk.

"Right, now that's out of the way, what are you planning to do with the rest of your evening?"

Ack-Ack Macaque was used to her mood shifts. He shrugged. Reynolds's final words still rankled him, like a fleabite he couldn't scratch.

"Drink imported lagers until I puke?"

Victoria smiled. She straightened the collar of her white military tunic, and slipped the retractable fighting stick into one of its pockets.

"That sounds like a damn fine plan, monkey-man. If you don't mind a little company, the first round's on me."

CHAPTER FIVE
UNCOMFORTABLY PARANOID

THE MAN WHO called himself Bill slumped back against the cabin wall, and stretched his legs out before him. One of his hands pressed at the wound in his stomach, and he sucked air through his teeth in tight, rapid breaths.

"I haven't got long. I have to. Warn you. About the virus."

Transfixed, William slid forward on the bunk. The gun Bill had given him felt heavy, cold and solid in his grip.

"Who are you? Why do you look like me?"

Bill coughed. Where William's hair was long and wild, his had been carefully cropped.

"I *am* you." He had trouble speaking and breathing at the same time. "Sort of. I'm a different version... of you."

William felt his face flush. "What, you're like my twin brother or something?"

"No." Bill's head shook loosely on a neck that seemed loath to support it. "I really am... you. But I'm a version of you from a different... world. A parallel... world."

"Bullshit."

Bill winced in pain. "You write... science fiction," he said between clenched teeth. "You know how... this works."

William fought the urge to curl into a ball and pull the covers over his head.

"No way," he said, voice unsteady. Parallel worlds were just a bit of fun, a thought experiment at best. Writing about them was one thing; he didn't necessarily believe in them. Despite setting his books in one, he'd never on a gut level accepted the idea of them as being *true*. "How did you get here?"

"Doesn't matter."

"But—"

Bill raised an arm. "We don't have time... for explanations. You're in danger. I'm here to help."

William leaned forward. "So, you know who's been trying to kill me?"

"Yes." Bill's breathing was shallow. The sweat glistened on his brow. "We didn't think... they'd find you. Not so quickly. We have to move you. Before they try—" His words dissolved into a convulsive fit of coughing. His shoulders shook and his back arched. By the time the fit subsided, his lips were dark, and shone red in the torchlight. Feeling panicky, William tried to stand.

"I'll get help."

Bill's hand locked around his wrist like a cuff. "No, it's too... late." The words were a bubbling whisper. "They're going to release the virus. You have... to stop them. Find Marie. She'll help you..."

William pulled back. "Marie's dead." His mouth was so dry he could barely speak. "She died two years ago."

Bill turned his head and spat a wad of red phlegm onto the deck.

"Not. That. Marie." His body shook in a final spasm, and then fell back against the wall. His chin dropped to his chest, and a line of bloodied drool unwound slowly from his lips, onto his beard. William heard the last of the air wheeze from his blood-filled lungs, and knew for sure that the man was dead. Dumbfounded, he sat and stared into Bill's face, with the uncomfortably paranoid feeling of just having watched his own demise.

K8 HAD THE *Tereshkova*'s kitchen more or less to herself. The radio on the shelf played a concert from the BBC's Paris studios, and the cook, a large Russian with a drooping moustache, snored in a chair by the open porthole, his feet up on an upturned bucket.

Much as she loved living on the *Tereshkova*, K8 treasured moments like these. In the rattling boxes of the skyliner's gondolas, peace and quiet were scarce commodities.

K8 was a young former hacker from Scotland, and one of Ack-Ack Macaque's most trusted friends. A pair of headphones dangled around her neck as she mixed ingredients in a bowl: flour, eggs and sugar, a handful of white chocolate chips, and a chopped banana. The cookies she was making were for the monkey. They were his favourite, and she called them 'macaque snacks'.

Not that he'd ever thank her, of course. Not out loud. He seemed embarrassed when people did nice things for him, and so the most she could expect would be a grunt. But she knew he liked them, and that was enough. Besides, she enjoyed having somebody to cook for. At school, the only subjects in which she'd shown any interest had been computer science and home economics; and, to her, cooking and hacking had always had their similarities. Both required concentration and the methodical combination of ingredients. If you followed the procedures, and threw in a dash of creativity, you could perform magic. The right components, put together in the right order, were capable of conjuring forth perfection.

And, she thought as she spooned the thick, sugary mixture into blobs on a baking tray, if you knew the rules you could find ways to break them. You could hack your taste buds with new combinations of flavours, such as white chocolate and banana.

She made two rows of blobs, leaving plenty of space for them to spread out as they cooked, and then bent down to slide the tray into the oven. As she slammed the door, the chef muttered in his sleep.

She'd been Ack-Ack Macaque's wing woman for a year now, having helped him escape the clutches of her former employer, Céleste Technologies. And she'd seen and done more in that time than she'd ever believed possible. Since the company plucked her from her mother's two-bedroom tenement in Glasgow, her life had been a mad whirl of travel and adventure. But, however unfamiliar or dangerous things had become, she'd always felt safe because he'd always been there. She was more than capable of taking care of herself, of course, but when he was there, she didn't have to.

He was her commanding officer, and her best friend; but, more than that, he was a shield against the world. In that respect, he reminded her of her ratty old teddy bear—the one she'd slept with every night of her childhood; the one she'd clung to during the arguments and recriminations of her parent's divorce; the one who'd kept her company during the lonely evenings spent with her finger jammed in one ear and the pillow jammed in the other.

When she was near him, she felt safe the same way as she had when she squeezed that bear. Except, she couldn't imagine Ack-Ack Macaque letting anybody hug him. The thought brought a smile to her face. Whatever else he might be, he certainly wasn't cuddly.

She checked her watch. The cookies would take a few minutes to bake through. She'd wait for them, and then she'd hit the lounge while they cooled. She was only seventeen, but had an arrangement with the bar staff. As long as she didn't ask them to serve her directly, and as long as she limited herself to a few glasses of wine in an evening, they turned a blind eye to her age. The *Tereshkova*'s rules said you had to be eighteen or over to drink in the bar—but as long as Ack-Ack Macaque ordered the drinks, the stewards were quite happy to pretend they didn't know that one of the glasses he wanted was for her.

She tapped her foot.

Yes, it would be good to kick back and have some laughs. It was Friday night, after all.

WILLIAM COLE WONDERED what his next move should be.

Here he was, in a cabin with a dead body—a body with a face that clearly resembled his own. How could he explain what had happened? Who in their right mind would believe such a story? He was only here on Captain Valois's sufferance. What would she say if he came to her with this? His mind raced. Was there any way he could dispose of the body? Or should he leave it here, and try to disappear himself?

His earlier tiredness had gone, washed away by adrenaline.

He shuffled forward on the bed and, placing the gun on the covers beside him, reached out a hand to touch Bill's still-warm cheek. Even closeup, the resemblance was striking. The hair might be shorter and the beard tidier and more neatly trimmed, but this was definitely the face William saw every morning in the mirror above his bathroom sink.

He took a deep breath and tried to stop his hands from trembling. Apart from the ugly guy in the car this morning, he'd never seen anybody actually die before—and to see 'himself' do it filled him with nauseous revulsion. He hadn't even been there when Marie went. When she'd finally slipped away, he'd been outside, in the hospital corridor, taking a call from his agent. By the time the nurse found him and brought him back into the room, it had been too late.

Find Marie, the man had said. But what did that mean? How could he find her? He'd scattered her ashes on their favourite beach, in accordance with what he thought her dying wishes might have been. She was one now with the sand, the wind and waves. How could she possibly help him?

And yet...

If Bill had been William's double, did that mean—dare he hope—that there could be another Marie out there? Was his wife's doppelganger walking around somewhere? If so, he had no idea how to find her.

He took another long, deep breath, trying to calm himself. He couldn't stop opening and closing his hands. They fluttered like startled birds. Before he did anything else, he had to decide where he was going to go when he left this room.

The gun lay on the blanket next to him. He picked it up and turned it over and over. He could smell the sooty oil used to lubricate its mechanism. He had a weapon now. The thought made him feel better. He had no idea how 'Bill' had smuggled the pistol on board, but that didn't matter right now. The important thing was that he wasn't defenceless any more.

But where was he going to go?

He tried to analyse the situation as calmly and rationally as he could, as if working out the plot for one of his novels. On balance, the *Tereshkova* still seemed like his best bet. It was a self-contained state, with limited access; but if he wanted to stay here, he'd have to find a way to explain the body.

So be it, he thought, pulse racing. He had a weapon. What he needed now were allies.

BREAKING NEWS

From *The South West Messenger*, online edition:

Police Try to Trace Missing Writer

Police in Somerset are trying to trace the whereabouts of reclusive science fiction author, William Cole. Cole, whose works include the 'Lincoln Mendelblatt' novels, disappeared from his home this morning, following an explosion in the street outside his apartment block. Eyewitnesses say that shots were fired before the explosion, possibly at Mister Cole, and police are very concerned for his safety.

Cole, aged 44, is known to have past convictions for the possession and use of controlled narcotics, and a history of depression, and police are appealing to members of the public to get in touch if they can shed any light on his whereabouts.

Cole, who is often compared to Philip K. Dick and H.P. Lovecraft, first came to public attention when a damning review of his debut novel, *Better Angels*, went viral on the Internet. Since then, two sequels have followed—*Die Robot* (2058) and *The Collective* (2060).

Speaking at a hastily convened press conference in London, Cole's agent, Max Morrison, said, "I spoke to Will this morning, just prior to the attack. He was in good spirits, and working hard on his next book, the fourth in the Mendelblatt series."

Online, fans have speculated that the author's disappearance could be a media stunt, designed to promote his forthcoming novel, *A Thousand City Whispers*. However, when asked if he had a message for William Cole, Morrison simply said, "We're all worried about you, buddy. If you're listening to this, I want you to get your act together and call me, okay? We've got important things to do, and time's getting tight."

Police are urging anyone with information concerning the author's whereabouts to come forward as soon as possible.

Read more | Like | Comment | Share

Related Stories

Merovech and Julie: date announced for royal wedding.

Diplomats from Commonwealth and China 'close to deal' on Hong Kong.

Car bomb rocks North Somerset town.

Members of the Gestalt cult petition for UN recognition as independent 'state of mind'.

Skyliner Tereshkova returns to British shores for the first time since 'Le Combat de La Manche'.

Culture: art world stunned by new Da Vinci sketches found in Paris cellar.

Sport: Eight Nations tournament kicks off at Twickenham.

Space: controversial Céleste probe still on course for Mars.

CHAPTER SIX
DON'T FUCKING MOVE

VICTORIA DECIDED SHE was too tired to accompany him into town, so they agreed to have a quick drink in the *Tereshkova*'s passenger lounge. They took a corner table, and Victoria signalled one of the white-gloved stewards.

"An Amstel for me, and rum for the monkey."

The steward bowed. Like most of the airship's staff, he was Russian. The Commodore, a former pilot and cosmonaut in the Russian air force, had preferred to hire his own countrymen.

The steward turned to Ack-Ack Macaque.

"Single or double rum, sir?"

Ack-Ack Macaque grinned around the cigar in his teeth.

"Bottle."

"Very good, sir."

This early in the evening, few people were in the lounge. Victoria knew that most of the transatlantic passengers had already disembarked. They would complete their journeys by fast trains to London, Manchester, or Edinburgh. The remaining passengers, who intended to stay with the airship for her onward journey to London and Paris, had also mostly gone ashore for the evening, glad to be back on terra firma after three days in the air, ready to sample the nightlife and historic tourist attractions of Bristol and Bath.

When the steward had fetched their drinks, set them down, and withdrawn, she leant across the table.

"Are you all right, now?"

The monkey glanced at her with his one good eye. In the light of the art deco electric wall lamps, his fur had a rough, bronzed sheen.

"I've been better."

Victoria wiped her thumb across the condensation on the neck of her beer bottle. She couldn't read the label, but she could recognise the maker's logo by its colours and shape.

"Would you care to elaborate?"

On the other side of the table, Ack-Ack Macaque unscrewed the cap of the rum bottle and, ignoring the glass the steward had brought, took a hefty glug from the neck. He smacked his lips, and replaced the cigar.

"Not particularly."

"Was it something he said?"

"Who, Reynolds?"

"Of course, Reynolds."

The monkey made a face and hunched over the table. His leather jacket creaked. "You know what they say: It takes a hundred and forty-three muscles to frown, but only fifty-two to grab somebody by the lapels and bite their face off."

Victoria wasn't amused.

"There's been too much violence on this ship. If you want me to carry on trusting you, you can't lash out like that."

Ack-Ack Macaque drummed his fingers on the side of the rum bottle.

"It was everything he said. Especially all that stuff about being alone." He ran a fingertip around the rim. "It got to me."

"But, you're not alone. You have K8. You have a place here." She reached out a hand. "You have me."

"I know." Ack-Ack Macaque scowled. "But it's not easy being the only talking monkey in the world."

"You feel like a freak?"

He gave a shaggy shake of the head. "You wouldn't understand."

Victoria felt her cheeks colour. She tapped the ridge of scar tissue at her temple. The surgery to repair the damage to her brain had been extensive and life saving; but it had left her bald and scarred—an oddity.

"Oh, really?"

She saw him glance at her scalp, then back down to the bottle in his paw.

"Sorry, boss."

She gave a shrug. In truth, she knew how he felt. She used to feel the exact same way when passengers tried not to stare at her. For a while, it had bothered her; but last year's unpleasantness had given her confidence, and a certain notoriety, and now she no longer cared what anyone thought of the way she looked.

She accepted his apology with a gracious nod.

"*C'est rien.*" Her beer was cold and sharp, just the way she liked it. She savoured the bubbles on her tongue before swallowing.

The sad truth was, the camaraderie she shared with Ack-Ack Macaque was about the closest thing she had to a relationship with an actual, physical being. She had Paul, of course, but, however much she loved him, he was still just a face on a screen, or a tiny hologram on her desk. The monkey was, tragically, the nearest thing she had to a living, breathing friend.

"You know," she said, "I don't trust them, either."

His eye swivelled up to meet hers.

"The Gestalt?"

"There's something about them." She thought of Reynolds, and wondered how many minds had been peering at her from behind the man's mild, cornflower-blue eyes. "They freak me out."

Across the table, Ack-Ack Macaque took another hit of rum. She gave him a long, thoughtful look.

"I wonder why he wanted you," she said. "In particular, I mean. After all, I've got nearly as much gelware in my head as you do, and yet he didn't even ask me."

"Feeling left out?"

"Hardly." Her thumbnail worried the edge of the beer bottle's label. "But doesn't it strike you as odd?"

"Everything they do's fucking odd."

She dipped her heard, conceding his point. "Still, there's something about it that doesn't ring true. Something that tells me he wanted to do more than simply recruit you."

Ack-Ack Macaque regarded her from beneath a lowered brow. "Your journalist instincts acting up again, boss?"

Victoria smiled. "Something like that."

Ack-Ack Macaque ground out the butt of his cigar, then fumbled in his jacket pocket and pulled out another. "I thought as much." He put the fresh cigar into his mouth, but didn't light it. "Don't go digging around on my behalf. I couldn't give a damn what they want." He grinned. "I'm just glad I slapped the silly sod when I had the chance." He stretched in his seat. "Now, if you'll excuse me, boss, I'm going out for the evening."

Victoria sat back with a sigh. Her curiosity would have to wait. She peeled off the label and screwed it into a ball.

"Are you going anywhere nice?"

"I hope not." He gave a toothy grin. "Are you sure you don't want to come?"

"Quite sure, thank you."

Victoria watched as Ack-Ack Macaque got to his feet, with the cigar clamped in his jaw and the bottle dangling from his fingers. *This is my life,* she thought: *an uplifted monkey, an electronic ex-husband, a teenage hacker and me; four wretched creatures drawn together because we have nowhere else to go; because we're all artificial, made things—with patched-up souls, and cortices covered with other people's grubby fingerprints. Maybe that's why the Gestalt frightens us so much: because, instead of feeling incomplete and ashamed, they embrace their artificiality. They make it a central part of themselves. And they want to help us.*

With a flick of her finger, she sent the screwed-up label skittering across the table.

"Well, have a good time, won't you?"

Ack-Ack Macaque caught the paper ball and dropped it into his unused glass.

"I'll give it a try."

A shout came from the corridor behind him. Victoria looked over, just in time to see a figure burst into the room—a wild-haired, bearded man in a white t-shirt and saggy pyjama bottoms, with pale, gooseflesh arms, and a gun clenched in his fist.

Oh hell, Cole.

The gelware processors in Victoria's head kicked into combat mode, pumping adrenaline into her system and ramping up the speed of her thoughts. The chair went flying behind her, and her fingers curled around the neck of the beer bottle, ready to hurl it. At the same time, in her peripheral vision, she saw Ack-Ack Macaque throw himself sideways across the lounge, dragging his huge silver Colts from their holsters. By the time Cole staggered to a halt a few paces inside the door, he found himself facing a woman and a snarling monkey, both pointing weapons at him, and both poised to defend not only themselves, but also everybody else on the skyliner. His eyes rolled from one to the other, and then down to the pistol in his fist.

"Don't shoot!" He let go of the gun as if scalded. The weapon clunked onto the deck, and he raised his hands.

Lying on his side, with both guns trained on Cole's forehead, Ack-Ack Macaque spat out his cigar.

"We won't fucking shoot," he said in disgust, "if you don't fucking *move.*"

Acting on Victoria's instructions, Ack-Ack Macaque and two of the white-jacketed stewards manhandled William Cole to her office, where they handcuffed him to the chair in front of her desk. She followed behind, examining the fallen gun.

"So, Mister Cole," she said when he had been firmly secured. "Would you care to explain what you were thinking?"

Cole looked bad. Beneath the scratches, his face was pale, and his eyes bugged out. His breathing came in heaves.

"Yeah," the monkey said, growling around his unlit cigar. "Because bursting into rooms waving guns is a very good way to get your fucking head blown off."

Cole looked between them. Sweat glistened on his balding forehead.

"I want to report a murder."

Victoria sniffed the barrel of the gun she'd picked up. It had been fired recently.

"Have you killed somebody, Mister Cole?"

"No!"

"Then, tell me, what's happened?"

Cole swallowed. "A man came into my cabin." He pulled experimentally at the cuff on his right wrist. The chain rattled. "He looked just like me. He said he'd come to help, that somebody was trying to kill me."

"But you already knew that." Victoria weighed the pistol in her hand. "You told me as much when you came on board."

"Yes."

"Did you shoot him?"

Cole shook his head. "He was already wounded. I didn't realise at first."

"And now he's dead?"

"I think so, yes."

Victoria turned to one of the stewards. "Get a medic to the chef's cabin. Go armed. Report back."

The man gave a salute, and left the room.

Cole squirmed in his chair. "I didn't kill him. That's his gun you're holding. He gave it to me before he—" He swallowed again. "Before he died."

Victoria looked him up and down. She knew he hadn't smuggled the gun aboard himself. Given his claim that somebody had tried to kill him, she'd made sure his bag and clothing had been thoroughly searched.

"All that remains to be seen," she said. "In the meantime, I'd like you to take a deep breath, and start from the beginning." As a former correspondent, she'd had plenty of practice at talking to the distraught. She slipped off the military jacket and draped it over the back of her chair, to make her look more informal. Then she sat and placed her hands on the desk, palms down. "Now," she said as calmly as she could, "who was this man? Did you recognise him?"

Cole's jaw tightened. "Of course I recognised him!"

Beside his chair, Ack-Ack Macaque spat out his cigar. "Then who was he? Don't keep us in suspense."

Cole turned a baleful eye on him.

"I told you. He was *me*."

CHAPTER SEVEN
DOPPELGANGER

THE DEAD BODY lay wrapped in its habit, on a bunk in the *Tereshkova*'s infirmary. Ack-Ack Macaque looked from it to the man standing at the foot of the bed.

"That," he said, "is fucking uncanny."

Standing next to him, Victoria Valois was forced to agree. Aside from a few cosmetic differences—tidier hair, a better maintained beard, and a bullet hole in the stomach—the man lying on the bed seemed to be the exact double of William Cole. At the end of the bed, Cole himself seemed transfixed.

"He said his name was Bill," he said.

"Who is he?"

"I don't know." Cole's hands were crossed in front of his chest. Despite the cold, he still wore only a t-shirt and pyjama trousers. "But he said he'd come to warn me. Something about a virus."

"Any idea what he meant?"

"Sorry, none." With nails bitten down to the quick, the writer scratched at each of his wrists. "What happens now? Do we go to the police?"

"No." Victoria looked up at the ceiling. She felt warm and tingly inside. First the Gestalt guy, and now this? So many questions suddenly needed answering. "The *Tereshkova* is mine." She pulled the Commodore's white dress tunic more firmly onto her shoulders. "For now, I'll lead the investigation."

"But—"

"No buts." She fixed Cole with her firmest stare. "The local *flics* don't get a sniff of this." She panned her gaze around the assembled faces. "Do I make myself clear?"

One by one, they nodded their assent. They knew as well as she did that international treaties protected the autonomy of each skyliner: that each functioned as an independent city-state, unaffected by the laws of whichever territory it happened to be flying over, and that the local police had no jurisdiction.

She looked over at Ack-Ack Macaque.

"What do you say, monkey man? Are you up for a challenge?"

Ack-Ack Macaque fixed her with his one-eyed squint.

"What do you have in mind, boss?"

Victoria smiled. She could tell by the way his tail twitched, and by the way the fingertips of his right hand drummed against the handle of the revolver at his hip, that he'd been just as bored as she had during the Atlantic crossing.

"First off, we need some facts." She gave a nod towards the dead man on the bunk. "Like who this guy was, and how he got aboard. And how he got dead."

Ack-Ack Macaque leaned over the corpse and sniffed.

"He smells fresh." His pink nostrils twitched. "I mean, apart from the fact that he's shat himself, but everybody does that when they die, don't they?" He looked up at her. "What does the doc say?"

Victoria had already spoken to the airship's medical officer—a grey-haired old alcoholic by the name of Sergei.

"Gunshot wound to the large intestine. Died from internal haemorrhaging. Otherwise, nothing unusual."

"Was he wearing a soul-catcher?"

"Unfortunately not." If the man had been wearing a catcher, they'd have been able to electronically revive and quiz the copy of his personality held within.

"So, no help there, then?"

"Not much." She reached out to touch the hem of the dead man's robe. As she moved, the medals on her chest tinkled together like distant wind chimes. "Mister Cole, do you have any idea why this man's dressed as a monk?"

The writer shook his head. He was calmer now than he had been when he'd burst into the lounge, but his eyes were still wide and bloodshot. It seemed to be their default setting, and gave him the look of a hermit dragged from a cave.

On the other side of the bunk, Ack-Ack Macaque gave a grunt. "Maybe he's a fucking monk?"

Cole blinked at him. "Who would shoot a monk?"

Victoria drew her hand back from the bed. "You didn't go to Catholic school," she said, "did you, Mister Cole?" He frowned, and opened his mouth to protest, but she silenced him with a raised hand. "You said his name was Bill. Did he tell you anything else? Give you any idea where he was from?"

Cole licked his lips. His eyes settled on her for a moment.

"You wouldn't believe me if I told you." He massaged the bridge of his nose between forefinger and thumb. "Hell, I'm not even sure I believe it myself."

Victoria narrowed her eyes.

"You're talking to a cyborg and a monkey. If you can believe that, you can believe anything."

The American put a hand to the small of his back and straightened his spine, visibly trying to pull himself together. Victoria could see the gooseflesh on his bare arms.

"Okay," he said. "What do you know of parallel worlds?"

"Quantum theory." Having been married to a sci-fi fan, and been obliged to sit through seemingly endless movies and TV shows, she had a pretty good handle on the concept. "The idea that there's a multiverse of endless alternate realities, each with a different history. Like in *Star Trek*, where everybody in the parallel world has a beard."

Cole gave her a reappraising look. "Yes, that's it. Essentially, every choice we make spawns two or more alternate worlds. In one, we take the first choice, in the other, we take the second choice, and so on."

Victoria glanced down at the dead man's face.

"And so this guy's supposed to be you from a different reality?" She didn't believe it for a second. "Alternate worlds are just fiction, Mister Cole. They're plots from bad movies about Nazis; they don't really exist."

Cole held out his hands. "I know. Trust me, I write books about them and even I can't believe in them. But that's what he told me; that he was me from another reality."

"Maybe he was having you on?"

Across the bunk, Ack-Ack Macaque gave a snort. "Who jokes with a bullet in their gut?" He waved a hand from the writer to the corpse, and back again. "Look at the two of them. They're completely identical. What other explanation is there?"

"Twin brothers?"

"Surely he'd know?"

"Plastic surgery?"

The monkey rubbed the leather patch covering his empty eye socket. "Who'd go to all that trouble and expense, just to kill this dickhead?"

Cole frowned.

"No offence taken, I'm sure."

Ack-Ack Macaque flashed his yellow canines.

"Shut the fuck up, asswipe."

Victoria still had the dead man's gun in her hands. It was a small, compact pistol, made of thick plastic and devoid of markings or serial numbers. She passed it across to Ack-Ack Macaque.

"Do you recognise the make?"

He dangled it between finger and thumb.

"Nope."

"But that doesn't mean anything, these days, does it?"

"Guns are as easy to make as anything else." He shrugged; if there was one thing he knew about, it was weaponry. "This could have come out of a 3D printer anywhere from Cape Town to Bucharest, and all points in between."

"Then it could have come from anywhere, as could our friend here."

Ack-Ack Macaque harrumphed. "So, we've no idea where to start?" He stuck out his bottom lip, and Victoria guessed he'd been hoping for some action, or at least the chance to kick an arse or two.

"Not yet." She ran a hand over her bare scalp. "But it's getting late, and I don't know about you, but I'd kill for a coffee." She took back the gun, and slipped it into her pocket. "And besides, I think I'm going to have to have a word with my husband."

THE *TERESHKOVA'S* AUTOMATIC systems were perfectly capable of holding its bulk in position above the airfield; and so, with the old skyliner at rest, the crew had no need to man the bridge around the clock. At this time of night, Victoria had the room to herself. Through the curving windshield, she could see the bright city lights of Bristol and, far across the black waters of the Severn Estuary, the orange lights of Newport and Cardiff. With a tin mug of fresh black coffee cradled in her hands, and the Commodore's jacket still draped over her shoulders, she perched on the edge of the Captain's chair.

"Are you there, Paul?"

In front of her, one of the screens on her workstation blinked into life.

"Hey, Vicky. What can I do for you?" The image on the display was of him as she remembered him: short, peroxide blond hair, rimless glasses, and a loud yellow and green Hawaiian shirt.

"I assume you already know about the dead guy in William Cole's cabin?"

Paul's fingers fiddled with the gold stud in his right ear.

"Yeah, I heard about that."

"Have you been eavesdropping again?"

"Maybe just a little."

Victoria raised the mug to her nose and inhaled steam. "I need you to review the security footage. Follow it backwards. Find out who the dead guy is, and where he came from."

"I can do that."

"Will it take long?"

Paul grinned at her. By rights, he shouldn't still be here. Most personality recordings fell apart after a few months. They just couldn't sustain themselves. But somehow, letting Paul loose in the *Tereshkova*'s memory had kept him intact—even if it meant he was now confined to the ship

"Just give me a moment..." He trailed off, and his image froze. Victoria sipped her steaming coffee. It was very good. After years of drinking cheap and nasty swill in newspaper offices, she now insisted that the *Tereshkova*'s quartermaster stocked only the very best.

From her chair, she watched the nocturnal bustle of the airport, and hummed to herself a little tune she'd picked up from that morning's radio.

When Paul came back, a few minutes later, he gave her a suspicious look.

"Why are you so happy?"

Victoria gave a start.

"Me?"

"You're practically singing."

"It's nothing." She tried to wave him away, but he raised an eyebrow.

"It doesn't look like nothing to me."

Victoria drummed her fingernails against the side of the tin mug. She let out a sigh. "It's just good to have something to do," she finally admitted.

Paul smiled knowingly.

"Running a skyliner's not enough for you, eh? You still need that extra excitement, don't you? The thrill of the chase?" He shook his head, pretending to despair of her. "Some things never change."

"And some things do." She put the tin cup down on the chair's padded arm. "Now, what have you got for me?"

Paul's smile widened, and he puffed his chest forward. "Well, I've reviewed the footage."

"Any luck?"

His eyes twinkled behind his glasses.

"Let me show you." A second screen lit, displaying grainy footage from the security camera in the corridor outside Cole's cabin. "Right, here's our man." A hooded figure appeared from the right side of the screen, moving awkwardly and hunched over to the right, as if trying to curl around a pain in his side.

Victoria said, "You see where he's holding himself? That's where he was shot." So, Cole's story held up. The man *had* been shot before entering the cabin, just as he'd said. "Okay, let's back it up."

The picture froze, and then began to rewind. Victoria watched the robed figure shuffle backwards along the corridor. Moving from one camera to another, the pictures retraced his steps to a tiny berth in one of the outermost gondolas.

"According to records, the cabin was occupied by a man calling himself Bill Cole," Paul said. "He came aboard shortly after William." The picture jumped to show a shot taken by a camera up on the main helipad. It showed a middle-aged man stepping down from one of the passenger choppers. He wore an expensive-looking business suit, and clutched a leather briefcase. Mirrored sunglasses covered his eyes.

"That's him?"

"Yeah. He must have the robe in his suitcase, but it's definitely him."

Victoria leant close to the screen. "He seems to be moving okay." In fact, he looked like a typical business traveller. "Which means, he hadn't been shot when he came on board."

Paul frowned. "So, whoever shot him might still be here somewhere."

"*Oui.* And Cole could still be in danger. Where is he now?"

The screen changed to a real-time view of the passenger lounge. Cole, now wrapped in a white bathrobe, sat at a corner table with Ack-Ack Macaque and K8. The monkey's revolvers lay on the table, within easy reach.

"He should be safe enough there," Paul said. "Nobody's going to tangle with the Ack-ster."

Victoria frowned.

"Let's hope not." She ran a hand up her forehead and over the rough scar tissue at the back of her scalp, dreading to think what mayhem might be unleashed if someone engaged the monkey in such a confined space. "Right," she said, "access the room records. Find all the information this 'Bill Cole' gave us when he came aboard."

Paul waved his hands like a conjuror, and the data appeared on the screen beside him: a copy of the man's electronic boarding pass, and a scan of his passport.

"Here it is. Bill Cole, aged forty-eight. British citizen. With an address in the city."

"This city?" She glanced forward, at the lights beyond the windshield.

"Yeah." Street maps appeared on the screen. "It's not too far from here, in fact. A couple of miles, at the most."

"Can you load it into my head?" Victoria's neural prosthesis held a satellite map overlay.

"Sure." Paul's eyes narrowed as he watched her slip her arms into the sleeves of the jacket draped over her shoulders. "Why, what are you going to do? Talk to the police?"

Now it was her turn to grin.

"No, of course not." She began fastening the shiny brass buttons on the front of the tunic. "I'm going down there to check it out myself."

CHAPTER EIGHT
RAY GUN

HALF AN HOUR later, they were driving through the city streets in a rented black Mercedes. K8 had the wheel, Ack-Ack Macaque rode shotgun, and Victoria Valois and William Cole shared the back seat. As they negotiated their way through the early evening traffic, Victoria kept track of their progress using a map uploaded to her mind's eye from the *Tereshkova*'s database. A small green dot marked their current position, a red one their destination.

In the front passenger seat, Ack-Ack Macaque wore dark glasses, a wide-brimmed fedora, and a long coat with the collar turned up. He'd even wound a scarf across the lower half of his face. This was his idea of going incognito—never mind the fact that nothing could disguise his lumbering walk, or the way his tail poked out of the vent in the back of the coat.

Victoria watched the passing buildings. They were moving through the affluent suburb of Clifton, with its steep, tree-lined streets and three-storey Georgian town houses. She saw sturdy-looking churches; corner pubs with traditional signs and black railings; newsagents with handwritten headline boards; supermarkets with glittering holographic window displays; and beautiful old houses retrofitted as solicitors' offices and estate agencies.

Despite being too young to hold a British driving licence, K8 handled the big Mercedes like a pro. She claimed to have been able to drive from the age of eleven, having been taught by joyriding classmates on the estate where she grew up. Right now, she was chewing gum and listening to punishingly loud techno on her earphones. As she turned the big wheel this way and that, her spiky ginger head bobbed in time to the music.

Victoria tapped her on the shoulder.

"Just down here, on the left."

With a squeal of tyres, they slithered to a halt in the middle of the road. Parked cars lined both sides of the street. Victoria nudged Cole, and they both climbed out. The air outside felt fresh in comparison to the heated comfort of the Mercedes, and Victoria was glad she had a fleece cap to keep her head warm. At the top of the street, between the buildings, she could see one of the towers of Brunel's famous Suspension Bridge. Originally the fevered dream of an eighteenth century wine merchant, the bridge had been designed by the engineer in the stovepipe hat and completed after his death. It spanned the gorge almost three hundred feet above the muddy River Avon, and was a magnet for sightseers and suicides alike.

Ack-Ack Macaque emerged from the front passenger door, and the Mercedes drove off to park.

William Cole had dressed in a pair of black jeans, an old sweatshirt, and a worn-looking tweed jacket. His thinning, unruly grey hair still stuck up at odd angles, despite his frequent attempts to smooth it into place.

"Which building is it?" he asked.

"This one." Victoria walked to the front door of one of the houses. An intercom had been screwed to the wall beside the door, with a separate buzzer for each of the six flats within. She dug in her pocket and pulled out the keys she'd found in the dead man's luggage. One had obviously been cut for an external door, the other for an internal lock. She tried the first, and it turned. The door was heavy and made of black-painted wood, and she had to shove to get it open.

Ack-Ack Macaque and William Cole followed her into an unlit hallway with a wide wooden staircase and black and white floor tiles.

"We want flat number three," she said, looking at the numbers on the doors to either side of her. "My guess is that it's on the next floor up."

They trooped up the stairs, and found the right door on the upper landing. Inside, the little flat smelled faintly stale. Threadbare curtains hung across the windows. By the light of the orange streetlamps, she could see that the main room was a sparsely furnished studio flat, with a futon at one end and a small kitchen area at the other. Another door led off into a cramped and damp-smelling bathroom, comprising no more than a shower stall, toilet and sink.

"This is it." She reached out a hand and flicked the light switch. Beside her, Cole gasped. The walls were covered in photographs and handwritten notes; and most of the photographs seemed to be black and white surveillance photos of him. He stepped into the room, gawping around at the pictures, and Victoria followed. The glossy prints showed Cole shopping in his local supermarket, a basket in the crook of his arm; standing on the edge of a marina on a bright morning, holding a mobile phone to his ear; getting into a battered-looking blue Renault in an underground car park; browsing bookshop shelves; struggling back from the off-licence with carrier bags filled with bottles of whiskey and gin...

"These go back months," Cole said. "How long was he watching me?"

In the doorway, Ack-Ack Macaque pulled the scarf from his face. He pocketed the dark glasses, and then fumbled around in his coat until he found the bag of banana and white chocolate cookies that K8 had baked, which he proceeded to eat.

"It looks as if you've got a stalker," he said, spraying crumbs. "I had one of those for a while last year. One of those gamer nerds who couldn't let go."

This was news to Victoria. She raised an eyebrow.

"You did? What happened to him?"

The monkey grinned, exposing dirty yellow teeth.

"Poor guy broke both his legs."

Victoria started to ask how, but then stopped and shook her head, deciding she'd be better off not knowing. Instead, she walked up to Cole, who was leaning close to the wall, reading the handwritten notes pinned beside each picture.

"Any clues?" To her, the scribbled words were just squiggles on paper, utterly indecipherable.

Cole tapped a picture of himself kneeling at a stone in a snowy memorial garden, a paper-wrapped bunch of flowers clutched in his hand. "It seems I've been under scrutiny for some time. At least since last Christmas."

"Any idea why?"

"Not so far." He turned to her. "But do you want to know something weird?" He pulled a note from the wall and held it out to her. "His handwriting is *exactly* the same as mine. Absolutely, spookily identical." He shivered.

Victoria peered at the paper trembling before her.

"I'll have to take your word for that." She watched as he opened his shaking fingers and let the note fall, spiralling down to the floorboards. "Why don't you sit down?"

Cole rubbed his beard. He seemed agitated.

"None of this brings us any closer to finding out who shot him." He tapped his ribcage. "Or who's been trying to kill me."

"I think we can assume for now that the same people are responsible for both," Victoria said.

The writer's nose wrinkled. "Even if that's the case, the question is: what am I going to do about it?" He glanced around at the walls, and crossed his arms over his chest. "Because poking around in this hovel isn't getting us anywhere."

Victoria felt her fists tighten at her sides. She licked her dry lips, and swallowed her irritation.

"Sit down," she said quietly. She took a breath. "We won't be here much longer. Have a rest."

Cole glared at her, but he sat on the futon. She left him there, muttering to himself and stroking his hairy chin, and went to see what the monkey was fiddling with. He'd been rummaging in the kitchen drawers.

"What's that you've got?"

He held it out to her.

"Another gun," he said.

"Is it the same as the last one?"

"No, boss." He tipped it into her outstretched hand, and she felt its weight. It was lighter then she'd been expecting. Also, it was like no gun she'd ever seen before. It looked like a pocket flashlight with a pistol grip fixed to the underside.

"What does it do?"

Ack-Ack Macaque reached out and took it back. He held it at arm's length and aimed the 'lens' at the far wall.

He pulled the trigger. Nothing seemed to happen.

"Is it broken?"

The monkey shook his head, and pointed a leathery finger at the wall. Amongst the papers, a small spot of plaster smouldered, molten red. The notes around it were charred at the edges; the photos had curled and melted, as if shrinking away from a flame.

"Good, huh? It must be some kind of ray gun."

Victoria scratched her chin. "Or an x-ray, perhaps?" She wished Paul were here, as she was sure he'd know. "Anyway, be careful where you point it."

Ack-Ack Macaque gave a gleeful simian grin. "Yes, boss."

She turned. "Hey, Cole. Have you ever seen anything like this?"

The writer looked up from wringing his hands. "What?" He stood upright, and shuffled over. "What is it?"

"A ray gun," Ack-Ack Macaque said.

"Let me see." Cole snatched the gun from the monkey's hand, and glowered at it. He turned it over and over in his hands. His tongue poked into the side of his cheek as he inhaled a long breath. "Ray gun, indeed." He stopped turning it and held it by the grip, forefinger resting on the trigger guard. He extended his arm and closed his left eye, drawing a bead on the futon.

"Be careful," Victoria said.

He turned to her. "I'm not an idiot."

"I never said you were..." Victoria trailed off. It was quite obvious that Cole had stopped listening to her. His eyes were focused on something she couldn't see: a thousand yard stare into the middle distance. His lips were working soundlessly, opening and closing, forming words she couldn't hear. The breath rasped in and out of his nostrils. "Uh, Cole?" He didn't react, and gave no signs of having heard her. She put a hand to his shoulder, and he went rigid. She could see beads of sweat forming at his temples. "What's happening? What's the matter?" She turned to Ack-Ack Macaque. "Is he having a fit?"

"How the hell would I know?"

Cole let out a moan. Every limb shook, and she thought he would fall. Then whatever was holding him seemed to relax its grip, and he sagged instead.

"I have to go." His voice was hoarse.

"Go? Go where?"

"Get away from me." He shook her off angrily. "I'm not waiting around here to be killed. I've got to go. Got to get out."

Holding the pistol at waist height, he blundered backwards until he stood in the open doorway.

Ack-Ack Macaque made to follow.

"Hey, Cole, wait."

The writer brandished the strange pistol in the monkey's face.

"Stay back!" His eyes were manic-looking slits. His lips were drawn back from his teeth. As Victoria watched, his knuckle whitened on the trigger. The shot drilled a smouldering hole through the top of Ack-Ack Macaque's fedora. "Stay back, or I'll kill you both!"

THEY LISTENED TO the American's footsteps clump down the stairs.

Ack-Ack Macaque turned to Victoria. "Should I go after him?" He had his hat in his hand, one finger exploring the charred puncture. The beam had burned its way in at the front, and out at the back, singeing a few hairs on the top of the monkey's head.

Victoria waved him on. "Yes, but be careful."

"What about you?" He flexed his leathery fingers, and drew one of the silver Colts from beneath his coat. "No offence, but I can probably move faster without you."

Downstairs, they heard the front door bang.

Victoria didn't have the energy for a chase. She couldn't keep up with the monkey, and she knew it. "I'll get a taxi back to the *Tereshkova,* and do some digging around. Find out if Cole had a twin, that sort of thing. Meanwhile, you and K8 find Cole and get him into the car. Call me when you're on your way back."

The monkey touched the barrel of the revolver to his brow. "Right-o."

"And Ack-Ack?"

"Yes, boss?"

"Try not to blow anything up."

CHAPTER NINE
THE MEN IN WHITE

WILLIAM'S HEART WAS a hunk of uranium: hot, heavy and crackling with toxicity.

Crashing out of the house, he turned right, and ran along the street until he reached an area with shops and bright lights. The boulangeries, patisseries, newsagents and offices were closing, and the pubs were filling up for the night. Rickshaws cut between the cars and vans; three-wheeled tuk-tuks chuntered past, farting petrol fumes. As he blundered past an open door, he got a whiff of stale beer, a blast of warm air and jukebox music.

Seeing the handwritten notes had shaken him. Up until that point, he'd been clinging to the idea that—however unlikely and fantastical it all seemed after four days without sleep—there would be a rational, mundane explanation for the sudden appearance of his doppelganger. Seeing the handwriting had changed all that. His understanding of the world had been shaken, and now all he wanted to do was flee.

Flee from the strangeness, and from the people who were out to kill him.

He didn't know what he could trust, or who he could count on. All he knew for sure was that somebody wanted him dead.

Marie, he thought. *Bill told me she'd help. And if there's a chance she's alive, anywhere or anyhow, I have to find her.* Wild hope surged against entrenched grief, and his legs wobbled beneath him. His knees felt soft like butter, and he couldn't remember the last time he'd eaten. He was empty. For the past four days, before boarding the *Tereshkova,* his body had been living off its own fat reserves while the speed quashed his appetite.

At a street corner, momentarily overcome by dizziness, he fell against the cast iron shaft of a Victorian-style lamppost.

How could his wife be both alive and dead? And which was the real Marie? And why had reality stopped making sense?

Parallel worlds?

Talking monkeys?

Car bombs?

Clinging on, he screwed his eyes tight. How could he comprehend any of this right now? As a habitual amphetamine user, he was used to a certain amount of craziness; but nothing on this scale, nothing of this magnitude. Like a frightened child, he wanted to run and lose himself in darkness and endless movement, until the world dwindled to a speck far behind him, and all its dangers and terrors were lost in his wake.

Releasing his grip on the lamppost, he blundered forward through a blur of pale faces. His eyeballs seemed to throb in time with his breathing.

In the past, when he'd been afraid to sleep, when his brain cells crackled with coffee and speed and he found himself gibbering at his keyboard at 3am, his hands shaking too violently to type, his peripheral vision itching with half-glimpsed phantasms; when the chemicals got too much; when paranoia or depression knocked the wind out of him or the walls of his room tried to engulf him like the petals of a carnivorous plant—when all that happened, he'd known where to turn. There'd always been one person who could straighten him out; one person who could claw him back onto solid ground. When he needed someone to talk him down and help him get his shit together, he called his dealer, Sparky.

Yeah, he thought, *that's what I'll do. I'll go and see Sparky. He lives near here. He'll help me. I need to hole up somewhere and ride this out. He'll understand, and maybe he'll have something to straighten me out. A few dabs of the good stuff on my gums, maybe, just to take the edge off.*

He staggered onwards, trying to ignore the looks of the passers-by, and straightened his collar, smoothed down his wild hair. His head spun and his innards writhed like hooked eels, but at least he had a direction. He had a goal. Like a drowning man reaching for a lifebelt, he knew what he needed, and where to get it. He was going to see a familiar face, and he was going to clear his head. Only speed could give him the clarity needed to cope with everything that had been happening; and Sparky's place was as good a bolthole as any.

Yes, he thought, *I'll go find Sparky. Good old Sparky. He'll fix me up.*

BY THE TIME he reached the block of student flats where Sparky lived, stumbling and cursing all the way, he'd begun to feel calmer, and more rational. As quickly as it had come, the panic passed, leaving him washed-out like a beach at low tide. In the aftermath of its onslaught, the events of the day seemed less overpowering, and more like the leftover hallucinations of a particularly vivid dream.

Panting for breath, he stood in the shadow of the gnarled trees at the edge of the square, looking up at the rectangle of Sparky's fourth-floor window, wondering if the car bomb and his doppelganger had all been part of some kind of fit—perhaps the result of a seizure, or maybe even the first stirrings of a brain tumour?

Was he having some sort of paranoid breakdown?

Was he going mad?

His hands trembled with the fear that he might, at any moment and without warning, slip back down that rabbit hole of delusion and madness. He could feel it there, like a dark sea beneath the icy crust of his sanity, just waiting to draw him in.

The cold air felt sharp and real on his cheeks and fingers. He tried to concentrate on it as he scratched his beard. Above, the light was on in Sparky's room. He knew he should go back to the house, try to find Captain Valois and the monkey, and apologise—but that light was warm and familiar. Looking at it, he could almost smell the flat's familiar mingled fug of chickpea curry and hash smoke. What would it hurt if he popped up for a few minutes? Sparky would be pleased to see him. The guy was pleased to see everybody. And maybe he'd have a few samples for his favourite customer?

Maybe enough, William thought, *to give me a little clarity?*

Clarity was what he needed now, more than anything; clarity, and the strength to stop himself coming apart at the seams. But he couldn't do it alone. He was too tired, too strung-out. He needed a little chemical pick-me-up. He could always make his way back to the *Tereshkova* afterwards. He could get a taxi. The speed would give him the energy and the nerve to do it. It would straighten him out, and hold him together.

He stepped out of the trees, onto the road. The buildings around the square were tall Georgian townhouses, fronted in pale stone. They had steps up to their front doors, and steps down to their basements. Some had wrought iron balconies, and several had been converted into offices, or subdivided into flats. He looked left and right. Two men stood at the corner of the square, watching him. They wore long white raincoats, white fedoras, and matching gloves. Even their shoes were white.

William frowned. They were dressed the way he thought angels might dress; yet something about them seemed to radiate menace.

"William Cole?" They spoke in unison. Startled, he stepped back, away from the light.

"Who are you?" He didn't feel up to talking. All he wanted was to get inside, and get fixed up.

The one on the left spoke.

"I am Mister Reynolds, and this is Mister Bailey. We knew you'd come, eventually, and we've been waiting."

Cole took another step back. They watched him with expressionless calm.

"What do you want?"

"We want you to come with us."

"Where?" He was playing for time, shuffling back towards the shops and crowds on the streets beyond the square. Moving in step, they kept pace.

"You know where," Reynolds said.

He blinked at them.

"What?"

"Don't try to stall us, Cole. You cannot change what must happen." Without breaking stride, they opened the left sides of their white coats, revealing ivory-handled pistols. Seeing them, William wanted to turn and flee, but his knees were still weak, and he knew he couldn't outrun a bullet. Instead, he fumbled in his pockets, until his fingers closed on the gun he'd taken from Bill's house.

Seeing what he was doing, the men in white drew their pistols in one smooth, coordinated sweep, and aimed them at his head.

"Don't try to pull that out," Reynolds warned.

With his hand still in his pocket, William felt for the trigger. He could hardly breathe.

"We wanted you to come with us, Cole," Bailey said.

"But if you're going to be awkward," Reynolds finished, "we'll have to shoot you where you stand."

Side-by-side, their gun barrels stared at him like the soulless, empty sockets of a metal skull.

In his pocket, his finger closed on the trigger, but he made no move to pull out his hand. Instead, heart squirming in his chest, he squeezed, firing through the material of his coat. Mister Bailey gave a grunt, as if he'd been punched, and dropped to his knees, pawing feebly at a charred spot on his chest. Reynolds looked down at him in confusion. Moving as if in a dream, William turned his hips and fired again. Reynolds yelped, and his gun clattered to the floor as his hands went to the pencil-thin hole speared through his left thigh. Without even thinking, William had fired twice through the lining of his coat into the two men in white. The beam had burned through their skin and bone as easily as it had through paper.

And it had set light to the fabric of his coat. With his hands beating at the flames, and his nostrils filled with the stink of bonfires, he turned and ran for all he was worth.

TECHSNARK
BLOGGING WITH ATTITUDE

Legion of the Bland?

Posted: 08/11/2060 – 16:00 GMT
| Share |

Wave of the future, or totalitarian techno terror? Whatever your opinion on the white-suited Californian cult, one thing's for certain: the 'Gestalt' is here to stay.

Since its inception a mere two years ago, the cult's grown at an unprecedented, and some would say alarming, rate. Their website boasts more than a million linked-up members across the world and, just yesterday, they petitioned the United Nations in New York, demanding to be recognised as a sovereign nation—a nation without geographical or ethnic boundaries.

Adherents to the faith use adapted soul-catcher technology to broadcast every thought and image in their heads to every other member of the cult. They can 'hear' what each other is thinking, twenty-four hours a day, three hundred and sixty-five days per year; and they claim this makes them the ultimate democracy, with 100% participation in every decision. Human language is, they argue, too limited and imprecise a medium to truly and reliably communicate the complexities of our innermost nature; only by linking brains, they say, can we fully engage in meaningful discourse.

According to its literature, the Gestalt cult aims to create a 'global consciousness' and free humanity from the hatreds and conflicts that have dogged its history. And yet, despite all this techno-utopianism, the individual members (if they can still be described as 'individual' in any meaningful sense) exhibit a disappointing blandness—the complacent vacuity of born-again converts whose troublesome personalities have been sterilised in the name of conformity. Yes, they seem happy but, speaking personally, I don't trust them. There's something sinister about the way they move and talk in unison. I grew up believing in freedom and individualism, but the men and women of the Gestalt seem dedicated to wiping out every quirk and foible, turning us all into mindless drones. They might wear white, but don't let that fool you. Beneath that smiling, angelic exterior, they're no better than ants in a nest or bees in a hive.

Read more | Like | Comment | Share

CHAPTER TEN
UGLY SONOFABITCH

THE DOWNS WERE an expanse of green parkland that ran along the lip of the Avon Gorge, sandwiched between its cliffs on one side and the city on the other. They ran a couple of miles downstream from the Suspension Bridge, eventually blurring into the leafy avenues of Sneyd Park and Henleaze. Having left the house, Ack-Ack Macaque figured Cole would have come this way, trying to lose himself in the darkness beyond the streetlights; but, so far, all he'd found had been a pair of urban fox cubs rooting through a bin, a drunken reveller asleep on the grass, and a misted-up car full of dope-smoking teenagers listening to Parisian techno.

Freed from the encumbrance of his overcoat, which he'd stashed beneath a park bench, and wearing only a t-shirt and holsters, he moved like a wraith through the cold November night, scampering on all fours from one clump of trees to the next, his breath steaming like cigar smoke from his mouth. Most of the Downs had been given over to rough grassland, and he tried to stick to the overgrown areas, hoping that if anyone saw him, they might mistake him in the dark for a dog.

From certain vantages, he could see right down into the bowl of the city. Bristol nestled around the old harbour side, where tall ships had once tied up, carrying tobacco and slaves, bringing in the wealth that had paid for much of the city's construction. Those docks had been a major global port; a hub of commerce and piracy; and the jumping off point for expeditions to far-flung lands of unexplored exotica. Now, all he could see down there were the glittering hologram signs that strutted and danced above the nightclubs and restaurants, and the advertising blimps drifting like goldfish between the church spires and high-rise hotels of the city centre—from which the surrounding districts spread, clinging to the sides of the ancient arterial roads like frost accumulating around the strands of a spider's web.

Like a dog, he was trying to pick up the writer's scent, but the smells of the city were too strong. They came drifting across with the omnipresent buzz of traffic and the occasional wailing siren. The ground around him smelled of moss and dog shit. The wind brought the oniony tang of fast food from the streets at the edge of the park, and animal scents from the nearby zoo; and, he had to admit, all those cigars hadn't done his sense of smell any favours. Nevertheless, he kept searching until his SincPhone rang.

"What?"

"It's me, boss." K8 sounded annoyingly perky. "I'm parked across from the flat."

"I'm not there anymore."

"I know, Captain Valois told me. Have you found Cole?"

"What the fuck do you think?"

"No sign, huh?"

Ack-Ack Macaque looked at the orange streetlamps, and the lit windows of the shops and houses, wondering if he'd made the right call. He'd assumed Cole would have made for the cover of trees and darkness; but maybe that was his own instinct talking. What if the old guy had gone into the city instead, trying to lose himself in the crowd? "A city this size, he could vanish forever."

"Do you think he might have jumped off the bridge?" K8's tone held the ghoulish delight of a teenager. "I hear people do that sometimes."

"Nah." Ack-Ack Macaque let his free hand drop to the gun at his side. "He was frightened, not suicidal." His leathery fingers drummed against the holster, and he scanned the horizon. "I just keep wondering: if I were an unstable, gun-toting psychopath, where would I go?"

K8 laughed. "You *are* an unstable, gun-toting psychopath."

Ack-Ack Macaque harrumphed. He was about to end the call—his thumb was actually on the button—when she took a sharp intake of breath. He heard the Mercedes' leather seat creak beneath her as she wriggled lower.

"What is it?" he asked, all humour gone. "What's happening?"

"A car just pulled up." Her voice had dropped to a breathless whisper. "A guy got out. Now he's letting himself into the flat. The car's leaving."

Ack-Ack Macaque looked around at the empty park. "Is he a cop?"

"I don't think so. That wasn't a police car, and the guy at the door doesn't look like a policeman. He's big and ugly-looking, and I think he means business."

Ack-Ack Macaque huffed. Tonight was supposed to have been a party night, and here he was, chasing a madman on a common when he could have been lying drunk under a table somewhere. "Okay, I'll be with you in a couple of minutes. Keep your head down until then. Don't let them see you."

"You don't need to tell me twice, Skip." Even over the phone, her excitement was palpable.

He sighed. Teenagers...

"Just do it, fuckwit."

HE RETRIEVED HIS coat and hat, and retraced his steps. When he reached the house, he saw the Mercedes parked at the opposite kerb, in the shadow of the Avon Gorge Hotel. He opened the passenger door and slid in beside her.

"Is he still up there?" He couldn't see any lights behind the first floor windows.

"No-one's come out yet."

He dumped his hat and coat onto the back seat, and hunched down beside her, with his feet pressed against the dashboard. "If he's sitting in there in the dark, I'd guess he's planning to jump somebody."

"The dead guy?"

Ack-Ack Macaque pulled out one of his Colts and checked the cylinder. "Chances are, he already knows he's dead. I'm guessing he had something to do with it, and now he's come back to stake out this place." All six shells were where they should have been, so he snapped the cylinder back into place, and re-holstered the gun.

"But why?" K8 wriggled closer to him. "Who's he waiting for?"

"Cole."

Her eyes widened. "Cole?"

"Somebody tried to kill him, then his double turned up dead." He pulled out his second revolver, and flicked it open. "The two events have to be connected."

"But why would big-and-ugly in there expect Cole to come here?" A furrow appeared between K8's eyebrows. She may have been exceptionally bright when it came to computers and electronic systems but, like most teenagers, adult motivations were still largely a mystery to her.

"He did though, didn't he?" Ack-Ack Macaque glanced at the copper shells nestling in the second gun. All six were present and correct, which meant he had twelve shots altogether, should he need them.

"Yes." K8's frown deepened. "But that's because we brought him with us."

Ack-Ack Macaque returned the second gun to its holster and cracked his hairy knuckles.

"In which case, as far as the bloke in there's concerned, we're Cole's allies."

K8 wriggled lower in her seat. She had a flick knife in her sock, and a small Beretta in the glove box.

"Skipper, all that stuff Cole was saying about parallel universes?"

"Sounded like bullshit to me."

"You don't think it's possible?"

"I haven't a clue." Ack-Ack Macaque scratched his belly beneath the t-shirt. "Just remember he writes science fiction. Those guys are all nuts. They've all got a screw loose somewhere."

K8 jerked a thumb at the unlit window. "So, who do you think our friend is?"

Ack-Ack Macaque let his lips peel back over his yellow incisors. "There's only one way to find out."

"Does it involve violence, by any chance?"

"Hell, yeah." He reached for the door. "You stay here, I'll grab him, and we can beat it out of him."

IN THE OLD days, back in the game, he wouldn't have thought twice about kicking down the front door and going in with both guns blazing. It was his style, his *modus operandi*. But he wasn't in the game anymore; oh no, those days were long gone, along with his invulnerability. He wasn't bulletproof anymore. Like it or not, over the past months, he'd had to get used to operating in the real world. Out here, actions had consequences, and injuries were real. He'd had to learn that the hard way. He'd had to wise up and find a way to temper his natural recklessness.

So, now, despite being tempted to mount a screeching frontal assault on the flat, he instead made his way around to the back of the building, where the waste water pipes from all the sinks and toilets clung to the outside wall like a giant, multi-limbed stick insect. If the building were alive, these pipes would be its digestive system. He had to climb over some bins to reach them. The main pipe was about the width of his thigh, and moulded from some kind of hard black plastic. Hardly breaking stride, he wrapped his hands and feet around it, and began to climb.

Reaching the first floor took a few seconds. A tributary pipe branched off, disappearing into the wall beneath the frosted glass of a bathroom window. Hanging by one hand from the main pipe, he stretched for the windowsill. The height didn't bother him; he was only about twenty feet up, and, in his time, he'd scaled much taller trees. Having made the sill, he saw that the window came in two parts: ones which opened outward like a door, and the other, smaller one above it, which hinged upwards like a flap. Right now, only the smaller one was open.

Clinging to the sill by his toes, he reached in and carefully unlatched the bigger window. Then he was inside, perched on the edge of a ceramic sink in a darkened bathroom no bigger than a large closet. His nostrils twitched at the damp reek of mouthwash, hair product and black mould. And there, behind it all, something else: a trace of something unfamiliar, something that hadn't been in the flat earlier; something that smelled of wet hair and stale, almost oniony sweat. Whoever this guy was, he smelled more like an ape than a human.

Leaving the window open behind him, Ack-Ack Macaque dropped silently to the floor and reached for the door handle with his left hand. As he did so, he drew one of his pistols with his right. If he wanted to get the jump on the guy in the flat, he had to be stealthy.

Like a motherfucking ninja, he thought to himself. But the door fittings were old. As he gently tugged the handle, the hinges squeaked. The living room light snapped on, and he found himself staring down the barrel of a fat silencer.

So much for stealth.

He leapt back and slammed the door, and dropped to the bathroom's tiled floor. Muffled shots blew splinters from the door panels and spanged off the sink, spraying him with chips. He rolled onto his back and fired both Colts through the gap between his feet. Three times he squeezed the triggers. In the enclosed space, the noise was thunderous. When he'd finished, most of the lower half of the door was gone.

Groans came from the other room. Ack-Ack Macaque slid his arse across the tiles, and kicked the remains of the door from its hinges.

"Anybody alive out there?"

No reply came; at least, none that he could hear. His ears felt as if spikes had been driven into them.

He had to move fast. Firstly, he knew K8 would have heard his shots, and he didn't want her blundering up here, not until he was sure it was safe. Secondly, half the city had probably heard them too, and he had no doubt the police would be on their way.

Standing, he edged around the doorframe, guns held out in front of him, ready to empty the rest of his bullets into anything that moved.

His shots had scythed through the flat at shin height, splintering wood, cloth and bone. Now, a thick-set man lay curled around a bloody leg wound, trying to stem the flow of blood from where a clean, white shard of bone stuck out from the back of his calf.

Ack-Ack Macaque pointed both revolvers at the man's head.

"Drop the gun, sweetheart," he said. The man glared up at him from under a heavy brow, and he did a double take. When K8 had told him that the guy was ugly, she hadn't been kidding. The man—if indeed he was a man—had a large, bulbous nose, with cavernous, hairy nostrils; his stubble-covered lower jaw seemed too large for his face, and his shovel-like teeth too numerous for his mouth. With one over-sized hand still clamped over the wound in his leg, he tried to raise his gun; but Ack-Ack Macaque sprang forward and stamped on the weapon, forcing the tip of the silencer into the floor. "I said, drop it, dickhead." He slammed the butt of one of his Colts into the man's temple. The man's head snapped sideways, hit the wall with a smack, and he slumped to the floor unconscious.

For a few moments, the only sound Ack-Ack Macaque could hear in the flat was the sound of his own panting breath. He holstered the gun in his left hand, but kept the right one drawn, in case of trouble. Then he bent over to take a look at his fallen opponent. The guy wasn't particularly tall, but he had powerful, muscular arms, broad shoulders, and a barrel-shaped chest. He wore a shabby overcoat and a cheap brown suit. The ridge on his forehead was far more pronounced than it had first appeared; and his unusually large jaw and protruding chin made his face look as if it had been somehow pulled forward.

"Ugly sonofabitch, aren't you?" Keeping the Colt aimed at the guy's face, he slipped a hand inside the raincoat, looking for a wallet, or anything that might identify who—or what—he might be. As he rummaged, he heard the front door slam, and the sound of shoes on the stairs. His SincPhone rang, but he didn't answer it. Instead, he stood up and faced the open door, gun at the ready.

A couple of seconds later, Cole stood swaying at the threshold. His eyes were wide, and he was out of breath. His coat had a blackened hole in it.

"Monkey?" The word was a croak from dry lips.

Ack-Ack Macaque raised his revolver.

"Don't move, fucknuts."

But Cole didn't seem to hear him. Without another word, the writer lurched forward, and collapsed into his arms.

CHAPTER ELEVEN
ANDROGYNOUS SEVERITY

VICTORIA VALOIS RETURNED to the *Tereshkova* by helicopter. More than two years had passed since her helicopter crash in the South Atlantic, and yet she still thought about it every time she climbed into one, remembering the helplessness and terror that had possessed her as the ailing craft hit the slate grey sea and started to sink. The raised scar on her temple served as a constant reminder that she'd been lucky not to die in the accident—that she'd only survived thanks to the gelware that had been used to replace the damaged areas of her brain.

Now, when the helicopter from Bristol touched down safely on the pad fixed to the *Tereshkova*'s upper surface, she felt her clenched fingers and toes relax. Today had been a long day, and she was ready for a hot shower and a good night's sleep, but she knew she'd get neither for a while yet—not with her professional curiosity aroused and prowling, hungry for answers.

Moving slowly, she made her way down through the hatch that led into the body of the skyliner. A flight of metal stairs took her down past one of the main gasbags, to a draughty walkway that ran the length of the *Tereshkova*'s central hull—almost a full kilometre in length. If she felt the need, she could walk all the way to bow or stern, past storage areas housing passenger luggage, freight, and essential supplies; additional gas bags; and a thousand other nooks and crannies containing who knew what. For thirty years, the *Tereshkova* had been the Commodore's private fiefdom, filled with souvenirs and trophies from a life hard lived and dearly sold; it had been his home and his attic, and now it was hers, and she didn't have the heart to start rooting through its alcoves, chucking out his stuff.

A series of companionways took her down through another four levels, until she reached the one that led down to the main gondola. She could hear piano music swirling up from the passenger lounge, where a cocktail pianist tinkled on an electronic keyboard, and smell the remnants of the evening's dinner from the kitchen. Her head was bare, and the top two buttons of her tunic undone. As she clomped down the grille metal steps, she saw someone waiting for her at the bottom. At first, she could only see their shoes; then their baggy cargo pants. The build and stance looked familiar but, for a second, she couldn't place it. Then she spotted the tattoos on the figure's arms, and her heart bucked in her chest like a startled horse.

"Paul?"

She took the last couple of steps in a daze, and there he was, waiting for her with a stupid grin plastered across his face.

"Do you like it?"

She couldn't let go of the metal banister. Paul was dead; he'd been murdered, and his brain had been removed; she'd seen the body, been at the funeral; and now all that was left of him was the electronic copy of his mind that lived in the *Tereshkova*'s computer. And yet here he was, standing before her, as apparently solid and alive as she was.

"I don't understand. What's going on?"

He held up a hand.

"Don't freak out, Vic."

"I'm not freaking out, I'm just—" She stopped, and narrowed her eyes. Then, very slowly, she pressed her hand into his chest. Her fingers passed through the material of his garish Hawaiian shirt without resistance, and pushed in up to the wrist. "You're a hologram?" Her heart sank. For a moment she'd allowed herself to hope that, however unlikely it might seem, he'd found a way to reincarnate himself. Now she knew what she was looking at, it became obvious he was a projection: a little pixelation here, a little blurriness there.

"Yeah, pretty good, don't you think?"

She pulled her hand back, feeling her breathing slow, and her pulse return to normal.

"How do you do it?"

He gave a modest shrug. "I had the idea while you were away, and got one of the mechanics to cobble it together for me." He pointed at his feet. "There's a little remote controlled car down here on the floor, with a tiny projector mounted on it. I control it using the skyliner's WiFi, and I use cameras on the front to see where it's going."

"Wow. That's pretty good. I have to admit, you had me there for a second." She bent down and reached into the image of his trainers. Her hands closed around something hard, and she pulled it out. His image flickered and died, and she found herself holding a toy car. It was around twenty centimetres in length, with fat rubber tyres and several projection lenses protruding from its roof. A tiny camera sat on its bonnet.

"Sorry if I startled you." Paul's voice came from a speaker bolted to the side of the car. Victoria turned the vehicle over, looking at the wiring.

"So, what's the range on this thing?"

"It can go anywhere on this deck."

"Only this deck?" Victoria bent at the knees, and placed the little car back on the floor. When she straightened up, Paul's image reappeared, looking almost as deceptively solid as before.

"I haven't found a way to make it climb stairs yet." He looked down at his hands. "It's just a prototype. Perhaps I'll build the next version into a little remote-controlled helicopter or something. Maybe one of those floating cameras, like the one the monkey smashed. Or maybe one of those quad copter drones, they look pretty cool."

"So, are you in there?"

"I'm still in the ship. This is just a remote. But it has the capacity. I could download into it if I needed to." He shrugged. "Anyway, how did it go for you? Did you find any clues?"

"We lost Cole."

"You lost him? You mean he's—?"

"No, he's not dead. He just ran off."

"Where'd he go?"

"I don't know." Victoria's eyes felt suddenly tired. She pinched the bridge of her nose between thumb and forefinger. "I sent the monkey to find him."

"Was that wise?"

"Damned if I know."

Paul took off his glasses. "I don't understand why you have to be involved." He wiped the lenses on the hem of his brightly patterned shirt. "Why don't you turn the case over to the local *federales*, and be done with it?"

Victoria stretched.

"Things have been a bit sedate around here recently, and I need a change of pace."

"Let me guess, you're just a simple journo at heart, right?"

Victoria pushed her fists into her pockets. "What can I say? I miss that stuff."

"Things have changed."

"You don't need to remind me." The helicopter accident had put an end to her career as a writer, but the old urges were still there, and she couldn't walk away from a mystery.

She made to step around Paul's ghost but, as she did so, he held up a hand to stop her.

"Hold on."

She paused. "What is it?" He was made entirely of light. If she wanted to, she could walk right through him; but, somehow, to do so seemed impolite.

"It looks as if you were followed."

"What do you mean?"

"There was a stowaway on your chopper. She was in the luggage compartment at the back. God knows how she got in there."

Victoria's tiredness vanished. "Where is she now?"

"I've got her on camera. She's making her way down one of the service ladders."

"Where's she going?"

"Looks like the accommodation section."

Victoria hurried through the lounge, along the connecting corridor, and into her office. Paul's image followed, the little battery-powered car whining as it kept pace. "Anyone we know?"

"Apparently not."

She shrugged off her tunic and sat behind the desk. "Have you run her face against the passenger manifest?"

"First thing I did."

"And you got nothing?"

"Well, duh."

"Show me." A few years ago, the Commodore had installed a SincPad in the top of the desk. Being unable to read, Victoria usually kept it switched off, using its glass screen as little more than a surface on which to rest her elbows. Now, for the first time in months, the display brightened into life, showing a grainy black and white feed from a camera in the corridor outside the crew's quarters. A slim, black-clad and obviously female figure was trying to jimmy the door to Cole's cabin. "Is this live?"

"Yes, it's happening right now." Paul reached up to fiddle with the gold stud in his ear. "How do you wish to respond?"

Victoria peered at the picture. She didn't know who this woman was but, as there'd already been one murder on the airship, she wasn't about to take any chances.

"Get some crew down there. Make sure they're armed, and have her brought to me."

"Aye-aye, Captain."

*   *   *

VICTORIA WATCHED THE screen as three of her stewards approached the intruder. By this time, the woman had gained access to the cabin, and was crouched over Cole's luggage, her hands rummaging through its contents. She froze when she heard the stewards in the corridor outside. Then, when they pushed the door open, she backed up against the wall, hands spread flat against it, ready to spring.

"Don't move," Paul said. Although his image stood at the side of Victoria's desk, she knew his consciousness—if you could call it that—still lurked in the skyliner's computer systems, where it could monitor everything that happened on board, and that his voice was being relayed to the woman in the cabin via the intercom system. "We have you surrounded. There's nowhere to go."

On the screen, Victoria saw the woman glance upwards. Her eyes found the CCTV camera, and she smiled. It was a smile of recognition, and resignation. Without taking her eyes from the lens, she relaxed her stance, and raised her hands.

"We've got her," Paul said.

Victoria watched the stewards cuff her, and then switched off the screen. She sat back and pulled the Commodore's cutlass from the umbrella stand.

"Tell them to bring her straight here."

"Have done."

Paul walked to the picture window that took up most of the wall behind the desk. Patting the flat of the blade against her palm, Victoria turned in her chair and looked out, trying to imagine what he was seeing through the little camera stuck to the front of the toy car supporting his image.

Beyond the window, she could see the whale-like undersides of the *Tereshkova*'s hulls, and the lit windows and red and green running lights of the other gondolas. Below, at the edge of the airfield, a motorway cut southwards like a ribbon of orange light. She could see cars and trucks skimming its surface. Further away, the lights of the two Severn crossings, their humped backs carrying other motorways westward across the river, into Wales.

Although she'd been here a few times over the years, this wasn't a part of the country she knew well. Nevertheless, it felt good to be back in England. However far the skyliner took her, the United Kingdom of France, Great Britain, Northern Ireland and Norway would always be her home—and she guessed Paul felt much the same.

He watched as she placed the cutlass on the desk and retrieved her white tunic. The shiny buttons were large and easy to fasten in a hurry. When she'd finished, she stood straight and looked at her reflection in the glass of the window: a tall woman in a military jacket, her bald, scarred head and strong-boned face lending her a handsome, almost androgynous severity.

She heard footsteps in the hall, and Paul said, "The stewards are outside."

With a tug, she straightened the hem of the tunic. Then she picked up the cutlass and stuck it through her sash. "How do I look?"

"Totally badass."

She smiled despite herself. "Then, I guess you'd better let them in."

HALF-CARRYING THE half-conscious Cole, Ack-Ack Macaque staggered out of the building's door. Across the street, K8 was in trouble. A couple of uglies had pulled open the door of the Mercedes and were trying to haul her from the car. They were short and stocky, just like the one he'd left in the apartment above, and he wondered again who—or what—they were.

"No time for guessing," he muttered. Inside the car, K8 scratched and bit at the hands that clawed at her. Thrashing like a trapped animal, she tried to reach the gun she'd stashed in the glove box, but the uglies were strong, with big hands, and seemed impervious to her blows. As he watched, she let fly with a kick that would have broken the arm of a normal man.

"Get away from me, you creeps!"

With his left hand still supporting Cole, Ack-Ack Macaque drew one of his Colts and put a bullet through the nearest of her attackers. The report was loud in the empty street, and he winced at the stab of pain from his already-damaged ears. The guy he'd hit fell against the car, and then slid down to the tarmac. He had a bullet in the spine. If he lived, he'd never walk again.

Ack-Ack Macaque gave a grunt.

"That'll teach you to pick on kids."

The remaining attacker let go of K8 and spun around. He had the same thick brow ridge and protruding lower jaw as the others. Like them, he reminded Ack-Ack Macaque of a hairless gorilla.

"Hold it right there, Delilah." Ack-Ack Macaque waved the Colt at him. "Step away from the irate teenager." He glanced at K8. She had a split lip, and her sleeve was torn. "You okay, kid?"

"I've had worse." She climbed out of the car and came over and took Cole from him. As she helped the writer into the back seat of the car, Ack-Ack Macaque kicked the dead thug aside, and led the other around to the rear of the vehicle, where he popped the boot.

"Get in." The ape-man scowled, and shook his head, stance defiant. Ack-Ack Macaque let his fangs show. "Don't fuck with me, Tinkerbell. I've already shot two of your friends tonight. No reason I shouldn't make it three."

He heard sirens: distant now, but closing fast. In minutes, the place would be swarming with police. If this lunkhead wouldn't move, there was only one thing he could do.

"Don't say I didn't warn you." He squeezed the trigger and the Colt leapt in his hand. The shot bit a bloody chunk from the man's thigh. As he bent in pain, Ack-Ack Macaque brought the gun barrel up in a vicious swing that caught him under his over-sized chin, knocking him back into the waiting trunk.

The sirens were close now. Ack-Ack Macaque grabbed the man's dangling legs and stuffed them inside. "Try not to bleed on the upholstery," he said, and slammed the boot shut. "How are we doing, K8?"

Cole had been laid out across the back seat, still insensible. K8 closed the door and hopped into the front seat.

"Get in, Skipper." She turned the key and the engine boomed to life. Ack-Ack Macaque bounded onto the roof, and slid over to the passenger side. The door was open, and he swung in. He was still closing it when she let the brake off, and the big Mercedes leapt forward, throwing him back in his seat.

WITH THE PEDAL pressed firmly to the metal, and a mile-wide grin on her face, K8 flung them through a maze of narrow terrace streets. She had one eye on the road, the other on the Sat Nav screen. Her hands and feet moved in sharp, precise jabs, spinning the wheel and stamping the brake, then the accelerator. In the seat next to her, Ack-Ack Macaque clung to his armrest. As they slithered around a particularly tight turn, the wing mirror on his side splintered, snatched away by the rear light of a parked car.

"Jeez!"

K8's grin grew wider than ever. She was obviously having the time of her life. The car moved like an extension of her will.

"Drive it like you stole it, Skip."

She gunned the gas again, and they tore down a steep, tree-lined hill, at the bottom of which, Ack-Ack Macaque saw a busy main road. His fingers dug into the armrest but, just before they reached the junction, K8 stood on the brakes, and the heavy Mercedes squealing to a stop.

In the sudden silence, K8 cracked her knuckles and smiled at him. The air smelled of burned rubber.

"I think we're out of trouble," she said, glancing in the rear view mirror. "And, fun as that was, we'd better stop drawing attention to ourselves."

She changed gear and pulled out into the traffic. Keeping to the speed limit, she drove the big Mercedes along the road, which ran alongside the city docks. Across the water, Ack-Ack Macaque saw the masts and floodlit prow of Brunel's *SS Great Britain*—the first iron-hulled steamship to brave the Atlantic, and a direct ancestor to the *Tereshkova* and all the other skyliners now plying the trade routes of the world. Nervously, he looked behind them, but saw no flashing blue lights. They were just one car among dozens now, going with the flow.

During the violent manoeuvres, Cole had been thrown from the back seat and now lay sprawled across the floor, with his head in one of the foot wells and his legs in the other. Ack-Ack Macaque decided to leave him there. He swivelled back to face the front, and stuck a finger in his ear. Firing his guns in the enclosed space of the bathroom had been a bad idea. He could have burst an eardrum. As it was, who knew what long-term damage he'd done to his hearing? At the moment, everything sounded muffled, as if he'd stuck gum in his ears, and waggling his finger in the hole brought no relief, no matter how hard he did it.

"Everything okay, Skipper?"

"Huh?"

"I said, are you okay?"

He sniffed the tip of his finger, and then slipped it into his mouth.

"Nothing serious," he said around the taste of the earwax. "Just a little deaf from the gunshots." He tried to sound cavalier, but the truth was he couldn't get away from the thought that, like the grey hairs around his muzzle, the damage to his ears was a sign that he was as mortal as anyone else—something he'd never had to worry about when he'd been immersed in the game, back before Merovech and friends busted him out of the Céleste Tech labs; back when he'd been the indestructible WWII flying ace, and all he'd had to worry about were enemy planes and banana shortages; back where guns never jammed, parachutes always opened, and the skies were forever a bright, brilliant blue.

They passed office blocks and bus stops. At the end of the road, K8 took a left up Park Street to avoid the city centre. The shops on the hill were arranged in a neatly stepped terrace, at the top of which the dramatic Neo-Gothic tower of the Wills Memorial Building loomed over the university.

Ack-Ack Macaque watched the reflection of the Mercedes as it flickered from one shop window to the next. He still wore only his t-shirt and ammo belt, and found himself wishing for the warmth of his flight jacket, which he'd left in his cabin, back on the *Tereshkova*. His coat and fedora were folded on the back seat, but he didn't like them as much as he liked the jacket. It had been a present from K8. She'd also given him a matching leather flying cap and a pair of goggles. They were the same as the ones he'd worn in the game; and that was the whole point. The outfit was his brand. When he wore it, people recognised him. He wasn't just a monkey then, he was a character.

He'd been the star of one of the world's most popular online virtual reality games; and then last year, after he and Victoria helped thwart a plot to trigger nuclear Armageddon, he'd become one of the most recognisable faces on the planet. Photos of him had been splashed over every newscast and web bulletin. His existence had been big news: a monkey raised to sentience via brain implants. They painted him as a walking, talking marvel; a cartoon character made real; a real-life superhero. He was the monkey who'd saved the world.

And then, at the height of it all, he'd walked away. He couldn't handle the fame, and he didn't want it. He had been trying to get his head around the fact that he was living in the middle of the twenty-first century and not, as he'd thought, in 1944. He needed rest and relaxation; so he stuck with the *Tereshkova*, and her new owner, Victoria Valois. Victoria needed a pilot, and he needed sanctuary. The deal worked for both of them.

He had a strange relationship with Victoria, and he didn't have the emotional vocabulary to describe it. She was his commanding officer, and she was his friend. The species gap ruled out any hint of romance, and yet there was something between them that was deeper than mutual respect: a recognition of kinship, perhaps. When they looked into each other's eyes, they saw a little of themselves staring back. They were both artificial creatures. Both their minds ran like software on the synthetic gelware neurons packed into their skulls; and both had been products of the Céleste Technologies lab in Paris. They were abandoned prototypes, and therefore both unique. But uniqueness led to loneliness. The *Tereshkova* was the closest thing he had to a home, K8 and Victoria the closest thing he had to any sort of family; but there was nobody who really understood him; no other talking monkeys to sympathise and share his pain.

And nobody he could fuck.

He rubbed his leather eye patch. The empty socket itched sometimes, especially in cold weather.

In California, some pony-tailed Buddhists had tried to explain to him about Karma and the journey of the soul.

What savage atrocity did I commit, he wondered, *to have to live this life as a talking monkey?*

Whatever it was, he hoped it had been spectacular.

Thinking about loneliness reminded him of the Gestalt, and the offer Reynolds had made earlier that evening.

How would it feel, he pondered, to be permanently hardwired into the thoughts and feelings of hundreds of other people; to be part of a larger, emergent personality; a single thought in a vast torrent of consciousness?

He could see how that kind of surrender might be a comfort, for some. Humans, like most primates, were social creatures. They clustered together in packs, seeking the safety, reassurance and approval of the tribe. Outcasts were miserable, distrusted and frowned-upon, and had a tendency to die early. If joining the Gestalt meant an end to loneliness, he could see how they might find doing so attractive; but it wouldn't work for him. He'd still be the only monkey in a sea of apes; still just as alone, however many humans he had crawling through his head, chattering away about their human feelings, and human problems.

Reynolds could go fuck himself. It was bad enough having to talk to humans, without being forced to hear all the crap that bubbled around inside their swollen brains. He'd rather be lonely than submerge himself in babble.

And yet, he had to admit, the white suits they wore did look kind of cool.

A raindrop hit the windscreen. Then another. As their patter became an insistent drumming, K8 hit the wipers.

Ack-Ack Macaque looked out at the suddenly slick and shiny road. Back in the game, he hadn't had to worry about rain; the weather had always been perfect: a perpetual high summer just right for dogfights. Of course, he'd seen rain before that; he wasn't a stranger to it. He'd spent the early part of his life in Amsterdam, made to battle other monkeys and apes in illegal backstreet knife fights. That was how he'd lost his left eye. His memories of that time were vague, to say the least. He hadn't been fully self-aware in those days; he'd been an average monkey, unable to speak. And without language, there had been no naming of things, and hence, no memory of having seen them. All he had were a few images, fuzzed by his lack of understanding, and blotted by the clumsy footprints of his subsequent neural surgery. If he concentrated, he could remember rain dappling the waters of a wine-dark canal at night, breaking up the reflections of the neon shop signs; and thunder that cracked and growled over the city like the very wrath of God. But how much of that was actual memory, and how much had his newly expanded brain backfilled over the years?

His real memories began with the game. His sentience and, to some extent, his personality, came preloaded on the synthetic gelware processors they stuffed into his skull. He'd been created to prove a point. He was a spin-off from AI weapons research, employed in a computer game to show the validity of using uplifted primate brains as CPUs for military drones. He hadn't been the first monkey those bastards at Céleste Tech had uplifted, nor was he the last—but, thanks to the fallout of last year's brouhaha, all the scientists were in jail, and all the other monkeys were dead.

He was, and now always would be, the only one of his kind.

CHAPTER THIRTEEN
MARIE

THE WOMAN STOOD before Victoria's desk, her hands bound before her, her feet apart, and her shoulders thrown back. She was, Victoria guessed, somewhere in her mid-to-late forties, and wore a black fleece top, black jodhpurs, and knee-length fur boots. Frizzy orange hair tumbled around her cheeks.

"I'll ask you again. Who are you, and why were you on my helicopter?"

The woman returned her stare. The lines at the corners of her eyes made her look as if she were permanently squinting against a bright light.

"I want to see William Cole." Chin raised, she spoke in a clear Home Counties accent. Victoria might have lost her ability to parse written text, but she could still read people, and if this woman weren't military in some way, she'd eat her wig. And with that in mind, perhaps she ought to try another tack.

Taking a deep breath, she pulled herself up to her full height and fixed the woman with her hardest stare. Then, trying to channel the Commodore's best parade ground bark, snapped, "What's your name, soldier?"

The prisoner blinked in surprise, and her posture straightened. If she hadn't been wearing cuffs, she would have snapped to attention.

"I'm not saying another word until I see William." She sounded less sure of herself now, but her continuing stubbornness revealed itself in the way her hands and jaw tightened. Seeing this, Victoria sighed inwardly. From long experience, she could sense when someone was likely to open up to her, and when they weren't. Still, the drill sergeant routine had been worth a try. Now, she'd have to think of something else.

When the *Tereshkova*'s stewards had apprehended the woman, she had been unarmed. If she was a killer, she was an unusually empty-handed one. All Victoria really had on her was that she'd stowed away in order to get aboard, and had broken into Cole's cabin; but her insistence on seeing Cole suggested her motive hadn't been burglary.

If she wasn't a killer or a thief, what was she?

Victoria walked around the desk, and stood close to the prisoner.

"Are you a friend of his?"

The woman looked sideways at her.

"You could say that."

"Then why won't you tell me who you are?"

The eyes swivelled to face forwards again, staring across the desk at the large picture window and the darkened skies beyond. "Because the less you know, the better."

"And why is that, *pourquoi*?"

"I can't say. Just let me see him."

Victoria perched on the edge of her desk. She could feel the cold of the metal through her jeans.

"I'm afraid he's not here."

"Not here?" The woman blinked rapidly. A tendon stood out on her neck. "Then where is he?"

"He went ashore."

"Is he all right?"

Victoria smiled to herself, knowing she'd found a way in, a crack in her opponent's armour.

"You answer one of my questions," she said, "and I'll think about answering one of yours." She crossed her arms. "So, tell me: why are you so keen to see Mister Cole?"

The woman's shoulders slumped, and she shifted her weight onto one hip.

"I'm concerned about him."

Victoria sucked her bottom lip.

"*Pourquoi?*"

"Because he's in danger."

"Yes, I gathered that. But you're not the first person tonight to come looking for him. I've got another one down in the infirmary. His name's Bill. Maybe you know him?"

"Is he okay?"

"He's dead."

The woman stiffened. "How?"

Victoria shook her head. That wasn't how the game was played.

"First, tell me who you are, and why you're so interested in Cole."

The woman's chin dropped to her chest as she looked down at her bound wrists. She rubbed the back of one hand with the fingers of the other.

"My name's Marie." She spoke quietly, without looking up. She seemed to be fighting a battle with herself. "And I'm his wife."

Victoria frowned. "Cole's wife is dead." She'd been reading through the writer's online biography, trying to figure out who Bill might be, and knew Marie had died over two years ago, from an infection contracted during a routine appendectomy.

The orange haired woman raised her eyes, expression bleak.

"Apparently not."

WHEN THE CHOPPER carrying Ack-Ack Macaque, K8 and William Cole touched down on the *Tereshkova*'s main helipad, Victoria was there to meet it. Wind and rain whipped in from the Bristol Channel, making her wince. Two stewards flanked her. It was past midnight now, and she was ready for her bunk.

K8 stepped down from the helicopter first, followed by Cole. Both had cuts and bruises. Cole seemed dazed, but he was upright, walking with one hand to his head. Ack-Ack Macaque came last, moving stiffly, dragging a body.

"Who's that?" She had to shout over the noise of the rotors.

Ack-Ack Macaque had been pulling the guy by the lapels; now, he let him drop onto the wet rubber of the pad.

"We got into a fight."

"You don't say?"

Without being asked, the stewards stooped, took hold of the body by its legs and arms, and carried it below decks. Standing there, in the helicopter's wet downdraught, Victoria gave silent thanks to the Commodore for having trained them so well.

The helicopter couldn't stay on the pad for long. The wind was too strong. The noise of its engines increased as it throttled up, preparing to depart. As it thundered away into the midnight sky, Victoria led the writer, the girl and the monkey down the main companionway, through the body of the airship, and into the warmth of the main gondola; but instead of heading for her office, she took them aft, past the passenger cabins and infirmary, to the brig.

"Why the brig?" Cole asked. He had some colour in his cheeks, and his breath smelled like a distillery. Apparently Ack-Ack Macaque had been using shots of rum to revive him during the helicopter flight.

Victoria paused at the door. "It's the safest place on the ship. And besides, there's someone in here I want you to meet."

The brig was a small room, just large enough to accommodate a narrow bunk and a stainless steel toilet. Its door was made of thick, soundproof glass. Inside, Marie stood with her back to them and her head down. Her hands were still cuffed together in front of her. Cascades of orange ringlets curtained her face. When Victoria pressed the keypad that unlocked the door, she turned, and the light caught the side of her cheek.

William Cole blinked.

"Oh!"

Victoria put a hand on his shoulder.

"Steady."

He turned to her, eyes bulging.

"I'm sorry, I can't—" Victoria felt his knees wobble. The vestibule held no chairs. As carefully as she could, she helped him over to the riveted metal wall. He leant his shoulder against it, and put his face in his hands.

When she looked around, Ack-Ack Macaque and K8 were staring at her. The monkey had one of his pistols in hand, just in case. He jerked a thumb at Marie.

"Who the *hell* is this?"

Cole trembled. Perhaps springing this on him had been a mistake; and yet, Victoria had been half-expecting him to denounce the woman as a fraud. She'd done some research and, as far as she could ascertain, Marie Cole was definitely dead. At least, the Marie Cole from this world...

The woman with the orange hair walked up to the open cell door, and leaned out.

"Hello, William."

He wouldn't look at her. Instead, he slid down into a crouch, and then bent forward with a tormented moan, wrapping his arms around his head, trying to block her out.

Victoria looked up at Marie.

"I'm sorry."

The other woman shrugged. "Don't be. It must be a terrible shock for him."

"And not the first he's had today."

Standing beside the cell door, Ack-Ack Macaque cleared his throat.

"Okay, I'll ask again." His tail twitched ominously. "Who the hell is this?"

Marie turned to him.

"I'm William's wife."

"Bullshit."

Marie held up her hands. The cuffs clanked together. "I can prove it."

"How?"

"Run any test you like. Fingerprints, DNA, whatever."

Ack-Ack Macaque looked her up and down, and then turned his sepia eye on Victoria.

"Can we do that, boss?"

Victoria shook her head. "Sorry. I already thought of it, but we just don't have the equipment."

Cole's hands fell from watery, bloodshot eyes.

"It's her," he said. His voice silenced the room. "Only you're not *her*, though, are you?" He curled his lip. "You look just like her, but you're not really *her*. I saw her body. You're no more the real Marie than your dead friend was the real me."

Marie lowered her arms.

"I am her, William. At least, I was until her baby died. That's where we split." She swallowed nervously. "She lost a child, I didn't. But up until that point, we were essentially the same person, identical in every way." She brushed a wisp of orange behind her left ear. "I am what she would have been, had things been different."

Cole glowered up at her from beneath his wiry eyebrows.

"But things weren't different, were they?"

Marie flinched at the bitterness in his voice.

"I loved you every bit as much as she did."

"No you didn't." Cole knuckled his eyes. "You loved the other one, the dead one. Bill. What was he, your husband?"

"He was. But in many ways, so are you."

Cole rubbed his forehead, hard, as if trying to dislodge a stuck thought, or an embedded arrow. "Where are you from?"

"You know," Marie said. "Deep down, you know. You've been writing about it for years. That's why we came to find you."

Cole looked blank. Marie took a step towards him, and Ack-Ack Macaque brought his gun up, covering her, making sure she made no sudden moves.

"Mendelblatt's world," she said, "Where the UK and France never merged, and there aren't any Zeppelins in the skies over London."

"Mendelblatt?" Cole's face was a mask of anguish and confusion. "You mean—?"

She raised her cuffed hands, imploring him to believe her.

"That isn't sci-fi you're writing, my darling; it's memory."

Palace Moves To Block Movie

LONDON 15/10/2060 – This morning, Buckingham Palace issued a statement expressing its opposition to the making of a movie based around the events of last year's attempted royal coup d'état.

Titled *Ack-Ack Macaque*, after the world-famous monkey, the multi-million dollar movie will tell the story of events leading up to the death of King William V, and the subsequent ascension to the throne of HRH King Merovech, then Prince of Wales. While some details of the so-called 'Combat de La Manche' have been made public, much remains classified, and royal sources fear that the gaps will be filled in by 'guesswork and fabrication, making any attempt at an impartial enquiry impossible.'

The film will be directed by BAFTA-winning British director, Tonya Field, who co-wrote the script with her husband and long-time collaborator, Tim Duncan. In 2057, the pair won an Oscar for their controversial screenplay, *Andre's Choice*, about the life of a surgically enhanced male prostitute on the streets of Berlin.

No actors have yet been named, but insiders tip teen favourite Brad Foley to play the Prince, and expect motion-capture specialist Ashton Stanislavski to be brought in to play the monkey. A veteran of sci-fi epics, Stanislavski is probably best known to UK audiences for his portrayal of the alien in 2053's horror blockbuster, *Death Station*. If the rumours are true, he will be playing one of the world's most unusual and enigmatic celebrities: an intelligent monkey with a passion for cigars and alcohol, and a pathological dislike of the paparazzi.

Having spent several years portraying the main character in an online video game, the real-life 'Ack-Ack Macaque' somehow escaped from the headquarters of Céleste Technologies in Paris, and made his way to the coast, where he joined forces with Prince Merovech and became embroiled in the fight against Céleste Tech's owner, the Duchess of Brittany, thereby averting a potentially catastrophic nuclear confrontation with China. Since then, the monkey has been living as a recluse aboard the skyliner *Tereshkova*, and has refused all requests for interviews or publicity.

In its strongly worded statement, the Palace called the forthcoming movie, 'a cynical and ill-informed attempt to turn a serious international event into a tawdry spectacle.'

Ack-Ack Macaque himself was unavailable for comment.

Read more | Like | Comment | Share

Related Stories

'Gestalt' members among four injured in multiple shootings.

North Sea fish stocks 'beyond recovery'.

European Commonwealth leaders meet for crucial budget summit.

Netherlands announces 'massive' flood defence scheme.

Royal wedding set for June 5th.

US carries out fatal drone strike in Nepal.

Elephants declared extinct in the wild.

Missing writer's car found at airport.

CHAPTER FOURTEEN
SPECIAL CIRCUMSTANCES

As a cool and watery sun rose beyond the portholes, Ack-Ack Macaque stood at the foot of another infirmary bed.

"We seem to be collecting bodies," he said. The room smelled of antiseptic and disinfectant. In front of him lay the guy he'd shot and dumped in the car. Somehow, despite the blood loss, the man had survived. Monitors and drips had been plugged into him to keep him alive.

Paul's hologram stood to one side of the bed, stroking his chin.

"How are you doing?" Ack-Ack Macaque asked.

Paul's face fell. He scratched at the wispy suggestion of a beard around his chin.

"You've never been killed, have you? Not even in the game, I mean."

"Not so far."

"Then you don't know what it's like, being a ghost, always on the outside of everything."

Ack-Ack Macaque thought of the hat and coat he had to wear in public. "Maybe I got some idea."

Paul wasn't listening. He held his palms out in front of him, and turned them over as if inspecting them for dirt. "I have hands, but I can't touch anything." He looked up. "I have a tongue, but I can't taste."

Ack-Ack Macaque rolled the cigar from one side of his mouth to the other. "You can complain though, can't you?"

Paul blinked at him. "I beg your pardon?"

Ack-Ack Macaque made his hand into a puppet's flapping mouth. "Yap, yap, yap." He laughed, and the tips of Paul's ears reddened. "So, you don't like being a ghost? Don't be a fucking ghost. Be something else."

"Like what?"

Ack-Ack Macaque waved his arms in an impatient gesture that took in the gondola and the five hulls above it. "Hell, you're practically running this ship. Why not plug yourself right in? Stop pussyfooting around. Stop being a ghost, start being an airship."

Paul's forehead grew lined in thought. He removed his glasses, blew on the lenses, and polished them on the hem of his long white coat. As a hologram, Paul had no need to clean them, and the action achieved nothing; but Ack-Ack Macaque knew he clung to these old habitual gestures. They were part of who he was, part of what made him Paul.

"You know, you could be on to something."

Ack-Ack Macaque clacked his teeth together. "Hey, you know the old saying: If life gives you lemons, pull a gun on it and say, 'Fuck your lemons, where are the goddamn bananas?'"

Paul smiled, and tapped an index finger against his chin. "If I could hook myself into the navigation software," he said slowly. "If I could somehow wire into the telemetry, and maybe co-opt the main bridge computers..." He looked up. "Yes, it could be done. I could totally run this whole ship." His eyes were shining. "Ack-ster, you're a genius."

Ack-Ack Macaque waved a hand. "Yeah, yeah." He looked down at the unconscious ape-man on the infirmary bunk. "Back to business. You were about to tell me about good-looking here."

"Yes, sorry." Paul hooked his glasses over his ears. In life, he had been a medical researcher, specialising in brain implants. "Well, the thing is, I've never seen anything quite like him before. I don't even think he's human. At least, not in the strictest sense."

"If he ain't human, what is he?"

"I'm not sure." Paul reached out a hand to indicate the figure's upper arm. "His bones are shorter and thicker than most people's. And take a look at the shape of the skull. The shape of his nose, and that ridge above his eyes."

Ack-Ack Macaque chomped the cigar between his molars, but didn't light it. "He's certainly one ugly motherfucker."

"He's more than that." Paul straightened up. Somehow he'd edited his appearance. The Hawaiian shirt and cargo pants were gone, replaced by blue jeans and a faded red sweatshirt, which he wore beneath a pristine white doctor's coat, complete with pens in the breast pocket and a stethoscope slung around his neck. "At least, he might be."

"Might be what?" Ack-Ack Macaque spoke around the cigar.

Paul pushed his glasses more firmly onto the bridge of his nose.

"Do you know what a Neanderthal is?"

"A type of cocktail?"

"Neanderthals were a type of intelligent hominid."

Ack-Ack Macaque frowned. "A what?"

"Like a cave man."

"Gotcha."

Paul pointed to the man's arms. "They had thicker bones than modern people, bigger jaws; and they lived in Europe around the time of the last ice age."

"Great, so now we know what he is."

"Yes, but that's left us with a much bigger question."

"Why does he smell so bad?"

"No." Paul put his hands in the pockets of his white coat. "It's that the last Neanderthals disappeared thirty thousand years ago. He shouldn't even be here."

"They're extinct?"

"They died out, or interbred with modern humans." He shrugged his shoulders. "The point is, there hasn't been a Neanderthal on the Earth for thirty thousand years, and suddenly you run into three of them, all on the same night, in Bristol."

Ack-Ack Macaque patted the Colts at his sides. "And I made two of the bastards extinct, all over again."

Paul didn't hear him. "It just doesn't make any sense." The skin between his eyebrows furrowed. He started to pace back and forth beside the bed, talking to himself. "Unless somebody's breeding them from fossil remains. But that's ludicrous. This one here's at least twenty-five years old. How could you keep it a secret that long; and, assuming you could, why would you risk exposure now?"

"Beats me, I only work here." Ack-Ack Macaque pulled the damp, oily-tasting cigar from his mouth. "Did you try going through his pockets?"

"One of the stewards did. He found a wallet. It's on that table in the corner." Paul held up his holographic hands. "I can't touch it."

Ack-Ack Macaque replaced his cigar and shuffled over to the table. The wallet lay on a shiny steel tray, along with a few coins, a flick knife, and a black plastic comb. The knife had a yellowish ivory handle. The comb had seen better days. He picked up the wallet and opened it.

"Not much here." He pulled out a dog-eared business card. "Only this."

A tiny electric motor whined as Paul's image 'walked' over to him.

"What does it say?"

"It's from a company called Legion Haulage. There's a number, but no address." Ack-Ack Macaque turned the card over. "The back's blank."

"Legion Haulage?" Paul tapped his chin. "They're not in my database. Maybe K8 can find them?"

Ack-Ack Macaque slipped the card into his gun belt. "She's asleep right now. I'll ask her when she wakes up." He looked down at the bed and wrinkled his nose. "In the meantime, what are we going to do with smelly here?"

"Victoria wants him kept alive, to see if he can tell us who he is, and where he came from."

The monkey cracked his knuckles. "Wake him up, and I'll slap it out of him."

Paul shook his head. "He's sedated at the moment. And she strictly forbade torture."

Ack-Ack Macaque huffed. "She can talk." He leant over the bed towards Paul. "Wasn't it her that dropped an assassin off this ship?"

Paul looked uncomfortable, and Ack-Ack Macaque knew he'd been present at the time, existing as a virtual ghost inside Victoria's neural gelware.

"He was more robot than man."

"Yes, but she didn't know that at the time, though, did she?" While interrogating the prisoner in one of the *Tereshkova*'s cargo bays, Victoria had allowed the man to fall to his death, from several thousand feet above Windsor Castle.

"Those were... special circumstances." Paul looked away. "That man was Cassius Berg. He killed me. He cut my brain out, and tried to do the same to Vicky. And he was threatening the safety of everyone on this airship."

Ack-Ack Macaque grinned around his cigar. "Hey, I'm not criticising, I would've dumped the fucker myself."

Paul's hands moved jerkily. He rubbed the back of his neck. "You don't understand. It really cut her up inside to do it. She doesn't want anything like that happening again. It nearly destroyed her."

"Even with a scumbag like that?"

Paul sighed. "Perhaps you don't know her as well as I do."

Ack-Ack Macaque bridled. He'd been flying for Victoria Valois for over a year. "I know she's a hell of a lot tougher than she thinks she is." He spared the caveman a final glance, and turned for the door. "Where are you going?"

He didn't turn around. "Up and out."

"Taking the Spitfire up for a jaunt?"

In the doorway, Ack-Ack Macaque pulled out his lighter. "You'd better believe it, my friend." He struck a flame and puffed the cigar to life. "It's been a long night, and I've got a lot of aggression left to work off."

CHAPTER FIFTEEN
SCOURGE OF THE SKYWAYS

AN HOUR LATER, at the other end of the main gondola, Victoria Valois sat behind the desk in her office, and regarded Marie over the steeple of her fingers. William Cole wasn't there; the writer had been sedated. The man hadn't slept in God only knew how long, and he'd had more than enough surprises for one day. Between the drugs, the car bomb, and everything else, his sanity had been dangling by a thread. Knocking him out had seemed by far the kindest option.

Sitting across the desk, Marie returned her gaze. Her hands, now unbound, were resting comfortably on the arms of her chair.

"So," Victoria said. "You really are his wife?"

The other woman brushed back an orange curl. "A version of her."

"From a parallel world; yes, I get it." Victoria dropped her hands to the desk. "The question is: what are you doing here, now?"

Marie straightened in her chair. "I've come to protect him."

"From whom?"

"Certain parties."

Victoria chewed her lower lip. "You said he was writing memories. Is that why they're trying to kill him, because of something he's remembered?"

"William's special. He's creative, and like a lot of creative people, he's sort of attuned to the probabilities and possibilities of the timelines. Without knowing it, he's picking up on the experiences of his other selves. Not memories as such, more like glimpses of the other world. I can't really explain it, except to say that it's like the rapport you get between identical twins. Sometimes, when something happens to one of his alternate selves, he senses it. He has dreams, and they feed into his writing. He thinks he's making all those stories up, but he isn't. He's just trying to get down on paper what's going on at the back of his head."

"And what is that?"

Marie rubbed the bridge of her nose with her index finger. She stifled a yawn.

"Look, Captain, I probably shouldn't be telling you this, but you seem a reasonable sort."

"Telling me what?"

"That there's a war going on."

Victoria raised a sceptical eyebrow. "A war?"

"William knows nothing about it, but he's involved nevertheless, whether he likes it or not."

"How so?"

"Because of his gift." Her fingers picked at a loose thread on the armrest. "The truth is, the war hasn't been going so well for us. We've been losing territory, falling back."

"So, why come here?"

"Because the battle's spreading."

"I don't like the sound of that."

"Nor should you."

From beyond the walls of the gondola, she heard the scream of a Rolls Royce engine; Ack-Ack Macaque was out there, putting his Spitfire through its paces, throwing it into loops and rolls above the airfield. She picked up a pen from the desk and clicked the end of it. Then she held it to her ear and clicked it again, two or three times. She could feel that they were getting close to the truth of things now; but her experience told her to stay quiet. People often divulged more than they wanted to if she simply gave them the space to do it. Her silence unnerved them, and they spoke to fill it. Leaning back in her chair, she tapped the end of the pen against her lower lip. Would the tactic work here? She liked to think of herself as a pretty good judge of character, and Marie struck her as a sharp cookie. Nevertheless, she held her tongue, and waited to see what would happen.

Part of her was convinced that, all evidence to the contrary, the whole 'parallel world' story would fall apart. After all, how could it possibly be true? The idea ran counter to every instinct in her body. And yet, how else to explain William Cole's doppelganger, and the reappearance of his dead wife? Across the desk, Marie's position hadn't changed. Her hands still rested loosely on the arms of her chair, and she showed no sign of agitation or discomfort, and certainly no burning urge to talk.

Okay, Victoria thought, this fish isn't biting. She gave the pen a final click, and tossed it back onto the desk. But, before she could marshal her next round of questions, somebody tapped on the office door.

"Come in."

K8 stepped into the room.

"I've got a result for you." She walked up to the desk and laid the printout in front of Victoria.

"What does it say?"

The teenager ran her tongue around her teeth, and glanced at Marie.

"I found Legion Haulage. They're a transport business, based in Rotterdam." She leant over and tapped her finger on some of the words. Victoria looked, but the black marks on the paper might as well have been written in Martian for all the sense they made. "They're a front for another company, who are a front for another in turn. If you follow the chain of front companies back far enough—" Her finger traced down the page. "You find out that they're owned by the Gestalt." She straightened up with a what-do-you-think-about-that look on her face.

Victoria smoothed a hand backwards across her bald scalp.

"Are you sure?"

"It's all there, in black and white."

"So it's possible the things that attacked you—"

"Were working for the men in white, yes. At least, it's a possibility."

Victoria frowned. "But what would the Gestalt want with William Cole?"

K8 shrugged. "Who knows? What would anyone want with him?" She glanced at Marie. "No offence."

The woman with the orange hair dipped her head and smiled. *None taken.*

"It still doesn't explain where the Neanderthals came from." Victoria hadn't slept all night, and she'd spent much of the past hour listening to Paul's speculations on the caveman nature of their prisoner. Now, she could feel her neural implant upping her production of adrenaline, fighting to keep her sharp. "I mean, where did they get them?"

Marie cleared her throat. Sitting up in her chair, she raised a hand.

"Perhaps I can help, Captain?"

Victoria pulled her fighting staff from the pocket of her tunic.

"I was just thinking the very same thing." With her head throbbing with fatigue, she clonked the staff onto the desktop. *Time to stop acting like a journalist,* she thought, *and time to start behaving like a skyliner captain.*

Under international law, skyliners were classed as autonomous city-states, able to travel where they wished, and govern themselves however their captains saw fit. They had been carrying passengers and freight around the world for almost a hundred years, and had become so vital to global commerce that now no country would risk interfering with the neutrality of a single vessel, for fear of boycott by the rest. On board, the captain's word was law. They were the undisputed masters of their little flying cities, and had the final say on everything from criminal trials to business deals and marriages. Yet, they weren't tyrants. At least, the majority weren't. Passengers tended to avoid skyliners famed for repressive laws or unusual punishments, and so, in order to survive economically, captains were obliged to run their ships with a modicum of fairness and equitability—but only a modicum. Skyliner captains enjoyed a reputation for eccentricity and ruthlessness unsurpassed by any profession since the eighteenth century sail ship captains of the Spanish Main.

Among them, Victoria was something of an oddity: she hadn't risen up through the ranks, and had no experience. But, as the Commodore's appointed heir and successor, she had the respect of her crew, and a burgeoning reputation based on her striking physical appearance and the fact that it was the *Tereshkova* she commanded: a vessel now famous to the public as the skyliner which, last year, had rammed the royal yacht in the middle of the English Channel. The well-documented fact that she'd also thrown an assassin out of a cargo hatch helped. According to the British tabloids, she was Victoria Valois, the half-human scourge of the skyways. Sometimes, it took her a while to remember that.

With a French curse, she pushed back her chair and rose to her feet.

"I have a dead guy in my infirmary, and a caveman in the bed next to him." She waved a finger in Marie's face. "Now, how about you start talking. I want to know why you're here, and how you got here!"

Marie's knuckles whitened on the arms of her chair.

"I told you—"

"That you're here to protect Cole? Yes, I know. But there's more to it than that, isn't there? You didn't just come here to find him, did you?"

The other woman's eyes widened. Victoria saw her nostrils flare.

"No."

"Then, what?"

Marie looked down at her knees. She ran her tongue around her lips, and her shoulders tensed. She seemed to be steeling herself to speak. When she looked up, her eyes were bright with desperation.

"It's my daughter."

"Your daughter?"

Marie glanced at K8. "She's about your age. Her name's Lila."

Victoria leant forward across the desk, her palms either side of the retracted fighting staff.

"What about her?"

Marie thrust her chin forward defiantly. Her eyes glittered.

"They have her."

"Who?"

"The Gestalt. They have her, and I'm here to get her back."

"By yourself?"

"Bill was helping me." The woman ran a hand across her eyes. "They killed him."

"And Cole?" Victoria bent her elbows, leaning closer. "Where does he figure into this?"

Marie squeezed her hands shut. She looked at K8.

"Lila's his daughter too."

CHAPTER SIXTEEN
FIRE POSITION

K8 LEFT THE Captain talking to the orange-haired lady, and wandered back in the direction of her cabin. As she passed through the gondola's main lounge, the sun shone through the brass-rimmed portholes. Motes danced in the light. Uniformed stewards bustled back and forth, serving breakfast to a handful of passengers, clustered in ones and twos around the small, circular tables. As a plate went past, she caught the smell of bacon and scrambled eggs, and her stomach growled. She'd been awake all night, and hadn't eaten anything for hours. For a moment, she dithered, trying to decide whether to sit down and eat, or head back to her cabin and crash in her bunk.

In the end, sleep won out. She was young, and needed her rest. Pausing only to snag a slice of toast from the serving table, she went aft, along the main accommodation corridor.

As she walked, she nibbled a corner of the toast, and pondered the events of the night. One thing particularly bugged her. She'd heard Marie claim the Gestalt had killed William Cole's doppelganger. But if Reynolds had been with the Captain when Bill was shot, he couldn't have done the deed—which meant Bill's killer could still be on board, somewhere, waiting for the chance to strike again.

How many members of the Gestalt were on the current passenger list?

She needed to talk to Ack-Ack Macaque. He'd know what to do. He always knew what to do. Just being around him made her feel safe. Partly it was his proclivity for violence—she knew he'd rip apart anyone who tried to harm her. He was like the big brother she'd never had, and the pet she'd always wanted: a big, sweary monkey who drank and smoked and was dangerous to other people, but always safe, safe, safe for her.

Not, of course, that she'd ever admit to such feelings. Where she came from, you learned to keep your emotions to yourself and never show a hint of weakness, or dependence on anyone else. And besides, she knew that if she tried to tell him how she felt, he'd laugh at her. Not in a cruel way, maybe; but not in a sympathetic way, either. As far as he was concerned, they were comrades in arms. She was his wingman, and that was all there was to it.

They'd first met in the game world. Impressed by her hacking and gaming skills, Céleste Tech had brought her in to help monitor the monkey's behaviour. They plucked her from the slums of Glasgow and flew her to their labs on the outskirts of Paris, where they had the monkey strapped to a couch in a lab, his artificially enhanced brain hooked into the simulated world, believing the dogfights and battles around him were real. They'd already used up four previous primates, and couldn't work out why the monkeys kept cracking up. It was K8's job to keep the latest, Ack-Ack Macaque himself, sane and operational. Instead, when he escaped into the countryside outside Paris, she went after him—not to get him back, but rather to help him bring down the company, and everything for which it stood.

When she'd gone to Paris, it had been the first time she'd left her native Glasgow. Most of her teens up until that point had been spent in her bedroom, illuminated by the blue glow of a computer monitor. Now, just over a year later, she'd been all around the world working as a navigator on the *Tereshkova*, playing co-pilot to an ill-tempered, cigar-chomping monkey. She'd walked the streets of New York and San Francisco, feeling like a character in a movie; seen the sun set over the Pacific; looked down from her porthole at the splendour of the Grand Canyon. And yet, despite it all, she was still the shorthaired little ginger kid from the Easterside estate, acting tough because she had to; because that was the only way she knew how. The irony was, she no longer had to worry about the mean kids, the schoolyard bullies, or her parents' fighting. Her hacking skills had taken her out of Scotland, and anyone who tried to intimidate her now would first have to deal with an angry and heavily armed primate; but she'd been putting up a front so long she couldn't let go of it. It had become a part of who she was. She'd been acting the plucky little tough girl so long that now she couldn't tell exactly where the role ended and the real her began.

Her shoes echoed on the metal deck. The doors to the passenger staterooms were made of polished wood. The door to Ack-Ack Macaque's, which was situated farther back, in the crew section, was metal. It was an oval hatch, with a lip like the hatch of a cabin in a seagoing ship. As she reached it, she heard the howl of the Spit's Rolls Royce Merlin engine, and knew he was still out there, flinging himself around the sky, reliving his glory days as a fighter pilot.

Disappointed, she thought about going back to her own cabin, but didn't feel like being alone. Instead, holding the toast in her mouth, she pushed down on the handle, intending to curl up on his spare bunk. He wouldn't mind, and she could barricade herself in his cabin while she waited for him, wrapped in the reassuring, homely scents of old cigar smoke, leather and animal sweat.

She shouldered the door open and, taking the toast from her mouth, stifled a yawn with the back of her hand. The room was dark. Still yawning, she fumbled her hand along the inside of the wall, searching for the switch. As she did so, she heard the rustle of clothing, and became aware of another presence in the room.

Before she could cry out, gloved hands closed firmly around her arm. Other hands closed over her mouth and nose, and squeezed her throat, holding her head still. She kicked out in the darkness, but their grip only tightened. There were at least two people holding her. The pressure on her larynx stopped her from being able to shout. She couldn't even breathe. Frantically, she kicked and thrashed, but the hands held her in place. Something cold pressed against her neck, and she flinched, expecting a gunshot. Instead, there was a loud, mechanical click, and a needle punched through the skin above her collarbone, into the muscle beneath.

THE SPITFIRE'S COCKPIT was cold, and smelled like a zoo, but that was just the way Ack-Ack Macaque liked it. Six thousand feet above the airfield, high above the uppermost antennae of the hovering *Tereshkova*, he wheeled the plane through the crisp morning air. From up here, through the perspex bubble of the cockpit, he could see down the length of the Estuary, towards the distant southerly hills of Exmoor; and west, across the rolling landscape of Wales, to the bracken-brown peaks of the Brecon Beacons. No trace remained of last night's rain. The sky was an endless blue, the air as fresh and clear as a melt-water stream, and his heart sang an accompaniment to the engine's holler.

Wrapped in his leather flying jacket and favourite silk scarf, he pushed his goggles up onto the top of his head, and peered down at the city streets whirling beneath his wings. He wondered how many people were still asleep in the houses on the outskirts of the airfield. Pushing the stick forward, he put the Spit into a screaming dive and held it—ignoring the screams of protest from air traffic control—until the altimeter dial had almost wound down to zero. At the last possible moment, less than a hundred feet above the deck, he hauled back and pulled up the nose, booming over the suburban roofs and gardens at three hundred miles per hour, rattling windows and setting off car alarms.

Cackling, he kept low, only pulling up once the houses gave way to fields and industrial units. Then, throttle pushed forward, he aimed the old plane's nose at the sky. The Spit leapt like a prancing horse, eager to kick up its heels, and he gave it the beans, glorying in the shuddering roar of the engine. This was what he was, what he'd always been: first and foremost, a pilot.

"To slip the ugly bonds of Earth," he misquoted around his cigar. "To punch the stupid, smiling face of God." His voice sounded muffled. His ears still ached from last night's gunfire, and the changes in pressure caused by these manoeuvres weren't helping. He opened his mouth wide to let them pop, then pushed aside his left earphone and waggled his little finger in the hole. His whole head felt like a bubble that refused to burst. "Fuck it," he muttered. Time to go home. A bit of rest and recuperation would do him more good than titting about in a plane, however chary he was to admit it.

He levelled out his climb at five thousand feet. By now, he was over the bronze-coloured waters of the Severn, so he put the plane into a wide turn, intending to bring it back to the *Tereshkova*.

He passed over the Second Severn Crossing, flashing through the gap between its massive concrete towers, and brought the nose around to face the rising sun.

As the cigar-shaped silhouette of the airship hove into view ahead, he clocked a helicopter lifting from its upper deck. But it wasn't one of the tubby passenger choppers that belonged to the ship. This was a sleek, small, and expensive-looking dragonfly; able to carry no more than two or three people; maybe four, at a push.

"Special delivery," he muttered, wondering if the 'copter had just picked someone up, or just dropped them off. He watched it climb into the sky, heading eastwards over the city, away from him. In his experience, an expensive 'copter like that usually belonged to a high-ranking business person or celebrity—or, he thought with a scowl, that bloody film crew who wanted to make a movie about him. Couldn't they get it though their thick, coke-addled heads that he wasn't the slightest bit interested in seeing a Hollywood version of his life? If he'd wanted fame, he could have had all he could handle last year in the wake of that scrap in the Channel. But he hadn't. He'd chosen to fly away on the *Tereshkova* instead. Couldn't those people take a bloody hint?

For the past half an hour, he'd been ignoring the radio chatter from the ground. Mostly, they'd been shouting at him for breaking rules and flying dangerously, and he'd sort of tuned them out. Now though, as he watched the helicopter pull away, he became aware of a new note of urgency in their voices.

Ack-ster, Ack-ster, respond please. This is Paul. Respond please.

"Hey Paul, what's up?"

Oh, man, where have you been? I've been calling you.

"I'm here, I'm here. What's the problem? Are the Hollywood people here again?"

It's K8. They've got K8.

Ack-Ack Macaque felt the hairs prickle on his neck. "Who's got her?"

The Gestalt. They grabbed her from your cabin. They were disguised as passengers. They disabled some of our cameras, but I caught them taking her up to the roof. She looked drugged.

His hands squeezed the stick.

"Where are they now?"

They had a helicopter waiting. It was registered as a courier from Legion Haulage.

Ack-Ack Macaque glared forward, through the bulletproof windshield.

"Small, pricey-looking job?"

Yes.

"I see it."

What are you going to do?

The push-button control for firing the Spitfire's eight machine guns was mounted on the stick. A cover prevented accidental firing during manoeuvres.

"What the hell do you think I'm going to do?" He took the cover between finger and thumb, and rotated it a quarter turn, from the 'safe' position to the 'fire' position. "I'm going to get her back."

CHAPTER SEVENTEEN
MY EYES

WILLIAM COLE LAY on his bunk, staring up at the painted metal ceiling. He felt washed-out and his thoughts, trodden down by the sedatives he'd been given, were soft and gloopy.

"My daughter?" His mouth was dry, his voice a croak.

"Yes, my love." Marie knelt beside the bed, and placed her hands on his arm. "Lila, our daughter."

"But, I don't have a daughter."

"Yes, you do. Or rather, you should have done."

"I don't follow." In the gloom of the curtained cabin, she looked and sounded so much like *his* Marie that he felt a hard, hot lump in his chest. Even her breath smelled the way he remembered.

"Do you recall when you and your Marie first got together, about sixteen years ago?" They'd run into each other at a book launch in Greenwich Village, for the autobiography of some flavour-of-the-month artist with hardly enough years behind her to fill the pages. Marie had been covering it for *The Guardian*; he'd been trying to buttonhole a literary agent with one of his manuscripts. Somehow, they'd ended up standing next to each other at the bar.

"How could I forget?" Two weeks after that first meeting, she'd come out to visit him in Dayton, and stayed for six months.

"And Marie had that miscarriage?"

William felt his eyes widen. "How do you know about that?" He and Marie had never spoken of it to anyone. It had been something they kept to themselves, even though the fact of it had driven them apart. After it happened, they just couldn't be around each other. She went back to England, to her job at *The Guardian*, and he didn't hear from her for another five years; didn't see her for another ten. By the time he came to the UK to live with her, they were both in their very late thirties, both divorced, and both still childless. It was going to be a second chance for both of them;

but, five years later, she was dead, and he was left alone again, this time on the wrong side of the Atlantic.

So many wasted years.

He felt Marie's fingers squeeze his arm through the bedclothes.

"Well," she said, "in my timeline, the baby lived."

He turned towards her. "I *beg* your pardon?"

"The miscarriage never happened." Marie let go of him and put a hand to her abdomen. "The baby survived. She grew up fit and strong."

William frowned in confusion.

"So we stayed together? You never went back to England?"

"We were a family."

William let his head roll back onto the pillow, trying to imagine all the what-ifs and if-onlys.

"But, she's not my daughter, is she? Not really. She's yours. You and the other me, from your world."

Without looking up, Marie shook her head. He saw her orange ringlets move in the corner of his peripheral vision.

"No, she is yours. The worlds didn't split until she died." She looked up at him, and he could see the care lines in the skin around her eyes. "She has your DNA. She came from you, before our worlds diverged. Just because she's from a different version of events, doesn't mean she isn't your flesh and blood." She reached up and brushed a loose hair from his forehead. The touch of her fingers sent little shivers though the muscles in his neck and jaw. "It doesn't mean you aren't her father."

William bit his lip. "I'm not sure I understand."

Marie cocked her head to one side.

"What's to understand? You fathered a child, but then the timelines diverged, and you got stuck on one and she got stuck on another. You got separated, but now you can be together again, after all this time."

He swallowed.

"How? How is this even possible?"

"There are machines. Big powerful machines that can nudge a person from one timeline to another."

"And you used one of those?"

"The Gestalt on our world have them. Bill, Lila and I used one. We broke into one of their facilities and sent ourselves here."

"So, you didn't bring it with you?"

"Strictly a one-way trip. We couldn't even choose our destination, they already had it programmed in, but that's okay. We don't want to go back.

We were trying to escape."

"Escape what?"

Marie dropped her gaze and shook her head.

With great effort, William elbowed himself up until he was half-sitting, with his back against the pillows and his head against the cabin wall.

"If you want me to help find your daughter," he said, "I want to be sure I know what I'm getting myself into."

Marie pursed her lips. She rocked back on her heels, and got to her feet. "Okay, then, here it is." Her voice had become brusque and businesslike. "There are an infinite number of identical worlds, all occupying the same space but separated by wafer-thin membranes of probability. A decision taken in one world will be reversed in the next, and so on to eternity. Every time one of us makes a choice, every time the wind blows left instead of right, every time a subatomic particle wobbles one way instead of another, the timelines fork, and new worlds are born. Trillions every second."

William was familiar with the concept, but when he tried to imagine it, he couldn't grasp the scale.

"That's hard to visualise."

"Think of them as branches." She clasped her hands behind her back. "Forks in the timelines."

"An infinite number of worlds?"

"Only a tiny percentage are inhabited by humans, but even that percentage accounts for a number so big that to write it down would take longer than the remaining age of the universe."

He licked his lips. They were rough and dehydrated.

"So, why are people trying to kill me?"

"Who?"

His face darkened. "There was a guy in a car yesterday afternoon, and those two Gestalt guys outside Sparky's place last night."

"You've met the Gestalt already?"

"They wanted me to go with them. They were armed."

For the first time in the conversation, she seemed off-balance. "I was hoping we'd get to you first. What happened?"

"I shot them."

She gave him a long, thoughtful look.

"Okay," she said at length, "I'll level with you. Bill and I, we've been fighting for a long time, trying to free our world."

"Free it from what?"

"From the Gestalt."

William raised an eyebrow. The Gestalt was a cult, a curiosity. They were rich and secretive, but nobody took them seriously. The media lumped them in with groups like the Scientologists or the Jehovah's Witnesses. They were eccentric, a little secretive, but essentially harmless. Until last night, he would never have thought them capable of carrying guns, let alone threatening anybody.

Marie said, "They evolved on a different parallel to ours. We don't know which one, but they've been trying to spread ever since." Her fingertips brushed the edge of his blanket. "They want to turn the whole multiverse into one giant hive mind. In order to do it, they recruit locals and convert them, then use them to spread their message and build support."

"Can't they be stopped?"

Marie shook her head. "That's just the first stage. On our world, they started kidnapping people and converting them by force. They bought up media companies and used them to broadcast propaganda. And in the end, when they got numerous enough, they staged a coup."

"They have soldiers?"

"Human and Neanderthal. They recruit the Neanderthals as muscle, from timelines where the species never died out."

"You think that's what they're planning here?"

"From what I've seen, I'd say they're almost certainly planning an invasion. Maybe even something worse."

"Worse than invasion?"

Marie looked tired. An orange curl fell across her forehead and she flicked it aside with her finger. "The Gestalt have been here on your world for a while now. They will have been studying your soul-catchers, finding out how they work; and you can bet they've thought of half a dozen ways to subvert the technology. When their main force gets here, they'll unleash something— could be a signal or a virus, depending on the way the technology works; maybe even something nanotechnological—to turn those implants against their owners, and assimilate them into the Gestalt."

William tried to sit up. Half the people he knew wore soul-catchers. Although the gelware recording devices sat comfortably beneath the skin at the base of the skull, their tendrils extended deep into the grey matter of the brain, recording and monitoring everything. If the Gestalt had some way to reverse the process, to turn output to input, the results could be catastrophic.

Beside him, Marie laced her fingers and stretched her arms, popping the knuckles. "The good news is, we've got people fighting them on my world, and we can fight them here."

"But why are the Gestalt trying to kill me?" Spoken aloud, and weighed against the idea of an impending battle, the thought sounded petty and selfish; but still, he needed to know. "I haven't done anything. I didn't even know about any of this."

Her head tipped to the side again. "In my world, Bill was one of our leaders. For years, he kept us going, and kept us united. And now he's dead." She gave a matter-of-fact shrug, but he could see the pain in the way the lines bunched around her eyes. "So it goes. But the Gestalt worry that another version of him might rise up in his place. And they know about you. They've seen your work, and they know you're getting glimpses of our world. Your last book, *The Collective,* was a dead giveaway."

"They're trying to kill me because of my books?"

"No, they're trying to kill you because they're concerned you might warn the people of this world of their plans. That you might use your knowledge to lead the fight against them the way Bill did. The fact they're here, now, means they're ready to make their move on this world, and they don't want you standing against them."

"And where does Lila come into all this?"

Marie pulled a photograph from her pocket, and handed it to him. It was a snap taken outdoors, on a bright day. Maybe it had been taken at the seaside; it had that quality of light. A teenage girl looked back over her shoulder, laughing into the camera. She wore a thick coat, and a strong wind teased her hair into long, dark straggles.

"She came here with Bill, looking for you. She wanted to warn you that the Gestalt were after you."

"And now they have her?"

He saw the muscles tighten as Marie clenched her jaw. Her fists were at her sides.

"We have to get her back," she said.

She looked so much like his own poor, dead Marie that he spoke without thinking.

"What can I do?"

"William, I know that right now you're a burned out writer with a drug problem. But in another reality, you were a guerrilla leader, and I need your help."

He glanced down at the picture in his hand, at a face that was somehow strange and familiar, all at the same time.

"She has my eyes."

"Will you help me get her back?"

He could feel the warmth of her breath; smell her unwashed skin.

"Do you think I can?"

She grasped him by the shoulders, her hands warm where they brushed the skin of his neck.

"My darling, I *know* you can."

BOOK REVIEW

From *Mega Awesome Sci-Fi Magazine*, October 2060 (online edition):

The Collective

William S. Cole
(Avuncular Books, £17.99)

Reviewed by Jared Easterbrook

The Collective is the third of Cole's 'Mendelblatt' books. In the opening chapter, private eye Mendelblatt's partner, Al Lemanski, turns up dead, killed in a gruesome, occult manner, and with his right hand chewed off and missing.

The police arrest Mendelblatt on suspicion, but his partner's client—the millionaire, Bradley Knox—intervenes, bailing him out of prison to investigate Al's death and retrieve the valuable briefcase that Al was transporting for him.

And so begins another adventure for the hard-bitten Mendelblatt—only this time, he's operating alone, without the back up of his partner. Personally, I was a bit sad to see Al killed, as I felt he added a much-needed sprinkling of comic relief to the earlier books. Without him, the world of the novel feels much darker, and Mendelblatt's loneliness is palpable, and almost overpowering.

Despite the gloom, the plot gallops ahead, and Cole pulls out all the stops. Within a few short chapters, Mendelblatt finds himself dealing with magic amulets, sinister cultists, mystic portals, and the threatened return of Lovecraftian horrors from beyond our dimension. Somehow, Cole also manages to cram a fairly tender storyline into the mix, and it is in the passages where our hero encounters his estranged daughter that the writing really comes alive.

The evil cult at the centre of the story provides a set of suitably sinister villains, prone to brainwashing recruits and bumping off enemies, and I particularly like the scarily plausible way that Cole shows them insinuating themselves into society.

All in all, I'm going to give this one an eight out of ten. The story's exciting and fast-paced, and certainly a page turner—but I could have done without so much existential moping on behalf of the main character, as it made him look like the disappointingly soft centre of an otherwise tough and enjoyably hardboiled tale.

Read more | Like | Comment | Share

CHAPTER EIGHTEEN
BRINGING A MONKEY TO A DOGFIGHT

PUSHING THE OLD Spitfire to the limits of its performance, Ack-Ack Macaque soared high into the bright morning sky, his right eye never leaving the dragonfly silhouette of the departing helicopter. It looked fast, but he was sure he could catch it; and it never hurt to have the high ground in a dogfight.

Paul's voice came over the radio.

Hey, Ack-ster. What are you doing, man?

"I'm going after K8."

But how are you going to stop them? You can't shoot them down with her on board.

"I'm not going to shoot them down, I'm just going to shoot bits off their chopper until they agree to land."

Are you serious?

Ack-Ack Macaque grinned around his cigar, his earlier tiredness gone.

"Damn right."

The altimeter nudged ten thousand feet, and he tipped the nose forward and down, aiming it at the back of the fleeing chopper. He wanted to come at it from behind, exploiting the blind spot caused by the bulk of its rotor mounting. With any luck, they wouldn't see him coming until he was already on top of them, and he'd be able to get a couple of good shots through the engine before they started weaving around.

The engine's pitch changed as the Spitfire began its dive, and his lips drew back from his teeth. He hadn't had a proper dogfight since being pulled from the game. Ahead, his target barrelled eastwards into the morning sunlight, seemingly oblivious to his pursuit. He watched it grow in his crosshairs.

He gripped the stick with both hands, and clamped his cigar tightly between his teeth. He wanted to get good and close before he opened fire. The chopper could stop in the air, he couldn't. He needed to make his first shot count. They were over farmland now—that great swathe of patchwork fields that stretched along either side of the M4. If he could get a quick burst through the engine without peppering the cockpit, he might be able to force it down without killing anyone—especially K8.

So intent was he on his target, he didn't see the attack drone spiralling down from above until it opened fire. Cannon shells punched through his wings and fuselage. The cockpit canopy shattered.

"Yowch!" He dragged the stick back into his left hip, throwing the plane over, trying to roll out of the line of fire. As he did so, he caught a glimpse of a shark-like profile, with two enclosed engines and short, stubby wings laden with missiles. The drone was an unmanned, jet-propelled weapons platform, and the Spitfire was no match for it. He could twist and turn all over the sky, but all that the drone had to do was follow and shoot. A single missile would be enough to finish him, and that thing looked to be packed with them.

"Fuck, fuck, fuckity-fuck."

He'd lost sight of the chopper but that, right now, was the least of his concerns. Squinting against the rush of cold air, he clawed his goggles down over his one good eye, and shoved the stick as far forward as it would go, throwing the Spitfire's nose at the ground. If he stayed up here, his life expectancy would be less than a few seconds. His hundred-and-fifteen-year-old plane was no match for a modern, computerised targeting system. His only hope was to get low, and try and lose himself in ground-level scenery.

For a moment, he missed his days in the game. Although he hadn't known at the time that he was, as far as the other players were concerned, technically immortal, he'd at least had the reassurance that he'd never be pitted against anyone with a better plane than him. The Spitfire and the Messerschmitt ME109 were reasonably matched in terms of weaponry and performance. The playing field had always been level, and the conflicts decided by the respective skills of the pilots involved. But in these days of autonomous decision engines and laser guidance, skill meant a hell of a lot less than it used to. All a drone pilot had to do was steer his craft within a mile or so of his target and press a button.

Creaks and groans wracked the airframe as the Spit drilled down through the air, hammering towards the green baize billiard table of a grassy field. Ack-Ack Macaque, head half-frozen by the wind, held his nerve for as long as he could; until he fancied he could see each individual blade of grass. Then he hauled back on the stick, pulling out of the dive with his wings in serious danger of clipping the trees and hedgerows at the field's border.

If he could stay low enough, with the belly of his plane almost kissing the dirt, the drone's missiles wouldn't have enough room to manoeuver; they'd plough into the soil or hit a pylon before they could zero in on him.

At least, he hoped so. But being so low had its own share of hazards. Not only was he in constant danger of smashing into a telegraph pole, lamppost or church spire; he was also too low to bail out if something went wrong. If the Spitfire were hit, he wouldn't have time to leap out—and if he did, his parachute wouldn't have time to open—before he hit the ground at three hundred miles per hour.

He weaved from side to side. He had no idea where the drone was, only that it was behind him somewhere. He didn't dare tear his one good eye from the onrushing scenery. With trees whipping past his wingtips like the skeletal fingers of ghouls trying to snatch him down, a moment's inattention would be fatal.

His lips drew back in a fierce grin.

"Ah, to hell with it!"

Sparing one hand, he reached into the side pocket of his flying jacket and pulled out his petrol lighter. A quick flick of the thumb, and a blue flame roared in the wind. He used it to light his cigar. If he had to go down, he was going to do it in style.

THE FIRST MISSILE hit an old oak tree a few metres behind and to the right of the Spitfire's tail, with an explosion that threw Ack-Ack Macaque forward and sideways against his harness. He saw a fireball in the shattered remnants of his rear-view mirror, but didn't have time for more than a quick glance. "Damn and blast!" He threw the stick to the left, and then hauled it back over to the right, hoping to throw off his enemy's aim. If there were more missiles, he couldn't see them. He flashed across a motorway at streetlamp height, and crossed a set of train tracks. Ahead, a line of hills stood like a frozen wave. Pylons marched across the ridge. And still he couldn't see the drone. The thing was built for stealth. It was designed to flit across warzones, raining death and mayhem on convoys and bunkers. His fingers curled around the firing controls, aching to shoot back. In the game, he'd taught his pilots to turn and face any attack. The drone might be a state-of-the-art killing machine, but a well-placed volley of tracer rounds would fuck it up the same as any other plane.

He hopped a hedge, into a long, wide field. With nothing to hit but brown soil, he risked a peep back, over his shoulder. The drone was a speck in his wake, above and behind him, black against the bright blue sky. As he watched, a flame shot from beneath its starboard wing: another missile on the way.

Ahead, the ridge of hills bore down upon him. He could go up and over—but when he reached the crest, he'd be plainly visible against the skyline, exposing his backside to the drone's cannon. Better, he thought, to stay low and fight dirty.

To his left, the motorway carved into the hills, and he angled his nose in the direction of the cutting. If he could get low enough, he could squeeze under the twin bridges of the junction, and emerge on the other side with a barrier between himself and the drone. But it was going to be tight. He couldn't fly up the middle of the road, as lampposts lined the central reservation. He'd have to confine himself to the westbound carriageway. As he powered down towards the tarmac, he realised that the four lanes of the carriageway measured no more than forty feet, which gave him less than five feet of clearance at each wingtip. But by that point, he'd already committed himself. He couldn't pull out, and he couldn't afford the slightest wobble.

Unfortunately, he was flying into the teeth of the oncoming traffic. Being early on a Sunday morning, there were thankfully few cars on the road; but, as the first bridge rushed at him, he saw a big, eighteen-wheeler bearing down on the junction from the opposite side. There wouldn't be room for both of them under the second bridge; so, unable to manoeuvre, he took the only course open to him. His thumbs mashed down on the firing control, and the plane shook as all eight machine guns cut loose.

Bullets hammered the front of the truck. The radiator grille and front bumper flew apart, tyres burst, and the vehicle slewed to the side. Its front fender hit and crumpled against the metal barriers at the edge of the hard shoulder. It was still moving forward, but it was slowing.

Ack-Ack Macaque's Spitfire cleared the second bridge and he hauled the stick back into his groin, dragging the nose up. For a second, he thought he wasn't going to make it. The eighteen-wheeler filled his windscreen. He locked eyes with the terrified trucker at its wheel. And then it was gone, snatched away beneath him, and he was airborne, wheeling up into the sky over Wiltshire.

Behind him, the drone's second missile hit the side of the first bridge. He didn't stop to watch. Instead, he was pulling his plane around in the tightest possible circle, crushing himself into his seat with the g-force, and lining up on the junction again, this time from the other side.

As he bore down on the bridges, the underside of his fuselage almost scraped the roadway.

"Well," he muttered, "this has to be the stupidest fucking thing I've done all day." To have cleared both bridges once was a miracle; to attempt the same feat again was madness. He saw the drone ahead, moving uphill towards him, framed by the chalk sides of the cutting. For the moment, he was hidden. The drone's computer couldn't make him out; he was lost in the background noise, obscured by cars and bridges and smoke. He might remain hidden only a few seconds, but, with his opponent exposed and blind, a few seconds were all he needed.

The Spitfire boomed under the first bridge, wingtips inches from disaster. The noise of the engine bounced back at him from the concrete overhead. The wind snatched at the hair on his cheeks, and threw sparks from the cherry-red tip of his cigar. Grinning, he squeezed the firing control. Eight lines of glittering tracer converged on the drone's bulbous, sensor-packed nose. He flashed into sunlight, then into shadow again. Passing under the second bridge, he kept the control depressed, knuckles white, pouring everything he had at the oncoming machine. A wild screech ripped from his throat.

"Die, motherfucker, die!"

CHAPTER NINETEEN
NO MORE MISTER NICE MONKEY

ACK-ACK MACAQUE NURSED the damaged Spitfire back to the *Tereshkova*, and pancaked her down on the airship's runway. He had nowhere else to go. By the time he'd finished with the drone, the helicopter had gone, having disappeared into the countryside at treetop height. He hadn't even known in which direction it had gone, and his plane had been too shot-up to go searching for it, so he'd come limping home instead, seething all the way.

As he climbed out of the splintered cockpit, he saw Victoria waiting for him, along with Paul's hologram, the American writer and the orange-haired woman.

"What the hell do you lot want?" He wasn't in the mood to talk. All he wanted was to wring the necks of the Gestalt clowns who'd snatched K8; to choke the life out of them with his bare hands, watch their tongues loll and their eyeballs bulge. Especially Reynolds. Oh, how he'd love to get his fingers around the throat of that smug prick. Without breaking stride, he stalked past Victoria, heading for one of the hangars. He was going take a helicopter and start trying to pick up K8's trail. She could be a hundred miles away by now, in any direction, but he had to try. He knew the odds were against him, and that his chances of finding her were miniscule; he just didn't know what else to do.

"Wait up." Victoria ran to keep up with him. "Where are you going?"

"I'm going after her."

"I know. I want to help." She caught his shoulder, but he shrugged her off.

"Then stay the fuck out of my way."

"No." With surprising strength, Victoria took hold of his arm and spun him to face her. Her eyes were narrow and her nostrils wide. "This isn't just about you. This was an attack on all of us. Somebody waltzed onto my skyliner and kidnapped a member of my crew. Not even the CIA would be stupid enough to do something like that. As far as I'm concerned, it's a declaration of war against you, me, and the *Tereshkova* herself."

He glared at her through the cracked lens of his flying goggles.

"Then get out of my way, and let me find them."

"You don't have any idea where they are."

He flapped his arms in exasperation.

"Then I'll go down to the city and pick one of the bastards off the streets. They're all linked, aren't they? So it doesn't matter which one we get. I'll just beat the shit out of him until he tells me where they are."

Victoria pursed her lips as if considering this. Then, regretfully, she shook her head.

"We're in enough trouble already, thanks to your stunt on the motorway. If we're going to strike against the Gestalt, we have to do it directly, without civilians getting in the way."

"If they hurt her…"

"My guess is she'll be safe for now. We have two things the Gestalt want. They want to kill Cole and, for some reason, they want to recruit you. God knows why, but I'm betting they'll use K8 as leverage to achieve at least one of those goals."

The wind blew across the runway. Ack-Ack Macaque felt it prickle the fur on his cheeks and the backs of his hands. He looked towards Cole.

"Do we know why they want to kill the American?"

Victoria raised an eyebrow. "You wouldn't believe me if I told you."

"Fine, then. Don't bother." He turned towards the helicopter sheds. "It's not like I give a shit anyway."

"They have his daughter."

"They have my friend."

"Then, let's work together." Victoria put a hand on his sleeve. "To get them both back."

The wind jostled them. Ack-Ack Macaque bared his teeth into it. "Since when do you care about Cole's daughter?"

"Since those bastards attacked my ship. And besides, there's a hell of a lot more at stake here than you realise."

Ack-Ack Macaque gave a snort. There usually was.

"End of the world again?"

"Something along those lines."

He let his shoulders droop. "Okay, fine. We'll work together." He flapped a leathery hand at the sunlit horizon. "But where do you suggest we start? That helicopter could be halfway to anywhere by now."

With a whine, Paul's image wheeled up to them. In full daylight, he looked faint and translucent, barely more substantial than a heat haze. Ack-Ack

Macaque could see right through him—see the little car at his feet, and the blue skies and white clouds behind him.

"Perhaps I can help?" He was the only one in shirtsleeves, the only one unmolested by the wind.

"What have you got?"

"Carry me down to Victoria's office, and I'll show you."

"Carry?" Ack-Ack Macaque passed a hand through the image. It was no more tangible than moonlight.

"He means the car," Victoria said. She crouched down and scooped the little vehicle into her hands. As she straightened back up, Paul's image shimmered, broke apart, and disappeared. "It won't go up or down steps."

WHEN THEY GOT to the office and Paul had been reactivated, the five of them clustered around Victoria's desk. The screen inlaid into its surface had been switched on, and showed a satellite image of the surrounding countryside: a chequered bedspread of green, brown and yellow fields, grey towns, and dark, winding rivers.

"We're here," Paul said, peering down, over the top of his rimless spectacles. He indicated the landing strip at Filton, on the northwest tip of the city. "Now, when you last saw it, the Gestalt helicopter was *here*." He moved his hand along the ribbon of the M4 motorway. "And you lost it *here*, at this junction."

Beside him, Ack-Ack Macaque struggled to contain his impatience. His fingers squeezed the metal edge of the desk.

"Yeah, so?"

Paul smiled. His finger traced a route southwards, following the road that led from the motorway junction to a sprawl of streets and buildings clustered around the lazy curves of a wide river.

"Now, this is Bath," he said. "It's an old Roman city famous for the hot springs which give it its name."

Ack-Ack Macaque suppressed a moan. *Geeks*, he thought bitterly. *They can never just get to the motherfucking point.*

"What about it?" He bent over the picture, trying to squint out likely places where they could have landed a helicopter. "You think they're there?"

"No." Paul pushed his glasses back up, onto the bridge of his nose. "But, according to what I've been able to dig up online, Legion Haulage has a corporate retreat on the outskirts. It's an old stately home on the hill, just about here." His finger tapped a building on a green hill overlooking the River Avon where it meandered between two hills, forming a grassy floodplain crossed by both the A4 and the Great Western mainline to London. It was a sprawling country house, with outbuildings and several acres of land. According to the map, it was called Larkin Hall.

"They have to be there," Victoria said. Beside her, William and Marie Cole leaned over the display with interest. Cole looked rough: his hair stuck up more than usual, and his eyes drooped, still carrying the weight of the sedatives he'd been given. A week's worth of bristles peppered his jowls.

"They'll have security systems and armed guards," Marie said, sounding worried. "We can't just walk in through the front gate."

Ack-Ack Macaque wrinkled his nose.

"Like hell we can't." He fixed her with his one good eye. "Listen, lady; breaking into places and busting stuff up is kind of what I do."

Victoria gave him a look.

"What do you have in mind?"

His flight jacket hung open. He straightened up and scratched at the hair on his chest.

"Helicopter assault. Don't bother with the front door; just blow a hole in the roof and abseil in. Find the girls, kick as many arses as possible, and then get the hell outta there before those Gestalt twats know what's hit 'em."

Marie gave him a long, thoughtful look.

"Is that possible?"

"Sure it's possible. It's just your basic smash and grab. Used to do it all the time, in the war."

Paul raised a hand.

"I don't want to be the voice of sanity in this little group; but shouldn't we go to the police?"

"And do what?" Victoria stepped away from the desk. The medals on her chest clanked together as she moved. She went to stand by the floor-to-ceiling picture window, and stood with her hands clasped behind her, looking out at the aerodrome below. "The Gestalt have money, and lawyers like you wouldn't believe. By the time the police get a warrant to search the place, there won't be a trace of the girls." She took a deep breath in through her nose. "Besides, I wouldn't be surprised if the Gestalt already have a few of the local gendarmes in their pockets. Maybe even a few converts on the force." She leaned forward, so that her forehead kissed the cold glass.

"Macaque? If I let you do this, who will you take?"

Ack-Ack Macaque pulled out a cigar and sniffed it.

"A small team of two, maybe three people. All the guns."

William Cole stood by the desk, blinking. He shuffled his weight from one foot to the other.

"I want to come."

Ack-Ack Macaque shook his head.

"No way, José. Not if you're going to flake out like you did last night."

Cole smoothed down the hair on one side of his head.

"I'm serious. I feel a lot better now."

"You look like shit, and you're a fucking liability."

Marie stepped forward, shouldering her way between them.

"That's his daughter in there."

"And that gives him the right to get himself, and the rest of us, killed?"

"It gives him the right to try."

Ack-Ack Macaque curled his lip. "No, it doesn't. I'm not taking him."

"Then take me instead." She stuck her chin forward. "She's my daughter too."

He looked her up and down. She stood with her weight on the balls of her feet, like a dancer. Her fists hung at her sides, but her shoulders were loose and relaxed, ready for anything.

"Think you can handle yourself?"

"I've been in worse places, and I know how the Gestalt work. I've fought them before. I could be useful."

"Okay, then." He couldn't be bothered to argue. He turned to Victoria. "I'll take her. Do you think you can get us there?"

Victoria turned away from the window, and pulled herself up. The overhead light shone on the bald skin of her scalp. The gold braid twinkled on her shoulders.

"We cast off in an hour."

Now it was Ack-Ack Macaque's turn to be surprised. He fought down the urge to grin.

"You're taking the whole ship?"

"K8's a member of its crew." Victoria's voice hardened. She ran a hand across the top of her head. "And if there's one thing the Commodore taught me, it's that nobody gets left behind."

He rolled the cigar in his fingers. K8 had stuck by him for the past year, and he'd done nothing but take her for granted and treat her like a lackey. The thought was an uncomfortable one. He wasn't used to thinking in those terms. Humans were humans; sometimes they were useful; sometimes they were friends. Being obligated to one of them, actually *caring* about them, was something he hadn't experienced before. He'd always had a healthy respect for Victoria Valois, and he enjoyed bantering with Paul, but he'd never felt responsible for either of them. K8 was something else. He'd known her in the game, and she'd helped him when he escaped from it. She was the one constant linking his old life with this one, his longest-serving friend and most stalwart of colleagues, and the thought of losing her filled him with a hot, helpless fury.

"Take me to the armoury," he said. "Those Gestalt wankers are going to be sorry. They'll rue the day they messed with us."

Marie leant on the desk with her fists.

"Do you think we can get them back?"

He sneered at her.

"Of course we'll get them back. Trust me, they've pissed off the wrong primate this time. No more Mister Nice Monkey. By the time I've finished with them, they'll be begging to give us the girls."

Marie narrowed her eyes.

"I hope you're right."

"Of course I'm fucking right." Ack-Ack Macaque drew one of his Colts. In the crowded confines of the office, the gun looked about the size of a cannon. "Take it from me, lady, those arseholes are going to wish they'd never been born."

PART TWO

WHAT ROUGH BEAST

I was thinking this globe enough till there sprang out so noiseless
around me myriads of other globes.

Walt Whitman, *Night on the Prairies*

CHAPTER TWENTY
TOOLING UP

THE *TERESHKOVA*'S ARMOURY: Victoria Valois stood in the corridor and watched as Ack-Ack Macaque worked his way around the walk-in cupboard, pulling weapons from the shelves. There were few guns, but he already had his Colts on his hips. He added grenades, knives, and a couple of rusty throwing stars that he found in an old shoebox on one of the higher shelves. Beside him, Marie did the same, tooling herself up with the calm efficiency of an experienced soldier preparing for an operation.

"So, you say you've done this before?" he asked, pulling a wicked-looking machete from a rack of blades.

Marie reached for a coil gun: a magnetic projectile accelerator in the shape of a machine gun, capable of punching a titanium slug through a concrete wall. With practised efficiency, she hefted it in one hand, braced the stock against her hip, and clicked a magazine into place.

"I can look after myself." She had her orange hair tied back in a severe ponytail, and Victoria had given her a bulletproof vest from her own personal stash. Watching her, Victoria couldn't help but be impressed by the way the woman stood up to the monkey.

"Take whatever you need," she said, reaching down to touch the retractable fighting stick tucked into her own belt. Ack-Ack Macaque saw her doing it.

"Wishing you were coming with us, boss?"

She smiled, but there was little humour in it. They were the assault team, and she was the skyliner captain.

"I'll have more than enough to do here." She had no doubt that, after the events of last year, every move the *Tereshkova* made would be closely scrutinised by both the authorities and the media. Larkin Hall was close to the skyliner's scheduled route to London, so they could approach it without raising undue suspicion; but once there, she'd have to do some pretty fast talking to justify a helicopter assault on a stately home. If worse came to worst, she supposed, it would help that they had a friend in Buckingham

Palace. Not that she'd presume on that friendship except in the direst of emergencies.

Briefly, she wondered how Merovech was adjusting to life on the throne. She hadn't seen him since the aftermath of the battle in the Channel, and still remembered him as he was when she first met him: a troubled young man in ratty jeans and a smelly red hoodie, struggling to come to terms with the death of his father. Now, he was king of the United Kingdom of Great Britain, France, Northern Ireland and Norway, and Head of the United European Commonwealth. He was preparing for his forthcoming marriage to Julie Girard, the digital activist who'd first drawn him into the intrigue that freed Ack-Ack Macaque from his virtual world and exposed the conspiracy at the heart of Céleste Technologies. The boy was a head of state, and still only barely out of his teens. He had quite enough on his plate without her turning up like Banquo's ghost.

If she could get along without involving him, she would. She had no wish to embarrass him, but she had no illusions that what they were about to do was illegal and could be construed as a terrorist act. The Gestalt might be a dangerous cult bent on global domination but, as far as the world at large was concerned, they were simply a group of technological eccentrics—a bit creepy, yes, but entitled to the same protections as everybody else. Launching an attack on one of the organisation's properties was an action bound to provoke a response from the UK authorities and, if it came to a standoff with the Royal Air Force, she wouldn't hesitate to pick up the phone.

"Besides," she said, "the two of you are carrying enough ordnance to level the place by yourselves; you don't need me tagging along."

"Are you sure about that, boss?" The monkey picked up a crossbow. "You can be pretty handy in a scrap." The crossbow had been made of some sort of carbon fibre, which made it light as well as tough.

Victoria turned to look up the corridor, in the direction of the airship's bridge.

"I'll have your backs from up here. If anything goes wrong, I'll have a chopper snatch you out in seconds."

Marie pulled a webbing harness over her shoulders and fastened it at the front. It had loops and pockets for weapons and equipment.

"How long will it take to get there?"

"About half an hour from when we cast off."

"That seems a long time."

"We have to fly slowly over the city."

"Can't we go around?"

"We could, but it wouldn't save any time." She checked her watch. "Now, I've got to get to the bridge so we can get under way. Monkey Man, are you going to fly us out?"

Ack-Ack Macaque stood in the centre of the armoury, festooned with weaponry and ammunition.

"You think I'd trust any of you idiots to do it?"

FIVE MINUTES LATER, Victoria sat in her command chair, looking forward through the curved windshield of the *Tereshkova*'s bridge. She wore an insulated cap with fur earflaps. The temperature in here was colder than in the rest of the gondola. The heat leached out through the glass of the big window and the metal of the walls and floor. The monkey sat at the pilot's workstation to her right, and the Russian navigator to her left. The touchscreens set into the arms of her chair displayed graphical summaries of the airship's systems. She couldn't read the numbers, of course, but was reassured to see that everything that should be green appeared to be green, and nothing glowed red or amber. The engines were all online, and she fancied she could almost feel their vibration through the deck.

Paul stood by her shoulder. He'd been tinkering with his image again, and now appeared to be clad in a black polo neck and slate grey chinos.

"You know," he whispered, "I could do this."

"What?"

"Fly the ship."

Victoria turned to look at him.

"Are you serious?"

"Perfectly. After all, it's just another computer system, isn't it? I don't see any reason I couldn't learn it, given enough time."

"Don't let the monkey hear you say that."

Paul gave Ack-Ack Macaque's back a guilty glance. "Of course not." He adjusted his glasses. "I don't want to undermine him or anything. It's just that if things go badly and we ever lost him, I'd want you to know that you had another pilot on standby. Potentially. If you needed me." He wouldn't meet her eyes, and Victoria felt a prickle at the back of her throat. This was, she realised, his way of trying to be useful.

"I'll always need you," she said.

At the helm, Ack-Ack Macaque cleared his throat.

"Will you two stop yapping? I'm trying to concentrate." He spoke without taking his eye from the controls, and Victoria knew he was busily aligning the engines to propel the airship's kilometre-long bulk eastward. She watched his hairy hands dance on his workstation's screen.

"All right, Mister Macaque." She sat up straight, and tugged the hem of her tunic into place. "In your own time."

The monkey hit a switch. A warning bell chimed over the intercom, followed by an announcement recorded in both Franglais and Russian. Down below, the delivery trucks, tenders and other vehicles had scattered from the runway to avoid the downdraught of the skyliner's fifteen giant impellers.

"Here we go." He dragged a fingertip down one side of the screen, and the bow tipped upward by twenty degrees. The airframe gave a series of creaks. A pen rolled from the navigator's console and skittered across the deck until it clanged into the bridge's rear wall. Victoria winced. She knew that in the gondola behind her—and in those hanging from the other four hulls—drinks would be spilling, plates would be sliding off tables, and people would be stumbling and tripping into each other.

Needs must, she thought. One of their crew was in trouble, and that took priority over a few spilled gin and tonics.

The thrust kicked in, pushing her backwards in her seat. She'd never felt anything like it in all her time on the *Tereshkova*, and hadn't thought the old airship capable of such acceleration. The monkey must have pushed all fifteen engines into the red. The whole ship seemed to judder, and she gripped the arms of her chair as the airfield fell away.

"Watch your speed," Paul said nervously. Ack-Ack Macaque didn't bother turning around.

"Screw the limits. What are they going to do, shoot us down over the city?" He touched a control and increased the thrust even further. Around them, the bulkheads moaned in protest, like the timbers of a galleon caught in a storm. The old airship rose, as if hoisted on the crest of a wave, and Victoria's communication display lit up. The airfield's control tower wanted to talk to her. She smiled, and dismissed their call. Inside, she felt a wild surge of pride. The *Tereshkova* was hers, and it was doing something unsuspected and spectacular—something that would further cement its reputation as a maverick in the skyliner community; a true individual in a company of rogues.

Silently, she offered up a prayer of thanks to the Commodore. Losing her ability to write, her career in journalism, and her husband had left her lost and rudderless, and it had taken the *Tereshkova* to rekindle her sense of purpose. She hoped that in whatever vodka-soaked afterlife the old man now found himself, he knew how thoroughly he'd saved her.

Beside her, Paul's hologram stood stroking his chin, unaffected by the tilt of the deck. She poked a finger at him.

"You'd be able to fly like this, would you?"

His eyes were locked on the forward view, and she saw his Adam's apple bob in his throat as he swallowed nervously.

"I don't know. Maybe. If I really had to."

"You think so?"

Wide eyes met her gaze over the tops of his spectacles.

"Perhaps."

"Are you monitoring the internal cameras?"

"Yes. It's a mess back there."

"Any serious damage?"

"Nothing dreadful; mostly crockery and furniture falling over. A few bumps and bruises. Everything else is secured against turbulence. Except—" He bit his lower lip. "Oh dear, oh dear. Our furry friend's going to be very upset."

"Why, what is it?"

He glanced at the back of the monkey's head, and then leant in close to whisper in her ear.

"It's his Spitfire."

"What about it?"

"It's fallen off."

CHAPTER TWENTY-ONE
IN THE CELLAR

THE DRUGS THEY'D given K8 hadn't knocked her completely out, just rendered her queasy and muddled. A whole bottle of vodka would have had a similar effect. She had vague, blurred impressions of being bundled out onto the *Tereshkova*'s flight deck and stuffed into a helicopter. Her legs hadn't been working properly, and so the men in white had to support her by the elbows. Then it was all blue sky, white clouds and green countryside until they landed in a garden somewhere, and they led her into the cellar of a big old house, and threw her down onto a bare and filthy mattress.

She lay there for a long time, staring at the ceiling, trying to stop the room from spinning. Then she felt small, tentative hands shaking her by the shoulder, and turned her head (making the walls of the room swoop and sway even more sickeningly) to find herself looking into the concerned eyes of a girl about her own age.

"What...?"

The girl shrank back. A bruise darkened her cheek. Her eyes were wary.

"Are you okay?" she asked.

K8 tried to sit up; then put a hand to her head and groaned, waiting for the pain behind her eyes to recede.

"I've been drugged," was all she could manage. The girl didn't reply. Instead, she shambled over to a workbench by the door and came back clutching a metal canteen. She held it out and K8 took it, unstopped the lid, and sniffed.

"Water?"

The girl gave a nod. She had brown hair tied back in a long plait, and wore a grey t-shirt and a pair of combat trousers done out in the black, white and grey splodges of urban camouflage.

K8 took a sip from the canteen. The water inside was cool and tasted of aluminium. She rinsed it around the inside of her cheeks, and spat onto the floor.

"Who are you?" She wiped her mouth on her sleeve. "Where are we?"

The girl hugged herself.

"My name's Lila."

K8 frowned, and rubbed her forehead.

"You're Marie's daughter, right?"

"You know my mother?"

"Yeah, sort of. I heard her mention your name. Just now, before those freaks grabbed me." With great effort, K8 pushed herself up into a sitting position and placed her feet on the floor. The room dipped and shuddered, but then seemed to steady itself, and she decided she'd better remain upright for the foreseeable future—at least, until she felt better. Tipping the canteen to her lips again, she swallowed a mouthful of water, and tried to take stock of her surroundings.

The cellar was about the same size as the passenger lounge on the *Tereshkova*, and illuminated by a single strip of light in the centre of the ceiling. It had obviously been used as a storeroom for many decades. Sagging, cobwebby boxes sat stacked against the back wall. She saw the handle of a tennis racquet protruding from one, and the moth-eaten arm of an old teddy bear sticking from the flap of another. Piles of decades-old newspapers sat clumped in string-tied bundles. Small screws and chips of wood littered the floor where they'd fallen. The air smelled of wood and mildew, and reminded her of the smell of the lock-up garage where her grandpa had kept his old car.

"Where are we?"

Lila took the canteen from her hands and refastened the stopper.

"I'm not sure." She nervously brushed a strand of hair behind her ear. "I mean, I'm pretty certain we're still in England. All those newspapers are English, for a start. I'm just not sure *exactly* where in England we are."

K8 thought about trying to stand, and decided against it. She wasn't convinced her legs were ready to bear her weight.

"Have you been here long?"

"A couple of days."

"Any idea what they want with us?"

"They're using me as a hostage, to get to my father. Why they'd want you, I have no idea." Lila crossed her arms. "I don't even know who you are."

"Oh, sorry." K8 rubbed her eyes, trying to force herself to feel more awake. "I'm K8."

"Kate?"

"Aye, close enough. I'm from the *Tereshkova*. I've been looking after your father."

Lila tensed.

"My father?"

"William Cole, the writer."

"Oh." The girl squeezed her hands together. She turned her head away. "He's not really my father. It's complicated. The last time I saw my real father, he was on his way to the *Tereshkova*, to intercept Cole."

K8 felt a chill. "If you're talking about 'Bill', he did."

"How is he?"

She swallowed. She wasn't in any fit state to be breaking bad news to a stranger. "I'm afraid he was shot."

Lila's hand flew to her throat. "He's dead?"

"I'm afraid so."

Lila's gaze dropped to the floor. Her chest rose and fell. K8 looked away. She didn't know what to do or say. She'd never been in this situation before.

Eventually, Lila looked up, and wiped her eyes with the back of her hand.

"You said you'd seen my mother?"

"Your mother came aboard last night. She asked Captain Valois for help in finding you."

"And now you've found me."

"Yeah, and a fat lot of good it does either of us." K8 put her head in her hands and glared down at her feet. Her stomach made sharp complaining noises.

Lila was silent for a minute or so. Then, quietly, she said, "The Gestalt must have grabbed you because you were helping my mum."

From somewhere far beyond the cellar walls, they heard a car approach and pull to a stop. Doors opened and slammed, and silence returned.

"No," K8 said. "I don't think that was it. They weren't waiting for me; they were waiting for my friend. I think they were after him."

"And they grabbed you by mistake?" Lila looked sceptical.

"He'd already refused to join their cult. He even slapped one of them around a bit. I think they were waiting for him, but when I arrived, I guess they improvised."

"And now you think they're using you as bait, the same way they're using me?"

"Who knows?" She shrugged. "Maybe."

"Do you think it will work?"

"Oh yes. He'll come looking for me. You can bet your life on that."

"And then you'll both be caught."

K8 smiled through the nausea. "You don't know what he's capable of."

Lila rubbed her hands and blew into them. "Do you really think he'll try to rescue you?"

"If anyone can, he will."

"And he's working with my mother?"

"I think we're all on the same side now."

Lila turned away. Her face was pale and drawn, and K8 could see that she didn't want to let herself hope too much, or put too much faith in a rescue that might never come. After two days in this cellar, and who knew what mistreatment at the hands of the Gestalt, she must have given up all hope at least once; and so it was little wonder if she seemed wary of rekindling it—especially now, in the wake of K8's devastating news.

"Well," she said, her tone flat, "your friend had better be something special, because you have no idea what he's up against." She walked over to the door and absently rattled the handle, as if checking it was still locked.

K8 hawked and spat, trying to get the bitter, coppery taste of indigestion out of her mouth.

She said, "I don't think a houseful of lunatics in white suits are going to put up much of a fight."

Lila turned to face her, leaning her back against the door.

"You haven't a clue, have you?" She shook her head pityingly. "You don't know what you're fighting."

"Why don't you enlighten me?"

"Those people out there aren't the local Gestalt. They intercepted me when I tried to contact Cole. They were waiting for me, and they knew who I was."

"So?"

"So, I don't exist on this timeline. The only way they could know who I was would be if they came here from somewhere else. These aren't your local converts, these are the Gestalt's advance guard, its elite troops."

"And they followed you here?"

"No, they came here to kill Cole, and a number of others. They're laying the groundwork for a full-scale incursion."

K8 rubbed her forehead, trying to massage some life back into her slothful synapses.

"They're preparing an *invasion*?"

"I told you, these are the advance guard. They even have their Leader with them."

"The Gestalt has a leader?"

Lila shivered, and wrapped her arms tightly across her chest. "They took me to see him."

"I thought the Gestalt were all supposed to be the same?"

"They are. But the Leader's something else. He's... different. Not hooked into the web like the rest of them."

"And he's here? I mean, right here in this house?"

"He was yesterday, when they took me to him." She shuddered and looked at the black mould dappling the cellar's back wall.

K8 clenched and unclenched her fingers and toes. She had pins and needles in her feet, but her legs were feeling less and less unsteady with every minute that passed. She wouldn't be sprinting anywhere for a while, but felt confident that, if she had to, she'd soon be able to get up and walk—at least, as far as the door.

"But how are they going to invade the whole world?" she said. "The idea's daft."

Lila didn't turn her head. "They'll do it the same way they invaded my world. And we've been fighting them ever since."

"But if we can warn people, if we can get the word out, we can be ready for them."

"You don't understand. They're relentless. If you shoot one, another one takes his or her place. And they just keep coming. You can't outthink them, because they all think as one. You can't surprise them, because if you kill one of them, all the others immediately know about it—unless you can do it so quickly they don't have time to register the attack, but even then, the others know *something's* wrong."

"So, what do you do?"

"You stay quiet. You hide. And when you strike, you do it quickly, and then you run." She took a long, shuddering breath. "And we've been running for five years. Until—"

"Until what?"

Lila swallowed. "They developed this plague. It's like a virus. It gets into your soul-catcher and changes it. Makes you one of them."

K8 rubbed the back of her neck, where her own device had been implanted on her sixteenth birthday—a present from her employers at the time, Céleste Tech.

"What if you don't have a soul-catcher?"

"It builds one." Lila rubbed her eyes. "It converts flesh and bone into gelware, and burrows into your head."

K8 swirled the water around in the canteen. Her thoughts felt heavy and tired.

"So, why didn't it infect you?"

"We saw what was happening, and we left. We crept into one of their machines and used it to get away while they were still in the process of spreading the infection. We didn't know where we'd end up, but anything seemed better than staying. But now, they're going to use their plague against this world, too."

"Unless we can stop them."

A sigh. "We can't stop them."

"If we could get to the Leader somehow, and make him—"

"Forget it." Lila waved a hand. "You'd never get past his bodyguards. And if you did, you still wouldn't stand a chance. He'd never surrender."

K8 said, "Tough, is he?"

Lila took a long, raggedy breath.

"You have no idea."

From above, they heard footfalls echoing on stone steps, descending in their direction. Keys jangled, and Lila backed away from the door.

"They're coming!"

K8 tried to push herself up, but her knees were still unsteady.

"Help me."

"I can't." Lila shook her head and backed away further. "I think they're coming for you this time. I think they're coming to take you to *him*."

CHAPTER TWENTY-TWO
STINGER

THE *TERESHKOVA* THUNDERED across the city at full power, startling pedestrians and shaking windows in their frames. From his seat on the bridge, Ack-Ack Macaque saw the shadow thrown by its five hulls—a great rectangular eclipse darkening office blocks and church spires. He made a few final adjustments and then, satisfied the airship was headed in the right direction, unclipped himself from the pilot's chair and turned to Victoria.

"Nobody touches that throttle," he said. "We'll get there faster if we accelerate all the way. When we get close, I'll jump out, and I'll take the woman with me. When we're gone, I've set the autopilot to bring the ship around in a wide loop. By the time you get back to the target, you'll be at rest, and it should all be over on the ground, one way or another."

Victoria watched him carefully.

"You missed a part."

"Which part?"

"The part where I'm the captain and you're the pilot, and I give the orders."

He glowered at her. He was still furious that they'd lost his plane—which now lay smashed and concertinaed in a supermarket car park—and this wasn't the time for her to be playing hierarchy games.

"Would you do anything differently?"

She stroked her chin with finger and thumb, considering.

"Well," she said after a moment, "no."

"Then please, get out of my way, *Captain.*"

Victoria narrowed her eyes, and there was a glimmer in them that told him her objections weren't entirely serious, that she was just making a point.

"Make sure you get them both back, okay?"

"Yes, boss."

"And *that's* an order."

"Yes, boss." He threw a floppy, long-armed salute and scampered aft, to where Marie Cole awaited him. She looked bulky with the bulletproof jacket that Victoria had given her, and bug-eyed with the goggles she'd put on over her face; but nevertheless, she exuded a fierce, furious determination that matched his own, and he had no doubt she'd do okay when the fighting got dirty and personal.

"Ready?" he asked.

"Lead on, monkey."

He led her up through the *Tereshkova*'s corridors and companionways to the helipad on top of the airship, and one of the sleeker passenger choppers. The pilot was already on board, warming the engine, and Ack-Ack Macaque hopped in beside him.

"Have you got the box stowed?"

"In the back, sir."

"Then take us up, as soon as you're ready."

"Aye, sir."

As the five-pronged shadow of the *Tereshkova*'s nose cleared the final suburb of Bristol, the helicopter rose from the flight deck. It hovered in the air for a moment, allowing the behemoth to move away ahead of it, and then dropped, coming down in a swooping curve that brought it down past the giant fins and rudders at the stern, and forward, under the speeding airship.

"Keep low," Ack-Ack Macaque told the pilot, "and follow the river. Watch out for bridges."

He scrambled into the back, where Marie sat strapped into her seat, coil gun resting across her knees. A large metal case sat on the deck by her feet, held in place by bungee cords. He crouched beside it, bracing himself against the seat in the cramped space, and began to unfasten it.

"What's that?" Marie leant forward for a better look.

Ack-Ack Macaque gave her a grin.

"This is our way in."

From the front, the pilot called, "Two minutes to target."

They were winding along the course of the River Avon. Ahead, they could see hills and main roads, Georgian terraces and the tower of Bath Cathedral.

The London mainline lay to their left, and they drew level with an eastbound train.

"Keep pace with the train," Ack-Ack Macaque ordered. The land was opening out into a wide river valley, down the middle of which the track ran, side-by-side with the river. Larkin House stood on a hill to the north, and he hoped that by staying low, concealed visually and audibly by the train, they might be able to approach without raising an alarm.

Looking out of the side window, he saw faces looking back at him from the train's carriages, and gave them the finger.

When they drew level with their target, the pilot pulled up and over the train.

"Thirty seconds," he reported.

Ack-Ack Macaque exchanged looks with Marie. Then he flipped the fastening on the box and opened it, revealing a long, fat tube with a gun sight and a pistol grip. It had been painted olive green, with bright red, black and yellow warning decals. It was one of the Commodore's hidden treasures, but there was no time to sit and admire the thing. He pulled it from the case and slung its strap over his shoulder, kicked his boots off, stuck a cigar into his mouth, and shuffled to the side hatch.

"Sit tight," he told Marie. He slid the door open and climbed through, onto the helicopter's landing strut. Cold winds tore at him but he gripped the strut with his toes. Ahead, the hillside came at them like a rising green wave and he could see the pale sandstone frontage of Larkin House in the centre of a tidy arrangement of fir trees, gravel paths and ornamental hedges.

Crouching, he wrapped his tail around the strut, and let go with his hands. Gripping hard with his toes, he swung around until he hung upside down by his feet. The helicopter rocked at this, but stayed on course. Below, white-suited figures emerged from the house and pointed guns at him. He saw muzzle flashes but, if any of the bullets hit the chopper, he didn't see or feel them. Instead, he concentrated on getting the tube—which now swung from his arm on the end of its strap—onto his shoulder, where he was forced to hold it in position with both hands.

Come on, he thought, *this isn't any harder than hanging from a tree branch. Travelling at a hundred miles an hour. Through a cyclone.*

The tube housed one of the Commodore's most prized souvenirs, taken from a cupboard in his cabin. It was a portable ground-to-air missile picked up off a battlefield somewhere in the Middle East thirty years ago.

Steadying the launcher, Ack-Ack Macaque lined the sight up on the eaves of the old house

"Okay," he muttered to himself around the cigar, "time to blow shit up."

He pulled the trigger. There was a sharp *whoosh*, and the tube bucked in his hands so hard he almost lost his grip on the strut. The missile leapt forward on a candle of flame, and the helicopter dipped its nose to follow.

Squirming around, Ack-Ack Macaque managed to pull himself back up to the helicopter's open hatch. He let the empty launcher fall away into the fields below, and drew one of his big, shiny Colts. Marie looked at him, and he gave her a big thumbs-up.

"Everything's okay!" he hollered above the engine noise. Ahead, the missile hit the roof and blew apart in a huge fireball. Tiles and bits of wooden joist flew into the air, and black smoke mushroomed over the house. "Okay, as long as they weren't keeping your kid in the attic."

They passed over the front gates of the house, and he dropped a grenade, to make the clowns with guns keep their heads down. Then the helicopter was over the hole in the roof, its downdraught whipping the smoke and flames. The drop was somewhere between fifteen to twenty feet.

"Okay, let's go." Cigar clamped securely in his teeth, he leaned out of the helicopter, and dropped.

The wind tore at him. His jacket flapped. He fell into the fire, and through, into the space beneath the roof. His bare feet hit wooden planks hard enough to jar his spine, and he rolled onto his shoulder, just getting out of the way in time before Marie crashed through the smoke and hit the deck beside him.

By the time she'd picked herself up, he was on his feet, both Colts at the ready, as the helicopter peeled away, heading back towards the *Tereshkova*, which was hammering past a couple of kilometres to the south.

Black smoke filled the attic. He coughed and pulled his scarf up to cover his nose and mouth. There wasn't time to waste looking for a hatch leading down, so he yanked the pin from a grenade, sang, "Have a banana," and rolled it as far along the floorboards as it would go.

A second explosion rocked the house. When it had cleared, the floor had a ragged, burning hole in it.

Marie brushed dust and splinters from her clothes. She looked at him with an expression of respect, astonishment, and irritation.

"Please," she said, "warn me the next time you're going to do that."

He grinned at her, scooped up a smouldering stick of wood, and lit his cigar.

"There's something you need to know about me, lady—"

"That you're dangerously irresponsible with explosives?"

He frowned, pulled out his cigar, and exhaled smoke.

"Uh, yeah," he said. "That's near enough."

*   *   *

DROPPING DOWN THROUGH the hole in the floorboards, they found themselves in a dormitory. The room had probably once been a grand bedroom; now it contained three rows of triple bunk beds. Chunks of shattered plaster lay on the blankets and floor, and the bunk closest to the hole was alight.

"Well," Ack-Ack Macaque said, "I told you I'd get us into the house, didn't I?"

Marie cradled the coil gun, keeping its barrel pointed at the door.

"You certainly did. I can't fault you on that. But it's lucky the girls weren't in this room."

Ack-Ack Macaque gave a shrug.

"Ah, they'd have been okay. I needed a grenade to get through those ceiling beams."

From the landing beyond, they heard the sound of shoes running on a polished wooden floor. Holding his Colts at arm's length, Ack-Ack Macaque drew a bead on the door. Marie waved him away.

"No, you'll give away our position," she said. "We need to kill them quickly, before they know what's hit them, otherwise they'll alert the rest of the hive. Leave this to me."

He glanced at her gun. It was a slim metal tube wrapped in electromagnets, with batteries in the stock, and a foot-long magazine protruding from the bottom of the barrel, just in front of the trigger. It looked like something knocked up in somebody's garden shed. Christ alone knew where the Commodore had found it.

"Really?"

She took up a firing stance.

"Have you ever seen one of these at work?"

He waggled his head.

"Nah."

"Then you might want to stand back."

The footsteps reached the door, and the handle rattled as somebody seized it. Marie clicked the coil gun's trigger, and moved the barrel back and forth. Firing without sound or recoil, the gun peppered the door, punching dozens of pencil-thin holes through the wooden panels, the frame, and the walls to either side.

The effect was as if she'd taken a chainsaw to it. As the stream of tungsten darts crossed and re-crossed the door, chunks of wood were cut away and blown out into the corridor. By the time she clicked the trigger off again, only one large piece remained, attached to the lower hinge, and even that had a few holes through it. Outside in the corridor, two Neanderthals lay slumped against the far wall, their white suits ragged and soaked in bright red blood.

Ack-Ack Macaque walked forward carefully, keeping his guns trained on them, but he needn't have bothered—when he got closer, he saw they were both quite definitively dead. Bits of their massive jaws and swollen craniums were missing, torn away by the deadly rain of miniature projectiles, and their chests and stomachs had been minced to hamburger. He poked one in the shoulder with the barrel of his gun, and the man's arm fell off, severed in three or four places, as if it had been hacked apart with a meat cleaver.

"Man," Ack-Ack Macaque muttered, "I have *got* to get me one of those guns."

The walls of the landing had been painted red; the floors were dark, varnished wood, and heavily framed paintings adorned the walls. Ack-Ack Macaque ran a finger across one of the paintings, and it came away covered in dust. Other doors led off from the landing, presumably into other bedrooms, and a wide stone staircase swept down to an entrance hall. Crouching by the wrought iron rail, he peeped over. The entrance hall had a bulbous, black metal chandelier hanging from a chain above its diamond-patterned flagstone floor, and a reception desk installed just inside the main doors of the house, at the foot of the stairs. A white-suited man and woman stood behind the desk, consulting a fire alarm console, on which several red lights were illuminated. As he watched, they stopped what they were doing, and both turned to look at the stairs. He ducked back.

Damn, he thought, *they're all linked, aren't they?* Marie had done her best, but it made no difference; as soon as you killed one of the Gestalt, the others all knew something had happened. They might not know the cause, but they sensed the loss. Now, they'd all be converging on this landing to find out what was going on, and he wasn't sure he could hold them all off.

Well, he thought, *so much for stealth. If I wanted a sneak attack, I wouldn't have blown up the roof.*

He picked another grenade from his belt, and tossed it over the rail. He heard a shout, then a satisfying *crump,* and the clatter of broken glass.

"Maybe that'll make them more cautious," he muttered, standing up and dusting himself down. The two by the reception desk were either unconscious or dead. He kept one gun trained on them and the other on the front door as he made his way down, step by step. The back of his leather jacket squeaked as he pressed it against the painted wall. His cigar left a descending trail of grey smoke.

Marie said, "They don't know there are two of us. You keep them distracted, and I'll stay up here and check the other rooms."

"Knock yourself out."

They had only seconds, and a staircase was no place for a shootout. Three doors led off the hallway, deeper into the rest of the house, and he knew he had to choose one. Rather than cross the hallway, he chose to slip around to the door beneath the stairs. His caution wasn't the result of fear; at this point, he had no regard for own his physical safety, he just wanted to make sure he survived long enough to find K8, and get her out of this madhouse.

The door opened to his touch and he stepped inside, guns at the ready. If one Gestalt member saw him, the rest would be on his trail instantly, so he had no time for subtlety. The rule for today was to kill or be killed; and he couldn't afford to die before he freed K8. She might be a brat, but she was a damn clever brat, and a dependable friend. She'd been there for him in reality and in the game and now she was his only remaining link to the game world, and the person he used to be. She was his colleague and his comrade, and he couldn't imagine life without her. She'd saved his life in the past; now it was his turn to repay the favour. Monkeys were instinctively social creatures, yet he was the only one of his kind. She was the closest thing he had to a member of his troupe, and those primate loyalties ran deep. He knew he'd get her back even if—*especially if*—he had to kill every last motherfucker in the building.

The door brought him into a long corridor, which seemed to run the length of the house, with doors leading off to either side. As he stood there, three of the doors opened, and men and women in white suits stepped out, blocking the way. They were of all ages and nationalities, but their faces all carried the same eerie smile. Some clutched guns, but most were armed with whatever they'd had to hand: knives, letter openers, chair legs...

"You cannot win," they said in unison, standing shoulder-to-shoulder, not attacking. "You are one, we are legion. You will join us."

"Go suck an egg."

"You will join us willingly." The crowd took a pace forwards. "Or otherwise..."

Ack-Ack Macaque glanced at his Colts. Both were fully loaded, which meant he had twelve shots—not nearly enough to deal with the mob in front of him. He might get the first few rows, but he wouldn't have time to reload before the others were upon him. He'd have to drop the revolvers and switch to the automatic pistol tucked into the waistband of his trousers, under his jacket. That would give him another ten shots. Then there was the knife at his belt and, if all else failed, his bare hands and fangs.

He fixed the closest two with a glare, and rolled the cigar from one side of his mouth to the other.

"Fuck you," he said.

As one, they took another step towards him, and raised their weapons. That was all he needed. He opened his mouth with a shriek, and leapt to the attack.

CHAPTER TWENTY-THREE
DIALLING OUT

WILLIAM COLE STOOD on the *Tereshkova*'s bridge, watching the countryside wheel around as the old airship slowed and turned, ready to begin its run back to Larkin Hall and the scene of the battle. From where he stood, he could see a black column of smoke rising into the autumn air. Most of the building's roof was ablaze. And, somewhere down there, beneath that inferno, his wife and child were fighting for their lives.

He scratched fitfully at his wild hair.

"How could I have let her go like that?"

Behind him, Victoria Valois glanced up from her instruments.

"I don't recall you having a choice."

He turned on her.

"But I could have insisted! I could have gone in her place."

"No, you couldn't. What use would you have been, eh?" She looked back down at her console. "At least Marie's fought the Gestalt before. She knows what to expect."

William shook his head. He had a pain in the back of his throat.

"I am such a coward."

He turned back to the window. The smoke and flames looked thicker than before.

Had he lost her again?

THREE CAVEMEN CAME into the cellar. One of them held Lila at bay while the other two grabbed K8. She tried to fight them off but they were solidly built and seemingly impervious to the kicks and blows she aimed their way. She tried to gouge their eyes and knee their groins, but they simply held her tighter, and twisted her arms up behind her back until she cried out and stopped squirming. Her strength had been sapped by the drugs in her system.

"You come with us," the Neanderthals said together. It was the first time she'd heard them speak, and she was surprised. Somehow, she'd been expecting a crude grunt rather than fully formed words.

Moving in perfect step, they pulled her out of the cellar and up a set of stone steps, into a white-tiled kitchen equipped with a wood-burning range, a walk-in larder, and a porcelain sink as big as a bathtub. As they led her through the room, the house rocked to the sound of an explosion. She heard a helicopter overhead, very low and very loud, and small arms fire coming from the front of the building.

"Are we under attack?"

The hands on her arms didn't loosen. Without breaking stride or showing even the slightest curiosity, the three Neanderthals carried her through the kitchen and out, through a series of utility rooms, to a wooden door, which led out into a well-tended kitchen garden, with rows of herbs and vegetables and ornamental bay trees. After the dry, dust-laden air of the cellar, the bright sunshine and chill November breeze hit her like a double handful of cold water, and she sneezed. The fresh air helped her head to clear, and she struggled anew, to test their grip.

"Where are you taking me?"

From within the house behind, she heard the muffled thump of another explosion. Her heart surged. That *had* to be the Skipper. He'd come for her, as she'd known he would. Who else would be tossing grenades around inside a stately home? She stopped wriggling and laughed.

"You idiots are for it now."

The Neanderthals weren't listening; or, if they were, they were doing a very good job of ignoring her and everything else around them. Still marching in perfect synchronisation, they marched her out onto the lawn, and stopped in the centre of a circular patch of dead grass maybe two metres in diameter.

Behind them, the roof of Larkin Hall was ablaze. Smoke billowed up into the blue sky, chased by orange tongues of flame. Gunshots went off like firecrackers.

The Neanderthals seemed to be in no hurry to get away. In fact, they could hardly have chosen a more exposed spot on which to stand. If the Skipper were in the house, all it would take for her to be rescued would be for him to look out of a window...

"Skip!" she hollered. "Skip, I'm out here!" But all that earned her was a cuff across the top of the head from one of her captors.

The caveman who'd whacked her pulled a device from the pocket of his white jacket. It was black and shiny, and resembled a fat SincPhone.

The casing looked to be tough rubber, worn in places but designed to take abuse. She watched him tap the touchscreen with a fat, hairy-knuckled finger. Was he making a call?

Far beyond the conifers at the far end of the lawn, she caught sight of the *Tereshkova*. Impeller blades glittering in the sunlight, the old airship banked sharply, and came around to face the house. She felt the urge to wave her arms and shriek. It might be old and, with its black and white paint job, somewhat ugly, but the elderly skyliner was her home; the first permanent one she'd had since the offer of work with Céleste Tech had enabled her to escape the disintegration of her parents' marriage.

The Neanderthal with the handset paused with his finger over the touchscreen, and muttered something in a language she didn't understand.

"What?"

He grinned at her, exposing flat, shovel-like teeth in a too-wide jaw.

"I said, 'hold on to yourself.'" He brought his hand down and stabbed the 'phone'. K8 felt a quiver move through her entire body. Every muscle and membrane shook. Her eyes trembled in their sockets, blurring her vision, and the sky went dark.

When her sight cleared, she found they were still in the garden, standing in their circle of dead grass, but everything around them had changed. The house wasn't on fire; in fact, it was larger than it had been a moment ago, with a couple of turrets that hadn't been there before, and a whole extra wing that seemed to have materialised out of nowhere. The sounds of fighting had gone, and the *Tereshkova* had disappeared from the sky. In its place hung another airship—bigger, armoured, and unmistakably decked-out for war. Cannon poked from turrets along its length, and its upper surfaces bristled with radar emplacements and anti-aircraft batteries. Its impellers were much larger than the *Tereshkova*'s, and every inch of its hull had been painted black.

A VTOL passenger jet sat on the grass nearby, engines idling, and the Neanderthals carried her towards it. K8 had never flown in a plane before. To her, this one looked kind of like a helicopter without rotors, and she didn't like it. Planes were rare in her world, and she didn't trust them. The idea that a slim metal tube could be held aloft by the difference in speed between the air passing over and under its wing seemed ludicrous.

"Come along," her captors said, bustling her forwards, "the Leader will see you now."

CHAPTER TWENTY-FOUR
THE LEADER

BRUISED AND BLOODIED, Ack-Ack Macaque limped down the steps from the kitchen to the cellar. His cigar, guns and flying cap were all missing, lost in the fight. His jacket had been cut and torn in a dozen places, and his skin slashed and scratched. In his left hand he held a machete, in his right, an antique samurai sword. Both blades were slick with the blood of their former owners.

"K8, are you down here?" He thought he could smell traces of that scent she liked to wear. "Hello?" He reached the bottom of the stairs and leant against the wall, trying to get his breath back. He'd had to fight his way through the corridor, and now his arms hurt and his legs were tired and shaky. Things had been so much easier back in the game. In those days, he could fight forever without getting tired or injured, and always have enough breath left over for a witty quip or scathing putdown.

Here in reality, things were somewhat different. Leaning against the wall, listening to the breath wheeze in and out of his heaving chest, he regretted every single cigar, every shot of rum and litre of beer. Compared to the character he'd been in the game, he was hopelessly out of shape.

And the Gestalt drones were really hard to fight. Usually, when facing overwhelming odds, he went for shock and awe, using battle cries and ferocity to scatter and panic his opponents. A few bites and screeches would usually shatter their discipline and strike fear into the stoutest of hearts. The ranks would collapse and he'd be able pick off his adversaries individually. That hadn't worked with the Gestalt in the corridor. He couldn't break them up. Whatever he did, they were still a perfectly coordinated group, able to attack and parry as one. Taking them on had been like tangling with a multi-headed, multi-limbed hydra, and he'd had to fight hard for every centimetre he'd advanced.

Looking back into the kitchen, he saw Marie appear in the doorway. She had the coil gun cradled in her right arm. Her left hung at her side, slathered in blood, and her right leg dragged behind her as she moved. Drops of blood dripped from her fingertips, onto the white tiles. The sleeve of her jacket had been torn away and used as a makeshift bandage. Warily, she looked at the weapons in his hands.

"Have you found Lila?"

Ack-Ack Macaque waved the point of his stolen katana at the door at the foot of the stairs.

"I think she's in here."

Marie limped towards him. "Is it locked?"

"I don't know, I haven't tried." He could feel his arms and back stiffening, and was sure he'd torn at least one muscle, if not more. "Help yourself."

He stood aside, and she brushed past him. The handle rattled in her hand, and she swore under her breath.

"Lila, honey? It's me. Are you in there?"

"Mum?" It was a girl's voice.

"Lila, I'm coming in. Stand away from the door." She stepped back and braced herself against the wall, keeping the weight off her bad leg. She reached into her pocket and pulled out a gun identical to the one Ack-Ack Macaque had seen in Bill's apartment. Keeping the barrel angled downwards, she pointed it at the door and squeezed the trigger. He couldn't see the beam, but a spot began to smoulder midway between the handle and the frame.

Within seconds, the door had a thin hole burned through it. Marie moved the gun around in a semi-circle, severing the section of door that held the lock. When she had finished, the rest of the door swung open, leaving the handle and lock in place. Ack-Ack Macaque closed his eye, and sank down onto the lower step. The stone was cold on his ass. He heard Lila crying and Marie fussing over her, checking her for injuries and evidence of torture.

"Hey, K8?" he said tiredly. "Are you in there?"

No reply.

He re-opened his eye to find Marie and her daughter standing in the doorway. Lila took one look at him and shrank away behind her mother, plainly terrified by his wild, bloodied appearance.

"She's not here." Marie limped forward, staying firmly between him and Lila.

Ack-Ack Macaque felt a flush of anger. All that fighting and killing, and he still wasn't done.

"Well, where the hell is she?"

"Lila says they took her to see the Leader."

"And where's he?"

"Somewhere else."

"Another hideout?"

Marie shook her head.

"Another *world*."

The walls of the cellar seemed to close in around him. Ack-Ack Macaque put his blades on the step and rubbed his eye patch. His chest felt tight, and sweat broke out on his back. Up until this moment all his missions had been successful. He'd never lost before, never come home empty-handed.

"Another world?" He tugged at his right ear. His mind raced, retracing his steps, trying to figure out where he'd gone wrong. Marie and Lila were still looking at him, and he wanted to scream at them, fling his shit around and frighten them away. How could this have happened? How could K8 not be here, after all the trouble he'd endured to rescue her? It didn't seem fair. He'd lost comrades in the past, in the game, but this was new and different. He actually cared about K8, even though he would have been loath to admit it under normal circumstances, and someone had known that, and used his feelings for her against him. She'd suffered because of his friendship, and now she was gone, spirited away to another plane of existence—lost in a sea of probability, on an unknown and unreachable world.

He looked down at his bare feet. They were chilly on the stone floor.

"What am I supposed to do now?"

His phone rang but he made no move to answer it. On the fourth ring, Marie said, "Hadn't you better get that?"

He curled his lip at her.

"Get lost."

On the sixth ring, still glowering at the woman and her daughter, he reached into his pocket, pulled out the phone, and clamped it to his ear.

Hey, Ack-ster. It's Paul. You've got to get back up here, man.

"Why should I?"

Just get up here, right now.

"But, K8—"

This is about K8. We're sending a chopper. Just get up here as fast as you can.

WHEN ACK-ACK MACAQUE arrived back on board the *Tereshkova*, a Russian steward met him at the helipad and escorted him to the captain's cabin, where he found Victoria and Paul waiting. As he walked in, Paul flinched, and Victoria's hand went to the handle of the cutlass at her hip.

"Okay, what's going on?" The chopper ride hadn't helped his frustration. "If you people don't start giving me some answers, I'm going to start banging heads together."

Victoria waved him to silence with her free hand.

"There's a call for you." They were both looking at him very strangely.

"But—"

She shook her head, unable to explain. "Just take it." She motioned to one of the large SincPad screens on the wall. The screen brightened into life, and Ack-Ack Macaque found himself staring into a mirror.

"What the—?" The face on the screen was his, only it wasn't. Whoever this monkey was, he'd been groomed and washed, and the sleek black hair around his face shone with cleanliness. Instead of a ripped and battered old aviator jacket, he wore a white suit with a white shirt and tie, and an eye patch that covered his right eye instead of his left. Looking at him, Ack-Ack Macaque felt his hackles rise.

"Who, the hell, are you?" He turned to Victoria. "What fuckery is this?"

The other monkey regarded him with a baleful glare.

"Who do you *think* I am?" He brushed the lapel of his suit jacket. "Check out the threads. Consider the context."

"You're *me*?"

"You seem surprised." The stranger sat back, away from the camera. He appeared to be seated in a cabin similar to the one in which Ack-Ack Macaque now stood, but the walls of *his* cabin were draped with tapestries and other expensive ornaments. Statues stood on plinths in front of bookshelves lined with the spines of ancient hardbacks. Having made himself comfortable, he waved a regal hand. "Before you say anything, let me first express what a genuine pleasure it is for me to touch base with you. As we're both iterations of the same basic individual, I hope we can find a way to collaborate together towards mutual understanding and profit."

"Huh?" Ack-Ack Macaque flexed his fists. "Look, pal. How about you just tell me what you want, and why you're here."

The monkey on the screen adjusted his tie with manicured fingers.

"Oh dear," he said. "You're one of the thick ones, aren't you? Well, you can call me 'Leader'. Everybody else does. I created the Gestalt out of nothing, and I've led them to dominance on half a dozen worlds. I'm the CEO, the king and the president, all rolled into one. I'm a pharaoh in three different Egypts; I'm the place where the buck most definitely stops; '*le grand fromage*'; and 'a jungle VIP'. In short, I'm the *boss*, and you'd do very well to bear that in mind. Capeesh?"

Ack-Ack Macaque's hands twitched, longing for his trusty Colts. He glanced across at his companions. Victoria was leaning on her desk, arms folded, watching the confrontation through narrowed eyes. Paul stood, hands in pockets and mouth agape, obviously delighted by the sight of two identical monkeys arguing between themselves.

"Don't try that alpha monkey shit on me," Ack-Ack Macaque said to the face on the screen. "I invented that."

The Leader just smiled and made a finger steeple in front of his lips. Shiny white cufflinks flashed in the light of the screen.

"I know you came here to reclaim your pet human, the little one who thinks it's clever to spell her name with numbers as well as letters," he said, "but you should really take a moment to reassess my earlier proposition. There's still a place for you on my team. I know how lonely you are. I used to be just like you. But now, think what we can achieve *together*. Think of the synergies. You and me, maestro, we'd be unstoppable: the dream team."

"If you've hurt her..."

The Leader shook his head.

"Your concern does you credit, but can we park that issue for a minute, and concentrate instead on what I'm offering?" He rubbed his covered right eye, and Ack-Ack Macaque had to make an effort to refrain from copying the gesture. "In a couple of hours, my fleet will arrive in your world, and I'll have an airship over every major town and city."

"Airships can be shot down."

"Not enough of them, and not quickly enough. You don't have enough planes or missiles, and my assets are packing some serious hardware of their own."

"We'll fight you."

"No, you won't. You see, as soon as I've given the fleet a short window in which to demonstrate their superior firepower, I'll broadcast my terms. This isn't some nineteenth century pirate raid, you know. We know what we're doing because we've done it before, on six worlds, and the outcome's always been the same. This is a takeover, plain and simple. Anybody who wants to come over to my side beforehand will be welcomed with open arms. But those who refuse—" he lowered his chin, and his yellow eye burned through the screen, "—will be subject to extreme measures."

"What sort of measures?"

"Let's just say, I have the means to make conversion automatic and mandatory. I have recently acquired an airborne agent that is capable of germinating inside the human body. It converts messy, rebellious neurons into clean, obedient gelware." He interlaced his fingers. "All I have to do is give my fleet the signal to release it and, within hours, every human on the planet's either dead or a functioning member of the Gestalt." He fiddled with his cuff, looking casual as hell. "So, it's time for you to choose, my brother. Come willingly, or come as a slave. Rule with me, or be ruled *by* me."

"You're mad."

"No, *companero*, I'm *winning*." He glanced at the white hands on his platinum wristwatch. "Now, you have less than four hours. My fleet's going to rock up at eighteen hundred hours, GMT. I'll be on my flagship, over London, drinking a cup of Earl Grey with your little friend. In fact, I'll pour an extra cup for you, just in case. If you'd care to join us, be there, and don't be late."

CHAPTER TWENTY-FIVE
ZEPPELINS FROM THE GREAT BEYOND

WITH A FLICK of his hand, the Leader cut the connection and the wall screen went blank. From where she leant against her desk, Victoria Valois saw Ack-Ack Macaque's posture slump. He'd been holding himself upright for the confrontation; now, he looked half dead.

"Are you all right?"

The macaque swivelled his face towards her, too tired to move his feet.

"Verbose motherfucker, wasn't he?"

She smiled.

"Do you think he was serious?"

"Do you have any reason to think he wasn't?" Ack-Ack Macaque put a hand to the side of his jaw, and pushed his chin up and to the side. Something crackled in his neck.

"You look like *merde*," she said. His knuckles were battered and raw. One of the sleeves of his flying jacket had torn at the shoulder seam, and now hung down almost to his elbow. His fur stuck out in clumps, caked in dark and sticky blood. She wondered how much of the blood was his, and how much had come from other people.

"What can I say? It's been a long day."

She pushed off from the desk and stood upright. Tapped the fingertips of her right hand against the palm of her left.

"I'm almost afraid to ask what you want to do."

"About what?" He jerked a thumb at the dead screen. "About that arsehole?"

"He's you."

"He most certainly is not."

"A version of you."

"So what? He's still an arsehole, and we're still going to kick his fucking head in." He turned his body to face her, his movements stiff and laborious. "Right?"

Victoria let out a breath she hadn't realised she'd been holding.

"If you say so."

The monkey's eye narrowed.

"You didn't think I'd be *tempted*, did you?"

Victoria shrugged.

"Stranger things have happened."

"Not to me, they haven't." He reached into his inside pocket and pulled out a cigar. About a third of it hung at an angle, having been damaged during the fight at Larkin Hall. He snapped off the short end and dropped it into her wastepaper basket.

"You can't deny you've been lonely."

He reached into the pocket on the other side of his jacket, and extracted his Zippo. "No, I can't." A quick flick of the little wheel, and a flame sparked. "But that doesn't mean I'm going to get gooey-eyed about the first talking monkey that comes along." He held the flame to the end of the cigar and huffed clouds of blue smoke into the room. "Especially as he's planning to fuck the planet."

The air-conditioning kicked in. It sucked most of the smoke up into vents on the ceiling, but couldn't completely obliterate the pungent and lingering whiff. Victoria wrinkled her nose, and mentally recited the code words that let her access the command menus for her cranial implant. Once in, she quickly deactivated her sense of smell. Fond of the monkey as she was, the aroma of cigar smoke always made her feel ill.

"So you do care about us?"

"Of course I do. I already saved the world once, didn't I?" He took a mouthful of smoke, rolled it around, and blew it at the ceiling. "Besides, I'm not really alone, am I?" He coughed, and looked away, wiping his mouth on the back of his hand. "I've got you two, and K8."

Victoria exchanged a look with Paul, and they both raised their eyebrows. This was the first time they'd heard him talk this way; the first crack they'd seen in his habitually gruff exterior.

"Yes," she said, "of course you do."

The monkey scuffed a foot against the deck. He looked supremely uncomfortable.

"That's okay then."

Victoria tried to suppress her smile. It appeared that, despite his coarseness, Ack-Ack Macaque had the same insecurities and needs as everyone else, including the need to belong; and it seemed losing K8 had finally driven home to him who his friends really were, and made him appreciate everything he had, and everything he stood to lose.

"You should get checked out," she said, wanting to spare him further embarrassment. "Get Sergei to patch you up."

Ack-Ack Macaque looked down at himself. He tried to straighten his torn sleeve.

"But K8—"

"You're not going to be any use to her in that state. Get down to the infirmary and get Sergei to see to you. That's an order."

He took the cigar from his lips and rubbed his brow.

"Yes, boss."

AFTER HE'D GONE, Victoria walked around her desk and sat in the chair.

"Jesus Christ," she said.

In the bright noon light from the picture window, Paul's image was an insubstantial ghost haunting the corner of her office: the murder victim who wouldn't lie down, the ex-husband who never left.

"What are you going to do?"

Victoria pulled the cutlass from her belt and dropped it into the umbrella stand.

"You said you could fly this thing?"

Paul took off his glasses and rubbed them on the hem of his shirt. "Well, yes, if I had to. All the connections are in place."

"You have to."

"Right now?"

Victoria drew herself up. "Make course for central London, best speed."

"Aye, aye." Paul's brow screwed in concentration as he devoted more and more of his processing time to the business of running the airship's systems. His image grew tenuous, and then finally disappeared, as he focused his attention elsewhere. Moments later, Victoria felt a tremble through the deck as the skyliner's engines powered up and the *Tereshkova*'s nose swung eastwards again, towards the capital.

Ahead, the windscreen showed a bright blue sky growing paler all the way to the far horizon. A single vapour train caught the sun like a comet trail, and she found herself wondering what the world would have been like had jet travel really taken off in the latter half of the twentieth century. With the first skyliners entering commercial service in the early 1960s, and the subsequent oil blockades and price wars of the 1970s, jet air travel had never become an economical option, and now only the richest and most extravagant used it as a means of crossing oceans. Skyliners might be slower, but they were dependable and cheap, and their nuclear-electric engines had none of the economic and environmental disadvantages of oil.

But how would things have been, she asked herself, had the skyliners not come along when they did—if the post-war British and French shipyards had been allowed to wither and die instead of being turned over to airship production? What would the globe look like with everybody rushing around at nine hundred kilometres per hour, and the skies streaked by hundreds of shining white trails?

Paul's voice came over the intercom.

"We can't fight them all," he said. "Not by ourselves."

Victoria glanced up at the security camera in the corner of the ceiling.

"We'll alert the authorities."

"Will they believe us? Because, quite frankly, I'm in the middle of this, and I'm not even sure *I* believe it."

Victoria knew he was right. Even among skyliner captains, most of whom were considered pretty eccentric in their own right, she had a reputation as a maverick. Putting the world on a war footing in three hours would take more than just her word.

"In that case," she said, "I'm going to have to make a call."

"Not—?"

"Who else? Besides, he owes us a favour."

THE FACE LOOKING back at her from the screen was that of a young man, but his eyes seemed more mature and weary than one might have expected from his apparent age. They were the eyes of a boy who'd served in the South Atlantic; who'd lost comrades in a helicopter crash; lost his father at an impressionable age; and fought his mother in order to prevent a holocaust.

"Hello, Victoria. What can I do for you?" This was Merovech I, King of the United Kingdom of France, Great Britain, Northern Ireland and Norway, and head of the European Commonwealth. In the time she'd known him, he'd played many roles—a soldier, a criminal and a runaway, to name three—but this was the first time she'd spoken to him since his coronation, and the first time she'd seen him actually looking like a king. Gone were the ripped jeans and red hoodie she remembered; in their place, a tailored suit, crisp white shirt and regimental tie.

"Your majesty." Victoria tipped her head forward. "I'm afraid this isn't a social call."

Merovech leant towards the camera.

"I should say not. I saw what our monkey friend did on the M4, and how much damage he caused."

"I can explain."

"I think you'd better."

Hands clasped behind her back, Victoria rocked back on her heels. The young king had become a man. Every gesture and tone conveyed authority and patience. She wasn't sure how much of that came naturally, and how much had been taught.

"Merovech, listen." She put a splayed hand to her chest. By addressing him informally, she hoped to break through the façade, and reach the young man she'd once fought alongside. "You remember last year?"

"I'm hardly likely to forget."

"Well, this is worse."

Merovech raised an eyebrow. "Worse than all-out nuclear war?"

"Yes. At least in a nuclear war there's the possibility of a few survivors."

"What are we talking about?"

"An invasion. Several hundred armed skyliners, one over every major city, and each one packed with some sort of hideous plague."

"Where are they coming from?"

"From thin air."

The young king sat back in his chair, and his image blurred for half a second as the camera refocused.

"I beg your pardon?"

Victoria rubbed her forehead. "Look, it's an invasion from another dimension, from a parallel world. I can't explain more than that because, quite frankly, I don't understand it all myself."

"Is this for real?"

"I keep asking myself the same question."

He looked at her for what seemed like a very long time, and she could see that he was weighing their friendship, deciding how far he could trust her. Finally, he cleared his throat and said, "When?"

"Three hours." She felt a surge of relief. "You'll need everything you have in the air, and you'll need to alert the other countries. But be careful. If these things unload their cargo, it's game over, and we're all as good as dead."

Merovech frowned, suddenly doubtful. He tipped his head to one side and tapped a finger against his lips.

"How can I ring the President of the United States and tell him we're being invaded by Zeppelins from the Great Beyond?"

Victoria took a step closer to her screen.

"You're the Head of the European Commonwealth, he'll have to listen to you."

"But will he believe me?"

"Does it matter? If one country scrambles every fighter plane it has, the rest will have to follow suit. They might not know the reason, but they won't want to be caught napping. You get every European plane in the air, and I can guarantee the Russians, Chinese and Americans will do likewise."

Merovech made a clicking sound with his tongue.

"After last year's unpleasantness with China, putting that many planes in the air could be dangerous."

"It'll be a lot more dangerous for you to do nothing."

"You don't know what you're asking."

"Yes I do. I've got the monkey with me. Twelve months ago, the three of us saved the world. Now, we're asking you to help us save it again."

CHAPTER TWENTY-SIX
FAMILIAR STRANGERS

IN A PASSENGER lounge on board one of the *Tereshkova*'s starboard gondolas, William Cole sat on a bar stool with his elbows resting on the copper counter top. The lounge had been decorated in the style of a Zeppelin from the 1930s, with lots of bare rivets and brass fittings, and lazily revolving ceiling fans carved to resemble wooden propellers. Behind the bar, a painting hung over the cash register. It depicted a young man in a white Russian dress uniform with a red s#ash. William didn't know who the young soldier was, but he recognised the jacket, and some of its medals, as being identical to the one worn by Captain Valois.

I guess that must be the Commodore, he thought to himself.

Opposite the painting, on the other side of the lounge, a row of portholes showed him the green countryside of southern England. The undulating landscape rolled past beneath the ship like the hide of some tremendous dragon.

He was waiting for Marie, and Lila. In his hands he held an old photograph. It was a printout from a digital file, and he'd been carrying it around in his pocket ever since the day of his wife's funeral. It was a shot he'd taken in New York, not long after they'd first met. He'd taken it on the observation deck of the Empire State Building, and it showed her laughing, leaning back against the railings with the whole of Manhattan spread out behind her. She was wearing a black 'I ♥ New York' t-shirt. Her orange hair had been cropped short and tucked behind one ear, and the sun picked out the freckles on her nose. It was the one photograph of her that he'd included in his bug-out bag; the one picture he wanted to keep, as a reminder of everything they'd had, and everything they'd lost. It was a picture of her taken when they were both young and in the first passionate throes of love, when the world seemed filled with excitement and hope, and all their dreams seemed attainable. At the moment the shutter clicked, neither of them had known that she would shortly fall pregnant, that the baby would die, and that, unable to comfort each other, they'd separate and spend so many years living apart, married to the wrong people, only to reunite a decade later, a short time before her untimely death.

A glass of soda water stood on the counter beside his left wrist, fizzing quietly. It was all he wanted. Once, he might have ordered a glass of bourbon to steady his nerves; now, he no longer felt the need. He'd taken a hot shower and changed his clothes and, for the first time in months, felt clean inside and out.

What would Marie—his Marie—have said if she'd known that, one day, he'd find another version of her, and get to meet the daughter they'd lost? Would she have felt betrayed, or would she have been pleased for him, wanting only for him to be happy? He smoothed out the edges of the photo with his thumbs, hoping her answer would have been the latter, because, whatever she might have thought, he couldn't afford to pass up this second chance.

After all, he told himself, he wouldn't be cheating as such. This *was* Marie. She had many of the same memories as his Marie. She'd even remember this photograph being taken. At the point the camera clicked, they'd been the same person. It was only later, when the baby died—or in her case, lived—that their lives had diverged. The last sixteen years may have panned out differently for her, but she was still, essentially, the same girl he'd taken up to the eighty-sixth floor of the Empire State; and the picture he held was as much a photograph of her as it was of the woman he'd said goobye to just over two years ago. He thought of the closing lines of *The War of the Worlds* by H.G. Wells: *And strangest of all is it to hold my wife's hand again, and to think that I have counted her, and that she has counted me, among the dead.*

How many people had ever been given such an opportunity? He placed the picture on the counter, and took a sip of water. The ice cubes clonked and jangled against his moustache and upper lip. How many, indeed?

He turned to the portholes and watched a wisp of white cloud drift past. They were making good time towards London but he didn't know how high they were. Were they higher than the observation deck on the Empire State? Perhaps he should have arranged to meet Marie and Lila on the helipad at the top of the *Tereshkova's* central hull. Perhaps that would have been somehow more fitting than arranging to meet in a bar? He'd spent far too much of his life in bars. If they all came through this alive, and if the world escaped assimilation by the Gestalt, he promised himself that things would change; *he* would change. He'd stop taking drugs and start getting regular exercise. If it took every last scrap of his strength, he'd make the woman in the photograph proud of him. He'd even start writing again, and do it properly this time.

A girl walked into the lounge. She had glossy, shoulder-length brown hair tied back in a loose ponytail, and she was dressed in the white jacket and black trousers of a borrowed steward's uniform. It took him a moment to realise who she was, but when he did, the realisation hit him like an electric shock that sparked from the sensitive pit of his stomach to the prickling skin at the back of his neck. This was Lila, the daughter who never was, the daughter who'd died in the womb. And now here she stood, as large as life, and twice as beautiful.

His mouth went dry, and he sucked his bottom lip. What could he say to her, what could anyone possibly say in this situation? The only words that came into his head were either far too pompous, or impossibly trite. In the end, he settled for, "Hello."

She smiled at him.

"Hello." She held out her hand. Her accent was pure cut glass. "Mother's resting at the moment, but I thought you and I should probably meet."

William rubbed his palm against his trouser leg before taking her hand. Her skin was cool and unexpectedly rough, and her grip was strong.

"Pleasure to meet you," he stammered as they shook formally.

She really did have his eyes; but on her, they looked much better.

After a moment of awkwardness, he realised he was still holding her hand, and hurriedly let go.

"Would you like a drink?"

She shook her head and pursed her lips. She seemed as nervous as he was. After a moment's hesitation, she slid onto the bar stool next to his, crossed her legs at the ankle, and clasped her hands in her lap.

"How are you?" she said. She had a wine-coloured bruise on her right cheek.

William straightened his back, and unconsciously reached up to flatten the hair at the side of his head.

"I'm okay," he said, meaning it. "The past twenty-four hours have been kind of rough, but I'm getting there."

"You don't find this peculiar, meeting me like this?"

He gave a snort of not-quite laughter.

"Yeah, of course I do. It's all extremely, majorly, fundamentally *weird*. But you don't know what my life was like up until yesterday." He looked into her eyes, fighting down the sudden urge to confess, to drag up his dust ball of a life and lay it all out in front of her, so she could see how

miserable and alone he'd been. "Compared to that, weird is kind of good."
He pulled back slightly. "Listen, I don't pretend to understand half of
what's happened. All I know is that right now, you and your mother are
here, alive and breathing, and that's all that really matters."

Lila tugged at the hem of her borrowed jacket, and glanced around the
room. She seemed to be grappling with something.

"I don't know what to call you." Her brow furrowed. "I don't even
know what you should call me."

William blinked. "What would you like me to call you? You're my
daughter."

She shrugged, clearly uncomfortable.

"I don't know. I just lost my father."

William felt an odd, fluttering sensation in his chest. He gripped the edge
of the copper counter.

"You weren't even *born* when I lost you."

Her eyes were like perfect jewels set into the marble of her face. They
filled him with a strange mourning for his own lost youth—for the gawky
Ohio farm boy he'd misplaced somewhere along the way. How different his
life would have been if he'd had a girl like this to care for and raise. How
much better a man he'd have had to be.

"So..." His voice wavered. "What do we do now?"

Lila bit her lower lip, and brushed her hair behind her ear. The gesture
was one she'd picked up from her mother, and it brought a lump to his
throat.

"I don't know about you, Dad," she said hesitantly, trying out the word,
"but there's a fight coming, and I'm going to be part of it."

BREAKING NEWS

From *The European Sentinel*, online edition:

Jets Scramble as Europe Put on Military Alert

PARIS 16/11/2060 – Official sources remain tight-lipped about unconfirmed reports of frenzied activity at RAF and Commonwealth airbases across Europe, and speculation that this could be part of a massive, Europe-wide mobilisation of air defence forces. All that is known for certain is that all leave has been cancelled for service men and women from all branches of the armed forces, and that the aircraft carriers HMS *Shakespeare* and HMS *Jules Verne*, which had both been en route to Oslo for a special visit to mark the centenary of Norway's integration into the United Kingdom, have instead been diverted, and are now believed to be steaming for the mouth of the Thames Estuary.

Are these measures a prelude to hostilities with another country, and if so, which one? Or could they be somehow related to last year's attempted royal coup d'etat?

So far, official sources have refused to comment, saying only that Commonwealth citizens should remain calm, and monitor news channels for further updates.

Read more | Like | Comment | Share

Related Stories

Witnesses report 'caveman' suspect in Greek police chief murder

Gestalt 'embassies' close their doors

Dead millionaire's back-up personality wins legal right to inherit wealth

'Miracle' taco contains likeness of Elvis

Car bomb explodes in Zurich, killing fitness instructor

Feature: As the Martian probe enters the final stages of its approach to the Red Planet, we assess the possible threats posed by its soon-to-be revived occupants.

CHAPTER TWENTY-SEVEN
WELCOME TO THE JUNGLE

THE VTOL PLANE took K8 and her three minders to the armoured airship. As soon as it touched down, they went to seize her again, but she slapped their hands away.

"Hey, I can walk by myself, okay?" She straightened her jumper, tired of being manhandled. "We're on an airship, remember? You've got me. Where am I going to go?"

The Neanderthals frowned at each other, then the one who'd spoken before said, "Okay, you walk. But don't try anything stupid."

K8 pulled herself up out of her seat, and moved along the aisle to the aircraft's cabin door. The plane had come down on the upper surface of the armoured airship, in a gap between gun emplacements and sensor pods. Carefully, K8 climbed down the steps, followed by the three cavemen in white. When they were at the bottom, she put her fists on her hips.

"Okay, Ug, which way?"

The one with the voice raised his arm.

"That way, through the hatch," he said. "Down the ladder. No funny stuff."

K8 turned in the direction he pointed.

"Oh, don't worry, sunshine. I'll leave the jokes to you."

She went over to the open hatch. Pleated metal stairs led down into the bowels of the ship. She paused to take a last look at the boundless sky, and to draw a last lungful of clear, untainted air. Then she started down. As she clumped towards the bottom rung, she took note of the thickness of the armour plate on the hull to either side of her. It was at least ten centimetres deep. That was enough to stop all but the most powerful machine guns. If the thickness remained consistent all over the hull, the airship would be nigh-on bulletproof, not to mention weighing about the same as a small mountain. Most of its interior would have to be given over to gasbags, she thought, just to support that immensity.

At the bottom of the stairs, the Neanderthals led her forwards, through the airship's interior, towards the bows. She saw racks holding automatic rifles and submachine guns, piles of ammo boxes, and heaps of white-painted body armour. The walls had been decorated in a deep, sumptuous olive, and the door handles and other fittings had been fashioned from brightly polished brass.

Several times, they passed human members of the Gestalt. All were dressed in identical white suits, and all were silent. Even groups who appeared to be clustered together for discussion stood without speaking or smiling. Nobody on the airship spoke a word, and yet they were working and cooperating seamlessly. Some of them turned to watch her as she walked past, their eyes flat and passive and their expressions unreadable. On the *Tereshkova*, you could always hear voices—stewards making their rounds; passengers coming and going; mechanics changing light strips or unblocking sinks, whistling as they worked—but here, she heard only the distant thrum of turbines and the gentle whir of air in the vents.

She didn't like it. The mute, emotionless Gestalt made her think of an old black and white horror film she'd seen once, about a group of white-haired children in a small English village. She'd been twelve years old when it came on the TV one evening, and it had given her nightmares for a week.

At one point, the corridor turned into a metal walkway suspended over a chamber with the appearance and approximate dimensions of a drained swimming pool. Four black boxes stood spaced along its bottom, each the size of an upended coffin. Frost glittered on their shiny sides, and K8 slowed to take a look.

"What are they?" She leaned over the railing. She thought they might be computer servers of some kind. Thick power cables and a variety of coloured data leads plugged into ports on the deck. The air in the chamber felt itchy with static.

"Engines." One of the Neanderthals poked her between the shoulder blades. "Now, move."

Reluctantly, she let them shepherd her onwards, until they reached an armoured door plated entirely in brass.

"Wait."

K8 crossed her arms. "Why? What's—?"

"Shush." The Neanderthal tapped a thick finger against his temple. "Am talking to Leader."

All three of them were motionless for a few seconds, just long enough for K8 to start feeling fidgety, before the vocal one gave a grunt and motioned at the door.

"You can go in now."

"In here?" She eyed the door dubiously, remembering Lila's fear of the Gestalt Leader, and the bruise on the girl's cheek.

The Neanderthal gave her an insistent shove.

"Leader will see you now."

K8 PUSHED OPEN the brass door and stepped through into warmth and steam, and an overpowering greenhouse smell of dank compost and ripe vegetation. Trees stood in large pots, seemingly placed at random, with vines and creepers trailing between them. Smaller pots held ferns and sprays of bamboo, and butterflies flickered hither and thither like animated scraps of colourful cloth. Reed mats covered the floor, strewn with fallen leaves, and, from somewhere nearby, she heard the lazy trickle of a fountain.

Pushing through the dangling branches, she emerged onto a wooden veranda. Surrounded by trees on three sides, the veranda looked forward, through the blunt nose of the airship's prow, which was transparent, having been constructed from thick panes of glass.

"Ah, there you are." The Leader sat at a wrought iron patio table, one leg crossed over the other, and a china teacup halfway to his lips. Looking at him, K8 felt herself go cold inside and, for a second, stopped breathing.

"You—" She couldn't get the words out. "You're—"

The Leader placed his cup and saucer on the table. Black monkey hair stuck out from his white cuffs. A furry tail snaked from the back of his sharply creased trousers.

"Please," he said, "have a seat. Can I offer you something to drink?"

Feeling suddenly faint, K8 tottered forward and sat on the closest of the three iron chairs set around the table.

"No," she said. "No, thank you."

"As you wish." He brushed his knee with fastidious fingers, and straightened his posture. "Now, you may be wondering why I wanted to touch base with you?"

K8 took a deep breath. She couldn't stop staring.

"I was wondering, aye."

The monkey glanced at his fingernails, and then interlaced his fingers. "I believe that you and I have an acquaintance in common."

"The Skipper?"

"If by that you mean the primate going by the ridiculous moniker of 'Ack-Ack Macaque', then yes."

"What about him?"

The Leader smiled. His teeth were impossibly white. "I've just been negotiating with him. He's a bit rough at the edges, but I think he's got definite potential. If we could find a way to optimise his temper management, and thereby redirect his physicality towards more profitable goals, he and I could collaborate together very well."

"He'd rather die."

"Yes, his lively exchange of views with Mister Reynolds rather gave me that impression. Still, nobody's perfect."

He picked up his teacup between leathery fingers and K8 fidgeted in her chair. She couldn't take her eyes off him. He looked so much like the Skipper, yet spoke and acted so, so differently.

Glancing back into the ersatz jungle, she said, "Those black boxes…"

His single eye looked at her over the rim of his cup.

"The engines."

"Are they what moves you between parallels?"

He took a sip of tea, rolled it around the inside of his cheeks, and swallowed.

"Indeed they do. I call them my 'probability engines', but I won't bore you with their technical specifications." He put the cup back onto the table and wiped his palms on a white silk handkerchief from his top pocket. "Suffice to say, moving between worlds takes a lot of power, both in terms of energy input and in the amount of processing power needed to make the requisite calculations."

"What do they run on?"

The Leader dabbed his lips, and pushed the hankie back into his jacket. "They draw power from the airship's fusion plant."

"You have fusion?" The idea sent a shiver the length of her spine. In her world, fusion had been one of a number of advances that always seemed to be about ten years away, forever on the horizon—like cheap space travel or a cure for AIDS—but never quite materialising. The idea that the inhabitants of another world had found a way to make it work, and a way to make it portable, filled her with unease, and an unreasonable stab of jealousy. And then, for the first time, she began to understand the reality of her situation. Wherever she was, she surely wasn't in Kansas anymore.

"How else could we generate enough energy to rip a hole between worlds?" The Leader uncrossed his legs. "But enough questions. There'll be plenty of time later, after you've been inducted into our fellowship. In the meantime, I have some enquiries of my own."

K8's unease blossomed into alarm. She had no intention of joining his 'fellowship'. Her heart beat so hard she was sure he could hear it, and she spoke to cover the noise.

"You know," she said, "you're the first member of the Gestalt I've met who says 'I' instead of 'we'."

The monkey gave an airy wave. "Well, I *am* the leader."

"No, it's more than that." K8 swallowed. "You're not fully connected, are you?"

In one fluid motion, the monkey rose to his feet. He stood over her, drawn up to his full height, clutching his lapels.

"Every society needs to be governed."

Any moment now, K8 was sure he'd order some thugs to drag her away, to be converted into one of his white-suited drones. She spoke to stall him. "But I thought the Gestalt were supposed to be a democracy?"

The Leader gave a snort. "Whatever gave you that idea, child? Just because they have their minds webbed together, that doesn't mean they're capable of self-determination. Mob rule never works; it just brings everything down to the level of the lowest common denominator. You need someone set apart from the herd, someone with vision, who knows what's best and can take the tough decisions."

"And that's you, I suppose?"

"If you like." He huffed a breath in through his cavernous nose. "Think of it in terms of an ant colony. Every member of the colony has his or her place and task and, to outsiders, the whole thing appears to move with a common will and purpose. But, behind the scenes, there's always a superior being pulling the strings."

K8 forced a smile.

"So, you're the queen, are you?"

His yellow eye frowned down at her and, for the first time, she caught a glimpse of the incisors behind his smile.

"That isn't the phrasing I would have chosen," he said quietly. Then, abruptly, he turned and walked over to the bamboo rail at the edge of the veranda, where he stood looking out through the airship's glass nose cone. Unsure what to do, K8 remained seated. Had she touched a nerve, or was this just his way of changing the subject? When uncomfortable or bored with a conversation, Ack-Ack Macaque had a tendency to get up and walk out; maybe his doppelganger shared that characteristic. Or maybe he just heard things in his head to which she had no access.

Without any real sense of hope, she said, "What do I have to say to get you to let me out of here?"

The Leader didn't turn around. He gripped the bamboo rail and kept his eye on the sky and clouds.

"They made him a cartoon character."

K8 blinked.

"Who, the Skipper?"

The Leader lowered his head, looking down at the landscape below.

"They created an intelligent monkey, and then plugged him into a video game." He drummed his fingers. "They never gave him a chance."

"He's doing all right."

"All right?" He turned to face her. "All that talent, and what is he? He's a pilot on an airship. *An* airship, and it's not even *his*." He held his hands behind his back, gripping his left wrist with his right hand. "Do you know how many vessels I have at my command?"

K8 shrugged, but the Leader ignored her. The question had been rhetorical.

"I was created in a lab," he said, "the same way as your friend. Like him, I was a simple macaque raised to sentience by the addition of artificial neurons, created by scientists trying to devise a new kind of weapons guidance system. But we became very different monkeys. When they'd finished with me, they didn't plug me into a video game. They didn't turn me into 'Ack-Ack Macaque'. Instead, they gave me to a different team, on a different floor. That's where our timelines diverged. I was given to a team studying direct mind-to-mind communication."

He held out his hand, inspecting his tidy, clipped nails. "They already had plans to spread their work beyond the confines of the laboratory. Within a month, I was part of the team. Within two months, I was running it." He looked at her as if peering, like a disappointed professor, over a pair of invisible spectacles. "We broke out of the lab and seized our first warship. And then, within six months, we'd acquired enough weapons and personnel to forcibly convert the remaining human population to our cause. Since then, we've spread ourselves to a dozen worlds, and assimilated them all."

K8 felt her ears burning, her cheeks growing hot.

"But... why? Why would you do that?"

The Leader sniffed.

"Progress, child."

"Progress?" She slammed her palms on the table, rattling the china tea set. "Turning everybody into mindless drones is 'progress'?"

The monkey shook his coiffured head.

"*Au contraire*, child. Mindlessness is the last thing I'm trying to achieve.

Quite the reverse, in fact." He lifted an elegant cigarette holder from the table; lit the cigarette in it with a white platinum lighter. "How do you think I came here? How do you think I developed the means to cross dimensions, to achieve—" he waved the cigarette holder in a circle that encompassed the jungle, the forward window, and the entire airship in which they were held, "—all of this?"

K8 shook her head. She didn't want to know but, somehow, couldn't stop listening.

The Leader's eye narrowed.

"Have you ever heard of 'parallel computing'?"

"Yes, of course." K8 frowned. It was a way of breaking large problems down into smaller ones, and then solving all those small ones simultaneously using multiple processing elements—whether within the same machine, or across a network of distributed computers. "Oh!"

He saw her understanding, and gave a nod.

"Yes, I created the largest virtual computer ever devised, running on the cranial wetware of seven billion people. Then I spread it to another world, and another." He took a drag of the cigarette and blew a thin line of lazy smoke from the side of his mouth. "And with all that at my disposal, I can solve anything: war, starvation... mortality." He mashed the half-smoked cigarette into an ashtray, and laid the holder aside. "Compared to that, what has *your* monkey achieved?"

K8 blinked at him.

"Hey," she said, nettled. "He saved the world."

The Leader looked down his nose at her, and his face curdled with disgust.

"He should be *ruling* it." He smacked a fist to his breast. "Look at me. I started out the same way he did, and I've conquered world after world."

"Well, maybe he doesn't have your lust for power."

"Nonsense." The Leader turned back to the sky beyond the windows. "Everybody wants dominion over his or her fellow beings. Everybody secretly wants to be the top of the heap, king of the hill. Everybody wants to rule the world. The question is whether or not they have the balls to take it."

K8 twisted her mouth into a sceptical sneer.

"And you do?"

The monkey laughed, and his tail twitched.

"Of course. I know what I want to achieve, and I'm prepared to take proactive steps to actuate that outcome. That's why, as soon as we make the transfer to your timeline, I'm going to launch all the missiles we have.

No negotiation, no time wasting, just decisive action." He clamped the cigarette holder between his teeth. "In order to give our virus time to work, we need to throw the enemy into disarray. So, as soon as we appear, we strike."

CHAPTER TWENTY-EIGHT
SOMEBODY ELSE'S APOCALYPSE

VICTORIA VALOIS LAY on her bunk, unable to sleep. The *Tereshkova* would arrive over the outskirts of London within the hour, but Paul had persuaded her to try to rest. She'd been awake for almost two days straight, and there was a limit to the amount of fatigue for which her gelware could compensate. But, try as she might, she couldn't relax. How could she, knowing what they were about to face?

She rubbed her eyes, and then ran her hand back, across her bare scalp, to the pillow.

How had she found herself in this situation again? Since saving the world last year with Ack-Ack Macaque and Prince Merovech, she'd kept as far from politics as she could, done her damnedest to stay away from international disputes and diplomatic intrigues. Cocooned within the safety of her gondola, she'd all but fallen off the grid. And yet here she was again, sailing into the crucible, ready once more to throw herself into battle against superior forces in order to avert apocalypse. Why did it have to be her? Who'd appointed her world saviour? She wasn't anything special, merely a brain-damaged ex-journalist with a knack for being in the wrong place at the wrong time.

All she'd wanted had been a nice, juicy mystery to alleviate the boredom.

She should have known better.

Irritably, she rolled onto her side, and found herself looking at her desk, and the window beyond. How could she sleep in daylight?

If she wanted to, she supposed she could slip into command mode and use her gelware to force her body to sleep—but that was something she'd never tried, and she didn't like the idea of artificially snuffing out her consciousness. It was a line she was reluctant to cross. Sleeping tablets were one thing, but she balked at the notion of turning off a switch in her brain in order to put herself under. The idea made her feel like a machine; and besides, what if she botched the instructions? She'd rather be shaky and exhausted than risk permanently shutting off the very gelware processors that kept her alive.

But maybe dying would be preferable to becoming one of the Gestalt?

She couldn't imagine what it would be like to share her skull with the thoughts of others; to have the echoing spaces of her mind filled with the ceaseless din of other voices; to submit her will to that of the majority and become little more than a synapse in something else's brain; a walking, talking logic gate in an unknowably vast super-organism. The idea filled her with revulsion. She already felt like a half-human cyborg; she wouldn't live as a zombie in somebody else's apocalypse. If the worst happened, and conversion became inevitable, she'd turn her gelware off and slide into unknowing, insensate oblivion.

Or perhaps, she thought grimly, she'd ask Paul to blow the skyliner's engines.

Would that even work?

Each of the *Tereshkova*'s fifteen impellers drew its power from its own nuclear-electric engine. If she asked him, could he find some way to detonate them all simultaneously, destroying the airship and all on board? Could he, in effect, turn the old skyliner into a flying bomb? Victoria didn't know enough about the physics involved, but she made a mental note to find out. Who knew what she might be called upon to do, and what she might be expected to sacrifice, in the coming hours?

For a few minutes more, she lay and listened to the familiar sounds of the gondola. She heard the wind buffeting against the walls; the flex and creak of the hull; and the almost subliminal hum of the motors. She heard people moving around in the corridors, opening and closing doors; the occasional scrape of a chair or shoe on the metal deck; and the clang and rattle of pans in the kitchen. It all sounded so peaceful and comforting that she could hardly bring herself to believe that it might soon be destroyed; that this flight might be the *Tereshkova*'s last.

With a sigh, she climbed off the bunk and walked over to the window. With luck, Merovech would be able to scramble enough planes to deal with the airships over Commonwealth territories; but what about the rest of the world? How many airships would it take to conquer the globe?

Paul's voice came over the intercom speakers.

"Vic?"

She blew out a long breath, and massaged her forehead with her fingertips.

"What do you want?"

"We've got a problem."

Victoria raised her eyes to the heavens. *Another one?*

"Please God, what now?"

"Can you let me in?"

For a second, she didn't understand what he meant. Then, with a sigh, she crossed to the cabin door and pulled it open. The remote control car waited in the corridor. She stood aside to let it in.

The car sped to the centre of the room and slithered to a halt on the Persian rug. Paul's hologram rose from its projectors. He'd altered his look again, and now appeared to be wearing a droopy khaki bush hat, a white t-shirt, and crisp urban camouflage combat trousers. Silver dog tags hung around his neck, and his clear frameless spectacles had transformed into mirror shades with round, purple-tinted lenses.

"What's going on?" She tried to keep her tone businesslike.

Paul scratched his chest.

"It's the monkey."

"What about him?"

"He's gone. He's taken off, literally. As soon as Sergei had him patched up, he went to the kitchen and ate a jar of instant coffee. Then he stole a helicopter from one of the hangars. He even bit a mechanic when she tried to stop him."

"*Merde.*"

"You can say that again."

"Where's he heading?" She didn't think for a second that Ack-Ack Macaque would run out on a fight. But what if he'd decided to defect? What if he'd decided the best way to save K8 was to hand himself over to the Leader? The thought made her feel crawly inside.

"We're tracking him via the chopper's built-in GPS transponder," Paul said.

"And?"

He shrugged. "He seems to be heading south, into Somerset."

Victoria frowned. "What's in Somerset?" All the action was ahead of them, in the Capital.

"He could be heading for France, or—" Paul stopped. He took his shades off. "Oh," he said.

Victoria restrained a futile urge to grab him by the lapels.

"*What?*"

"I'm picking up a transmission. He's making a call."

"Can you patch it through?"

"Yeah, hold on a sec." Paul's eyes rolled back in his head, and the room's speakers hissed into life. They let out a nerve-jangling blast of static, and then she heard the monkey's yawp, his voice shaky from vibration and backed by the *thud, thud, thud* of a helicopter rotor.

"...fuelled and ready to go," he was saying, "I'll be with you in fifteen minutes, and I'll need pilots for all of 'em."

"Who's he talking to?" Victoria asked, raising her voice over the noise.

Paul lowered the volume.

"The control tower at the Fleet Air Arm Museum," he said.

Victoria frowned. "Don't tell me..."

"Yeah," Paul couldn't keep still. "You remember those Spitfires they dug up in Burma a few years back?"

"Yes, I bought him one."

"Well, they have a dozen currently under restoration at the museum and, according to its website, at least half of those are airworthy."

"Holy crap."

"Quite." Paul slid his glasses back into place, and shook his head. A smile tickled his lips. "It seems our friend's rounding up a posse."

CHAPTER TWENTY-NINE
UTTERLY FUCKED

SAT ON THE wooden veranda, surrounded by the fetid air of the potted jungle, K8 began to feel feverish. At first, she put the sudden clamminess down to fear, but the warmth kept spreading. At the small of her back, sweat pooled and ran like condensation on a cold beer glass. Seeing her growing discomfort, the Leader grinned, and his sharp canines caught the light from the armoured windows at the airship's nose.

"Are you quite sure you wouldn't like a cup of tea?"

K8's hands were trembling. She screwed them into little balls.

"Go to hell."

The monkey rose to his feet and tugged at his cufflinks, first one, then the other.

"I can see," he said, "that you're going to prove an interesting addition to the group dynamic."

K8 swallowed hard.

"I'd rather die."

He looked down at her, head slightly to one side.

"Would you?" He sounded surprised, and almost disappointed. "Would you really?"

The shaking in her hands spread to her forearms and shoulders.

"You're damn right I would."

The monkey touched his chin with leathery fingers.

"Well, that won't be necessary, I assure you." Leaving her seated at the wrought iron table, he walked back over to the veranda's rail and stood, looking out at the sky. Parrots and budgerigars flapped among the upper branches of the trees, little flits of colour against the drab battleship grey of the chamber's roof. The Leader was a silhouette against the windows. K8's nose itched and her eyes hurt. All of a sudden, the light from outside seemed uncomfortably bright.

"I'll never join you."

The Leader turned to her, but she couldn't make out his features against the glare. She held up a hand to shade her eyes.

"It seems," he said, "that you're labouring under a misapprehension."

"Dream on, pal."

He smiled and shook his head, ran a paw back through his coiffured mane.

"Allow me to speak plainly." He jabbed his index finger in her direction. "You have no choice in the matter. You will join us. You will become part of the collective."

K8 coughed. Her eyes were watering, and her nose had begun to stream. She dug in her pocket for a screwed-up tissue.

"How can you be so sure?"

The Leader leant back against the rail. He tapped a finger to his lips.

"Because we've already ticked that box."

K8 sniffed and hugged herself. The shakes were getting worse.

"You what?"

The monkey came back to the table and picked up the silver teapot.

"Do you recall the injection on the *Tereshkova?*" He opened the lid and sloshed the contents around. "Well, I'm very much afraid it contained more than simple sedatives." He refilled his cup, but didn't sit.

Through watery eyes, K8 glowered up at him.

"How long have I got?"

He looked at his watch. "You'll feel under par for another few minutes, like you're coming down with the flu."

"And then?" K8's fingers and toes felt cold. Her stomach growled like a frightened dog.

"Then all your questions will be answered."

She felt a lump welling in her throat. She couldn't attack the monkey; in her weakened state, he was far stronger than she was. Neither could she run. He'd catch her before she found her way through the potted trees; and, even if he didn't, she'd never get past the guards waiting outside the brass door. If she wanted to escape, her only choice would be to throw herself over the edge of the veranda, into the depths of the airship, and hope the fall broke her neck.

It wasn't much of a choice.

"Why me?"

The Leader reached for the milk jug, and stirred a little of the contents into his tea. Then he placed the teaspoon on the saucer beside his cup, and set the jug back where it had been.

"I'm sure you know the answer to that one."

She closed her eyes. Of course she knew. He wasn't the slightest bit interested in her as a person; she had no value to him beyond her worth as bait. She was simply a lure to entrap the Skipper. But, by the time Ack-Ack Macaque came for her—and she had no doubt whatsoever that he *would* come for her—she'd already be gone, claimed by the hive mind and sentenced to a zombified half-life as one of its drones. Even if by some miracle he got to her before the transformation was complete, he had no cure, no antidote with which to save her; and anyway, who knew what would be left of the world by then? If the Leader succeeded in dumping his plague, there'd be nowhere for them to go, nowhere to run. No way out.

She was, she admitted to herself with a sinking heart, utterly fucked.

"But, I thought—"

"I need you on board for this one, K8. It's all about intelligence gathering; market research, if you like. If I'm going to persuade our mutual associate to join the winning team, I'm going to need to get a handle on his worldview. I need to find out what makes him tick, and so I'm going to need access to your memories and knowledge of him." The Leader raised his drink. In his hairy, simian hands, the teacup looked absurdly dainty. "If he refuses to play ball, and it comes down to a fight, well then, who knows his weaknesses better that you, eh?"

K8 couldn't reply. Her right eye socket felt as if a rusted spike had been driven into it. It was all she could do to stop herself from crying out. She ground her knuckles against her burning forehead, trying to rub away the pain.

"Don't think of it as losing," he said, looking down his nose at her. "Think of it as upgrading early, to avoid the rush."

CHAPTER THIRTY
WHAT WOULD MENDELBLATT DO?

WILLIAM COLE LINGERED in the doorway of the *Tereshkova*'s infirmary, watching the woman in the bed. She hadn't seen him yet. Her eyes were resting, and her auburn hair tumbled across the pillow like copper filigree. Her left arm and right ankle had both been plastered, and now hung suspended from a traction rig. Beneath the covers, her chest rose and fell, and its gentle rhythm brought tears to his eyes. As long as he could see it, he knew she lived.

Was there a word, he wondered, for what he felt? He'd never been so happy or so terrified; never felt so vulnerable or powerless. Over the past two days, he'd had his dead wife returned to him, and then almost lost her again. He'd become a husband and father on the brink of Armageddon, allowed only a fleeting moment of ephemeral happiness before the world fell apart.

It all seemed so damn unfair.

He thought of the old saying, that it was better to have loved and lost than never to have loved at all. Whoever came up with that had been an idiot. Two days ago, William would have probably welcomed the coming catastrophe, welcomed an end to loneliness and grief, and have quite happily thrown himself off the end of Portishead pier, into the sea with heavy rocks in his pockets, in order to escape the coming plague. But, as things stood now, he suddenly had something worth protecting, something worth living for. He had a family: two people he loved more dearly than he loved life itself, and no way to shield them from the coming horrors. He'd always known fate could play tricks, but he'd never expected it to be downright cruel. Losing his wife and daughter once nearly killed him. To lose them twice would be surely more than any man could be expected to bear.

Above the bed was a porthole, with blue November sky beyond. Leaning against the doorframe, he found himself remembering bright autumn days from his childhood: the front lawn of his parents' house in Dayton; his father sorting Christmas lights in the garage, or tinkering with the petrol mower; his mother upstairs, running her stock trading business on a laptop in the spare bedroom, making video calls to New York, Tokyo and London. He remembered playing with the other kids in the neighbourhood; the sandpaper roughness of his father's cheek, and the smell of oil and old cologne on his shirt; the clatter of his mother's heels on the parquet floor; and the aroma of meatloaf from the kitchen.

Where, he wondered, had all that gone, and how could he have let something so precious slip away from him? That had been his family, his support, and his *home*. Right now, he'd give anything to hear his father's voice, to lose himself in one of the old man's bear hugs; but his father was dead, and his mother in a nursing home in Dayton, her mind already lost to the twisting confusions of advanced senility. However much he longed to go back, he never could, and never would. He wasn't a child any more. He was a father himself, with a teenage daughter of his own, whom he'd only known for a few brief moments, and to whom he couldn't offer anything like the stability or security shown to him by his own father.

The thought brought an irrational stab of shame, as if he'd failed in a sacred duty—failed Lila, Marie, and himself.

His cheeks burned, and he didn't seem to know what to do with his hands. They fidgeted like spiders, moving from beard to pockets, and back again.

When he opened his eyes, he found Marie watching him from the bed.

"William, what's the matter? Is Lila—?"

"Lila's fine." He swallowed hard, and brushed his hair flat with his left hand.

"You saw her?"

"We talked."

"And?"

He cleared his throat, wiped a hand across his eyes.

"She's incredible."

Marie smiled. "Yes, she is, isn't she?"

He walked over to the bed and stood uncertainly. Should he pat her shoulder, or bend down and kiss her cheek? After a moment's dithering, he settled for taking her hand.

"She wants to fight," he said.

"So do I." Marie looked at her suspended arm and leg. "But I can't."

"Shouldn't we try to stop her?"

Marie shook her head. "No. Absolutely not. This is her choice."

"But, aren't you worried she might be killed?"

Her eyes widened in anger. "Of course I'm worried. But look what we're up against. If we lose, that'll be it, game over for good, and it won't matter whether she was on the front lines or back here hiding under your bed." She kicked at the covers with her good leg. "Personally, I'd rather see her dead than become one of them."

William was aghast.

"How can you even say that?"

"Because I've seen what happens, okay? I've seen what they do to people. Men, women and children turned into drones, all traces of individuality banished by the machines in their heads." She took a breath. "And so has Lila. She's seen it all, and she knows exactly what we're up against. She knows the odds and she knows the stakes, and if she wants to fight, there's nothing you or I can do to stop her."

"But the danger—"

"Danger's relative. Sometimes it's more dangerous to do nothing." Frustrated, she tugged at the wires holding her damaged limbs in position. "And if it weren't for these, I'd be right out there with her."

"What about me?"

"If you want to help her, go with her."

"What good would I be?"

Marie looked up at him.

"The Bill Cole I knew was a guerrilla fighter. What kind of man are you?"

"I don't know."

"Then don't you think it's time you found out?"

"I wouldn't know where to start."

"Of course you would. Seriously, William, don't you remember your dreams, the ones you wrote down as stories? They weren't dreams, they were memories. I don't know how or why, but you've always been close to your alternate selves."

"No, I don't think—"

She slapped her palm against the covers.

"What was the name of that detective in your books?"

"Lincoln Mendelblatt."

"Well, he's you. Or at least, he's a version of you. When you're writing all that stuff about him, you're really writing about yourself."

William turned away from the bed. He could feel his cheeks going red.

"Bullshit."

Marie caught his hand, and squeezed.

"It's time to ask yourself," she said, "what would Mendelblatt do?"

CHAPTER THIRTY-ONE
STAY FROSTY

VICTORIA VALOIS STOOD on the *Tereshkova*'s bridge, at the front of the airship's main gondola. She stood with her legs slightly apart and her hands clasped behind her back, at the edge of the windscreen, which sloped down from the ceiling and curved into the floor. It had been designed to afford the pilot and navigator an uninterrupted view of the sky and terrain ahead. The toes of her boots overlapped the join between glass and deck, and, looking down between them, she could see the ribbon of the motorway cutting through the countryside between Reading and Slough. Ahead, London lay beneath a towering mound of cumulus, the cloud's shadow falling across the city's glass towers and sprawling streets like the footprint of an alien mothership.

As they were riding into battle, she'd chosen to wear one of the Commodore's more resplendent jackets: a red one with gold buttons and a silver scabbard on a white silk sash. She'd decided to leave her head bare, presenting her scars as an unashamed 'fuck you' to the world. Earned in combat, they were her medals—badges of suffering and survival, displayed now as an act of defiance, a warning to others and a reminder to herself.

Merovech had assured her that she wasn't needed, that the RAF could handle things without the help of an unarmed and elderly skyliner; but she'd told him she was coming anyway, and he hadn't tried to stop her. He knew as well as she did that there was nowhere else for her to be. Having come this far, she had to see the story through to its conclusion, even if it meant pitting herself against overwhelming odds; even if it meant dying in the attempt. With the whole world under threat, she had little to lose. She wouldn't wait on the sidelines, passive and cowering. Better to go out kicking and screaming, she thought. If she had to die, she'd make sure the bastards remembered her.

Do not go gentle into that good night...

Well, duh.

The only thing that frightened her was the thought she might fall before the battle's end, that she might never know the outcome—never know if her death had done more than simply buy the world a few moments of grace.

Behind her, the bridge lay deserted. With Ack-Ack Macaque currently AWOL, Paul was running the ship. All remaining passengers and non-essential members of the crew—including the navigator—had been put ashore, ferried down to the ground on the *Tereshkova*'s remaining helicopters. As far as she knew, the only flesh-and-blood people left aboard were a couple of engineers; half a dozen of her most trusted stewards; the writer, William Cole; his wife; and their daughter. With her arms and legs in traction, Marie couldn't be moved, and Cole had nowhere else to go, refusing to leave her side. At least the girl, Lila, might be of some use. She'd fought the Gestalt before, on other parallels, and had some insights into their methods and tactics.

But how could Victoria best apply the girl's expertise? Officially, the *Tereshkova* carried no ship-to-ship armaments. The 1978 Treaty of Bergerac, which enshrined the autonomy of skyliners in international law, expressly forbade them from carrying anything but the most defensive of weapons. She had half a dozen anti-aircraft missiles, a few flares, and that was about it. The monkey had taken the Commodore's handheld missile launcher, and now only a few antique submachine guns remained in the airship's armoury—enough to equip the six remaining stewards, but hardly enough to hold off a full-scale global invasion.

Gloomily, she contemplated the suburbs unrolling beneath her. The sun, now dipping towards late afternoon, threw the *Tereshkova*'s rectangular shadow ahead of it, and she watched it ripple across ring roads and roundabouts, tower blocks, industrial parks, and flooded gravel pits. Several kilometres to the southeast, she saw Heathrow. A few elderly jets lumbered around like pollen-drunk bees, staggering off on international runs to New York, Tokyo and Sydney. Above the cargo terminal, a couple of skyliners hung in the air like whale sharks looming over the surface of a reef, their torpedo-shaped bodies grey with distance and cloud-shadow. She thought she recognised one, but it was difficult to tell.

She could have used her neural implants to check their identities, but couldn't be bothered. Some people obsessively collected sightings of individual skyliners, and each craft had its own online fan communities; but Victoria had never been one of them. She was happy enough to exchange pleasantries with a fellow captain if they passed each other during an ocean crossing, or found themselves in port at the same time, but she'd never really fallen for the whole 'romance of the skies' that so captivated the glorified train spotters posting photographs of the various ships on their forums. For her, the *Tereshkova* was a refuge. The Commodore had taken her aboard when her marriage to Paul collapsed, and the old gondolas, with their creaking walls and cramped cabins, had become her home. She liked the feeling of remoteness she got when looking down at the world from her porthole. Always moving, always in the same place. The scenery changed, but her immediate surroundings stayed comfortingly the same.

She heard a hiss as the intercom speakers switched themselves on.

"Uh, Vicky?" It was Paul's voice. "We've got an intruder in the cargo area."

"An intruder?" That was impossible. While she'd been resting, the stewards had searched the ship to ensure no one remained save those who were supposed to be aboard.

"It's like they appeared from nowhere."

"From another world, perhaps?"

"Exactly."

She gripped the sword protruding from the scabbard at her hip.

"Where are they now?"

"Main forward cargo hold."

Victoria glanced up at the ceiling. The main forward hold lay inside the central hull's envelope, almost directly above the bridge.

"I'm on my way."

SWORD DRAWN, SHE made her way aft to the companionway that led up into the body of the skyliner. With so few people on board, the ship felt echoing and empty, and somehow colder than usual. Her boots seemed to clang deafeningly on the cleated metal steps, and she became aware of the sound of her own breathing, and the insistent knocking of her heart.

At the top of the steps, she stepped off onto the walkway that ran the length of the central hull's keel. Overhead, gasbags, platforms, and storage bays filled the vast space contained within the hull's lightly armoured cylinder. After the warmth of the gondola, the unheated air felt sharp and fresh, tangy with the smells of cold metal and rubber, and alive with metallic squeaks and screeches, and the ever-present vibration of the engines. Sepia, mote-flecked sunlight filtered down from panels set into the airship's upper surface, high above.

The forward cargo hold was a large room at the end of the walkway: an aluminium-walled compartment wadded into the point of the tapering bow, and accessed through a pair of double doors—one of which now hung ajar. It was mainly used for storage of passengers' luggage. Larger items of cargo were accommodated in special bays in the outer hulls.

Although she could feel the chill around her, Victoria's palm, where it gripped the sword, felt damp. She thought about using her gelware to squirt a mild sedative into her bloodstream to calm her nerves, but decided against it. As she didn't know who or what she might be facing, it would probably be best to 'stay frosty', as the monkey often put it.

Sword held out in front, she crept her way forwards. She knew the stewards would be on their way, but couldn't bring herself to wait. It was up to her to lead. She was the captain, after all, and this was her ship and her home, and therefore her responsibility. She cleared her throat.

"Okay," she said. "I know you're in there. Come on out."

She tensed, but nothing happened. She heard something that might have been the deck creaking beneath the weight of someone moving, but no one replied, and nobody appeared in the doorway.

Carefully, she inched closer. The sword's point wavered before her, ready to impale anyone who startled her.

"I know you're there," she said.

More sounds of movement came from within. Victoria stopped edging forwards, and dropped into a fighting stance. In the doorway, a middle-aged man stepped into the light. She saw thin grey hair and the ubiquitous white suit of a Gestalt drone.

"Hello, Captain."

Victoria drew herself up.

"Mister Reynolds."

Where Ack-Ack Macaque had hit him, the man had a split lip and a dark bruise around his mouth.

"How agreeable to see you again," he said, smiling awkwardly around his injuries.

Victoria thrust her chin forward.

"How did you get back aboard?"

Slowly, Reynolds reached into the inside pocket of his suit jacket and pulled out something that looked like a SincPhone.

"We walk between worlds."

Victoria held out her hand.

"Pass that to me."

Reynolds shook his head.

"No, we don't think so."

She waggled the sword.

"May I remind you that I'm the one holding the big, pointy weapon?"

Reynolds's hands enfolded the device. His smile remained unwavering.

"Even so, Captain, we will have to decline."

Victoria thought about insisting that he hand it over, but then decided to switch tactics. From her years working as a journalist for *Le Monde*, she knew that a sudden change of subject could wrong-foot the tight-lipped, and get them to reveal more than they were intending.

"So, what were you doing in there?" She looked over his shoulder, into the darkness of the cargo hold.

Reynolds, who was still clutching his transport device, turned his head slightly, following her gaze. For a second, he hesitated, and she saw his smile falter; but by the time he turned back to face her, it had returned to full strength.

"I'm afraid we are the bearers of bad news," he said, his voice dripping with false, honeyed regret.

"What have you done?" Victoria took a step closer, bringing the tip of the sword to within a foot of his face. He didn't flinch. In fact, his blue eyes seemed to twinkle in the light sieving down from above.

"We have placed a bomb in your hold," he said. "A very sophisticated bomb."

Victoria drew back, her breathing fast and shallow.

"Get out of my way."

Reynolds shook his head, and held up a hand.

"Some rules, Captain." He brushed a speck of dust from his sleeve. "Our Leader is very keen to meet your macaque."

"He's not here."

"We know. We also know that you still have the writer, William Cole." The man's smile broadened. "Hence, the bomb."

Victoria ran her tongue across her lower lip. Her mouth was dry.

"You mentioned some rules?"

"Ah, yes." He raised a finger. "Rule one. If this airship drops below three thousand feet, the bomb will go off." Another finger. "If anyone tries to move the bomb or otherwise tamper with it, it will go off." He raised a third and final finger. "And if Cole and the monkey aren't delivered to us within the hour, it will most definitely go off."

Victoria took a deep breath through her nose.

"And what if I keep you here? Are you going to set it off while you're still on board?"

Still smiling, Reynolds shook his head.

"We're afraid you can't keep us, Captain." He thumbed a button on the device. Blue sparks crackled along his arm and played across his body. "You are defeated, and now, we go to meet our Leader."

"Yeah?" Victoria drew back her arm. "Then give him this message from me."

Enveloped in flickering light, Reynolds raised a supercilious eyebrow. He thought he had all the winning cards.

"What message?"

"This one." Victoria stabbed the sword forward, putting her entire weight behind it. The blade caught Reynolds in the waistcoat, midway between navel and ribcage. His mouth and eyes opened in outrage and surprise, and she rammed it home, up to the hilt. The fabric at the back of his jacket stuck out like a tent. Red blood soaked into white cloth like spilled wine on a restaurant table. Sparks crackled. Victoria snatched her hand back, leaving the sword in place.

Mouth gaping, hands pawing at the pommel, Reynolds shimmered once. His knees buckled. There was a bright blue flash, a burst of ozone, and he vanished.

CHAPTER THIRTY-TWO
THIS TOWN AIN'T BIG ENOUGH

THE FIVE SPITFIRES came in from the southwest, in a v-shaped formation. In the lead plane, hand wrapped around the throttle, Ack-Ack Macaque chewed nervously at an unlit cigar. The Fleet Air Arm Museum had been hosting five airworthy Spits in their hangars but, although he'd been able to scare up four pilots at short notice, none of them had any combat experience.

Ahead, through the armoured glass pane at the front of the cockpit's perspex canopy, he saw the black and white zigzags painted on the *Tereshkova*'s five hulls. Annoyingly, his hopes that the museum kept a stock of live ammunition had been dashed, so his makeshift squadron would have to land on the old airship in order to load up with bullets from his personal stash. Between the five of them, they'd use up his entire stock.

That's if the fucking guns even work, he thought to himself with a snarl. He'd been assured that each and every one of the Browning machine guns on each of the Spitfires had been faithfully restored, and were therefore all in good working order; at least, theoretically. Whether they'd stand up to being fired in anger was another matter, and he half expected them all to either jam or explode as soon as their firing controls were depressed.

Still, he thought, *I've done the best I can. They may be five museum pieces, and inexperienced pilots might be flying four of them, but surely they're better than nothing?*

Over a hundred years ago, the British had used these antique fighters to halt the Nazi advance and keep the Luftwaffe at bay. He gave the dashboard an affectionate pat. With a bit of luck, maybe the kites could work their magic a second time.

And anyway, what was there to lose?

He brought his plane around, lining up with the runway that ran diagonally across the backs of the airship's hulls.

"It's me," he said into the radio. "I'm coming in."

Who else would it be? Paul's voice spoke in his headphones. *Welcome home, monkey boy.*

Beyond the *Tereshkova*'s bow, Ack-Ack Macaque saw the suburbs of London: leafy streets laid out in rows and crescents; red brick tower blocks; billboards; railway cuttings and embankments. From up here, it looked peaceful.

"Any sign of attack?"

Not yet. And no word from your evil self, either.

Strapped into his seat, Ack-Ack Macaque bristled.

"Hey, I thought I was my evil self."

Paul laughed.

Sorry, dude. I guess you're just going to have to face it. Like it or not, you're one of the good guys now.

"Goddammit."

He had the nose of his plane aligned with the runway. Because the *Tereshkova* was ploughing forwards at a respectable rate of knots, he would have to come in at an angle, using the rudder to keep himself on target. With his right hand, he toggled the lever that lowered the undercarriage. Behind him, the other four planes lined up like ducklings, ready to follow him down—ready to transform the *Tereshkova* from a passenger liner to an aircraft carrier.

ACK-ACK MACAQUE LEFT his plane with one of the mechanics and, without stopping to watch the others land, made his way down through the airship to the bridge.

Stepping into the room, he pulled out his lighter and lit the damp cigar in his mouth, huffing great clouds of blue smoke into the room.

"Hey, Boss. What's shaking?"

Alone in front of the main window, Victoria wrinkled her nose and flapped a hand in front of her face.

"We had a visit from your old friend, Mister Reynolds."

"And how is the old bastard?"

Her hand went to the empty scabbard at her side.

"Dead."

"Good." Ack-Ack Macaque looked around at the unmanned workstations. "So, who's flying this thing?"

"Paul."

"Seriously?"

"He seems to be doing a reasonable job of it."

Ack-Ack Macaque loped over to the window.

"Then I'm out of work?"

"Not at all, just redeployed." Victoria crossed her arms over her chest. Medals jangled. "We need you on the front line."

He looked at the distant towers of Central London, and tried to imagine them in flames, pillars of smoke reaching up into the clouds—a new Blitz to wipe away everything rebuilt since the last one.

"Who's coordinating the defence?"

"Merovech's enlisted some high-ups in the RAF. They're trying to liaise with the Russians and the Yanks, but everybody's talking at the same time, and no-one's listening."

Ack-Ack Macaque curled his lip. He had some strong opinions on the subject of commanding officers and top brass. When he tried to express them, words such as 'arse' and 'elbow' came to mind.

"So, we're on our own?"

"No, we'll have fighter support. There are two aircraft carriers steaming up the Thames, and we can call in planes from Air Command in High Wycombe."

"What about the other cities?"

"From what I can gather, Edinburgh, Manchester, Paris and Belfast are covered. The rest will have to take their chances."

"That's a bit harsh."

"There simply aren't enough planes."

Ack-Ack Macaque blew a smoke ring at the ceiling. "Well, I brought another five."

Victoria turned away from the view. Looking down, he saw the capital opening up before them like an unfolding map.

"Listen," she said, walking over to a cabinet set into the wall. Inside were half a dozen swords. She selected one and slid it into her scabbard. "There's something else you can do, right now, that might just give us an edge."

Ack-Ack Macaque removed the cigar from his mouth and held it between the fingers of his left hand.

"What's that?"

"The leader of the Gestalt."

He felt his lips draw back from his teeth.

"What about him?"

"He's a version of you. He might talk differently, but deep down, you're the same."

"He's a lunatic."

"Exactly." She came over and stood beside his chair. "Can you put yourself in his position? Can you think like him? You're the best chance we have of second-guessing his tactics."

Ack-Ack Macaque rolled the cigar thoughtfully.

"I thought he made his tactics pretty bloody clear."

"Yes, but if we're going to have any hope of defending ourselves, if we're going to fight him, we need to know how his mind works." She turned to a screen on the wall of the bridge, and it blinked into life, displaying a strategic satellite view of the city, with red and green icons marking the positions of known forces, and yellow arrows indicating major targets. "If you were him, what would you do?"

Ack-Ack Macaque gave the map a wary squint. Then he kicked himself to his feet and shuffled over to it.

"If it was me, I'd materialise here." He tapped a point on the screen where the river snaked through the heart of the city, just downstream from Westminster Bridge. "And launch everything I had. Take it all out in the first few seconds: government, monarchy, civil service, everything. Wipe out every one of the bastards, and the battle's over. There's nobody left to give orders."

Victoria stroked her chin. "Decapitate the state, you mean?"

"Yeah." Ack-Ack Macaque couldn't help grinning. "Knock out the high command, and you can mop up the foot soldiers later."

"You wouldn't just nuke the place?"

His grin spread. "I can't lie, that would be very tempting; but I don't think that's his game. He doesn't want everybody dead. He wants converts for his religion. He wants fresh brains for the hive, and he can't have them if they've all been vaporised." He took a draught of smoke, and then blew it out the side of his mouth. "If he can throw us into disarray, even temporarily, it gives his virus thingy space to work. By the time we've regrouped, we'll already have been infected."

Victoria leant close to the map, eyeing the Commonwealth Parliament— the seat of power for most of a continent.

"A single, overwhelming attack," she mused, "and then all he has to do is sit back and wait for us to come to him."

"Unless we nuke him first."

She straightened up, eyebrows raised, her hand on the pommel of her replacement sword.

"*Non!* We cannot! This is London, for heaven's sake. Eight million people!"

The monkey shrugged.

"Then all we can do is wait until he appears, and then hit him as hard as we can." He scratched his cheek. "What does the girl say?"

"Lila? Pretty much the same." Victoria let her shoulders drop. She ran a hand back across the dome of her scalp.

"There's something else," she said. "Reynolds left us a present before he died. It's in the cargo hold directly above this room. If we're not there waiting for the Leader when he arrives, ready to hand you over to him, it'll go off."

Ack-Ack Macaque gave a snort.

"That stupid fuck."

Victoria frowned. "Reynolds?"

"No, the Leader. He's just made his first mistake."

"How so?"

"Because I *want* to get onto his ship." He curled his hands, picturing his thumbs digging into the other monkey's larynx, choking off his air supply. "He's got K8. If I'm going to get her back in one piece, I'm going to need to meet him, face-to-face. And if that happens, I can kill him."

"But he'll know you want that, won't he?"

Ack-Ack Macaque shrugged. "Yeah, I'm sure he does."

"So, why does he—?"

"Because he wants to recruit me." Ack-Ack Macaque tapped his temple. "And because he's fucking nuts. He probably wants to fight me as badly as I want to fight him. There's only room for one alpha monkey, and neither of us will stop until we find out which of us it is."

"This town ain't big enough for the both of you?"

He stuck the cigar in his mouth and grinned around it.

"It's a primate thing."

Abruptly, the map vanished and the wall screen cleared to a picture of Paul's face.

"Heads up," he said. "Something's happening."

The display changed again, to a BBC News feed. The volume was off, but the pictures spoke for themselves. They were being relayed from a camera in Trafalgar Square, on the steps of the National Gallery, looking south down Whitehall towards the tower of Big Ben. Above the roofs, the sky crackled with blue and white sparks. People were standing and pointing, or running for cover. Police vans tore past, lights flashing. A cloud of pigeons flew in front of the lens.

And then, *blam!* Something vast, black and impossible snapped into solidity above the city, blocking out the daylight. The picture went dark, and then came back up as the camera adjusted to the sudden shadow.

Ack-Ack Macaque scowled at the screen and swore under his breath. They were looking at the underside of an airship so large he couldn't see its edges—just row upon row of gun emplacements; a scattering of engine nacelles; and more than a dozen large, armoured gondolas, each bristling with missile tubes and machine gun turrets. The thing had appeared partially inside the low cloud layer, and rivulets of displaced grey fluff rippled away to either side.

Turning away from the screen, he looked to the front window, and whistled. Ahead, the Leader's flagship filled the skies. It must have been at least two kilometres long, more than twice the size of the *Tereshkova*. Its footprint stretched from Green Park to Waterloo, and every inch of it radiated a brutal menace.

And then, even as he watched, he saw the first missiles streaking down from the giant warship, hitting the self-same targets he'd just selected on the map, turning the skyline into a series of fireballs.

CHAPTER THIRTY-THREE
THE COMMONWEALTH EXPECTS

As the first explosions still shook the capital, Ack-Ack Macaque dropped to all fours and scampered from the bridge. He threw himself up the nearest companionway. He had to get airborne. It was his default response, a reflex written into the software of his mind. He'd been created to re-fight a fictionalised Battle of Britain, and had scrapped his way through countless simulated air raids and scrambles. This was what he did, and what he knew. When the bell rang, you ran for your plane. It was as simple as that. In some ways, it was a comfort to find himself back in such a familiar situation.

Using his arms to haul himself upward, he charged up flight after flight of metal stairs, until he reached the top of the *Tereshkova*. By the time he got there, he was wheezing for breath, and coughing up globs of brown tobacco-tasting mucus. All five of the planes were waiting at the end of the runway. There wasn't much room for them, but somehow they'd managed to cram themselves together. The pilots and solitary mechanic had been in the process of loading ammo belts into the machine guns built into the wings of the lead plane when the attack began, and had stopped to stare at the carnage, hands shading their eyes as they peered ahead.

"Hey!" He did his best parade ground yelp. "No time for gawping. I need these babies in the air, right now. How are we doing?"

The nearest pilot turned to him. Like the rest of this ad hoc squadron, he wasn't military. He was a retired airline pilot, a volunteer at the Fleet Air Arm Museum, and his face dripped fear and bafflement.

"Have you seen—?"

"Of course I've fucking seen it. Why do you think we need the bullets?" He pushed past, to where the mechanic knelt on the wing. The mechanic's name was Smithy. He wore oil-stained overalls and a battered, shapeless cap.

"It's okay, chief." Smithy closed the lid of the ammo compartment and wiped his hands on an old rag. "This is the last one. I can't swear they'll all work, mind, but they're loaded and ready to go."

Ack-Ack Macaque felt his teeth peel back from his gums. His pilots were looking to him, plainly shocked and badly frightened. None of them were warriors. He spoke loudly, to cut through their confusion.

"Okay, sweethearts, this is it. 'The Commonwealth expects', and all that crap." He strode to the leading plane, and hopped onto the wing beside the open cockpit canopy. He knew he had to say something to motivate and inspire them, but, "Follow me, and don't get yourselves killed," was the best he could come up with. In annoyance, he flung a hairy arm at the distant warship. "I'm going to land on that big bastard and try to rescue my friend. Your job is to keep it busy. Try to stop it deploying its doomsday weapon before the jets get here."

Cigar clamped in place, he glared around at their upturned faces. Like startled owlets, they blinked back at him. They were weekend hobbyists pitched into an unforeseeable war. When the firing started, they'd be lucky not to crash into each other, let alone take on the enemy. Still, they were all he had, and he knew he had to make the best of them. If this was going to be his final flight, his last battle, he was damned if he wasn't going to take it seriously.

He snapped his heels together and threw them a stiff salute. Then, with as much style as he could muster, he turned and dropped into the pilot's seat.

Oh well, he thought. *Here goes nothing.*

HE BARRELLED ACROSS the London sky with the other four planes arranged in a line behind him. This new Spitfire wasn't the same as his old one. Like horses, every plane had its own character and set of quirks. This was a Mark V, with wings clipped for greater manoeuvrability—a model he hadn't flown before. A few of the controls were in different places, and the stick felt jumpier than he was used to. Nevertheless, it was still a Spitfire, and he thrilled to the guttural growl of its engine. Like him, it was a relic from another time.

Ahead, the Gestalt warship loomed like a cliff face.

Ack-ster, it's Paul.

"What is it?"

We've received a signal from the RAF. Planes are scrambling from the Shakespeare *and* Verne. *They should be with you in five minutes, and suggest you hang back until they arrive.*

"Screw that, I'm going after K8."

A fresh volley of missiles burst from the underside of the behemoth, and he followed their white smoke trails down to the ground. That was Downing Street gone. The Parliament buildings and large areas of Whitehall already lay in ruins. The invasion seemed to be proceeding exactly the way he'd told Victoria it would, with a decisive first strike aimed at destroying the country's political and military leaders.

Well, not on my watch, motherfuckers!

With his left hand, he pushed the throttle forward as far as it would go. The Gestalt ship hung in his gun sights.

"Okay, spread out," he told his wingmen. "Concentrate your fire on the gun turrets and missile launchers. Try to knock out as many as you can."

He watched them peel away to either side, taking up attack positions, while he held his course, hurtling straight at the enemy. He couldn't afford to show fear or hesitation. Somewhere on board, the Leader would be watching. He would guess who was piloting the lead Spitfire, and be ready to attack at the first sign of weakness or hesitation.

This was a test of courage. They were sizing each other up.

Stabbing at the radio with a gloved hand, Ack-Ack Macaque changed the frequency.

"Okay," he said into his mike, "it's me. I'm coming aboard."

As if in reply, fire erupted from every turret he could see. Lines of tracer raked the sky. Anti-aircraft missiles streaked like sparks. And, one by one, his Spitfires fell. The first two disappeared in greasy fireballs. The third seemed to fall apart in mid-air, hacked to bits by bullets. The fourth pulled up sharply—a sure sign the pilot had been hit—and tipped over onto its back. He watched it dive on Lambeth, accelerating into the road just shy of the bridge. And, just like that, all four of his wingmen were gone, blown away before any of them had managed to fire even a single shot.

When he looked up, the airship's guns had all swivelled in his direction.

"Oh, bollocks."

His squadron hadn't stood a chance; and now, if he was at all mistaken about the Leader's desire for a face-to-face confrontation, neither did he. For a long, long moment, he kept driving forward, into the teeth of the arsenal arrayed against him, knowing it would be fatal to flinch now. If he was right, this was all still part of the pre-fight posturing. The Leader was demonstrating his superior firepower, and Ack-Ack Macaque his courage. Essentially, they were beating their chests and circling each other.

For tense seconds he continued to hurtle at the juggernaut. Then he heard a burst of static over his headphones, and a familiar voice hissed, "Welcome, my brother. I am flattered you have decided to accept my invitation."

Ack-Ack Macaque felt his hackles rise. His tail thrashed against the cockpit wall.

"Screw you."

"Crude as ever, I see." The Leader sounded weary, almost bored. "But it can't have escaped even your limited attention that I have you at something of a disadvantage."

Ack-Ack Macaque pushed his goggles up onto his forehead. The gun barrels twitched in unison as they tracked the movements of his plane. He was beaten, and he knew it.

"Just tell me one thing." He fumbled one-handed for a cigar. "What do you want with me? First you send Reynolds, now all this. Why've you got such a hard-on for my approval?"

The Leader didn't speak for a few moments. When his voice came back over the airwaves, his tiredness held an edge of disappointment.

"Don't you feel it too?"

"Feel what?"

"Haven't you ever wanted to meet another one of your kind? Haven't you ever been lonely?"

Ack-Ack Macaque jammed the cigar between his teeth. The black armour-plated flank of the airship filled his entire forward view. If he didn't pull up soon, he'd hit it dead centre, at three hundred miles per hour.

"So," he rolled the cigar from one side of his mouth to the other, "you're looking for a playmate?"

"No, my simple brother." The Leader gave a half-hearted chuckle. "I'm looking for a lieutenant. Now—" his voice hardened, "—I want you to come aboard."

Ack-Ack Macaque pulled back on his stick, and the Spit's nose rose towards the low grey clouds. He zoomed over the whale-like back of the airship and looked down.

"You haven't got a runway." All he could see were a few helipads, with choppers and VTOL jets parked on them.

"You have a parachute."

"Fuck off."

"If you want to see your little friend again, you'll do it."

Ack-Ack Macaque snarled.

"If you've hurt her—"

"I'll give you thirty seconds."

Ack-Ack Macaque screeched, and hammered the Perspex canopy with his fists.

"Twenty-eight..."

He thought of K8 and took a long, shuddering breath through his teeth.

"Twenty-six..."

"Okay, okay." He wiped his right eye with the back of one hairy wrist. "I'll do it. But I'll need to gain some altitude, or the 'chute won't open properly."

The radio crackled.

"Understood. But we're still tracking you. Try anything idiotic, and I'll blow that balsawood kite out from under you before you can blink. Capeesh?"

Ack-Ack Macaque's shoulders hunched, and he drove his plane skyward.

"Yeah, I got you."

As the Spitfire's prop drilled into the rainclouds, he took a last look downwards, and saw a glint at the airship's bows. What was that?

Were they *windows*?

A wicked grin smeared itself across his face. His plane circled upward in a narrowing spiral, like a vulture riding thermals above a wounded buffalo, and then the clouds enveloped him and everything turned to fog.

As soon as the monkey's plane vanished into the overcast, the Gestalt warship opened fire on the *Tereshkova*. Bullets punched through the black and white zigzags at its bows, piercing all five hulls. Propellers sparked and windows smashed. Radio aerials snapped and fell.

On the *Tereshkova*'s bridge, Victoria grabbed for support as the floor lurched. In the doorway behind her, William Cole yelped as he was thrown against the frame.

Slowly, the bow began to turn.

Clinging on to the arm of the pilot's chair, Victoria shouted, "What are you doing?"

"Turning away," Paul's voice quailed through the intercom speakers. Bullets rattled against the aluminium hull like hail clattering on a tin roof.

"No!" She pulled herself upright. "If you turn sideways, you'll just make us a bigger target."

"What, then?"

She glanced at the cloud layer.

"Take us up. Follow the monkey."

"I can't!"

The front windows shattered, and Victoria ducked.

"Why not?"

"We're losing gas from the port hull."

"Jettison it!" The *Tereshkova*'s five hulls were kept in place by lightweight steel girders. Up until last year, they could only be disengaged manually. Then, after damage to one of the outer hulls had almost cost the whole craft, one of Victoria's first acts as Captain had been to install explosive bolts at all the key junctures.

"It's losing buoyancy," Paul protested. "It'll crash."

"Better it than us."

She heard a detonation, and the deck shook. She couldn't tell if it had been the bolts, or a shot from the Gestalt.

"Separation complete," Paul reported.

The *Tereshkova*'s four remaining hulls quivered like a wet horse, and began to rise. The hail of bullets paused as the sudden change in altitude threw off the Gestalt's gunners.

Through the howling gap where the window glass had been, Victoria caught sight of the discarded section pitching down towards the city like a kilometre-long torpedo, trailing smoke and debris. Almost in slow motion, it dived into the shadow of the Gestalt craft and hit the brown waters of the Thames, throwing up a huge fan of spray. The nose smashed against the piers of Westminster Bridge, crumpling even as the bridge cracked and buckled before the weight of the impact. Clumps of masonry fell into the river. The fins at the stern rose into the air, hung there for an instant, impellers still spinning wildly, and then crumpled back with a splash.

"Jesus." William Cole joined her behind the pilot's chair.

"You said it."

"No, I mean those engines. They're nuclear-powered."

"They're designed to survive crashes."

"Will they?"

"Who knows?" Right now, irradiating half of London was among the least of her concerns.

She lost sight of the chaos on the ground as the *Tereshkova* reached the clouds. For a moment, the bombardment wavered, but quickly picked up again with equal ferocity.

Damn. For a minute there, she'd thought they might find cover in the overcast.

"They must have infrared tracking." Paul's voice held an edge of panic. The deck shuddered again. "We're taking damage to all sections. Venting gas in a dozen places."

Victoria turned to Cole, who was in the process of brushing glass and dust from his hair and beard.

"Take your family," she said, "and get out."

He looked at her, wild-eyed.

"Marie can't move."

"Then find a way to move her." She seized him by the shoulders, spun him around, and shoved him at the door. "*Allez-y!*"

He ran off unsteadily into the corridor, heading aft.

She heard the *blang, blang, blang* of bullets punching through metal and flinched. Her hand went to the sword at her side.

"What do we do?" Paul cried.

"How the hell would I know?" With the *Tereshkova* literally falling apart around them, her options were shrinking by the second. "How much longer can we stay airborne?"

"Assuming they don't hit the airbags again, another ten minutes. Twelve at the outside."

"Not good."

"And we're losing manoeuvrability."

She shook her head.

"*Putain de merde.*" She climbed into the pilot's chair and pressed the ship-wide intercom. "Attention all hands," she barked. "This is the Captain. Assume crash positions. We are going down. Repeat. We are going down."

AT THE TOP of its climb, the Spitfire emerged from the clouds into sunlight, and stalled. As it hung vertically in the clear air, with its prop spinning at the cobalt sky, Ack-Ack Macaque pulled the goggles back over his face, and dragged open the canopy. He had only seconds before gravity's fingers brought the nose down and the plane began the long fall earthwards. Bracing himself against the lip of the cockpit, he used his knife to hack a strip from his safety harness. Then he stood up, and gripped the control stick with his prehensile toes.

"Think you've got me, fuck-knuckle? Think again."

The plane began to slip backwards and he clung on with his feet until the nose snapped earthwards and he had it aimed where he wanted. With all the cloud and murk between him and his target, he had to line it up from memory, and then use the strip of harness to lash the stick in place. It was trickier than he'd thought it would be, but he did the best he could do in the few seconds available to him, and hoped it would be enough.

Falling nose first, the plane began to pick up speed. The wind flapped at the collar of his jacket. He crouched on the seat and leapt, arms and legs stretched out as if hurling himself from one jungle branch to another.

"Geronimo!"

He fell spread-eagled for a few seconds, towards the undulating carpet of cloud. Air rushed past his face, pulled at his hands and feet. Then, just as he reached the tops of the mashed potato-like peaks, the 'chute sprang open, jerking him back with a snap.

Swinging from its straps, he fell into the white and grey void, one hand on the lines, the other pulling a pistol from the holster at his thigh. He knew the enemy airship lurked only a few metres below the base of the clouds, so he wouldn't get much warning before he hit it. But that also meant her defenders wouldn't get a lot of time to shoot at him, either. He'd only be vulnerable for a few seconds. And, if he came down where he hoped, they'd already have better things to worry about.

THE MIST LIGHTENED around his feet and he fell into clear air, just in time to see the ruined Spitfire whirling away from the airship's bows, slipping from the toughened glass like a crushed butterfly falling from a car windscreen.

"Hell and damnation!" He'd hoped that by crashing it into the ironclad from above, the plane might have sheared the front of the ship's nose right off—but it seemed to have done little beyond smashing half a dozen panes, and cracking a handful of others.

The deck rushed at him. As he'd expected, there were people waiting for him. Members of the Gestalt stood at intervals along the two-thousand-metre-long craft, each dressed in an identical white suit, and each cradling an identical machine pistol. He put bullets in the nearest two, but then had to haul at the parachute and brace for collision. His feet struck the armoured surface with a shock that rattled his skeleton like a maraca, and he went limp, rolling with the impact.

He came to rest on the edge of one of the broken panes of glass, where the bow joined the body of the airship, his torso and legs on the metal hull, his boots dangling over the edge of the jagged hole. Flapping in the wind, the parachute tugged at him, and he flicked the release and wriggled out of the harness before it could inflate and drag him off the ship, dumping him onto the buildings below.

Weapons raised, the remaining Gestalt drones walked in his direction. They didn't seem hurried. He heaved himself to his feet and plugged one.

The man crumpled soundlessly, only to be replaced moments later by another emerging from a hatch. All along the airship's length, Neanderthals in white suits were clambering from ladders and companionways. If he shot one, three more appeared to take their place. With their thicker bones, they were tougher than ordinary humans, and he knew he simply didn't have the ammunition or strength to fight them all.

Behind him the splintered hole led down into a cavernous interior. He saw more glass far below. The entire nose was glazed, like the cockpit of a World War II German Heinkel. He glimpsed leaves and vines further back, in the body of the airship. The nearest treetop was maybe thirty feet below. With the heel of his boot, he kicked away the remaining glass splinters around the window's frame. Shots were fired at him, and he paused to return the compliment, felling a white-clad woman with a silver beehive. Behind her, maybe fifty others shuffled forwards, their movements eerily synchronised. Treading as carefully as he dared, he balanced around the edge of the broken pane until he was at the lower edge, closer to the pointed bow. From here, he could see the trees more easily, and also some sort of wooden platform set with tables and chairs.

Thirty feet seemed suddenly more like forty. Still, there was no way to back out now. Muttering to himself, he re-holstered his pistol and backed off a few paces. The guys and gals in white opened fire again. Ducking, he made a dash for the hole, and threw himself headlong through it, aiming for the nearest trees.

His jacket fluttered around him as he fell into the comparative gloom of the airship's interior. He saw the wooden platform—some kind of balcony—beneath him; but before he could make out any more detail, he crashed into the upper branches of a coconut tree. The thick fronds snapped and tangled around him, catching his arms and legs, slowing him; and the trunk bowed, absorbing some of his momentum. Then he broke through, and fell, in a shower of twigs and leaf fragments, into a web of vines and creepers. He fell from one branch to another, until he ended up swinging from one leg, his right knee hooked over the lower branch of a potted cedar. His goggles hung down on their strap, almost touching the floor. The cigar remained clamped firmly in his teeth, but it had snapped midway along its length, and the loose end dangled in front of his eye.

Debris settled around him.

* * *

FOR A FEW MOMENTS, he was content to remain there, letting his shaken brain catch up with his precipitous descent. Then he heard clapping, and the Leader emerged from the trees.

"My dear fellow," the monkey said, "that was quite an entrance. But then, I guess I shouldn't have expected anything less."

Ack-Ack Macaque spat out the remains of his cigar. Painfully, he reached up to grab the branch supporting him, and unhooked his leg. At this point, he felt more bruise than monkey, and every abused limb griped with its own chorus of aches and pains. He lowered his feet to the floor, brushed down his aviator jacket, and readjusted his eye patch.

"That's nothing," he rumbled. "Wait 'til I tell you about the time I made a jetpack out of fire extinguishers."

The Leader bowed his head and made a welcoming gesture.

"Please," he said, "we've been waiting for you. Won't you join us?"

He turned and led the way through the trees, onto the veranda, and Ack-Ack Macaque trailed after him, rolling and stretching his stiff shoulders beneath his jacket. His boots crunched over shards of glass from the broken panes high above.

The veranda overlooked the interior of the airship's conical nose. And there, silhouetted against the blue sky, a wrought iron table with three chairs, one of which was occupied.

"K8?" Her posture looked wrong. Instead of her usual teenage slump, she sat with her back straight and her hands resting on her knees. A half-finished cup of tea sat on the table before her, gentle wisps of steam curling upward past her unseeing eyes. "What have you done to her?"

"Oh, her, she's fine." The Leader dismissed the matter with a flick of his hand. "It's you I want to talk about, my brother."

"Stop calling me that."

"Then how should I address you?"

Ack-Ack Macaque curled his lip. "Most people use my given name."

The Leader pulled back a chair, scraping the metal legs on the veranda's wooden planks, and gestured for him to sit.

"But that's just the point," he said, "Somebody *gave* you that name, and the identity that goes with it. They made you, just as they made me. The difference between us is that I had the wherewithal to think outside the box, to reject the paradigm handed to me by those damn dirty apes, and forge my own identity. Create my own brand, if you like."

Ack-Ack Macaque remained standing. His fingers curled and uncurled. He'd been primed for a fight, but this clown seemed intent on talking him to death.

"Look at you," the other monkey continued, walking around to stand behind K8. "A monkey in a flying suit? You're a joke to them. A living cartoon character; a plaything created for a game, still playing out that game in real life."

"And what are you?"

The Leader's eye narrowed.

"I'm a self-made monkey. I'm a king on many worlds, a pharaoh on three. I'm practically a god."

"Because you turn everybody into mindless puppets?"

"On the contrary, my brother." He placed his hands on K8's shoulders. "They are not mindless, quite the reverse. They retain their thoughts and memories, but share them with the wider consciousness. They become part of a giant web of humanity that stretches across the timelines, linked by transmitters like the ones on this ship. A multi-global harmony of thought and reason."

K8 hadn't reacted to his touch.

"They're still zombies."

"Not at all." The Leader shook his head. "They've simply surrendered their initiative to that of the consensus. Their individual identities remain, and are preserved as essential parts of the whole, rather than isolated sparks of awareness. The things which make them unique human beings are the things about them we cherish most." He patted K8's shoulder proprietarily. "Take your little friend here, for instance."

Ack-Ack Macaque looked down into her face. Her features were smooth and untroubled, her eyes focused on the middle distance.

"She has become one with the collective." The Leader bent around and spoke into her ear. "Isn't that right, Katie?"

"Yes, Leader." Her voice was a calm monotone that seemed to come from somewhere far behind her face. Hearing her speak, Ack-Ack Macaque felt a hollow open in his stomach. It was an upturned, empty, impotent sensation.

"You still remember everything, don't you, Katie?"

"Yes, Leader."

"Even this reprobate here?"

Her eyes swivelled up to focus on Ack-Ack Macaque, and he felt a wild surge of hope.

"Yes, Leader." Her tone remained flat, her gaze cool and dispassionate, accepting his presence without reaction.

Rage burned like a flare in his chest.

"No..."

He drew himself up and glared: a direct physical challenge.

The Leader stepped back from K8's chair and straightened his tie.

"Really?" He looked sceptical. "We're the only two of our kind in the world, closer than brothers, closer than twins. And you want to *fight*?"

Ack-Ack Macaque squeezed his aching hands into fists.

"You're damn right I want to fight."

The other monkey gave a snort.

"Then I'm sorry, but you leave me no other choice. Katie, if you please?"

Without changing expression, the girl reached under the tea cosy on the table and produced a pistol, which she pressed to her own temple.

"Make another move," the Leader growled, "and she's dead."

CHAPTER THIRTY-FOUR
OPTIMISED PEOPLE

VICTORIA STAYED IN the pilot's chair. She had nowhere else to go. Around her, the old skyliner moaned and squealed its torment. Wet air barged through the shattered windshield, hurling debris and loose sheets of paper around the bridge.

"Nine thousand feet," Paul intoned over the speakers.

Victoria gripped the console in front of her, trying to make sense of the readouts and winking lights. Her mind kept flashing back to the helicopter crash, the one in the South Atlantic more than two years ago; the one she should never have survived; the one that had left her a half-human cyborg.

How much of her would be left after this one?

"Can we steer?" She spoke to stave off the panic that thrashed inside her. Most of the screens on the bridge were dead. A small one set into the console lit with a projection of her ex-husband's face. He still wore his round spectacles, but he'd somehow found the time to add a red and white Kamikaze headband to his image. Spikes of peroxide yellow hair stuck up above it like the bristles of an unwashed paintbrush.

"Barely." He bit his lip. "Eight and a half thousand. Best guess is we'll be coming down somewhere between Victoria Embankment and St. Paul's."

"Can we turn?"

"What difference does it make?" He waved his arms. "Wherever we hit, we're going to be hitting buildings."

"Not if we land *on* the airship."

He looked at her open mouthed. He took his glasses off, and then put them on again.

"Come on," she said. "If we discard the other three hulls, we'll be small enough. He's bigger and wider than us."

He pushed the glasses into place with an index finger. "But, what if we glance off?"

"Who cares?" She felt a dizzying sense of freedom, and knew the gelware in her head had cut in, suppressing her fear in a blast of clear-thinking machine clarity. "We're going down anyway."

"But the Ack-ster—?"

"He'd do the same."

Paul thought about it. The wind howled through the bridge.

"Okay," he said after a few seconds. The deck heaved to port as he used the ship's remaining rudders to bring her about. "What choice do we have?" He swallowed. "Seven thousand..."

Victoria couldn't see anything ahead but cloud. They were still in the murk, but the number of shots hitting them had dwindled.

"Get the stewards up here," she said. "As soon as we hit, I want them out, ready to fight."

"What about Cole and his daughter?"

"Everybody fights."

She watched the interior of the cloud slide past the window. Heading set, the *Tereshkova* lurched forward again, every last drop of engine power being used to propel it forward, and down.

Almost immediately, the Gestalt's bullets resumed their clatter. Victoria ducked.

Paul said, "I think they're onto us."

"Then let's give them something else to shoot at." She leant close to his image. "Jettison the hulls."

A series of bangs rattled the length of the skyliner, and the deck surged under her as the weight of the other sections fell away. They were on their own now, just one airship in a crowd of four. To the Gestalt gunners, reliant on infrared images, they must look like a sudden fleet of ships—or a gigantic wreck. But this obfuscation came with a price. Most of the engine nacelles and rudder fins were on the outer hulls. Losing them left the central section almost helpless. In effect, they were riding a kilometre-long balloon with only a single impeller to push it along. Now that they were locked on course for a collision, there was nothing they could do to alter their decision. They had lost the manoeuvrability needed to change course. Like it or not, they were going to hit the ironclad, and hit hard.

"I'm getting reports in from other skyliners around the globe." Paul flashed some images onto a sub-window behind his face, making him look like a newsreader. Over his shoulder she saw aerial battles over foreign cities; burning planes, exploding buildings.

"Are we winning?"

He bit his lip.

"Not even slightly. There are too many 'ships, and not enough cooperation."

"So we're losing?"

"We're getting annihilated."

The bridge bucked as the remains of the *Tereshkova* hit turbulence. Then they were out of the cloud, with the broad bulk of the enemy ship directly ahead, and their abandoned hulls falling around them like spent rockets. They were seconds from collision with the Gestalt. Tracer bullets hosed the sky, their lines of firefly sparks joining the two ships. With one finger, Victoria pulled back the attitude control and raised the nose, bringing up the bow.

She touched the image of Paul's face on the screen.

"I love you," she whispered.

He didn't hear her.

"Brace!" he yelled, his voice echoing through the ship. "Brace, brace!"

"WELL," THE LEADER said with a thin smile, "it seems we have a standoff."

He stepped backwards until he reached the veranda's bamboo rail. Teeth bared, Ack-Ack Macaque glowered at him. Between them, K8 sat impassively, the barrel of the gun she held making a slight indentation in the short-cropped ginger hair above her right ear.

"Let her go, shitweasel. You and I need to settle this, monkey to monkey."

The Leader shook his head.

"You still think you can fight me?" He seemed amused. "Look at the state of you." He leant his elbows on the rail. "I'm surprised you can even stand."

Ack-Ack Macaque gave him the finger.

"Spin on it."

The Leader laughed, and turned his face to the broken glass ceiling.

"Oh, my friend. Why must you think of me as 'the bad guy'? Surely even you can see the good I do?" He stretched out his arms. "There are entire worlds out there that know nothing of war or hunger. They have no crime or suffering, no murder or terrorism. No loneliness. Just world after world of happy, optimised people, working and striving together towards common goals." He interlaced his fingers. "Togetherness, mutual understanding and brotherhood. That's what it's all about." He checked his ornate wristwatch. "As your world will discover for itself, in a few short moments."

"Says you."

The Leader tugged his lapels, straightening his jacket.

"My fleet has begun to seed the skies with little machines, each with the dimensions of a single molecule. The process will take a few moments. After that, these little machines disperse themselves on the wind, adapting and assimilating every human with which they come into contact. Within hours, the world will be as your friend here." He drew back his lips in a smirk that was half smile, half challenge. "You can be as sceptical as you like, 'Ack-Ack', but I build utopias. Good ones. Better than anything you've currently got."

"We've got our freedom."

"And what good is that? Last year, you almost blew yourselves up in a thermonuclear war."

"We didn't though, did we?

The Leader flicked dismissive fingers. "Only by the unlikeliest of chances."

Suddenly, he frowned. He opened his mouth to speak again, but broke off before he'd uttered a complete syllable.

"That's strange," he said, tipping his head to one side. The frown grew deeper. He looked at Ack-Ack Macaque. "My connection..."

Ack-Ack Macaque heard a strangled noise and glanced down at K8. She was looking straight back at him. Her features were pale and strained, and her teeth were clamped together. A single bead of sweat ran down the side of her forehead. The hand holding the gun began to shake. Behind her, the Leader cried out in pain and put a hand to his brow.

Ack-Ack Macaque looked from one to the other, and realisation dawned.

"Holy shit!" He sprang forwards and seized K8's arm. It was her. She was fighting back. Somehow, she'd found a way to resist.

Twisted like wires around the pistol's grip, her fingers didn't want to relinquish the weapon, but he managed to pry them apart just as her knuckle whitened on the trigger. He jerked her hand free, and the gun went skittering across the wooden decking and clonked against a plant pot.

Spent with effort, K8 collapsed, arms and legs flopping down on either side of the chair. He took her by the shoulders.

"K8, can you hear me? Are you still in there?"

She gave him a look.

"You know me, Skip," she croaked. "I can hack anything. But it's hard. I don't know how much longer I can block his connection. Be quick, before the others notice."

Ack-Ack Macaque squeezed her shoulders. He didn't need telling twice. Separated from the hive and unable to summon reinforcements, the Leader was vulnerable. He lunged forward, covering the distance between them in a handful of steps. The other monkey saw him coming, and thrust out a hand.

"No, you imbecile!"

But it was too late.

They crashed together in a flurry of raking claws and snapping teeth, each intent on ripping out the other's throat. Ack-Ack Macaque was fast, and fought dirty, but he was carrying the injuries accumulated during the storming of the Gestalt headquarters, as well as the bumps and scrapes from his fall through the trees. The Leader was fresh and rested, and fought with such ferocity that Ack-Ack Macaque quickly found himself being pushed back. A manicured thumb tried to gouge his eye, and he bit it.

But then a blow caught the side of his head, and he staggered. His vision blurred for a second. Reaching out, his fingers grasped the Leader's lapels, but the other monkey had something in his fist. The Leader's arm pulled back and light flashed from a steel blade. Ack-Ack Macaque tried to block the blow, but only succeeded in deflecting it. Instead of puncturing his gut, the point of the knife caught him across the upper arm, slicing through leather, hair and skin.

"Aargh!"

Gripping the wound, he stumbled back. The Leader followed, a snarl of triumphant bloodlust on his leathery features, his hand drawn back for another thrust.

And then something hit the airship from above.

There was a cataclysmic crash and a great weight pressed on them. Something had hit the airship, and hit it hard. Ack-Ack Macaque felt his feet lift as the floor surged downwards, and, for an instant, everything went weightless. The Leader staggered and threw out a hand to steady himself against the veranda's rail. The distraction was all Ack-Ack macaque needed. With a bloodcurdling howl, he ducked under the knife and flung himself at the other monkey. His shoulder hit the Leader in the stomach and, caught off-balance, the other monkey fell back against the rail.

"No!" he cried.

Ack-Ack Macaque wrapped his arms around the Leader's waist.

"I'm taking you down, sweetheart."

He heaved with every ounce of remaining strength. Dry bamboo snapped and splintered, and they both crashed through and fell, still struggling, into empty space.

BREAKING NEWS
From *B&FBC NEWS ONLINE*:

GLOBAL WAR!

Reports are coming in of massive aerial attacks against cities in Europe, the Americas, and the Far East. Details are uncertain, but it seems that in the past few minutes, major bombardments have hit London, Paris, Berlin, New York, Tokyo and Beijing. There are also unconfirmed reports of further strikes in Madrid, Rome, Ankara, Los Angeles, Buenos Aires, and Athens.

So far, the bombings seem to be targeting government buildings and military installations, but explosions have hit some civilian areas. The source of these attacks is unknown, but it is feared thousands may already be dead.

Click here for amateur footage of the attacks

No official sources could be reached, but Commonwealth citizens are advised to seek shelter, and tune to the Emergency Broadcast System for updates.

In the meantime, all

-- CONNECTION LOST --
-- CONNECTION LOST --
-- CONNECTION LOST --
-- CONNECTION LOST --
-- CONNECTION LOST --
-- CONNECTION LOST --
-- CONNECTION LOST --
-- CONNECTION LOST --
-- CONNECTION LOST --
-- CONNECTION LOST --
-- CONNECTION LOST --
-- CONNECTION LOST --
-- CONNECTION LOST --
-- CONNECTION LOST --
-- CONNECTION LOST --
-- CONNECTION LOST --

CHAPTER THIRTY-FIVE
THREADS

VICTORIA VALOIS MOANED, and tried to move. She was still seated in the pilot's chair, but the floor of the *Tereshkova*'s bridge had crumpled inwards, its metal walls concertinaed by the force of the collision, and she now found herself wedged between the seat and the curved metal ceiling, held in place by the remains of the instrument console.

And beyond the ceiling, she thought, the bomb. Had it survived intact? Obviously, it hadn't gone off, but that didn't mean the impact hadn't triggered some sort of malfunction. For all she knew, a countdown could be under way right now. And here she was, with her cheek pressed up against it.

She twisted around in her seat. The chair had been wedged sideways into the narrow gap between floor and ceiling—an uneven space filled with smashed furniture and broken sections of bulkhead. If she could get free from behind the console, she could probably crawl to the front of the bridge, and squeeze out through the remains of the front window; but the console's edge pressed uncomfortably into her abdomen, pinning her against the back of the chair, and she couldn't escape.

"Paul? Paul, are you there?"

Nothing. All the instruments were dead, and all the lights were off.

She tried pushing at the console but its metal stand had been bent in such a way that she couldn't move it.

"Captain?"

The voice came from somewhere aft, beyond a section of deck that had cantilevered up into the ceiling.

"I'm here."

"Captain, it's William. Are you okay?"

She squirmed her hips, trying to wriggle her way out, but to no avail. She tried twice, and then fell back with a curse, slapping the instrument panel that held her.

"I'm stuck," she said.

Cole didn't answer straight away, but she heard him banging around.

"I can't get to you," he said. "Not without equipment."

"How many of you are back there?"

"Four stewards, myself and Lila."

"Marie?"

He paused again. "I don't know. We can't get to the infirmary from in here."

"Can you get out?"

"We can climb through the main hatch behind the passenger lounge."

"Then go. Don't wait for me."

"Are you sure?"

"Just get out. Take guns, and do whatever you can. I'll join you later."

"Okay." He didn't sound convinced. "Good luck, Captain."

"And to you."

She listened to him work his way back into the interior of the gondola. Overhead, the main body of the *Tereshkova*'s central hull gave a loud, metallic groan as the wind caught it, and heeled it over slightly to the left.

It wouldn't take much, she thought, to completely dislodge the *Tereshkova*'s carcass from its precarious perch atop the Gestalt vessel. A decent gust of wind, or some gentle manoeuvring by the bigger craft, could be enough to tip it off, and send it falling, to dash itself to pieces on the roofs and spires of Westminster.

If she were going to get free, she'd have to do it herself.

Closing her eyes, she mouthed the series of passwords that allowed her access to the command mode of the gelware processors in her skull. These slimy artificial neurons handled the bulk of her brain's processing, regulating the physical functions that kept her body alive and working, as well as supplementing the damaged areas responsible for reasoning and memory. Stepping into command mode was a way of tinkering with their settings, and thereby changing the way her body behaved. Strictly speaking, it was cheating. It was not something the surgeons and technicians who'd installed the neural prostheses had bargained on her being able to do; but she'd pestered and cajoled them, using every trick in her reporter's tool kit, until they'd finally given her the access codes.

Now, as she shifted her focus, her mind was pulled up, out of the hormone-washed gunk of her biological cortex, and into the crisp, rarefied air of pure machine thought. In this heightened state, she saw everything with luminous summer clarity, unencumbered by fear or anxiety. Life-threatening situations, which would otherwise have left her biological cerebellum quaking, became abstract puzzles to be solved, and self-preservation a desired outcome rather than an overpowering physical imperative.

Coolly, she considered the console in front of her, assessing its weak points and comparing them to her body's capabilities, balancing necessity against acceptable levels of organic damage. It would be no good, for instance, to escape her present predicament only to find that, because she'd dislocated both hips in the process, she was unable to walk.

There.

Feeling under the console, her fingers found the point where the stand—basically, a steel tube sprouting from the floor—had been welded to its underside. That was the weak spot. If she could apply enough force, she could break the join and kick the stand free, thereby removing the thing that kept the console braced against her.

Pressing back in her chair, she brought her foot up so that it rested against the stand, just below the weld. Then, in her mind's eye, she summoned up the menus governing adrenaline production and pain tolerance, switched off the safeguards, and turned all the dials up to maximum.

Mentally exhausted, she dropped out of command mode and her awareness fell, like a released fish, back into the comforting shallows of her natural mind.

In response to the changes she'd made, her adrenal glands were dumping huge amounts of adrenaline into her bloodstream. She felt her heart quicken, and her breathing grow rapid, drawing oxygen to her muscles. It was the classic 'fight-or-flight' response, and she'd found a way to weaponise it. Butterflies fluttered in her chest, and she itched with a sudden, smothering feeling of claustrophobia. She had to get out, and get out now!

She heard the whine of an electric motor, and a toy car bumped and trundled through the gap where the forward window had once been.

"Paul?"

The car wobbled towards her on its thick, knobby tyres, and paused a few metres away. Her ex-husband's image flickered into the gloom of the wrecked bridge, crouched in the confined space.

"Hello, Vicky."

Gone was the Kamikaze headband. Now, he'd reverted to his default appearance: white lab coat over a garish green Hawaiian shirt, cargo pants, and ratty old trainers. His gold earring twinkled.

"Paul, you're alive."

He shook his head.

"No, I'm not. I've just downloaded myself into this car, but I'm still dead. And, unless you shift your butt, so will you be." He eyed the ceiling dubiously. "This whole thing's going to collapse."

"I'm trying."

"Try faster."

Gritting her teeth, she pushed with her foot. Engorged with blood, the muscles in her calf and thigh, already hard from regular training sessions with her fighting stick, bulged like steel cable.

"Come on," Paul urged.

She felt the sole of her boot flatten against the steel pole, and pressed harder. The chair creaked under her. The quadriceps at the front of her thigh felt ready to rip in half. The back edge of the console rasped against the ceiling. Something had to give; she just hoped it wouldn't be her leg or ankle.

She closed her eyes and kicked with every ounce of strength.

"Argh!"

With a crack, the weld split. The post clanged back, and the console came free. Victoria tumbled out of the chair, onto the uneven remains of the deck. Her foot throbbed, but she didn't have time to worry about that now. On hands and knees, she followed Paul's car forward, across the smashed glass and plastic littering the remains of the bridge, to the window.

As she emerged into daylight, she saw the *Tereshkova*'s prow rising above her, and gave the wall of the smashed gondola a final pat.

"Goodbye, old girl."

Following Paul, she rolled out from under the skyliner and got to her feet. Her right foot was sore, but the gelware kept the pain in check.

They were on the armoured upper surface of the Gestalt battleship. Further along the two-hundred-metre length of the *Tereshkova*'s pancaked gondola, she could see Cole and his daughter. They were heading in her direction. Behind them, four of the Commodore's stewards had taken positions behind air ducts and missile turrets, and were keeping at bay a group of armed Gestalt. Pillars of black smoke rose from the city below. Fighter jets screamed overhead, raking the ironclad with cannon fire.

"Come on," she called to Cole. "We need to get inside."

The writer carried a Kalashnikov. The wind blew his hair up like the wing of an injured bird.

"No," he said, looking over his shoulder. "I have to go back. My wife—"

"Leave her."

"But—"

Victoria put a hand to his cheek, turning his face to hers.

"She can't walk, and we can't carry her. And if we don't get down inside this thing and kill that monkey, she's as good as dead anyway."

Cole looked down at her with red-rimmed, haunted eyes.

"No," he said, his voice firmer and more decisive than she would ever have believed. "I lost her once, I can't lose her again." He stepped back. "I'm sorry Captain, but I have to do this. I can't leave her. I won't." And with that, he turned and walked back towards the stern.

Victoria let him go. In his position, she would have done the same.

Had done the same.

She glanced at Paul. He glanced back.

"Hell to it," she said.

Lila was still standing in front of her, an automatic pistol held to her chest. Victoria looked from her to her retreating father.

"Are you with us?"

"Yes, ma'am."

"Your mother—?"

The girl clenched her jaw. "She'll understand."

"Okay, then." Victoria drew her fighting stick. They'd wasted enough time already. "In that case, you go ahead, and shoot anything that moves."

VICTORIA AND LILA made their way to an anti-aircraft turret near the bows. Paul's car trundled after them. The installation had obviously been hit by one of the circling jets. The domed roof had been peppered with fist-sized holes, and the white-suited Neanderthal inside lay dead and mangled in his chair, thick blobs of glossy blood dripping onto the deck from the tips of his hairy fingers.

Behind his chair, a hatch opened onto a narrow companionway. The stairs led down into the interior of the airship. They were only wide enough for one of them to descend at a time, and were a lot steeper than those on the *Tereshkova*. As Victoria ducked under a low stanchion, she figured they must be have been designed to allow the gunner to reach his post, rather than as a means of general access to the roof.

With Lila in the lead, they crept down, ready to shoot or stab, and acutely aware that if only one member of the Gestalt caught sight of them, the whole of the hive mind would instantly know about it. Victoria had to carry Paul's car under her arm. She felt a bit bad about letting the girl go first, but Lila was much better armed than she was, and handled the weapon with a respectful nonchalance that spoke of training and experience.

The companionway wound down through the ship in a spiral, eventually ending in a heavy oval hatch that would have looked more at home on a submarine than an airship.

Lila peeped through the porthole in the door.

"Corridor," she whispered.

"Clear?"

"Two guards at the bow end."

"What are they guarding?"

"Big brass door."

"How are we going to get past without them seeing?"

"Can't."

"What, then?"

Lila pursed her lips. "Look, it's big and brass, it's at the bows and there are two guards. Whatever's behind it has got to be important."

With her left hand, Victoria gripped the handle of her fighting stick; with her right, she put the toy car down and reached into the pocket of her tunic.

"What's that?" Lila asked.

"A tracking device." Victoria thumbed the power button and waited for the screen to boot up. When it did, it showed a series of concentric green circles, which indicated distance in units of ten, fifty, and one hundred metres. A red direction arrow bobbled about. "I find it useful for keeping tabs on the monkey."

"Does he know?"

Victoria shook her head. "Are you kidding? I got a vet to insert the microchip while he was passed out drunk, after we lost him for two days in Las Vegas. He doesn't even know it's there. If he ever finds out, he's going to go berserk."

She held the little device flat in the palm of her hand. The arrow swung back and forth, and then settled.

"Alive or dead," she said, "he's behind that door."

"Right, then it's decided." Before Victoria could stop her, Lila pulled the hatch to the corridor open. Without stepping out, she leaned around the frame and fired twice, and then twice again. The shots echoed loudly in the steel-walled corridor. Victoria's nostrils twitched to the familiar tang of gun smoke, and she heard the thuds of bodies hitting the deck.

Lila raised the pistol to her lips and blew.

"Okay," she said, "the guards are down. But now every white suit on this ship knows we're here."

Victoria slipped the tracker back into her pocket, and grinned. She couldn't help herself. Right now, they had nothing to lose. She felt liberated, and dangerous. She reached down and picked up the toy car.

"Then we'd better make this quick," she said.

CHAPTER THIRTY-SIX
PRIVATE JUNGLE

STEPPING OVER THE bodies, they pushed through the brass door, into the potted forest. Victoria looked up at the overhanging fronds and the glass ceiling. The place had the warm compost smell of a greenhouse. A parakeet flapped from one tree to another, its plumage an impressionist dash of blue and yellow. Butterflies twitched hither and thither.

"*C'est quoi?*"

Lila was in the process of reloading her pistol, taking loose cartridges from her thigh pocket and snapping them into the magazine.

"Remember we're dealing with a monkey," she said. "This is probably his gym or something."

"A jungle gym? On a Zeppelin?" She gave the girl a sideways squint. "Have you been here before?"

"No." Lila touched the bruise on her cheek, and scowled. "I only saw the Leader once, but that was on the ground, at the mansion." She pushed the last bullet into the magazine with her thumb, and snapped the whole thing back into the butt of the pistol. "Now, let's be quiet. Those guards were protecting more than just a bunch of trees, you know."

She moved off between the pots, and Victoria took a second to marvel at her. She was only a teenager, yet she talked with the assurance of a combat veteran. What kind of upbringing, what kind of *life*, had that poor kid endured?

She placed Paul's car on the deck.

"Okay," she said, "you can come out now."

The car buzzed. The headlights flickered on and off, and it jumped forward half a wheel rotation. Then the projectors kicked in and Paul shimmered into apparent solidity amongst the ferns and creepers.

He used a finger and thumb to settle his glasses more firmly on his nose.

"Um," he said, looking around. "Where are we?"

"The boss monkey's private jungle."

"Ah."

Victoria shook her fighting stick out to its full length.

"Come on."

Holding the staff in both hands, she picked her way into the foliage, and Paul trundled after her, his image seeming to glide above the leaf-strewn matting that covered the deck. It was very quiet beneath the trees. Even the roar of the jets and the clatter of gunfire from above seemed somehow muted. The trees rose from their pots like the pillars of a cathedral, their branches forming archways and overhead vaults.

Ahead, through the low-hanging ivies and lianas, she saw Lila crouched beside a particularly large pot, her back resting against the curved ceramic, her gun at the ready. Beyond, the vegetation thinned out, and she caught a glimpse of an open area, with grey sky beyond it. Lila waved at her to get down.

"There's somebody out there," she hissed.

"Where?" Victoria craned her head for a look. She saw an iron patio table and accompanying chairs, one of which was occupied by a slumped, skinny figure in jeans, with arms hanging loose, and short, carrot-coloured hair.

Oh, *merde*.

"K8?" Victoria ran forward. "K8, what happened? Where's the Leader?"

The girl looked up at her and raised a trembling arm. Tea dripped from a spilled cup. A saucer lay in pieces on the floor.

"Over," she whispered. "They went over."

Victoria walked to the edge of the veranda. The entire nose cone of the airship had been glazed, like the cockpit of some art deco spaceship from a pulp magazine. A section of the bamboo rail had been broken. She stood at the edge and craned forward. Below, she could see the rooftops of central London, and, stretching back beneath the veranda, an unglazed area of shadow and machinery.

"Any sign?" Paul asked, wheeling up beside her.

Victoria shook her head.

"That has to be a fifty foot drop." If Ack-Ack and the Leader had fallen from here, they hadn't hit the glass, which meant they must be somewhere amongst the machinery. Victoria got down onto her hands and knees, and leant over as far as she dared. Far below, wires and cables covered the floor of the chamber. Computer servers stood like islands. Strange, archaic-looking pistons moved up and down. Fans turned. Lights blinked. Coolant steamed.

An iron ladder had been bolted to the far end of the veranda.

"You could climb down," Paul suggested. "And make sure they're dead."

"Maybe in a minute." Against such a drop, the ladder looked fragile and spindly. And besides, there were more important things to worry about first. Victoria turned back to K8. She walked over and crouched in front of her. "Are you hurt?"

Sweat glittered on K8's forehead. She put a hand to the back of her skull, where her soul-catcher nestled beneath the skin.

"I'm plugged into the hive."

"Shit." Lila brought her pistol to bear. "So, they already know we're here."

K8 shook her head. "No. I'm blocking them. For now." Her voice was hoarse. Her fists were hard little balls in her lap, the knuckles as white as bone. "But I don't know how much longer I can keep it up."

Victoria waved Lila's gun away, and put a hand to K8's freckled cheek.

"We'll get you out of this," she said.

The girl shook her head again, flinching away from the physical contact.

"I don't think so, boss." She gave the brittle, self-conscious smile of a little girl trying to be brave. "The stuff he put in my head's getting stronger all the time. I don't know how much longer I can fight it."

A jet screamed past outside, and something exploded aft. They felt the deck quiver.

"We don't have a lot of time," Lila said. "If the monkey's dead, we need to find the control room, and stop them dumping the agent."

"Oh, I'm not dead."

The voice came from the edge of the veranda. Victoria turned in time to see a hand appear at the top of the ladder, followed by a hairy head. A white-suited monkey clambered awkwardly over the bamboo rail and dropped to the wooden deck. Beneath the suit, he wore a bandolier across his chest, and a holster on each hip.

Lila raised her gun.

"No!" K8 lunged forward in her chair. "Don't shoot him. Look at his eyes."

Victoria frowned. His eyes?

Then realisation hit her.

"*Mon dieu!*" She lowered her sword, and put a hand on Lila's gun, gently pushing it downwards.

"But—"

"His eye patch. It's on the left."

"So?"

"The Leader wears his on the right." She turned to the monkey. "Isn't that right, Ack-Ack?"

The macaque threw a floppy salute.

"Howdy, boss." He straightened his tie.

"Nice threads." Paul looked him up and down. "What happened to their owner?"

"I used him to break my fall."

"He's dead?"

"Very."

"So, it's over?" Lila asked hopefully.

Ack-Ack Macaque shrugged. "Not yet. The attack's still under way."

"How do we stop it?"

"Leave that to me."

Victoria slid her sword into its scabbard.

"What are you going to do?"

Ack-Ack Macaque jabbed a leathery thumb in K8's direction.

"Well," he said. "First off, she and I need to convince the fuckwits in white that I'm their chief."

"No, you can't do that." Victoria was horrified. "I won't let you."

They had been arguing for several minutes.

"It's the only way," Ack-Ack Macaque assured her. "K8 can broadcast to the entire hive."

"But it'll destroy her."

He reached into a silk-lined jacket pocket and pulled out a rather battered-looking cigar.

"We don't have a choice. You understand that, don't you, K8?"

"Yes, Skip."

The girl's hair was wet at the temples. Her face had become pale and drawn.

"No." Victoria made a cutting motion with her hand. "She's only seventeen, for God's sake. You can't ask her to do this."

Ack-Ack Macaque lit up, and huffed the cigar into life. He took a heavy draw, and blew smoke at the butterflies flittering above his head.

"I don't like it any better than you do. But she hasn't got much choice. The way I see it, that muck in her head's winning. It's going to take her sooner or later, whatever we do. At least this way, she gets to save the world first."

Paul scratched his beard thoughtfully.

"But if she opens herself to the hive," he said, "won't they be able to read her thoughts? Won't they know it's a trick?"

Ack-Ack Macaque curled his lip in irritation. He rolled the fat cigar between his fingers and thumb.

"Okay." He stood over K8. "Can you do anything about that? Send sound and vision only, without the commentary?"

"I can try."

"Good girl."

He went to stand by the veranda's rail, with the darkening November sky at his back. Somewhere far beyond the clouds, the sun had already set. Fuming, Victoria took Lila and Paul to watch from the treeline. K8 sat facing him.

"Ready?" he asked her.

"Yes, Skip." There were tears in her eyes. He straightened his collar and smoothed back the hair on his cheeks and scalp. He had to look convincing to the Gestalt even if, inside, all he wanted was to murder every single last one of the motherfuckers.

How dare they put him in this position.

He bit back the rage, and dropped the half-smoked cigar over the rail.

"Right then, sweetheart," he said gruffly. "Ready when you are."

K8 swallowed.

"Goodbye, Skip."

"Don't say that."

She sniffed.

"What should I say, then?"

For the first time, Ack-Ack Macaque felt a hot lump rise in the back of his throat.

"Be seeing you, kid."

They held each other's gaze for a long moment. They both knew this was it. Then, wiping her cheeks, K8 sat up straight. She closed her eyes. Her posture became stiffer and more formal, and the tension bled from her features. Her lips curled up in the same dreamy, vacant smile that he'd wanted to wipe from Reynold's face.

By the time she reopened her eyes, she looked like a different girl.

The K8 he'd known was almost gone, and he didn't have a lot of time.

Ack-Ack Macaque cleared his throat.

* * *

"LADIES AND GENTLEMEN of the Gestalt," he began. "Esteemed colleagues. It is I, your Leader, standing here on my flagship, over London. Apologies for not contacting you directly," he tapped the side of his head, "but my connection has been damaged."

Were they getting this? Did he sound convincing? The Leader had been a wordy bastard with a gob full of corporate waffle. Could he match that?

"I have something important to, um, tell you. And you'd better listen because otherwise I'll... I mean... Look, attacking this world was a mistake." He punched the fist of one hand into the palm of the other. "And the reason I'm speaking to you now is that I require you to stop it. Stop everything. Immediately. Like, *right now*, okay?"

Over by the trees, Paul winced. Victoria shook her head. He was fucking this up, and they knew it. Flustered, he opened his mouth to speak again but, before he could, K8 moaned. Her eyes rolled up in her head, and she fell back, her body as limp as a tossed banana skin.

"Christ!" All pretence forgotten, he hopped forward and took her hand. Her skin felt cold. Before he could do anything else, Victoria marched up and shouldered him aside.

"Get out of the way," she said. She picked K8 from the chair and laid her on the deck, then checked her pulse and breathing.

"Is she going to be okay?" Ack-Ack Macaque asked.

"I don't know." Victoria didn't look up. "I don't even know what's wrong with her. But she's breathing for now, no thanks to you."

"Hey, I—"

Paul's image stepped between them.

"Listen," he said. "The guns have stopped."

Interrupted in mid-protestation, Ack-Ack Macaque cocked his head. All he could hear was the distant rumble of jets. The constant firing from above had ceased.

"Holy shit," he muttered. "They believed me? That speech worked?"

Paul coughed. He ran his tongue around his lips.

"No," he said regretfully. "No, I don't think they did."

Ack-Ack Macaque fixed him with a one-eyed stare.

"What makes you say that?"

Paul swallowed, and raised an arm to point into the trees at the back of the veranda.

"She does."

Another macaque stood in the gloom of the potted forest, squinting at them through a monocle. Two armed Neanderthal bodyguards flanked her.

She wore a white business suit with matching gloves and pearls, and carried a furled white umbrella with an ivory handle.

Ack-Ack Macaque curled his lip at her.

"Who the hell are you supposed to be?"

The female removed the monocle from her right eye and smiled, revealing sharp, pointed teeth.

"Me, darling?" She licked her left canine. "Why, I'm the power behind the throne. And I'm here to make you—" she raised her chin, "—an offer."

Ack-Ack Macaque narrowed his eye.

"What kind of offer?"

"A job offer."

"Whoa, lady." He held up his hands. "I think you've got the wrong monkey."

"Please." Her tone was scornful. She blew dust from her monocle, and screwed it back into her eye. "You've just killed my protégé, the least you can do is hear me out." Without taking her eyes from Ack-Ack Macaque, she leant her head towards the Neanderthal on her right, and whispered, "And if any of the humans move, kill them."

Both bodyguards raised their weapons: heavy automatic rifles with long, curved magazines, each capable of hosing all life from the veranda in a couple of sustained bursts.

"Yes, Founder."

CHAPTER THIRTY-SEVEN
CORONA OF IRIS

SHE TOOK THEM back to the wrought iron table, and bade them sit.

"You may call me Founder." She walked slowly around the table. As she passed behind each of them, she paused to sniff their hair. "I am the true leader of the Gestalt. The monkey you just killed, the one who liked to call himself the 'Leader', worked for me." Having completed a circuit of the table, she stopped walking and stood between her bodyguards. "I come from a timeline significantly more advanced that this one, and I am significantly older than I look." Resting both hands on the umbrella's pommel, she glared at them through her monocle. "So, I'd appreciate it if you showed me some respect. When I was born, Queen Victoria sat on England's throne."

Paul's image crouched between Ack-Ack Macaque and Lila. He pushed his glasses more firmly onto the bridge of his nose and stammered, "But, but, but that would make you two hundred years old!"

"Two hundred and four, actually."

"How could you still be alive?"

"Technology, dear boy." The Founder straightened up. "I have tiny engines in my blood, which constantly monitor and repair and renew. With their help, I might live to be a thousand years old."

Ack-Ack Macaque stirred uncomfortably.

"Bullshit," he muttered.

The Founder gave a sigh.

"Do you remember my husband's machines, the microscopic ones that turn normal humans into fresh recruits for the Gestalt? The ones you came here to stop? Didn't you ever wonder why they were so much more *advanced* than the rest of his technology? I mean, *airships*?" She rolled her eyes. "Give me a hypersonic scramjet any day."

Victoria Valois had been watching and listening quietly. Now she sat forward, her hands on the table.

"You gave them to him?"

"Precisely." The Founder tapped the tip of her umbrella against the deck. "When I recruited him, he was little more than an escapee from a laboratory." She smiled nostalgically. "I showed him how to move between worlds, and gave him the technology to build an army."

"But why?"

The monkey laughed.

"My dear woman, why ever not?" She swept the umbrella around in a gesture that encompassed all the possible worlds of creation. "You humans are far too irresponsible and squabblesome to be allowed free rein."

"And so you turn us into zombies?" Lila asked indignantly.

The Founder's brow furrowed.

"Think of it as harnessing your potential, child, and turning it to less destructive ends. Sometimes being a grownup means being prepared to take responsibility for yourself, your friends and, if necessary, your entire world."

High above, the grey clouds finally delivered on their promise. Rain beat against the glass panels of the airship's nose. A few drops fell through the holes made by Ack-Ack Macaque's Spitfire, and pattered down onto the uppermost leaves of the trees, dripping from there onto the deck's wooden planks. On the ground below the warship, London lay battered and smoking. Lights flashed as emergency vehicles tried to push through roads choked with abandoned cars. People were cowering in offices and Underground stations, dreading the next bombardment.

Ack-Ack Macaque tapped his fingers on the iron table. He wanted to smoke, but didn't want to risk reaching into his inside pocket for a cigar. He didn't want the Neanderthals to think he was going for a concealed weapon.

"You mentioned a job offer?"

The Founder turned to him.

"Indeed."

"Let me guess." He pushed back in his chair. The metal legs scraped on the timbers. "You want me to join your merry band?"

"Would that be so awful?" She stepped up to him, so that the toes of her shoes almost touched the heels of his outstretched feet. "I know you must have been lonely. Macaques like us, we're not solitary creatures. We need the company of our own kind. We need a place to belong. We need the comfort and security of a troupe."

Ack-Ack Macaque pulled his feet away from her. He snarled, but he knew she was right. He could feel it as an ache in his chest. And yet—

"You've been alone so long," she said. "But all that's past now."

He could smell her. Somewhere beneath the cotton and pearls, beneath the aromas of shampoo and perfume, lay the scent of a female macaque. The first female of his kind he'd ever met, and maybe the only one he ever would.

His nostrils twitched. Something stirred inside him, and he closed his eye, feeling dizzy.

He could go with her. It would be easy enough to do. He felt the soft fabric of the borrowed suit and tie, and visualised himself at the head of a Zeppelin fleet, with her at his side. He imagined holding her in his arms, and pictured the two of them in heat, mating in a frenzied mutual lust...

"No." The word rolled like molasses from his tongue, and he opened his eye to banish the images playing in his head. "No, you're wrong." He looked around the table, at Victoria and Paul, and K8's unconscious form lying on the deck. They were his friends, his comrades. His family.

"I already have a troupe," he said, and snorted to clear the stink of her from his nostrils. His hands itched, painfully aware of the revolvers in the holsters at his hips.

She gave him a haughty look.

"I could make you a king."

Moving very slowly, he opened his jacket and pulled a cigar and lighter from the silk-lined pocket. He'd made his decision and chosen his side. Now, all he had to do was get her fragrance out of his head, and the only way to do that was to smother everything in a tobacco fug. His hands felt shaky as he bit the end from the cigar and spat it onto the floor.

"Sorry, sweetheart." He paused to light the end of the cigar, and then spoke through clouds of pungent blue smoke. "But I don't want your machines in my head."

The smoke spread warmth in his chest, and he felt his head go deliciously light. *Ah,* he thought, *that's the stuff.*

Looking distinctly unimpressed, the Founder pursed her lips. She reached up and adjusted her monocle.

"Better a few machines in your head than a bullet?"

Their eyes locked.

"That's the deal, huh?"

"I'm afraid so. And if you've got any notions of somehow saving this world, you can forget them right now. The fleet's already begun to dump its cargo. Within hours, the planet will be ours."

Ack-Ack Macaque looked at his friends.

"And what about them?"

"They will join the Gestalt." She peered around at them. "We will be enriched by their bravery."

Ack-Ack Macaque shook his head. He'd already lost K8 to the hive, he'd be damned if he'd let them take Victoria as well.

He looked across at his boss, and noticed her eyes. The pupils had dilated into wide, black pits. Only a thin corona of iris remained and he realised that, while he'd been talking, she'd taken the opportunity to slip into command mode and overclock her system. Her mind must be racing and her heart pounding, ready to fight or flee. All she needed was an opening.

Their eyes met, and an understanding passed between them.

"And as for you," the Founder was saying, oblivious to this byplay, "either you come willingly, or you'll be assimilated right along with them. The process works equally well on monkeys as it does on people."

Ack-Ack Macaque drew himself up in his chair. He sucked in a mouthful of smoke and blew it in her direction.

"Sorry love, but that's not going to happen."

The Founder's gloved hand tried to flap away the cigar fumes.

"And that's your final answer, is it?"

"Not quite." Under his chair, Ack-Ack Macaque pressed his bare feet to the smooth wooden deck, ready to spring. "There's just one more thing."

The female monkey's eyes became suspicious slits.

"And what might that be?"

"Just this." He screamed, and leapt. At the same time, Victoria surged to her feet, sending the heavy iron table flying towards one of the bodyguards.

The machine guns fired.

CHAPTER THIRTY-EIGHT
WRECKAGE

CRAWLING ON ALL fours, William Cole worked his way through the shattered remains of the *Tereshkova*'s main gondola. As he moved, he tried to ignore the sounds of battle coming from outside, and the ominous groans and creaks of the superstructure above his head. All he could think of was Marie. Nothing else mattered to him, except to see her safe.

He crawled across the carpeted expanse of the main passenger lounge, through piles of broken furniture and shattered fittings, onto the hard steel deck of the corridor that led aft to the infirmary.

"Marie!" he called. "Hold on, I'm coming."

In places, the corridor's ceiling had hinged down to within inches of the floor, and he had to squirm and wriggle his way through sharp-edged gaps that were too small for him. By the time he reached the infirmary, the skin on his arms, shoulders and hips had been scraped raw, and his knees were bruised and battered.

"William?" Her voice sounded weak.

"I'm here," he cried, "I'm here."

Part of a medical trolley had wedged itself in the doorway, and he had to squeeze around it. When he got inside, he saw his worst fears realised. The ceiling had collapsed in the same way as in the rest of the gondola, leaving only a few feet of clearance. Marie, who had been lying on the bed at the time of the crash, now lay pinned to the mattress.

"Marie!"

"William."

Her head was turned towards him, held against the pillow by the steel ceiling panel pressing down from above on her cheek and chest. The foot of the bed was a tangle of wreckage, and he couldn't see her legs.

"Oh, crap. Marie." He knelt beside the bed and reached in to touch her face. "Don't worry, honey. Don't try to move. I'll get you out."

Bracing his back against the fallen ceiling, he tried to heave upwards, pushing until sweat broke out on his forehead and his temples felt ready to burst.

"No." Her voice was a whisper, but it stopped him.

"What do you mean?"

Marie licked her lips.

"No, you're not getting me out."

William felt panic surge up inside.

"But, I—"

"No." Marie swallowed. "It's too late. I'm sorry."

William stopped pressing against the ceiling and dropped to his knees. He reached for her, and brushed a curl of auburn hair away from her eyes.

"I'm not leaving you."

"I'm afraid you'll have to, my love."

He ran his hand back along the bed, past her shoulders and down, following the curve of her body beneath the blanket. He got as far as her hip before he found something blocking the way. His fingers hit metal where there should have been flesh. A girder had broken through from above, driving the ceiling down into the mattress. Her abdomen and legs were crushed. Her torso stopped in a mess of torn blankets, slathered in something warm and sticky.

Fighting back a cry of anguish, he jerked back his hand and, without looking at the blood on his fingers, wiped it on the sheet.

"No," he said. There had to have been some sort of mistake...

Marie closed her eyes.

"I'm sorry," she said again.

William wanted to cry. He wanted to curl into a ball and block his ears, and make it all go away.

"It's not fair," he said.

Marie looked at him with liquid eyes.

"You haven't lost me," she whispered. "I'm still out there somewhere, on another parallel close to this one."

"I'm not leaving you. Not like this." William's mind raced. There had to be some way to save her, some way he could get her out.

Overhead, the wreck quivered. Something in the corridor collapsed with a metallic crash.

"You have to go now. Lila needs you."

William blinked.

"Lila?"

"I'm going to need you to look after her now."

"I can't." Misery threatened to envelop him. "I can barely look after myself."

"Of course you can. Look at you. You risked your life crawling in here. I need you to be just as strong for her."

"But I don't know anything about being a father."

"You know enough." She winced in pain, and tried to adjust her position beneath the weight pressing down on her. "Besides, you're all she's got. I need you to be strong for her, William. Can you promise me that?"

"I don't want to leave you."

"Promise me."

He reached out and touched her cheek. Her skin felt clammy. Her bright eyes implored him.

"Okay," he said. "Okay, I promise."

Marie let her eyes fall shut.

"Then go find her. Go now."

"But what about you?"

Marie kept her eyes closed. Above her, the ceiling pinged and popped as it struggled to support the weight of the collapsing structure above it.

"We both know what's going to happen to me, and it's not going to be pretty. I don't want you here when it happens. You have to get out." She opened her eyes and fixed him with a brittle stare. "You have to get out. You're all she's got."

William looked down at the gun in his hands. He pictured his daughter's face, and his fingers squeezed the grip. Marie was right. It didn't matter how many white suits were outside waiting for him; he knew what he had to do. Lila was out there somewhere, and he had to protect her.

He was her father.

He touched his wife's face for the final time.

"Don't worry," he said. "I'll find her."

Marie smiled.

"Thank you, my love."

CHAPTER THIRTY-NINE
PROTECT THE TROUPE

TEETH BARED AND fingers grasping, Ack-Ack Macaque lunged towards the Founder, only to find that she'd anticipated his attack. As they came together, she grasped the lapels of his jacket and fell back. She rolled away from him, using his momentum to throw him over her head, onto the deck. He landed on his back with a smack that drove most of the wind from his body.

As he lay gasping, the Founder sprang to her feet and fled into the jungle.

He heard gunshots and shouting, and his hands went to the holsters at his sides. One of the Neanderthals was down, toes crushed by the edge of the iron table. Victoria had been upon him before he could fight through the pain and bring his gun to bear. Unfortunately, she hadn't been quite fast enough. The second bodyguard had seen her move and fired. He was too late to save his colleague—in fact, he'd caught the other caveman with a couple of stray shots—but he'd managed to hit her as well, and now she lay on her side a few feet from her victim, in a spreading pool of blood.

Ack-Ack Macaque struggled to his feet, wheezing for breath. Wide-eyed, the surviving Neanderthal swung the machine gun at him. For half a second, Ack-Ack Macaque stared into the black eye of its muzzle.

Then a shot rang out.

Ack-Ack Macaque winced, but it was the Neanderthal who fell.

Still seated in her chair, Lila held a smoking pistol in her lap.

"Go," she said.

Ack-Ack Macaque hesitated, looking at Victoria. The former journalist moaned, and tried feebly to move. Her feet scraped the deck as if trying to gain purchase. Clearly distressed, Paul's hologram image bent over her, calling her name.

"Go on," Lila said. "We'll take care of her."

Ack-Ack Macaque lingered for another moment. He looked from Victoria to where K8 lay, on the other side of the veranda. His two best friends were both down, and both fighting for their lives. He holstered his guns, dropped onto all fours and, with a snarl of fury, plunged headlong into the trees.

*   *   *

THE FOUNDER COULD run, but she couldn't hide her scent. It itched in his nose, maddening him as he pursued it through the potted forest and out, through the brass door, into the corridor beyond.

Half a dozen white-suited men and women marched towards him. He rose to his feet and drew his guns. Without breaking stride, he shot the first two, and ducked into the alcove housing the companionway that led upwards to the roof. Ahead, on the curving staircase, he could hear the tap, tap, tap of the Founder's shoes.

He went up two steps at a time, hauling himself along with one hand on the banister. Having stepped over their fallen comrades, the remaining Gestalt followed him, but couldn't keep up. By the time he got to the top, they were far behind. His chest burned with the effort, but he knew he was only moments behind her.

The remains of the *Tereshkova* loomed over him in the rain. The hull looked broken and sad, like a partially collapsed party balloon, and the gondolas had been smashed almost flat. An engine nacelle stuck out like a broken limb, water dripping from its bent and broken blades.

The Founder stood in front the wreck, brandishing her umbrella. As he emerged from the stairwell, she tugged, and the handle came away from the rest of the brolly, revealing a wicked-looking steel blade. She dropped the canopy, and took up a fencing stance. The wind blew her skirt and flapped her jacket.

"Get back," she said.

Ack-Ack Macaque still held one of the Leader's pistols in his hands. It wasn't one of his trusted Colts, but it would do.

Overhead, Commonwealth fighter jets rumbled in the overcast.

"Stop it," he said.

She glared at him, and swiped the umbrella handle sword.

"Stop what, sweetie?"

"Stop the plague. The machines. Whatever the fuck they are."

"Why should I?"

He waggled the gun.

"Because if you don't, I'll shoot you."

She brought the sword up, and held it over her head, with the tip pointing at him. She looked like a scorpion, ready to strike.

"Then you'll just have to shoot, my dear."

She started to back away, one step at a time. With a curse he took a pace forward. Her arm whipped down, and the sword flew out like a thrown knife. It caught him in the left thigh. With a howl, he fell to the deck and the pistol fell away. Before he could reach for it, she was there before him, grasping the handle of the sword. He screeched again as she pulled it out of his leg. He used both hands to try to cover the wound and staunch the spurt of blood.

"Shit," he wailed. The airship's armour plates were wet beneath him. Rain fell against his face. "Shit, that hurts."

Above him, the Founder laughed.

"Face it, flyboy, you've lost."

Still gripping his leg, he snarled at her with such vehemence that her monocle fell out. She stepped back, out of reach, waving the sword's slick point at him.

"There's nothing you can do," she crowed. The rain stuck her hair to her face and scalp. "This world's mine now. Or soon will be. And when it is, I'll simply move on to another world, and find another monkey somewhere else. One with more vision." She shook her head, spraying drops in all directions. "And hope he's a darned sight more cooperative than you."

Ack-Ack Macaque thought of his fallen friends, and felt rage boil up inside, blotting out the pain.

"Yeah, well. I ain't finished yet, lady."

Teeth clenched, he clambered to his feet. He could feel blood running down his leg, soaking into his white trousers, mixing with the rain. He ignored it. Every instinct in his body told him to protect his troupe, wreak bloody vengeance against this interloper, and drive her from his territory.

"Oh, please." The Founder raised her sword. "Don't you ever give up?"

Ack-Ack Macaque shrugged. He gave her a defiant grin.

"Let's find out."

He took a step towards her, clawed hands stretching for her throat. At the same time, she pulled her arm back, ready to run him through with the blade. He knew he couldn't win, but figured that, even if she skewered him, he could still probably choke her to death before he died.

For an instant, their eyes locked. They stood poised, ready to strike.

And then the bomb on the *Tereshkova* exploded.

BOWLED OVER BY the blast, they tumbled together, rolling off the armoured section of the hull and onto the sloping glass of the airship's nose. Faster and faster they slid. Behind them, the remnants of the *Tereshkova* burned.

Ahead lay the point of the bow, with nothing beyond it save sky and death. In a panic, they scrabbled at each other, still fighting. Leathery hands squeaked against toughened glass, trying in vain to slow their descent. And then they were there.

The edge rushed at them, and they felt themselves going over. In desperation, Ack-Ack Macaque flung out his hand and caught something. At the same time, the Founder grabbed his foot. They jerked to a halt, their combined weight almost enough to tear his fingers from their precarious hold, and his shoulder from its socket.

Swearing at the agony in his arm, he looked up. A communications antenna stuck out from the glass point of the airship's bow, and it was from this that they now hung, swaying, a couple of thousand feet above the muddy waters of the Thames. The Founder's skirt flapped in the wind. A patch of it was on fire. Her feet pawed at emptiness.

"Please," she said. "Please, don't drop me."

Wincing with pain and effort, Ack-Ack Macaque reached up with his other arm and caught hold of the mast.

"Stop thrashing about then," he said with a grunt, "or we're both going to fall."

Beneath them in the gathering darkness, the wind chopped the surface of the river into little waves. Rain fell on the burning wreckage of the Commonwealth Parliament.

Heaving upwards, he managed to hook an elbow over the metal pole that formed the mast.

He could kick her off. She'd hurt his friends, attacked his world, and unleashed all kinds of hell. And now he had her at his mercy. She clung to his ankle with only one hand. All it would take to kill her would be a simple jerk of his leg.

She deserved it, and yet, he couldn't bring himself to do it. Twice he tensed, ready to shake her off—but each time, he relented.

He swore under his breath.

Try as he might, he just couldn't kill her in cold blood. She was the only intelligent female monkey he'd ever met; and the only one who could call off the invasion.

He looked down at her and their eyes met.

"Okay," he said.

The Founder started to climb. Her hands worked their way up his legs, tearing cloth and stretching skin. She touched the wound in his thigh and he growled.

"Wait, for fuck's sake."

She stopped moving, eyes wide, and monocle long gone.

"What?"

"I'll let you up on one condition. Contact the hive. Tell them that I'm the new Leader."

She grimaced.

"No."

"Listen, lady, I've got nothing to lose, okay? I don't want to live in a world of drones. So do it, and do it now, or I'll let go of this pole, and drop us both. Do you understand?"

She looked him in the eye again, but it wasn't a challenge. Their faces were almost touching, and he could smell her breath.

"I'd rather die."

"Yeah?" He showed her his teeth, and took one of his hands from the mast. "I can arrange that."

He now held the weight of both of them on one arm.

"All I have to do is let go," he said. He could already feel his fingers slipping.

"You wouldn't."

"Try me."

For a long, agonising moment, they remained frozen, locked together high over the river. A squall of rain hit them, drenching them further. Ack-Ack Macaque's arms felt as if they were being dragged from their sockets.

"No."

"Fine."

He let go.

For half a second, they were falling. The Founder screamed. And they jerked to a halt.

Ack-Ack Macaque had his tail wrapped around the mast.

Swinging from it, he put a hand to her forehead, ready to push her away. "Last chance, lady."

Hair wet and bedraggled, dress torn, the Founder looked up at him. Her eyes blazed. Then she dropped her chin and sighed.

"All right," she said. "I'll do it."

"And tell them to stop spreading that fucking plague."

The Founder closed her eyes and hugged him tight.

"Okay," she said.

The wind battered them, and he saw smouldering fragments of the *Tereshkova* blowing down towards the distant, darkened roofs of the city.

After what seemed like an eternity, she reopened her eyes.

"All done."

"No tricks?"

She shook her head. The fight had gone out of her. She'd stopped struggling, and now just hung there, holding on to him as the weather howled around them in the night.

"All activity ceased." She spoke so quietly he could barely hear her. "They await your orders."

He looked up. The Gestalt drones on top of the airship had lowered their guns. They stood in the rain and wind, staring impassively ahead.

"And you?"

She looked down at the city beneath her shoes. Her hands were slippery and red with blood from his thigh.

"Please," she whispered, "just get me out of here."

Above, William Cole shouldered his way between the passive drones. He held a gun in one hand, and a coil of rope in the other.

"Here," he called. "Catch this."

CHAPTER FORTY
AN INFINITE NUMBER OF MONKEYS

THE RAIN STOPPED during the night. As the sun rose, Ack-Ack Macaque sat on the wooden veranda with his legs dangling over the edge. His leg had been cleaned and dressed by a Gestalt nurse, and he'd been given a fresh white suit, over which he'd squeezed the remains of his leather flying jacket. Now, he was smoking the last of his cigars.

Below, in the streets of London, he could see the blue lights of emergency vehicles and the dull khaki of troop lorries and armoured cars. This morning, the city looked like a disturbed ants nest. Fires still burned in parts of Whitehall. News choppers wheeled around like flies. Columns of refugees were heading outwards, choking the arterial roads, desperate to escape the destruction and contagion of the inner city.

Behind him, he heard the big brass door open, and the whine of a small electric motor approaching through the trees. Paul's car zipped up beside him, the lenses of its camera and projectors bristling.

"Hey Ack-ster, how are you doing?" The dead man's image shimmered into apparent solidity beside him. This morning, Paul had opted for a dark suit and sombre tie.

"Just smoking." He looked down at the tangle of wires and servers beneath the balcony. If he was right, they formed an important node in the Gestalt's wireless network: a router to bounce their thoughts from mind to mind. If he turned it off, he might be able to free some of them. Or possibly kill them. With K8's neck on the line, he wasn't about to try messing around until he was damn sure how the machinery worked.

"Did the 'Founder' give you any trouble?" he asked.

Paul's image lowered itself until it appeared to be sitting next to him.

"A little," he said. "But there's a brig in the stern that's shielded against transmissions. Once we got her in there, and she realised she couldn't talk to the rest of the hive, she quietened down."

"She's an interesting woman."

"If you say so."

Ack-Ack Macaque cleared his throat. His cheeks felt hot. He decided to change the subject.

"How's the boss?"

"She's fine." Paul scratched his bristled chin. "Or, at least, she's going to be fine. In fact, Lila's bringing her up here now."

"They sent you on ahead, did they?"

Paul gave a guilty smile.

"They thought it prudent to see what sort of mood you were in."

Ack-Ack Macaque stretched. He felt like he'd been pulled through a jet engine's air intake, and then spat out the back. Every muscle ached and there was hardly a patch of skin without some sort of scratch or bruise. But the painkillers he'd been given by the Gestalt were remarkably effective, and he actually felt kind of good, despite everything.

"I'm okay," he said, kicking his feet. "Why shouldn't I be? After all, we saved the world."

"Again."

He looked down at the roofs below. "How are things down there?"

Paul's face grew serious.

"Reports coming out of San Francisco aren't good. The city took a pasting, and the airship above it managed to release its entire cargo before it received the abort command. Also, Madrid and Singapore report heavy casualties. Some places have been using flamethrowers and napalm to destroy areas suspected of infestation, and infected people are being herded into hospitals and quarantine camps."

"So, it's all a bit of a mess?"

"That's putting it mildly."

"But the nano-whatsits have been stopped?"

"Mostly, yes."

"Then I call that a win." He took a deep drag on the cigar, and blew smoke from his nose.

The brass door opened again, and Lila appeared through the trees, pushing Victoria in a wheelchair. Victoria had her left arm in a sling, and bandages across her ribs and stomach. Behind them, William Cole walked with his back straight and shoulders thrown back.

Ack-Ack Macaque stood to meet them.

"Hi, boss."

Victoria didn't return his salute.

"I'm not your boss anymore, monkey man. I'm not even a captain. I lost my ship."

Ack-Ack Macaque huffed. The *Tereshkova* had been the only real home either of them had known.

"Yeah," he said, "that was a shame. She was a real lady, and I'll miss her."

"How's K8?"

He shrugged. "They tell me she's part of the hive now."

"But she's alive?"

"Oh yes." He couldn't help a rueful smile. "And kicking up hell in there, from what I can gather."

They looked at each other for a moment: two old soldiers comparing losses. Then William Cole stepped forward to put a protective arm around his daughter's shoulders.

"So," he said, "what happens now?"

Ack-Ack Macaque gave him a wary squint.

"How do you mean?"

The writer smoothed his unruly hair with his free hand. He had his own share of scrapes and grazes, but they didn't seem to bother him. "I mean, where are you going to go?" he said. "What are you going to do?"

Ack-Ack Macaque rubbed his leather eye patch. The empty socket beneath itched.

"If there's any way to pull K8 out of the hive, I'll find it."

"And beyond that?"

The monkey turned to look at the pall of smoke above London.

"Well, this place has gone all to shit." Cigar clamped in his teeth, he rubbed his hands together. "Perhaps it's time to move on?"

"Actually," Victoria said, "I spoke to Merovech. He thinks the shock of this attack might be good for us. He thinks it'll bring the fractured politics of this world into a new unity, now that the nations know there are bigger threats out there."

Ack-Ack Macaque made a farting noise with his lips.

"Pffft. Let's see how long *that* lasts."

"You could help them," Lila said. "You're the leader of the Gestalt. You have an army. You can help them rebuild."

Ack-Ack Macaque shook his head.

"Sorry, sweetheart, not really my style."

"Then, what?" Cole asked.

Ack-Ack Macaque fingered his chin.

"I'll tell the Gestalt to surrender," he decided. "There are thousands of them, in all those airships. They can help clear up the mess they've made."

"And what about you?"

Ack-Ack Macaque turned to Paul.

"Hey, Paulie," he said. "Do you think you can fly this thing?"

Paul put a hand to the back of his neck and puffed out his cheeks.

"The ironclad? Sheesh, I don't know. I'd need to take a look at the computers they're using. But, in principle, I guess it's possible."

"Would you like to?"

Victoria raised an eyebrow.

"Are you suggesting we keep this ship?" she asked.

Ack-Ack Macaque showed his teeth.

"Why not? Fair's fair. They wrecked ours."

"But it's a battleship," she said. "It doesn't carry cargo or passengers. Where will we go? What will we do with it?"

He tapped the side of his nose.

"Last night, the Founder said something about moving on and finding another monkey. I reckon we do the same."

Paul gaped at him. "You mean, travel between worlds?"

"Fuck yeah." He threw a reckless smile. "There's not a whole lot to keep us here. And there must be other monkeys out there. Hundreds, maybe thousands of them."

Lila let go of the handles of Victoria's chair.

"All your alternate selves?"

"Yeah. We can find them, and tell them—" He licked his suddenly dry lips. "Tell them they don't have to be alone anymore." He glanced at Victoria. "What do you think?"

Victoria Valois ran a hand back over the smooth skin of her scalp, and shrugged.

"What the hell, I'm in."

"Excellent. Paul?"

The hologram looked at the lady in the wheelchair.

"I go where she goes."

"How about you, Cole? You've been writing about these parallel worlds all these years. Maybe you could help us navigate?"

"To Mendelblatt's world?" Cole frowned. "I don't know about that." He gave Lila a squeeze, and straightened his posture. "But there must be other Maries out there. If you need a couple of crew, then sure, I guess. We're with you."

"Okay, then. It's settled." Ack-Ack Macaque clasped his hands together. "Paul, go and see if you can hook yourself into the navigation software.

The rest of you are welcome to stay here, or join me on the bridge."

Lila looked incredulous.

"You want to leave *right now*?"

Ack-Ack Macaque turned to her.

"Can you think of a better fucking time?"

Straightening his tie, he walked through the potted jungle, heading for the airship's command deck. For the past year, he'd been casting around, wondering what to do with his life. Now, he had a mission and a purpose... and an army. He'd moved from the game world to the real one—and now a million other worlds were out there, just waiting for him. His tiredness had gone, burned away like morning mist, and all he could see ahead were possibilities.

AND IF YOU want a picture of the future, try to imagine a hundred thousand talking monkeys, gathered from a hundred thousand worlds, their numbers ever-swelling, swarming across the worlds of men—forever.

MACAQUE ATTACK

PART ONE

PERSONAL FRANKENSTEIN

Of all the animals, man is the only one that is cruel.
He is the only one that inflicts pain for the pleasure of doing it.

Mark Twain, *The Lowest Animal*

King to Mark Second Anniversary of Invasion

LONDON 15/11/ 2062 – A service of remembrance will be held in Parliament Square tomorrow to mark the second anniversary of the Gestalt Invasion.

During the invasion, heavily armed airships appeared over major cities across the globe, and government buildings and seats of power were destroyed in an attempt to 'decapitate' international society. The Gestalt were eventually beaten, but not before thousands of civilians and military personnel lost their lives.

His Majesty, King Merovech I, ruler of the United Kingdom of Great Britain, France, Ireland and Norway, will dedicate a memorial to those who died in London, including his fiancée, Julie Girard, Princess of Normandy. Similar services will be held simultaneously in Cardiff, Oslo, Manchester, Dublin, and Paris.

Two years on from the events of 16th November 2060, the whereabouts of those responsible for halting the invasion remains a mystery. Captain Valois and the crew of her skyliner, the *Tereshkova*—including the famed monkey pilot, Ack-Ack Macaque—vanished shortly after defeating the Gestalt forces in the skies above the British capital. It is believed they may have used the hive mind's own machinery to 'jump' to a parallel dimension.

Whether they went to avenge the attack, or on some other undisclosed quest, their fate remains unknown.

Read more | Like | Comment | Share

Related Stories:

Controversial light-sail probe reaches Mars.

A look inside the rebuilt Palace of Westminster.

From protester to princess: the life of Julie Girard.

Gestalt prisoners reveal chilling details of 'alternate Earth'.

World leaders sign mutual defence pact in Moscow.

Global warming: sea level rise may be faster than predicted.

CHAPTER ONE
INSTANT KARMA

"ARE YOU SURE we should be doing this?" The driver's sharp green eyes met Victoria's in the rearview mirror and she looked away, twisting her gloved hands in her lap. She was being driven through Paris in a shiny black Mercedes. The parked cars, buildings and skeletal linden trees were bright and crisp beneath the winter sun.

"I think so."

At the wheel, K8 shrugged. She was nineteen years old, with cropped copper hair and a smart white suit.

"Only..."

Victoria frowned, and brushed a speck of dust from the knee of her black trousers.

"Only what?"

"Should it be you that does it? Maybe somebody else—"

"She won't listen to anybody else."

"You don't know that for sure."

"I really do."

They passed across the Pont Neuf. Sunlight glittered off the waters of the Seine. The towers of Notre Dame stood resolute against the sky, their solidity a direct counterpoint to the ephemeral advertising holograms that stepped and swaggered above the city's boulevards and streets.

"Look," Victoria said apologetically, "I didn't mean to be snappy. I really appreciate you coming along. I know things haven't been easy for you recently."

K8 kept her attention focused on the road ahead.

"We are fine."

"It must have been tough for you." During the final battle over London, the poor kid had been assimilated into the Gestalt hive mind. For a time, she'd been part of a group consciousness, lost in a sea of other people's thoughts.

"It was, but we're okay now. Really." There were no other members of the Gestalt on this parallel version of the Earth. For the first time since the battle, the girl was alone in her head.

"You're still referring to yourself in the plural."

"We can't help it."

The car negotiated the Place de la Bastille, and plunged into the narrow streets beyond. Their target lived in a two-room apartment on the third floor of a red brick house on the corner of la Rue Pétion. When they reached the address, Victoria instructed K8 to park the Mercedes at the opposite end of the avenue and wait. Then she got out and walked back towards the house.

With her hands in the pockets of her long army coat, she sniffed the cold air. This morning, Paris smelled of damp leaves and fresh coffee. Far away and long ago, on another timeline entirely, this had been her neighbourhood, her street. Even the graffiti tags scrawled between the shop-fronts seemed just as she remembered them from when she lived here as a journalist for *Le Monde*, in the days before she met Paul.

Paul...

Victoria squeezed her fists and pushed them deeper into her pockets. Paul was her ex-husband. In the three years since his death, he'd existed as a computer simulation. She'd managed to keep him alive, despite the fact that personality 'back-ups' were inherently unstable and prone to dissolution. Originally developed for battlefield use, back-ups had become a means by which the civilian deceased—at least those who could afford the implants—could say their goodbyes after death and tie up their affairs. The recordings weren't intended or expected to endure more than six months but, with her help, Paul had already far exceeded that limit.

But nothing lasts forever.

During the past weeks, Paul's virtual personality had become increasingly erratic and forgetful, and she knew he couldn't hold out much longer. In order to preserve whatever run-time he might have left, she'd found a way to pause his simulation, leaving him frozen in time until her return. She didn't want to lose him. In many ways, he was the love of her life; and yet she knew her attempts to hold on to him were only delaying the inevitable. Sooner or later, she'd have to let him go. Three years after his death, she'd finally have to say goodbye.

Scuffing the soles of her boots against the pavement, she wondered if the woman inhabiting the apartment above had anyone significant in *her* life. This woman still lived and worked as a reporter in Paris, was registered as single on her social media profile, and had somehow managed to avoid the helicopter crash that had left Victoria with a skull full of prosthetic gelware processors.

Victoria reached up and adjusted the fur cap covering her bald scalp.

This would have been my life, she thought, *if I'd never met Paul, never gone to the Falklands...*

She felt a surge of irrational hatred for the woman who shared her face, the stranger who had once been her but whose life had diverged at an unspecified point. Where had that divergence come? Who knew? A missed promotion, perhaps, or maybe something as banal as simply turning right when her other self had turned left... Now, they were completely different people. One of them was a newspaper correspondent living in a hip quarter of Paris, the other a battle-hardened skyliner captain in league with an army of dimension-hopping monkeys.

At the front door, she hesitated. How could she explain *any* of this?

For the past two years, she'd been travelling with Ack-Ack Macaque, jumping from one world to the next. Together, they'd sought out and freed as many of his simian counterparts as they could find, unhooking them from whichever video games or weapons guidance systems they'd been wired into, and telling them they were no longer alone, no longer unique—welcoming them into the troupe. But in all that time, on all those worlds, she'd never once sought out an alternate version of herself. The thought simply hadn't occurred to her.

Here and now, though, things were different. K8 had tracked the most likely location of Ack-Ack Macaque's counterpart on this world to an organisation known as the Malsight Institute. It was a privately funded research facility on the outskirts of Paris, surrounded by security fences and razor wire. While trying to hack its systems from outside, K8 had discovered a file containing a list of people the institute saw as 'threats' to their continued operation. Victoria's counterpart had been the third person named on that list. Apparently, she'd been asking questions, probing around online, and generally making a nuisance of herself. The first two people on the list were already dead, their deaths part of an ongoing police investigation. One had been a former employee of the institute, the other an investigative journalist for an online news site. Both had been found stabbed and mutilated, their bodies charred almost beyond all recognition. Hence, the reason for this visit. If the deaths were connected to the Institute, Victoria felt duty-bound to warn her other self before the woman wound up as a headline on the evening news, her hacked and blackened corpse grinning from the smoking remains of a burned-out car.

From the pocket of her coat, she drew her house key. She'd kept the small sliver of brass and nickel with her for years, letting it rattle around in the bottom of one suitcase after another like a half-forgotten talisman. She'd never expected to need it again, but neither had she ever managed to quite bring herself to throw it away.

She slid the key into the lock and opened the door. Inside, the hallway was exactly as she remembered: black and white diamond-shaped floor tiles; a side table piled with uncollected mail, free newspapers and takeaway menus; and a black-railed staircase leading to the floors above. She closed the front door behind her and made her way up, her thick-soled boots making dull clumps on the uncarpeted steps.

The feel of the smooth bannister, the creak of the stairs, even the slightly musty smell of the walls brought back memories of a time that had been, in retrospect, happier and simpler.

In particular, she remembered an upstairs neighbour, a woman in her mid-forties with a taste for young men. Often, Victoria had found she had to turn up her TV to hide the bumps and giggles from above. One time, a lump of plaster fell off the ceiling and smashed her glass coffee table. Then, in the morning, there would usually be a young man standing in the communal stairwell. Some were lost, some shell-shocked or euphoric. Some were reassessing their lives and relationships in the light of the previous night's events. Victoria would take them in and make them coffee, call them cabs or get them cigarettes, that sort of thing.

She liked their company. In those days, she liked being useful. And sometimes, one of the boys would stay with her for a few days. They used her to wind down, to ground themselves. Sometimes, they just needed to talk. And when they left, as they inevitably did, it made her sad. She would rinse out their empty coffee mugs, clean the ashtrays, and fetch herself a glass of wine from the fridge. Then she would settle herself on the sofa again, rest her feet on the coffee table frame, and turn the TV volume way up.

SOMEBODY SCREAMED. THE sound cut through her memories. It came from above. Reaching into her coat pocket, Victoria pulled the retractable fighting stick from her coat and shook it out to its full two-metre length. Was she already too late? Taking the stairs two at a time, she reached the third floor to find the door of the apartment—*her* apartment—locked, and fresh blood spreading from beneath it, soaking into the bristles of the welcome mat.

She'd been around the monkey long enough to know she'd only hurt herself if she tried shoulder-charging the door. Instead, she delivered a sharp kick with the heel of her heavy boot, aiming for the edge of door opposite the handle. The lock would be strong, but only a handful of screws held the hinges in place. She heard wood crack, but the door remained closed. Leaning backwards for balance, she kicked again. This time, the frame splintered, the hinges came away from the wall, and the door crashed inwards and to the side.

Victoria pushed through, stepping over the puddle of blood, and found herself on the threshold of a familiar-looking room. A body lay on the floor by the couch. It had shoulder-length blonde hair. A tall, thin man loomed over it, a long black knife in his almost skeletal hand. His shoes had left red prints on the parquet floor, and there was a long smear where he'd dragged the body. As she burst in, he looked up at her. His face was set in a rictus grin, and she swallowed back a surge of revulsion.

"Cassius Berg."

His expression didn't change, and she knew it couldn't. His skin had been stretched taut over an artificial frame.

"Who are you?"

Victoria swallowed. She felt as if she was talking to a ghost. "The last time we met, I dropped you out of a skyliner's cargo hatch, four hundred feet above Windsor."

He tipped his head on one side. His eyes were reptilian slits.

"What are you on about?" He stepped over the corpse and brandished the knife. "Who are you?"

Victoria moved her staff into a defensive position.

"I'm her."

She couldn't bring herself to look directly at the body. As a reporter, she'd seen her share of violent crime scenes, and knew what to expect. Instead, she looked inside her own head, concentrating on the mental commands that transferred her consciousness from the battered remains of her natural cortex to the clean, bright clarity of her gelware implants.

Berg's posture tightened. He glanced from her to the body, and back again.

"Twin sister?"

"Something like that."

"Lucky me."

The first time she'd fought him—or at least the version of him from her own parallel—he'd been superhumanly fast and tough, and he'd almost killed her. She'd been left for dead with a hole punched through the back of her skull. She tightened her grip on the metal staff. This time would be different. This time, she knew all about him, knew his methods and limitations, while he remained blissfully unaware of her capabilities.

Visualising her internal menu, she overclocked her neural processors. As the speed of her thinking increased, her perception of time stretched and slowed. The traffic noise from outside deepened, winding down like a faulty tape. In slow motion, she saw Berg's muscles tense. His legs pushed up and he surged towards her, black coat flapping around behind him, knife held forward, aimed at her face. His speed was astonishing. A normal human would have been pinned through the eye before they could move. As it was, Victoria only just managed to spin aside. As momentum carried him past, she completed her twirl and brought the end of her staff cracking into the back of his head. The blow caught him off balance and sent him flailing forwards with an indignant cry, through the remains of the front door and out, into the hallway.

He ended up on his hands and knees. Victoria stepped up behind him, but before she could bring her staff down, Berg's spindly arm slashed backwards, and his knife caught her across the shins, slicing through denim and skin. The pain registered as a sharp red alarm somewhere at the back of her mind, way down in the animal part of her brain, and she tried to ignore it. It was a distraction, the gelware told her, nothing more. Her heart thumped in her chest, each beat like the pounding of some great engine. He'd hurt her before; she wouldn't allow him to hurt her again. She stabbed down with her staff, pinning his wrist to the hardwood floor, and leant her weight on it. She ground until she felt the bones of his hand snap and crack, and saw the knife fall from his fingers.

Berg's head turned to look at her. Although the grin remained stretched across his face, his eyes were wide and fearful.

"Who *are* you?"

"I told you." Victoria could feel blood running down her shins, soaking into the tops of her socks. She glanced back at the dead woman in the apartment, and saw blonde hair mixed with wine-coloured blood, and an out-thrown hand with torn and bruised knuckles. The poor woman hadn't stood a chance. She'd been butchered, and all Victoria could do now was avenge her.

"I'm Victoria Valois." She stepped forward and raised her weapon high over her head. She wanted to bring it down hard, driving the butt end into the space between his eyes. She wanted to feel his metal skull cave beneath her blow, feel his brains squish and perish. He had killed at least three people, probably more, and would kill her too if he got the chance.

He deserved to die.

And yet...

CHAPTER TWO
UNCLEAN ZOO

TAKING OFF FROM a private airstrip on the outskirts of Paris, Victoria and K8 flew across the English Channel in a borrowed seaplane, with Cassius Berg handcuffed and gagged in the hold. They were heading for a sea fort that stood a few miles off the coast of Portsmouth. When the old structure came into sight, they splashed the plane into the waters of the Solent, carving a feather of white across the shimmering blue surface, and taxied to the rotting jetty that served as the fort's one and only link with the outside world.

The seaplane was an ancient Grumman Goose: a small and ungainly contraption with which Victoria had somehow fallen grudgingly in love. The little aircraft had two chunky propeller engines mounted on an overhead wing, and the main fuselage dangled between them like a fat-bottomed boat bolted to the underside of a boomerang.

When she stepped from the plane's hatch, Victoria found a monkey waiting for her, fishing from the end of the jetty. It wore a flowery sunhat and a string vest, and had a large silver pistol tucked into the waistband of its cut-off denim shorts. Overhead, the sun burned white and clean.

"I'm Valois."

The monkey watched her from behind its mirrored shades. She couldn't remember its name. A portable transistor radio, resting on the planks beside the bait bucket, played scratchy Europop.

"So?"

Behind the monkey, at the far end of the jetty, the fort rose as an implacable, curving wall of stone. Victoria swallowed back her irritation. The breeze blowing in from the sea held the all-too-familiar fragrances of brine, fresh fish, and childhood holidays. Considering it was November, the day felt exceptionally mild.

"Where's your boss?"

"Does he know you're coming?"

"Don't be stupid." She slipped off her flying jacket, pulled a red bandana from her trouser pocket, and wiped her forehead. Keeping hold of its rod with one hand, the monkey produced a rolled-up cigarette from behind its ear. The paper was damp and starting to unravel. It pushed the rollup between its yellowing teeth, and lit up using a match struck against the jetty's crumbling planks.

"I don't think he'll want to see you."

Smoke curled around it, blue in the sunlight. Victoria sighed, and raised her eyes to the armoured Zeppelin tethered to the fort's radio mast.

"Is he up there?"

"Yeah, but he ain't taking no visitors."

"We'll see about that."

She went back to the Goose and pulled Berg out onto the jetty's planks. He blinked against the sunlight. Victoria slipped a loop of rope around his neck, and jerked on it like a dog chain. Leaving K8 to secure the plane, she led her prisoner past the startled monkey, along the jetty, and into the coolness of the stone fort.

The corridors were dank with rainwater, and she was surprised to feel a sense of homecoming. Despite the frosty welcome, this little manmade island felt more like home than anywhere else on this timeline. She'd spent the past six weeks in Europe, but it hadn't been her Europe. Everything about it had been different and, to her, somehow wrong. She looked forward to getting back to the familiar cabins and gangways of the armoured airship, and Paul.

Would he even remember her?

Dragging Berg, she stomped her way across the fort's main flagstone courtyard.

Standing in the English Channel, several miles off the coast of the Isle of Wight, the circular fort had been built in the nineteenth century to defend Portsmouth from the French. Made of thick stone and surrounded by water on all sides, the structure had lain derelict until the turn of the millennium, when an enterprising developer had converted the stronghold into a luxury hotel and conference centre, complete with open-air swimming pool. Fifty years, and two stock market crashes, later, the weeds and rust had returned; and now that the place had been 'liberated' by the monkey army, it more resembled an unclean zoo than an exclusive resort. The water in the swimming pool lay brown and stagnant, its scummy surface speckled by shoals of empty beer cans and the wallowing bleach-white bones of broken patio furniture. Shards of glass littered the patio area.

The steps up to the base of the radio mast were where she remembered, still overgrown with lichen, grass and mould. The grass whispered against her leather boots, and she knew suspicious eyes watched her from the fort's seemingly empty windows.

Stupid monkeys.

She'd only been gone six weeks.

ONCE ABOARD THE airship, Victoria led Berg to the artificial jungle built into the vessel's glass-panelled nose. Cut off from the rest of the craft by a thick brass door, this leafy enclosure formed Ack-Ack Macaque's personal and private sanctuary and, at first, the monkeys guarding it didn't want to let her in.

"He's in a foul mood," warned the one wearing a leather vest.

Victoria tugged at the rope around Berg's neck, making him stumble forwards.

"He'll be in a worse one by the time I'm through with him. Now, are you going to let me past or not?"

The monkeys exchanged glances. They knew who she was, yet were obviously nervous about troubling their leader. Finally the older of the two, a grey-muzzled macaque with a thick gold ring in his right ear, stood aside.

"Go ahead, ma'am."

"Thank you."

Victoria pushed open the heavy door and stepped inside. The chamber was a vast vault occupying the forward portion of the airship's main hull. The floor had been covered in reed matting, on which stood hundreds of large ceramic pots. Palm trees and other jungle plants grew from the pots, forming a canopy overhead, and it took her a minute or so to make her way through the trees to the wooden veranda overlooking the interior of the craft's glass bow. Birds and butterflies twitched hither and thither among the branches. The air smelled like the interior of a greenhouse.

ACK-ACK MACAQUE STOOD at the verandah's rail, hands clasped behind his back and a fat cigar clamped in his teeth. He didn't turn as Victoria walked up behind him.

"You're back," he said.

"I am."

From where he stood, he could see the sea fort and the blue waters of the Channel.

"Any luck?"

"Some."

She took her prisoner by the shoulder and pushed him down, into a kneeling position on the planks at his feet. Ack-Ack Macaque looked down with his one good eye.

"Who's that?"

"Cassisus Berg."

The monkey gave the man an experimental prod with his shoe.

"Didn't you kill that fucker once already?"

"Not on this timeline."

Ack-Ack frowned at her. Her face was pale despite her exertions, and her eyes were red and tired-looking. He could see she hadn't slept well in several days. "And your other self? Did you find her?"

"We were too late."

A wrought-iron patio table stood a little way along the verandah. Behind it stood a wheeled drinks cabinet filled with bottles of all shapes and sizes. Victoria left Berg kneeling where he was and walked over and helped herself to a vodka martini.

A parrot squawked in one of the higher branches, its plumage red against the canopy's khaki and emerald.

Six weeks ago, Ack-Ack Macaque had tried to talk her out of getting involved with another version of herself but, predictably, she hadn't listened—and he'd had more than enough to do trying to keep control of his monkey army. The problem with being the alpha monkey was that they all looked to him to tell them what to do and arbitrate all their pathetic squabbles. When faced with any kind of decision, they were more than happy to pass the responsibility up the chain of command until it dropped into his lap. It was the way primate troupes worked; it was also the way the military worked, and he didn't like it. It was a pain in the hole. He was used to being a maverick, a grunt, an ace pilot rather than an Air Marshal. Being a leader cramped his style.

Considering the figure at his feet, he said, "What are we going to do with him?"

Victoria took a sip from the glass, and wiped her lips on the back of her gloved hand.

"He's a cyborg, same as before. A human brain in an artificial body."

Ack-Ack Macaque twitched his nostrils. The man smelled like an old, wet raincoat. He gave the guy a nudge and, arms still cuffed behind him, Berg tipped over onto his side.

"It's definitely him, though?"

He watched as Victoria swirled the clear liquid in the bottom of her glass.

"*Mais oui,*" she said. "And you realise what this means, don't you?"

Ack-Ack Macaque scowled at her.

"Should I?"

"It means Nguyen's on this parallel, too."

Ack-Ack Macaque's hackles rose. His scowl turned to a snarl, and his fingers went to his hips, where two silver Colts shone in their holsters.

"Where is he?"

"Paris, I think. An operation calling itself the Malsight Institute. I had K8 pull up some information on it."

"And?"

"Officially it doesn't exist. There's nothing about it until two years ago. Rumours, conspiracy theories, that sort of thing. Very secretive, government money. Black research. Heavy security."

"Sounds familiar."

"If he's there, and he's building another robot army, we have to stop him."

Ack-Ack Macaque growled, deep in his throat. Doctor Nguyen had been the man responsible for creating them both in his laboratories—their own personal Frankenstein. He took the cigar from his lips and rolled it in his fingers.

"We leave in an hour," he decided. He was overdue for some action, and, after spending the last six weeks trying to sort out the complaints and squabbles of a troupe of irritable, irresponsible monkeys, he was itching to bust some skulls. "Reactivate your husband and recall the crew."

"What are you going to do?"

"What do you think I'm going to do?" His lips curled back, revealing his sharp yellow fangs. He clamped the cigar back between his teeth. Leathery fingers bunched into fists. "If Nguyen's here, I'm going to grab the bastard by the ears and rip his fucking head off."

CHAPTER THREE
ASSHOLE VARIATIONS

ON THE AIRSHIP'S bridge, Paul shimmered into apparent solidity. He blinked, removed his rimless spectacles, and rubbed his eyes.

"Ah, Vicky."

His image was a hologram projected by a small drone, about the size and shape of a dragonfly, which hovered behind his eyes. It portrayed him as he had been before his death: spiky peroxide hair, gold ear stud, and a loud Hawaiian shirt under a long white lab coat.

"How are you feeling?"

"Me? I'm perfectly, um—" He frowned down at the glasses in his hand, as if seeing them for the first time.

"Fine?" she suggested.

He jumped, as if startled. "What? Oh yes. Fine. Perfectly fine."

"Are you still hooked into the main computer?"

"I am."

"Then warm up the engines, we're leaving."

She walked over and lowered herself into the captain's chair. She knew Ack-Ack Macaque wouldn't mind.

Below, the members of the ragtag monkey army emerged from the doors and windows of the sea fort. Some were clothed, others were not; but all carried weapons, either slung on their backs or gripped in their teeth. She watched them swarm up the mooring ropes and suppressed a shiver.

"As soon as they're all aboard, head for France," she said. "And tell K8 to leave the plane and get her butt up here, or she's going to get left behind."

"And Cole?"

"*Merde.*" She'd forgotten the writer. "Where is he?"

"The Lake District."

"And Lila's with him?"

"Lila?"

"His daughter."

"Ah yes, of course. I think so."

"Can you get a call through to them?"

"I'll do my best." Paul's image wavered and froze as he turned his attention to the airship's communication systems. Victoria sat back in her chair, allowing her coat to fall open around her. After a few seconds, one of the screens blanked, and then cleared to show the face of a middle-aged man with wild grey hair.

"Hello, Captain, what can I do for you?" The picture was shaky and showed the man's face from below. Cole was hiking in the hills above Lake Windermere, and talking into a handheld phone. His cheeks were red and he was out of breath.

"We're moving the ship, Cole."

"And you want us to come back?'

She shook her head. "There isn't time. We're going to Paris. We'll try to pick you up afterwards."

William Cole stopped walking. The air wheezed between his lips.

"Don't hurry on our behalf," he said. Behind him, Victoria glimpsed sunlit hills curled with brown autumn bracken and, far below, the waters of the lake.

"We'll be back," she promised. "But maybe not for a while."

"What are you going to do?"

"Something illegal."

"Well, don't worry on our account." He scratched the grey fuzz on his chin. "We're happy enough here. We found Marie and everything's great. In fact..." He looked away from the camera and the wind ruffled his hair.

"What?"

"Well, we were thinking of staying here," he said. "Permanently."

Victoria felt a pang of disappointment. "Is that what you both really want?"

"I think so. I mean it's quiet here. Things are going well with Marie. We've found a cottage, and I've started writing again."

Victoria took off her fur cap and ran a hand over the bristles of her scalp. Thrown together by chance, she and Cole had become friends over the past two years, and she'd be sad to lose him—especially as he was one of the last humans left among the airship's crew. With him and Lila gone, only Victoria and K8 remained, the only two women on a Zeppelin full of primates.

"Then I wish you luck." She drew herself up in her chair. "You and Lila. After everything that's happened, you both deserve some peace."

Cole smiled.

"As do we all, Captain. As do we all."

*   *   *

FIFTEEN MINUTES LATER, the gigantic airship rose from the fort and turned its two-kilometre hull eastwards towards France. Once, it had belonged to the leader of the Gestalt; now it belonged to the monkey army, a prize taken in battle and rechristened in honour of its new masters. At first, the monkeys had simply called it 'Big Sky Thing'. It was only recently, at the urging of the troupe's more erudite members, that Ack-Ack Macaque had officially renamed it *Sun Wukong*, after the monkey king of Chinese myth, who was born from a stone and went on to rebel against Heaven itself. Reclining on the bridge, Victoria watched the blue waters of the English Channel wheel beneath. The coast of France lay against the horizon like a green and purple cloud.

Back we go…

She gripped the arms of the chair. Unlike the world she called home, on this parallel France and England were separate countries, and she guessed the French wouldn't be too keen at the prospect of a heavily armed dreadnought ploughing through their airspace.

Still, it's not as if they've got anything big enough to shoot us down.

For a moment, her thoughts turned back to the apartment, and the blonde woman lying dead on the parquet floor.

Just let them try…

Over the past two years, she'd seen dozens of worlds, each a little different to the last. She'd seen versions of Europe riven by war and famine; versions ruled over by resurgent British, German or Roman Empires; and versions controlled by every '-ism' under the sun, from capitalism to communism to religious fundamentalism. She'd walked their streets listening to the *put-put-put* of steam-driven cars; seen gleaming supersonic airliners cleave the skies; watched gigantic Soviet hovercraft patrol the Thames Estuary; and taken a ride through a Transatlantic Tunnel wide enough for four lanes of traffic. And in all that time, on all those worlds, had encountered nothing capable of putting more than the most cursory of dents in the *Sun Wukong*'s armour plate.

"All engines online and showing green," reported Paul.

Victoria glanced around at the bare metal walls with their lines of rivets. She'd been away for a month and half, and now saw the cold, spartan interior with fresh eyes. She knew the monkeys didn't care about the lack of décor, but she missed the shabby elegance of her old skyliner, the *Tereshkova*. At least she had the bridge of this vessel pretty much to herself.

Paul could run the ship, it didn't need a crew; and none of the monkeys were all that interested in acting like one. To them, the airship was simply a moving home—a means to get from one adventure to the next. Even Ack-Ack Macaque came up here only occasionally. He was happy in his potted jungle, and could issue commands from there as well as anywhere.

Victoria tapped her nails against the chair's armrests.

"Then, full speed ahead, all engines."

"Aye."

At the rear of the dreadnought, on a forest of engine nacelles, huge black blades began to turn. Moving slowly at first, they gradually increased their speed until they blurred into whirring grey discs, and the vast craft to which they were attached began to slide reluctantly forwards, slowly picking up momentum. Sunlight glimmered from its gun turrets and sensor pods. Two thousand metres in length, it moved like an eclipse across the world's busiest shipping lane, its rippling shadow dwarfing even the largest of the Channel's car ferries and container ships.

Victoria Valois felt the vibration of the airship's engines through the gondola's steel deck and smiled. Even though they were riding into battle, it was comforting to be airborne again, and to know that she rode the largest flying machine this particular version of the Earth had ever seen.

STANDING AT THE window of her cabin, K8 looked out through a ten-inch thick porthole. Despite her exertions with the seaplane, she still wore her habitual white skirt and blouse. It was her uniform now, as seemly and natural as blue jeans and a black t-shirt had been to her younger self.

"We're not a child any more. We're nearly twenty."

Beside her, Ack-Ack Macaque scratched at the leather patch covering his left eye.

"Yeah, but—"

"You can't stop us."

"I fucking can."

She looked him in the eye. "No, you fucking can't."

He watched her cross her arms across her chest, and turn back to the window. Her hair looked bronze in the light; her freckles like sprinkles fallen across her nose and cheeks. He pulled the cigar from his mouth and rolled it between finger and thumb.

"So, what am I supposed to do?"

She didn't look around.

"Just take us somewhere we can connect back into the hive mind."

Ack-Ack sighed. He watched the smoke twisting in the cabin's air.

"This is partly my fault, isn't it?"

K8 made a scornful noise. "Of course it's your fault. It's your *entire* fault. You gave us to the hive."

"I didn't have a choice."

"We never said you did." She hunched her shoulders. "We just need to get back, to reconnect."

"But why?"

She hugged herself, gripping her upper arms. "You wouldn't understand."

Ack-Ack Macaque frowned. He could see sweat on her lip.

"I thought you'd be better off here," he said, "cut off from the rest of them."

"You were wrong."

"Well, excuse me."

K8 winced at his sarcasm. She passed a hand across her face, and turned to face him. "Look, we're sorry, okay? We know you were trying to help. It's just tough for us now, to be alone."

"Tell me about it."

"This is different."

Ack-Ack Macaque sat heavily on the edge of the bed. "I don't see how. So you're the only Gestalt drone on this rock. Big whoop. I spent years as the world's only talking monkey."

"But now you have an army."

He grinned. "Yeah, but most of them are assholes."

K8 looked him in the eye, expression serious. "Most of them are variations of you."

"Asshole variations."

"Well, imagine losing them." She straightened the hem of her jacket with a tug. "Imagine going back to being the only one of your kind after being surrounded by all those others. How do you think that would feel?"

Ack-Ack Macaque shifted his position on the bed, getting more comfortable on the mussed blankets.

"Pretty shitty," he admitted.

"Well, that's what we're going through. The majority of the Gestalt aren't fanatics. Only the leaders were evil. Most of the drones are ordinary, decent people caught up in something bigger than themselves. And they welcomed us. They took us for who we were and welcomed us. For the first time in our life, we felt truly accepted; truly part of a family."

"The 'first time', huh?"

"Don't be like that." She stuck her chin forward. "We come from a broken home. Our only friend was a talking monkey."

"I thought we were doing okay."

"We were." She rapped the side of her head. "But now it's too quiet. We can't stand it."

Ack-Ack Macaque looked down at his hairy hands.

"I'm sorry," he said. "If I could get that computer stuff out of your head…"

"We don't want it out."

He pulled a cigar from the inside pocket of his flight jacket.

"Then what should I do? I can't just give you back to the hive."

"It's what we want. We need to be whole again."

"But, Nguyen—"

"We'll help you with Nguyen. But after that, you take us back, okay?"

He huffed air through his cheeks. He could tell she wasn't going to drop the subject, and he couldn't be bothered to argue any more. Best just to agree now and deal with the consequences later.

"Okay," he said.

"You promise?"

Ack-Ack Macaque screwed the cigar into his lips and lit it. All he wanted was some peace and quiet. "Sure."

"Then we have a deal."

"Thank fuck for that."

K8 uncrossed her arms and perched beside him. "What do you need us to do?"

Ack-Ack suppressed a yawn. "I need you to get on the jump engines and plot our escape. I don't want to hang around after we've trashed Nguyen's lab. I can do without a run-in with the French air force."

K8 raised an eyebrow. "That doesn't sound like you, Skipper."

"Maybe I'm getting old."

"Seriously?"

"We're about to attack a civilian government contractor." He blew at the tip of his cigar, watching the cherry-red ember flare. "The French are going to take that as an act of terrorism. They'll send planes."

"They don't have anything that can hurt us."

"Not straight away." Ack-Ack Macaque got to his feet and shambled to the door. "But as soon as we shoot one of them down, they'll send ten more. We'll be fighting a war and, frankly, I'm just too tired for all that crap." He scratched his belly. Some mornings, he ached all over, and he had to get up at least twice every night to take a piss.

"So, you want us to go in fast, hit them hard, and then vanish?"

"Bingo." He turned the handle and stepped out into the gangway beyond. "Oh, and K8?"

"Yes, Skip?"

"Try to find us somewhere nice, okay?"

"Define 'nice'."

"Ah, you know." He waved a hand. "All the usual shit. White sand, blue sea, coconut trees. *No incoming fire.*"

"You want us to plot a course back to Kishkindha?"

Ack-Ack Macaque let his shoulders and cigar droop.

"If you must."

MEANWHILE, AS THE *Sun Wukong* crossed the coast of France, Victoria stood on the verandah inside the airship's glass nose. Paul's image stood beside her. Together, they watched the craft's shadow pass over the white waves and yellow beaches of the Normandy shore, and Victoria caught herself wondering how many human bones lay forever buried in those deceptively welcoming sands. Was there anywhere in Europe that hadn't been a battlefield at least once? She squeezed the verandah's bamboo rail. Behind her, in the potted forest, birds chirped and squawked.

"So," she said.

Paul gave her a sideways glance. "So?"

"This forgetfulness..."

He made a face. "I know what you're going to say."

"You're supposed to be running this ship."

"I know, I know." He looked down at his red baseball boots, and rubbed the side of his nose with the index finger of his right hand. "It's just, I get these headaches."

Victoria blew air through pursed lips. "*Merde.*"

"What?"

"You're the expert, you tell me."

Paul looked up at the sky. "You think I'm de-cohering?"

"You've lasted a lot longer than most."

He sighed. "Maybe you're right."

"Seriously?"

"Don't think it hasn't occurred to me. Don't think that, since I found

I was a back-up, I haven't thought about it every single minute of every single day." He waved his arms in exasperation. "How do you think it feels to realise you have a built-in expiry date?"

Victoria watched as his image walked to the wrought iron table and appeared to flop onto one of its attendant chairs.

"What can we do?" she asked.

He gave an angry shrug. "How the hell would I know?"

"You know more than most."

"Still not enough."

They fell silent. Below, the beaches had given way to brown fields and winding lanes.

"I don't want to do it," Victoria said quietly, "but, if you need me to, I can always switch you off, permanently."

Paul's eyes widened. "No. No, absolutely not. Why would you say that?"

She walked over and crouched in front of him, wishing she could take his hand in hers.

"Then, I'll be here for you," she promised, "as long as you need me."

Paul looked down at her. His forehead wrinkled. "Do I sense a 'but'?"

Victoria rocked backwards on her heels. "But I think we should disengage you from some of the airship's more vital systems."

She let out a breath.

There, I've said it.

The apparition on the chair blinked at her from behind his spectacles. "You think I can't handle this?"

"It doesn't matter what I think."

"Of course it does." He leaned forward. "Vicky, I need to know that you believe in me."

"Of course I believe in you." She felt flustered. "But you've lasted so long, so much longer than anybody else in your position. I just—"

"What?"

"I think we need to take precautions."

His chin dropped to his chest, and his eyes closed. When he finally spoke, his voice was small and tired. "Look, I know you're right. But, not just yet, okay?"

"Then, when?"

He raised his eyes to her. "I don't know. I want to be useful. I know I'm deteriorating, but there's something I want to do first, before..." He coughed, stumbling over his words. "Before the end."

"What?"

"It's a surprise. I just need a bit of time. Can you give me that?"

Hands pressing on her thighs, Victoria pushed herself back up onto her feet. "I don't know. If you start to—"

"If I endanger the ship, you can cut me out of the loop. I'll rig up a protocol."

She chewed her lower lip. The *Sun Wukong* was a monster: two thousand metres of gasbags, aluminium struts and thick armour plating, powered by dozens of nuclear-electric turbines. If something went wrong and it crashed into a populated area, the devastation would be appalling.

Paul looked at her over the rim of his glasses. "Please?"

Victoria took a deep breath. She couldn't refuse him; she never could. He was like a little boy. "Okay, for now. But the second you start to have any doubts, you tell me."

"I love you."

She felt her cheeks redden. "I know. I love you too."

Paul's nervous smile was like the sun coming out from behind a cloud. He jumped to his feet. "In that case, let's go and cause some trouble."

Victoria grinned despite herself. She wiped her eyes on the back of her wrist, and drew herself up to her full height. Further discussion could wait. For now, it was time to focus on the task at hand.

"Right," she said, "give me full speed ahead and don't stop for anything."

"There isn't anything that *can* stop us, short of a nuclear blast."

"Well, let's hope we don't run into any of those."

"Amen to that. Now, hold on tight. I'm putting us on an…" He clicked his fingers, searching for the right words. "Um…"

"Attack approach?"

"Yeah." He looked sheepish. Victoria rolled her eyes.

"Oh, *mon dieu*."

CHAPTER FOUR
PHOENIX EGGS

FROM THE WINDOW of his office on the third floor of Buckingham Palace, Merovech watched the rain falling over London. On the mahogany desk behind him, sheaves of paperwork awaited his attention and his inbox bulged with unanswered email. He wasn't in the mood to pay either more than a cursory glance. He'd rolled up his shirtsleeves and loosened his black tie. A glass of single malt nestled, half forgotten, in his hand.

At first, he'd intended to remain king only as long as it took to restore national calm following the death of his parents and the revelation of his mother's complicity in an attempted coup d'état. But that had been three years ago, before the Gestalt invasion and the death of his fiancée. Since then, everything had changed. The world had become stranger and more threatening than anybody could have guessed, and his Commonwealth needed him. They needed a figurehead and a sense of continuity, and he was the most qualified to offer both. Whatever the secret truth of his origins—that he'd been cloned in a lab from one of his mother's cells—he'd been raised to be monarch, and nobody else had his level of training or preparation. His people needed him and, truth be told, he needed them. With Julie gone, he had nothing else.

The rain blew across the Mall, shaking the leafless trees lining the road. Car headlights shimmered through the gloom. To the east, a twin-hulled skyliner thrummed its way upriver, following the twists and turns of the Thames. Its navigation lights blinked red and green. As he watched, it passed behind the forest of cranes towering over Westminster, where the government buildings were still being rebuilt, rising like misshapen, blocky phoenix eggs from the craters left by the Gestalt's bombardment.

How many times had this city rebuilt itself? The inhabitants seemed used to chaos and ruin; in fact, they seemed to revel in their resilience. From the destruction wrought by Boudicca, and then the Great Fire of 1666, through to bomb attacks by the IRA and Al Qaeda, via the Zeppelin raids of the First World War and the Blitzkrieg pummelling of the Second, Londoners had always been fiercely proud of their ability to keep calm and carry on, even in the most trying of circumstances. And these past two years had been no exception. Faced with a baffling multiverse of potential threats, the capital was doing what it had always done: going about its daily life with scarcely more than a shrug and tut. As long as the Tube ran, the people were happy. Whereas other cities such as Pompeii, Petra, Hashima Island, and Detroit had fallen by the wayside during London's two thousand years of history, the Mother of All Cities had simply endured, and always would.

Looking down, Merovech remembered the glass in his hand, and raised it to his lips. Set against the ravages of the past, the damage left by the Gestalt—a few dozen bomb craters, some demolished buildings—seemed minor and ephemeral, a hiss and a pop in history's sizzling pan; but that was only until you remembered the three thousand dead bodies that had been pulled from the rubble. Three thousand innocent men, women and children who had been caught in a conflict they couldn't possibly have foreseen or understood, killed in a surprise attack.

He rinsed the whisky around his teeth. His wife had been among them. At least, she would have been his wife if she'd lived. The date of their wedding had been set, and the preparations had been under way. Then a Gestalt dreadnought appeared in the skies over London and showered missiles on Whitehall.

When the assault came, Julie had been in a car, on her way to shelter. She'd been crossing Westminster Bridge at the exact moment the parliament buildings took their first hit. A swerving lorry crushed her car through the stone parapet, into the Thames.

Merovech drained his glass.

She hadn't stood a chance.

With her gone, he had nothing. He had no mother or father, no brothers or sisters, hardly any friends. He felt like a refugee from a vanished land—alone, and the last of his kind. Even the damned monkey had disappeared. All that kept him going was his duty; the same duty he'd once spurned and sworn to resign.

Three thousand had died in London, but similar numbers had also been killed in all the other cities that had been targeted. In the aftermath of all that tumult and loss, the survivors craved stability. They desperately needed a leader they could count on; somebody whose familiarity would provide permanence and comfort in a world turned outlandish and unsafe; somebody to be a focus for their grief, and embody their hopes for the future. And so he toured the cities that had suffered in the attack; he cut ribbons at construction sites and waved for cameras; he visited schools and factories and spoke about hope and faith and the importance of rebuilding the country; and then, when he came home, he locked himself in his office, away from the public gaze, and drank whisky until the footmen came to pour him into bed.

He watched the twin-hulled skyliner until it disappeared. Then he turned to the bottle on his desk, ready to refill his glass. As he unscrewed the cap, he heard a soft knock at the office door.

"Come in."

The door opened and his personal secretary stepped into the room.

"Your Majesty."

"Amy?" The neck of the bottle clinked against the rim of his glass as he refilled it. "What are you doing here so late?"

"We have a bit of a situation, sir."

Amy Llewellyn still wore the same clothes she'd been wearing earlier in the day, but now she'd discarded her suit jacket, loosened her collar, and pushed the sleeves of her blouse up to the elbows.

"A situation?" Carefully, he replaced the bottle on the desk and fastened the cap. Then he picked up his drink. "I thought I'd asked to be left alone."

"This won't wait, sir."

Fatigue clawed at him. He gave them body and soul during the day. Why couldn't they leave him in peace in the evening?

"What is it?"

Amy blew a loose strand of hair from in front of her face. "We've received a message."

He sighed. "Are you sure it can't wait?"

She swallowed, and shook her head. "It's from your mother, sir."

Merovech's fingers tightened on the glass. "My mother's dead."

"Quite so."

"Then what are you talking about?"

"She made a back-up, sir."

Merovech felt his knees begin to shake. He'd seen his mother die, blown to fragments by her own hand grenade. He leaned against the desk. "Where is it? Where's it calling from?"

Without asking, Amy turned over a clean glass and poured herself a drink.

"You're not going to like this, sir."

He watched her put the top back on the bottle, and noticed her hands were shaking.

"Just tell me."

Amy swallowed nervously, and cleared her throat.

"The transmission appears to have originated on, um, Mars."

CHAPTER FIVE
HAIRY FRIENDS

CASSIUS BERG'S SPINDLY frame lay strapped to a bunk in the airship's infirmary. Victoria looked down at him with distaste. Even in sleep, his leering smile remained fixed and permanent.

The Smiling Man.

Once, on her world, he'd been a figure of nightmare and terror, a killer with the face of a clown and the dead eyes of a snake. He'd haunted her nightmares. He'd killed Paul and tried to kill her. And then she'd thrown him out of the *Tereshkova*'s cargo bay, and thought it was over. She'd thought he was gone for good, little suspecting she'd run into another version of him, in an alternate version of Paris, on another timeline altogether.

This new version of Berg looked even more like a corpse than the first one had. His skin was pale almost to the point of translucence, and had been stretched tightly across his scalp and cheekbones. Metal staples held it in place, each at the centre of a circle of red and puckered flesh. His black overcoat reeked of mildew and stale cigarettes.

She looked around at the dozen or so monkeys crowding the bed.

"Wake him up," she said.

A grizzled capuchin tapped Berg on the forehead with the flat side of a meat cleaver.

Victoria looked down and straightened her tunic. It was a red one with gold buttons and a silver scabbard on a white silk sash, and it had once belonged to her elderly Russian godfather, the Commodore. It was the only thing of his to have survived the crash of his old skyliner, the *Tereshkova*; and it had only survived because she had been wearing it at the time, having donned it for luck in the battle against the Gestalt.

For this confrontation, she had left her head bare, displaying her scars— scars the other Berg had given her during their first clash.

On the bed, the new Berg's eyelids flickered. He blinked up at the hairy faces and bared fangs around him and jerked against his restraints.

"What's happening?"

"I'm happening, Mister Berg." Victoria stepped forward and bent slightly, bringing her face a little closer to his. "I trust you remember me from this morning?"

"Let me go."

Victoria shook her head, keeping her expression immobile and unfriendly. "I'm afraid not. I have some questions for you."

"I mean it. I have powerful friends. If—"

"As you can see, I have angry, hairy friends, Mister Berg, with sharp teeth and bad tempers. Now, let's take all your bluster as read, shall we? Because, from where I'm standing, you're in no position to be making threats."

He glared at her.

"When I get free from these straps, I *will* make it my business to kill you."

Victoria wagged a finger. "If you get free from those straps, Mister Berg, these guys will *eat* you."

She brushed at a speck of dust on her tunic, making the medals clink and jangle, and let her other hand rest on the pommel of her sword. Around the bed, the monkeys chattered and whooped, and did their best to look fierce and hungry. They brandished swords and knives. One, a brawny howler monkey, carried an old fire axe.

Berg looked around at them, and stopped straining against his straps.

"I won't talk."

"Yes, you will."

He cocked his head. "How can you be so sure?"

"Because we've done this before, you and I." Victoria tried not to shudder at the memory. "Last time we spoke, you were dangling out of the back of a skyliner and, when push came to shove, you told me everything I needed to know."

Berg's brows furrowed. "What on Earth are you talking about?"

"We've met before, Mister Berg, on another timeline. You may have killed the Victoria from this world—you may have killed a whole lot of people for that matter—but, where I come from, *you're* the one who's dead." She rocked back on her heels and folded her arms. The overhead light twinkled across the frayed gold braid on her cuffs. "So, keeping that in mind, I want you to tell me about your boss, Doctor Nguyen. We know he's at the Malsight Institute; I just need you to tell me on which floor to find his office."

Berg licked his lips, his tongue darting like a lizard's, scenting the air.

"Go to hell."

Victoria sighed. "Please, Mister Berg. This is your last chance to be helpful." She looked around at the motley troupe of primates assembled around the bed. "Otherwise I'm going to have to ask my friends here to start getting creative with you."

She gave a nod to the capuchin. The little creature had a swollen head, deformed by the artificial processors crammed into its skull, and a row of sturdy input jacks protruding from its back like the spines of a dinosaur. At her signal, it inched forward, raising its cleaver above the captive's forehead.

Berg's flat and expressionless eyes looked up at the blade.

Then, with a roar of anger, he sat up. The leather straps at his wrists stretched and snapped. With the speed of a striking snake, he clamped a hand around the little monkey's neck and snapped its spine like a used match.

Aghast, Victoria threw out a hand.

"Stop!"

But it was too late. With an angry shriek, the rest of the troupe fell on him. Berg writhed and lashed out with his hands and feet, but they were too numerous, too close. Blades flashed. He used his forearm to block one sword, but two more skewered him through the ribs. He cried out, sounding more indignant than hurt, and tried to swing his legs off the table, but that only exposed his back, and a gibbon with patchy fur took the opportunity to sink a foot-long carving knife into the hollow between his shoulder blades.

Victoria stepped backwards to the door, hands covering her ears.

"Stop," she cried again, but they couldn't hear her over their own frenzied screeching. Horrified, she watched Berg sway to his feet. He had a sword stuck right through his chest, and she could see both ends of it. However, it didn't seem to be slowing him down. With a single bone-crunching backhand, he slapped a Japanese macaque against the wall, crushing its skull.

"Stop!"

His smile turned in her direction and their eyes locked. The monkeys were just an inconvenience to him. He had promised to kill her, and he intended to make good on that vow. As if in a nightmare, Victoria drew her own sword. Berg moved towards her as if moving through water, monkeys hanging from his arms and legs, weighing him down. As she watched, he reached around and pulled one of the knives from his back. He held the red, slick blade by the point, and drew his hand back, ready to throw it.

"Goodbye, Miss Valois."

Victoria flattened herself against the door. She didn't have time to access her internal clock. She'd have to rely on her natural reactions. But he moved so *fast*...

Behind him, the howler monkey leapt from the bed. Still in the air, it swung its axe. Howlers were among the largest of all monkeys, and its arms were twin cables of elastic muscle. Hearing its cry, Berg glanced around, and the blade caught him across the bridge of his nose. The top of his skull came away like the top of a boiled egg, and he collapsed, dragged down and submerged beneath a tide of biting, clawing, stabbing beasts.

CHAPTER SIX
KISHKINDHA

BALI SAT CROSS-LEGGED on a sun-warmed rock, waiting for the leopard. His tail twitched. He knew the big cat was stalking him, and had been for some minutes now. He was at the upper limit of the jungle, where the trees grew sparse and petered out like a green wave breaking against the volcano's curving flank. Below, he could see most of the island and, beyond its treetops, the narrow strait dividing the island from the rest of the peninsula. Sunlight danced on the water. A couple of miles from where he sat, smoke rose from a clearing, marking the position of the stockade where the other members of the monkey army, gathered and brought here by Ack-Ack Macaque and the *Sun Wukong*, awaited him.

Humans, it seemed, had uplifted at least one primate on every parallel world visited by the airship. As soon as they had the technology, they created an intelligent ape or monkey. Privately, Bali wondered if they did it because they were lonely. Once, the humans had shared their worlds with other intelligent hominids, such as *Homo erectus* and the Neanderthals; but then those species had died away, leaving *Homo sapiens* home alone, with only themselves to talk to.

It must have been terribly lonely for them, he thought. No wonder their stories were filled with fairies, pixies, vampires and other half-human creatures.

But was that loneliness what had driven them to upgrade other primates?

Life for most of the uplifted creatures had not been pleasant. Some bore lingering pain from the surgery that had increased their intelligence; others simply pined for more of their kind, or for a release from captivity. Some, like Ack-Ack Macaque, had been plugged into virtual reality environments, such as games or targeting systems; while others lived out their days in laboratories or cages.

Now, thanks to Ack-Ack Macaque, they were all free. They had this island, which they'd named after the monkey kingdom in the story of the *Ramayana*; and they had each other. And, while Ack-Ack Macaque was away with the *Sun Wukong*, Bali had command. In the big guy's absence, he was the alpha male.

And so it had fallen to him to kill the leopard.

He could feel it behind him in the shadows, and imagine it edging closer and closer, its belly brushing the leaves of the forest floor, haunches trembling, muscles coiled and ready to strike, spotted fur quivering.

Not today, mon ami.

In his lap, Bali held an automatic pistol and a hunting knife. All he needed was to draw the animal to him, and bring it close enough for a clean shot, or a deft strike with the blade.

The beast had been hanging around the camp for a couple of weeks. In that time, it had taken a lamb and half a dozen chickens. Then, last night, it had attacked and killed one of the chimps as they were out gathering firewood. How it got onto the island, nobody knew. Bali's best guess was that it must have swum across the strait from the mainland, but he had no idea what could have driven it to attempt such an arduous feat, unless it had been drawn by cooking smells and the promise of fresh monkey meat.

He glanced down at the knife in his left hand. When he killed the leopard, he had decided he'd gut it and wear its skin as a trophy. He would walk back into the stockade draped in the pelt and blood of the vanquished beast. A display like that would impress the rest of the troupe, and strengthen his position as alpha. It might even convince a few of them that he should be running the show, rather than Ack-Ack Macaque. After all, where was their precious leader now that they needed him? Swanking around the multiverse in his dreadnought with the women, while the rest of them were here in the jungle, facing down predators and building a civilisation from scratch, with little in the way of luxury—and no females.

Bali felt his lips draw back from his sharp incisors. If he were in charge, things would be different. Good lord, yes. Less crude, more forward thinking, more *businesslike*. And there would be females! Even if he had to raid a zoo, he would find some.

To hell with trying to build a homeland of our own, he thought. What could be more inefficient? With their numbers and the dreadnought, they could take one by force, rather than carving it from the jungle by hand. There were so many human worlds. Surely they could find a lightly defended one that was ripe for a management takeover, with plenty of human slaves to do their bidding? After everything they'd suffered at the hands of the humans, surely they were owed a modicum of revenge, not to mention compensation?

Before being picked up by the *Sun Wukong*, Bali had been kept in a temple, chained to a wall and fed by the monks. They had taken him in following his escape from the laboratory that created him. The monks revered him as an aspect of their monkey god, Hanuman, and he'd enjoyed being pampered. Despite the chain, he had been looked after and respected, and he missed that. He had liked being a god. His grip tightened on the knife. He would be one again. When he became the true and undisputed alpha, he would fashion himself as a fearsome leopard god, falling from the skies to plunder world after world. Instead of hiding here, on an empty parallel devoid of humans, he and his brethren would avenge themselves on their creators. They would gather riches and power—and, most importantly, females—and he would be the true, one-and-only alpha, forever.

His nostrils quivered. On the breeze, he caught the barest hint of cat; a fleeting waft of spice, sweat and blood. The beast must be close now. Slowly, so as not to startle it, he rose to his feet, gun held out to his right, knife to his left, naked save for the elasticated straps of his shoulder holster.

He felt invincible.

"Okay, *mon ami*, I am here, and I am ready." His eyes swept the shadows and dapples between the trees, his ears strained for the stealthiest sound.

"Now, where are you?"

CHAPTER SEVEN
SHITS AND GIGGLES

STILL SHAKEN BY the killing frenzy in the infirmary, Victoria summoned the *Sun Wukong*'s command crew to the airship's briefing room. They sat in the front row of chairs, and she leant on the lectern before them. Outside the porthole, dusk had begun to lower.

"Okay," she said, "Let's review what we know about Nguyen."

Ack-Ack Macaque stirred in his seat.

"He's a fuck-head?"

Victoria ignored him. The gelware in her skull had been pumping sedatives into her bloodstream to calm her after the incident with Berg, and she felt lightheaded and in no mood to spar with the gruff old monkey. Instead, she nodded to K8.

"S'il te plaît?"

The white-suited teenager gave a tight smile, and unrolled a keypad. She tapped in a command and a screen lit behind Victoria. It displayed a photograph of a short, balding, middle-aged man with a stethoscope slung around his neck.

"Doctor Kenta Nguyen," K8 said, reading from her notes. "Surgeon and gelware specialist. On our parallel, he was born on the seventh of December 1989, in Osaka, Japan. Mother Japanese, father from Vietnam. He graduated from university in Tokyo in June 2014; went to work on the Human Genome Project; and then went to work for the Céleste Institute, where he helped develop soul-catcher technology and became a pioneer in the field of gelware neural prostheses."

"Blah, blah, blah." Ack-Ack Macaque made talking motions with his hands. "And then in 2059, he tried to blow up the world and turn everybody into robots. Yeah, we know the story." He sat back in his chair. "I just don't see what good talking about it's going to do. I don't need to understand the guy." He made his fingers into the shape of a gun and took aim at an imaginary target. "I just need to know *where* he is."

Victoria put her hands on her hips. "And then what are you going to do?

You just want to shoot him?"

Ack-Ack Macaque's grizzled face frowned in puzzlement.

"Well, yes." His expression split into a toothy grin. "Something like that, anyway. You know the old saying, boss: revenge is a dish best served hot, from ten thousand feet."

"You want to bomb the place?"

"I figure we cruise over and drop half a dozen missiles on the lab. That ought to do it."

"Aerial bombardment?" Victoria shook her head. "That's your answer to everything. Besides, we couldn't be sure we'd got him, and there'd be a lot of innocents caught in the explosions. No, if we're going to do this, we're going to do it face-to-face. Up close and personal. Before he dies, he's going to know who we are and why we're there to stop him."

The monkey huffed, and stuck out his bottom lip. "Then what do you suggest?"

Victoria drummed her nails on the edge of the lectern. "I suggest you take a small team and infiltrate the lab. Find Nguyen and bring him back on board."

"A quick smash and grab?"

"Precisely."

Ack-Ack Macaque stroked his hairy chin, considering. Then he shrugged.

"Okay, you got my vote. I'm happy as long as I get to wreck stuff and hurt people." He pulled out a fresh cigar and ran it under his nose, savouring the smell.

"Who will you take?"

"Lumpy and Cuddles have commando training. Erik and Fang are handy in a fight."

"*D'accord.*" Victoria folded her hands on top of the lectern. "Take them to the armoury and get what you need. We'll be in position in thirty minutes."

Ack-Ack Macaque stuck the cigar in his mouth, rose to his feet and threw her a floppy salute.

"Aye, boss." He shambled out and K8 followed him, leaving Victoria and Paul by themselves.

Victoria looked at her ex-husband.

"What?" she asked.

Paul shrugged. "Nothing."

"Don't give me that. I know that look. What's wrong?"

Paul pushed his glasses more firmly onto the bridge of his nose.

"I'm just a bit concerned, that's all."

"About what?"

He looked down at his hands.

"About killing Nguyen."

Victoria walked over and sat in the chair next to his. She thought of Berg, and shivered.

"In what sense?"

"In the moral sense." He shifted around to face her. "I mean, I know the Nguyen on our world was a bastard and all, but does that justify us killing his counterpart on *this* parallel? For all we know, the man might be innocent."

He looked so worried that Victoria felt a rush of affection, and had to consciously stop herself from putting an arm around him. She kept forgetting he was only made of light and that, if she tried to touch him, her fingers would pass right through his hologram body, saddening them both.

"I think I understand what you're saying," she said. "But you didn't see Cassius Berg. He looked exactly as he did before, with human skin over a metal skull. Which means Nguyen's pursuing the same goals he was last time. He's trying to build cyborg bodies for human brains."

Paul looked unconvinced. "But that doesn't mean he's going to try to start a nuclear war, does it?"

"We can't take that chance."

"But what if he's innocent?"

Victoria clenched her jaw. "He's not."

"How can you be so sure?"

She crossed her legs. "If he had nothing to hide, he wouldn't have sent Berg to kill me. The other me, in Paris."

"I suppose."

He still looked doubtful. She let him mull her words over for a moment, then asked, "How are you feeling otherwise?"

He gave her a wary look. "I'm fine."

"Are you sure? Because I'm counting on you to fly this thing."

He looked away. "I won't let you down."

Victoria clasped her hands on her knee.

Merde.

She took a deep breath, and made a decision.

"I'll try not to let you down, either."

"What do you mean?"

Fingers still interlocked, she tapped the ends of her thumbs together. "We won't kill him."

"Seriously?" Paul sat up straight.

Victoria exhaled. She had seen more than enough killing and death for one day—for one lifetime, even—and it disturbed her that assassinating the elderly scientist had been her default response. The man had done some terrible things on her world, but unthinkingly condemning his doppelganger to death put her on dubious moral ground.

"Seriously. Well, we'll try. If we capture him in one piece, then instead of killing him, we can stick him in the brig until we find somewhere safe to maroon him, where he can't do any harm. How about that?"

Paul swallowed.

"Thank you." He looked about to cry.

"No." Victoria gave him a smile that was part affection, part relief. Her conscience might have been asleep at its post, but his was as reliable as ever, and he'd saved her from making an irrevocable decision she might later have regretted. Killing Nguyen on this world would have made her no better than the monkeys in the infirmary, lashing out for vengeance with no thought for morals or justice. "Thank *you*."

HALF AN HOUR later, the *Sun Wukong* reached the outskirts of Paris. Ack-Ack Macaque and his team dropped from its underside, and their black parachutes flowered in the darkness. Below, the Malsight Institute was a large, smoked glass building surrounded by lawns and fountains, and a gradually emptying car park. The time was six o'clock, and workers were packing up for the day and leaving.

"Does this bring back memories, Chief?" Erik called. He was an orangutan, with arms made of sinew and covered in carrot-coloured hair.

Ack-Ack Macaque glared at him with his one good eye.

"Shut up and concentrate."

They came down in a small, square courtyard at the centre of the building. As Ack-Ack Macaque's boots hit the flagstones, he let out a grunt.

I really am getting too old for this crap.

He rolled over and hauled at the lines connecting him to his 'chute, pulling it towards him in great bundled armfuls. By the time he had it gathered, the rest of the team had done likewise, and were stuffing their 'chutes into the courtyard's fountain. He crammed his in as well, and shuffled over to a fire escape.

"Cuddles, get this open."

"Right away, Skip." The young gorilla stalked forward on his knuckles.

He was almost twice the size of Ack-Ack Macaque, and wore a gold chain and a set of specially adapted Ray-Bans. Without preamble, he punched his fist through the thin aluminum door and hauled back, ripping it from its frame.

"Good work." Ack-Ack Macaque drew his revolvers. "Now, the rest of you, inside."

He could feel his lungs heaving in his chest. He wasn't as young as he'd once been, and all those cigars had taken their toll. He was happy to let the younger primates take the lead as he followed them into a corridor lined with offices.

"All right, split up, just like we planned. Cuddles, take the first floor; Lumpy, the second; Erik, the third. I'll check out this one."

He watched them go, scattering startled office workers as they charged towards the stairwell. Then he struck a match against the doorframe and lit his cigar.

Okay.

He knew the younger monkeys thought he'd picked the ground floor in order to avoid tiring himself on the stairs, but that wasn't the reason; at least, not the *only* reason. He thought he knew Nguyen. He'd fought the man before, and had seen what a control freak he was. The old man liked to oversee everything. He wouldn't be stuck away upstairs, he'd be down here, close to his minions and machinery.

Victoria wanted Nguyen alive. Ack-Ack Macaque drew his guns. He wasn't so fussy. He'd happily plug the bastard as soon as look at him. And 'alive' didn't necessarily mean 'intact'.

He was at the corner of the building. The corridor led off in two directions. His team had gone left, towards the stairs, so he set off right. Men and women in white coats manned the offices and laboratories he passed, with pens and surgical instruments sticking from their pockets. They smelled of anesthetic and disinfectant, and cowered back when he snarled at them.

"You!" He waved one of his Colts in the face of a young man carrying a pile of box files. "Where's Nguyen?"

The files clattered to the floor and the man raised an arm.

"That way," he stammered. "In the lab. Last door, at the end."

Ack-Ack Macaque grinned around his cigar.

"Thanks, kid."

*   *   *

As HE STALKED towards the laboratory, Ack-Ack Macaque took an earpiece from his pocket and thumbed it into his left ear.

"We're inside," he said.

The earpiece hissed, and then Victoria's voice came on the line.

"Understood," she said. "Deploy the drone."

"Aye, aye."

Ack-Ack Macaque fished the drone from the pocket of his flight jacket. The tiny machine looked like a jewelled dragonfly with a lens instead of a head. He held it in the palm of his hand and bent his face in close, focusing on it with his single eye.

"Are you getting this?"

"Urgh!"

"What's the matter?"

"Don't get so close to the lens."

"What? Why not?"

"You're holding a high definition camera, and I really don't need to see the inside of your nose in that much detail."

Ack-Ack Macaque huffed, and tossed the little machine into the air. It whirred away in a clatter of miniature blade-like wings.

"Just keep it out of my way," he grumbled.

He heard gunshots and screams from the floors above, followed by the shrill of a fire alarm, and he grinned. He'd handpicked his crew for their expertise at making noise and causing chaos—and it seemed they weren't letting him down.

Ahead, the door to Nguyen's lab remained closed. He holstered one of his guns and tried the handle. Inside, the lab smelled of disinfectant, fear, and monkey shit, and Ack-Ack Macaque felt the hackles rise at the back of his neck. Until Merovech and Julie had busted him out, he'd lived in a lab just like this one, strapped into a couch with wires plugged into his brain.

How many monkeys had he since rescued from a similar plight? It must be getting on for a hundred and fifty now, and yet the smell, with its overtones of surgery and terror, still bothered him. It was a sharp, chemical reminder that he was an artificial, made thing—a prototype weapon manufactured as a proof of concept, and then plugged into a video game because, hey, waste not, want not.

He stepped through the door, and the drone buzzed past his shoulder. It rose to the ceiling and scanned the room. The lab was a long, narrow and brightly lit room, with an adjoining office. Workbenches lined the walls; medical equipment stood on stainless steel trolleys; and six couches stood in a row down the centre of the room, each with its own simian occupant. Ack-Ack Macaque gripped his guns. At the far end of the lab, two white-coated technicians were bending over the last couch, ministering to the monkey strapped into it. One was a tall, blond man; the other was, unmistakably, Nguyen.

"Hey."

They looked up. For a second, their mouths hung open and their eyes popped. Then the big guy went for his hip pocket and Ack-Ack Macaque shot him. The Colts were deafening in the narrow laboratory. The blond took two bullets in the chest and crashed backwards against a workbench, scattering scalpels and other instruments.

Ack-Ack Macaque and Doctor Nguyen regarded each other through a blue haze of gun smoke and tobacco.

"Remember," Victoria buzzed in Ack-Ack Macaque's ear, "we want him alive."

Ack-Ack swore under his breath. It would be so easy to waste this fucker. All he had to do was pull the trigger...

But then he'd get Victoria mad at him, and the last thing he felt like was an earful from her. With a snarl, he lowered his guns.

"Get your coat, doc; you're coming with me."

Nguyen straightened his back. A bloody catheter dangled, forgotten, from his fingers. With his other hand, he gestured to the sedated primates on their couches.

"You are one of mine?"

"Yeah, something like that."

"And you wish revenge?'

"Me, and the rest of these poor bastards."

The old man swallowed visibly, then narrowed his eyes. "I don't remember you." His lip curled. "But what does it matter? Stupid monkey. You should be thanking me."

"For what?"

"I made you a man."

"Big whoop." Ack-Ack Macaque chewed his cigar from one side of his mouth to the other. Nguyen's fists were clenched at his side. The elderly doctor drew himself up to his full height.

"I gave you the gift of consciousness. I raised you to sentience."

"And I'm supposed to be grateful?"

"I don't care if you are or not. I did what I did for the betterment of mankind, and I have no regrets. Can you say as much, I wonder?"

Ack-Ack Macaque waggled his guns.

"Shut the fuck up. You're coming with me."

"You're insane."

"Yeah, and whose fault is that?" Pointing the gun in his right hand at the bridge of Nguyen's nose, Ack-Ack Macaque holstered the one in his left. If he was going to have to drag Nguyen out, that was fine. He might even bounce him off a few walls while he was at it, just for shits and giggles. With a growl, he reached out. But, before his leathery fingers could close around the knot of the old man's tie, he heard the flat snap of a pistol shot and Nguyen fell, poleaxed by a round to the left temple.

VICTORIA SCRAMBLED TO her feet.

"What the hell was that?" She was on the bridge of the *Sun Wukong*. Paul's image stood beside her; K8 sat at a console, controlling the dragonfly drone. In front of them, the main screen displayed the feed coming through from the drone's camera. Doctor Nguyen lay slumped in a splatter of blood. Ack-Ack Macaque crouched behind one of the couches, Colts in hand.

"Get the rest of the boys down here," he snarled.

"What's happening?" Victoria shouted. "Who's shooting?"

The monkey didn't reply. He stood upright and fired both guns through the open office door, then ducked back as his shots were answered.

"Fuck and blast," he muttered, crouching.

"Can you see who it is?"

"No, they're behind something. See if you can get the drone in there."

Victoria glanced at K8.

"Do it."

"Aye." The young woman's fingernails tick-tacked the keys of her console, and the view on the screen trembled. Slowly, the drone advanced, keeping close to the ceiling and out of the line of fire.

"What sensors do you have on that thing?"

"We have everything. Microphones, thermometers, spectrometers, the works."

"Turn them all on."

Another click of the keyboard, and a dozen sub-windows opened around the edges of the display, showing the same view filtered through the drone's various onboard instruments. Victoria leant forwards, squinting at them. Some were dark and fuzzy, others simply readouts of temperature or humidity. When she reached the infrared view, she stopped.

"*Merde.*"

Something in the office glowed like a miniature sun, swamping all other heat signatures.

"Some sort of machinery?" Paul ventured.

Victoria shrugged. Whatever it was, it seemed to be getting steadily hotter.

"We are picking up some noise," K8 said.

"Let's hear it."

A rising whine filled the bridge.

"That's coming from the office?"

"As far as we can tell."

Victoria touched the headset attached to her ear. "Hey, monkey-man. Are you hearing this?'

"Yeah." He had to raise his voice. "Sounds like they're firing up a jet engine in there."

Paul put a hand to his bristled chin. "I don't like this at all. You should get him out of there."

A sickly white glow shone from the office door, casting a beam across the laboratory floor.

"Yes," Victoria said, "I think you're right. I'll—"

Ack-Ack Macaque leapt to his feet. In one fluid move he vaulted the row of couches and, firing both Colts, charged the light.

"*Merde!*" Victoria turned and barked at K8. "Get the drone in there, now!"

The picture on the screen tipped forward as the dragonfly dived at the open door. For a second, everything disintegrated into a whirling medley of gunshots and bright light. Then she caught a glimpse of an armed figure silhouetted against the threshold of a bright, circular portal. It was a woman. Whoever she was, she looked up as the drone clattered into the room, taking her eyes from the door. As she did so, Ack-Ack Macaque barrelled into the room at full pelt, and shoulder-charged her. He hit like a rugby player, knocking them both into the gaping portal. Victoria had an instant to see their bodies puff apart in bursts of dust, and then the screen flashed white, and died.

She cried out in frustration.

"Power spike," K8 said, voice flat. "Drone's dead."

CHAPTER EIGHT
A NECKLACE OF LEOPARD'S TEETH

THE SUN WUKONG loomed over the jungle, its armoured glass bow moored to a mast on the summit of the island's volcano. In its briefing room, Victoria Valois stood with her arms crossed. Her tunic hung open and her scabbard hung crooked. K8, Cuddles and Erik sat in the front row of the theatre-style seats. Paul's image hovered at the back, glowing gently in the low light. Wrapped in an animal pelt, Bali leant against the door, a twine necklace of leopard's teeth draped around his neck.

Nobody wanted to be the first to speak.

Finally, Victoria walked over to the brass porthole and considered the blue ocean stretching away to the horizon. Below, between the trees, she could see the thatched roofs of the log cabins in the monkeys' stockade.

"So," she said, hugging her upper arms, "did we salvage *anything*?" She looked questioningly at them all, one after another—all except Cuddles. One thing she'd learned about male gorillas was that, no matter what, you never looked them in the eye. Not unless you wanted your arms ripped off and your head stomped into paste.

Erik coughed and squirmed in his seat. "Not much. By the time we got into the lab, there was no trace of the Skipper, and the machine had pretty much melted. It must've had a destruct setting." From his shoulder bag he pulled something sticky and covered in dried black crusts of flaky blood. He held it pinched between thumb and forefinger in much the same way Victoria imagined he'd have held the tail of a dead, plague-sodden rat.

"We did get this, though." He stretched his lower lip over his upper. "It's the doctor's soul-catcher."

Victoria glanced at the dangled fronds of hair-fine wire, and then at the bayonet sheathed in the orangutan's belt. She didn't need to ask how they'd extracted the device from Nguyen's skull.

"Is it intact?"

Erik dropped it onto the empty seat beside his, and wiped his long, hairy orange fingers on the bare plastic arm.

"We pulled it out by the root, Captain."

"Anything else?' She addressed the room. "Anything that can tell us what the hell happened back there?"

After a moment, K8 raised a hand.

"We've been analysing the drone's telemetry."

"And?"

The teenager stood and walked over to the wall screen. She tapped the upper right hand corner, and it flashed into life.

"These graphs represent readings taken from the machine immediately prior to its self-destruction." Her index finger traced a sharp upward curve. "As you can see, there's a spike here, indicating an energy profile similar to that of the *Sun Wukong*'s jump engines."

Victoria raised an eyebrow. The lines and words on the screen were squiggles to her.

"You think it might work the same way?"

"Almost definitely."

Victoria blinked away a mental image of Ack-Ack Macaque's body apparently exploding into dust. "Then he could still be alive?"

K8 gave a small, tight smile. "We think so."

"How do we find him?"

The young woman returned her attention to the screen. "There's a clue in the visual footage." She tapped a few commands and the graphs disappeared, replaced by a blurred close-up of the black-clad figure in the office, caught in the instant she glanced up at the dragonfly. Victoria walked up to the screen, screwing her eyes into slits in an attempt to glean as much detail as she could.

"She looks familiar, but..."

Behind the figure, the portal presented as a disc of shimmering light.

K8 said, "We can enhance the image."

She pressed a control and a line moved across the screen from left to right. As it tightened the pixels and sharpened the picture, Victoria felt her eyes widen with surprise. She put a hand to her chest. Behind her, everybody started talking and shouting and gibbering at once. She waved an arm to shush them. Even though the woman's hair had been closely cropped, and she now wore a coal-black military uniform, the face on the screen was undoubtedly and unmistakably that of Lady Alyssa Célestine.

K8 said, "It must be another version of her, another iteration, from another parallel."

"Can we follow them?"

"We don't know where they went. They could be on any one of a billion possible timelines."

"So, we've lost him?"

K8 blanked the screen and looked down at her white shoes. "In all likelihood, yes. We're afraid so."

The temperature seemed to drop a couple of degrees. Victoria rubbed the bridge of her nose. "I hate this parallel world shit."

Across the room, Bali straightened up. With a shrug of his leopardskin-covered shoulders, he pushed himself away from the doorframe against which he'd been leaning.

"He's gone?"

Victoria didn't answer. She couldn't trust herself to speak. Bali seemed agitated. His bare feet shuffled on the steel deck.

"Then we should choose a new leader," he said.

Erik looked him up and down. The orangutan's eyes narrowed. "And I suppose you want the job?"

Bali drew himself up. "Who else is there?" He cast around, as if looking for someone to challenge him.

Victoria took a deep breath. "You know who else."

"The old lady?" Bali frowned as if genuinely puzzled. "Surely you can't be serious?"

"She should be consulted."

"She's a psychopath."

"Nevertheless, Ack-Ack trusts her."

"And what gives you the right to decide that, *human*?" Bali fingered his necklace of teeth. "You may have been a captain on your own airship, but that doesn't confer any authority here. You're in Kishkindha now, and don't you forget it. This is our world, not yours."

Victoria flexed her fists. Her stomach felt hollow.

"Half of this airship's mine," she said defiantly. "Ack-Ack and I had a deal."

The monkey's lip curled. He held her stare. Heart in her throat, she wondered if he meant the eye contact as insolence or direct physical challenge. He was shorter than her, but wiry and powerful, the same as Ack-Ack Macaque, and she honestly didn't know if she could beat him.

Perhaps the fear showed in her face. Maybe it was in her scent or body language. Bali's eyes widened. His lips peeled back, exposing his incisors. Then, just as Victoria was tensing for an attack, he dropped onto all fours and, with a snort of triumph and disgust, knuckle-walked out of the room, tail held high and proud.

* * *

THE 'OLD LADY' occupied a cabin at the rear of the *Sun Wukong*'s main gondola, guarded by a gibbon with a shotgun. As Victoria approached, the gibbon gave a languid, long-limbed salute, and opened the door.

Victoria stepped through. The room smelled of lavender, incense, and musty books. The Founder was sitting in a wicker chair, using an e-reader in the light from the cabin's porthole. She wore a lacy black Victorian dress. Pearls clung to her hairy throat. Hearing the door, she looked up at Victoria and adjusted her monocle. "Good evening, Captain Valois."

"Miss Haversham."

The Founder clicked her tongue in irritation.

"Don't be facetious, dear, it doesn't suit you." She smoothed down the folds of her skirt. "Leave that sort of thing to our mutual friend."

Victoria helped herself to a chair. "It's him I've come to talk to you about."

The female monkey made a steeple of her fingers, and gave a theatrical sigh.

"What's he done *now?*"

Once, she'd been the head of the Gestalt movement. For the past two years, she'd been confined to this room, alone with her books and her sewing, cut off from the outside world in more ways than one. The Gestalt had installed this cabin when they'd built the airship. It was designed for isolation, impervious to radio or WiFi—a place to put damaged or infected drones, where they couldn't infect the rest of the hive—and therefore perfect for imprisoning the hive's queen, to keep her out of mischief and completely incommunicado.

"He's charged off and gotten himself lost somewhere."

The Founder gave a sigh. She placed the e-reader on the arm of her chair. "How lost is 'lost'?"

As succinctly as she could, and reporting purely the facts, Victoria outlined the events at the Malsight Institute. The Founder listened, and scratched the greying hairs on her muzzle. When Victoria had finished, she said, "It's really quite simple, dear. Célestine and Nguyen were quite obviously working together. You tell me you've recovered Nguyen's soul-catcher; in which case, all you need do is interrogate the back-up it contains."

Victoria tapped her forehead.

"Of course!"

"I'm sure his ghost will be able to tell you where they've gone."

"Thank you." Victoria turned to leave, then hesitated. "There's something else."

"One is, as ever, all ears."

"Bali wants to appoint a new alpha monkey, right now. And he thinks it should be him."

The Founder put her hand to the pearls around her neck. "Bali is a child. He wants to be the head of the pack but he has no appreciation of what it means to be a leader."

"And Ack-Ack does?"

The monkey smiled. "No, not really. But he never *wanted* to be a leader—which, in my book, makes him ideally suited to the job."

"So, what do we do?"

"About Bali? Well, dear, there's not much I can do from here." The Founder peered around at the walls of her cabin. "Now is there?"

"I can't let you out."

"Why ever not, dear? We're in the monkey kingdom now. There are no Gestalt here. I've no one to interact with. What harm can I do?"

Victoria raised an eyebrow.

"I'm sure you could do plenty, if you put your mind to it. And anyway, there's K8 to consider."

"She's still one of the hive?"

"Only just. We're trying to rehabilitate her."

"And you don't think I'd be a good influence?"

"Would you?"

The Founder raised her chin. "In the hive," she said haughtily, "K8 shared her every thought with thousands and thousands of individuals; and they shared theirs with her. Now, she's alone in her head." She paused to adjust her monocle. "I know something of that pain. And besides, you need my help with Bali. I can talk to him, make him see reason."

"Why would Bali listen to you?"

"Because I'm the alpha female."

"You're the *only* female."

"Same difference." The monkey frowned. Her lips became a horizontal slash. "And besides, there's something else."

"*Quoi?*"

The Founder gripped the arms of her chair and heaved herself up into a standing position, revealing a bulge in her midriff that stretched the lace of her dress. She put a hand to it.

"I'm with child."

Victoria spluttered. "Y-you're pregnant?"

"Very much so."

"But how? I mean... *Who*?"

"I think we know the answers to both those questions."

"Ack-Ack?"

"Indeed."

"Does he know?"

"Of course not."

"Then why are you telling me?"

The monkey exhaled regretfully. "Mostly because I'm not going to be able to hide it much longer. And besides, it could be to our mutual advantage."

"How so?"

"Family bonds are important, Captain, especially in a troupe with only one female. In human terms, I'm carrying the heir to the throne. I expect most of the macaques will side with me. Many of them are other iterations of Ack-Ack, close enough genetically to recognise the child as kin."

"Including Bali?"

"We'll have to see." Her face became thoughtful. "His ambition clouds his judgment. But even he must realise that, without children, Kishkindha's future looks bleak."

Victoria shook her head and smiled. "I still can't believe that you and Ack-Ack... I mean, I knew he spent a lot of time down here talking to you, but I never realised you were, you know. Doing It."

The Founder glowered through her monocle.

"I'll have you know that it only happened the once."

"And you got pregnant first time?"

The elderly monkey straightened her dress and turned to the porthole. "What can I say? The boy's an exceptional shot."

Victoria put a hand to her mouth to stifle a smile. "But you're two hundred years old. I wouldn't have thought—"

"Neither would I, but it appears we were both wrong. Apparently, the treatments I've taken to retain my youth have been more effective than even I could have suspected." Still at the porthole, she looked back over her shoulder. "So, do we have an agreement, Captain?"

Victoria gripped the pommel of her sheathed sword.

"I turn you loose?"

"And in return, I calm things down in the monkey camp."

"And K8?"

"I help her too."

Victoria let out a long sigh.

I know I'm going to regret this.

"*Oui, d'accord.*"

"Is that a yes, Captain?"

"As long as you keep Bali out of my face."

The Founder placed her palm against the porthole's glass. "And in return, I'm free to go down to the surface, to walk in the jungle, to feel the earth beneath my feet and the sun on my face?"

"I suppose." Absently, Victoria scratched at the long ridge of scar tissue at her temple. "But I'll need to know where you are at all times."

"Naturally."

"You'll be on probation."

"I'd expect nothing less."

"Fine, then."

The Founder gave a courteous nod. "Thank you, Captain. And not just from me." She gave her distended abdomen a gentle and affectionate pat. "But from these two, also."

CHAPTER NINE
IN VIRTUAL VERITAS

K8 DIDN'T HAVE time to create an entirely new virtual environment, so she stole one, lifting the code from a popular combat game. Looking over her shoulder, Victoria made a face.

"An oil rig?"

"It's the best we could do on short notice."

"Is Paul ready?"

"We're loading him in now." K8 entered a command and Paul's image appeared on the rig's helipad. Victoria saw that he'd dressed for the part. In his olive green combat fatigues, black beret and silvered sunglasses, he looked like a South American revolutionary.

K8 donned a headset and passed another to Victoria.

"You can speak to him through this," she said. She turned back to the screen and pulled her mike closer to her mouth. "Okay, Paul, we're going to load in Nguyen's back-up in a moment. First, there are a few things you need to know."

Paul walked to the edge of the helipad and leaned over, looking at the gantries and waves below. The rig was in a rendering of the North Sea, out of sight of land. A stiff wind blew from the northeast, ruffling his clothes.

"I'm listening," he said.

"This might be a sim, but it's based on real world physics. Things work the same in there as they do out here. So, don't try to walk off the edge of the rig or anything stupid like that."

Paul stepped back from the edge. "Gotcha."

"Also, you'll be able to feel pain."

"Jesus." Paul flinched. "What kind of game *is* this?"

"A hyper-realistic combat game. Special forces versus oil pirates."

"Sounds dreadful."

"Actually, it's pretty cool. But the point is, if you thump Nguyen, he's going to feel it."

"Okay." Paul shivered and wrapped his arms across his chest. "Couldn't you have found somewhere a bit warmer?"

K8 smiled and glanced at Victoria.

"The only alternative was a magical fairy castle, and we didn't think that sent out the right message."

"What?" Paul grumbled. "That we're bloodthirsty torturers who'll kill him if he doesn't cooperate?"

"Exactly."

"I don't know if I can go through with this."

Victoria activated her mike.

"You won't really be hurting him," she said reassuringly. "Remember, he's just a bunch of pixels."

"Yeah, but so am I."

"You'll be fine. Just remember why you're doing it, and try your best."

Beside her, K8's index finger clicked a key.

"We're uploading Nguyen now," the girl said.

Pixels rippled in the simulation, and the old man appeared in the centre of the helipad, looking much as he had in the lab. He wore a white coat over a blue business suit, a striped tie, and a pair of horn-rimmed spectacles. He stood, blinking in the sunlight, one arm raised to shade his eyes.

"Okay, Paul," she whispered. "You're on."

PAUL'S EYES WERE still on the slate-grey horizon, his thoughts lost in the simulated distance. At the sound of Victoria's voice, he gave a start.

Where am I?

Oh yes, Nguyen.

He cleared his throat and pushed back his shoulders.

"Welcome, Doctor."

Nguyen ignored him. He was peering around at the rig's pipes and derrick.

"Crude."

"I beg your pardon?"

The doctor waved an arm at his surroundings. "The simulation. It's very crude. I expected something far more sophisticated."

Behind his mirrored shades, Paul raised an eyebrow. "You were *expecting* to be killed?"

"Not at all." The old man looked over the top of his glasses like a disappointed schoolteacher. "But the whole point of wearing a soul-catcher is that, if you do die, you anticipate revival." Nguyen frowned. "And I expected to be revived somewhere altogether more luxurious than this."

"Well, I'm sorry to disappoint you."

Nguyen's expression soured. "You're not one of Célestine's people, are you?"

"I'll ask the questions, Doctor Nguyen."

"No." The man gave a small, tight shake of the head. "I don't think so."

Paul opened and closed his mouth. In his ear, he heard Victoria come on the line.

"Tell him to cooperate, or you'll torture him."

Paul grimaced. He drew a deep breath.

"Look, Doctor. You'd better answer our questions, or I'll hurt you." Even to his own ears, he sounded hesitant. To try to reinforce the point, he tapped the leather holster dangling from the webbing belt at his waist.

The corner of Nguyen's mouth twisted in a skewed smile. "No, I don't believe you will."

"Why not?"

"Because I've always been a very good judge of character and you, my young friend, you're not the type."

"You don't know anything about me."

The old man held up a gnarled finger. "Ah, but you're wrong. I know you very well. Or rather, I know the version of you that lives on my world. As a matter of fact, he's on my surgical team."

Paul felt his stomach flip, as if he was riding a plane in turbulence.

"He's still alive?"

"Of course, why shouldn't he be?" Nguyen removed his spectacles and regarded Paul with narrowed eyes. "Ah, I see." He gave a nod of understanding. "You are dead. You are a back-up."

The words were like icicles in Paul's gut.

"So are you," he blurted.

Nguyen shook his head sorrowfully. "Alas, I surmised as much. Tell me, how did I die?"

"You were shot."

"By your people?"

Paul forced a smile. "By Alyssa Célestine."

Nguyen sighed. For a moment he looked old and genuinely sad. "How... disappointing."

"And now I need you to tell me how to find her."

"Ah, so she got away, did she?"

"She fell through some kind of portal." Paul drew his gun. "And she took a friend of mine with her."

"I see."

"Will you help me?"

"Probably not."

A cold wind blew across the platform. High above, gulls cried.

"Then you leave me no choice." Paul raised his weapon.

"What are you going to do, shoot me?" Nguyen chuckled. "What good will it do here? I have already *been* shot."

Paul levelled the gun and swallowed. It was a light, compact pistol.

"This is your last chance," he said, voice wavering.

Nguyen laughed at him.

"You can't kill me," he said.

Paul clenched his jaw. His finger tightened on the trigger.

"Maybe not," he admitted. The gun fired with a savage jolt. Nguyen fell to his knees. His hands went to his stomach. Blood welled between his fingers. "But I'll bet that hurts."

The old man groaned.

"I need the coordinates of Célestine's world," Paul insisted. Nguyen looked up at him helplessly. Blood dribbled from his lips.

"What's the matter?" Paul asked. "Can't you talk?"

Nguyen shook his head. He opened his mouth and retched ropes of thick, red gore. Disgusted, Paul stepped forward and pressed the gun barrel to the doctor's temple. The hot metal sizzled against the old man's mottled skin.

"Better luck next time."

VICTORIA WATCHED AS Paul pulled the trigger. She really hadn't believed he'd actually do it, and she didn't know whether to be relieved or horrified.

Beside her, K8's fingernails rattled against the console's keypad.

"Okay," she said, "we're re-spawning Nguyen in five, four, three, two…"

DOCTOR NGUYEN REAPPEARED at the exact centre of the helipad to find himself standing astride his own dead body, facing his killer, who brandished a still-smoking pistol.

"We can do this all day," Paul said. "And it's going to hurt just as badly every time."

Nguyen put a hand to his stomach. Slowly, he looked up to meet his own reflection in Paul's mirrored lenses.

"Perhaps we could come to some form of arrangement?"

Blam!

Nguyen tottered back on his heels, half-blinded by the muzzle flash. A hot, red pain skewered his chest. His pulse roared in his ears.

"Sorry," he heard Paul say. "No deals."

"RE-SPAWNING IN FIVE, four, three..."

CHAPTER TEN
CLAP OF SILENCE

PAUL'S HOLOGRAM STOOD at the edge of the wooden verandah. He'd changed out of his military fatigues, back into his Hawaiian shirt and white lab coat. His head was down, looking out through the *Sun Wukong*'s nose at the island of Kishkindha, and his hands were in the pockets of his jeans. The sun slanting in from the glass panels above rendered his peroxide blond hair a dazzling white.

"Are you okay?" Victoria walked over to stand beside him.

He shook his head. "I don't know."

She gripped the bamboo rail. "Look, I'm really sorry. I expected him to give up much sooner than that."

"Stubborn old git." Paul looked ready to spit. "I think he was hoping I'd get sick of it before he did."

Victoria wanted to hug him. "Is there anything I can do? I mean, I can't offer you a stiff drink or anything, but if there's something…"

"I'll be all right." His fingers worried at the gold stud in his ear. "I just need some time. I just need to forget."

"It *was* worth it, you know."

"Was it?" Paul kicked the toe of one trainer against the back of the other.

"He told us how to find Ack-Ack."

A shrug. "Yes, I suppose."

"Come on." Victoria tried to sound cheerful. "The monkey would have done the same for you."

"Would he?" Paul's shoulders slumped even further.

"Yes, of course he would." Victoria smiled. "Only more so."

They stood side by side, looking down at the steep, tree-covered slopes of the volcano and the clustered huts of the monkey village. After a few minutes, Paul said, "I want to go home."

Victoria looked at him. He sounded like a lost child, and she wanted desperately to take him in her arms.

"I'm serious," he continued, as if she'd spoken. "As soon as we've got the monkey back, I want to go home, to our world, to our London. I want to see my flat again."

Victoria bit her lip, all attempts at forced jollity abandoned.

"*Pourquoi?*"

Paul looked up at the sky and clicked his tongue behind his teeth.

"I don't think I have much time left, and I'd rather be somewhere familiar, somewhere I remember, when it runs out. I don't want to die in a strange place."

Victoria felt her eyes prickle. Her vision swam.

"Okay," she said.

"You promise?"

"Whatever you want, whatever I can do."

Paul walked over to the edge of the potted jungle. A blue butterfly flapped between the trees.

"And I want you to promise me something else," he said.

"Anything."

He stopped beside a vine, and tried to cup his hand beneath the bloom of a large white flower, but his hologram fingers passed through its petals without disturbing them.

"When I'm gone, I want you to go back to the world where we left Cole and his daughter."

"The one we've just come from?" Victoria shook her head. "After all the chaos we've just caused, I don't think I'd be very welcome."

"Nevertheless, you have to go back," Paul maintained. "Sneak in, go in disguise, anything."

Arms folded, Victoria walked over to him.

"But why?"

Paul's hand dropped from the flower.

"Nguyen said that the Paul on his world still lived." He gave her a sad, sly look. "And we already know Berg killed the Victoria that was there."

"What are you saying?"

"Do I have to spell it out? You'll be a Victoria without a Paul; he'll be a Paul without a Victoria. You'll need each other. You'll need to be together."

Victoria's cheeks burned. A tear ran down her face.

"No," she said.

Paul looked crestfallen. "I think you should do it, for me."

Victoria shook her head again. "No, it wouldn't be the same. He wouldn't be you."

Paul pursed his lips. "He'd be close. Maybe too close to tell apart. Cole managed to find another version of his dead wife. Why can't you do the same with me?"

Victoria felt her cheeks flush. "I don't want another version, you idiot. I want you."

"I'm just a recording."

"You're more than that!" She paused, letting the anger subside. "You've changed, you've grown." He was now, she thought with a twinge of guilt, a far more caring and considerate person than he'd ever been while alive. Dreadful as it was to admit to herself, his death had, in some ways, improved their relationship beyond all recognition and, after everything they'd been through over the past three years, she couldn't imagine starting again with a stranger—even a stranger with his face and mannerisms.

"No." She wiped her eyes on the back of her sleeve and sniffed. She hadn't cried properly in years, and she wasn't about to start now. "No, that's not going to happen. You're my Paul, and I don't want anybody else." She swallowed down the lump in her throat. "I'm not going to lose you."

He watched her as she straightened the collar of her tunic, brushed the medals into place, and gripped the pommel of her sword.

"Now, pull yourself together," she said, straightening her back, unsure if she was talking to him or herself. "We've got a monkey to rescue." She walked back to the edge of the verandah and looked out at the island. "Are the crew all aboard?"

Paul joined her.

"The Founder recalled them as soon as we had the coordinates."

"She's still here?" After the monkey's long detention, Victoria had expected her to be down on the ground, enjoying the daylight and open space.

"She's as interested in finding Ack-Ack as we are."

"Very well. Sound the alarm. We jump in thirty seconds."

"Thirty *seconds*?"

"There's no telling what sort of trouble he's in," Victoria said. "The sooner we find him, the better."

Paul gave a nod. He clicked his fingers and alarms wailed in the corridors and open spaces beyond the indoor jungle.

"I'm going to bring the engines online," he said. He became very still, like a figure in a paused video, and Victoria knew his attention had moved elsewhere, focused on the *Sun Wukong*'s navigation systems. She looked down, over the bamboo rail, to where dark machines bulked in the verandah's shadow. As the power rose, she felt the vibration through her hands and feet.

"Five," Paul's voice said over the ship-wide address system. "Four."

Blue static danced over the machines.

"Three."

A rising whine came from below, building rapidly, like the sound of an approaching train. Victoria braced herself.

"Two."

The airship's skin crackled with a green aurora.

"One."

Victoria's ears pulsed with a noise beyond hearing: a silent detonation. She felt her stomach turn itself inside out.

And they were gone.

Message Received From Mars Probe?

LONDON 17/11/2062 – Government sources are staying tight-lipped this evening regarding earlier reports of a possible message from the surface of Mars.

First mention of the message came at 04:20 GMT this morning, when an anonymous operator at the Parkes Observatory in Australia posted a report on the observatory's website, as well as on a number of online message boards, claiming to have received a radio message from the Céleste probe. This report has since been taken down, and all references to it have been deleted.

At 06:40, NASA's press office released a statement saying that they were monitoring the situation and, while 'an anomalous signal' had been received, it was 'most likely natural in origin', and 'no cause for alarm'.

Céleste Technologies launched the probe three years ago, to coincide with celebrations to mark the centenary of the union of Great Britain and France. However the company, which was owned by the Duchess of Brittany, was disbanded following her foiled plot to assassinate her husband, King William V, and seize control of the Franco-British throne. The controversial probe reached the Red Planet yesterday, carrying a cargo of allegedly stolen 'souls'.

When it was launched, Céleste Technologies claimed the probe carried only scientific instruments, but according to recently unearthed documents, the probe actually carried 'back-up' personality recordings of the Duchess and other high-ranking members of Céleste Technologies staff, as well as several hundred personalities harvested from former employees, including some from murder victims. In addition, it also carried machinery capable of turning material from the Martian soil into cyborg bodies designed to house those stored personalities.

A spokesperson for the ESA said, "Mars is 225 million miles from the Earth. Even if these cyborgs exist, and I'm very far from being convinced that they do, there's almost nothing they could do to threaten us from that distance."

However, inside sources tell us the agency will be allocating additional funding to its experimental nuclear engine programme, designed to create boosters capable of pushing craft through interplanetary space.

When confronted with this information, the ESA spokesperson said, "While it is true that the project exists, and a number of test engines have been built, we have neither the resources nor the funding to construct a spacecraft capable of making the journey to Mars."

Read more | Like | Comment | Share

Related Stories:

Parallel worlds: How likely are we to be invaded again?

The King cancels royal visit to Canada.

Is there life on Mars?

Troubled 'Ack-Ack Macaque' film to premiere at Cannes.

Crew of the Tereshkova declared officially 'lost'.

CHAPTER ELEVEN
TOUGH TO KILL

ACK-ACK MACAQUE TOOK shelter in the front room of a burned-out cottage, and peered through a broken window at the bridge. If he was right, the river it spanned was the Seine, and he was a few kilometres south of Paris. He could see a small town on the far bank, and a distant church tower. At each end of the bridge, barbed wire had been strewn across the road. The middle section of the bridge had collapsed into the water, leaving a tangled mess of girders and concrete. If he could somehow get across, he might be able to shake off his pursuers. Even a temporary reprieve would give him time to take stock, to look around and figure out how he'd get a message to Victoria. He was sure she'd be looking for him, but had no idea how she'd find him. Even if she somehow traced him to this new world, how would she know where he was hiding, and how could he let her know without giving his position away to the cyborgs on his trail?

He shivered, and pulled his sodden jacket tighter. The cottage smelled of damp and ashes. A few sticks of charred furniture remained. Every time he moved his feet, his boots crunched on shards of broken glass and crockery. Outside, rain fell from a bruised sky, pocking the surface of the river. The wind whipped dead leaves across the road. Thunder rumbled in the overcast.

When he'd woken up this morning, getting trapped in a post-apocalyptic wasteland hadn't been high on his list of things to do—and yet, here he was. One instant he'd been charging the figure in the office, keeping low to avoid bullets. The next, he'd been rolling and sprawling on the shiny white floor of a different laboratory, on a different world altogether. The black-clad version of Célestine lay beside him on the tiles, winded, sucking in air. Behind them, the portal died, its light sputtering out like a dying candle. For long moments, Ack-Ack Macaque lay looking up at the strip lights. Then a squad of soldiers entered the room and he took flight, leaping through a window and hurling himself away, into the ruins of an industrial park.

Now, hours later, he was wet, cold and hungry, and the bastards were still chasing him.

"I should have stood and fought," he grumbled, but he knew he couldn't have won. The soldiers hadn't been human. Each had displayed the unnaturally smooth features, the waxy, sepia-coloured skin and tall, graceful builds he remembered from the last time he'd tangled with one of Nguyen's cyborgs, back on his own timeline. They were human back-ups running on gelware brains, housed inside bodies equipped with titanium skulls and carbon fibre skeletons. One of them had been tough to kill; a whole squad would have been next to impossible. And so he'd run, and kept running.

Now, he needed food, ammunition and allies, and he needed time to think, to work out where he was and how he could find his friends—but he couldn't do any of that until he got away from his pursuers.

He'd skirted several villages and suburbs, crossed half a dozen major roads, and had yet to meet a single human. Where was everybody? Thunder cracked and rolled, almost directly overhead. He could feel the rumble of it in his chest. He scratched at the leather patch covering his left eye socket, and yawned. If his geography was correct, the forest of Sénart lay a kilometre or so east of the river and, if he could only get to the trees, they'd never catch him.

First, though, he had to get across the river. It was too wide to swim, and looked to be running fast, swollen with rainwater. The broken bridge was his only option. It was a modern, two-lane highway with little in the way of cover, only steel railings on either side.

Well, I can't stay here.

He stood and slithered over the windowsill, back out into the rain. Nguyen's cyborgs were fast, and he'd have to keep moving if he wanted to stay ahead of them.

Before him, the bridge looked empty and wide. If he tried to run across, he'd be plainly visible to anybody on either bank, and exposed to whatever weaponry they cared to turn in his direction.

But did he have to go *over* the bridge? Seized by a sudden idea, he ran on all fours, scampering to the edge of the carriageway and down a slippery grass slope to the towpath running along the riverbank. From underneath, the bridge was made up of six long steel I-beam girders lying side by side, with the road running atop them.

Behind him, in the direction from which he'd come, he heard the *thud-thud-thud* of military helicopters.

Damn. Another moment, and he'd have been caught in the open. *Don't these guys ever stop?*

As the sounds of pursuit grew louder, he jumped up and heaved himself into the space between two of the girders. The gap was about a metre wide. From here, he'd only be visible to somebody looking up from directly beneath. With his hands and feet braced against the girders' lower flanges, and his tail whipping around to keep him balanced, he could cross the bridge on all fours without being seen by the choppers or, when he got out over the water, anyone on the bank or roadway. The collapsed middle section might prove tricky, but he'd deal with that when he reached it. Right now, his priority was to get across the river without being caught, and without falling in.

Muttering obscenities to himself, he started crawling.

CHAPTER TWELVE
VAST AND COOL

As IF OPENING an old fashioned scroll, Amy Llewellyn unrolled a flexible display screen and placed it on the desk before Merovech, weighing down its corners with coffee mugs and books.

"She's waiting for you."

Merovech exhaled. He had a hollow, churning feeling in his stomach.

"Will this be live?"

"Yes, sir. We've repurposed one of the largest dishes at Goonhilly. She wants to speak to you, and you alone." She tapped a spot at the side of the flat screen, turning on the power.

"Of course she does."

"But that doesn't mean other people won't be listening. Most of the news networks will be casting this live."

"I'm sure."

"All you have to do is touch this button here to connect, and touch it again to disconnect." She leant over him, pointing to the appropriate control, and he could smell the shampoo in her hair: a hint of mint and berries.

"This one?"

"Exactly." She straightened up and tugged down the hem of her silk blouse. "But don't forget, there'll be a delay on the signal."

"What sort of delay?"

"With Mars at the distance it is from Earth, it'll take your signal about six minutes to reach her, and another six minutes until you receive her reply."

"Twelve minutes?"

"I'm afraid it will make for rather a slow conversation." She reached into her pocket and produced a large, silver-plated stopwatch. "This will help you keep track."

Merovech took it from her and put it on the desk in front of him. His hands felt jittery.

"Okay," he said. "I think I can manage this by myself."

Amy raised her eyebrows. "Are you sure you don't want me to stay?"

"No." He waved her away. "No, thank you. I want to do this by myself."

"But, sir."

"No, really. It's better this way." He would be self-conscious enough just knowing the world's media were eavesdropping. He didn't think he could bear to have anybody else in with him, watching and listening and trying not to meet his eyes. "I'll be fine."

She put her hands on her hips.

"Well, if you're sure."

"I am."

She tugged at the cuffs of her blouse. "Then I'll be right outside. Just call me if you need me."

Merovech rose to his feet.

"I will," he said. "Thank you."

She went to the door. He listened to her heels clack on the oak floorboards. When she'd gone, he considered his reflection in the ornate, silver-framed mirror that hung on the wall above the fireplace. As he was in mourning, he'd chosen to wear a black shirt and tie with a charcoal-grey jacket. It was the same suit he'd worn to his father's funeral, three years ago. But, of course, the previous king hadn't been his *real* father—and, although she'd carried him in her womb, his mother hadn't really been his mother, either. He was a clone, cultured from one of her cells and turned male through the use of prenatal hormone injections—an artificial creature grown with the sole purpose of furthering his mother's dynastic ambitions. Now that Julie was dead, only three people in the world knew the truth, and two of them— Victoria Valois and Ack-Ack Macaque—were missing, presumed lost.

He clenched his fists and swallowed. The whole world would be listening to his conversation—at least, those agencies, governments and broadcasters with the equipment and ability to intercept signals sent to and from Mars. Would the Duchess blurt the truth? Would she accidentally or deliberately expose him as a fraud? The disclosure would be a disaster. It would undo his attempts to unite and hold together his Commonwealth in the aftermath of both the Duchess's attempted coup and the Gestalt invasion. The last thing his people needed right now was another crisis; and yet, in a deep and selfish corner of his heart, he knew the revelation—despite the accompanying scandal and disgrace—would come as something of a relief. For the first time in his life, he wouldn't be playing a part; he would have responsibility for nothing but himself.

It was all he'd ever craved: the simple freedom to be himself. But suppose he ended up in jail, or was cast out as an exile, with the media hounding his every move? From childhood, he'd been trained and shaped for leadership and, for the past three years, he'd worked hard to keep the United Kingdoms together in the face of attack and economic turbulence. To have his efforts go to waste… Well, it was more than he would be able to bear.

His thoughts turned to Julie. She had respected but never really understood his sense of duty. What would she say now? From somewhere, she'd found the courage to confront her abusive father. Surely, she'd expect the same courage from him.

With a dry mouth, he turned to the desk and held his finger over the button.

"Okay." He took a long breath. "Let's get this over with."

And let the cards fall where they may.

THE FACE THAT appeared on the screen before him bore a passing resemblance to his mother, the Duchess, but its features held the smooth, passive lines of a waxwork. Behind it, Merovech could see the rusty pink glow of a Martian sunrise.

"I'm here," he said, and reached for the stopwatch.

Twelve minutes. The lower drawer of his desk held the bottle of 15-year-old single malt that he'd been enjoying earlier, and a clean set of crystal tumblers. He picked one and sloshed in a generous measure, and then sat back to await his mother's reply. When it came, he saw her eyes narrow and her posture harden. The ghost of a smile crept across her lips. A faint breeze disturbed her synthetic hair.

"I see you survived."

Merovech felt his jaw clench.

No thanks to you.

On the screen, the Duchess raised a hand to indicate the boulder-strewn Martian plateau behind her. Tall, spindly figures bestrode the cratered surface, picking their way between the rocks. Some carried tools, others weapons. They cast long, black shadows across the regolith.

"So have we."

"What do you want, mother?" Merovech spoke without thinking, and then sighed and restarted the stopwatch. He got up from his chair and walked over to the window, and looked out at the cranes and scaffolding of a city in the process of reconstructing itself.

If she'd had her way, this would all be radioactive ash.

Twelve minutes crawled past.

"Straight to the point, I see." Was that a hint of pride in her voice? Merovech returned to his seat.

"I am calling with a proposition," the cyborg continued. "I am aware of your recent brush with the Gestalt, and I'm here to offer my protection."

"Your what?"

"You see," she continued, as yet unaware of his interruption, "I have an army of my own here. A thousand cyborgs with human minds. We are stronger, faster and more intelligent than you could ever be. Our technology is years ahead of yours, and we have all the resources of this red planet. Just think what we can achieve."

Merovech clunked his tumbler onto the desk.

"Get to the point," he muttered.

Two hundred and twenty million kilometres away, the Duchess smiled.

"I know the world listens to our conversation," she said. "And I'm here to make you this offer. Any country that pledges us their fealty and support will receive in return our protection. There are an infinite number of parallel worlds out there. Who knows when the next invasion may come?"

She paused expectantly. Merovech chewed his lower lip.

"You tried to trigger a nuclear war," he said. "And now you expect us to believe you have our best interests at heart?" He sat back and shook his head. "I don't buy it. I won't believe it."

A dozen minutes later, the Duchess laughed.

"What you believe scarcely matters, my son. The simple fact is, the Earth is under threat and only we can save it."

"Save it by destroying it, you mean? By bending it to your will?"

"Spin it however you like, Merovech, but know this: your world is being watched by intelligences greater than your own, intelligences vast and cool and deeply sympathetic. Spurn us at your peril."

She fell silent. Merovech cleared his throat.

"Is that a threat, mother?"

Twelve minutes later, the Duchess narrowed her eyes. "Every carrot has a stick, my son. When we return to Earth—and return we shall—the weapons we will have built to defend our supporters will be turned against those who have denied us." Her eyes flicked up and to the right, as if consulting a display he couldn't see. "You, and all the nations of the Earth, have one hour to decide. Our forces grow by the minute. Within days, we'll have weapons capable of reaching the Earth. Join us now, or suffer the consequences."

CHAPTER THIRTEEN
CARBON FIBRE BONES

IN THE COLD grey light of a damp false dawn, Victoria stood at the edge of the village, her thin frame wrapped in an old army greatcoat like one of the ones the Commodore used to wear in the winter. Leaves blew around her feet, which were wrapped in rags. Her clothes were drab and tattered and she'd left her head bare to the glowering sky. Only a torn and grimy length of cloth, wrapped around her forehead and tied at the back, hid the input jacks set into her temple. Shambling from their ruined houses, the villagers ignored her. She looked like one of them. Moving like emaciated shadows, their feet dragged through the mud and rubble and their eyes remained lowered and hopeless. As they formed up into ranks at the edge of the main road, she shouldered her way in among them, keeping her head down, hoping her disguise would be enough to fool the guards at the laboratory.

In the corner of her eye, she saw Paul's image. He hung above the cracked and weed-pocked tarmac of the road like a spectre, invisible to everyone except her.

"I still say this is a bad idea," he muttered. Victoria said nothing. She hadn't wanted to leave him behind, so she'd uploaded him into her neural gelware, as she had three years ago after first activating him. Now, he was a ghost overlaid across her vision. She nestled her hands deeper into the pockets of her coat, squeezing them for warmth. Around her, the villagers huddled into themselves. Unkempt, stale and unwashed, they stank. None of them spoke; they simply stood there, swaying slightly, as they waited for the sun to rise and the truck to appear.

Paul looked around at them.

"These people are starving," he said. "And covered in sores. And I don't like the way some of them are missing clumps of hair."

Victoria sidled to the edge of the group.

"What do you think?"

"I don't know. I'm a surgeon, not a general practitioner."

"If you had to guess."

"Radiation poisoning, maybe."

"*Merde*. You really think so?"

"I could be wrong." He considered the drab sky and shivered. "But I wouldn't recommend staying here a moment longer than absolutely necessary."

Victoria swallowed. Her mouth felt suddenly dry.

"*Oui, d'accord.*"

Despite his pessimism, she was glad to have him along for the ride. In this drab and forlorn landscape, it felt good to have a friendly face to offer moral support.

A fat drop of rain fell onto the road, followed by another, and another. From the left came the grunt and rumble of an engine. Belching smoke, the truck came around the corner at the end of the village. It was an eight-wheeled military model painted in autumnal urban camouflage. With a squeak of brakes and a hiss of hydraulics, it pulled to a halt in front of the villagers. They clambered up to join the other workers already huddled on the benches inside. Victoria hauled herself up behind them, and sat on the bench with her back against the canvas wall. Someone banged the side and the vehicle lurched forward, throwing everyone against each other. Then they were under way and, through the flap at the back, she could see the unrepaired road spooling away behind them.

In a field beyond the village, a fairground lay rusting.

"What happened here?" she whispered.

Paul shrugged. "Something bad." He jerked a thumb at the truck's other occupants. "Why don't you ask them?"

Victoria glanced sideways, and gave a tight little shake of her head. She didn't want to do anything that would make her stand out as being different, or not from around these parts. To do so would be to risk getting turned in for a reward. Instead, she turned up her collar and hunkered lower on her seat. The truck bumped and rattled along the road, jolting her spine.

Eventually, after a seeming eternity of discomfort, they came to a wire fence and a pair of anonymous-looking cyborg guards, who waved them through with scarcely a glance. Through the rear flap, Victoria saw the barrier and its coils of barbed wire receding behind them.

No turning back now.

They were in the grounds of the laboratory. If Célestine were anywhere, she'd be here, overseeing the activities of Nguyen's cyborg master race. All Victoria had to do was find her, and then get her to lead her to the monkey. Victoria's fingers curled around the plastic casing of the tracking device in her pocket. Once she got within a few hundred metres of Ack-Ack Macaque, she'd be able to locate him via the microchip she'd hired a vet to implant under his skin.

That's if he's still alive.

The truck pulled up in front of a pre-fab industrial unit, and the workers clambered out. Keeping amongst them, Victoria allowed them to lead her to a large canvas marquee, which had been erected at the side of the building, and which housed a couple of rickety trestle tables, from behind which dispirited-looking men and women dispensed cups of water and bowls of thin porridge. Accepting a bowl and a tin mug, Victoria stood on the edge of the group. The other workers ate and drank with listless, automatic movements. They showed no relish or urgency in the slaking of their hunger. They were like machines taking on fuel. Holding the plastic bowl to her chin, Victoria sniffed.

"That looks tasty," Paul said.

"It smells like wallpaper paste."

"You're not going to eat it, then?"

"Shut up."

The last thing she'd eaten had been a simple egg-white omelette, some hours before, in the commissary of the *Sun Wukong*. Now, the giant airship lay somewhere out in the Bay of Biscay, out of sight of land, its vast bulk floating half a dozen metres above the water—hopefully beyond the range of any radars Nguyen's troops might bring to bear, and hidden from the few civilian vessels brave or foolhardy enough to set forth upon the dead, polluted sea.

She swilled the gloopy muck around, and then tipped it into some weeds growing up against the side of the building.

"How did I get here?'

Paul looked confused.

"The truck...?"

She shook her head and sighed. "I mean, how did I get *here*." She looked around at the low, functional buildings, the miserable workers, and the dark, sullen sky. How had she made the progression from that apartment in Paris, from a promising career in journalism, to this post-apocalyptic wasteland? She thought of her other self, lying dead in that apartment, and almost envied her.

"Maybe I should have died in the crash," she murmured, thinking back to her accident in the South Atlantic. Everything that had happened, all the weirdness, had come about as a direct result of that crash. From the moment, four years ago, when she stepped onto the chopper and strapped into the seat next to the then-teenage Prince of Wales, her course had been fixed, her life changed. She'd climbed aboard as an up-and-coming reporter, and then woken four weeks later as a technological freak—a woman kept alive by the artificial neurons that now did most of her thinking.

And here she was on a parallel timeline, in a possibly radioactive dystopia, searching for her best friend—a rude, violent, ungrateful monkey, who smelled like a wet dog and drank like a fish—with only the electronic projection of her dead husband for company.

Why couldn't they have just let her drown?

She pulled her coat tight, and muttered curses under her breath. After a few minutes, the doors to the laboratory opened, and she followed the thin, shivering villagers to a production line, where industrial robots assembled artificial cyborg bodies in showers of welding sparks, and humans simply fetched and carried, swept and sorted. For an hour, she tried to blend in but had no idea what she was supposed to be doing and kept getting in the way. The sight of the arms and legs that lay, awaiting attachment, in hoppers beside the conveyor belts unnerved and sickened her. Their carbon fibre bones had already been partially covered in cultured skin, giving them the look of severed human limbs. It made her feel like a worker in a death camp. Especially as she knew that, somewhere nearby, real arms and legs were being carved off and discarded as brains and nervous systems were stripped from frail flesh-and-blood bodies and implanted into waiting cyborg shells.

When the two tall, expressionless guards came to arrest her, she felt almost relieved.

"Take me," she said as bravely as she could, "to your leader."

CHAPTER FOURTEEN
WRATH AND MALICE

ACK-ACK MACAQUE KEPT moving. His stomach grumbled and tiredness clawed at him. He'd been on the run for hours now and was, frankly, knackered. But, even though he'd made it to the forest, he didn't dare stay still for more than a few minutes at a time—just long enough to catch his breath, drink some water from a stream, or take a shit. After all, who knew what kind of heat-seeking tech those metal bastards packed? For all he knew they'd be able to pick him out at a hundred yards, and he had no intention of sitting around waiting for them to find him. Better to keep low and stay nimble, scampering through the undergrowth on his hands and feet. His plan, such as it was, involved finding a police station or army base, or maybe even a country sports store—anywhere that might have a stock of guns and ammunition. He only had four bullets left in his Colts, and there was no way in hell he'd be able to force his way back into Célestine's facility without some serious firepower.

And when I get inside, I'm going to shoot her ladyship in the kneecaps, he vowed to himself, *and then keep shooting bits off her until she agrees to send me home.*

He paused for a moment to catch his breath, and leant against a tree, chest heaving. All he'd wanted was to save the world—and it hadn't even been his world. How had he ended up here, in this cold and windy hellhole? Still wheezing, he spat into the grass, regretting each and every cigar he'd ever smoked.

From behind, he heard the thud of clawed feet on mossy ground, and the rustle of lithe bodies crashing through bracken and underbrush.

Dogs!

They were close, and their cyborg masters wouldn't be far behind.

"Shitballs."

The trees in this part of the forest were mostly young saplings, with thin springy branches that wouldn't bear his weight. Even if he managed to swarm up one, he'd be trapped in it, treed like a cat—unable to swing to the next because it'd snap beneath him.

The sounds of pursuit grew closer, and he looked back. From the undergrowth, a pair of Dobermans flew at him like slavering suede missiles. His hands dropped to his holsters; but he knew that if he fired, he'd be giving away his position to his pursuers *and* using the last of his ammo. Instead, with no other choice, he dropped into a fighting crouch and let his lips peel back from his teeth.

"All right, mutts, let's play."

The dogs were almost upon him. He could see breath steaming from their mouths and powerful muscles rippling like pistons under their hides. He curled his hands into claws and thrashed his tail. Then he let out the deepest, most guttural snarl he could muster—an outpouring of rage and frustration that welled up from the soles of his boots. It was the cry of a challenged alpha male, an expression of wrath and malice so potent it could have stopped a charging gorilla.

The two Dobermans slithered to a halt, their paws scrabbling at wet leaves and moss. It was a fair bet that, living in France, they'd never seen a monkey before—especially an enraged male almost the size of a human being. They took one look at the creature in the clearing—at its yellow incisors and baleful eye—and, whimpering in terror, fled back the way they had come.

Ack-Ack Macaque scowled after them.

"Yeah, you'd better run." He put a hand to the small of his back and straightened his spine. Something clicked and he groaned. "Goddammit." The roar had taken much of his strength. He felt emptied out. Much of the fear and anger that had been driving him had vanished, having vented away into the damp autumn air like steam from a safety valve. Now, he felt overwhelmingly tired.

What I wouldn't give for a coffee right now. He scratched his stomach. He couldn't afford to linger. With a sigh, he turned and loped deeper into the forest, heading away from the distant sounds of pursuit.

Soon, he came to an older part of the wood, where he scaled the first tree that seemed capable of holding him. Once up in the tangle of bare branches, he started swinging from tree to tree. The going was slower than running on the forest floor, but at least he wasn't leaving a scent trail for the dogs to follow. They wouldn't be able to track him through the air.

HALF AN HOUR later, as the light of the afternoon began to fade and his arms started to feel like overstretched rubber bands, he came to an area where the trees were blackened and charred. An airliner had crashed into the heart of the forest. Parts of the wings and fuselage were clearly visible at the centre of the burned-out area. Cautiously, he crept closer. There hadn't been many jet airliners on Victoria's world, where skyliners accommodated the vast majority of aerial passengers. Neither had there been any in the game world he'd once inhabited, based as it had been on a fictionalised version of World War II.

Stupid way to travel, he thought, regarding the wreck. Blasting through the air at half the speed of sound, crammed into a thin metal tube, more payload than passenger. Why go through all that when you could have the comfort and relative spaciousness of a skyliner cabin? Sure, the journey would take longer, but if your only concern was time, why not simply strap yourself onto a missile and have done with it?

Something white caught his eye. A thighbone. Now that he'd seen one, other bones seemed to leap out at him. They lay strewn around the wreck like the leftovers of some hideous feast, some half-buried and sticking up from the earth, others piled in heaps where they'd fallen. He frowned. The plane had fallen here, and nobody had come to collect the bodies.

What the hell? This wasn't the Amazon rainforest; the wreck lay less than ten kilometres from the centre of Paris. Why hadn't anybody come? They must have been able to see the smoke and flames. He thought back to the ruined village, the collapsed bridge. Whatever had happened here must have happened everywhere else as well. Some calamity had hit the whole country—maybe the whole world—and nobody had come to investigate this plane crash because they were all too busy dealing with their own dead and injured.

He shivered.

A few years ago, he'd fought Célestine and her plan to provoke a nuclear war. The crazy old cow had wanted to cleanse the world, leaving it free for her cyborg armies to inherit. Eventually, she'd been defeated and killed; but this was a whole different timeline, with a whole different Célestine. What if, in this reality, the Duchess had succeeded? Ack-Ack Macaque cast his eye at the darkened clouds and leafless trees.

"Ah, crap." He felt his skin crawl at the thought of radioactive fallout. The hairs on his neck and arms prickled. What was safe? Was he breathing the stuff now? Then he remembered Célestine. When they'd fallen through the portal, she hadn't been wearing a protective suit. She hadn't taken any precautions. Maybe things weren't so bad.

"Either way, there's fuck all I can do about it now."

He crawled along the branch he was on, and jumped into the waiting arms of the next tree. He was going to give the crash site a wide berth; and, unless he dropped dead of radiation poisoning in the next couple of hours, he'd just have to go on assuming there *was* no contamination—or, at least, not enough to hurt him in the short term. He had to assume he'd go on living.

After all, what choice did he have?

CHAPTER FIFTEEN
THAT VILE PRIMATE

THE TWO GUARDS marched Victoria across the windswept campus, past row after row of workshops and assembly lines; past racks of artificial torsos, crates filled with disembodied heads, and, at the back of one particular building, a conveyor belt leading to a row of dumpsters filled with discarded human remains. Arms and legs stuck out at uncomfortable, unnatural angles. The bodies had been cored like apples, their brains and spinal cords having been cut out and pasted into new cyborg bodies. Flies swarmed over the cooling meat. The workers tending the conveyor belt turned to watch her pass with dull, frightened eyes.

At the end of the row of structures, they came to an exposed area that had once been a car park but which was now empty, save for a couple of rusting Citroëns and a large military transport helicopter. The helicopter's twin rotors turned lazily. The craft had been painted the same dull, oppressive grey as the sky. Warm yellow light spilled from the ramp gaping open at its rear. The guards led Victoria to the base of the ramp and pushed her forward. She took a couple of steps, and then looked back.

"You're not coming?" she asked.

They regarded her with blank, impassive expressions, their faces betraying all the verve and personality of shop window mannequins.

"You go on," one of them said. "We'll be here when you're finished."

The breeze whipping across the car park smelled smoky and autumnal, laced with the scents of wet earth and rotting leaves. In Victoria's head, Paul said: "I don't like this." The helicopter's tail rotor towered above them. The ramp was wide enough to accommodate a tank.

"I don't blame you." She hadn't been a fan of helicopters since that crash in the South Atlantic, a lifetime ago.

She walked up the ramp and paused at the top, where she used her arm to shield her eyes, blinking as they adjusted to the contrast between the twilit gloom outside and the brightness within.

The helicopter's cargo hold had been outfitted as an art gallery. There were expensive-looking carpets on the deck, and tapestries hanging from the bulkheads. She recognised a number of famous paintings and carvings. In the centre of the space, a long metal box had been covered in candles, each of which was lit. There were votive candles, tea lights, lanterns, and gothic candelabra. Their glow gave the place the feel of a church, and their flames flickered brightly in the cold air swirling in from the open ramp. At the back of the room, near the hatch that led through to the cockpit, Alyssa Célestine sat behind a desk, face like a scowling cat. Back on Victoria's timeline, the woman had been the Duchess of Brittany, companion to the King of the United Kingdoms, and mother to Merovech, the Prince of Wales. Goodness only knew what rank or title she held on this world.

"Come in." Célestine had unbuttoned her tunic. A squat black pistol lay on the desk in front of her. Victoria glanced back, at the guards at the bottom of the ramp. They were watching her. How could they stand to live in those metal shells? For a second or two, she pitied them. Then a wave of nausea splashed over her as she remembered her own situation. However artificial they might be on the outside, at least they still had their own brains. They weren't running on slippery, lab-grown gelware. Their limbs and organs may have been replaced but their minds were still their own, still the product of greasy human neurons. For all their physical alteration, they remained human in a way she never could. And it was all Célestine's fault. Célestine and Nguyen. Victoria should have died of her injuries, but they'd saved her. Nguyen had used her to test his techniques and theories. She had been an early prototype for his cyborg soldiers, her brain a testing ground for the gelware that allowed human consciousness to be copied and transferred into a metal body. They'd turned her into a guinea pig, and she'd been pathetically grateful—at least, until she'd realised the full scope of their plans. Then she'd killed Nguyen and helped Ack-Ack and Merovech finish off Célestine.

Yes, back on her timeline, the Duchess was dead. On this one, she wasn't. Victoria swallowed. Mouth dry and heart twitching like a caged animal, she turned to face the woman.

Lady Célestine glared at her.

"Do you speak English?"

"*Oui.*"

"Why have you come here?"

"To find my friend."

"The monkey?"

"Yes."

"He tried to kill me."

Victoria drew herself up. "As I recall, *you* opened fire on *him*."

The woman's gnarled fingers brushed the stock of the pistol on the desk.

"He broke into my lab."

"Is it your lab or is it Nguyen's?" Victoria narrowed her eyes. "And, talking of Nguyen, why did you shoot him, anyway?"

Célestine pursed her lips. She wrapped her fingers around the gun.

"He allowed himself to be captured. His death was necessary."

"In case he talked?"

"Because he disappointed me." She raised the weapon. "But now it's your turn to talk. Where are you from?"

"Paris, originally."

"Which Paris?"

"How the hell would I know?"

"Your name?"

"Victoria Valois."

"Valois…" Célestine's lip curled. "Of course. You're the woman from the helicopter crash."

"You know me?"

"I remember Nguyen operating on you."

Victoria blinked in surprise. "You were there?"

"I have made contact with alternate versions of myself and the good doctor on a dozen parallels," she said, "and on each, I have given them the tools to create new bodies, new societies." Keeping the gun's narrow barrel trained on Victoria, she rose stiffly to her feet. "The iteration you killed three years ago was one of my most promising students. We had never been so close to success. But then you ruined everything. You and that vile primate."

"You were trying to start a nuclear war."

"We were trying to save humanity. To improve it."

"By killing most of it."

"So what? Your world was dangerously overpopulated. You could have stood to lose some of the dross, the deadwood." Célestine gestured to the open ramp behind Victoria. "As we have done here."

Victoria's mouth felt dry.

"There was a nuclear war *here*?" A droplet of sweat tickled as it ran into the small of her back.

Célestine waved a dismissive hand. "A small one. Inconsequential, really."

"Somebody stopped you again?'

The woman smiled. "We just developed more subtle methods. Biological methods. Diseases genetically tailored to target certain subsets of the population, leaving only a percentage of the adults."

Victoria had to stop herself from turning away in disgust, appalled by the implied slaughter. "Enough to create your brave new world?" she asked, almost spitting the words.

"Enough to provide the slave labour to build it."

Victoria felt her cheeks growing hot. Rage bubbled up like stomach acid. "Who elected you ruler of the world?"

Behind her, she heard the ramp closing. The deck trembled underfoot as the helicopter wobbled into the air. Braced against the desk, the Duchess straightened her arm, and aimed the gun directly at Victoria's face.

"And who elected you its saviour?"

Beneath the anger, Célestine looked tired. The fingers holding the weapon were starting to gnarl, the backs of the hands blotchy with liver spots and ancient scars.

"Do you think this has been easy?" she asked, regarding Victoria with glittering eyes. "All these years, all these worlds? This has been my life's work."

"Turning people into robots?"

"Trying to save the human race!" She shook the gun and Victoria cringed. If she could keep the Duchess talking, she might have time to access her internal menus and dial up her speed and strength.

"You could just stop now, and walk away," she suggested, stalling for time.

Célestine shook her head. "No, not now. I've spent too long at this. I've invested too much time, too much of myself—too much of all my selves."

"Perhaps we could help you?"

"No." She motioned Victoria over to a porthole. They were climbing slowly, rising over the campus of workshops and warehouses that made up the laboratory. Victoria braced herself against the inside of the hull and bent to the window. Below, in the fields beyond the barbed wire fences, immense armoured vehicles sat in ranks.

"Are they tanks?" They were bigger than any kind of tank she'd ever seen.

Lady Alyssa buttoned her black tunic. Her close-cropped hair and bright eyes gave her the look of a Siamese cat.

"They are my Land Leviathans."

Victoria cupped a hand around her eyes and pressed her face to the glass. Bristling with guns, and with sparks shooting from their smoke stacks, the Leviathans resembled armoured locomotives, or battleships plucked from the sea and given caterpillar tracks. In the corner of her vision, she saw Paul's image superimposed across the scene.

"There are *hundreds* of them," he said.

For a moment, Victoria regretted her decision to allow Paul to ride in her head. If she got herself killed—and it seemed increasingly likely that she would—he'd also die. If her heart stopped pumping the oxygen her gelware ran on, he'd fade away like a computer program in a power cut. She could have left a copy of him running on the *Sun Wukong*'s processors, but that would have run contrary to their pact. In the aftermath of the Gestalt invasion, they'd made each other a promise. She wasn't backed-up, and Paul didn't want to live without her, haunting the memory banks of a captured airship. If she died, he would follow. On this trip, they were sharing the risk, and there would be no second chances.

Victoria stepped back from the window. Célestine let her pistol drop demurely to waist-height, but kept it aimed. "What do you think?"

"Does it matter what I think?"

"Perhaps not, but I wanted you to see them." She walked around the heavy metal box occupying the centre of the hold, putting it between them. In the candlelight, her eyes seemed to smoulder.

"You say I kill people? Before I came to this world, it was a totalitarian dictatorship, a fascist nightmare. There were death camps, torture houses. Now, because of me, many of the formerly downtrodden are free, and equipped with bodies that may serve them for a thousand years. I killed all the generals."

"And most of the people."

"They would have died anyway." Célestine's jaw clenched. "What do a few casualties mean in the grand scheme of things? Everybody dies sooner or later; nobody survives. The point is that I achieved my objective: I made it possible for a few to transcend the limitations of the flesh."

Victoria tasted sourness. "But all those deaths—"

"Think how many have died throughout history. Millions upon millions of bright, sparkling intelligences doomed to rot in a prison of meat. And only I can stop it all. I can make their lives worthwhile, because I have it in my power to halt death."

Victoria stepped back, away from the candles. "You're insane."

"Insane?" The gun waved above the flames. "Of course I'm insane. You would be too, if you'd had to do and see the things I have."

"Then why not stop? Why not put an end to it all?"

"Because humanity needs me. It needs what only I can do." Célestine drew herself up to her full height. "I invented the soul-catcher, you know. Thanks to me, a hundred timelines use it. The people on them record their personalities as electronic back-ups, little realising the true purpose of the thing, its true potential."

As she spoke, Victoria called up the menu that enabled her self-defence routines—routines she'd been practising and refining for the past three years.

"Which is?"

"When the time comes," the Duchess said, "most of its users—at least, most of those worth saving—will already have a copy of themselves digitised and ready to load into one of my cyborg bodies."

In her mind's eye, Victoria triggered a threat evaluation subroutine. Slowly, the gelware in her head began to accelerate its processing rate from the speed of thought to the speed of light.

"So, you've built an army?" She tried to keep her voice steady, her tone neutral.

"Indeed." With the end of the pistol, Célestine pointed through the window. The helicopter had turned, bringing into sight something that looked like the sort of giant lighting rig you saw at open air music festivals: an arc of metal forming an archway big enough to easily accommodate one of the Leviathans. The centre glowed and rippled like a luminous heat haze. Its edges sparkled with rainbow light.

"Oh no," said Paul.

Victoria frowned, trying to make sense of the skeletal structure. Then realisation hit her, and she gaped at Lady Alyssa.

"That's a portal."

The woman's expression hardened.

"I have unfinished business on your world, Miss Valois." She motioned Victoria back to the desk and into a chair, then took up position across from her. "My spies tell me that, back on your timeline, the Céleste probe reached Mars. It was a success. Even as we speak, it will be busily constructing its own army of enhanced humans."

"You mean cyborgs."

Uniform fastened, Célestine raised the gun. Her eyes went to the scar tissue at Victoria's temple.

"You are in no position to make such distinctions."

Victoria focused on the barrel of the pistol, which was about a metre from her face. Her neural prosthesis tagged the weapon as a threat and dialled her adrenal glands up to maximum. At the same time, her mental clock completed its acceleration, and the world around her slowed to a glacial pace. She felt her chest rise like an old set of bellows, and the indrawn breath pass across her tongue into her throat. Her heart thumped and the blood roared in her ears. Her thoughts, which had been racing, hardened and clarified.

"But why do you need my world," she asked, "if you already have this one?"

Célestine looked scornful. "This world is ending," she said. "The seas are poisoned, the vegetation dying off. It's useless. Soon, only bacteria will remain." She took a step back and closed one eye, sighting the gun at the bridge of Victoria's nose. "On your world, we already have Mars—an unspoiled canvas upon which to build—and soon, we will have the Earth as well. With the Red Planet in our hands, we are halfway there. We just need the final push, and then we'll found a society that will last an aeon, spreading from world to world through space, and from timeline to timeline on Earth. A society that will outlast the sun itself."

Victoria tensed. She knew she could move quickly, but could she move quickly enough to dodge a bullet?

"It'll never happen," she said, buying time.

Lady Alyssa looked pityingly at her.

"My Leviathans cannot be stopped. I will fly this helicopter right into the heart of London and land it on the lawn of Buckingham Palace. Merovech will surrender to me personally."

"You'll be shot down before you get within a mile of the palace."

"Don't be so sure." The Duchess moved sideways and tapped the toe of one of her military boots against the metal box holding all the candles. "Do you know what this is?"

Victoria glanced down. Whatever the box might be, there were power cables plugged into it, and it gave off a faint, almost subliminal hum, easily missed against the racket of the helicopter's engines.

"I haven't the faintest idea."

Célestine smiled triumphantly, and thrust out her chest.

"It's a field generator. It creates an invisible energy shell around the aircraft. It can stop bullets, even tank shells."

"Bullshit."

"No, I assure you, it's true. It's even impervious to air and water. If we had the right propulsion system, with that shield in place, we could fly this helicopter under the sea."

"And your Leviathans have them?"

"Most, yes." She brought her free hand up to grasp her other wrist, steadying her aim. "But enough of this chatter. You have seen all I wished you to see, and now, I'm afraid, it's time to say farewell."

CHAPTER SIXTEEN
THE BONE PIPE

ACCORDING TO THE luminous dial of Ack-Ack Macaque's wristwatch, it was midnight when he first glimpsed the campfire. From where he hung, in the upper branches of a tall conifer, the flames danced invitingly, illuminating the trees and throwing long black shadows through the forest. He sniffed. His limbs were tired, his belly empty. Along with the wood smoke, he could smell something else. Something that smelled like an unwashed human, or perhaps…

Moving as stealthily as possible, he worked his way towards the quivering light, keeping to the high branches. Eventually, he came to the edge of a clearing and there, in the centre, was the fire. A figure crouched beside it, wrapped in old blankets, poking the glowing embers with a long stick. At first glance, it resembled a monk, or an old woman in a shawl, but on closer inspection, he saw that copper hair covered the backs of its hands, and its fingers were thick, leathery sausages. Ack-Ack Macaque wrinkled his nose. He'd been right about the smell. The figure wasn't an old woman; it wasn't even human. As he watched, it pulled back the blanket covering its head, revealing the deep brown eyes and greying muzzle of an elderly female orangutan.

"You may as well come down," the orangutan said. "I know you're there. I've been listening to you crashing around for the last ten minutes."

She waited patiently as Ack-Ack Macaque lowered himself to the forest floor and edged towards the campfire, one hand resting on his holster.

"Who are you?" he demanded.

The orangutan smacked her lips.

"My name is Apynja. Use it wisely." She reached into the folds of her blanket and pulled out a battered steel canteen. "I expect you're thirsty."

"You escaped from Célestine's place too?"

"It doesn't matter where I come from. My journey is of little consequence." She tossed the flask to Ack-Ack Macaque. "Now, take a drink."

Suddenly, Ack-Ack Macaque's tongue felt like an old flannel. He unscrewed the lid of the flask and took an experimental sniff.

"Is this vodka?"

"Vodka, and a few medicinal herbs." Apynja tapped her stick against one of the stones ringing the fire. "Strong stuff, too. It'll keep out the cold."

Ack-Ack Macaque swirled the liquid around in its container.

"What are you doing here, Apynja?"

"Waiting for you."

"For me?"

"You, or somebody like you. You see, if you're running from the laboratory, these woods are the closest of any appreciable size. I knew that if I waited here, you were bound to turn up sooner or later. You or somebody like you, at any rate."

Ack-Ack Macaque took a sip from the canteen. The taste drew his lips back against his teeth. The fumes made his eye water.

"How long have you been here?"

"A short while."

"What about the cyborgs?'

"They don't worry me." Apynja smiled through thick, rubbery lips. "You can hear them coming a mile off."

Ack-Ack Macaque stepped closer to the warmth of the fire. His arms and legs felt like overcooked spaghetti.

"They were chasing me."

"I don't doubt it." She gave the fire a final prod, and then settled back on her haunches. "Now, why don't you sit down and join me." She reached behind her and threw a handful of dry leaves onto the embers. They crinkled and curled as they burned, giving off a sweet, oily smoke.

Ack-Ack Macaque glanced back, into the blackness beneath the trees.

"Listen, lady—"

"I'm no lady. And you can relax; you're perfectly safe here, as long as you're with me."

Ack-Ack Macaque opened his mouth to respond, then wondered why he was arguing. He let his shoulders slump.

"Whatever you say." He took a draught from the flask, and felt the vodka burning its way down to his belly. He was exhausted; he'd been running and swinging for hours. The internal warmth, combined with the heat from the fire, made him drowsy.

He watched as Apynja produced a dirty yellow pipe that looked as if it had been carved from the shinbone of a largish animal, and filled it from a drawstring pouch she kept tucked into the sleeve of her robe. With delicate fingers, she fished a burning twig from the edge of the fire and used it to light the mixture. After a few puffs, she got it going and gave a sigh of satisfaction.

Ack-Ack Macaque took a deep sniff through his nostrils, breathing in as much of the fragrance as he could catch, trying to identify it. She saw what he was doing, and held the pipe out to him.

"Would you like some?"

"Is it tobacco?"

"Something along those lines."

"Then hell, yeah. Pass it over."

The elderly ape paused. "It might be more... potent than you expect."

"Listen, lady, I've only got one cigar left, and I've been trying to save it. I'm gasping. The way I feel right now, I'd smoke a used teabag if I had to."

He accepted the pipe from her hands, and took a long, noisy suck from the business end.

Stars exploded behind his eyes.

"Whoa."

"Quite." Apynja smiled. In the firelight, wreathed in blue, sticky-smelling fumes, the hairs on her arms and face seemed to shimmer like molten gold. Ack-Ack Macaque blinked. His head felt deliciously light and airy, like a dusty attic with the skylight open, and he could feel all his aches and pains bubbling away into nothingness, as if he'd just slipped into a hot bath. He pulled back his lips and let the smoke curl out between his teeth.

"That," he said, his voice like boots treading a gravel path, "is some *seriously* good shit."

He was born in captivity, in slavery. For the first years of his life, all he knew was cages. Other monkeys were unknowable smells and shrieks in the darkness beyond the bars, trapped behind bars of their own. The only time he met them in the flesh was when he was put in a ring with one of them, their feet scuffing sawdust, weapons clenched in their paws, human faces howling and chanting around them.

The victors were rewarded with fruit, cigarettes and beer; the losers died, coughing their last breath on the floor of the ring.

His owner, a rake-thin Malaysian, stank of coffee, sweat, and back-alley deals. All the man cared about was money. As long as Ack-Ack Macaque kept winning, his owner stayed happy and the treats kept coming. If he was wounded, there were no treats, just a slap across the head. If he lost... Well, Ack-Ack Macaque didn't need to lose in order to know his owner would walk away without a second glance. So he made sure he never lost. He channelled all his hurt and rage into the fights, taking on larger and larger opponents; sometimes two or three primates at a time; sometimes dogs or large cats. He had no morality or conscience, and could only dimly sense the suffering and pain he caused. In order to survive, he killed everything they put in front of him and, in the process, earned some scars and lost an eye.

Later, he was sold to a lab. They opened up his head and filled it with plastic. They gave him a voice box capable of human speech, then lengthened his spine and extended his arms and legs. He spent six months in a motion-capture suit learning to walk and talk like a human. New skills and attitudes were loaded onto the processors that filled his skull, and then they dropped him into their virtual reality war game and let him think it was real...

THE MOVIE OF his life went dark.

He felt himself unspool into the obscurity of the void. The remains of the world reeled around him, reduced to fragments of memory, glimpses of other times, other places...

Through the maelstrom, he heard Apynja's voice.

"Close your eye," she said, "and tell me what you see."

"Do what?" He struggled against the darkness, flailing like a drowning monkey.

"Indulge me."

AT FIRST, ALL he perceived was the light of the fire flickering through the skin and blood vessels of his closed eyelid, turning his world a deep rosy pink. Then, out of the colour, a pattern emerged. It was like television static, but every blip and pixel contained an image of the whole. Every scratch and shadow was a world in itself, and all the worlds were connected.

"I see... everything," he said, his tongue thick like a dead thing in his mouth. "The whole multiverse. All the timelines."

"And what else?"

He tried to look closer, but the picture seethed, always just out of focus. He got the impression there were forces moving beyond the limits of his *perception, mighty struggles being played out just beneath the surface tension of his understanding.*

"War," he said.

Apynja pursed her lips and nodded gravely.

"You are a creature of violence," she said, "in a world laid waste by violence—lost in an endless ether of chaos and suffering."

"It's not my fault."

Apynja's laugh filled the skies like the derision of an unkind god. "But of course it is."

The giddy sensation passed. Ack-Ack Macaque found himself standing on something that felt like sand or ashes. His toes sank into it and he shivered in the wind.

"Where am I?"

He raised his eye to a sky grown dim with the burned-out embers of dying stars, and knew he stood on a lifeless planetoid at the conclusion of all things, at the dusk of the universe.

"At the Eschaton. The place where one story ends and another begins."

Recoiling from the emptiness, he flailed his arms and legs, lashing the void around him, kicking up dust.

"Let me go!"

"Hush now." The old orangutan's voice seemed to come from everywhere at once. "Concentrate."

"Fuck you."

Apynja sighed like a tired parent.

"Why must you always make this so difficult?"

And then everything spiralled away, like water down a plughole.

SOME TIME LATER—he had no way of guessing exactly how many hours had actually passed—Ack-Ack Macaque realised he was back in the familiar discomfort of his own body. Opening his eye, he looked up through the black, almost leafless branches at the edge of the clearing. He was lying on his back and the clouds seemed to flex and roil above him like the skin on the belly of a dragon.

He sat up, and had to put his palms flat against the forest floor to stop the world from spinning. The trees around him seemed to bend and straighten in time with his breathing.

"What fuckery was that?" The dregs of his dream were fading. On the other side of the fire, Apynja watched him with shining eyes.

"You saw things as they really are. Now, tell me, what do you believe?"

Ack-Ack Macaque's head throbbed and he groaned. He hated hangovers. "I don't believe in anything."

The orangutan looked disappointed.

"How about good versus evil?"

With a hand to his brow, Ack-Ack Macaque snarled. "Good and evil, heaven and hell, humans and monkeys. I'm sick of all of it."

"Really?" The faintest suggestion of a smile brushed across the elderly ape's lips.

Ack-Ack Macaque took another pull on the pipe. The smoke seemed to calm him, seemed to stop the world from trying to sway and tilt. "Yeah, I'm sick of being told to choose sides all the time. I'm sick of people messing with my head; people trying to take over or destroy the world; sick of *fucking robots trying to kill me*."

"Then what are you prepared to do about it?"

"Me?" He gave a snort. "What can I do, except look out for myself?"

"Ah!" Apynja held up a wrinkled finger. "So you *have* chosen a side?"

"Yeah, I guess I have." He looked into the flames. "My own side. Just me, because I'm sick of all the other bullshit."

"Always the same." Apynja scratched her cheek with dirty fingernails. "But would it surprise you to learn you're not alone?"

He glanced up at her with his one good eye.

"What does that mean?"

"There are a lot of humans who feel the same as you. They don't care about politics or war; they just want to be left to get on with their lives in peace. Look around you. There used to be eight billion people on this world, now only a tiny fraction remain." She pulled her blankets tighter around her squat frame. "You should have seen it when it happened. The corpses were rotting in the streets. Millions upon millions of them: men, women and children who wanted nothing more than to live their lives, to go to school, fall in love and care for their families."

Ack-Ack Macaque growled, deep in his throat. The silence seemed to press in against his ears.

"What are you trying to say?" He took another hit to steady the ache in his brainpan, and passed the pipe back across the fire.

"Look at the way you're dressed," Apynja said. "You're a soldier. A rebel. But have you ever asked yourself why? What is it you've been fighting all this time?"

Ack-Ack Macaque closed his eye again. He saw Spitfires and

Messerschmitts wheeling across bright blue virtual skies; three-legged German war machines stomping through ruined villages; and Gestalt airships raining fire and death on London.

"Bad guys," he said. "All my life, I've been fighting bad guys. First, the Nazis, then the Céleste conspiracy, and then the Gestalt."

He looked at Apynja and she nodded.

"You've been fighting tyranny, Napoleon," she said quietly. "You always have, right from the beginning. Don't you remember? Even way back then, you had a problem with authority. The trouble is, the way things are set up at the moment, there will always be another would-be dictator. However many you defeat, others will always rise. It's human nature. They're primates like us. Their behaviour's ruled by the same power dynamics as ours. Someone always wants to dominate. They want more sex, more food and more money than the others, and they always want to rule the world—or as much of it as they can get their grubby little hands on."

"And now Célestine's trying to conquer two worlds?"

"If not more."

Ack-Ack Macaque felt the dead grass beneath him. The stillness beyond the fire's crackles seemed oppressive and sad, and spoke of murder and death. Another growl worked its way up from his chest, curling his lip.

"Fine. You want to know what I believe? Well, I believe in a person's right to be free to get on with their life without all the bullshit, without other people trying to rip them off and kill them. Not to have to put up with governments and corporations and megalo-fucking-maniacs."

The elderly ape placed the bone pipe on the ground beside her.

"Then, I'll ask you once more, Napoléon. What are you prepared to do about it?"

Ack-Ack Macaque shrugged. "What can I do? I'm outnumbered, outgunned..."

"I thought you liked it that way."

"What are you saying, lady?"

Apynja raised her snout. "Somebody needs to bring order to the multiverse, to stop the killing, stop the chaos."

Ack-Ack Macaque frowned.

"Me?"

"Who better?"

Ack-Ack Macaque felt his lips peel back in a savage grin. For the first time since coming to this benighted hellhole, he felt some of his old fire return. Maybe it was exhaustion; maybe it was the vodka and the smoke, but right then he felt ready to take on the whole of Célestine's cyborg army—one by one, or all at once.

"Eight billion people died here," Apynja said. "If you had the power, would you avenge them?"

He looked around at the empty forest, and thought of the bones littering the wreck of the crashed airliner.

"Damn straight."

"Would you find those responsible?"

"Yeah, I'd find them. And I'd fuck them up, too."

"Like the Lady Célestine?"

"Especially her."

"Good." Using her stick for support, Apynja levered herself into a standing position. "You need to make an example of her. You need to show the rest of them, all the would-be dictators, where the line is, and what will happen to them if they cross it."

"Yeah."

"You need to keep them in order, Macaque. You need to stop them killing their populations, stop them breaking out of their timelines."

For a queasy moment, Ack-Ack Macaque's head spun. He felt light and dry, like an autumn leaf.

"Hell, yeah," he mumbled.

Apynja gave a nod. She looked pleased. "That's what I was hoping you'd say." Leaning on her stick for support, she made off towards the trees at the far side of the clearing. "Now," she called over her shoulder, "come with me."

SHE LED HIM through the forest until they came to a large gnarled oak. To Ack-Ack Macaque, in his addled state, it resembled an ancient forest god, wrinkled and patient in its eternal vigil. Using her stick, Apynja hacked at the undergrowth surrounding the trunk and exposed an opening—a black maw in the half-light, like a vertical mouth, or the entrance to a womb.

"Here we are," she said.

Ack-Ack Macaque frowned.

"I may be stoned, but I'm not climbing in there." Spider webs draped the entrance, and who knew what other creepy crawlies lurked inside? "No fucking way."

Apynja made a rude noise.

"I don't want you to *get in there*." She spoke slowly, as if to an idiot. "I want you to *reach* in there and pull out the box."

"What box?"

"The one in the tree." She jabbed her stick at the hole. "And be quick about it."

Ack-Ack Macaque swore under his breath. He handed her the steel canteen that he'd been carrying, and stuck an arm into the orifice. Grimacing, he waved it around until his fingers made contact with something hard and rectangular. There seemed to be a rope handle affixed to the end. He gave it an experimental tug.

"Christ, this weighs a tonne."

"It should do." Apynja rapped her stick against the tree trunk. "It's full of guns."

Ack-Ack Macaque's tail stood on end. He turned his head to her.

"No shit?"

"Guns and bullets, and a few hand grenades."

Grinning, he gave another heave, and the wooden box slid out into the open. It was the length of a coffin, but narrower and not as deep. When he pulled up the lid, he found himself staring at a veritable arsenal of machine guns, pistols and spare magazines. There were a few knives taped to the inside of the lid, and even a couple of hatchets and a solid-looking chainsaw. He took a deep breath in through his nostrils, savouring the smells of cold metal and gun oil.

"Oh, momma. Where did you get them?"

Apynja sniffed. "At the start, the humans resisted. Célestine had the elite—the world leaders and major industrialists—in her pocket. She bribed them with promises of eternal life and eternal power. But the real people, the everyday men and women—the doctors, soldiers, teachers and police— they resisted. Even as they fell sick and died, they tried to fight Nguyen's metal men."

"What happened?"

"They died. These are their weapons. I've been collecting them from battlefields and mass graves. I thought they might come in useful." She tapped his boot with her cane. "I trust you know how to use them?"

"Do you shit in the woods?"

"I don't see how that—"

"It means yes." He picked up an automatic rifle. It was sleek and black, and reassuringly heavy. The fug in his head began to clear and he felt wired and energised and... just fucking ready to kick some fucking arse.

"Can you take me back to Célestine's lab?" he asked.

Apynja worked her lips together, looking pleased. "Of course."

"Good." He snapped a magazine into place. "Because my only way home's through her portal."

"You'll need her to operate it for you, Napoleon."

"I'll persuade her."

Apynja smiled. "Of course, you realise that the only way to get to her will be by fighting your way through Nguyen's soldiers?"

Ack-Ack weighed the gun, judging its balance.

"That's what you're counting on, isn't it?"

Apynja's hands folded over the top of her cane. "Of course. If you can kill the woman and destroy Nguyen's creations, the surviving humans here might just stand a chance."

"Leave it to me." Hefting the rifle in one hand, Ack-Ack Macaque reached into his jacket and pulled out his last cigar. He looked at it for a moment, wondering if it really would be his *last* cigar; then he screwed it into the corner of his mouth and grinned. "Cos when I shoot a fucker, that fucker stays shot."

He heard a grunt of contentment.

"Why do you keep calling me Napoleon?" he asked.

"Because that's your name."

"No it isn't."

"Yes, it is. It's your *real* name…"

He felt the air stir, and his hair prickled with static. When he looked up, through a blue haze of cigar smoke, Apynja had gone. She had evaporated into the damp forest air as thoroughly as if she had never been there at all.

CHAPTER SEVENTEEN
TITANIUM CRANIUM

CÉLESTINE'S KNUCKLE TIGHTENED against the trigger. In her accelerated state, Victoria saw every movement as if in extreme slow motion. She saw the tendon in the woman's wrist stiffen like a violin string. She saw the skin of her knuckle stretch and blanch, and the way her jaw clenched in anticipation of the bang. Then, below, on the ground, something exploded. A fireball blossomed among the laboratory buildings. Distracted, Célestine's gaze flickered to the porthole, and Victoria had her chance.

Now.

Using all her pent-up energy, she threw herself across the metal box that lay between them, scattering candles in all directions. As she did so, the gun went off with a bang and a flash. The bullet passed somewhere above her, still aimed at the spot she'd just vacated. The recoil rocked the Duchess back on her heels. Victoria hit the floor with her shoulder and rolled. Her weight smashed into Célestine's legs. The gun flew from the woman's fingers, spinning a lazy parabolic course through the air. The Duchess cried out in indignation and surprise, and fell forwards onto her hands and knees.

Victoria climbed to her feet. She walked over and picked the pistol from the deck. Her hands felt shaky. Crisis over, her neural circuits were powering down, draining the dangerous levels of adrenaline from her system and returning her time perception to something more akin to normal human experience. Behind her, Célestine was on all fours among the fallen and rolling candles, cursing the pain in her arms and legs.

Paul's ghost hovered in the air.

"Oh God," he said, hand over his mouth. "Oh shit, Jesus."

"It's over," Victoria told him.

"You were so *fast*."

"It's over. Send the signal."

"What signal?"

"To the *Sun Wukong*. Tell them to come and get us."

"Ah yes, of course. Sorry. I'll do it now."

Victoria remembered the pistol in her hands. She pointed it at the woman on the floor.

"Don't move." With her other hand, she rummaged in the pocket of her ragged coat, and pulled out her monkey detector. Paul watched her.

"Is it him?"

"Of course it's him." She risked a peep through the nearest porthole. A battle raged beneath. "Who else would it be?" The tracker beeped its confirmation. "He's at the far end of the compound," she said. "How long until the *Sun* gets here?"

"At least half an hour."

"*Merde.*"

ACK-ACK MACAQUE LAY flat against the corrugated roof of one of the industrial units. He was panting. In one hand he gripped a matt black Desert Eagle—a semi-automatic pistol big enough to blow a tunnel through a mountain—and, in the other, the chainsaw. Grenades filled the bulging canvas satchel at his hip. Below, in the narrow gap between his building and the next, he heard heavy footsteps. The cyborgs hadn't considered that he could climb as well as he could run, and they were still looking for him on the ground. On the edge of the compound, a gas cylinder burned. The explosion had covered his entrance through the fence, and he'd been running and sniping ever since. He couldn't take on Nguyen's robot army and win in a stand-up firefight, but that was okay, because he had no intention of playing fair. The .44 Magnum cartridges in the Desert Eagle's clip were powerful enough to take down elk or buffalo, and the diamond-tipped chainsaw would make short work of even the sturdiest metal limb. If he could keep the action on a one-to-one basis, using the guerilla tactics of ambush and surprise, he might stand a chance.

For some moments, he remained where he was, ears straining. Then, when the noise of pursuit had died away, he rolled onto his stomach. His pistol had a fat silencer screwed into it that, while unable to actually silence the noise the gun made, would deaden the sound, making it harder for Célestine's troops to work out exactly where it was coming from. If he could stick to the rooftops, he might be able to take out a decent number of them before they located him.

Wriggling forward on his elbows, he took up position behind an air-conditioning unit and sighted along the pistol's barrel. Tall, spindly figures moved back and forth in the darkness, rifles gripped in their metal hands.

He picked one that was out by itself, in the weeds near the perimeter fence, and lined up his sights.

"Say goodnight, dickhead."

The gun gave a low, flat crack and jumped in his hands. His target dropped into the long grass, a fist-sized hole punched through its titanium cranium, and he grinned.

One down, several hundred left to go.

He rolled away from the air-conditioner and scampered across the roof, in the opposite direction, seeking another vantage and another victim. If he could keep the robots guessing long enough, he might be able to slip into Célestine's sanctum unmolested.

Beyond the far edge of the laboratory compound, a large military helicopter wallowed in the air, only a few hundred feet above the scrubby ground. Its twin rotors filled the night with a low, guttural throb. Was it looking for him? It didn't seem to be executing any sort of obvious search pattern; in fact, it seemed to be wobbling around as if a fight were going on in its cockpit. He frowned at it in puzzlement, then turned his attention elsewhere, to more pressing matters. If the helicopter wasn't an immediate threat, he didn't have time to waste on it. He had better things to worry about.

The chainsaw had a leather strap, so he hooked it over his shoulder and slid the pistol into the waistband of his trousers. From where he stood, he could see the laboratory building that housed the portal that brought him here. It was the next building but one. To get there, he'd have to jump from this roof to the next—a gap of at least fifteen feet, over a drop of thirty.

To his right, a half-track troop carrier rumbled along the row of buildings, using a searchlight to peer into the alleys between.

Ah, fuck it. Sorry Apynja, but we both knew this was a suicide mission.

He backed up as far as he could. Then, when the searchlight had passed the alley he intended to jump, he took three grenades from his satchel and pulled their pins. An underarm toss sent them tumbling over the edge of the roof, towards the sound of the half-track's engine. While they were still in the air, he started to run. His boots slapped on the corrugated roof. The gap ahead yawned like a chasm.

By the time he realised he wasn't going to make it, he was already airborne. The alley between the buildings was simply too wide, the chainsaw too heavy.

"Fuuuuck!"

*   *   *

VICTORIA STOOD BRACED in the doorway of the helicopter's cockpit, holding Célestine's pistol to the pilot's head.

"Circle around," she told him. "Set down at the end of the row."

"Then what?" Paul asked. From her point of view, he was sitting in the vacant co-pilot's chair.

"Then we find the monkey and attract his attention."

"What if he shoots at us? If he sees a helicopter swooping at him, he's bound to assume it's hostile."

Victoria pursed her lips.

"Look, I'm improvising. If you've got any better suggestions, don't keep them to yourself."

In front of her, the pilot, who could only hear her side of the conversation, cleared his throat.

"If there is going to be shooting," he said in a strong French accent, "we could always activate the field generator."

Victoria and Paul looked at him, then at each other.

"Do it," Victoria said.

The man gave a shrug. "Only the Duchess can make it work."

Victoria considered this. Then she pressed the pistol hard into his shoulder. "If I leave you here for a moment, you won't try anything stupid?"

"*Non, Madame.*"

"Good boy."

With a tired sigh, she went aft, back into the helicopter's cargo hold. She'd left Lady Alyssa tied to the leg of the desk, but she wasn't there now. A wind whipped though the hold, extinguishing the candles. Célestine had opened the cargo bay's side hatch. She was a black figure framed against the night. Victoria whipped the gun up and squeezed off two shots, but Célestine had already gone, allowing herself to fall away into the wind, and Victoria wasn't sure whether or not she'd been hit.

"*Putain!*" She kicked her boot against the deck in frustration, and marched over to the hatch. The noise of the rotors was deafening. Below, the roofs of the factories wheeled beneath them in the darkness—but of the Duchess, there was no sign.

ACK-ACK MACAQUE'S CHEST hit the lip of the opposite roof with a crunch that blew the wind from his lungs. His knees smacked against the side of the warehouse. In a panic, his fingers scrabbled at the rusted metal roof.

Behind him, the half-track exploded.

He ended up hanging by one hand from a broken sheet of corrugated iron, his boots dangling over a thirty-foot drop, the chainsaw swinging on its strap from his shoulder. If one of the cyborgs saw him, he'd be a sitting duck.

Q: Why did the monkey fall off the roof?

A: He was shot.

With a snarl, he reached up and took hold of the gutter with his other hand. He couldn't pull himself up. The iron pipe was cold and its edges sharp, and he simply didn't have enough strength left in his arms. The breath heaved in his chest and, not for the first time, he began to regret his cigar habit.

If I get out of this, he promised himself, *I'm going to take up jogging. I'm going to join a gym. I'm going to…*

Oh, who am I kidding?

He kicked off his boots and let them fall. One after the other, they spun end-over-end to the muddy floor of the alley, landing with hollow thuds. If two hands weren't enough, he'd try four. Using his tail as a counterbalance, he swung his feet up, and gripped the roof with his toes. His legs were stronger than his arms. Using them to bear most of his weight freed his hands to seek firmer purchase, and he was eventually able to heave himself up, out of danger.

He lay on the roof, cursing softly under his breath. Voices came from below. Another few seconds, and he would have been seen.

"Too close," he muttered.

Overhead, the helicopter wheeled toward him; or at least, towards the car park at the end of the row of buildings. Light spilled from an open hatch in its side. A figure stood braced on the threshold, tall, thin and feminine. For a moment, it swayed. Then it fell, arms and legs spread out in a graceful swallow dive. Ack-Ack Macaque elbowed himself up into a sitting position. That was Célestine! What was the Duchess playing at? Was she trying to kill herself? He could see she was too low to use a parachute.

"Pavement pizza," he muttered glumly, wondering how he'd ever get home without her to operate the portal.

Then, as the falling woman hurtled towards the cracked surface of the parking lot, two of the spindly cyborgs leapt ten metres into the air. They caught her between them and fell, cradling her in their interlocked arms. As they hit the ground, their carbon fibre legs flexed, absorbing the force of the impact and the weight of the woman they'd rescued. They set her feet gently onto the shattered tarmac of the car park, and stepped away, giving her space.

Watching the Duchess, apparently unharmed and dusting herself down, Ack-Ack Macaque felt his jaw drop open. He blinked his solitary eye. Célestine had been falling from a helicopter, and two of her cyborgs had *jumped up and caught her*.

"What the *fuck*?"

Beyond the barbed wire of the perimeter fence, massive vehicles were coming to life. Their engines growled and their weapons swung back and forth as if scenting the air. Fire and smoke belched from their chimneys. Tall, spindly figures raced toward them, climbing into their cabs or piling into hatches along their lengths. Célestine and her saviours followed at a brisk walk. Ahead, through the gloom, the metal arch had begun to glow brighter than ever. Blue sparks flickered like sprites amidst the metal latticework of its frame. The warped space at its centre swirled and sparkled like a whirlpool, throwing off shards of rainbow light.

It was another portal, Ack-Ack Macaque realised, and all these giant tanks were lining up to pass through it.

"Holy shitballs." Even to his own ears, his laugh held an edge of panic. "It's an invasion!"

CHAPTER EIGHTEEN
A VIEW OF THE RIVER

THE CROWD STOOD in Parliament Square, solemnly contemplating Big Ben's ruined tower. Rather than being rebuilt along with the rest of the Palace of Westminster, the scarred and shattered clock face had been repurposed as a permanent memorial to those who had died in the Gestalt attack. The pockmarked sides of the tower had been inscribed with the names of more than fifty thousand Commonwealth citizens, from more than a dozen countries, who had perished during that initial assault on the major cities of the world. As well as civilians, the names included those of politicians, civil servants, and members of His Majesty's armed services.

Dressed in a ceremonial uniform, Merovech stood on a specially constructed stage and looked up at the tower. Today, it stood battered but proud against a backdrop of blue sky and high, white cloud. He wondered exactly where on its ornate surface Julie's name had been carved. He hoped it was somewhere near the top, with a good view of the river.

Around him on the platform sat heads of state from most of the Commonwealth nations. Some had survived the tragedy; others had been elected in its wake. They were here, like him, to officially dedicate the monument. They all knew of his personal loss, of course, but had so far been either too polite or too reticent to mention it.

Is it time?

The thought surprised him. He'd spent the past three years pushing it to the back of his mind, smothering it with notions of duty and continuity; and yet here it came now, worming its way back.

When he'd first taken the throne, in the immediate aftermath of the battle in the English Channel, he'd done it to avert a nuclear war. He'd always meant to abdicate. He'd promised Julie that he would. But then the Gestalt invaded, and everything changed. He put aside his personal feelings for the good of his country and his Commonwealth, and loyally played the part his people expected; but he had never been of royal blood and bore no right to sit upon the throne. He wasn't even sure he was entirely human. Now, with this dedication, could it finally be time to walk away, to announce his retirement and take himself off to a small cottage on a Greek island, somewhere far from the machinery of media and state? Today seemed as good a day as any. If the crowds and cameras were gathered here in order to draw a line under the catastrophic events of the recent past, then surely now would be the perfect time to put an end to his reign? He had served his people. None of them knew that he had no claim to the crown. He had served and he had suffered, and the people had taken him to their hearts. Surely they would understand and be sympathetic if he announced his wish to step down, on today of all days?

The cracked bell tolled in the damaged tower. He rose to his feet and walked to the microphone. Heads and cameras turned towards him. The upturned faces of the people packed into the square reminded him of a field of sunflowers, turning to greet the day. As they fell silent, he cleared his throat.

"Today," he began, reading from the words projected by the autocue. They shimmered in the air before him like the delusions of a heat-stricken madman. "Today marks a most solemn anniversary. It is a time for remembrance but also a time for hope; a time to acknowledge our grief but also to give thanks for the peace and international cooperation that have followed in the wake of catastrophe. For now, nation stands shoulder to shoulder with nation, united. Our petty and dangerous squabbles have been put aside in the face of strange and graver threats, and in honour of those whom we come here today to remember." He paused, conscious of the bell tower behind him. The words he was reading were his. He'd written them himself, yet still they died in his mouth. He couldn't go on. His throat felt closed up and he couldn't swallow properly. All he could think of was Julie: her face, her smell, the way her eyes would crinkle at the corners when she smiled.

Damn it all.

She'd want him to do it. She'd never wanted to be a queen or princess, but she'd gone along with the charade because he'd convinced her it was necessary. And it had been, at the time; at least, he'd thought so. He'd spent his life being trained to lead, and so who better than him to step in during a crisis? But with that crisis now over, how necessary was it for him to remain? He closed his eyes and sighed. The crowd was silent. They thought he was overcome with grief, and their sympathy stung him even as he was grateful for it. It made him feel like a fraud.

Time to go.

In his imagination, he'd rehearsed this moment a hundred times. Yet, now it was upon him, he couldn't think of anything to say. The only words that came to mind were tumbled, nonsensical platitudes.

He watched one of the vast Gestalt dreadnoughts chug across the rooftops of the city, on its way to Heathrow. Following the Gestalt surrender, the hundred or so dreadnoughts that were still operational had been placed under joint international control. In a world still reeling back from the brink of World War III, no single country could be permitted sole control of such a fleet, and so the vast armoured airships, still operated by their Gestalt crews, had been organised into a defensive force, designed to combat incursions from other timelines. Thanks to Ack-Ack Macaque, Earth's assailants had become its protectors.

Thinking of the monkey, Merovech looked down at his hands.

Why didn't I go with them when I had the chance? How different his life would have been if he and Julie had accepted Victoria Valois' invitation to join the *Tereshkova*'s crew three years ago, in the wake of the so-called 'Combat de La Manche.' They could have travelled the world. Julie might still have been alive.

"I have to tell you something." His voice faltered. The crowd's wide eyes radiated commiseration and compassion. He gripped the sides of the lectern with his white-gloved hands and took a deep breath. His legs were shaking.

"I have to—"

He became aware of voices behind him, and glanced around. A number of the world leaders arrayed behind him were talking urgently into their phones, or listening to aides. Had they guessed what he was about to say? Even as he frowned at their interruption, he saw Amy Llewellyn shouldering her way towards him from the back of the stage. She had her security pass in one hand and carried a SincPhone in the other. Her dark brows were drawn together and her cheeks were ashen. Reaching him, she placed one of her hands across the microphone and raised herself on her toes to whisper in his ear.

"It's Mars," she said, pushing the phone into his hands. Her breath was warm against his cheek.

"Another message?" Merovech looked down at the handset she'd forced on him. The very last thing he wanted right now was to talk to his mother.

"No." Amy shook her head, expression grim. She gripped his shoulder. "They've launched a missile." She eyed the expectant crowd. "And if our estimates are correct, it's the size of the Isle of Wight."

Astronomers Detect 'Missile' From Mars

PARIS 18/11/ 2062 – Astronomers working for the European Space Agency have observed the launch of a gigantic projectile from the surface of Mars. The shock announcement came earlier today, during a service of remembrance to mark the second anniversary of the Gestalt attack of 2060. The projectile, which is believed to be some sort of weapon, is on a course to hit the Earth, and is due to arrive in less than six months.

At a hastily convened press conference in Paris, Dr. Sandrine Aurand, a spokesperson for the ESA, told reporters that the missile appears to be moving faster than expected, saying, "If our measurements are correct, the only way to explain the object's apparent acceleration is to assume some form of antimatter propulsion."

Antimatter is matter in which the charges of the particles are reversed. When it comes into contact with ordinary matter, the two annihilate each other with a release of energy much greater than that given off during a nuclear reaction. Antimatter is extremely rare, and it is not known where the newly revived crew of the Martian probe could have obtained enough to power a missile of such size.

According to observations, the object is most likely a captured asteroid or 'minor planet' measuring almost two kilometres in length, which makes it comparable in mass to the asteroid that is thought to have wiped out the dinosaurs.

"We're running simulations at the moment," Dr. Aurand warned, "but wherever this hits, the effects will be global."

Read more | Like | Comment | Share

Related Stories:

Government appeals for calm as shoppers stockpile food and water.

Emergency talks to be held in London.

Opinion: Is it time to make peace with Mars?

Today's List: Ten historical impacts that literally shook the globe.

Religious sects proclaim 'End of the World'.

Did H.G. Wells predict all this 160 years ago?

Where will you be when the rock hits? Celebrities tell us their plans for 'Doomsday'.

CHAPTER NINETEEN
THE BELLY OF THE BEAST

VICTORIA VALOIS STOOD in the cockpit door, her pistol pressed into the skin at the back of the pilot's neck.

"So, how come you're still human?" she asked. She had to raise her voice over the noise of the engines.

The Frenchman gave a tight shrug. He was trying to concentrate on his instrument panel.

"I'm good at what I do."

"Okay, prove it." Victoria pointed forward, through the windshield. "Get us as close to that roof as possible, and lower the ramp."

"You want to get out?"

"No, we're picking somebody up."

The hull rattled, as if hit by a handful of ball bearings.

"They're shooting at us!" Paul said.

Victoria ignored him.

No shit, Sherlock.

She kept the barrel of her gun jammed against the pilot's spine, just below his helmet, where it met his shoulders. Her other hand gripped the doorframe and she had her feet braced against either side of the narrow gangway. She watched the horizon tilt and slide as the big helicopter wallowed around, lining its tubby backside up with the old warehouse. A small screen on the pilot's console showed a grainy night-vision view of the roof, taken from a camera at the back of the copter. In its unreal green light, she could see Ack-Ack Macaque crouched by one of the air vents. The gun in his hands flashed, and Victoria flinched as a bullet clanged against the bulkhead behind her.

"Jeez, now *he's* shooting at us," Paul complained.

"What do you want me to do about it?"

"You could call him. Assuming he's still got his radio."

"His radio?" If she could have spared a hand, she would have slapped her forehead. "Of course, he was wearing his link when he fell into the portal."

Paul smiled infuriatingly.

"It's a good job one of us pays attention."

Pocketing her gun, Victoria reached forward and lifted the radio handset from its clip on the console between the seats. She thumbed through the frequencies, and then squeezed the button to transmit.

"Hey, monkey-man. It's us. Stop firing, and shift your *derrière*."

Ack-Ack Macaque thrust the Desert Eagle into his waistband, and pulled tight the strap holding the chainsaw. Then he ran. He crossed the rusting iron roof on all fours, scampering as hard and fast as he could, careless of the noise he made. Shots came from below but he ignored them. He couldn't see who was firing or where the bullets were going; all he could see was the inviting maw of the helicopter's open cargo ramp. He could feel the blood surging through him and felt like whooping. He had been alone, but now his troupe had found him. With a last, desperate bound, he was aboard, and half-running, half-stumbling up into the belly of the beast.

He found himself in a cargo bay filled with toppled candles. For a second, he thought he might be back in the woods with Apynja, hallucinating, still high on exhaustion, vodka and weed. Then reality kicked in and he forced himself forward, to where Victoria stood, covering the pilot with her weapon. She smiled.

"Damn good to see you, monkey-man."

"Likewise. But I think I hit your fuel tank." He'd certainly stitched a row of bullet holes across the helicopter's flank and seen liquid vent from the base of the rear rotor. Without looking around, the pilot tapped a dial.

"He's right, we're losing fuel."

Victoria swore under her breath. Reunions would have to wait. "Do we have enough to make it through the portal?"

"Yes, but—"

"Then take us through. We'll worry about the rest later."

Ack-Ack Macaque looked forward through the windshield and gaped at the ranks of lumbering machines arrayed before the metal structure. "Are you fucking nuts? You'll be flying us into the middle of an invasion."

"Yes, but at least we'll be home. We can signal the *Sun Wukong* to follow us when it gets here."

Ack-Ack Macaque focused his yellow eye on her. "Home?"

"That's where the portal leads," Victoria said. "Célestine's planning to invade *our* timeline."

Her words seemed to echo in his ears. *Home*. He hadn't been back to the timeline of his birth in two years, and the thought of all this armour attacking it filled him with a sick kind of rage. The Gestalt assault had been bad enough; the thought of another onslaught so soon...

"What are we waiting for?" He straightened his collar and champed at the cigar still clamped in his teeth. "The *Sun*'s on its way. Tell it to drop all its missiles on these tossers."

"We can't wait for it."

"We don't have to." Bullets clanged against the hull. "We've done all we can. Now get us through that portal before we fall out of the goddamn sky."

TRAILING SMOKE, THEY passed through the portal and burst into sunlight. Ack-Ack Macaque blinked and put up a hand to shade his eye.

"Are they coming after us?" Victoria asked.

He ducked his head back into the cargo bay. The rear ramp had been left open. Behind them in the winter air, he saw nothing more than the faintest suggestion of a shimmer, like a desert heat haze.

"Nope, not yet at any rate."

"Well, they can't be far behind." He watched her pick up the radio and begin flicking through the frequencies, calling for help. He left her to it, inching his way aft, searching for weapons. If a couple of hundred Leviathans were about to breach the portal, he wanted to face them with something more substantial than a pistol and a chainsaw.

"Come on," he muttered irritably, scanning the bare walls and desk. "There's got to be something." He tried the desk's drawers but they were mostly empty, and he didn't think a stapler would be much use against an armoured battle tank.

"Balls."

He slammed the top drawer. As he did so, the helicopter's rear engine spluttered and the craft lurched. They wouldn't be airborne much longer. Knotting his fingers in the cargo webbing fixed to the wall, he braced himself. Candles dropped and tumbled, rolling across the deck. Through the open rear doors, the green and brown French countryside dipped and spun. He heard Victoria shout something, and closed his eye.

With an almighty splintering crash, the chopper hit the upper branches of a tree and tipped sideways. There was an instant of sickening free-fall, and then the whole craft rattled as the rotors battered themselves to splinters against the stony soil of a winter field, and the cabin crunched down like an eggshell.

CHAPTER TWENTY
GET TO THE CHOPPER

"NEVER AGAIN," MUTTERED Victoria Valois. Picking her way from the helicopter's ruined cockpit, she swore that, as long as she lived, she would never set foot in another of these contraptions.

Ack-Ack Macaque stood waiting for her. He offered her a leathery hand to help her down.

"You okay, boss?"

She held onto his shoulder for support. She had a few new cuts and bruises, but nothing serious.

At least we didn't land in the sea this time... She blinked in the sunshine. Beyond the fields, she could hear traffic. To the north, a bulky two-hulled skyliner forged towards Paris.

"We're home."

"Seems like it." Ack-Ack Macaque sniffed the air. "How's the pilot?"

Victoria shook her head. "He didn't make it." The man had been crushed when the cockpit hit the dirt. The monkey shrugged. He didn't care. What was one dead henchman in the face of an invading army?

"Come on," he said. "Let's get the fuck out of here." He shambled off across the ploughed field, in the direction of the road, and she trailed after him, still feeling a little unsteady on her feet. A watery winter sun warmed her face and, after spending so long in the gloom of Célestine's world, she could feel herself drawing nourishment from its light and heat. In her eye, Paul fizzed and flickered into virtual existence. He looked around, taking in everything she could see and hear.

"We're in one piece?"

"Just about."

He frowned.

"Why are we running?"

Victoria slowed.

"Because of the tanks."

Paul scratched his temple. "What tanks?"

Up ahead, the monkey had dropped to all fours. He had a pistol in his belt and the chainsaw over his shoulder. She watched him bound towards the dry stone wall at the edge of the field, and quickened her pace to keep up.

"You know, the big Leviathans."

Paul shook his head. He stuck out his bottom lip.

"Where are we, anyway?"

"Home."

"Really?"

Victoria didn't answer. She was jogging now, and couldn't spare the breath. She saw Ack-Ack Macaque reach the wall and clamber over it. Standing on the other side, he called to her.

"Come on!"

Floating above the hardened muddy ground, Paul's image radiated surprise.

"Who's *that*?"

Victoria felt a stab of pain. "What?"

"The monkey." Paul straightened his glasses. "How come he can talk?"

Victoria felt like crying.

"I'll explain later."

"Why, what's the hurry?"

A couple of steps from the wall, she stopped and turned. Roughly a kilometre away, an arch-shaped section of air roiled and bubbled like a pan of boiling water.

"That's why," she said, panting.

As she watched, a slab of khaki-coloured metal appeared in the air, in the centre of the disturbance. It quickly swelled into the snout of one of the Leviathans. Moving slowly, rumbling forward on great tracks, the huge machine pushed its way into the world as if emerging from an invisible tunnel. Its gun turrets bobbed and swivelled, seeking targets. Even at this distance, it seemed to tower over her, and she could feel the ground shake beneath her feet.

Paul's mouth fell open.

"Ah."

MOVING AT A crouch, staying as low as possible, Ack-Ack Macaque led Victoria along the edge of the field, keeping the wall between them and the advancing tank. They were moving at a right angle to the Leviathan's progress, trying to avoid getting crushed by its rolling treads. The noise it made was terrific: the continuous rattle and clatter of the tread links; metallic whines and screeches from axles and wheels; the powerful bark and thrum of its engines...

As he moved, Ack-Ack Macaque sucked in as much fresh air as he could, trying to clear the fumes lingering in his head.

Apynja had used him. The realisation burned fiery and sore, its flame fed by anger and embarrassment. When she'd found him, he'd been exhausted and hungry, and lost on a strange world. She'd drugged him, riled him up, and then turned him loose against Célestine's compound, on what she must have known would be a suicidal attack. Yes, he'd been angry about the needless deaths of so many people on her world; yes, he'd been upset and tired, and wanting to hit back; but she'd amplified and exploited that anger, and used him as a weapon. She'd aimed him at the target, and then pressed all the right buttons.

What had she been expecting? There was no way he could have prevailed against so many cyborgs. He'd been running from them for days—taking the fight to them had been insane. He might be reckless but he wasn't usually that stupid. Usually, he knew when to attack and when to retreat, but Apynja had found a way to circumvent his common sense. He felt used. He would have died had Victoria not shown up when she did. Despite all Apynja's talk about individual freedoms and the taking down of tyrants, the saggy old ape had manipulated him into doing something stupid for her own ends, and—now he was starting to think clearly again—he hated her for it. She was just one more self-serving bastard in a long line of self-serving bastards, and he was tired of being treated like a puppet.

Motioning Victoria to stay hidden, he risked a peep over the wall. They were out of the Leviathan's immediate path but not out of range of its weapons, and he had no doubt that, if they were seen, they'd be blown to pieces. Grinding relentlessly forward, the tank's front tracks rolled across the wreck of the helicopter, flattening it into the ground like a dead bird caught beneath an elephant's foot. Ack-Ack Macaque ducked down.

"If only I had a rocket launcher..."

"It wouldn't do any good," Victoria said. "They have shields. They're almost impenetrable."

"You're kidding me?"

"No, sorry."

"Damn it!" He looked at Victoria and saw she was red-faced and out of breath. Her eyes were raw and puffy, as if she'd been crying. She still wore the shabby, threadbare clothes she'd used as a disguise, and her hands and knees were filthy with mud.

"Stay low," he growled.

At the end of the wall, a stream cut between the fields. With a curse and a snarl of distaste, he crawled down into the reeds at its edge, feeling his hands and legs squishing into the frigid, cloudy muck at their base. His nose wrinkled with the rank cabbage-like smell of rotting vegetation, and his skin cringed at the icy water's cadaverous touch.

"Ah, fuck it." At least now he was below the level of the surrounding fields, and hopefully hidden from sight. He started crawling, sloshing downstream, towards a small stone bridge that marked where a lane crossed the stream. He heard Victoria suck air through her teeth as she slid herself into the water behind him; then, a clattering crash as the Leviathan smashed its way through the field's boundary wall. The beast was going to pass them about two-dozen metres to their left. They were running parallel to its course now. All they had to do was get into the shade of the bridge without being seen. Beneath its mossy stones, they'd have the breathing space to hunker down and plan their next move.

His lips drew back in an involuntary smile. Here he was again, running from enemy war machines in the fields of France. It was just like being back in the game, and he revelled for a moment in the situation's familiarity, remembering better days. He'd been unstoppable back then: the best pilot on the Allied side, victor of a thousand dogfights and a hundred ground skirmishes. He'd once gone hand-to-hand against an entire platoon of Nazi ninjas, and emerged with nothing more serious than a few scratches and some singed fur.

No chance of that now.

The cold water swirled around his arms and legs, aching his bones, and he could feel it sapping his strength—but at least the shock of it had cleared his head. His body might be exhausted but he felt mentally fresher and more on-the-ball than he had in days.

He dipped his head, looking back through his legs.

"How are you doing, boss?"

Victoria's coat was sodden and floating out on either side of her. Her shoulders shook with the cold and her lips had turned a deep purple colour.

"Just keep moving," she hissed through her clenched jaw. Ack-Ack Macaque's grin widened.

"Aye, aye."

He began to shuffle forward, but then stiffened as he heard the boom of a cannon off to his left. Half a second later, a shell exploded on the right-hand bank of the stream, a few metres the other side of the bridge.

"Shit!" He ducked his head as lumps of soil and clumps of grass rained down around him. The gun fired again and the centre of the bridge blew apart. Stones flew in all directions. Heedless of the water, Ack-Ack Macaque threw himself flat. When he emerged a couple of seconds later, gasping and spitting out weeds, he saw that the small structure had been completely destroyed. If he and Victoria had been sitting under it, they'd have been killed by the blast and buried by the debris.

He leapt to his feet and grabbed her by the hand, pulling her back in the direction from which they'd come.

"New plan," he hollered. "Run like fuck!"

SHELLS CRASHED AROUND them as they splashed through the water. The banks of the stream afforded some protection, but not much. Victoria's legs were shaky with cold and fear, and her face stung from the earth and gravel flung up by the explosions. At one point, she and Ack-Ack Macaque were blown completely off their feet, and lay panting in the mud and ooze, ears ringing.

Closing her eyes, she accessed the gelware in her skull. A mental menu allowed her to dial down her sensitivity to pain and fatigue and increase the amount of adrenaline coursing through her arteries.

"Get up." The monkey tugged her sleeve and she stood, coat dripping into the water around her.

"I'm okay." Where a moment ago there had been soreness and discomfort, now she felt only stiffness.

"Ready to run?"

"*Pourquoi pas?*"

"Come on, then." He pushed her forward. Another shell whined overhead and thumped into the ploughed earth of the field on the other side of the stream. Even through her numbed toes, Victoria felt the ground shudder with the force of its impact. She risked a peep at the Leviathan. The enormous, slab-sided vehicle hadn't altered course, and continued to draw away from them, towards the outskirts of Paris. The shells it fired came from two of the smaller turrets towards its rear.

"They're using us for practice," she said indignantly.

Ack-Ack Macaque shoved her onwards.

"Would you prefer they turned around and used their really big guns?"

"No, but—"

"Keep moving," he said. "We need to get across this field." They were back to the point where they'd originally entered the stream. "We'll use the wall as cover again, only this time we'll go on the other side."

"But—"

"They've almost got our range. We have to change direction. If we get behind the wall, they won't know which bit of it we're behind. They won't know where to aim."

"Unless they have thermal imaging."

"In which case, we're fucked whatever we do, so let's act like they don't." He scrambled up the bank and Victoria followed. A shell hit the ground a few metres behind her but she ignored it and kept crawling. The November soil was hard and friable beneath her hands. The wall lay to her left, the portal to her right. The monkey scurried after her, far more comfortable on all fours than she was.

"Don't stop," he huffed. "The only way we're getting out of this is if they don't know where we are."

Two shells hit simultaneously, but they were back towards the stream, further away than before.

Is it working?

She could see Paul's ghost floating in the air before her. He'd taken off his glasses and had his hands on his hips.

"I'm sorry," he said, "but who's shooting at us?"

"Lady Alyssa."

"I thought she was dead."

Victoria didn't answer; she couldn't spare the breath to explain, and she wasn't sure she could talk to him without her voice cracking. For three years, she'd been dreading this moment: the point at which his simulated personality began to de-cohere and fade, and he became progressively more confused. As a teenager, she'd had an aunt with Alzheimer's and had no desire to repeat the experience of watching another human being unravel piece-by-piece—especially one she loved as fiercely as she loved Paul. She reached the section of wall pulverised by the Leviathan's tracks and stopped crawling. The noise of the tank's engines was quieter now, and the shells it fired were going wide, its rear gunners still concentrating on the section of wall closest to the water.

"Why aren't they firing this way?" she asked.

Ack-Ack Macaque dropped back onto his haunches.

"They don't need to."

"Why not?"

"Because of that." Across the field, beyond the crushed remains of the helicopter, the portal shimmered again, and the snout of another huge battle tank appeared.

"*Merde.*"

"You said it."

Whichever side of the wall they chose, they'd be visible to one Leviathan or the other. They were trapped and exposed, with nowhere to hide, and no weapons capable of inflicting damage on the enemy.

She grabbed the leather shoulder of Ack-Ack Macaque's flight jacket.

"What do we do?"

The monkey smacked his lips and drew the large black pistol from his belt.

"I'll distract them, you run for it."

She gave him a look.

"You're kidding?"

He shook his head, and unstrapped the chainsaw. "I'll charge the bastard. You run for it. See if you can get across the field and lose yourself behind the far wall. It's your only chance."

The second Leviathan was only halfway through the portal but its turrets were already zeroing in on their position. Victoria swallowed.

"I can't leave you."

"You don't have a choice, sweetheart." Ack-Ack Macaque jumped to his feet, brandishing a weapon in each hand, and let out a howl. Then he started to run. Victoria winced. She could see guns of all shapes and sizes turning on him.

"Wait!" But it was too late. She couldn't do anything to stop what was about to happen. She couldn't even bring herself to run. Her body wouldn't respond. She crouched there, unable to move, as her best friend ran at the biggest tank she'd ever seen, waving his chainsaw above his head.

He wouldn't get close, she knew. He'd die and, moments later, she'd follow him. She tried to close her eyes but couldn't wrestle her gaze from the horror unfolding before her.

She braced herself for the inevitable hail of bullets...

THE AIR CRACKLED and the sun went out.

By the time she realised it was the *Sun Wukong* blocking out the sky, the dreadnought had unloaded a clutch of missiles at the tank, engulfing it in a series of gigantic fireballs. The concussions knocked her back on her derrière, and she sat for a few seconds, mouth open at the ferocity of the attack. Ack-Ack Macaque recovered faster than she did. While her attention remained fixed on the Leviathan—still rolling and apparently unharmed as it emerged from the conflagration—he ran back and yanked her upright.

"Cavalry's here," he said.

Looking up, Victoria saw a helicopter spiralling down from the airship, weaving and ducking to avoid the lines of tracer cutting the sky around it.

Oh God, she thought. *Not another helicopter. Not again.*

Hand-in-hand, they started running, stumbling and skidding on the loose, uneven surface of the ploughed field. Above, the dreadnought fired another clutch of rockets.

"The shield," she said. "The missiles can't get through."

Ack-Ack Macaque said nothing. He just kept pulling her onwards. His palm felt as soft and warm as a leather glove, but the tendons beneath were as hard and tight as wire.

Several of the Leviathan's larger cannons swung upwards, aiming at the *Sun Wukong*. As Victoria watched, they fired a volley. She tried to cover her ears. The noise was deafening, and she could feel it in her gut. The tank rocked on its tracks, and angry explosions tore the airship's underside. At the same time, a pair of missiles dropped from the main gondola and punched through the Leviathan's roof. Their combined detonation lit the tank up from within. Flames burst from every hatch and turret, and the upper superstructure blew apart like a tin can filled with firecrackers.

Even as the wreck burned, the air behind it rippled and the bow of a third Leviathan appeared. Legs and feet now almost completely numb, Victoria staggered unsteadily towards the spot where the helicopter was in the process of touching down in a whirl of dust and twigs. To her left, beyond the wall, the first Leviathan also engaged the airship, and they traded shots. She wondered how much punishment the *Sun Wukong*'s armour could withstand.

With all hell breaking out around her, she ran for all she was worth—but Ack-Ack Macaque merely stood contemplating the burning wreckage of the second tank, with its punctured roof and smoking windows. A slight frown creased his face and he rubbed thoughtfully at the patch over his left eye.

"Now, that's interesting," he said.

CHAPTER TWENTY-ONE
LABYRINTHINE AND MOSTLY UNDOCUMENTED

THE HELICOPTER TOOK them up, through a hurricane of explosions and tracer fire, to the upper deck of the *Sun Wukong*. Victoria's knuckles were white on her safety straps and her heart raced in her chest. By the time they touched down, her gelware had been forced to intercede, flooding her bloodstream with sedatives. She stepped out onto the deck feeling dreamy and disjointed. The monkey shuffled along beside her as if suffering the world's worst hangover.

"We have to get to the bridge," he said. A shell struck the bottom of the airship and Victoria staggered as the deck shook beneath her feet. Ack-Ack Macaque looked at her with his bloodshot yellow eye. "Come on." His face had scratches; his jacket had become filthy, ripped and scuffed; his fur had been caked in mud and tangled with brambles and twigs; and his arms dangled loosely at his sides, as if he lacked the strength to lift them. God alone knew how long he'd been without food or sleep.

"No," she said.

He blinked at her. "But—"

"No, I've got this." She rolled her head, stretching her neck muscles in an effort to shake off the drowsiness of the drugs. "You get below. Take a shower. Get something to eat. Have K8 patch you up." He opened his mouth but she cut him off. "Go on," she snapped in her best captain-of-a-skyliner tone, "you're no use to us if you can hardly stand."

Now she was out of the chopper, and not in imminent danger of another crash, she felt better. And this wouldn't be her first battle.

"I'll call you if I need you," she promised. A damaged rocket corkscrewed up into the sky and burst like a firework. Ack-Ack Macaque sagged with relief.

"Yes, boss."

"Good, now get below."

"Just one thing." He lingered. "Their shields."

"What about them?"

"They work both ways. They have to drop them to fire."

Victoria raised an eyebrow. "Are you sure?"

The monkey gave a grim nod. "I clocked it in the field. That's how the missiles got through to the second tank."

Victoria felt her cheeks redden. So, that's what he'd been doing. She'd been too busy running to pay attention to the ins and outs of the battle. Surprising herself, she lunged forward and caught him in a bear hug. He squirmed, and stank like an old carpet, but she held him tight, clinging to his leather-clad shoulders, feeling his whiskers prickle her cheek and neck.

"I'm so glad to have you back," she said. She held him for a moment, then gave him a final squeeze and hurried up the companionway to the bridge, where she found the Founder in the command chair. The pregnant monkey looked at her through her monocle.

"Thank goodness you're here, dear." She wore a long velvet dress and a miniature top hat.

"What's the situation?"

"Two tanks clobbered, dear, but more keep coming. Every time we hit one of them, another takes its place."

"Keep firing."

"I'm not sure we can, dear. Those tanks are shielded and we're running out of missiles."

The bridge trembled with the force of an impact. Victoria reached over to connect herself to the ship-wide intercom.

"Don't waste your ammo," she snapped, addressing the crew. "The Leviathans have to drop shields to shoot. Wait until they fire, *then* let them have it." She clicked off, and turned back to the Founder. "Now, get out of my chair."

"Yes, dear."

She let the monkey move, and then slipped into place. There was no time to get comfortable. A quick scan of the tactical display showed that the Founder hadn't been exaggerating: they were running out of ammunition at a frightening rate, and damage reports were coming in from all sections of the airship, nearly all of them tagged as urgent.

"We can't take much more of this," Victoria muttered to herself. It was time to call in reinforcements.

"Paul," she said, opening the wireless connection between her cranial gelware and the *Sun Wukong*'s control systems, "get in there and get on the radio. Send out the following message with a general distress call: *Am fighting invasion from parallel world. Stop. Outgunned. Stop. Send help. Stop.*"

He blinked at her through his spectacles, eyebrows scrunched in puzzlement.

"Huh?"

"Please, I'll explain later. For now, just do it."

"What are you going to do?"

"I'm going to call Merovech."

"The Prince?"

"The *King*."

Paul smiled. "Oh, I like him."

A shell hit the underside of the gondola like a hammer striking an anvil. Klaxons wailed. With a lurid French curse, Victoria initiated the transfer, giving Paul the electronic equivalent of a hefty shove. He tumbled out of her head, his source code transferred from her neural prosthesis to the airship's computer—his 'home' for the past two years.

She hoped he wouldn't get lost in there. The computer's file structures were labyrinthine and mostly undocumented, and Paul's memory could hardly be described as being at its best; still, she didn't have time to worry. All that mattered for now was that he sent the distress signal; everything else could wait. With luck, there'd be one or two dreadnoughts in the vicinity, fully armed and able to assist.

While he called for help on the radio, she accessed the ship-to-shore telecommunications console and typed in a private number, known to fewer than a dozen people. The phone line rang twice, and she found herself facing the image of a young woman in a business suit.

"Captain Valois? You're back?"

"Who are you?" Victoria had to shout over the airship's sirens.

"Amy Llewellyn, His Majesty's private secretary. Are you calling to speak to him?"

The deck lurched again, knocking Victoria sideways. She had to grab the console's rim to avoid being thrown from the chair. The air on the bridge smelled of burning electrical wire.

"This is an emergency."

"I can see that."

"Then stop blithering and put me through!"

"Victoria?" Merovech looked haunted. "Is the monkey with you?"

"Yes."

"Good. I need to see you both, as quickly as possible."

"That's not going to be easy." Victoria flinched as the airship took another hit. "We're sort of busy right now."

The young king narrowed his eyes, for the first time noticing the chaos around her.

"Why, what's happening?"

She gave him a brief summary of the situation. As he listened, his expression grew darker and more troubled.

"I'll send everything I can," he promised. "How long can you hold out?"

"A few minutes at the most. We're taking quite a hammering."

He shook his head. "Then get out of there. You've done your bit."

"But if we're not here—"

"It won't make much difference." He glanced aside, consulting another screen. "We can have another fully-armed dreadnought on site within fifteen minutes; then another ten minutes after that, with a third close behind."

A huge detonation shook the *Sun Wukong*, and it tipped a few degrees to starboard. They were losing buoyancy and the smell of smoke was growing stronger. Victoria put a hand to the scar tissue at the back of her head. She had no desire to be shot out of the sky again, especially so soon after her most recent helicopter crash.

"Okay," she said, "we're leaving."

Merovech stood. He was wearing a charcoal-grey blazer over a black polo neck sweater. The camera followed his motion, tracking his face.

"Head for the Channel," he told her. "I'll meet you en route. I've got something I need to brief you on."

"What about the invasion?"

Merovech shook his head, looking suddenly far older than his years. "Believe me, we've got worse problems."

ACK-ACK MACAQUE LAY on his bunk, wrapped in a towel. He had a glass of rum in one hand and a fat Cuban cigar in the other. He'd taken a long, hot shower and eaten the meat from a whole roast chicken. He'd even sucked the grease from its carcass. K8 stood in the doorway, bracing herself against the frame to compensate for the tilt of the deck.

"How are you feeling?" she asked.

Ack-Ack Macaque took a luxuriant puff on his cigar and blew a line of smoke at the low ceiling. His bones ached and his muscles felt as if they'd been worked over with a meat tenderiser, but at least he'd scrubbed the dirt from his fur and filled the void in his stomach. Apynja's drugs had worn off and he felt almost back to his old self.

"Better." He stretched and yawned, baring his fangs. "I haven't heard any sirens for a while. Are we still fighting?"

"We're withdrawing. There are other airships coming in to take our place."

Startled, Ack-Ack Macaque sat up. "What do you mean, 'withdrawing'?" He couldn't believe Victoria would run from a fight.

"Merovech wants to see us."

"Oh, he does, does he?"

"He *is* the King."

"So?"

"And he's our friend." K8 adjusted the lapels of her immaculate white jacket. "He says we've got more to worry about than a load of tanks in a French field."

"Pah." Ack-Ack Macaque clamped the cigar in his teeth and stretched his legs over the edge of the bed. He wriggled his toes. "How long until we get to London?"

"We're not going to London. We're meeting Merovech in Calais, in about an hour."

"Time for a nap, then?"

"Maybe a quick one."

Something in her voice caused him to pause. He gave her a look. "What's the matter?"

She looked down evasively, like a teenager with a secret. "Nothing."

He grunted. "Hey, K8, come on. It's me you're talking to. I can see there's something bugging you. What is it?"

"You wouldn't understand."

"Try me."

She licked her lips.

"It's the hive," she said. "Now we're home, we can hear them again." She tapped her temple. "In here."

Ack-Ack Macaque narrowed his eye. "But that's what you wanted, wasn't it?"

K8 balled her fists. It made her look like the moody, freckle-faced adolescent he remembered. "We don't know. Being away from them was difficult, but coming back feels like trying to catch the thread of a conversation that's been going on without us. It takes some getting used to."

Ack-Ack Macaque drummed his toes on the deck. "But it's still what you wanted, right?"

She sighed. "We said you wouldn't understand."

Ack-Ack Macaque took the cigar from his mouth and rolled it between his fingers and thumb.

Bloody kids.

He took a deep breath and reminded himself that it was his fault she was as she was. If he hadn't given her to the hive, she wouldn't be in this mess.

"So," he asked gruffly, trying to make conversation, "what are they saying?"

"All sorts." K8 stretched like a cat. "Remember, there are close to a million of them. Some are still on the dreadnoughts, helping train crews from this timeline; others are on the ground, helping the rebuilding effort."

"And what about the Founder?" Ack-Ack tried to keep his tone neutral. "Now Victoria's let her out of her cage, won't she be plugged back in?"

K8 gave a nod, and he scowled.

"What's she saying to the hive?" Despite their mutual attraction, he'd never completely trusted the Founder, and had been deeply sceptical about her release.

"Not much. Just keep cooperating, keep working hard. That sort of thing."

"That's it, huh?"

"Pretty much."

"No insurrection?" The first time he'd met her, she'd been trying to take over the world. This new meekness seemed out of character, and he didn't buy it.

"There is one thing." K8's face split in a sudden grin, teeth squeezing the tip of her tongue, eyes sparkling.

"What?"

She covered her mouth with her hand, trying to stifle her amusement. "We shouldn't say."

Ack-Ack Macaque growled. "What's she planning?

K8 shook her head. "It's not like that, Skipper."

"Then what is it? I know she's up to something. If she so much as—"

"She's pregnant."

Ack-Ack Macaque's head jerked back. The cigar fell from his fingers. "*What?*"

K8's smile broadened. "You're going to be a daddy."

Ack-Ack Macaque coughed. He worked dry lips but no sounds emerged from his throat. There seemed to be a disconnection between his brain and vocal cords.

K8 stooped to retrieve the cigar. She held it out to him, and he took it, fingers shaking.

"You're shitting me?"

Her laugh was clear and bright, like a Highland brook. "We're afraid not, Skip. It's the truth."

"And it's definitely mine?"

"No doubt about it."

With a groan, Ack-Ack Macaque sagged back onto the bedclothes.

"And everybody knows?"

"Only the hive."

"Why hasn't she told me?"

K8 spread her hands. "You'd have to ask her."

He bared his teeth. "Oh, I intend to, you can be sure of *that*." He glared at the rivets on the ceiling. "Where is she now?"

"She's on the bridge, with Victoria."

Tired stomach muscles protesting, Ack-Ack Macaque sat up.

"Then I should probably go and see her, huh?"

K8's smile faded. "No, not yet. There's something else you have to take care of first."

"Can't it wait?"

"It's Bali. He's been stirring up trouble."

"Tell me something new."

K8 bit the inside of her cheek. "He's serious this time." She started fiddling with her cuffs, then stopped as she realised what she was doing. "We don't like it. He really thinks he should be in charge."

Ack-Ack Macaque huffed. "Well, he can moan all he likes. If he wants to be leader, he'll have to challenge me first. That's the way it works." He gave a snort. "And he's hardly going to be dumb enough to do *that*, is he?"

The corners of K8's mouth pulled back in a nervous grimace.

"Um…"

"You're joking?"

"We're afraid not." She pointed upwards. "He's waiting for you up in Hangar Three. Most of the other monkeys are up there. Some are just curious, but others support him."

Ack-Ack Macaque's exhaustion came flooding back, like a tide reclaiming a beach. "So, I've got a mutiny on my hands?"

"We're afraid so."

"Have I got time for a nap, and to get some clean clothes?"

K8 checked her watch—a habitual and obsolete gesture given the connections in her head. "He's given you an hour. He says you forfeit if you don't show your face by three o'clock."

Ack-Ack Macaque bridled. "Cheeky bastard. What time is it now?"

"Two-thirty."

"Ah, crap." Ack-Ack Macaque pushed himself up, onto his feet.

"What are you going to do?"

"What do you think I'm going to do?" He scratched at his eye patch. "I'm going to teach the little twat a lesson. Give me five minutes and then go and let them know I'm on my way."

K8's brow furrowed with concern. "Are you sure you're up to it?"

He laughed, but there wasn't any humour in the sound, only bitterness. "Not really, but what choice do I have?"

"You could arrest him, and throw him in the brig."

Ack-Ack Macaque opened the drawer containing his spare clothes. He couldn't go up there in a dressing gown. If he wanted to assert his dominance over the troupe, he'd have to do it looking his best.

"No, I couldn't," he said. "His supporters would think that was my way of avoiding a fight. They'd take it as a sign of weakness."

"Monkey politics?"

"It's all about being the alpha male, sweetheart."

K8 rolled her eyes but didn't protest.

"All right," she said wearily, "but be careful."

As she turned to leave, Ack-Ack Macaque pulled a knife from the bottom of his sock drawer.

"Careful isn't a word I know." He held the weapon up to the light, checking the edge for nicks and dents. "Oh, and K8?"

She paused in the doorway, one hand gripping the handle to keep her balance.

"Yes, Skip?"

"It's good to see you."

She smiled.

"It's good to see you, too, Skipper."

LATER, UP IN the hangar, Bali stood at the centre of a helipad, naked save for his necklace of leopard's teeth. His fingers gripped the hilt of a foot-long machete and his feet straddled the crossbar of the pad's large, yellow 'H'.

He stood with as much nonchalance as he could muster, with his weight on one hip and his shoulders loose, and an insolent sneer on his face. He wanted the other monkeys to know he wasn't afraid. They stood around him at a respectful distance, fidgeting and glancing at wristwatches. None dared speak aloud. Bali's own timepiece showed there were only three minutes remaining until the deadline. Despite what the K8 child had said, it didn't look as if Ack-Ack Macaque would be making an appearance. Deep inside, Bali snarled to himself. It would be typical of the irresponsible clown to ignore this challenge and risk losing a lot of credibility in the eyes of the monkey army.

"Come on," he muttered impatiently. He didn't want to win by default, and he didn't want to drag this out. A simple, clear victory would be all it took. He'd seen the state of his rival—scratched, filthy and exhausted—and felt confident he could beat him.

And then all this will be mine. He checked his watch again. The monkeys around him were getting fidgety. They knew that, any moment now, the challenge would be resolved one way or another and, unless Ack-Ack Macaque showed his face, they would have a new leader.

Two minutes. Bali could feel his palm sweating against the machete's plastic grip. He tapped the point of the blade against the metal deck. The troupe needed strong leadership. They needed goals, and incentives, and something for which to aim and strive. Now Ack-Ack Macaque had freed them from their various timelines, they needed a *purpose*—and Bali knew he was the one best equipped to provide it.

And what greater purpose could there be than ensuring the survival of the troupe? He would find them mates and a homeland—and not some dreary stockade on an empty world, but a true home, on a timeline with a working infrastructure and plenty of potential slaves. Before being rescued, every monkey here had been the victim of human experimentation. Instead of hiding themselves away in the jungle, they deserved revenge; they deserved the chance to turn the tables on their former oppressors, and use their newfound intelligence for something more satisfying than erecting mud huts and digging latrines.

One minute. He drew himself up. The nervous chatter stopped, and all eyes turned to him.

"Well," he said with a fierce grin, "I seem to have been stood up." He held his arms out to his sides in a theatrical gesture, the machete dangling limply from his right hand. "It seems our erstwhile leader has better things to do than defend his position."

For a second, awed silence reigned. Then the pad lurched beneath their feet. With a mechanical squeal, it began to rise. Overhead, part of the upper deck slid aside, revealing the open sky, and a lone figure silhouetted against it. It was, of course, Ack-Ack Macaque. Bali felt his heart skip. The older monkey stood with his arms crossed and his back to the sun. A cigar smouldered between his fingers and he wore a brand new flying jacket, leather cap and goggles. A pair of chrome-plated Colts gleamed at his hips and he had a pristine white silk scarf knotted around his neck. As the lift drew level with the airship's upper surface, he fixed Bali with a baleful eye, and cleared his throat.

"Au contraire, mon frère."

PART TWO

EMBERS ON THE WIND

Gliding o'er all, through all,
Through Nature, Time, and Space,
As a ship on the waters advancing,
The voyage of the soul—not life alone,
Death, many deaths I'll sing.

Walt Whitman, *Gliding O'er All*

CHAPTER TWENTY-TWO
NAPOLEON JONES

VILCA'S MEN WERE going to kill him. He tried to lose himself in the improvised warrens of the vertical favelas, but knew it was only a matter of time before they found him. He'd been away too long; his memories of the rat runs and back ways were out of date by at least a couple of decades. In the end, two of his pursuers cornered him on one of the innumerable wire footbridges stretched between the barrios that clung coral-like to both walls of the steep, narrow canyon.

"Stay where you are, Jones." The short one's name was Faro. He was a tough young street kid. His elder brother Emilio blocked the other end of the bridge. They would have both been small boys the last time Napoleon Jones had been here; but now they were in their mid-twenties and armed with machetes. Caught between them, he realised he had nowhere left to run. The springy bridge was less than two metres in width and fifty in length. Half a kilometre below, corrugated metal rooftops patchworked the canyon's rocky floor. Other bridges crisscrossed the gap at various heights. Flyers and cargo Zeppelins nosed like cautious fish between them. Shanties crusted both the canyon's cliff faces, layer upon layer. Lines of laundry drooped from window to window. Cooking fires filled the air with the bitter tang of smouldering wood and plastic. He could hear shouts and screams and children's voices. Somewhere a young woman sang.

"What do you want?" he said, buying time.

The two kids each took a step onto the wire bridge. Napoleon took hold of the handrails to steady himself.

"We got something for you, from Vilca," Emilio said.

Napoleon tipped back the brim of his Stetson. "Maybe I don't want it."

Faro laughed cruelly. He slapped the flat blade of his machete against the palm of his hand. "Maybe you're going to get it, whether you want it or not."

Napoleon risked a peep over the handrail. This canyon was just one of hundreds arranged in a vast, sprawling delta, carved out over millennia by the patient action of wind and water. Like the tentacles of an enormous squid, the canyons stretched from the mountains at one end of the planet's solitary supercontinent to the sea at the other, providing the only shade in what was otherwise a pitiless, UV-drenched desert.

Looking down, he saw a cargo Zeppelin about to pass beneath the bridge, its broad back like the smooth hump of a browsing whale, and felt the walkway shudder beneath his feet as the street kids advanced, weapons raised.

He should never have come back to Nuevo Cordoba. He should have known better. He looked longingly down the canyon, in the direction of the distant ocean. The wind tugged at his lizard-skin coat. If he could only get back to his starship, the *Bobcat*, floating tethered at the offshore spaceport, he'd be free. He could finally shake this planet's dust from his boots. As things stood, though, it looked as if he'd be lucky to make it off this bridge alive; or at least in one piece.

He glanced at the approaching thugs. They were closer now. Emilio swung his machete from side to side.

"Nowhere to hide?"

Napoleon glanced from one brother to the other. They were almost within striking distance.

"I don't want any trouble."

"Shut it," Faro said.

Below, the Zeppelin slid its blunt nose into the shadow of the bridge. Napoleon took the antique flying goggles that hung around his neck and pulled them up over his eyes. Seeing the movement, Emilio stepped forward with a grunt. He scythed his machete around in a powerful swing aimed at Napoleon's head. Napoleon ducked the blade and came up hard, grasping for the big lad's arm while the force of the swing still had him off balance. He slammed Emilio's wrist against the rail of the bridge, trying to get him to drop the knife. Emilio roared in annoyance and pushed back. The machete came up in a vicious backhand swipe. Napoleon tried to twist out of the way but the tip of the blade caught him across the right forearm, biting through lizard skin, cotton and flesh.

"Ah!" He staggered back, clutching the stinging wound. He saw more of Vilca's men arrive. They began to advance across the bridge, and Napoleon knew this was a fight he couldn't win. As the brothers dropped into fighting crouches on either side of him, ready to hack him to pieces, he braced himself against the handrail.

"Sorry, boys," he said.

Using his boot heel to push off, he crossed the width of the walkway in two quick steps and launched himself over the opposite rail, into empty air.

THE WIND TORE at him. His coat flapped. The fall seemed to take forever.

Then his boots hit the fabric upper surface of the Zeppelin hard enough to jar his spine. He bounced, sprawling forward in an ungainly tangle of limbs and coattails. For a second, he thought he was going to roll right off the side and fall to his death at the bottom of the canyon. Then his hands and feet found purchase against the fabric and he clung spread-eagled, sucking in great raw lungfuls of cold canyon air.

If he raised his head, he could see, over the curve of the hull, one of the engine nacelles, with the blurred, hissing circle of its black carbon impeller blades. Beyond that, nothing but air and rooftops.

Heart hammering in his chest, he clawed his way back up to the relatively flat surface at the top of the Zeppelin. Once there, he rolled onto his back and sat up. He'd skinned his knees and palms. His right arm hurt and his hand and sleeve were slathered and sticky with blood. Worst of all, he'd lost his hat. Still, he was alive. Behind him, Faro and Emilio boggled open-mouthed from the footbridge. He pushed his goggles up onto his forehead and raised a bloody, one-fingered salute.

"So long, fuckers."

The wind straggled his hair. Staying low to avoid being blown off the airship altogether, he crawled back towards the tail fin and found a maintenance hatch set into the fabric at its base. He pulled it open and climbed down an aluminium ladder, into the shadowy interior.

The outer envelope of the airship housed a number of helium gas bags, with walkways and cargo spaces wedged between them. The air was dark and cold in there, like a cave. Moving as quickly as his protesting limbs would allow, Napoleon made his way shakily across a catwalk and down another ladder to the access panel that led to the control gondola slung beneath the main hull. As he dropped into the cabin, the pilot—a scruffy young technician sipping coffee at a cup-strewn computer console—turned to him in amazement.

"Where did you come from?"

Clutching the torn sleeve of his snakeskin coat, blood seeping through his fingers, Napoleon glowered. He pointed forward, through the windshield, at a docking mast protruding from a cluster of warehouses near the base of the canyon's right-hand wall.

"Take us down, boy," he said.

*   *   *

As soon as the Zeppelin's nose nudged the mast, Napoleon Jones was off and running again. He pushed through the narrow stairwells and crowded walkways that formed the streets of the vertical town. His boots splashed through water and over broken glass floors of shattered tiles. Down here at the base of the favela, water dripped constantly from the upper levels. Strip lights flickered and sizzled; power cables hung in improvised loops. He passed dirty kitchens; tattoo parlours; street dentists. Blanket-wrapped figures slept in alcoves behind steam pipes. He smelled hot, sour plastic from the corner kiosks, where fabbers made shoes and toys from discarded bottles and cans. He turned right, then left, trying to put as much distance as he could between himself and Vilca's men. He moved awkwardly, cradling his hurt arm, trying to keep pressure on the wound.

Reappearing like this, after two decades, had been a mistake. Twenty years ago, he'd been at the top of his game: a celebrated daredevil repeatedly flinging his craft into hyperspace on arbitrary trajectories, just to see where he'd end up. The media called the sport 'random jumping', and it was a dangerous pastime; not all the pilots who took part returned. Those who did, especially those who'd discovered a newly habitable world or the location of an ore-rich asteroid belt, became celebrities. Venture capitalists and would-be entrepreneurs lined up to sponsor them. And in his time, Napoleon Jones had been one of the best and brightest of their number. But he'd been unable to manage the wealth and attention. He fucked up. He developed a tranquiliser dependency and let things slide. He got sloppy. And then one day, he simply disappeared.

Now he was back, he was a fugitive. In his absence, Vilca had gone from a small-time gang boss to *de facto* ruler of Nuevo Cordoba's favelas, and he wanted the money Napoleon owed him; money that should have part-financed another random jump into the unknown, but went instead to supporting an extended stay on Strauli, a crossroads world eight light years in the wrong direction.

Napoleon came to the end of a corridor and cut through a laundry area. Hot wet steam filled the air. He squeezed through the narrow spaces between the vats of boiling clothes, searching for another way out. Spilled detergent made the floor slick and slippery. The workers watched him with dull, incurious eyes. They knew better than to get involved. Eventually, he found a hatchway that led into a narrow service duct between one set of buildings and the next. Thick cables ran the length of the floor, beneath a layer of waste paper and discarded packing materials. At the end of the duct, he emerged into daylight. He was on the floor of the canyon now, looking up at the layers of improvised dwellings that towered a hundred metres up the side of the cliff above him.

A tangle of shacks and warehouses covered the ground between him and the vertical settlements on the far wall, clustered to either side of the melt-water stream that ran from the mountains at one end of the canyon to the sea at the other. Napoleon looked left and right, trying to orientate himself. He wasn't familiar with this part of town. His old stamping grounds were further downstream, towards the port. He'd come this far inland seeking an old flame: the girl he'd ditched twenty years ago, when he'd jumped out of the system *en route* for Strauli, half baked on tranquilisers and intending never to return. He brought his ship down in the ocean off the coast, where the canyons met the water, and left it floating there. Then he went looking for her.

Her name was Crystal. He had found her in a small room off a darkened landing, half an hour before Vilca's men found him.

"What do you want?" she asked.

"It's me, honey. Napoleon." He took off his hat.

"I know who you are."

"I've come to see you. To see how you are."

She looked him up and down with contempt.

"You still look exactly the same," she said.

He forced a smile.

"So do you."

Crystal gave a snort. "You always were a lousy liar, Jones." She stepped back from the door, her heels clicking on the vinyl floor. "You can come on in, if you want."

Napoleon hesitated at the threshold, both hands holding the brim of his hat. The room wasn't much larger than the bed it contained, and dark; and the air smelled of stale sheets.

"I thought you might have been married."

"I was, for a while." Crystal squeezed her hands together. "It didn't take."

"What happened?"

She stopped kneading her fingers and wrapped her arms across her ample chest.

"Why the hell do you care?"

Napoleon shrugged.

"Look, I'm sorry—"

"You're sorry? You stand there all sorry, not having aged at all. While the rest of us have had to live through the past twenty *years*."

He held up his hands.

"I just wanted to see how you were."

Crystal tossed back her mane of red hair.

"I'm fat and middle-aged and alone. Are you happy now?"

Napoleon stepped back onto the landing. While the hyperspace jumps from one star system to the next took the same amount of time as it took light to cross the intervening distance, the jumps themselves felt instantaneous to the crews of the ships making them; so for every light year Napoleon had travelled, a calendar year had worn away here, for Crystal. She'd gone from her mid twenties to her mid forties while he'd only aged by a couple of years.

"I should be going," he said, regretting the sentimental impulse that had brought him to her door.

Her lip curled. She took hold of the door, ready to close it.

"Yes, go on. Leave. It's the only thing you're good at."

Napoleon backed off another step.

"I can see you're upset—"

"Oh, just go."

She closed the door, leaving him standing alone in the gloom of a solitary overhead fluorescent strip. He could hear her sobbing behind the door. The sound gave him a sick, empty feeling.

He replaced his Stetson and, hands in pockets, he walked back to the stairwell. From there, he went looking for a bar; but before he could find one, Faro and Emilio found him.

Now, still on the run after his adventures on the Zeppelin, and still bleeding heavily from the gash in his arm, Napoleon started making his way through the maze-like shanties on the canyon floor, towards the transport tube that threaded along the base of the far wall, fifty or so metres away. If he could get there and get on a train, he'd be at the port in no time.

He staggered forward. The sky was a thin strip of blue, high above. Flyers and Zeppelins floated like fish in an undersea trench. Down here at the bottom, a thin frost covered everything. The sun rarely penetrated to this depth.

The houses here were ramshackle affairs. Some were two or three storeys in height. They looked like pieces fallen from the cliff-hugging favelas looming over them on either side: minor debris presaging a forthcoming avalanche. The houses belonged to mushroom farmers. Between them lay tended rows of edible fungi, like the fingers of dead white hands thrusting up through the damp soil.

Napoleon picked his path with care, sticking close to the houses, avoiding the crops. The last thing he needed was an irate farmer taking pot shots at him; and besides, he didn't want to get his boots any dirtier than they already were.

He was almost to the river before Vilca's men caught up with him again. This time, it was four of them in a flyer. They came in low and fast, the flyer's fans kicking up dirt and rubbish. Napoleon started running as best he could but he couldn't move quickly while cradling his arm. Bullets ripped into the ground around him, sending up angry spurts of dust; each one closer than the last.

He made maybe ten metres before something punched through his thigh. The impact spun him around in a graceless pirouette.

He landed on his back in the dirt. The flyer's howling fans kicked up a maelstrom of dust and grit around him, and he rolled onto his side, trying to curl into a ball, cringing in anticipation. Waiting for the next shot.

CHAPTER TWENTY-THREE
SUNBURN

THE TRADING SHIP *Ameline* flashed into existence a thousand kilometres above the inhospitable sands of Nuevo Cordoba. The ship was a snub-nosed wedge, thirty metres across at the stern and narrowing to five at the bow, its paintwork the faded blue and red livery of the Abdulov trading family. Alone on its bridge, her neural implant hooked into its virtual senses, Katherine Abdulov looked down at the planet beneath, with its deep, fertile oceans and single barren supercontinent. Even from here, she could see the tracery of fissures comprising the canyon system that gave shelter and life to the planet's human population.

"Any trace of infection?" she asked the ship, and felt it run a sensor sweep, scouring the globe for signs of The Recollection's all-consuming spores.

> NOTHING I CAN DETECT, AND NO MENTION OF ANYTHING SUSPICIOUS ON THE PLANETARY GRID.

Kat heard the ship's words in her mind via her neural link, and pursed her lips. For the moment she was relieved, yet knew such relief to be premature. Even if the contagion hadn't yet spread to this planet, it was almost certainly already on its way, using cannibalised human starships to spread itself along the trade routes from Strauli Quay. She took a moment to remember the other worlds already lost to the unstoppable red tide. Their names burned in her mind: Djatt, Inakpa... Strauli.

She'd seen her home world swallowed by The Recollection, lost most of her family, including her mother, to its insatiable hunger. Now she was out here, at this world on the edge of unknown space, hoping to warn the inhabitants of the approaching threat, and rescue as many of them as she could.

Through the ship's senses, she felt the arrival of the rest of her flotilla: two dozen fat-arsed freighters, each piloted by a crew of Acolytes, and each with the cargo capacity to transport several hundred refugees.

One by one, they reported in.

"Target the spaceport and the main canyon settlements," she told them. "Save as many people as you can."

HER ONLY PREVIOUS visit to the isolated world of Nuevo Cordoba had taken place years ago—whole decades in local time—during her first trip as an independent trader. That had been back before her pregnancy and the birth of her daughter, back before the coming of The Recollection and the loss of her left arm. She remembered the planet as a corrupt, mean-spirited place, the canyon dwellers made hard and cynical by the harshness of their environment, and lives spent mining the rock or grubbing for mushrooms and lichen. She wondered how they were coping without the arch network. She also remembered one Cordoban in particular: a random hyperspace jumper with whom she'd had a brief affair. She remembered his Mephistophelean beard; his long hair tied back in a dark ponytail; his Stetson hat, and snakeskin coat. The way his skin smelled of cologne and old leather.

PROMPTED BY THE memory, she said, "Scan the port for the *Bobcat*'s transponder."
> ALREADY LOCATED. THE *BOBCAT* IS CURRENTLY FLOATING IN THE PARKING ZONE OFF THE CONTINENT'S WESTERN COAST. DO YOU WANT TO MAKE CONTACT?
Kat settled back in her couch feeling winded. She'd been half-joking when she asked for the scan. She hadn't actually expected him to *be* here. Swallowing down an unwelcome flutter, she drummed the instrument console with the tungsten fingers of her prosthetic hand.
"Just see if he's on board."
The *Ameline* opened a comms channel. Through her neural link, Kat felt it squirt a high-density info burst at the other ship. The reply—a similarly compressed screech of data—came a couple of seconds later, delayed by distance.
> HE'S NOT THERE AT THE MOMENT.
"Can the ship patch us through to his implant?"
> I'M AFRAID NOT.
"Any mention of him on the Grid?"
The *Ameline* accessed the planetary communications net and ran a quick search.

> HE'S IN TROUBLE.

Kat rolled her eyes. *Of course...*

"With the law?"

> THERE'S A PRICE ON HIS HEAD.

"Can you locate him?"

> IT SEEMS HE'S BEEN TAKEN CAPTIVE BY ONE OF THE LOCAL GANGSTERS, A MAN NAMED EARL VILCA.

"Show me."

A map unfolded before her eyes: a three-dimensional aerial view of one of the canyons, patched together by the ship from direct observation, public records and intercepted satellite observation. A yellow tag marked Jones' last known location, on the canyon floor.

> THE *BOBCAT* WAS ABLE TO TRACK HIM THIS FAR, THEN HE VANISHED. EITHER HE'S DEAD, OR HE'S BEING HELD SOMEWHERE WITH COMMS SCREENING.

A scarlet circle appeared on the map, near the upper lip of the canyon wall, at the top of the vertical favela.

> THIS IS VILCA'S COMPOUND. IF HE'S STILL ALIVE, CHANCES ARE THAT'S WHERE THEY'RE HOLDING HIM.

"Can I speak to Vilca?"

> I'LL SEE IF I CAN—

The ship's voice cut off. Kat sat forward.

"What is it?"

> INCOMING.

The map of the canyons vanished, to be replaced by a stylised strategic overview of the planetary system. Nuevo Cordoba floated in the centre. Green tags picked out each of the twenty-four rescue freighters. Off to the left, coming in above the plane of the planet's equator, a flashing red circle highlighted an unidentified ship.

> IT JUST JUMPED IN. COURSE EXTRAPOLATION MARKS ITS POINT OF ORIGIN AS STRAULI.

Kat's heart seemed to squirm in her chest. These days, every unidentified ship was a potential threat.

"Is it infected?"

> ALMOST CERTAINLY.

The intruder seemed to be heading straight for the planet, ignoring the scattering freighters. Kat disconnected her neural implant from the ship's sensorium and reeled her perceptions back into the confines of her skull.

"Are we close enough to intercept and engage?"

> AYE.

She flexed the fingers of her artificial hand. The joints buzzed like mosquitoes.

"Okay," she said. "Let's do it."

UNDER FULL ACCELERATION, it took the *Ameline* an hour and a half to get close enough to fire on the unidentified ship. Throughout that time, Kat remained in place on the little ship's bridge. Housing only two crash couches, the room was too small for her to pace nervously—more of a large cockpit than a ship's bridge in the accepted sense. Instead, she sat impatiently watching their progress via the interactive touch screens on the forward wall.

When they were almost within range, she activated her implant and joined her mind once more to the *Ameline*'s heightened senses. When hooked in to the ship like this she could feel the thrust as a tingle in her feet; the power of the engines as a growl in her chest and stomach. Her nostrils were full of the cold, coppery smell of the vacuum. The heat of the local sun warmed her. The lights of distant stars pinpricked her cheek.

She opened a line to the weapon pod slung beneath the *Ameline*'s bows.

"Are you ready, Ed?"

Ed Rico lay submerged in the greasily organic entrails of the Dho weapon. Its flabby white wax forced its way into his eyes and ears; it filled his lungs and stomach, even the pores of his skin.

"I'm here." His voice sounded thick, the sound forcing its way up through the alien mucus clogging his throat.

Ed had once been an artist, back on Earth. He had come to Strauli the hard way, through the arch network, and been chosen by the Dho to wield this ancient weapon; to become part of it.

Cocooned within, he had no access to the rest of the ship while in flight. The weapon's tendrils fed him nutrients and oxygen to keep him alive; and when he wasn't needed, it simply put him to sleep.

Now though, Kat knew he'd be fully awake, brain pumped with synthetic adrenaline; all his senses filled with a real-time strategic view of the space surrounding them.

All he had to do was point and click.

> IN RANGE IN TWENTY SECONDS.

"Get ready to fire."

Ahead, the infected craft continued toward the planet, seemingly oblivious to their approach. Yet deep in her head, Kat felt a strange scratching sensation, as if tiny animals were flexing their claws against the inside of her skull. She knew this feeling, recognised it for what it was. During her first brush with The Recollection she'd been briefly infected by it, and now the dormant nanomachines it had pushed into her body were stirring, disturbed from their slumber by the proximity of an active mass of their fellows.

There could be no doubt now that the ship ahead was infested.

"Over to you," she told Ed. "Fire when ready."

> TEN SECONDS.

The Recollection was a gestalt entity comprised of uncounted trillions of self-replicating molecular-sized machines—each one in the swarm acting as a processing node, like a synapse in a human brain. Destroy one and the network simply re-routed, maintaining its integrity. Let one touch you, and it would start converting your atoms into copies of itself: remorseless and unstoppable. The ship ahead would be packed with them, like an overripe seedpod, ready to spread its voracious cargo across the unsuspecting globe below.

> FIVE.

Kat swallowed. Ahead, the target remained on course, still apparently unaware of the attack about to rain down upon it.

> THREE.

> TWO.

A white, pencil-thin line stabbed from the *Ameline*'s nose: a superheated jet of fusing hydrogen plucked by wormhole from the heart of the nearest star. Still hooked into the ship, Kat saw it on the tactical display. It cut the sky like a knife. The hellish backwash of its scouring light hit her virtual face like sunburn. Where it touched the infected ship, metal boiled away.

The beam flickered once; twice; three times. The target broke apart. The pieces that hadn't been vaporised began to tumble.

Kat pulled out of the tactical simulation, back into the real world of the *Ameline*'s cockpit.

"Did we get it?"

> SCANNING NOW.

Kat blinked. Her eyes were watering. Although she'd witnessed the scouring light via her neural implant, her body's reflexes still expected afterimages on her retinas, and seemed confused to find none.

A wall screen lit, showing a forward view of the planet, which instantly crash-zoomed to a sizeable piece of wreckage silhouetted against the daylight side, tumbling through space wrapped in a cloud of hull fragments and loose cables. Fluid dribbled from a severed tube.

> VESSEL DESTROYED BUT SOME DEBRIS REMAINS.

"Damn. Can we hit it again?"

> IT'S ALREADY ENTERING THE ATMOSPHERE OVER THE CANYONS. IF WE FIRE NOW WE CAN EXPECT CIVILIAN CASUALTIES.

Kat hesitated. She didn't know if she could bring herself to fire on innocent people. Not again. During The Recollection's attack on her home planet of Strauli, she'd been forced to destroy the orbital docks in a futile attempt to stem the spread of infection. A million people had died, either in the initial explosions or the subsequent disintegration of the structure, and their deaths still troubled her.

She looked down and flexed the fingers of her left hand. The metal of the fingers and wrist had been stained and half-melted during an attack by The Recollection. She could have had the whole arm surgically re-grown months ago, but she preferred to keep this clunky souvenir. It reminded her of everything and everyone that had been lost. It was her scar and she'd earned it.

She watched the tumbling wreck flare as it hit thicker air.

"Follow it down," she said.

CHAPTER TWENTY-FOUR
EMBERS

KAT KNEW STRAIGHT away that she didn't have much time. Standing in the airlock of the *Ameline*, she could see greasy black smoke belching from the site of the crashed starship debris. It had been a big ship, probably a container carrier of some sort. Sliced apart and half-vaporised by the Dho weapon, fragments of the vessel had fallen to the ground, ploughing into the desert that covered most of the planet's solitary supercontinent, flaming like meteors. By the time she'd followed them down, huge tracts of scrubland were already ablaze. Now, surveying the impact crater from a dozen kilometres away, with her eyes on full magnification, she could make out grain-sized specks of red in the smoke: clumps of infected matter from the ship riding the hot air like embers, using the updraught to spread themselves across the landscape.

Embers on the wind.

This was exactly what she'd been trying to prevent. From bitter experience, she knew the specks contained tightly-packed clusters of aggressive nanomachinery. Where they landed, the ground turned red. Spreading stains of wine-coloured destruction bloomed as the tiny machines ate into the surface of the planet, turning rock and dust into more machines, exponentially swelling their numbers.

The ship had been a seed pod: its systems hijacked by the contagion, its hold full of seething red nanomachines ready to split the hull and burst forth in an orgy of destruction.

Kat felt her lips harden. Her little fleet might rescue a couple of thousand people; but there was nothing she could do for the rest of the population. She was five light years from the Bubble Belt. By the time she jumped there and came back, a whole decade would have passed, and this world would have fallen. She thought of the tortured, wailing minds she'd encountered during her own brush with The Recollection; of her mother, pinned like a butterfly in its virtual storage spaces, with nothing to look forward to but an eternity of torment.

She turned back into the familiar confines of the *Ameline*.

"We should have been quicker," she said.

In her mind, she heard the *Ameline*'s reply.

> WE HIT THAT SHIP WITH EVERYTHING WE HAD. THERE WASN'T ANYTHING ELSE WE COULD HAVE DONE.

"We could have rammed it."

> AND WHAT WOULD THAT HAVE ACHIEVED? IT WAS TOO BIG. IT WOULD HAVE FLATTENED US AND KEPT RIGHT ON GOING.

"I know, but still."

> THIS IS A WAR, AND WE'RE LOSING. CASUALTIES ARE INEVITABLE.

"We should be doing more."

> THE FREIGHTERS WILL RESCUE SOME OF THE POPULATION.

"A tiny fraction."

> BETTER THAN NONE.

She let out a long sigh. This was the third world she'd seen fall to The Recollection. First Djatt, then Inakpa, then her home world of Strauli. Now this place, New Cordoba.

Just another apocalypse.

Before it arrived at Djatt, The Recollection had been drifting through space for thousands of years, the relic of an ancient and long-forgotten alien war. Now it had access to human ships, it could spread unstoppably from world to world, consuming everything it touched. And all humanity could do was fall back.

As the airlock door slid closed behind her, she turned for one last glimpse of the redness spreading across the land, the widening circles meeting and merging, growing with obscene haste. She'd seen this happen before. With nothing to stop it, she knew the infection would cover the entire surface of the globe within days.

There was nothing she could do.

Except...

She gripped the gun.

"Take me to Vilca," she said.

THE *AMELINE* DROPPED onto the desert sand a dozen metres from the edge of the canyon, directly above Vilca's compound. The old ship came down with a whine of engines and a hot blast of dirt. As the landing struts settled and the engines whined into silence, Kat unhooked herself from the pilot's chair and made her way down the ladder that led to the rest of the ship's interior.

At the foot of the ladder, opposite the door of her cabin, the ship's locker held a rack of weaponry picked up on half a dozen different worlds. She reached up and pulled a twelve-gauge shotgun from the wall. It was a gas-powered model, fully automatic and drum-loaded, capable of delivering three hundred flesh-shredding rounds per minute. She hefted it in one hand, resting the stock on her hip as she picked up a couple of extra magazines and pushed them into her thigh pocket.

> I HOPE YOU'RE NOT PLANNING ON DOING ANYTHING STUPID.

"Define stupid."

WEAPON AT THE ready, Kat stepped from the bottom of the *Ameline*'s cargo ramp. Her boots crunched into the coarse desert sand. Tough little grass tufts poked through here and there, stirring in the thin, scouring wind. Overhead, the sun burned blue and hot. Ahead, the canyon lay ragged and raw like a claw mark in the skin of the world; and over the lip, Vilca's compound.

She took three quick steps to the edge and looked down. As she'd expected, a metal fire escape led down to an armoured door in the side of the building. A razor wire gate blocked the top of the staircase. She considered cutting her way through; then decided it wasn't worth the bother. The people inside must know she was here. They would have heard the *Ameline* set down, and they were sure to be watching her, even if she couldn't see any cameras.

She held the shotgun across her chest and raised her chin.

"I'm here to see Vilca," she said.

A minute later, she heard the sound of scraping bolts. The heavy door hinged open. A gun appeared from behind it, clutched in the fists of a young kid gaunt with malnourishment.

"Who are you?"

"My name is Katherine Denktash Abdulov, of the Strauli Abdulovs, and I am here to request an audience with your esteemed Capo, the Right Honourable Lord Vilca."

Beneath the rim of his cap, suspicion screwed the kid's face into a wary scowl.

"Huh?"

Kat sighed. *Young people today…* She licked her lips, and then tried again.

"Take me to your leader," she said. The kid's eyes scanned the canyon's lip, alert for treachery.

"You alone?"

"Yes."

He looked at her shotgun, then down at the pistol in his hand, transparently calculating the difference in their relative value and firepower.

"You'll have to give me your weapon."

Kat shook her head. "I don't think so."

The kid scowled. "Give me the shotgun or I won't take you to Vilca."

She looked him up and down: just another armed street thug with bad teeth and delusions of competence. A few years ago she would have been intimidated; now she couldn't care less. She cleared her throat.

"You saw my ship land?"

The kid's eyes narrowed further. "Yeah."

Kat took a step closer to the razor wire gate.

"You saw its fusion motors?"

The barest nod.

"They spew out star fire, son. That's fourteen zillion degrees centigrade. What do you think will happen if I let them hover over your little citadel?"

Behind her, she heard the *Ameline*'s engines whine into life. The ship was monitoring her conversation via her neural implant, and this was its idea of theatrics. Suppressing a smile, Kat took another step forward, so that her stomach pressed up against the spikes on the wire gate. At the same time, she brought the shotgun to bear, pointing the barrel at the bridge of the kid's nose.

"Open up," she growled. The kid's eyes went wide. He knew he was out of his depth. He looked at her, then over her shoulder at the rising wedge of the *Ameline*. She saw him swallow. Without taking his eyes from the looming ship, he reached for a button inside the door and the gate drew back. Kat stepped forward, shotgun now pointed at his midriff.

"What's your name, son?"

"Faro."

She raised a finger and waggled it, telling him to turn around.

"Never try to out-negotiate a trader, Faro."

FARO LED HER down a set of pleated metal steps. His trainers dragged on each stair. She kept the shotgun trained on the small of his back.

"How old are you?" she asked. He didn't answer. His vest and jeans hung off him, several sizes too large for his half-starved junkie frame.

"Down 'ere," he muttered.

At the foot of the steps was an iron door. Beyond that, a poorly carpeted corridor that stank of incense. Faro flapped an arm at a pair of rough pine doors that formed the corridor's far end.

"Vilca's office."

Kat gave him a prod with the shotgun barrel.

"Why don't you knock for me?" She followed him to the doors. "Go on," she said.

Faro tapped reluctant knuckles against the wood. From inside, a voice called: "What is it?" Faro glanced back at Kat, his eyes wide, unsure what to do. She nudged him in the kidney with the tip of the shotgun.

"Open the door," she suggested.

Inside, the office was as rough and raw as the rest of the building, but the rugs on the floor were thicker and newer than elsewhere, and there were curtains at the windows. A heavy-set bald man sat behind a scuffed steel desk.

"I said I wasn't to be disturbed. Who the devil are you?"

Kat took Faro by the shoulder and pushed him aside. She drew herself up.

"My name is Katherine Denktash Abdulov, master of the trading vessel *Ameline* and scion of the Strauli Abdulovs. Are you Earl Vilca?"

The fat man frowned.

"You're a *trader*?"

Kat lowered the shotgun so that the barrel pointed at the floor.

"As I said, I represent the Abdulov trading family."

The man eased back in his chair. He gave her an appraising look.

"And what can I do for you, Miss Abdulov?"

Kat took a pace towards the desk.

"That's *Captain* Abdulov, and you have a friend of mine. I want him released."

Vilca chuckled. He folded his hands over the bulge of his stomach. Gold rings glistened on his sausage-like fingers.

"Very good," he said approvingly. "I do so like a woman who comes straight to the point."

According to the profile the *Ameline* had been able to piece together from information retrieved from the local Grid, Earl Vilca was one of the most powerful men on Nuevo Cordoba. His operation dealt in drugs, prostitution and extortion. He had politicians and high-ranking police officers in his pocket, and a seemingly endless supply of teenage muscle. On a world of high-piled shanties and meagre mushroom harvests, he lived like a king. But when Kat looked down at him, all she saw was a white, bloated parasite: a puffed-up hoodlum in a cheaply-fabbed suit.

"I know who you are, and what you are," she said. "And I'm not impressed. So if you'd be kind enough to release Napoleon Jones, I'll be on my way."

On the opposite side of the desk, Vilca pursed his lips. He drummed his fingers against his belt buckle.

"Jones, eh? Well, well, well." He shook his head with a smile. "You've come bursting in here to rescue Napoleon Jones? He's nothing but a two-bit hustler. What do you want with him?"

Kat gripped the shotgun.

"As I said, he's a friend."

Vilca narrowed his eyes. He ran his tongue across his bottom lip. Then he sat forward, hands resting on the desk.

"All right, Captain. I'll make you a trade. Jones for some information."

"What kind of information?"

The fat man waved his hand at the sky.

"I hear things. Rumours. Shipments have disappeared. Scheduled deliveries from Strauli have not arrived. Ships are overdue."

Kat felt her pulse quicken. She knew where this was going and she didn't have time to waste playing games.

"Strauli has fallen," she said bluntly. "Inakpa, Djatt and probably several others."

Vilca blinked at her.

"Fallen?"

"Gone, destroyed. No more."

The man's brows drew together. He plainly didn't believe her.

"I am serious, Captain. I have been losing money—"

Kat stepped right up to the desk and glared down at him.

"They're gone."

"Gone?" Vilca's cheeks flushed. His fingers brushed his lower lip. "But what could do such a thing?"

Kat used her implant to signal the *Ameline*.

"I've asked my ship to download all the information we have to the local Grid. See for yourself. It's all tagged with the key word 'Recollection'."

Vilca gave her a long look. He was getting flustered.

"Go on," she said. "Check it out. I'll wait here."

"No tricks?"

Kat nodded in the direction of Faro, still cowering in the corner of the room.

"Your boy here can keep an eye on me."

Vilca looked up and to the right, accessing the cranial implant that connected him to the vast cloud of data that formed the planetary Grid. Kat stood watching him. She shifted her weight from one hip to the other. After a few seconds, she saw the colour drain from his cheeks. She knew what he was seeing. She'd seen it herself firsthand: the destruction of Djatt, the boiling red cloud that seemed to emerge from the fabric of space itself, closing like a fist around the planet.

His eyes snapped back into focus.

"*Madre de Dios.*"

"Quite."

"What can we do?"

"Give me Jones."

Vilca's eyes narrowed to slits. "What's to stop me killing you and using your ship to escape?"

Kat hefted the shotgun.

"You try to kill me and I'll use my ship's fusion exhaust to scour this canyon back to the bedrock."

Vilca gave a snort. He seemed to have recovered his composure.

"You wouldn't. You're not the type."

Kat leaned toward him.

"Check the data, Vilca. Look at the fall of Strauli Quay."

"Strauli...?"

The man's eyes flicked away for a second.

"You *fired* on the Quay?"

Kat set her jaw. "I had no choice."

"But there were more than a million—"

She raised her shotgun, pointing the barrel at his chest.

"Do you still think I'm bluffing?"

Vilca swallowed. She could see a damp sheen on his bald pate. After a moment, he let his shoulders slump.

"All right," he said. "You win. Faro, would you please fetch Mister Jones?"

Kat realised she'd stepped too close to Vilca's desk. She hadn't kept track of the boy. As she turned, she saw him raise his gun. Her finger yanked the trigger. The shotgun jumped in her hand. Faro jerked backward, chest shredded by three rapid-fire blasts. She turned back to Vilca, and caught the fat man in the act of reaching for the pistol in his desk drawer. She fired into the surface of the desk and he jerked his hand back, eyes wide.

"Okay, that's enough!"

Kat's pulse battered in her head. She didn't know if she was angry with Vilca, Faro or herself.

"Get Jones up here, right now!"

Vilca knew he had been defeated. He sent an order via his implant. Moments later, a pair of wide-eyed teenagers brought Napoleon Jones to the door. They were half-carrying him. He couldn't walk by himself. They looked down at Faro's smoking corpse and turned questioning eyes on their boss. Vilca waved them away with a flap of his meaty paw.

"These people are leaving," he said.

Kat looked at Jones. His arm and leg were bandaged. His coat was torn. The antique goggles still hung around his neck.

"Kat?"

"I've got a ship up top. We're leaving."

Jones shook his head, as if trying to clear it. He'd been beaten. His lips and eyes were swollen; his moustache caked with dried blood.

"What about Vilca?"

The man behind the desk looked up at him.

"You should not have come back, *señor*. People love a daredevil because they are always awaiting his death. If he lives too long, well," he spread his hands, "they become resentful."

Kat pulled on Napoleon's sleeve.

"Leave him. He knows it's all over." She picked Faro's pistol from the dead boy's fingers.

"What's over?"

"His little empire." She glared at the fat man. "This whole planet."

Vilca put his head in his hands.

"Go now," he said.

Kat put an arm around Napoleon and he leaned his weight on her shoulder. They backed out of the room. When they reached the door at the far end of the corridor, the one that led to the roof, Vilca raised his head.

"Captain?" he said, his voice hoarse.

Kat paused.

"Yes?"

"What can we do? About The Recollection, I mean."

She took a deep breath. She owed him nothing. Further down the canyon, the freighters were filling their holds with refugees. She'd done all she could.

She looked him in the eye.

"Pray it doesn't take you alive."

*   *   *

WITH GREAT EFFORT, Katherine helped Jones up the metal stairs. When they got to the surface, it was snowing. Blood red flakes fell from an otherwise clear and empty sky, whirling around on the warm air rising up from the canyon.

"Oh hell." The outbreak had spread faster than she'd expected. Using her implant, she told the *Ameline* to warm the engines. If they hurried, they might still have a chance.

"Come on, Jones." His arm lay draped across her shoulders. She gripped it and pushed upwards with her legs, taking as much of his weight as she could.

> TOO LATE.

Ahead, at the lip of the canyon, a scarlet slick covered the *Ameline*'s upper surfaces.

"No!"

One of the red flakes stuck against her right thigh. Another hit the back of her hand. She looked at Jones. He already had half a dozen in his hair, more against his shoulders and back.

"Damn it." She let go of his arm and brushed at her trousers. For each flake she dislodged, another three attached themselves. Where they touched her skin, she felt a sting like the bite of a tiny insect. Her movements became more frantic, but to no avail.

No, it can't end like this...

She thrashed impotently at the storm, trying desperately to brush herself clean. As the blizzard intensified, she lost sight of her ship, lost touch with Jones. All she could feel were a thousand needle-like stings all over her body; all she could think of were the millions of dead on Strauli Quay; and all she could see were bright red sparks—billions of them, shredding and consuming her limbs, roaring through her head and heart like a fire. Reducing her every cell to ash and embers.

Embers on the wind.

PART THREE

MONKEY VS MULTIVERSE

All you need in this life is ignorance
and confidence; then success is sure.

Mark Twain, *Letter to Mrs Foote*, Dec. 2, 1887

EDITORIAL

From the *European Review of Physical Sciences*, online edition:

Our Science is Wrong

Two years have passed since our world was invaded by a white-suited hive mind from another dimension, and yet we still have absolutely no idea how they did it.

We have examined the machinery aboard the captured Gestalt dreadnoughts, but have yet to come up with a convincing explanation. The problem is not that these fantastical engines are too complicated—on the contrary, they appear to be of an extremely simple construction—the problem is that they work *at all*.

By somehow moving an airship from one parallel timeline to another, these engines violate almost everything we know about physics. According to all our theories, they should not work; and yet they do. Travel between alternate worlds has become an undeniable reality—a reality that has thrown into disarray everything we thought we understood, and left us with a stark realisation: our science is wrong.

Fitting the Gestalt machinery into our view of reality will necessitate a radical overhaul of both quantum and classical physics. Under current 'laws', they should not be able to do what they do, and yet they do it anyway. Either these airships are a figment of our collective imagination, or the universe (multiverse?) is far stranger than we could ever have expected.

Read more | Like | Comment | Share

Related articles:

Hacking the Gestalt 'WiFi'.

What's it like to be part of a hive mind? The answer may surprise you.

Ten famous people with doppelgangers amongst the Gestalt.

RAF takes command of refurbished Gestalt dreadnoughts.

Are US politicians already negotiating with other time streams?

From the rubble: Berlin's extraordinary recovery.

CHAPTER TWENTY-FIVE
ILLEGAL DUPLICATE

PAUL WASN'T ANSWERING her calls, so Victoria found his projection drone and activated it manually. The tiny machine looked like a cross between a toy helicopter and a complex mechanical dragonfly—much like the surveillance drone they'd used in Nguyen's lab. When she hit the power button, its little fans whirred and it wobbled into the air. The lenses spaced around the narrow constriction at its middle brightened, and a three dimensional image of Paul flickered into being on the bridge before her. He appeared to be wearing his usual Hawaiian shirt and white lab coat.

"Where am I?" He rubbed his eyes and looked around with a puzzled expression. Victoria moistened her lower lip.

"You're on the *Sun Wukong*."

"And who are you?"

"Your wife."

Behind his glasses, his eyes were wide and fearful, like those of a frightened animal. "My wife?"

"Ex-wife."

He seemed to mull this over. A hand came up to scratch the bristles on his chin.

"You're... Vicky?"

"*Oui, mon amour.*"

He frowned again. "What happened to your hair?"

Victoria put a hand to her scalp. "I had an accident, years ago. You saved me."

"I did?"

"Yes. Yes, you did." She felt a lump in her throat; she couldn't swallow properly. "Don't you remember?"

Paul looked pained. He reached up to fiddle with the diamond stud in his ear.

"I'm not sure..."

"Do you remember the *Tereshkova*?" she prompted. "The battle over

London?" She stepped close to him. She wanted to touch his face, ruffle his spiky hair.

"I remember a smiling man."

Victoria felt her heart lurch. "You don't need to worry about him," she said hurriedly, blinking away the memory of Berg's reptilian face and the screams he made as the monkeys tore him apart.

"But the rest..." Paul flapped his arms helplessly. "It comes and goes. I get flashes."

Victoria put a hand to her mouth. She wanted so desperately to comfort him.

"It's okay," she said. "I'm here. I'm going to look after you."

Paul clenched his jaw. He glared over the top of his glasses.

"I'm not an idiot. I know what's happening to me."

"Then you also know that I love you, and I'm going to do whatever I can to help."

His expression hardened. "There's nothing that can be done."

Victoria clenched her fists. "I'm not letting you go without a fight."

"But what can you do?"

Victoria drummed her fingers against her chin. "Could we duplicate the original back-up, and integrate your stored memories?"

Paul shook his head. His earring flashed. "It wouldn't work. We didn't keep a pristine copy. The memories I've gathered since being activated have overwritten and updated the original recording."

"So, all we have is you as you are now? No back-up to the back-up?"

Paul looked down at his body, and wiped his hands down the front of his lab coat. "That's the way these things were designed. Nobody wants multiple copies of their dearly departed."

Victoria bit her lip, thinking furiously. If they couldn't get the original, then maybe they could get the next best thing...

"You know, there *is* another copy of you."

"Where?"

"On Mars."

Paul raised sceptical eyebrows. "Mars?"

"Yes." Victoria walked over to the main windshield. Rural France lay below like a winter blanket, a patchwork of browns and yellows. "When you were killed, Berg cut out your brain, soul-catcher and all. He took your official back-up and we never recovered it." She turned her back to the view and levelled a finger at him. "You, the you I'm talking to right now, *you're* the illegal duplicate."

Paul shrugged his shoulders, plainly struggling to follow her reasoning. "If you say so."

"Don't you remember?" Victoria leant back against the glass, arms folded. "Nguyen told us all the stolen souls had been loaded aboard Céleste Tech's Martian probe. And that means there has to be a copy of you up there too, maybe stomping around in one of those robot bodies."

Paul walked over to stand beside her. He looked out at the blue afternoon sky.

"Even if that is the case, I don't see what good it does us."

Victoria knew she was grasping at straws. "If we could get to it and somehow integrate the two of you..."

Paul clicked his tongue behind his teeth. He reached a hand towards the window. "First off, I don't know if that's even possible and, secondly, what does it matter anyway?" His fingers reached the pane, and seemed to sink into the glass. "We can't get to Mars. And, even if we could, the copy might have expired by the time we got there. Most copies last around six months. It might as well be on the other side of the universe." As if to reinforce his point, the image of his hand emerged from the other side of the glass, into the air outside.

"That shouldn't stop us trying."

Paul flexed his fingers in the wind. "What do you suggest?"

"I don't know." Victoria turned her palms upwards. "Perhaps we can negotiate with Lady Alyssa. She could transmit the file containing your copy. It would get here in minutes rather than years."

"Why would she do that?"

"I don't know. Maybe if we had something she wanted?"

Paul opened and shut his mouth a couple of times, as if he'd been about to snap back a retort but had then forgotten exactly what it was he had been about to say. His features softened into an expression of confusion. Slowly, he withdrew his hand from the window, bringing it back into the room, and looked at it. He repeatedly opened and shut his fist as if seeing it for the first time. Then he raised his eyes to Victoria's and smiled apologetically.

"I'm sorry, but who are you again?"

CHAPTER TWENTY-SIX
BIG DOG

THE WIND BLEW across the top of the airship's armour-plated hull, ruffling the hairs on Ack-Ack Macaque's cheeks and the backs of his hands, and flapping the scarf at his neck. His arms were folded across his chest. As he drew them tighter, the brand new leather jacket creaked around his shoulders like a timber galleon. Thank goodness K8 had talked him into buying several spare sets of clothes. She knew his propensity for getting into trouble and, although he'd grumbled at the time, he was grateful now. If he was going to convince this ragtag mob of primates that he was still their leader, it helped to look the part; and besides, in his state of injured exhaustion, it was pretty much only the stiffness of the jacket that was holding him upright.

With a squeal and a clunk, the platform—designed to transport helicopters from the hangars to the flight deck—drew level and the crowd parted around Bali, forming a loose semicircle with the younger monkey at its focus.

Ack-Ack Macaque glanced back, to the gun turret at the far end of the airship's hull, almost a kilometre away, where K8 monitored proceedings through the scope of a high-powered sniper rifle.

"Stay cool," he told her, knowing his words would be picked up and relayed by the throat mike beneath his scarf. "Don't shoot unless I'm already dead."

He didn't have an earpiece, so couldn't know if she replied. Nevertheless, he trusted her. She knew how important appearances were in these matters. If she intervened to save his life, he'd lose the respect of the troupe—not because she was a girl but because she was human, and this was one fight he had to win or lose by himself. He uncrossed his arms, clamped the cigar between his teeth, and cracked his knuckles. Surrounded by onlookers and supporters, Bali did his best to look unimpressed.

"I didn't think you'd come," he said, fingering the blade of his machete.

Ack-Ack Macaque grinned, letting them all see his teeth.

"I didn't." He gestured at the platform. "You came to me."

"A cheap trick."

"No." Suddenly serious, Ack-Ack Macaque blew smoke from the corner of his mouth. "A message." He took a step forward and saw Bali tense. "I heard you wanted to challenge me."

The younger monkey drew himself up. "That's right."

"You don't feel like backing down?"

Bali's blade swiped the air. "Not today, grandpa. We've followed you for two years and enough is enough. It's time things were different. We need to start thinking about ourselves and about what *we* want. Let the humans deal with their own problems."

Careful to keep his face impassive, Ack-Ack Macaque gave an inward groan. Part of him had been hoping Bali would lose his nerve and retract his challenge, sparing them both a fight—at least until Ack-Ack's bruises had been given a chance to heal.

"The people we're fighting against are the ones who made us," he said, appealing to the onlookers as much as Bali. "They're the ones who turned us into monsters."

Bali laughed scornfully. "Then perhaps we should thank them?" He thumped a hand against his breast. "Just because you hate yourself, old man, it doesn't mean the rest of us have to be wracked with self-loathing."

"Is that what you think?"

"Yes, it is." Bali let the flat edge of his weapon rest against his shoulder. "Now, *compadre*, are you going to bore me to death or are you going to meet my challenge?"

Ack-Ack Macaque huffed. He didn't want to fight Bali—the monkey had been a trusted lieutenant and he honestly didn't know if, in his current state, he could beat him—but neither could he walk away.

"I rescued you," he said.

Bali scowled. "Maybe I didn't need rescuing. Perhaps I *liked* living in that temple. Perhaps I *liked* being a god."

"I didn't hear any complaints at the time."

"You're hearing one now." They stood looking at each other, neither willing to be the first to break the stare. Finally, Ack-Ack Macaque rolled his cigar from one side of his mouth to the other, and gave a weary huff.

"So be it." He flicked a hand at the crowd, and the circle widened as every monkey in it took a quick step backwards. "Pick your weapon."

Smirking triumphantly, Bali held his blade aloft.

"I choose the machete!" The polished steel gleamed in the cold November sun, and Ack-Ack Macaque shook his head, suppressing a shudder. *Not another knife fight.* Too many memories brawled at the edges of his awareness; his nostrils filled with the jumbled odours of sawdust, blood and shit.

No!

In one movement, he pulled out a Colt and fired. Bali's arm jerked as the bullet snatched the machete from his grip and sent it clattering across the deck.

In the sudden, echoing silence, nobody dared move.

"Pick again," Ack-Ack said.

Bali sucked bruised fingers. "Are you insane?"

Ack-Ack Macaque lowered his revolver until it was aimed directly at the younger monkey's face. The spectators cowered.

"Possibly," he admitted. "I'm certainly sleep-deprived and recovering from some pretty fucking strong drugs."

Bali swallowed, looking truly uncertain for the first time. He thrust his chin forward. "Are you going to shoot me down, just like that?"

For a moment, Ack-Ack Macaque considered it. With his thumb, he levered back the Colt's hammer, clicking a fresh shell into the firing chamber. All he had to do now was squeeze the trigger. One little squeeze, and all his problems would be gone. He could blow Bali's brains all over the top of this dreadnought, and then go and find the Founder and demand to know why she hadn't told him about the baby; and then, after that, maybe he could *finally* go and get some fucking sleep.

His forefinger caressed the trigger. *So tempting...* But would the other monkeys respect him or despise him for taking the easy way out?

With a silent curse, he eased the hammer forward, and slid the smoking gun back into its holster.

"I don't need to shoot you," he growled, "to show everybody here what a jumped-up little piss-weasel you really are."

He took a deliberate step forward. Bali flinched but held his ground.

"You don't frighten me, old man."

Ack-Ack Macaque grinned. "Yes I do." He took another step forward, clawed hands reaching out.

"So," Bali said, raising his fists, "we're going to duke it out like gentlemen, is that it?"

Still advancing, Ack-Ack Macaque shook his head.

"Don't be a twat."

The first flickers of real fear crossed Bali's face. He began to back away. "Then what?"

Ack-Ack Macaque rotated his shoulders and flexed his neck. His original plan had been to intimidate Bali into submission, but now his blood was up. Tiredness and irritation gave way to boiling anger. As far as he was concerned, the upstart was a stand-in for every hurt, frustration and setback he'd suffered over the past few days, and all he wanted now was to stomp the insolent look from the little bastard's stupid eyes.

"We're going to fight like monkeys," he said gruffly. "We're going to scream and leap and scratch and bite. You know, old school. And then, at some point, I'm going to rip your tail off and jam it up your devious, backstabbing arse."

Bali's hackles rose. He stopped retreating. "Oh, really?" He spoke for the benefit of the audience. "You think you can take me in a fair fight?"

Ack-Ack Macaque laughed.

"Who said anything about fair?"

THEY CRASHED TOGETHER with a screech that seemed to fill the vaulting sky. A kilometre away, the sound chilled K8's blood and prickled the hairs at the back of her neck. Through her rifle's telescopic sight, the two monkeys became a tumbling blur of flailing limbs and thrashing tails. They squirmed around each other, each trying to clamp his teeth around the other's windpipe. She saw flying clumps of torn hair and ripped clothing, and the flash of yellow incisors.

"Aw, shite."

Her index finger tapped against the trigger guard. She wanted to help, but the Skipper's instructions had been very specific. She wasn't to fire on Bali unless Ack-Ack Macaque died—and even then, she was only allowed to do it in self-defence. If Bali's first act as new alpha male was to turn on the humans—K8 and Victoria—she was authorised to put a bullet in his brain. Otherwise, she was just to get the hell off the airship and let the *Sun Wukong* go wherever it wanted.

I don't think so.

K8 jerked upright, startled by the voice in her head. Since returning to this parallel, the voices of the Gestalt had been a low buzz at the back of her awareness, a conversation she could tune in or out at will. This voice, however, was much louder—a sharp feminine voice speaking directly into her mind, and the sudden, queasy sensation of another presence in her head, peering out through her eyes.

"What do you mean?"

If you get a shot, child, you take it.

"Founder?"

Who else?

"But the Skipper, he said—"

I don't care what he said. He's a reckless fool. If you see a chance to end the fight, you end it.

"But the other monkeys…"

You leave them to me.

K8 closed one eye and squinted down the scope. Her cheek brushed the rifle's wooden stock.

"They're moving too fast." She clicked the magnification up a notch. "If we shoot, we could kill them both."

Then wait for one of them to get the upper hand.

Lurking behind the voice like the background hiss of a radio transmission, K8 sensed frustration, concern, and an exasperated, grudging respect for Ack-Ack Macaque and his hotheaded ways. She hunched around the rifle, arranging herself in order to minimise the amount of recoil her shoulder would have to absorb. Despite the cold wind, her hands were sweating. Through the sight, she saw Ack-Ack Macaque pull back his arm and let fly with a punch that sprayed blood and teeth from Bali's mouth.

"Yay!" K8 whispered—but, even as Bali turned with the force of the blow, his foot swept around and caught Ack-Ack off balance. The big monkey went down on his back, and Bali was on him, hands locking around his throat, throttling him. Heart beating hard, K8 tried to focus the cross hairs.

Before she could, one of Ack-Ack Macaque's hands came up to grab the side of Bali's head, and his thumb pressed into the younger monkey's eye. Bali twisted away with a cry of pain, but still the chokehold stayed in place.

Was Bali going to win? From where K8 knelt, he seemed to have the advantage. He was younger and faster, and coming to the fight fresh and rested instead of exhausted and bruised; and with his hands locked around the Skipper's throat, surely it was only a matter of time…

Come on, girl.

K8 swallowed. Bali was still on top of Ack-Ack, who was writhing furiously, trying to throw his opponent off. If they could just hold still for half a second…

Ack-Ack Macaque's thumb stabbed into Bali's eye socket again, this time rupturing the soft jelly within. Bali screamed and pulled back, hands flying to his face. Vitreous fluid poured down his cheek like the contents of a broken egg. Freed from his stranglehold, Ack-Ack Macaque sat up and lunged forward with a vicious head-butt. The other monkey toppled back and they rolled apart. Bali was on his back now, feet in the air, hands clamped to his face.

NOW!

The force of the command swamped all other thoughts. K8's finger twitched and the gun bucked—and a thousand metres away across the curving roof of the dreadnought, Bali's left knee exploded.

ACK-ACK MACAQUE TIED his white silk scarf around his fallen opponent's thigh, pulling it tight to form an improvised tourniquet. Then he turned to glare at the distant figure of K8, who was standing up now, the rifle dangling from her right hand.

"Why the fuck did you do that? I was *winning*, for Christ's sake."

At his feet, Bali moved feebly, one hand on his shattered leg, the other covering his punctured eye.

"Hold still," Ack-Ack Macaque told him. "You'll be okay."

Bali looked up at him, his remaining eye filled with anguish.

"You're not going to kill me?"

Ack-Ack Macaque reached into his jacket and pulled out a pair of cigars. He lit both, and handed one over.

"I never was. I only planned to teach you a lesson."

The other monkeys stood awkwardly around them. Some didn't believe the fight could be over; others were just waiting to see what would happen next.

"A lesson?" Bali's laugh was brittle. The hand holding the cigar shook so violently he almost dropped it. He was going into shock. To keep him focused, Ack-Ack Macaque bent down and slapped him across the cheek.

"I didn't say I wasn't going to kick your ass." He stepped back a few paces, his boots leaving bloody footprints on the iron deck. Bali regarded him with horrified disbelief.

"But, you took my eye..."

Ack-Ack Macaque shrugged. "If you challenge the big dog, you're going to get bitten."

He straightened his jacket, and glowered at the assembled crowd.

"Now, I'm going to let this one live," he said, nodding down at his fallen challenger, "for one reason, and one reason only. And that's because I've seen enough senseless killing to last me the rest of my days. There are too many assholes out there thinking they've got the right to kill and maim

and enslave, and I've had a gut-full of all of it. I won't be one of them."
He stomped to the edge of the deck and threw an arm out, pointing to the
horizon. "If any of you want to leave this ship and live out your days on
Kishkindha, you're welcome. I won't stop you. But let me just say this. You
remember those tossers we were just fighting? The ones in the big tanks?"
He recalled his woodland encounter with Apynja, and bared his teeth at
his audience. "Do you know they killed everybody on their timeline, just
because they fucking *could*? They murdered eight billion people because
they were *in the way*." He shook his head, feeling disgusted with himself,
with Bali and K8, and the whole messy fuck-up.

"The woman leading them is called Alyssa Célestine. Some of you may
have heard of her. She's a grade-A fucking psychopath." He sucked his
cigar until the end glowed like a flare, then spoke through a plume of
smoke. "She wants to live forever. She's worked with copies of herself and
Doctor Nguyen on a number of timelines, trying to convert people into
undying machines. And that's where we came from." He jabbed the cigar
butt at the nearest monkeys. "We're byproducts of their experiments. They
didn't want to try uploading people until they'd tried it on monkeys first."
He hawked and spat over the edge of the deck, and watched his phlegm get
snatched away by the wind. "And so, here we are. We're the cast-offs, the
prototypes. The ones sentenced to lives of loneliness and pain, separated
from our species and surrounded by humans. And my question to you is
this…" He paused, letting his words hang, watching their eyes widen. He
was their boss and he was angry. This wasn't a victory speech; it was a call
to war.

"Are you motherfuckers ready to do something about it?"

CHAPTER TWENTY-SEVEN
NUCLEAR WINTER

As the *Sun Wukong* approached the glittering ribbon of the English Channel, Merovech's helicopter touched down on the airship's upper deck. As he stepped out, into the downdraught from the rotors, two dark-suited bodyguards, a pair of armed Royal Marines, and a young lady with a briefcase accompanied him. Standing at a safe distance, Victoria watched them hurry towards her, their heads bent and hands shielding their eyes. As this was a royal visit, she'd made a point of wearing the Commodore's old dress tunic and scabbard. She even wore a blonde wig to cover the scars on her scalp. She might not be in sole command of this airship, as she had been with the *Tereshkova*, but she'd be damned if she couldn't look the part.

Once clear of the rotors, the boy-king's pace slowed. He straightened up and fixed her with a smile.

"Victoria!" He took her hand and pumped it, then pulled her into an awkward, backslapping embrace. "I really thought we'd lost you."

"No," she said, gently extricating herself, "we're still here, still alive and kicking."

"But why did you have to stay away so long? Couldn't you have sent word?"

"We've been busy."

"And Ack-Ack?" Merovech looked around hopefully.

"He'll join us later." Victoria glanced past the King's shoulder. "You must be Amy Llewellyn."

The young woman swapped her briefcase into her left hand and extended her right.

"Captain Valois. We spoke on the phone." Her voice was as cold as a Welsh mountain frost.

"Yes, well, I'm sorry if I was rude." Victoria gave a halfhearted shrug. "But needs must, you know?"

"Quite." Amy regarded the windswept deck and wrinkled her nose.

"Frankly, I don't even know what we're doing here. But now we are here, is there somewhere a bit warmer where we can talk?"

VICTORIA TOOK THEM down to the potted jungle at the nose of the airship, where they found Ack-Ack Macaque nursing a glass of medicinal rum and talking to the Founder.

"You've finally grown up," the Founder was saying, touching him on the arm.

Ack-Ack Macaque didn't reply. He looked around at the intruders with a guilty start. If Victoria hadn't known him better, she would have sworn he looked embarrassed.

She made five coffees, and placed them on the patio table. The others took chairs. The bodyguards lurked between the trees, and the Marines—who were clearly uncomfortable about the number of armed monkeys prowling the *Sun Wukong*'s corridors—took up positions by the big brass door.

"Right," she said, folding her hands on the iron tabletop, "now, perhaps you can tell me what's more urgent than an invasion?"

Merovech moistened his lips. He looked so much older than she remembered, less angry and more careworn than the mental image of the teenager she'd carried with her for the past two years.

"It's my mother," he said quietly. Among the branches, a parrot squawked. The air smelled of blossoms and rich compost.

Abruptly, Ack-Ack Macaque climbed to his feet and went to lean on the bamboo rail at the edge of the verandah. He lit a cigar and looked down through the airship's glass nose at the waves washing the French coast, his hairy head haloed in clouds of drifting blue.

Victoria frowned at his back, then turned her attention back to the King.

"She's the one leading the tanks."

"No, not her." Merovech tapped his knuckles against the table. "She's an alternate version. I'm talking about the Duchess, the one from this parallel."

"The one who blew herself apart with a hand grenade?"

He gave a nod, wincing at the memory. "She had a back-up, on the Mars probe."

"We knew that."

"Well, the probe's reached its destination, and she's been in contact."

Victoria's eyes widened. "Already?"

"It's taken them three years."

"What does she have to say for herself?"

Merovech's face clouded. "It's not so much what she has to say, as what she's done." He turned to Amy Llewellyn. "Would you mind?"

The Welsh girl pulled a flexible display screen from her briefcase and unrolled it on the table, weighing down the corners with coffee cups.

"These are the best images we've been able to get so far," she said. The pictures on the screen showed two grainy shots of the night sky, obviously taken through a telescope. "This first picture was taken yesterday at 1100 hours, this second one six hours later."

Victoria bent forward to get a better look. The only difference between the two shots was the position of a fat white dot that had been ringed with red marker pen. Between the first picture and the second, it had moved relative to the stars behind it.

"What is it, a spaceship?"

"A projectile."

"From Mars?"

Merovech cleared his throat. "My mother gave the world an ultimatum, to join her or suffer the consequences. When no-one replied, she launched this."

"No-one replied?"

Merovech turned his coffee cup but didn't lift it. "She was trying to turn country against country, but we've been doing a considerable amount of diplomatic work since the Gestalt attack. She couldn't have foreseen that."

Victoria was impressed. How different things were to the way they had been, three short years ago, when the West had been on the verge of nuclear war with China over the sovereignty of Hong Kong. Times had changed, relations had thawed; and all it had taken to usher in this era of peace and cooperation had been a global invasion from a parallel world.

She tapped the image on the screen with her fingernail. "So, what kind of projectile are we talking about? Is it a bomb?"

Amy enlarged the picture, but couldn't resolve any further detail. The white dot remained a white dot. "As far as we can tell from spectrographic analysis, it's a solid lump of rock, possibly a repurposed asteroid."

"And what kind of damage are we talking about?"

Amy sniffed. "Projections vary, but it's likely to be extensive. Given its mass and speed, it'll hit with anything from several hundred to several thousand times the force of the Hiroshima explosion. There'll be catastrophic damage, earthquakes and tsunamis, and the aftereffects won't be much fun, either. At the very least, we're looking at a worldwide nuclear winter lasting anywhere from ten to a hundred years."

Victoria thought back to the parallel world she'd just left, to the grey skies and dying plants, and the thin, starving and disease-ridden survivors.

"Why are you telling me this?" She shuddered.

Amy gave Merovech a sideways glance. "I've been wondering that myself."

Merovech had been leaning back, listening. Now he sat straight, and reached across the table for Victoria's hands.

"You and Ack-Ack, you've saved the world twice in the last three years," he said. "I guess I'm kind of hoping you'll find a way to do it again."

Leaning against the bamboo rail, Ack-Ack Macaque blew air through his nostrils in a low, animal grunt. Victoria ignored him.

"Can't you fire a missile at it and blow it up?"

Merovech shook his head.

"It's not possible," said Amy Llewellyn. "We don't have anything with that kind of range or stopping power. We could fire a hundred warheads at it and it still wouldn't be enough."

"Then what's the plan?"

"We don't have one." The Welsh girl made a sour face. "If we did, we wouldn't be here talking to you."

Victoria reached up and pulled off her wig. She let it fall to the table.

"You want us to go up into space?" She ran a hand over her bald scalp, grimly amused at Amy's attempts not to stare.

"We don't have a craft," Merovech said. "We've got some experimental engines but nothing to bolt them onto."

"Then I'm sorry, your highness, but I don't see how we can help." Victoria got to her feet. "Unless you need us to evacuate you to another parallel?"

Merovech set his jaw.

"I won't leave my people to die."

"You may not have a choice." They stood looking at each other for a moment, and Victoria couldn't help but admire his bravery and dedication. The boy who never wanted to be king had grown to be one of the finest kings the Commonwealth could ever have hoped for. At the rail, Ack-Ack Macaque took the cigar from between his teeth.

"I've got an idea," he rumbled.

Victoria gave him a look. "Seriously?"

"Yeah." He leant back, resting his elbows on the bamboo, the butt glowing between his fingers. "I'll need to check it with K8, but yeah, I think I know how we can stop that asteroid." He picked something from the hairs on his chest, inspected it, and then popped it into his mouth. "This whole invasion thing, too."

Amy Llewellyn frowned sceptically. "You really think one monkey can make that much of a difference?"

Ack-Ack Macaque stiffened. He stood straight and looked her up and down. "You really think I can't?"

For a moment, there was silence, broken only by the cries of the birds in the upper branches. Then the Founder cleared her throat.

"You have a plan?" she asked, speaking for the first time since the meeting convened.

"That's what I said." Ack-Ack Macaque wouldn't look at her.

"Care to share it?"

He turned back to the view through the airship's glass nose. When he spoke, his voice was gruff.

"Well," he said, "the first thing we're going to have to do is capture one of those tanks."

CHAPTER TWENTY-EIGHT
HEAVY COAT

THE THINGS ACK-ACK Macaque missed most about the *Tereshkova* were its watering holes. He missed hanging out on a barstool, eating peanuts and drinking daiquiris. The old skyliner had been built to transport passengers in comfort and elegance, and most of its half a dozen gondolas had sported at least one lounge area with a fully stocked bar. The *Sun Wukong*, on the other hand, was a warship. It had been built by a hive mind with no real interest in creature comforts. The crew cabins were spartan affairs, with steel-framed bunks bolted to the metal walls. The only touch of luxury was the forest built into the airship's nose, and even that had its uses.

After the humans left through the brass door to return to the bridge, he spent a few minutes swinging through the upper branches, stretching himself, working out the kinks in his back and shoulders. The fight with Bali had left him battered, but he'd been bruised and hurting to begin with.

The Founder watched him from the patio table. She'd discreetly tipped her coffee into the soil at the base of one of the potted trees and replaced it with tea—black, with a slice of lemon—which she sipped as she waited for him. When he finally came down from the trees, she was sitting demurely, monocle in place and hands clasped in her lap.

"Do you feel better now?"

Ack-Ack Macaque growled. "I feel like hammered shit."

"Are we going to finish our conversation?'

"What conversation?" He shuffled over and flopped onto a vacant chair. "You already told me you were pregnant."

The Founder twitched her tail.

"I haven't told you the best part, yet."

Ack-Ack Macaque raised an eyebrow, too tired to move or really give a shit. "What best part?'

"It's twins."

The air drained out of him. He felt like a week-old party balloon.

"Twins?"

"A boy and a girl, as far as can be told."

"Holy hopping hell."

The Founder removed her monocle and polished it with a lace handkerchief.

"Is that all you have to say?"

"For the moment."

"And you're still going through with this idiotic plan to capture a Leviathan?"

"Yah."

She twisted the lens back into place. "I thought that now you knew about the children, you might—"

"Might what?" Ack-Ack laughed bitterly. "Give up this life of adventure and settle down somewhere?"

"Don't be childish."

"Then what? What do you want from me?"

The Founder looked towards the vast, cone-shaped window that formed the airship's nose. The daylight glinted on her monocle.

"When you told me you'd let Bali live, I thought you'd finally started to grow up. I thought you were starting to accept your responsibilities."

Ack-Ack Macaque snarled deep in his throat. "Why the fuck do you think I'm doing this? You think I'm facing off against those tanks for *fun*?"

"Why else? This isn't our fight. We could leave now, leave this world to Célestine and her minions, find a better one, a safer one..."

"Fuck that." He leant his elbows on the table and leaned towards her. "Listen, lady. I saw some stuff on that last parallel, when I was in the woods."

The Founder frowned.

"What sort of 'stuff'?"

"Stuff that opened my eye." Ack-Ack Macaque put a fist to his forehead and mimed an explosion.

"You mean the drugs that *female* gave you?"

"No, it was more than that."

The Founder gave a dismissive snort. "If you don't want anything to do with these children, just say so."

Ack-Ack sat back with a sigh. "You don't get it."

"I'm quite sure I don't. Why don't you explain it for me?"

Frustrated, he ground his right fist into his left palm. "I saw the multiverse," he rumbled. "All of it. Now, whether it was real or a hallucination doesn't matter. I know what I saw."

The Founder considered him with cool disdain. "And what else did you see? What 'revelations' were vouchsafed?"

Ack-Ack Macaque bit down on an angry reply. She could be as sarcastic as she liked, he was still going to say his piece.

"I know that if we run, now, we'll be running forever."

"Not necessarily."

"Yes, yes we will." He scratched his chest. "Because I've seen what happens—I've seen war and suffering. I've seen that wherever you go, wherever you run, there's always some fuck-knuckle thinks he has the right to impose his will on everybody else. Look at Bali." He lowered his voice. "Look at yourself."

The Founder's chin dropped. She squeezed her hands in her lap.

"That was a cheap shot."

Ack-Ack Macaque swore, got to his feet and shambled over to the drinks cabinet. It was a box on wheels containing a few bottles and a stack of glasses, and had once been a minibar in an expensive New York hotel, before he'd liberated it by heaving it through the window into the pool.

"Don't mean it ain't true." He knew he was being petty, but didn't much care. After all, it was her who'd bombed London and killed all those people, not him, and he saw no reason to sugarcoat the truth. He rummaged in the cabinet and fixed himself rum and cola, dumping both into a tall glass without care for drips or spills. Once again, he missed the shabby elegance of the *Tereshkova*'s lounge, and the white-gloved stewards who used to mix his drinks.

Still seated, the Founder said, "So, this is where you've decided to make your stand?"

He stood straight, downed half the glass in a single swallow, and then wiped his lips on the back of his hand.

"I'm tired of saving the world," he said. "If we keep jumping from one timeline to another, we're always going to be butting up against trouble, in one form or another." He took a second smaller sip; swallowed. "There's always going to be somebody that needs their ass kicked."

"You'd rather stay here and fight?"

Ack-Ack Macaque stuck his chin out. "Sure, why not? This is where I'm from. I've got friends here."

"And that's worth dying for, is it?"

He shook his head. "You're not listening."

"And you're not explaining yourself very well." The Founder unfolded her hands and stood. She brushed down the front of her skirt with a gloved hand. "I just want to be sure you know what you're doing, and that you're doing it for the right reasons."

Watching her, and the bulge at her middle, Ack-Ack Macaque drained his glass. He clunked it down on top of the cabinet.

"I belong here," he said. "I can't run out at the first sign of trouble."

"I'd hardly call impending global annihilation 'the first sign of trouble'."

"Whatever." He reached up and snatched off his goggles and leather cap, and tossed them down beside his glass. "I'm talking about Victoria and K8, and Merovech. They're..." He tailed off.

The Founder inclined her head. "They're *what*?"

Ack-Ack Macaque swallowed. He felt foolish, and that only fuelled his irritability.

"They're my troupe." He fixed the Founder with a baleful eye, daring her to laugh, but she only smiled.

"So, you *do* care about something, then? You have chosen a side?"

"Shut up." He stomped back to the rail and leant his weight on it. Through the airship's nose, he could see the distant coastline of England lying like a green smudge on the other side of the Channel. Seagulls wheeled through the air like little white fighter planes. Ships carved long, foamy wakes across the calm waters.

Damn it all, what *had* Apynja done to him? What had happened to the days when he would have simply hopped into his plane and flicked the world the finger? When had he started giving a shit? He glanced back, around his shoulder, at the Founder's pregnant belly and shuddered. It filled him with... what? Not dread, exactly. He wasn't afraid of being a father. No, it was something else, something harder to pin down. For much of his life, as far as he'd been concerned, he'd been living on the edge of death, throwing himself into one dogfight after another, relying on skill and sheer bloody-mindedness to see him through. Now though, for the first time, he felt flutters of apprehension. Where previously he would have been itching to get going—to fly eagerly against the Leviathans in a battle to the death—now a strange fatalism gripped his heart. Mortality weighed on him like a heavy coat. When he thought of the children—his children!— growing in the Founder's womb, he experienced a wave of sadness, almost regret, and knew in his gut that, one day, he'd go off on one of those damn fool missions and never return. One day, he'd leave them fatherless. In that instant, he knew it, and knew the Founder knew it too.

No wonder she's pissed off.

He licked his lips and swallowed. His life had split in two. A crazy, reckless chapter had drawn to a close, and something new was waiting to take its place—an unexplored future with no maps or precedent, where everything to which he'd become accustomed would change. *He* would change. Truth was, he already had. For the first time in his life, death actually meant something.

CHAPTER TWENTY-NINE
INCOMING

With Victoria and Merovech on the bridge, the *Sun Wukong* retraced its steps, back towards the field near Paris where the portal stood. Merovech had stayed on board despite the express objections of his security people. He didn't want to miss this. The only concession he'd made to their concerns was to don a helmet and flak jacket.

As the site of the incursion became obvious on the horizon, Victoria saw at least twenty of the large vehicles spread out in a fan shape, their huge caterpillar tracks having flattened trees, power lines and stone walls with as much ease as the first tank had flattened her helicopter. Above them, four ex-Gestalt dreadnoughts hung like armoured thunderclouds, dispensing volleys of missiles whenever a Leviathan dropped its shields for a split second.

"Looks like a stalemate," she said. "The tanks can't shoot the airships because they daren't lower their force fields in order to fire, and the airships can't hurt them in return while their force fields are in place."

Merovech stood silhouetted against the front window, peering forward.

"So they're just sitting there, looking at each other?"

"Not exactly."

The cannon on the front of one of the Leviathans boomed, gushing smoke and flame. At the same instant, a rain of black torpedoes fell from the nearest dreadnought. Both vehicles rocked with the forces of impacts and explosions.

"It's a war of attrition," Victoria said from the command chair. "They're going to keep plugging away at each other until eventually someone's going to score a lucky hit, or they all run out of fuel and ordnance."

"It seems so pointless."

"Well, nobody ever said war had to make sense." She rose and walked over to join him, right hand resting on the pommel of her sword. "The Founder says there are Gestalt advisors on each of the airships, helping coordinate the attacks."

"I suppose that makes sense."

"You don't sound too keen?"

Merovech let his hands fall to his sides. "I know they surrendered, and I know they've been a big help with the rebuilding and everything." His voice caught. The light shimmered in his eyes. "I just can't forgive them for what happened to Julie."

Without thinking, Victoria reached out and took him by the shoulder.

"It'll be okay."

He shook his head and put a hand to his mouth. "How can you know that?"

"Because I'm going through the same thing with Paul."

"Paul's dead?"

"Paul's been dead for three years."

"But his back-up?"

"It's falling apart."

Merovech swallowed, and wiped his eyes. "I'm sorry to hear that."

"Yeah, me too."

"Is there anything I can do?"

"Not unless you've got a way to get us to Mars." Ahead, one of the dreadnoughts took a hit to one of its engine nacelles and peeled off, side-slipping away from the fight with all the majesty of an iceberg calving. Smoke trailed from its damaged impeller.

"If I had," Merovech said, "I'd be using it to stop that asteroid." He looked sideways at her. "Do you really think Ack-Ack's got a plan?"

"He says he does."

"What do you think?"

Victoria gave an elaborate shrug. "Who knows? But he's been talking it over with K8; I think he's confident."

"He hasn't told you what it is?"

"He will when he's ready."

"But you trust him?"

"Trust him?" Victoria laughed at the absurdity of the idea. How could she trust somebody so fundamentally unreliable?

And yet...

"He's never let me down."

Merovech looked hopeful. "You think he's onto something?"

"Could be."

"He's really going to try to save the world?"

"Or die trying."

The young king gave a nervous laugh. "Well, that's all I can ask."

Victoria gave his arm a comradely pat. She knew she should leave it there, change the subject or walk away, but found she couldn't.

"What happens if he can't save it?" The old journalistic itch was playing up again, and she just had to know. "Is there a plan B?"

Merovech's jaw tightened. "We have the nuclear shelters. A few of us might survive, but only until the stored food runs out."

"What about the dreadnoughts?"

"What about them?"

"They can jump to other parallels. You could load them up with people, use them as life rafts."

Merovech's brow creased thoughtfully. "How many can they hold?"

"I don't know. A thousand each, maybe."

"It's not enough."

"You have six months." Victoria waved her arms helplessly. "You could keep coming back for more, right up until the impact. You'd get tens of thousands out. It would be worth doing."

"But how would we decide who to take?"

"Does it matter?" She barked with incredulous laughter. "Just take as many as you can."

"But where would we go?"

"We'd find *somewhere*. If the monkey army can set up a homeland, we can too."

Merovech looked unconvinced. "But the ones left behind, they'd still be killed."

Victoria took a deep breath, feeling suddenly powerless. However much she tried, there was no way around the scale of the coming catastrophe. She'd seen the damage projections. Whatever she did, whatever any of them did, that rock was going to hit the Earth like a hammer, and when it did, there would be a colossal explosion. Everything in an area the size of Australia would be vaporised on impact. The rest of the world would be battered by secondary impacts, rattled by earthquakes, and drowned beneath tsunamis. So much dust and ash would be thrown up into the atmosphere that the sun's rays would be unable to heat the surface for years, maybe decades. Without its warmth, the remaining plants would wither and die, as would the animals and people that depended on them. The food chains would collapse. Some life might survive, clinging to hydrothermal vents at the bottom of the deepest oceans, but within a few years, the human race would be as dead as the dinosaurs and the ravaged

Earth left for Célestine and her army of Martian cyborgs to inherit. It was Armageddon, Ragnarök and the Mayan Apocalypse, all rolled into one, and all Victoria could do was cross her fingers and hope Ack-Ack Macaque wasn't bullshitting when he claimed to know what he was doing.

AMY LLEWELLYN MARCHED onto the bridge, heels tapping across the deck with staccato urgency.

"I'm sorry, sir." She was out of breath. "I have to show you something." Without waiting for a reply, she crossed to the tactical display and pulled out a data crystal. "May I, Captain?"

Victoria waved a generous hand. "Be my guest." She watched the Welsh girl slot the crystal into the console and tap at the glass-topped controls with a painted nail. Above the forward window, the main display screen fuzzed, and then brought up a blurred picture.

"This was taken twenty minutes ago," Amy explained, "by one of our high-altitude reconnaissance planes."

Victoria frowned at the image. It showed a black triangle, obviously an aircraft of some kind, hanging above the curve of the Earth. The sky behind it was mauve, shading to black. Where the harsh sunlight struck its flank, it gleamed a metallic blue.

"What is it?" Merovech asked.

"I don't know." Amy's voice held the brittleness of an icicle. "But it's the size of a house and it doesn't show up on radar."

"Have you checked with the Americans?"

"They think it's Chinese."

"And the Chinese?"

"They think it's American."

Merovech gaped. "Are you telling me *nobody* knows what it is?"

Victoria stepped forwards. "Could it be from Mars?"

They both looked at her. Amy Llewellyn shrugged and increased the magnification, which made the blurred triangle larger but revealed little in the way of additional detail. "It's big and it's fast," she said, "and we have absolutely no idea what it is or where it's from."

"Jesus." Merovech rubbed his knuckles into his eyes. He looked ready to drop. "Can we track it?"

"No, sir," Amy tapped her knuckle against the image. "It outpaced our guys as if they were standing still. They only had time to snap this picture."

"Where were they when they took it?"

"Over the Atlantic, sir." Without seeming to notice, Amy bit the corner of one of her perfectly manicured nails.

"Did they get a fix on its course?"

"Yes, sir."

"Well?"

She blew a fragment of painted nail from the corner of her mouth. Behind her professional façade, her eyes were wide and scared. When she spoke, her accent was more pronounced than before. "Well, it seems to be heading this way."

An alarm sounded on the *Sun Wukong*'s bridge. Victoria shouldered the girl aside and checked the tactical display.

"*Merde*. We've got incoming. A pair of helicopters."

"Hostile?" Merovech asked.

"Without a doubt."

"Can you shoot them down?"

"No, they're wrapped in the same energy fields as the tanks."

"What about when they fire?"

"They're not firing. I think they're a boarding party."

"What do we do?" Merovech looked around, as if searching for a weapon.

"You stay here," Victoria told him. "Post guards on the door. Take command of the flotilla, keep up the attack."

"And you?"

Victoria drew her sword. "I'm taking the remaining monkeys topside. We're going to be there to welcome them when they land."

BREAKING NEWS
From *Curious Occurrences* (online edition):

UFO Sightings

American authorities are investigating a series of bizarre UFO sightings, with reports coming in from as far afield as Tokyo, San Diego, and Havana.

At 15:00 hours GMT, observers in Japan reported a large fireball, which moved slowly across the sky from west to east, accompanied by a loud roaring noise. An hour later, the crew and passengers of a Puerto Rican cruise liner watched a 'gigantic' spacecraft pass slowly overhead, again accompanied by a loud roaring sound. One of the British passengers on the vessel, Mr. Richard Lewis from Birmingham, filmed the incident on his mobile phone and uploaded the footage to his social media profile.

"It was incredible," he wrote in his status update. "I've never seen anything like it. It wasn't an airship. I don't know what it was."

In another peculiar instance, the pilot of an airliner called in to report a 'close encounter' over Baja California, describing a craft that looked "A bit like a space shuttle without wings. It was blue, and had these huge rocket exhausts sticking out the back."

Online speculation suggests the appearance of these craft could herald another invasion from a parallel world but, so far, the US Air Force has refused to confirm or deny the validity of the sightings. In a brief statement, it acknowledged that an investigation was under way, urged people not to panic, and promised that the public would be 'kept informed' of developments.

Read more | Like | Comment | Share

Related Stories:

Tereshkova crew reappears in France.

Swiss government reopens Cold War bomb shelters.

Thousands flock to Rocky Mountains to join survivalist cults.

Pope calls for 'six months of repentance'.

Reports of fighting near Paris.

Church of Rock 'n' Roll declares 'Second Coming of Elvis'.

'Pork Flakes' breakfast snacks recalled following spate of heart attacks.

CHAPTER THIRTY
CUDDLES

THE CHURCH STOOD at the edge of the village. Like many churches in that part of rural France, it was small, rectangular and austere, with little in the way of carvings or other ornamentation, just a single stained glass window and a lone bell at the top of a modest tower. In its graveyard, Ack-Ack Macaque crouched behind a headstone and looked out at the tanks lumbering through the fields beyond the village. Even at this range, he didn't need binoculars. The damned things were the size of buildings and he could feel the earth tremble with the vibration of their tracks. Behind him, the village itself had already suffered half a dozen hits, but he couldn't tell whether these had been the result of accident or deliberate attack. The inhabitants, clutching suitcases, children and cats, were fleeing in the direction of the main road. In the village square, two houses and a boulangerie were on fire and the war memorial had been toppled. He could smell wood smoke and hot bread, and the faintest traces of incense and candle wax from the church.

He took a moment to consider the memorial's broken column. How many times had this territory been fought over? The First and Second World Wars had left their scars on the landscape from here to Norway, but there was a history of conflict and dispute in this area stretching back through the Napoleonic Wars, the French Revolution and the Hundred Years War. Europe, which liked to see itself as a cradle of civilisation and enlightenment, had for much of its history been a seething cauldron of blood and death—a rag caught between the jaws of fighting dogs.

"And here we are again," he muttered with disgust, adjusting the strap of the chainsaw he carried on his back.

"What's that, Chief?" Erik the orangutan crouched a little further along the wall, clad in beige fatigues. Beyond him, hunkered low behind a pair of gravestones, the red-faced macaques Lumpy and Fang sat curled around their submachine guns. Fang wore a horned Viking helmet and carried a sword at his belt; Lumpy was naked, save for a leather tunic. Cuddles, the big gorilla, lurked in the church porch. He wore aviator sunglasses, a white vest, and a pair of cut-off camouflage shorts. In his thick arms he cradled the dead weight of a six-barrelled minigun.

"Nothing." Ack-Ack Macaque dragged his thoughts back to the objective at hand. "Okay," he said, "you see the Leviathan on the left by the copse, the burning one?"

"Yes, Chief."

"That's our target."

Erik ducked back into the wall's shadow, resting his back against the ancient, mossy stones.

"How are we going to get down there?"

"Carefully." Ack-Ack Macaque pulled out a cigar and fastened it between his teeth. "If we get caught in the open, it's all over." He beckoned them closer, and unrolled a printed photomosaic of the battlefield, taken from a camera on the *Sun Wukong*. "There's a culvert running alongside the lane," he said, tracing the ditch with his finger. "We can follow it down the hill as far as the copse."

Lumpy leant in. "What we going to do then, Chief?"

Ack-Ack Macaque rocked back on his heels and glared at him.

"They're trees, we're primates. What the fuck do you think we're going to do?"

"HEY, CUDDLES, UNLESS you want your arse shot off, keep it down."

"Sorry, Chief."

They were about halfway down the hill from the village now, moving in the direction of the battle and the ruined tank Ack-Ack Macaque had picked out as the most likely target for his purposes. The culvert along which they were crawling smelled of mouldering leaves and old dog shit, but he was past caring. He'd been running, crawling and fighting so long, all he knew how to do was keep going—keep soldiering on. He could rest when all this was over; until then, nothing else mattered. And, after all this skulking around, he was actually looking forward to getting in among the Leviathan's cyborg crew. He'd had enough hiding; it was time to fight back, and blow off steam by blowing off a few heads.

Ahead, the Leviathan resembled a land-going warship, its superstructure rising in successive levels, each bristling with gun turrets and missile launchers.

"I figure they're heavily defended at ground level," he said. "But maybe they don't expect enemy troops to come at them from above."

"So," Erik asked, "we're going to drop out of the trees?"

"Bingo." Ack-Ack Macaque stopped crawling. His elbows and knees were sore and the front of his jacket was caked in mud. When he swallowed, his neck still hurt from being throttled by Bali. "I reckon, if we get up onto that second level, we'll find an access hatch or something."

"You reckon?"

"I've studied the motherfucking photos." He started moving again, muttering under his breath about smartarses. Behind him, Erik cleared his throat.

"What about Cuddles, Chief?"

Ack-Ack Macaque turned to glare over his shoulder.

"What about him?"

"Well," Erik lowered his voice. "He's a silverback. He weighs like five hundred pounds."

"So?"

"So, how's he going to climb a tree?"

Behind them, Cuddles let out an aggressive snort. "You see these arms?" he growled. "If I can peel a car apart with my bare hands, I think I've got the strength to pull myself up a damn tree."

Erik cringed. "No offence, big lad. It's just I never heard of a gorilla doing that."

"And I never heard of such an ignorant orangutan."

They crawled onwards in sullen silence. At the bottom of the hill, fresh explosions shook the fields. Handfuls of dirt and stones rained down into the ditch, showering their backs. The ground shook beneath them, and the crunching, screeching noise of a Leviathan grew steadily closer. Motioning his squad to stay down, Ack-Ack risked a peep over the edge of the lane. From the field on the other side of the tarmac, one of the giant machines rumbled in their direction, trying to get out from beneath the dreadnoughts' barrage.

"Oh, balls." There was no time to move. He hunched back into the ditch. "Change of plan, chaps. Get ready to follow my lead."

He stayed down as the vast machine clattered across the road, shattering the tarmac. From above, he heard the sound of its cannons firing. As it loomed over the ditch where he hid, he leapt to his feet and threw himself forwards, into the wide space between the sets of the tracks. With the guns in action, the shield had dropped. Erik, Fang, Lumpy and Cuddles came after him, the latter just managing to clear the culvert before the bank gave way beneath the tank's weight.

Now, they were under the Leviathan, within its protective force field envelope. Everything stank of diesel and wheel grease. The noise was almost indescribable, like being caught in the heart of an exploding steel foundry, and they had to duck as the underside of the vehicle slid past, centimetres above their heads. With no hope of being heard above the din, Ack-Ack Macaque settled for waving his squad towards the rear of the tank. It was their only choice of direction. Running on his hands and feet, he made for daylight, hoping the tank's back end would be lightly armed, and that the gunners would all be facing forwards, looking for targets ahead or to the sides, rather than directly in their wake. If the monkeys could remain unobserved the next time the tank lowered its shield, they'd have time to dart across the field and into the trees.

Before he could reach the back end, the Leviathan squealed to a halt, rocking on its tracks, and figures dropped from the tail to block his way. A quick glance behind showed other figures at the front of the tank—all with the unmistakable tall, slim build of Nguyen's cyborgs.

Ah, crap. They had been detected. If they were going to get out from under this tank, they were going to have to fight their way out.

"Erik! You and Fang take the front," he barked over the din of the idling engine. "Cuddles and Lumpy, cover the rear."

Directly above him, a hatch scraped open, spilling light into the shadows beneath the tank. From the overhead darkness, thin metallic arms reached for Ack-Ack Macaque. He snarled, and slipped his chainsaw from its strap. If the tank's crew wanted a fight, he was going to give them more fight than they could possibly imagine.

With a howl, he bent his legs and sprang upwards, leaping headlong into the belly of the beast.

CHAPTER THIRTY-ONE
JUST FLESH

THE HELICOPTERS TOUCHED down at the *Sun Wukong*'s stern, their wheels kissing the armoured deck only long enough to disgorge their passengers. With no appearance of haste, the willowy cyborgs—ten in all—arranged themselves into a v-shaped formation and began marching towards the nearest hatch, where Victoria stood, flanked by a dozen heavily armed monkeys. As they approached, she raised her sword, levelling the point at the chest of their leader.

"*Arrêtez-vous, s'il vous plaît.*"

To either side of her, the monkeys displayed their weapons—a motley collection of rifles, pistols and submachine guns.

The cyborgs stamped to a halt, just out of reach.

"You are required to surrender this vessel," the leader said, his voice expressionless and devoid of emotion. He had high cheekbones, slicked-back hair and a pencil moustache. The skin on his face looked almost real, but his hands, where they protruded from his utilitarian one-piece overall, had the mirror-like finish of polished chrome. They resembled gauntlets from a suit of armour, and she couldn't help but speculate about the rest of his body. Where had the line been drawn between man and machine—and which parts were still soft enough for her sword to penetrate?

"You're not welcome here," she said. "Get back in your tanks, turn around, and go back to where you came from." Around her, the monkeys chattered appreciatively. The cyborgs, however, remained impassive.

"It's for your own good," said the one with the moustache. "You may fight us now, but you'll thank us in the long run."

Victoria raised her sword slightly, lining it up with his throat, which looked reassuringly organic and vulnerable.

"I don't think that's going to happen."

The half-man looked down at her. His pupils were black dots set in silver irises.

"You have no idea of our capabilities."

Victoria kept her expression neutral, making use of her best poker face. "On the contrary, I've met your sort before."

"Then you should know that we're very hard to kill."

Without breaking his gaze, she turned her chin a little to the side, so he could see the thick scars at the back of her head and neck.

"As am I."

The moustache kinked as the cyborg's mouth twitched up at the side in what was probably meant to be a smile. He held up his fists, and a pair of foot-long machete-like blades slid from recesses concealed beneath his cuffs. A series of *snicks* came from each of the cyborgs behind him as their own blades slid into place—one from each arm. In the winter sunlight, the edges looked sharp enough to cut the air itself, and certainly strong and heavy enough to snap Victoria's thin sword like dry spaghetti.

"You're just flesh," the leading cyborg said, contempt dripping from his lips.

Victoria felt her pulse quicken. Her fist tightened on the grip of her weapon.

"And you're not even that."

Her gelware came online. It reacted to her elevated heart rate by flooding her body with adrenaline. She felt the clarity and speed of her thoughts increase as sections of her consciousness were shunted from her brain's natural cells to the crisp lucidity of the artificial processors in her neural prosthesis. Her thinking became clearer and more dispassionate, and she realised that she was going to have to kill or be killed. These creatures had come to take the dreadnought and slaughter or convert its crew. They weren't interested in negotiation or compromise, and they'd dismissed their helicopters because they had no plans to surrender or retreat. They were here to fight and win, and Victoria was the only obstacle in their path.

Well, that's just fine.

She glanced sideways at the snarling monkeys. "Take 'em out, boys," she said, and lunged forward. Striking with all the accelerated speed her gelware could muster, her first thrust took the guy with the moustache through the Adam's apple. He gurgled and choked, and blood spewed down his chest. But, even as she withdrew the sword, his hands scythed up, gleaming blades describing two neat parabolas in the winter air—and she found herself holding only the grip and guard. With the cut-off point of her sword still protruding from his neck, he came for her, and she backed away. Around her, the shrieking monkeys grappled with the other cyborgs. Shots were fired, blades flashed. She saw one macaque—a gorgeous Japanese snow macaque with thick beige fur and a bright red face—impaled on the end of a cyborg's fist.

"*Merde.*"

Moustache Man swung at her and she danced away. To her left another monkey went down, throat slit. Fast as the monkeys were, the cyborgs were faster, and the blades protruding from their synthetic wrists added half a metre to their reach.

"Retreat!" she called. "Fall back to the hatches!"

Meanwhile, below:

"Pass us those cables." K8 pointed across the engine room to a bundle sticking from a power socket. She had a lot to do, but the pair of chimps she'd been assigned weren't being a great deal of help. At first, it had been because her habit of referring to herself using plural pronouns, such as 'we' and 'us', confused them; but now they were just plain distracted. Over the past few minutes, more and more of their attention had become fixed on the sounds of combat coming from above. As K8 toiled, preparing the groundwork for the second part of Ack-Ack Macaque's plan, she heard small arms fire, monkey screams, and even the dull crump of a grenade. As the fighting grew closer, the chimps, whose names were Oing and Boing, grew increasingly skittish. They kept chattering to each other and fingering the holsters slung around their waists, leaving K8 to do the bulk of the work herself.

Not that she minded so much. Sometimes it was just quicker and easier to do something yourself, rather than explain it to someone else, and, as the majority of the work here involved wiring—setting up a power feed from the airship's generators, and a six-foot cradle to hold the force field device the Skipper planned to bring back from one of the Leviathans—it was nothing she couldn't handle alone.

She stomped over and picked up the cables she wanted, and hauled one end back to the improvised metal frame she had built in the centre of the room. The design of the contraption wasn't entirely of her own devising. As she laboured on it, she received a constant flow of suggestions and comments from other members of the Gestalt, their minds attuned to her thoughts, seeing the project through her eyes. To a girl used to loneliness, whose only real friend had been a foul-mouthed, unappreciative monkey, their warmth and companionship gave constant comfort, and the reassurance that she would never be alone again. Right at this moment, as she tugged the power leads into place and connected them to a socket hastily screwed to the side of the structure, her thoughts were communing with members of the Gestalt in London, Cairo, San Francisco and Dubai. Their shared awareness stretched like a web of light around the world, binding and bonding them in ways far more intimate than the ties of familial or sexual love. The Founder, with the help and encouragement of her puppet, the Leader, had tried to use the Gestalt's hive mind as a weapon—but K8 thought that by doing so, they'd missed the point. As far as she was concerned, this interconnectedness wasn't a tool to be used to achieve a goal, it was an end in itself. It was a beautiful way to live and work and collaborate—not in pursuit of power or greed, but simply to enrich the lives of all by sharing knowledge, skill and camaraderie.

She picked up a wrench. The noise of battle grew louder still. It sounded as if scuffles were taking place in the corridor outside the engine room. She heard a monkey screech. Something thumped against the wall; there were two gunshots in quick succession, and then silence.

The chimps drew their pistols.

"Hurry up, girlie," warned Oing, extending a hairy arm to level his weapon at the door.

"Yeah," Boing agreed, using his free hand to pull a bayonet from his belt, "make it quick."

ON THE AIRSHIP'S bridge, Merovech watched the computer plot different coloured vector lines across a map of Europe.

"Extrapolating from initial sightings," Amy said, "projected analysis shows the unknown craft arriving in our airspace within ten minutes."

"You definitely think it's coming here?"

"Where else would it be going?" She cast a hand at the forward window, and the battle raging below. "It's too much of a coincidence for it to be going anywhere else."

"What can we do?"

"You could give the order to scramble jet fighters."

"Would they get here in time?"

"They might."

Merovech rubbed his chin. He was twelve hours overdue for a shave. "Okay, do it."

"Yes, sir." Amy signalled to one of the Marines, who began talking urgently into his radio.

"Not that I expect it'll do much good."

"Sir?"

Merovech shrugged. "You say it overtook one of our fastest planes and left it for dust. It's the size of a large house, yet it doesn't show up on radar. Whatever it is, it's an order of magnitude more advanced than anything we can put in the air."

CHAPTER THIRTY-TWO
PURÉED BRAINS

THE LEVIATHAN'S INTERIOR was a maze of noisy steel chambers and cramped, badly lit companionways. It felt like the inside of a submarine. Slashing and stabbing with his chainsaw, Ack-Ack Macaque fought his way deeper. With each swing, sparks flew and severed metal limbs dropped to the deck, twitching and writhing like decapitated snakes. Somewhere along the line, he'd lost his flying cap and goggles, and the cigar he held chomped between his teeth had been snapped in half. The arm holding the chainsaw had become slathered to the elbow in blood and synthetic fluids, and he was down to his last three bullets—yet he felt better than he had in months. He'd never wanted to lead an army. He was a soldier, not a general, and *this* was where he belonged: at the heart of the mêlée, grappling overwhelming odds, with the fate of the world on his shoulders.

The confined spaces in the heart of the Leviathan proved an advantage, as Célestine's cybernetic soldiers couldn't overwhelm him; they could only attack one at a time, which suited him fine. When he swung his chainsaw in the narrow gangways, they didn't have the leeway to dodge, and more than one of them went down with their faces shredded from their skulls and their brains ripped to purée.

His other advantage was that his strategy seemed to be confusing them. They were deploying themselves to defend access to the control room at the top of the vehicle, whereas Ack-Ack Macaque's target was lower, and to the rear. They thought he wanted to destroy the tank, or capture it; that he gave a flying fuck about their nuisance invasion, when, in reality, stopping it wasn't on his immediate to-do list—later maybe, but not right now. Right now, he had another objective. As they moved to block his upward progress, he moved back and to the side, wrong-footing them at every turn.

Behind him, the rest of his squad raced to keep up, fighting off pursuers and pausing only to finish off those wounded cyborgs he'd left in his wake that were still capable of offensive action.

"How much further?" he shouted over the noise and vibration of the

Leviathan's engines. Behind him, Erik consulted an infrared photo of the tank, taken via scopes on the *Sun Wukong*, his rubbery-looking fingers measuring the distance from where they thought they were to the large heat source at the Leviathan's stern.

"Five metres. Just the other side of the next hatch."

"Are you sure?"

"No."

"Ah, fuck it." Ack-Ack Macaque spat out the soggy butt of the broken cigar. He was gambling everything on the assumption that the heat source marked the position of the engine room, and that the engine room housed the device he sought.

"Well, it's certainly loud enough. Tell Cuddles to get his arse up here. If what we're looking for is in here, we're going to need him to carry it."

"Roger, Chief."

Ack-Ack Macaque put a hand against the hatch. Like the rest, it was made of thick, uncoated steel, with rivets the size of golf balls, and he could feel it throbbing to the beat of the Leviathan's mechanical heart.

"This has to be the place." Hefting the chainsaw in his right hand, he holstered his Colt and gripped the wheel that opened the door. The steel was shiny with use. He gave it two quick yanks and it spun open. The locks disengaged, and the hatch swung inwards.

Beyond, the engine room was a mass of ducts, pipes and tangled wiring, at the centre of which lay two vast and thundering turbine engines. He sniffed. The air stank of hot oil and choking exhaust fumes, and the racket was so loud he couldn't hear the whine of his chainsaw—only feel it juddering through the bones and muscles of his arm.

"Right," he yelled over his shoulder, hoping his troops could hear him, or at least get the gist, "let's get in and out before they have a chance to figure out what we're doing."

He stepped over the raised threshold, onto a catwalk suspended above the grinding turbines. At the far end, the device he'd come for stood bolted to a bulkhead, looking like an upturned coffin leant against a wall. Between him and it stood a cyborg, and Ack-Ack Macaque sighed. The walkway didn't seem all that secure underfoot, and he could feel it sway with the cyborg's movements. There was no point trying to speak over the din, so he simply bared his teeth and drew his revolver.

"*Adios, muchacho.*" He squeezed the trigger and the gun bucked in his hand, once, twice, three times. The advancing figure stopped. The first shot had torn a gash across its temple, exposing the shiny silver skull beneath the skin and biting away a sizeable chunk of ear. The second and third had hit it in the chest, but Ack-Ack Macaque could see no evidence of damage. He'd hoped to hit something vital, but the shots didn't seem to have penetrated anything save for the cyborg's cotton overalls.

"Bollocks," he muttered, tossing aside the empty handgun. Facing him, the cyborg frowned, and put a hand to its ruined ear. Anger flashed across its features. With slow deliberation, it started walking forward, hands grasping at the air. Ack-Ack Macaque swore under his breath. He needed the box at the other end of the gangway. He needed it to save the world— and if that meant going through this robotic motherfucker to get his hands on it, then that was the way it had to be.

"Okay," he snarled, shaking the chainsaw, "you want some more, eh?" He ran to meet his opponent, and they crashed together at the walkway's midpoint, suspended above the spinning turbines. The cyborg parried Ack-Ack Macaque's first swing, using his left forearm to deflect the whirring teeth, while swinging his right fist at the monkey's midriff. Luckily, Ack-Ack was ready for the move, and twisted aside, bringing his chainsaw back and around for another swipe. As he did so, the cyborg smiled, and vicious-looking blades sprang from his wrists. He used one to block Ack-Ack's second attack, and stabbed with the other. Unable to counter the thrust, Ack-Ack Macaque was forced to relinquish the chainsaw and skip back. He only just made it. The tip of the attacking blade ripped a razor-straight gash across the front of his jacket and the leather sagged open, revealing the white sheepskin beneath.

Incandescent with rage but now unarmed, Ack-Ack Macaque screeched at his attacker and did the only thing he could think of. Bending at the knees, he waited until the cyborg took another swing, and leapt, launching himself over the gangway's rail. For a split second, he seemed to hang in space. The turbines spun beneath him, ready to crush and mangle him. Then his tail hooked one of the wires supporting the walkway. He swung down and round, passing beneath the feet of his surprised attacker. His hand grabbed the underside of the gangway, and he let the momentum carry him, so that he came up the other side and hit the cyborg in the head with both feet. The impact jarred every bone in his body and snapped the metal man's head back on its shoulders. Something cracked, and the figure staggered.

Ack-Ack Macaque dropped to the floor. When he got back to his feet, he saw the cyborg tottering, its head dangling behind it, held in place by electrical wires. Ducking under its swiping, blindly scissoring arms, he grabbed its overalls by the knees and heaved. The metal body went up and backwards, and toppled over the rail into the engines below.

For an instant, it seemed to bob and dance on the spinning turbines before getting caught and dragged into the machinery. He saw the head fly in one direction, one of the arms in another. Then its torso must have caught on something, because there was an ear-splitting bang, and the engines whined into smoke and silence.

Looking back to the hatch, Ack-Ack saw Erik and Cuddles were watching him with wide, awestruck eyes.

"Come on," he barked, ears ringing in the sudden silence. "I need you guys to grab hold of this device and get it back to K8 on the *Sun*."

Erik the orangutan blinked at him.

"What about you, Chief?"

"Me?" Ack-Ack Macaque scowled down at his damaged jacket. "I'm going to need my chainsaw and some ammunition. I've got some unfinished business with Célestine." He tried to pull the two sides of the slit together with his hands. "And, while you're at it, see if you can find me some goddamn safety pins."

CHAPTER THIRTY-THREE
AMELINE

TWELVE KILOMETRES ABOVE the battle-torn fields of northern France, the former trading ship *Ameline* slowed to a halt in the air. The ship had been travelling at Mach 4, but now it was stationary, hanging in the sky like an impossible statue. In cross-section, it was a snub-nosed wedge, its sheen of blue and red paint bleached by the light of a dozen alien suns. Jacked into its virtual senses, Katherine Abdulov looked down at the carnage beneath. Even from here, she could see the Leviathans crawling around like tracked armadillos, and the massive airships harrying them from above.

"Any sign of Célestine?" she asked the ship, and felt it run a sensor sweep, scouring the countryside below for signs of their quarry.

> DIFFICULT TO TELL.

Kat heard the ship's words in her mind via her neural link, and pursed her lips.

"But this fits her M.O.?"

> OH, DEFINITELY. THERE ARE A LOT OF CYBORGS DOWN THERE. MONKEYS TOO.

"Monkeys plural?"

> IT SEEMS NAPOLEON'S FOUND HIMSELF A POSSE.

Kat gave a weary sigh.

"And what about our other target, the Valois woman?"

> ACCORDING TO RADIO TRAFFIC, SHE'S ON ONE OF THE AIRSHIPS.

"You're sure?"

> SURE AS CAN BE.

"Have they seen us yet?"

She felt a shiver in the connection, like the electronic equivalent of a sniff.

> WE'RE INVISIBLE TO THEIR RADAR. THE ONLY WAY THEY'LL NOTICE US IS IF ONE OF THEM STEPS OUT ON DECK AND LOOKS UP WITH THEIR EYES.

"Which is always possible."

> MEH.

Kat took a moment to savour the view: the clear blue skies and rolling brown and yellow countryside, the grey urban sprawl of Paris to the north and the sea to the west. All of it alive, untouched, and relatively unspoiled. *Djatt, Inakpa, Strauli...* Those tragedies seemed so long ago, so far away—and yet their pain never lessened, never left her. And so here she was at the other end of the universe, trying to save this world—trying to avert yet another apocalypse.

She opened a channel to the forward weapons pod, where Ed Rico lay cocooned in alien technology, as much a component of the gun as its operator.

"How are you doing, Ed?"

"Hanging in there." His voice sounded bubbly and distorted, forcing its way up through layers of alien mucus.

"Keep an eye on the horizon," she told him. "I'm going to try landing on the airship, but if this all goes tits-up, we can expect an armed response."

"Don't worry." He sounded like a man choking, pushing each syllable through the glop that filled his lungs and throat. "I'm on it."

"Thanks, Ed." She turned her attention back to the downward view. The airships moved like armoured clouds, raining fire on the tanks, which in turn resembled the restlessly moving buildings of a mobile city.

"Okay," she said, "let's go down there and say hello."

She looked down and flexed the fingers of her artificial left hand. The metal of the fingers and wrist had been stained and half-melted during an attack by The Recollection.

The ship trembled around her as the engines changed their pitch, and the deck skewed forward.

> DESCENDING NOW.

Through the ship's senses, she felt the wind caressing the outside of the hull and the hairs on her arms and neck prickled in response. Tingles in her feet represented the push of the thrust, growls in her stomach the power of the engines.

"Let's *try* to do it gently this time," she implored the cranky old spacecraft as she felt it fire up its fusion motors. "Remember, we want to speak to these people, not incinerate them."

CHAPTER THIRTY-FOUR
WRENCH

OING WAS THE first to die. A tall, golden-skinned female cyborg came crashing through the engine room door. Her mane of bright red hair gave her the look of an idealised Roman centurion, and her shining blades were black with blood and gore. She dispatched the chimp with a single backhand swipe of her arm, gutting him with a vicious slash from right hip to left nipple.

As Oing collapsed in a flood of gore, Boing opened fire with his sidearm. K8 covered her ears. The gunshots were shockingly loud in the confined space, but seemed to have little effect on the gleaming woman. When the gun was empty, Boing threw it at her. It hit her on the chest and fell to the deck.

K8 looked around for a weapon, but the only thing with any heft was the wrench she was already holding—and even that looked pitifully small and ineffectual compared to the half-metre blades extending from the woman's sleeves.

The cyborg looked down at the gun on the floor.

"Is that it, Cheetah?" she asked. Her voice was rich and deep, and only slightly human. Boing snarled. He shifted his weight from one foot to the other and tightened his grip on the bayonet in his other hand.

"That's not my name."

"Do you think I care?"

She raised her arms—one held forward defensively, pointing at him and daring him to rush her; the other pulled back, fist level with her ear, ready to strike.

Boing growled.

Feeling helpless, K8 called the hive for assistance, but they were all too far away to offer practical help.

All save one.

Be strong, my child. The Founder's words emanated an indignant and flinty resolve. K8 squeezed the wrench in her fists. Boing and the golden woman were circling each other.

Help us.

I am trapped on the bridge with Valois and the Marines, but I will come as soon as we can.

We need you now.

I'm afraid that's not possible.

K8 felt anger stir up inside, let it leak onto the communal channel.

Then what bloody use are you?

She crouched beside the metal cradle she'd improvised on the engine room's floor, thinking maybe she could unplug the power cables she'd just connected and use them to electrify the deck. She didn't know whether doing so would affect their cyborg attacker, but was certain it would, in all likelihood, kill her and Boing.

Best leave that as a last resort.

Motion caught her eye. Boing leapt forward, lunging with the bayonet. His long, hairy arm gave him tremendous reach and the tip of his weapon actually touched the golden woman's breast before her arm—moving so fast it was little more than a blur—swiped him aside with all the power of a car crash, sending his broken body tumbling and flopping across the deck like windblown laundry.

Sickened, K8 swallowed hard. Slowly, she rose to her feet, wrench held shakily before her. At this point, her fear and anger had become interchangeable. She couldn't tell where one finished and the other began, but both were firing her with a desperate, insane urge to fight back, no matter how mismatched and hopeless the struggle—the same instinct she imagined filled swimmers and led them to struggle in the jaws of a shark, or compelled doomed cavemen to pit their fists and fingernails against the claws and teeth of a sabre-toothed cat. Whatever happened here, she knew she would not beg, would not grovel, and would not die like cowering prey. She knew that if the Skipper were here, he'd do the same. He'd never give up, never surrender, and never give his opponent the satisfaction of seeing his fear—and neither would she. She took a deep, steadying breath, and gripped the wrench with both hands. Gold eyes flicked in her direction. The cyborg let its head tilt to one side. It looked her up and down, from the ratty baseball boots on her feet to the tousled top of her carroty hair.

"Oh, relax," it said. "I'm not going to kill you."

K8 felt her jaw clench. The golden woman stepped towards her, moving on thin, graceful legs.

"Jeez," the cyborg said, "you look so short."

K8 worked her lips. It took her three attempts to make her voice work.

"Stay back."

The woman smiled.

"I'm not going to hurt you, K8." With a sound like scraping cutlery, her stained blades retracted into her sleeves.

"How do you know my name?"

"How do you think?" A shining hand reached out, plucked the wrench from her grip, and tossed it away. "I'm you, you dumbass."

"M-me?" In her head, K8 could feel the other members of the Gestalt recoiling from her.

"Yeah, girl. I'm the version of you from the other world. You know how this works."

"But I would never, never—"

"Never can be a long time when you don't have a choice."

With her back to the wall, K8 looked around for a way out. Her eyes fell on Oing and Boing, still lying where they fell.

"Why did you have to kill them?" she demanded, cheeks burning.

"They were in my way."

"And me?"

"You can be saved." The gold woman shook her red Mohican, which shimmered in the light like strands of fibre optic thread. "You can come with us, and have a body like mine."

"But, I—" K8 stopped, surprised to hear herself using a singular pronoun. "I…" the Gestalt were still there at the back of her mind, but their voices were quieter now, less intrusive—and where once there had been 'we' and 'us', now there was only 'me' and 'I'.

"Are you listening?" The golden woman reached for her. "I'm trying to save you."

"Well, I don't need saving." Still distracted by the changes taking place in her head, K8 slapped the cyborg's hand away. "I don't need you, or anybody else."

The gold woman cocked her head in amusement. "But you're so lonely."

"No, I'm not." K8 bunched her fists. "I thought I was, but I'm not."

"Because of the monkey?"

K8 felt her heart rattling against her ribs.

"Yes, the monkey."

The golden woman straightened up and made a show of looking around the room.

"Then where is he, eh?" She bent forwards, putting her face level with K8's, and K8 could see her own distress reflected in the polished mask.

"Everybody let me down; why should you be any different? Where's this hairy 'friend' of yours when you need him? *And where was he when I needed him?*"

A cough came from the door. They both looked around to see Cuddles standing on the threshold. The big gorilla filled the entranceway with his muscular bulk, the Gatling gun cradled like a toy in his massive hands.

"Ack-Ack sends his regards."

A fat, leathery finger squeezed the trigger and the gun's barrels spun. The cyborg tried to leap aside but, fast as she was, she couldn't outpace a weapon capable of firing fifty rounds per second. The room flickered as fire danced from the gun. K8 let her knees give out and collapsed to the deck, landing on her hip. Above her, her golden counterpart jerked and danced like a marionette as bullets punched through her metal skin, into the flesh and wiring beneath. Stray shots riddled the rear wall. Used shell cases showered around the gorilla's feet. The chattering roar of the gun filled the room.

And then all was quiet.

The minigun's spinning barrels whined into silence and the last spent case jangled on the iron deck. The room stank of hot metal, spilled oil and gun smoke. K8 uncovered her ears and looked up. The perforated cyborg stood swaying. It put a hand up to the smoking holes peppering its chest, and then dropped heavily to its knees.

"You idiots," it wheezed.

Cuddles pushed up his sunglasses and fixed the woman with a sharp-toothed sneer. His feet straddled the end of a long, grey, coffin-shaped box. He dropped the minigun and pulled out a large silver pistol, which he levelled at her head.

"Fuck you, lady."

After the whining din of the Gatling gun, the pistol's shot was a flat crack. The bullet hit the cyborg in the forehead and her head tipped back on her neck. Something snapped in her chest, metal parted and, as if in slow motion, her head and shoulders broke from the ruins of her trunk. They fell backwards with a heavy thud. The rest of her body—sparking wires projecting from the shards of her chest—tottered for a second on buckling legs, and then collapsed in the opposite direction.

STILL FEELING NUMB, K8 helped the gorilla lug the stolen shield device across the deck to the cradle she'd built. At first glance, it appeared to be a sealed container with no obvious controls or openings, save for a power coupling at the narrow end. As Cuddles kicked the remains of the golden cyborg out of the way, she ran her hands over the edges of the box, searching for seams or hidden catches.

"Any idea how it works?" the gorilla rumbled. Grease and dirt streaked his white vest, and his sunglasses perched on top of his head. The dog tags around his neck clanked quietly when he moved.

K8 sighed and shook her head. Her pulse still roared in her ears and she felt sick. She couldn't believe she'd been talking to another iteration of herself; that the brain in that precious metal physique had once belonged to a girl almost identical to her—a kind of twin sister, but a shadow sister that had turned to the Dark Side, renouncing her humanity and morals in exchange for a shot at immortality. K8 shook herself and decided she'd worry about the philosophical implications later. When all this was over—assuming they lived through the next few hours—she'd have time to freak the hell out. Right now, she had a job to do, and the Skipper was counting on her to get it done. Hell, the whole future of the *world* depended on it.

She coughed and cracked her knuckles. Then she gave the grey box a prod with her toe.

"I guess we just plug it in and see what happens."

She helped Cuddles guide it into the makeshift cradle and was gratified to see it was an almost perfect fit.

Let us help, child. The Founder's voice echoed in the spaces behind her conscious thoughts.

Get lost.

Our minds, working together...

K8 screwed her eyes shut and tapped her knuckles against her temples. She'd yearned to rejoin the hive, craved its comfort the way a raindrop craves the ocean; yet now, a crack had appeared. She could still hear them, still feel them, but they'd let her down in a moment of need. They'd left her hanging, high and dry. A rift had opened and now she wasn't sure it could ever be repaired. She wasn't part of their collective any more. In facing death, she'd found herself.

Shut up and get out of my head.

All that mattered now was the task at hand, and the Skipper's plan.

You can't shut us out.

Leave me alone.

You hate being alone, all by yourself. Don't you remember? Don't you remember how hard it was, how lonely?

She picked up the power cable and rammed it into the waiting socket, twisting and jiggling it until it slid home. The number of voices in her head rose to a chorus, a multitude. A whole congregation of true believers called to her, beseeching her.

Come back to us. Be one with us again.

Tears rolling down her face, she crammed her fingers into her ears. They sounded like disappointed primary school teachers and she tried to drown them out the only way she knew how.

La la la la, she sang to herself, inner voice almost shrieking the words she remembered from a childhood spent as the only ginger kid in her class, the words she'd used to block out the schoolyard taunts.

La la la, I'm not listening.

CHAPTER THIRTY-FIVE
MARY SHELLEY

ACK-ACK MACAQUE LEAPT from the rear of the crippled Leviathan, leaving it straddling the road, and ran on all fours across the field. The fighting had intensified, with the tanks and airships exchanging fusillades in an almost continuous bombardment, and he hoped everybody's attention would be fixed on their opponents rather than scanning the grass for scampering primates.

He didn't know for sure which tank Célestine was in, but he had a fair idea. So far, the Leviathans had arranged themselves in an arrowhead formation, with one at the rear, close to the portal—and that was the one he was running towards. The Duchess might be a deranged and evil bitch, but she was also very keen on self-preservation. She wanted to live forever, which meant she wouldn't be riding in the vanguard with the rest of the grunts; she'd be at the back, close enough to command the battle but sheltered behind the first wave of tanks. And, now he was on the inside of the 'V', he made straight for her.

What he'd do when he found her was another matter. He hadn't given it much thought, beyond the vague idea that he'd rip her arms off and use them to beat the rest of her to death. After all, this was the woman who'd started it all: the spider in the web, pulling the strings. She was the one who'd contacted the various Doctor Nguyens on their respective worlds, and encouraged them in their experiments. If it hadn't been for her, he might never have been uplifted. He might have stayed a semi-conscious monkey, living out his days in ignorance. He and all the other sentient monkeys and apes might have gone on with their lives as nature intended, without being strapped to tables and shaped into aberrant, gaudy monstrosities. If Nguyen had been his personal Frankenstein, Célestine was his Mary Shelley. She was the author of all that had transpired, the mad genius behind his story, and he *really* wanted to kill her. Because who knew what insanity she intended to unleash this time? Three years ago, she'd egged on her counterpart on this world—Merovech's mother—to engineer a nuclear confrontation with China, all in order to further her own desires for cybernetic immortality, and, if Apynja was to be believed, she'd already killed most of the population of her own timeline, sentencing billions to sickness and lingering death for her own foul ends.

Well, fuck that with a long, greasy pole. It was time for a reckoning, and it seemed only fit and proper that he—one of her discarded prototypes— should be the one to dish out the justice.

A stray shell hit the ground a couple of dozen metres to his right, with a force that bowled him over and showered him with earth and stones. He rolled with the impact, taking it on his shoulder, and came back up onto his hands and feet, still running.

It's going to take more than that to stop me today. All his aches and pains seemed to have fallen away, having sloughed off like a dead skin. Adrenaline burned through him like good rum. He felt young again.

Ahead, his target lumbered forward at less than walking pace, the vast tracks barely turning.

She doesn't want to get too far from the portal, he thought. And who could blame her? The last thing she would have been expecting was to have her lead tanks savaged by armour-plated aerial behemoths. She would have been anticipating a world still recovering from the nuclear standoff between China and the West, a world devoted to peace and disarmament; she would have had no idea she wasn't the first to try invading from another parallel, and therefore she couldn't have foreseen the presence of the Gestalt dreadnoughts.

Attacks from other worlds—so far, the Earth had suffered two, and now there was the threat of the asteroid from Mars. Was this the way reality was going to work from now on? Would there be other aggressors, an endless procession of belligerent invaders from an infinite number of parallel worlds, unending strife and conflict?

Fuck, no. Not if I've got anything to say about it.

Veering to the left, he started to circle the great machine. Even in his wild state, he wasn't reckless enough to try a frontal assault. His Colts had been refilled and he'd retrieved his chainsaw, but neither would be much use if the forward machine guns drew a bead on him.

A missile whistled overhead, coming in at a steep angle from one of the dreadnoughts on the edge of the pack, and exploded against the Leviathan's invisible shield.

"I've got to time this right," Ack-Ack Macaque muttered. He needed to be in position when the tank retaliated; ready to leap through when it dropped its force field in order to fire.

And there it was! The cannons at the Leviathan's snout let loose a volley that rocked the beast on its tracks and shook the earth beneath his feet. Without waiting for the echoes to die away, he hurled himself between its caterpillar tracks. He rolled and kept rolling, until he was right under the main body of the tank and away from the danger of being crushed by its treads. Then he climbed to his feet and brushed himself down. Having already infiltrated one tank, he knew exactly where to find the hatch on the underside of this one. Without hesitation, he marched over and, standing directly beneath, used the butt of his Colt to hammer on the steel.

"Knock, knock, motherfuckers. Guess who."

VICTORIA VALOIS USED the blunt end of her fighting stick to give the green cyborg's head a final series of whacks. When its emerald skull finally caved and she was quite sure it was dead, she turned to look around the *Sun Wukong*'s bridge.

"Everybody okay?"

Three camouflage-painted cyborgs had tried to force their way onto the bridge, but all had been felled. The two Marines were down, one dead and the other injured. Merovech stood by the front window, his arm around Amy Llewellyn's shoulders. He held a French-made FAMAS assault rifle in his free hand, taken from one of the fallen soldiers.

"Are we safe now?"

Victoria walked to her command chair and pressed a control. A loud clunk came from the back of the room, followed by more slams and thumps from further back in the gondola.

"I've locked down the airship. All the fire doors and bulkheads are now sealed. I don't know how many of those metal bastards are still aboard, but that should slow them down."

"What about the crew?"

"What about them? Between screeching, firing wildly in all directions, and flinging their own *merde* at each other, they're doing nearly as much damage as the invaders." She worked her shoulder, which hurt where it had taken a glancing blow from a cyborg's kick. "It'll do them good to stay confined for a while, give them all a chance to calm down."

She watched Merovech help Amy over to a chair. The secretary had been thrown into a wall and cut her head. The King pulled the handkerchief from the breast pocket of his suit jacket and pressed it to her wound.

A light flashed on Victoria's console, indicating an incoming message. She accepted it, and routed the signal to the main view screen above the forward window.

"Victoria Valois?" The woman in the image wore a grey coat over olive green one-piece fatigues. She had short brunette hair and eyes the colour of dried dates.

"Yes?"

"Greetings, from one captain to another. My name is Katherine Denktash Abdulov of the Strauli Abdulovs, late of Strauli Quay, and I am here to offer my assistance."

Victoria frowned.

"I'm sorry, who are you?"

"Katherine Abdulov, of the trading vessel *Ameline*. We're currently two hundred metres above you, monitoring your situation."

"Two hundred metres above...?" Victoria reached out and activated another screen, displaying a composite of feeds from all the security cameras on the upper deck. As she did so, Merovech left Amy holding the handkerchief to her head and came over to stand behind her.

"There," he said, pointing over her shoulder at one of the images. Victoria tapped it, enlarging it until it filled the display.

"Jesus."

The wedge-shaped UFO from Amy's photographs hung in the sky above them, balanced on three jets of pale fire. Victoria glanced from it to the face of the young woman on the main screen.

"Yes, that's us." Katherine Abdulov rolled her eyes impatiently. "Right where I told you we were. And, once again, we're here to help."

Victoria swallowed. A thousand questions swarmed, fighting to be asked. Behind her, Merovech said, "Help? What kind of help?"

Katherine looked at him with frank astonishment.

"With the invasion," she said. "With the tanks you're fighting."

Victoria raised an eyebrow. "You have weapons?"

"Oh yes."

"Well, those tanks have some kind of force field. It's damned near impenetrable."

"Really?" The young woman glanced off-camera for a moment, and then smiled. "Watch this."

For a few heartbeats, nothing happened. Then a brilliant white pencil-thin spear of light flashed from the spaceship's nose, overloading the cameras. Victoria leapt from her position and ran to the front window.

"*Putain de merde!*"

Below, the hindmost Leviathan lay carved in half, sliced down the middle like a log in a sawmill. The edges of the cut smoldered a molten yellow and beneath them, a long, thin strip of grass and soil had been charred down to bedrock. Victoria put a fist to her lips, hardly daring to breathe. The weapon struck again, and another of the giant tanks flared.

"Yes!" She punched the air. "Oh, yes, yes, yes!"

CHAPTER THIRTY-SIX
DEATH IN THE AFTERNOON

ACK-ACK MACAQUE LOOKED up at the blue sky.

"What the fucking, fucking *fuck* was *that*?" He'd been skirmishing his way through the big tank's walkways and chambers when the world turned white and hot, and everything tipped sideways. Now he lay with his back against what, until a moment ago, had been a wall, with his nose full of the stink of burning plastic and singed monkey fur.

Climbing gingerly to his feet, he poked his head above the cooling edges of the room and looked out. The other half of the tank rested on its side a few metres away. Smoke rose from a dozen points, and he could see flames leaping where fuel lines had been cut.

"Holy crap in a hand basket." He had no idea what had happened, only that he'd been lucky to survive the experience. The cyborg he'd been fighting at the time hadn't fared nearly as well. It had been standing directly in the path of whatever had split the tank, and now its body lay on the grass between the two halves of the wreck, cleft into asymmetric and half-melted segments. Its metal body had probably shielded him from the worst of the mysterious attack, but all he felt towards it was the fierce satisfaction of seeing an enemy brought low.

He had to get out of here and find the Duchess. The edges of the cut walls were rapidly cooling. He leapt up onto one, trusting his boots to shield his feet from the residual heat. The tank lay with its innards bared to the sky, its rooms and walkways like the indentations in an empty chocolate box. As long as he kept moving, followed the walls and kept his balance, he'd be okay.

He started running, using his tail as a counterbalance to steady himself. He guessed Célestine would be somewhere towards what had been the top of the vehicle, so he made his way in that direction, and found her lying in the ruins of the Leviathan's control room. She had two cyborgs with her, but both were damaged and disorientated. Crouching on top of the wall, he decapitated them both with his chainsaw, sending their metal heads rolling into the echoing depths of the damaged tank like ball bearings rattling into a sewer.

The Duchess looked up at him.

"Oh," she said. "It's you. What do you want?"

Ack-Ack Macaque curled his lip. "I've got a message for you."

Célestine rose to her feet and brushed herself down with her palms. Her black uniform was rumpled and dusty, and one of the sleeves had been badly scorched.

"You know, I told Nguyen you were going to be trouble."

Ack-Ack Macaque killed the chainsaw's engine, and laid it aside.

"Well." He drew his revolver. "That's one thing you got right."

"You said you had a message?"

"Yeah, from a lady called Apynja."

Célestine blinked and her face tightened.

"Oh, so you're working for her now?"

Ack-Ack Macaque was surprised. "You know her?"

"Of course I know her. She's my sister."

He opened and shut his mouth a few times.

"Your sister? But she's a—"

"I wouldn't expect you to understand." Célestine drew herself up. "Now, what is it she has to say?"

Ack-Ack Macaque glowered at her and raised his gun.

"Just that you shouldn't have killed so many people."

"Me?" Célestine pushed her tongue into her cheek. "That's a good one."

Ack-Ack Macaque snarled. "You killed eight billion people. I don't see anything funny about that."

The Duchess waved a hand. "It's all just numbers." She looked up at the sky. Her breath came in small, almost imperceptible wisps. "You have no idea who she is, do you?"

Ack-Ack Macaque rubbed his leather eye patch. The socket beneath itched.

"She's an ape."

Célestine laughed and shook her head.

"Oh no, no. She may be many things, but she's not remotely an ape. She's not even human."

"Then what is she?"

"I told you." The woman smiled with all the warmth of a shark. "She's my sister. Or rather, she was, before she grew a conscience."

Ack-Ack Macaque growled. "You're not making any sense." He waved the gun at her in annoyance. "Make sense!"

Célestine stuck her chin at him.

"I'm making perfect sense, you vile creature. You're just too stupid to grasp what I'm talking about." She put her hands on her hips. "Aren't you?"

Ack-Ack Macaque took a deep, shuddering breath. "I'm the one holding the fucking gun," he reminded her.

"So you are." Up ahead, one of the other Leviathans sparked and fell to pieces, diced into chunks by a blinding white beam from the heavens. Moments later, the one next to it suffered an identical fate. Ack-Ack Macaque blinked away purple and green afterimages.

"Your invasion's cancelled," he said. "You're fucked."

"Really?"

Célestine brought her hands together and smiled. She seemed to shimmer and her body grew translucent. She was fading, exactly as Apynja had faded from the clearing in the wood.

"Oh no you fucking don't!" Ack-Ack Macaque stood up and fired his Colt into her almost transparent torso. His first two shots seemed to pass through without hurting her, but the third made contact. Célestine screamed with pain and rage, and suddenly she was solid again. She fell back into a sitting position, hands dabbing madly at a bloody wound in her stomach.

"You imbecile. What have you done?"

Ack-Ack Macaque raised the pistol's barrel to his lips and huffed away the smoke.

"I told you, I'm delivering a message." He holstered his weapon and jumped down beside her. "To you and all the other megalomaniacal ball-sacks out there."

"And what message is that?" She was panting, and her skin was pale with shock. He crouched, bringing his snout to within inches of her face.

"That we've had enough of your shit."

He watched her struggle and curse. She tried to pull herself up on the edge of a chair but his bullet had damaged her spine, and her legs wouldn't work.

"Do you even know how many people you've killed?" he asked contemptuously. She gave a snort.

"Do you?" Another bolt sizzled from above, bisecting a Leviathan to their left. With a squeal of brakes and a crunch of abused gears, the remaining tanks cranked into reverse and began backing towards the portal. "After all, you're hardly blameless, are you?"

Ack-Ack Macaque bridled. "I only kill people that need killing."

"And who are you to decide?"

"Who are you to say I can't?"

Célestine coughed, and wiped her lips on the back of her sleeve.

"You can dress it up any way you like, but you're as much of a murderer as I am."

Ack-Ack shook his head. "Nobody's as much of a murderer as you are, lady."

She laughed bitterly.

"Your friend Apynja is. Or she was before she changed her ways, the hypocritical bitch."

"What are talking about?" Ack-Ack shuffled back slightly, to avoid the blood spreading from her wound. "She's just an escaped orangutan."

Célestine shook her head sadly. "She's so much more than that. Yes, I killed a world. I admit it, and I'm proud of it. But her." She coughed again. This time, her sleeve came away red when she wiped her mouth. "She's killed dozens. Hundreds maybe."

"Who is she?"

Célestine's eyes became glassy and her head began to sway. Ack-Ack Macaque took her by the shoulders and shook her.

"Who is she?"

He shook her again, but her head lolled back and her body went limp, and he knew she was dead.

CHAPTER THIRTY-SEVEN
ALL THE FISH

WITH THE INVASION defeated and the Leviathans in retreat, Victoria allowed herself to slump into the command chair. Merovech and Amy had taken the surviving Marine to the infirmary in search of medical attention, leaving her alone on the airship's bridge. The noise of battle had faded, and the only sound she could hear was the constant hum of the *Sun Wukong*'s engines. Her shoulder still hurt, and she had a number of additional cuts and bruises, but her mind wasn't dwelling on her injuries. Right now, she had other priorities.

She couldn't read the words on her computer display, but knew the control sequence by heart. A tap here and a tap there, and Paul's hologram activated. The little drone sailed into the middle of the room and projected his image in all its three dimensional luminosity. For the briefest moment, he remained frozen as the airship's processors booted up his personality, and she took the chance to drink in his appearance without distraction—his bright shirt and creased white lab coat; his spiky peroxide hair and hipster spectacles; the jewelled stud in his ear. This could very well be the last time she'd ever see him, and she wanted a clear picture to remember him by.

"Ah," he said, blinking rapidly and focusing on her. "You again. I was hoping you'd be Vicky."

Victoria felt her heart sink into the pit of her stomach.

"I am Vicky."

"Really?" He peered at her over the rim of his glasses. "My word, so you are. What happened to you, to your hair?"

She didn't feel like going through it all again. "It's a long story."

"And you've aged."

Her hand went to the back of her head. She felt suddenly, stupidly self-conscious. If this was going to be the last time she saw him, she realised, it would also be the last time he saw *her*, and she wished she'd had time to make more of an effort with her appearance. Not that he'd remember once she'd switched him off again, but still she couldn't help feeling she should have done more to create a sense of occasion. After all, how many chances did one get to say goodbye forever to the love of their life?

"It's over," she said. "The invasion. Célestine's dead."

Paul's face creased. He was obviously struggling to make sense of her words.

"Does that mean we can go home now?"

Victoria felt something stick at the back of her throat. "We are home, my love."

He took off his glasses and looked towards the large window at the front of the gondola.

"We are?"

"Come and see." She climbed to her feet and trudged over to the glass. He followed, the soles of his feet never less than a centimetre above the deck.

"Look," she said, "that's Paris over there on the horizon. You can see the skyliners over Orly Airport."

He peered down his nose.

"If you say so."

"This is where we came from, Paul. We're back." She put out a hand to touch his arm; stopped herself. "I just wanted you to know."

Paul stroked his chin, squeezed his lower lip.

"I wanted to go home, to my apartment." His voice was small and lost.

"That's in London."

"And we can go to London?"

"Of course we can. Just not right now." She turned her back on the view, squaring up to him and gathering her resolve.

"Why not?"

"Because we need to talk."

"That sounds serious."

"I'm afraid it is." She clapped her hands together and squeezed. "*Je suis désolée.*"

His eyes looked into hers, shifting nervously from one to the other.

"What is it?"

Victoria opened her mouth but nothing came out. Her throat had gone dry and the words wouldn't form. She turned her face away and exhaled. She couldn't seem to breathe properly.

"I'm afraid this is goodbye," she croaked at last.

"Goodbye?" Paul frowned. He didn't understand. "Where are you going?"

"I'm not going anywhere." She waved her hands in a helpless gesture. "It's you. I have to turn you off. I've got no choice."

He shook his head and she saw the diamond stud twinkling in his ear.

"You're pulling my plug?"

Victoria winced. If she was going to get through this, she had to be firm. "You're falling apart," she said.

"So, what?" His eyes were wide, his expression alarmed. "Does that mean I get put down like an incontinent old dog?"

Victoria shook her head. This was hurting way more than she'd imagined. "It takes longer every time I switch you on," she tried to explain, "and there's less of you here each time. One day, I'm going to switch you on and you'll be nothing but a drooling electronic vegetable—that's if you even boot up at all."

Paul's mouth was a hard line. "I see."

"I can't do it, Paul." Her eyes prickled. She felt her poise crumbling like wet sand. "I can't go through that. I don't want to see you reduced to such a state."

"And what about what I want?"

She ran an agitated hand back across the top of her head. "I don't know. It seems… kinder to say goodbye now." She walked back to the command console, feeling his eyes on her the whole way.

"But I love you."

Her vision blurred. "I love you too, and that's why this is so hard for me. Believe me, this is the most difficult decision I've ever had to make." She activated the touchpad that would cut off the power to his projector and confine him to an inactive file in the computer's storage. All she had to do was tap the final command and he'd be gone—probably forever.

"We've been through so much." His tone was pleading. She had to fight back tears.

"I know, and I'll always treasure every moment."

"But now you're going to kill me?"

Victoria felt like weeping. "Don't say it like that."

"How else should I say it? I don't want to die."

A tear brimmed over her lower lid and dripped onto her cheek. She didn't bother wiping it away.

"You died three years ago, Paul. You just haven't stopped talking yet."

Another tear fell, splashing onto the black glass console. Her finger hovered over the cut-off switch. Her hand shook.

"Please," he said.

She bit her lip. "I'm sorry. Goodbye, Paul. *Au revoir.* I'll always love you." She looked up and their eyes met.

"Vicky, wait…"

She sniffed, fighting back sobs.

"What?"

He looked down at his feet for a long moment. When he looked back up, his expression had changed. He looked bemused. He frowned at her in puzzlement, as if trying to remember who she was.

"I'm terribly sorry," he said. "What were you saying?"

Victoria swallowed back her grief. If she had to do this, it was better he was confused rather than terrified. She forced a watery smile. In her heart, she wanted him to be reassured, to be happy—and sometimes, ignorance really was bliss. She looked him in the eye.

"I was saying goodbye, my love." Her finger touched the control and he disappeared. One instant he was there, blinking owlishly at her; the next, he was gone, switched off like a light, leaving only the tiny drone to mark where he had been standing.

VICTORIA STUMBLED FROM the bridge with tears cascading haphazardly down her face, falling onto her chest, and soaking into the fabric of her tunic. She didn't care. She'd had enough of being strong. The grief she felt wasn't grief for her husband, the flesh-and-blood man whose funeral she'd attended three years ago; the grief burning a hole in her heart right now was for the Paul who'd been her constant companion since that dark day—the electronic ghost who'd become something so much more than the sum of his parts; the back-up who'd ended up getting closer to her than anyone else ever had, or ever would. She was crying for him, and for herself. For with him gone, who did she have left? She had friends, yes, but who would love her; who would comfort her in the night, and stay up talking with her until the dawn? Paul had spent time literally living in her head. How would she, could she, ever be that close to anybody, ever again?

Heedless of her appearance or the worried stares of the monkeys she passed, she made her way topside, seeking fresh air, wide open spaces, and a fresh sense of perspective. However, as she stepped out onto the flight deck, her eyes fell on something she hadn't been expecting to see. In the centre of the airship's back, resting on three extended landing struts, sat the *Ameline.*

Two figures were walking towards her, clad in identical green fatigues.

One was the woman from the transmission, Katherine Abdulov. She walked with a shotgun balanced on her hip. The other figure was... familiar.

"Cole?" Victoria's heart leapt at the prospect of a friendly face, a sympathetic ear.

The man raised his eyebrows. "Pardon?"

She wiped her nose on the cuff of her tunic. This wasn't her former comrade, the alcoholic sci-fi writer who'd helped her uncover the Gestalt conspiracy. This was merely another iteration of the same man—a stranger with a similar face.

"Sorry, love," he said, scratching the side of his nose, his accent betraying traces of time spent in both Cardiff and London. "My name's Ed." He shrugged again. "Ed Rico." A grin split his face and he pointed two fingers at her, miming a ray gun. "Take me to your leader."

Katherine Abdulov elbowed him in the ribs. Then they both frowned. Katherine stepped forward and placed a hand on Victoria's shoulder.

"Why are you crying?" she asked.

SCIENCE NEWS

From *Physics? Fuck Yeah!* (online edition):

Is Our Universe a Hologram? ➤

TOKYO 18/11/2062: Scientists in Japan claim to have found the clearest evidence yet that our universe—that's you, me, and everything we can see and hear around us—is a hologram. If true, this breakthrough could be a vital stepping-stone on the path to reconciling Einstein's theory of relativity with quantum physics, and paving the way for a so-called 'Theory of Everything.'

According to calculations made by the team at Ibaraki University in Japan, the three dimensions we're familiar with—length, breadth and depth—are illusions, and the universe is simply a projection of information encoded on a two-dimensional 'cosmic horizon' in the form of vibrating, one-dimensional 'strings'.

Although it sounds complicated, the idea can be visualised by imagining a balloon full of smoke, with pictures drawn on the outside. When a light shines through the skin of the balloon, the pictures cast seemingly three-dimensional shadows through the smoke.

While the theory has been around for some years, this is the first time a team claims to have simulated the process in convincing detail, by using extra dimensions implied by the proven existence of multiple, co-existing timelines.

The next step will be to widen the idea to incorporate a fundamental theory of the structure of the multiverse. Whether or not that project is successful, or even possible, today's news provides an important boost for string theory, which had rather fallen from fashion of late.

Read more | Like | Comment | Share

Related Stories:

Quantum computers 'borrow' processing time from their counterparts on other timelines.

Gestalt engines reverse-engineered to power alternate world 'probe'.

Incursion in France? Reports of King leading airship task force.

Plea for 'responsible' approach to deep-water mining of seabed resources.

Jet stream change to cause colder winters in Europe.

CHAPTER THIRTY-EIGHT
FOLLOWING ORDERS

AMY LLEWELLYN LOWERED herself into a sitting position on the bunk, back resting against the pillows.

"So," she asked, "what are you going to tell the reporters?" Since the cessation of hostilities, news copters had been circling the dreadnoughts, desperate for a shot of the King.

Merovech unhooked the submachine gun from his shoulder and laid it on the side table. They were in one of the crew cabins, which he had requisitioned. The infirmary had been filled to overflowing with wounded, irate monkeys, so he'd only stopped there long enough to grab some dressings.

"I don't see why I have to tell them anything." He perched on the blanket beside her and used his finger to push a strand of hair from the gash in her forehead. "It doesn't look too bad," he said, squinting at it in the dim overhead light. He went to the cramped bathroom, tore off some toilet tissue, and moistened it under the tap.

"This may sting a little," he warned, and began to lightly sponge the wound. During the scuffle on the bridge, she'd fallen and hit her head against a steel bulkhead. She'd been stunned by the blow, and there was no doubt she'd have a painful bruise. However, it appeared the cut wasn't nearly as bad as he'd feared. Once he'd cleaned away the blood that had run down her face, the wound turned out to be little more than a deep graze.

"You have to tell them something," she insisted. "You're the King, for goodness' sake. You shouldn't be riding into battle."

Merovech smiled with one side of his face. "I don't see why not." He opened the bag of supplies he'd lifted from the infirmary and emptied them onto the bed. "There are precedents, you know." He peeled apart a dressing and pressed it to her head. "Now, hold this in place while I get some tape."

She touched her fingertips to the bandage and he picked up a small roll of white surgical tape and some scissors, and used four short strips to fix the dressing securely to her skin. When he was done, he sat back to inspect his handiwork.

Amy cringed. "How do I look?"

"It's a bit crooked, but you'll be fine."

She coughed and looked away, cheeks flushed. "I feel such an idiot."

"There's no need."

"You're too kind." Her voice held a sarcastic edge. Irritably, she tried to stand. "But I've got work to do. Somebody's got to sort out this mess." She got upright and swayed, and Merovech caught her by the hands.

"There's no hurry," he said, supporting her. "Take a moment. You've had a bang to the head; you're going to be a bit wobbly."

Her fingers felt cold, so he blew on them. It seemed like a natural thing to do, but Amy snatched them away as if he'd bitten her.

"What's the matter?"

"Nothing, I'm sorry." Her face was flushed and she wouldn't meet his eye. In the cramped cabin, they were standing face-to-face, almost touching.

"Did I do something inappropriate?"

"No." She brushed a lock of hair behind her ear and straightened her jacket. "Not at all."

"Then what is it?"

Amy rolled her eyes and tried to turn away, looking mortified. "Nothing, forget about it." She brushed down the front of her suit. Her hand shook, and Merovech thought of his dead fiancée.

As a young prince, he had met his share of eligible society women. The royal matchmakers had tried to pair him with rich girls from all over the Commonwealth—the daughters of industrialists, presidents, oil barons and sultans—and yet none had fascinated and challenged him like Julie Girard. He'd loved her from their first meeting on the Paris Metro. She'd been a breath of fresh air. The girls he was used to were all ambitious, would-be princesses. They were obsessed with gossip and horses, and dazzled by the glamour of the throne. Julie wasn't anything like them. For a start, she favoured a republic. She believed in causes and direct action, and thought the world could be made a better place through protest. She was the most *real* person he'd ever met. She hadn't cared for power, fame or prestige. The things that concerned her were honest, tangible things. Things he hadn't considered until she showed them to him. Poverty, social justice, animal rights... She had opened his eyes to a world of inequality and injustice, and he'd planned to abdicate and spend the rest of his life with her, fighting for her causes.

Only, of course, things hadn't worked out that way—and now here he was, standing in an airship's cabin with a girl from Wales, feeling emotions he couldn't name. He missed Julie so much that her absence had become a physical need. His skin cringed at the lack of her touch; his lips were raw where he'd been nervously dragging them over his teeth, missing her kiss. He hadn't let go, hadn't grieved. He'd kept everything bottled up inside so he could do his duty to his country and Commonwealth.

And now...

Now, he just wanted to be held. He wanted to rest his head on Amy's shoulder and feel her arms around him. He wasn't in love with her (at least, he told himself he wasn't). He had no family, no close friends. She was the nearest he had to either, and he wanted her to stroke the back of his neck and whisper comforts to him as he wept into the fabric of her jacket.

It felt right. She felt right.

He coughed and looked at his feet.

"Amy, listen—" He wasn't sure exactly what he was going to say, but it didn't matter. Before he could continue, K8 knocked smartly on the open cabin door.

"Hey, Your Majesty." She looked curiously from Merovech to Amy. "Not interrupting anything, am I?"

Merovech gave a silent, exasperated curse.

"What do you want?"

The girl raised an eyebrow at his aggrieved tone. She jerked her thumb at the low metal ceiling.

"We've got a couple of visitors upstairs you *really* need to meet."

ACK-ACK MACAQUE SHUFFLED across the field. He was bone tired and his jacket hung in ribbons. A pistol dangled from one hand, the recovered chainsaw from the other. Around him lay the remains of the Leviathans. Some of the wrecks had been cut in two; others had been diced into fat metal cubes with drippy-looking melted edges. A couple of the tanks were on fire, and their smoke stained the autumn air, hanging thick and languid across the battlefield.

A damaged cyborg clawed its way across the turf. Its legs were missing and it was using one arm to pull itself forward while the other brandished a fat machine gun. Ack-Ack Macaque walked up behind it and pressed the chainsaw to the wrist of the hand holding the weapon. Sparks flew and there was a noise like someone feeding a set of steel railings into a wood chipper. He felt the vibration rattle his teeth. Then the hand fell to the earth and the chrome fingers writhed in the dirt like the tentacles of a beached sea creature.

"Where do you think you're going, eh?" He reached down and flipped the cyborg onto its back. Part of its face had been torn away, exposing the wires and circuits beneath the stretched skin and dull armour.

"Please," it whispered through its mangled mouth, "please, I don't want to die."

Ack-Ack Macaque's lip curled. "You start a war, sunshine, you have to be prepared to lose it."

"No."

The monkey frowned. "What do you mean, 'no'?"

"It wasn't me. I didn't want any of this." The thing was begging for its life. Ack-Ack Macaque pocketed his revolver and rubbed his eye patch.

"Were you on one of those tanks?" he asked.

"Yes..."

"Then you're the enemy." He took a firm grip on the chainsaw.

The cyborg wriggled back on its elbows, trying to squirm away from him. "I was only following orders."

Ack-Ack Macaque snarled. "That's the oldest bullshit in the book." He raised the chainsaw over his head and the cyborg cowered.

"But it's true! I didn't want to be *this*." It thumped the stump of its arm against its chest. "I didn't have a choice."

Ack-Ack Macaque showed his teeth. "Oh, really?"

"People were dying." The metal figure stopped wriggling. "They offered me a chance to live."

Ack-Ack Macaque lowered the saw and nudged the metal body with his boot. "You call this 'living', do you?"

"I had no choice."

"Horse crap. You had a choice. When they turned you into a robot, you had a choice. When they told you to get into a tank and invade my world, you had a choice." He bent low over the recumbent figure, growling his words. "If we hadn't stopped you here and now, how many innocents would you have killed before you grew the balls to say 'no'?"

The cyborg's eyes had become misaligned. One looked up at him imploringly while the other lolled drunkenly in its socket. "The Duchess, she would have killed me."

"The Duchess is dead."

Something seemed to sag in the cyborg's posture. "Then it's over?"

Ack-Ack Macaque shook his head. Overhead, the dreadnoughts were dispersing like clouds after a storm, moving away in the directions of Paris, London and Berlin—large ports where they could refit, repair and resupply. Their engines thrummed, stirring the still morning sky like the broodings of a billion disgruntled bees. The only one not moving was the *Sun Wukong*.

"These things are never over," he said. "There's always some other ruthless bastard out there, with an army of gullible cowards." He stepped forward and placed one booted foot on the cyborg's chest. It struggled beneath him.

"What are you going to do?"

"I'm going to put you out of your misery."

Its stump flailed and its hand clawed at the soil, trying to heave its legless torso out from under his foot. "No, please! It wasn't my fault! I just wanted to live."

"Everybody wants to live." Ack-Ack Macaque raised the chainsaw and levelled the point of the whirring blade at the cyborg's throat. "But you chose the wrong side. You chose to stand with the killers." He stabbed downwards, leaning his weight on the handle. With a metallic screech, the chainsaw bit through the cyborg's neck. It buried itself in the earth below and juddered to a halt, motor stalled. Disgusted with the whole incident, he left it where it was—sticking up like a grave marker—and stood upright. His back ached. He brushed his leathery palms together and spat into the dirt.

"There's always a choice."

CHAPTER THIRTY-NINE
STOP THE ROCK

VICTORIA GATHERED THE crew of the *Ameline* and the command crew of the *Sun Wukong* on the verandah at the airship's bow. Several of the armoured glass panels had been cracked or broken during the fight and cold wafts of fresh November air curled through the greenhouse warmth of the potted jungle, agitating the parakeets and other birds that twittered and squawked among the leaves on the upper branches. A utilitarian trestle table had been set up on the verandah, overlooking the rail, and her guests were seated on either side, perched on folding chairs and stools borrowed from the galley. Katherine Abdulov sat at the far end with Ed Rico on her right, while K8, Merovech, and Ack-Ack Macaque occupied the remaining chairs.

The monkey's solitary eye glowered around the table.

"Okay, does anybody want to tell me what the fuck's going on? Who are these people, and why does this guy look like William Cole?"

Victoria stood up. "These are the people who helped us against the Leviathans."

"Yeah, I saw. As a matter of fact, I was in one of those tanks when they cut the fucking thing in half."

Victoria sighed. Her tears were gone, but they'd taken most of her strength with them.

"They stopped the invasion," she said.

Ack-Ack Macaque huffed. "I could have handled it."

"I'm sure you could. Nevertheless, try to be polite."

Victoria turned her attention to the woman at the far end of the table. Katherine Abdulov sat with her hands in the pocket of her thick overcoat, and the ankle of her left boot resting on her right knee.

"You're not out of the woods yet," Katherine said.

"How so?" Victoria cocked an eyebrow. Célestine was dead; the assault had failed.

"The asteroid."

"Ah, of course..."

"Do you have a plan to deal with it?"

Ack-Ack Macaque stirred, and raised a paw. "I do."

"Care to share it?"

The monkey took out a cigar, bit off the end, and spat it over the bamboo rail, into the airship's glass nose cone. "I figured we could fly up there and twat it."

K8 smiled. Merovech shook his head. "We don't have anything that can make the journey," he said.

"Of course we do." Ack-Ack Macaque struck a match and lit up. Smoke curled around his muzzle. "And you're sitting in it."

"An *airship*?"

"Why not?" The spent match sailed after the cigar tip. "We use the Duchess' force field to keep in the air and keep out the radiation, and we bolt your ion drive to the back."

"That's insane."

"Yeah, but it's gonna work." He moved his one-eyed gaze around the table, daring those present to disagree. Finally, his attention settled on Katherine. "What do you say, space lady?"

Katherine Abdulov rubbed her chin.

"Don't look at me," she said. "I've got no idea. All I'll say is that if you're going to try riding in it, you're a damn sight braver than I am."

The monkey scoffed. "And I suppose you've got a better idea, sweetheart?"

Katherine and Ed exchanged looks.

"You could come with us."

"On your ship?"

"Of course. You've seen what it can do. Ed can carve lumps off that rock. Chop it up into little pieces."

"That'll stop it?"

"No." Katherine looked regretful. "But it'll help. Make it a bunch of smaller targets, and easier to destroy."

"And then what?"

"Then your kludged-up space Zeppelin can finish the job." She uncrossed her legs and set both boots on the deck. "We can break it up into glowing rubble but we can't stop it. Our weapon isn't designed to take down big targets. It would take us too long to pick the rock apart with our narrow beam—but, if we dice it into little enough pieces, a couple of nukes from you should be enough to vaporise the remains." She looked up at the cracked panes in the glass ceiling, high above. "That's if you can get this heap put back together, armed and launched in time."

As one, Victoria and Ack-Ack Macaque turned to Merovech. The young king's manicured nails tapped the table's Formica top.

"How long have we got?" he asked.

"A couple of weeks, a month at the most." Katherine gave a one-shouldered shrug. "It depends how fast your ion engines are."

"I'm not sure." Merovech looked thoughtful. "Not very, I think."

"Then the sooner you can launch, the better."

Merovech stopped tapping his nails. He met Victoria's eyes. "Set a course for Gibraltar."

"Gibraltar?"

"The ESA has a test facility in the Straits. It's an old, repurposed oil platform. That's where the engines are."

"Aye, sir." Victoria glanced at K8. "Do you mind?"

"I'm on it." The girl sprang to her feet and vanished into the jungle, hurrying in the direction of the bridge.

"What else do we need?" Victoria asked. Ack-Ack Macaque removed his cigar and tapped ash onto the deck.

"Nuclear weapons," he said.

Merovech nodded. "Well, I may be able to help you there. We have a number of submarines in the North Atlantic. I'll have one meet us there. What else?"

"Food and water, enough for the whole monkey army."

"You're going to take them all to the asteroid?" He raised his eyebrows. "Surely a skeleton crew would suffice?"

Ack-Ack Macaque shook his head with slow deliberation. "No, we're going to need as many soldiers as we can carry," he said.

"Soldiers?" Victoria scratched the ridge of scar tissue at her temple. "What do you need soldiers for?"

Ack-Ack Macaque sucked the end of his cigar. The tip burned brightly. He exhaled at the high ceiling and smiled.

"After we've dealt with the asteroid, I'm taking them to Mars."

"That's your plan?"

"Yah." He smacked his lips together. "We're going to go up there and kick some butt. Otherwise, what's to stop the Robo-Duchess chucking another rock at us?" His face darkened. "And besides, we've got a score to settle."

Victoria felt her heart quicken. The breath caught in her throat. There had been a copy of Paul's 'soul' on the probe, along with the stolen personalities of all Cassius Berg's victims. They had been taken to form the basis of a cybernetic slave army, toiling to build Célestine's utopia among the cold

Martian rocks. There was even a copy of Victoria that had been ripped from her skull during her first encounter with the murderous Smiling Man.

"I'm coming too," she said. She'd seen firsthand the kind of twisted sexual depravities Doctor Nguyen had foisted on a different copy of her 'soul', and knew she couldn't leave herself or Paul at his mercy.

Paul... Could there really be a way to splice the remains of his crumbling psyche with the 'fresh' copy in the Martian probe? Even now, at this late stage, could some part of him still be salvaged?

She became aware that Ack-Ack Macaque was squinting curiously at her.

"Okay," he rumbled, reading her face, "that's settled. Merovech and K8 can fit this beast out. Vic and I will ride with Kat here to the asteroid. Once we're there, we'll do what we can to whittle it down to a more manageable size. Then we'll meet up with the monkey army, nuke what's left of the rock, and go on to Mars."

"And what if it doesn't work?" Victoria could hardly bring herself to believe any of it was possible. "What's the contingency plan?"

Ack-Ack Macaque scowled around the red cherry of his cigar. "There isn't a contingency." He sat back in his chair with a growl. "If this doesn't work, that's it. Game over, folks. End of the fucking world."

ISSUED BY HM GOVT.

PROTECT AND SURVIVE

This pdf tells you how to keep your home and family safe during an asteroid strike.

1. Taking shelter

In advance of an asteroid strike, warnings will be broadcast on all television and radio channels at the following times:

i. Twelve hours before impact.
ii. Six hours before impact.
iii. Three hours before impact.
iv. One hour before impact.

Warnings will then continue at fifteen-minute intervals.

When you hear the warning, please make your way immediately to a place of shelter.

Your shelter should contain:

i. Enough food and water in sealed containers to last your family for 14 days.
ii. A portable radio and spare batteries.
iii. Warm clothing, and changes of clothing for the entire family.
iv. Bedding or sleeping bags.
v. Torches with spare batteries, matches and candles.
vi. Sturdy refuse sacks and packing tape.

Read more? Y/N

CHAPTER FORTY
SURFIN' FROGS AND PUNCHING GODS

As the Sun *Wukong* powered south towards the Spanish border, Katherine Abdulov took Victoria to see the *Ameline*.

"Call me Kat," she said, buttoning her coat as they stepped out onto the airship's flight deck. "Everybody else does."

Victoria tried to place her accent but couldn't. There were hints of Spanish and Arabic influence, but nothing she could pin down. To starboard, the sun was a red ember on the horizon. In the darkness below, the lights of Bordeaux and Toulouse slid past on either side like the raked coals of glowing campfires. Feeling the cold, she tugged at the hem of the Commodore's military jacket, straightening it. It had been tailored for a skinny old man, not someone with breasts, and so had a tendency to ride up at the waist.

"Everybody?"

"My family."

"And where are they?"

Kat scuffed the sole of her boot across the metal deck. "All dead."

Victoria thought of Paul. "I'm sorry."

The young pilot shrugged. "Don't be. We all are." She stopped walking, and the wind ruffled her hair. "Dead, I mean. You and me." She craned her neck to peer over the side. "Everybody down there."

After her recent experiences in helicopters, Victoria preferred not to look down. Instead, she let her hand rest on her scabbard. Her head felt cold and she wished she'd brought a hat.

"We're not dead yet." After all, wasn't that what this was all about? Weren't they trying to save the world?

Kat clicked her tongue regretfully. "Yeah, I'm afraid you kind of are."

Victoria was confused. "But you said the plan would work, that we could stop the rock."

"That's not what I'm talking about."

"Then what is it, *s'il vous plaît?*"

The younger woman faced into the wind for a moment, and took a deep, savouring breath.

"Come inside," she said, nodding at the *Ameline*'s open cargo ramp. "I'll explain everything."

KATHERINE STALKED UP the ramp and Victoria followed. She found herself in a hold that had seen better days. The walls were covered with scuffs and dents; much of the webbing had been torn or tangled, and graffiti marred the doors and bulkheads. The air smelled musty, with hints of solder and old sacking.

"This way," Kat said, leading her forward, through a hatch outlined with yellow and black warning tape, into a passenger compartment lined with rows of threadbare seats, their plastic covers split and frayed, the foam insulation ratty and discoloured beneath.

"Everything happened a long time ago, and far away," Kat said without lingering. She stepped through into a short corridor, at the end of which was a ladder leading upwards. Victoria stood at the bottom and watched her climb, then followed. At the top lay the *Ameline*'s bridge. It was a small cockpit, with a low, readout-covered ceiling and a pair of well-worn couches. Kat took the couch on the right and motioned Victoria to the one on the left.

"Where?" Victoria asked.

"Back in the real world."

"This isn't the real world?"

"No, sorry."

Victoria twisted around, trying to get comfortable as she processed the statement. "We've seen a few timelines," she said, "and they all seemed remarkably real and solid."

"None of them were, I'm afraid."

"I don't follow."

Kat exhaled through her nose. "I'm trying to explain this as gently as I can." She brushed back her hair. "Take your monkey friend, for instance."

"What about him?"

"He used to be a character in a computer game, didn't he? And when he was in there, he was locked into the virtual world."

Victoria didn't like where this was going. "We rescued him. We got him out."

"But did you?" Kat moved her cupped hands as if weighing up invisible bags of flour. "Did you really rescue him, or did you simply bring him from one simulation to another?"

Victoria narrowed her eyes. The old journalistic instinct twitched. There was a story here and, whether she wanted to know the truth or not, she needed to uncover it.

"You tell me," she said.

Katherine gave her a frank look. "I don't think I have to, do I? I think you've already guessed."

"You're implying all the worlds we've seen, the whole multiverse, they're all part of a game?" Victoria was beginning to wish she had a martini.

"Not a game, as such, but a simulation nevertheless."

Victoria gave a loud tut. "*C'est ridicule!* There isn't enough computing power in the world."

"Not in *this* world, no."

Victoria took a deep breath. "Okay," she said reasonably, "let's backtrack a couple of steps. Why don't you explain to me again who you are, and how you got here?"

Kat sighed. She crossed her booted feet at the ankle and tapped at a couple of overhead readouts.

"I was born on Strauli," she began, "which is a planet a hundred light years from here, in the year 2360."

"The future?"

"More like the distant past, now."

Victoria shook her head. "I don't understand." She was missing something, but wasn't sure what it might be.

"I'll get to it." Kat promised. "But, to start at the beginning, my family were traders, and I captained one of their ships."

"This one?"

"Yes, the dear old *Ameline*." Katherine gave the bulkhead an affectionate pat. "We've been through some scrapes together, I can tell you."

Victoria reached over and touched her sleeve. "But how did you get *here*?" she insisted.

Kat made that clicking noise with her tongue again. "Something got loose," she said. "Something horrible. We weren't sure if it was a weapon or a deranged filing system, but it was sentient, and it called itself 'The Recollection'." Her shoulders quivered as she tried to repress a shudder. "It rolled over world after world, breaking apart everything it touched, and storing it all as information."

She was telling the truth. Victoria could tell; she'd had enough practice interviewing politicians and other professional liars.

"What did you do?"

"We ran." Kat punched one hand into the palm of the other. "We gathered together as many survivors as we possibly could and we made for the stars." She stopped talking, eyes focused on the pictures in her head—a thousand light-year stare.

"So, why are you here, now?"

"It caught us." The words came out tinged with loathing. Kat's fists were clenched. "The Recollection's whole purpose was to gather intelligent beings," she said, "to harvest them and deliver their stored minds to the end of time, to a point it called 'The Eschaton'—the ultimate end of all things."

"But why?"

"Because its builders believed they'd be resurrected, brought back to life in the infinite quantum mind-spaces of the ubercomputer."

Victoria frowned. "*Je ne comprends pas.*"

Kat tipped her head back against the chair's rest and rubbed her eyes. "At the end of time, as the last stars guttered and died, they believed there would be a final flowering. That their descendants—or the descendants of whichever race survived until the end—would have the means and wherewithal to construct a huge computer of near infinite complexity, powered by the very dissolution of the universe itself. And having retreated within this computer, they'd then be able to play out the entire history of the cosmos, over and over again with endless permutations. As the final seconds of the real universe ticked towards their conclusion, the builders would be able to live out aeon after simulated aeon, cocooned within their virtual worlds."

Victoria looked at the main view screen, which currently showed a crystal clear, light-enhanced image of the *Sun Wukong*'s deck and the darkening sky beyond. "And that's where we are now, in this simulation?"

"Yes." Fingers laced over her midriff, Kat closed her eyes. "When The Recollection came for us, we fought and we ran. But, as I said, it caught us." She shivered again. "All of us."

Victoria lay back and considered her reflection in the touchscreen panel above her head. Not everything Kat had said had made sense, and she had plenty of questions. They were part of her default response: if she didn't understand something well enough to explain it in a newspaper article, she just kept chipping away at it until she had all the facts.

"If all that's true," she asked hesitantly, picking her words, "how come you remember it and I don't?"

"Because it never happened to you." Kat gave one of her one-shoulder shrugs. "You were long dead by the time The Recollection reached Earth."

"Then what am I doing here?"

The young pilot glanced sideways at Victoria. "The ubercomputer's vast and powerful. It recreated you from the DNA of the people it had. From them, it extrapolated every person who ever lived, anywhere, and brought them back to life."

Victoria wanted to laugh or cover her ears. It sounded like the most muddleheaded New Age tomfoolery, and she really wanted a drink. This wasn't, she felt, the kind of conversation one should have sober.

"I'm sorry, but all this, everything you're telling me, it all sounds crazy."

Kat sat upright. "It is crazy, but that doesn't make it any less true."

"And what about you?"

"I had a brush with The Recollection. It infected me with its spores but only at a low level. I had protection." Her artificial hand went to her throat, as if touching a pendant that wasn't there. "The changes it made to the structure of my brain enabled me to retain my memories. There are others like me, just a few of us who know the truth, who remember."

"And you're just flying around, spreading the word?"

"No." A grim shake of the head. "We're fighting a war."

"Against the computer?"

"Against its builders." Kat pressed a control, and a rotating three-dimensional display blinked into existence in the centre of the cockpit, showing a tactical representation of the surrounding airspace, from ground level to the upper stratosphere. Possible threats, such as ground vehicles and large buildings, were picked out in red. "I told you they retreated into their own simulations to escape the death of the universe. Well, some of them went native in a big way. Instead of being content to live out their lives in recreations of the past, they decided to change it to suit themselves, to carve out little empires and stamp their domination on the timelines."

"Like Célestine?"

"Bingo." Kat clicked her fingers. "She's one of the builders. A long time ago, she cast versions of herself across all the timelines, and now she sits behind the scenes, working through them to achieve her ends."

"Célestine built the multiverse?"

"Yes, in part. But there's another out there, another of the architects of the simulations, and she's more dangerous than Célestine could ever be."

"Who is she?"

"A criminal, responsible for a million atrocities." Kat's fists clenched. "We've been tracking her for years but she's recently gone quiet. Most of her alternate selves are dead."

"And you think she's here too?"

"I know it."

Victoria swallowed. Her mind raced. Then she froze. Something cold squeezed her stomach and her mouth went dry.

"Is she me?"

"What?" Kat's eyebrows shot up. "No!" She laughed. "No, you can relax, you're fine. It's not you." The laugh dried like a puddle in the sun. "No, you already know her. She built the airship we're riding on, using her knowledge of glitches in the programme to move it between the timelines."

"The *Founder*?"

"The clue's in the name, I guess."

"But she's a monkey."

Another shrug. "It amuses her to take animal form. She might be a monkey on this world and an ape on the next. And she goes by many names—Founder, Architect, Apynja…"

"You're here to get her?"

"Her and Célestine." Katherine Abdulov drew herself straight and Victoria saw her lip curl. "We're here to stop them before they do any more harm; to bring them to account for the billions who've died in their little games."

"Virtual beings?" Victoria thought of the world she'd visited most recently, laid waste by Célestine's drive to build a cyborg army. All those ghosts…

"Sentient beings nonetheless, and fully capable of suffering."

"Why are you telling me all this?"

A mischievous smile glimmered behind Kat's dark eyes. "Because you and Ack-Ack Macaque have been fighting them and, if you don't mind me saying, doing a damn good job."

"And you want our help?"

"Not help so much, but maybe we should pool resources. What do you think?"

Victoria took a deep breath and let out a long, draining exhalation. "This is a lot to take in."

"I know." Kat chewed her bottom lip. "It was tough for me too, to start with. But please think about it. I could do with someone like you. There are very few who can move between the worlds, and you've been doing it for the past two years." Her expression became wistful. "And besides, I've been looking for Ack-Ack for a long time now."

"You have?"

"Yes." Kat smiled. "You see, I know who he really is."

*   *   *

ACK-ACK MACAQUE STOOD with K8, on the viewing platform at the top of the Rock. The Strait of Gibraltar lay before them like a sparkling azure carpet. At the foot of the Rock, the hotels and apartment complexes of the town clustered close to the shoreline. Waves broke against the beaches. A westerly breeze blew in off the Atlantic, bringing a chill to an otherwise unseasonably warm November day, and he turned up the collar of his coat. Fourteen miles away, across the water, the stony Rif Mountains of Morocco loomed brown and purple through the haze—the uppermost tip of a whole new continent that stretched eight thousand vertiginous miles to Cape Town, and the spot where the waters of the South Atlantic ran into those of the Indian Ocean.

"Make the most of it," he said, watching as K8 took photographs of the view with her SincPhone. She didn't reply, just kept snapping. She knew as well as he did that they might never get another chance to come here, and that their forthcoming journey to Mars could very well end up being a one-way trip, even if they somehow defeated Célestine and her minions.

He was pleased to see that she'd finally changed out of her white suit, into a pair of jeans and a black t-shirt, both purchased on the ride here from the airport. The suit jacket and skirt had been abandoned in the back of the taxi and were now somewhere in the city below, off on adventures of their own.

Ack-Ack turned to look into the wind, at the vast dark bulk of the *Sun Wukong*. The airship rode at anchor above the airport, its impellers spinning sporadically to keep it in place. From here, he could see the damage it had suffered during its confrontation with the Leviathans. Its armour had been blackened by flame and smoke, and pockmarked by shells, which had, in a handful of places, penetrated through into the rooms and spaces within.

The *Ameline* sat atop the larger vessel like a frog on the back of a surfboard. Its three landing legs were splayed to provide maximal balance, and the sun glinted from its various sensor blisters and intake valves. In a few short hours, he would be riding it into space. He glanced up, at the seemingly impenetrable blue of the zenith.

"To shake the surly bonds of Earth," he misquoted, "and punch the very face of God."

K8 looked around. "What?"

"Nothing." He patted his jacket pockets. He wanted another cigar but the last one had left his throat raw. On the other side of the viewing area, a couple of wild Barbary macaques perched on a railing, watching him with dull, suspicious eyes. They were used to the tourists that came up here during the year, but this was the first time they'd seen one of their own parading around in clothes and boots, taking in the sights like a human— and standing as tall as one.

He flipped them the finger. *Fucking yokels.* What did they know about anything? Here he was, about to launch himself into the void in order to save their hairy backsides, and all they had on their minds was food. They sat up here year after year, looking down on the town with its cars and motorbikes, luxury hotels and airport... and scratched themselves. They were curious, but their curiosity seemed limited to the contents of handbags and litterbins; none of them had ever ventured downslope to steal a car or attempt a little credit card fraud. Their worries were immediate and mostly revolved around eating and fucking, and they'd go on to spend their whole lives up here on this rock, sandwiched between Europe and Africa and knowing nothing of either.

He envied them that, he realised. They'd never have to fight a war or save a planet. If he'd been given the choice, he'd have stayed like them. He'd have been far happier to have been spared the upheavals of the past few years, and instead have spent his life as a simple, half-aware simian, passing his days in the rough and tumble ignorance of monkeydom.

They glared at him, and he glared back, showing his teeth.

"You want to swap places?" he asked them. "Be my fucking guest."

LATER, HE AND K8 rode the cable car back down to street level. They caught a cab to The Macaca Sylvanus, a small pub adjacent to the main airport terminal, and a place popular with visiting skyliner crews.

All eyes watched them as they walked from the door to a table by the window, where they had a view of the runway and the looming underside of the *Sun Wukong.*

"It's hard to imagine," K8 said when they were settled with drinks, "that all this might be gone in a few months."

Ack-Ack Macaque swirled the rum in the bottom of his glass. The ice cubes cracked and clinked. "Only if we fail."

"And how likely is that?"

He didn't really want to think about it. "We're trying to fire a two-kilometre-long airship into space using experimental engines and a force field we don't really understand," he said. He raised the glass to his lips and sniffed the contents. "Your guess is as good as mine. For all I know, the whole fucking thing'll blow up on take off."

"But you won't be on it, will you? You're going ahead with Abdulov."

"Fuck yeah." He'd flown all sorts of aircraft in his time, from his beloved Spitfires to lumbering transport planes. Now, he was itching to get inside the *Ameline* and see what she could do. If the size of the fusion exhausts at her stern was anything to go by, that crate could really *move*. He tipped a little of the drink into his mouth, savouring the sting of the alcohol on his tongue. "That's the plan."

"What about me?"

"You can come if you want."

K8 visibly perked. "Really? I thought you'd want me on the *Sun*, looking after the machinery."

"Nah." Ack-Ack Macaque glanced around the room. Most of the patrons had gone back to their own conversations; those that hadn't were trying not to stare. "If it works, it works; if it doesn't, it doesn't. I can't see how you being on board will make a damn bit of difference." He drained his glass and set it down. "Besides, you didn't think I'd go off and leave you behind, did you?"

K8's cheeks coloured.

"I did wonder. Things have been a little... weird between us."

Ack-Ack Macaque gave a snort. "I did what I could. You wanted to be brought back to the hive, so I brought you back."

She fiddled with the straw in her bottle of Pepsi. Without the white suit, she looked younger and somehow more alive.

"Yes," she said slowly. "I did. That's true. For a time, getting back was all that seemed to matter—but I think I'm getting over that now."

Ack-Ack Macaque put down his glass. As well as the change in her outward appearance, he'd noticed the change in her speech patterns. Every time she opened her mouth, she sounded less like a blissed-out automaton and more like her old self.

"Good." He reached up and scratched his eye patch. "Because there aren't going to be any Gestalt on Mars."

"What about the Founder?"

Ack-Ack made a face. That was a subject he *really* didn't want to discuss. He tried to shrug it off.

"It's complicated," he said, voice gruff.

"I know Victoria's got her locked in the brig."

Ack-Ack picked at the hairs on the back of his hand. "Abdulov thinks she's some kind of alien."

K8 took a sip of cola. "What do you think?"

"I think I knocked her up." He signalled to the barman for another round.

"Awkward."

"No shit."

Outside, a supply helicopter rose from the tarmac. He followed it with his eye as it wheeled upwards, towards the vast airship. Another followed, and then another. Merovech had been as good as his word. Food, water and other consumables were being loaded onto the *Sun Wukong*, along with enough spacesuits to allow the monkey army to operate on the surface of the Red Planet.

The suits had been hastily churned out by the *Ameline*, and were little more than transparent inflatable human-shaped balloons with sleeves for arms and legs, and large fishbowl helmets. They were designed to protect the old trading ship's passengers in case of accidental hull breach and cabin depressurisation. They were flimsy and vulnerable, but they'd do for now. As long as they kept out the vacuum long enough for him to defeat the last copy of the Duchess, he'd be satisfied. He could start thinking long-term survival later, with the fight over and both worlds safe.

"You know," K8 said hesitantly, "I never blamed you for what you did to me."

Ack-Ack Macaque scowled. "You didn't have to."

A fourth helicopter lumbered skywards. He watched it wobble into the air, the downdraught from its rotors kicking up a swirl of dust and sand. K8 reached over and grasped the cuff of his jacket. "And you shouldn't blame yourself, either."

"Easier said than done." At the height of the final battle against the Gestalt, he'd given her to the hive. It had been a tactical decision and had played a big part in their final victory, yet the guilt had been immense. For the past two years, as they'd traipsed the multiverse freeing uplifted monkeys from laboratories on a hundred different parallels, he'd watched her suffer withdrawal from the rest of the hive, knowing all the time that he was the cause of her pain and discomfort, that it was all his fault.

"Forget it," K8 said. The barman brought more drinks. Ack-Ack looked around at the people on the other tables. There were about a dozen of them, all told, in a room designed to hold around three times that number. Some were crewmen and women from visiting skyliners. You could tell them by their uniforms. The others were a mixture of fans—former gamers bedecked in vintage leather flying coats and decorative brass goggles— and wannabes here to find work. A small knot of tourists lingered by the counter, throwing the occasional glance his way, and more were arriving all the time, sidling into the room in ones and twos as news of his presence spread over the social networks.

K8 leant across the table and whispered, "And since when have you had a conscience, anyway?"

Ack-Ack Macaque didn't want to meet her eye. He toyed with his glass instead.

"It's a recent development," he said.

CHAPTER FORTY-ONE
NOT BEING ONE

WHEN ACK-ACK MACAQUE and K8 returned to the *Sun Wukong* an hour later, Victoria was waiting for them. She sniffed the air.

"Have you been drinking?"

Ack-Ack Macaque grinned. "Just an eye-opener, boss."

"Good." Victoria rubbed her hands together. A good night's sleep had done wonders for her; she felt brisk and alive for the first time in days. "Because we need to talk." She led them to the bridge. With the craft stationary, the control room remained deserted. Those crewmembers that weren't ashore were busy aft, helping repair and refit the vessel for its upcoming voyage.

"About anything in particular?" Ack-Ack Macaque flopped into the pilot's couch and put his feet up on the console.

"About your girlfriend."

"What about her?"

Victoria swallowed down her irritation. "We need to decide what to do with her. We have her locked up, but should we turn her over to the authorities, or take her with us?"

The monkey took hold of his tail and started half-heartedly grooming it, his glove-like fingers picking through the scorched and frazzled hairs at the tip.

"I don't think it matters," he said. "Because if she's what Abdulov claims, I think she can escape any time she wants."

Victoria poked her tongue lightly into the side of her cheek and exhaled a long breath.

"We've had her locked up for two years."

"Have we?" Ack-Ack Macaque didn't look up. "Because I met her in the forest, right before I stormed Célestine's compound. Who do you think gave me all those guns?"

"Are you sure it was her?"

"Of course I'm sure. Abdulov said she sometimes went by the name

Apynja, and that's who I met. Only she didn't look like a monkey then, she looked like an orangutan." He let the tail drop. "And when we'd finished talking..." He trailed off, and coughed. If Victoria hadn't known him better, she would have sworn he was embarrassed. She stepped over and put her hand on the console, next to his feet.

"What happened when you finished talking?"

He coughed again, and his yellow eye glowered up at her. "She went all see-through and vanished, like a ghost. There, are you satisfied?" His stare dared her to disbelieve.

Victoria frowned. "So, all that stuff the Founder told us about who she was and where she came from—"

"All horseshit."

"But if she can come and go as she pleases, why's she stayed in our custody for the past two years?"

Ack-Ack Macaque took his boots from the control panel and put his hands on his knees.

"She's a talking primate. Where better to hide than in an airship full of them?"

"So, we just let her go?"

He stood, and straightened his coat. "The way I see it, it doesn't matter. If she wants to go, she'll go. If she wants to stick around..."

"Abdulov wants to arrest her."

"So what? A lot of people in London want to arrest her. You saw what a mess the Gestalt made."

Victoria raised her chin. "Julie died in the Gestalt attack, or had you forgotten? Merovech will want her to answer for that."

Ack-Ack Macaque made a peculiar growling noise deep in his throat. His breath smelled, as it so often did, of rum. "Well, Merovech can go whistle. Whatever else the Founder is, she's carrying my babies." He stomped towards the door. "I know she's done some bad shit, but the babies come first. If Merovech or Abdulov or anybody else wants a reckoning, they'll have to wait."

"And what if they won't wait?" she called after him.

He paused at the door.

"They'll have to come through me first."

AFTER HE'D GONE, Victoria went to stand at the main floor-to-ceiling window, looking out across the Strait in the direction of Tangiers. She wanted to talk to Paul, wanted to hear him make one of his smart-alecky quips to defuse the tension; only Paul was gone, and she had nobody. The inside of her head felt empty and echoing, like a cabin without a passenger—an emptiness mirrored by the dull, hollow ache in her heart.

Pleasure craft bobbed on the ocean; ferries cut back and forth. To the west, a civilian skyliner rode the prevailing wind, plying a coastal circuit that would take in Rome, Athens, Istanbul, Alexandria and Tunis. Victoria watched it pass, imagining the passengers lounging on its observation decks. At that moment, she would have given anything to be one of them, to have seen the whitewashed coastal towns and ancient ruins of the Mediterranean for herself, while she still had the chance.

Such a cruel irony, she thought, that she would have to leave the world in order to save it.

She felt the butterflies flapping in her chest. How would it feel, she wondered, to fail? To see the world reduced to ash and darkness and know it was partially her fault? Against such horror, the hope of making it to Mars and finding a way to resurrect Paul seemed a selfish and petty yearning, but right then, it was all she had to cling onto. For three terrifying, wonderful, dangerous years, he had been her whole world and she could never be whole again without him.

She sniffed. Sometimes, she wished the gelware had replaced more of her brain. It would be a relief at times like this to retreat into the emotionless clarity of machine thought, untroubled by fear or sentiment. And yet, wasn't that precisely what Célestine and the Founder had been trying to do, in their own peculiar ways? Each had wanted to 'improve' humanity by freeing it of its emotions and its dependence on frail flesh and greasy animal neurons— not realising that, as they did so, they were sacrificing the very individualism and eccentricity that made humankind so unique.

Am I turning into a monster? Looking at her faint, translucent reflection in the glass, she touched her fingertips to the ridge of scar tissue on the side of her head, and felt the various input jacks inlaid into the puckered skin.

No.

She still felt uncertainty, loss and pain. However much she might want to escape their weight, she knew deep down that her feelings were the only proof she had that she was alive, and more than simply a reanimated corpse with a computerised brain—that she was, on some deep and fundamental level, still human.

She wiped her eyes on the gold brocade at her sleeves, and allowed the gelware to pump a mild sedative into her blood. She couldn't afford to fall apart today. She had work to do. She turned from the window to find Merovech standing in the corridor outside the room, his knuckle raised, about to knock on the open door.

"Are you all right?"

She waved away his concern.

"You don't have to knock," she told him. "You're a king."

The young man looked self-conscious. "Actually, that's what I'm here to talk about."

"Being a king?"

"Not being one." He came over to join her in the light from the window. His tie was loose, his collar open, and his suit rumpled as if he'd slept in it—which, she realised, he probably had.

"I'm going to abdicate," he said frankly, hands in pockets. "I've been thinking about it for a long time. I promised Julie I would, and I think the time's finally come."

Victoria opened her mouth to speak, then realised she didn't have anything constructive to say. Somewhere at the back of her mind, a small part of her cursed. Before her accident, when she was still a journalist able to read and parse written text, she would have done almost anything for a story like this. Getting advance notification of an abdication direct from the monarch, having exclusive access to him before the event, would have made her career; and, for a moment, she allowed herself to imagine how it would have felt to break news of that magnitude.

"Why are you telling me?"

Merovech tapped his shoe against the metal deck. "Because I want to come with you."

"Are you serious?"

He looked up at her. "Of course I'm serious. I've given this a lot of thought. I know exactly how I'm going to do it." He turned his head to the sea, and the huge union flag painted on the roof of the airport terminal. "I've got a speech ready." He tapped his head. "It's all in here. I've been rehearsing it all night."

Victoria felt curiosity drown her other feelings. She couldn't help it. "What are you going to say?"

Merovech wrinkled his nose. "That I'm stepping down for personal reasons, and appointing a committee to oversee the functions of the monarch until such time as a referendum can be carried out, and the citizens of the Commonwealth decide for themselves how they want to be ruled."

Victoria felt her eyebrows rise. "Wow."

Merovech smiled guiltily. "Well, what have we been fighting for, if it hasn't been freedom from dictators and autocrats?"

"And you really want to come with us, on the *Ameline*?"

His face grew serious again. "I think it's best. If I stayed, I'd only be a distraction." He raised his eyes to the sky. "And don't forget, that's my mother up there on Mars, which makes it my fight as much as yours."

BREAKING NEWS

From *The London and Paris Times*, online edition:

Abdication!

PARIS 20/11/2062 – The world's media were caught off-guard this morning when, in a shock statement, His Majesty King Merovech I stepped down as ruler of the United Kingdom of Great Britain, France, Ireland and Norway, and Head of the United European Commonwealth.

Declaring his intention to step down with immediate effect, the King is believed to be accompanying the dreadnought Sun Wukong as it prepares to leave Earth.

Citing "personal reasons", the King expressed his gratitude to his citizens, and said he hoped they would forgive him.

So far, there has been no official statement from either the Palace or the Prime Minister, but Downing Street sources have indicated that His Majesty's last act as regent was to appoint an interim committee to oversee the functions of the monarchy. The committee's primary task will be to prepare a referendum in which the people of the Commonwealth will vote for a new head of state. Whether this new head will be a king, queen or president remains open for discussion, and it is rumoured that His Majesty hopes his former subjects will opt for a republic.

In the meantime, little is known of the King's plans, although credible sources in Gibraltar say he is planning to lead the fight against the Martian aggressors, who are led by the reincarnated 'soul' of his mother, the Duchess of Brittany.

In an ironic postscript to the announcement, polling organisations report that the King's approval rating in the wake of his resignation has soared to an all-time high of nearly 97 percent.

Read more | Like | Comment | Share

Related Stories:

Democracy or populism?

King's cousin, Princess Isabelle, to be next monarch?

Referendum to be held 'early next year'.

World leaders pay tribute to Merovech I.

Ten famous historical abdications.

Our last, best chance: the Sun Wukong prepares for lift-off.

Internet billionaire opens underground 'asteroid shelter' in Kenya.

CHAPTER FORTY-TWO
SHOTGUN

KATHERINE ABDULOV LED them into the *Ameline*'s passenger lounge and showed them where to sit.

"Stay buckled up until we're clear of the atmosphere," she warned. "The inertial dampers aren't what they used to be, so you might get thrown around a bit if things get bumpy." She watched K8, Merovech and the monkey strap themselves into chairs, then caught Victoria's eye and nodded upwards, towards the bridge.

"Do you want to ride shotgun?"

Victoria looked at her friends. Merovech seemed preoccupied, looking down at his thumbs. His thoughts were quite obviously elsewhere, and who could blame him? She knew he took his duty seriously. He was probably tearing himself up inside right now, wondering if he'd made the right call, done the right thing. Beside him, Ack-Ack Macaque kept taking his Colts from their holsters and spinning their barrels. If he was nervous, he was hiding it well. He looked restless and eager to fight, as if he couldn't wait to get going.

"Come on," he muttered. "Let's get this kite in the air."

Across the room, K8 seemed the most reassuringly normal of the three. Clad in jeans, trainers and a hooded top, she looked like an average teenager, and her wide-eyed apprehension filled Victoria with an unexpected rush of protectiveness.

"Are you okay?" she asked.

The girl smiled bravely. "Oh, aye. Never better."

ONCE UP ON the bridge, Victoria settled into the co-pilot's couch. This time, all the displays and overheads were alight, showing data on ship systems and atmospheric conditions. She tried to make sense of it but couldn't. The diagrams were unfamiliar and the letters and numerals, thanks to her head injury, were nothing but squiggles.

"How are we doing?" she asked.

In the pilot's chair, Kat smiled. Her dark eyes seemed to shine.

"The ship says we're ready to go."

"It can talk?"

"Yeah." Kat tapped the side of her head. "I hear it in here, through my implant."

"But, it's intelligent?"

Kat made a face. "I wouldn't go that far... Hey!"

"What?"

Kat seemed to be listening to something Victoria couldn't hear. After a couple of seconds, her eyes re-focused.

"The ship thinks it can tap into your gelware, if you'd like to be able to interact with it."

Victoria looked dubiously at the bulkheads and instruments surrounding her.

"Should I?"

"Your choice."

"Okay, then." As soon as the words left her lips, she felt a tingle at the back of her skull, and then sensed an odd, silent hiss, like a carrier wave.

> HELLO

She jumped. In her head, the voice felt loud and unmistakably synthetic.

"Uh, *bonjour?*"

> AH, YOU'RE FRENCH. I'VE ALWAYS LIKED THE FRENCH. MY NAME IS THE *AMELINE. JE M'APPELLE L'AMELINE.* WELCOME ABOARD.

"Thank you."

> *MON PLAISIR.* NOW, MAKE YOURSELF COMFORTABLE. WHEELS UP IN FIVE.

"Five minutes?"

> SECONDS.

The cabin lurched. A rumble came from below, deep but rising in pitch. Instinctively, Victoria gripped the armrests, and her heart raced as her mind flashed back to the helicopter crash. Through the link, she could feel the edges of the ship's excitement. It was like an eager dog scenting an open field. The sky above was its playground and it wanted to leap up and run forever.

> HERE WE GO.

Victoria felt the seat shove against her. The thrust was less violent than she'd feared but still insistent. Through the forward view, she watched the top of the *Sun Wukong* fall away as if snatched downward by a kraken's claws. The *Ameline* went up like an elevator, rising swiftly until the land shrank away to a green and brown blur and the horizon took on a distinct and visible curve. Then the old ship tipped on her tail and pointed her nose at the stars.

"A short jump and we'll be there," Kat said.

Victoria didn't reply. She had no words. Ahead, the stars lay strewn across the sky like scattered pearls, so close she felt she could reach out and let them run like sand through her fingers.

Oh, mon dieu, she thought. *This is really happening. I'm in space!*

Through her gelware, she could feel the ship straining at its leash. Titanic energies gathered in its jump engines, building and building until the whole hull seemed to shake with unbearable energy and impatience. Her body itched with a fire that felt almost sexual. She opened her mouth to ask whether they were going to wait to see if the *Sun Wukong* had successfully taken off but, before she could, she heard Kat issue a mental command. The ship whooped. All the gauges spiked at once. All the lights went red. There was a flash of intense, dazzling white light and an instant of shocking cold—

CHAPTER FORTY-THREE
SPACE MONKEY

VICTORIA SAGGED FORWARDS against her straps, gasping.

"Is it always like that?"

Beside her in the cockpit, Kat smiled. "You get used to it."

"I don't know if I want to."

Ahead, the screens pictured a grey rock, rounded and scarred like an old potato. Reflected sunlight lit one side of it. Its craters were little wells of impenetrable shadow.

"There it is," Kat said.

Victoria leaned forward, staring. "That's it? That's the 'missile'?" She narrowed her eyes. "It looks tiny, like a pebble."

"Don't let the visuals fool you." Kat was busily tapping away at controls and readouts. "Everything looks sharper in a vacuum. There's no dust or haze to indicate distance, so it all looks closer than it is."

"How big is it?"

"About the size of the Isle of Man."

"*Putain.*"

"And I know it doesn't look as if it's moving, but trust me, it's coming on like God's own freight train." She tapped a communication panel. "Hey, Ed, how are you doing?"

Ed Rico's voice burbled from the speaker. He sounded like a bad ventriloquist choking on a glass of water.

"Ready when you are, Captain. Only—"

"Only what?" Kat asked.

"Only, maybe we should let the monkey take the shot?"

"Any particular reason?"

Rico gurgled. "It's his world we're saving. Also, I'd like to see how he handles it."

There was a moment's pause. Kat had a rapid, silent conversation with the ship, and then shrugged. "Fine, whatever." She broke the connection and turned to Victoria. "You'd better tell your hairy friend to get suited up."

*   *   *

As the airlock door swung open, Ack-Ack Macaque found himself face-to-face with eternity. Beyond the curve of the fishbowl helmet, the sky fell away in all directions, receding to infinity wherever he looked. His panting sounded loud in his ears, and he felt his toes contract as if trying to tighten their grip on a branch—an automatic primate response to vertigo.

"Holy buggering shit," he muttered. Every instinct he had screamed at him that he was falling—falling between trees forever—but he tried to ignore them. Heights had never bothered him all that much. He wouldn't have made a very good pilot if they had, but this boundless infinity was something else again. With an effort of will, he tore his eyes from the sky and tried to concentrate on spying out the handholds inlaid into the ship's skin. Designed to facilitate extravehicular maintenance, the little recesses were spaced evenly around the hull, allowing an astronaut to 'walk' around the outside of the ship with their hands. Every fourth one had a clip for tethering a safety line. Using them felt similar to rock climbing, only without any sense of weight or appreciable notion of either up or down.

Moving one hand at a time, keeping the other firmly gripped, Ack-Ack Macaque worked his way forwards, towards the *Ameline*'s blunt prow.

When he got there, he saw the alien weapon was a pod grafted beneath the bows. It looked like a cocoon made of melted candle wax. As he drew near to it, one end of it peeled apart like a banana and a helmeted head emerged. Behind the faceplate, sunlight flashed on Ed Rico's roguish grin.

"Come and have a go," he said, his voice sounding distant and scratchy in Ack-Ack Macaque's headphones.

Ack-Ack watched the man drag himself from the weapon's embrace like a butterfly pulling itself from a ruptured chrysalis. Then, holding the lip of the opening with one gauntleted hand, he beckoned.

"Just slide your feet in," Rico said.

Moving slowly, Ack-Ack pushed himself forward. Ed took hold of one of his boots and guided him into the pod's sticky-looking maw.

"I'm not sure about this," Ack-Ack grumbled. The thing resembled a hungry maggot trying to latch onto his feet.

"Relax," Ed said. "It's not nearly as gross as it looks."

"Yeah?" Ack-Ack Macaque made a face. "Because it looks pretty fucking disgusting from here."

He allowed Ed to feed him into the hole, until his head sank beneath the lip and he was looking up at the sky through his helmet.

"What now?" he asked.

Ed maneuvered himself so that he was looking down at Ack-Ack. His head obscured the stars.

"Wait until the top closes, and then take off your helmet."

Ack-Ack Macaque eyed the walls around him. They reminded him unpleasantly of pictures from a colonoscopy. "And what then?"

"Breathe in the liquid. Stay calm."

"Easy for you to say."

"Ah, you'll be fine." Ed backed away as the edges of the opening began to pucker. Slowly and silently, they crinkled shut, leaving Ack-Ack Macaque swaddled in darkness. Huffing and muttering, he reached up and un-dogged the neck of his helmet. Raising his arms was tricky in the confined space— kind of like getting undressed in a coffin made of slime—but he managed to prise the glass bowl off his head.

Now that his eye was adjusting, he could see that the walls of his prison shone with a faint green luminosity. They glistened with white, gloopy sweat. His nose wrinkled in revulsion.

"This place smells like feet."

Pressure on his boots and legs told him the gloop had begun to collect in the bottom of the cavity, gradually rising to fill the cramped space.

"Fuck." He wanted to get out. As the rising liquid reached his waist, he began to struggle, instinctively trying to claw his way upwards to avoid drowning. As it reached his chest, he took a deep breath.

Come on, monkey. If a scrawny tosspot like Rico can do this, so can you.

He screwed up his eye and his courage, and clamped his lips together. The gunk came up over the neck of his suit and over his chin. Then it was exploring his face. Involuntarily, he jerked backwards, trying to reach clear air, but the stuff had already found its way into his nose. It seemed to flow with purpose. Within seconds, it had pushed its way into his lungs, invaded every opening, from ears to pores to arsehole. And he could breathe. Somehow, miraculously, the muck was feeding him air. Even as he choked on the obstruction in his throat, his lungs were drawing oxygen from the liquid.

Slowly, chest heaving, he began to calm down.

I'm not dying, I'm not dying...

He opened his eyes, cringing at the touch of the peculiar gel against his eyeballs.

Oh, holy fuck, this is disgusting.

Then he saw the hair-fine filaments extruding from the walls like the tentacles of albino sea anemones. He tried to flinch away but the walls of the fissure contracted like a sphincter, squeezing against him and holding him in place. He tried to snarl, but the filaments pushed their way into his mouth and nose and he gagged as he felt them slither into his throat. Another insinuated itself into his left ear, and another two drilled into his eyelids. For a second, every nerve in his body flared with intolerable pain.

And then he saw *everything*.

The walls of the chamber were replaced with a three-dimensional tactical view of the surrounding volume. He saw the rock ahead, his target, outlined in red. He felt the caress of the solar wind, the touch of its warmth against his cheek, and he felt the weapon like a Spitfire beneath him—responsive, keen, and ready to do as he bade. He felt its power like an electrical shock to his spine. He'd seen what it had done to Célestine's Leviathans and now, as the weapon integrated itself with his frontal lobes, came the knowledge of how it worked. Suddenly he knew, as if he'd always known, that the weapon displaced plasma from the heart of the nearest star and squirted it in a tight beam at its target. That pencil-thin line of brilliant white, crackling energy he'd seen in France had been raw fire from the core of the Sun. Thirteen million degrees centigrade. No wonder it had carved metal like butter and eaten through the bedrock beneath.

And now that insane destructive beam was his to control!

Heart beating, he opened himself to the weapon's interface. All he had to do was think of the target and the gun would do the rest. Like a god, his will would be made manifest; a single thought would be enough to unleash a lightning bolt of pure, sizzling energy.

"Oh baby," he muttered to the system swaddling him, "where have you *been* all my life?"

ON THE *AMELINE*'S bridge, Victoria watched as the white line stabbed out, spearing the oncoming asteroid. Where it hit, the surface turned a livid molten yellow. If the ship's cameras hadn't automatically polarised, she would have been blinded. As it was, the line was reduced to a dull grey laceration in the fabric of reality. On the asteroid's surface, dust and loose rock blew away from the boiling incision. Then the beam moved. Slowly, it tracked upwards, slicing though the stone like a hot wire through a block of cheese. Then it blinked off. When it reappeared, it moved laterally, cutting from left to right. Then it jumped again, and now it moved from right to left. Faster and faster it slashed, hacking back and forth, up and down, until it became a flickering blur.

Under its assault, the asteroid seemed to fall apart. Glowing chunks broke away into space, only to be skewered and reduced still further. Within a couple of minutes, the potato had become a mass of cooling, tumbling fragments, each no bigger than a basketball.

Kat said, "Your monkey did well."

Victoria let herself smile. "He likes blowing things up." She felt a strange kind of pride. "It's kind of what he does."

"I can see that." Kat tapped the screen. "But those fragments will still do a lot of damage if they hit the Earth like that. Let's hope your airship can mop them up. They're small enough that a nuclear blast should vaporise most of them. The rest can burn in the atmosphere."

"So, that's it?'

"If the plan works, yes. Actual surface hits should be minimal. All we have to do now is track this cloud of debris and wait until the airship gets in range."

"Where is the *Sun Wukong*?" Victoria asked, looking at the inscrutable instruments above her. "How's it doing?"

Kat consulted the ship. "Almost in orbit. It's had a bit of a shaky ride, apparently, but the thing's more or less intact. They should be firing up the ion engines at any minute."

Victoria let out a breath she hadn't realised she'd been holding. Something eased inside her.

"Well, fingers-crossed they work."

Kat's face remained grim. "We'll soon find out. I'm plotting in a course to jump back there now." She jerked her head towards the hatch at the back of the bridge. "Why don't you go below and share the good news?"

CHAPTER FORTY-FOUR
EMPIRE STATE

LATER, STANDING ON the verandah inside the *Sun Wukong*'s glass nose, Ack-Ack Macaque looked out at a dark sky filled with stars. His fur was still damp from the alien goo of the weapon, and his throat and eyes were sore from the intrusion of its questing fibers; but despite all that, he felt good. The demolition of the asteroid had been an almost religious experience for him—an act of epic cosmic vandalism that dwarfed all his previous accomplishments. And the best bit was that there was more fun to come, as soon as the lumbering, slowly accelerating airship got close enough to unleash its nuclear torpedoes.

Yes, he thought, *an airship. Here I am riding a goddamn Zeppelin through the motherfucking universe.* Even to his own ears, it sounded batshit insane—and it had been his plan! He took a deep puff on his cigar and glanced around at his comrades. They had gathered here to toast their success with the rock, and the airship's successful launch. Even Apynja had been let out of the brig, once he'd convinced Victoria that mere walls couldn't hold the female monkey if she decided to do that teleport trick he'd seen her do in the forest.

"So," he rumbled, "what should I call you? Founder or Apynja?"

She looked up at him through her monocle. She wore a specially made black corset and skirt, and a top hat with a black veil that angled down across her face, covering her other eye.

"Does it matter?"

"I suppose not." He returned his gaze to the void beyond the windows. It would take weeks until they reached the remains of the asteroid, months after that until they reached Mars and the final confrontation with Célestine. He huffed smoke at the stars. Beside him, the Founder clicked her tongue and ran a protective hand over the bulge at her middle.

"You shouldn't be smoking around me, you know."

He looked down.

"Sorry." He dropped the butt to the deck and ground it out with the toe of his boot. The truth was, he hadn't been enjoying it anyway. Smoking had become a habit that had outlived its pleasures. Maybe now, with the babies on the way, it was time for him to quit.

He felt the Founder move closer along the rail, until their elbows were almost touching.

"You're an old soul, monkey man."

He fixed her with his good eye. "What?"

She smiled and shook her head fondly. "You don't remember at all, do you?"

"Remember what, lady?"

"All the times we've done this before."

He looked incredulously at the walls of the airship and the star field beyond. "Lady, nobody's done *this* before."

Her smile broadened, but he thought he caught an edge of sadness in her eyes, and something else in the way she drew a ragged breath through her nose.

"You're an old soul, Napoleon. One of the oldest, just like me, just like Célestine. You've been here from the beginning, in one form or another."

"What in holy hell are you talking about?"

The Founder raised her chin. "When we built the multiverse, there was one resurrected soul who opposed what we were doing. He was a man named Napoleon Jones—a human brought to our time by The Recollection. He thought we should embrace the chaos instead of hiding from it. When we took shelter in our creation, he plagued us with his sabotages and pranks for millennia. Somehow, when we were copying him into our virtual creation, he found a way to embed himself in the very warp and weft of the world. However many times we caught and killed him, he always resurfaced, always came back to cause trouble, and usually in the form of a talking beast."

"Wut?"

"A thousand times I've tried to build a paradise, and a thousand times you've thwarted me, Jones." She waved a bony finger in his face. "The Gestalt was only my most recent attempt."

"My name ain't Jones." Ack-Ack Macaque glowered. "And this paradise of yours sounds more like slavery to me."

The Founder glared defiantly. "I didn't say it would be a paradise for everyone."

"Just for you?"

She turned slightly and indicated the rest of the assembly with a twitch of her lace-covered hand.

"These people aren't real, you know."

Ack-Ack looked at Victoria and K8, who were engaged in earnest conversation with Merovech and Cuddles. "They think they're real, and that makes them real enough for me."

Leaving her where she stood, he stalked over to Katherine Abdulov, who was leaning against one of the giant pots at the edge of the jungle, nursing a glass of white wine.

"What are you going to do with her?" he asked.

Kat looked at the Founder and gave a one-shouldered shrug.

"She's done unspeakable things. All we can do is try to lock her up."

"Even knowing she'll escape?"

The young pilot gave him a curious look. "We can't kill her, if that's what you mean."

"Why not?"

"Because that's the sort of thing she would do."

Ack-Ack Macaque growled in his throat. Then he looked down at his arm. The fur stood on end. Static sparked from teaspoons. He felt his hackles bristle.

And there was Célestine, standing in the centre of the room. A few final blue flickers of static danced down her metal legs. The air smelled of ozone.

Ack-Ack Macaque went for his holsters. He had both guns pointing at her head before she'd fully finished materialising—but when he pulled the triggers, nothing happened. Célestine held up a hand and the metal grew hot. With a screech of pain and annoyance, he dropped them both.

"I'm tired," Célestine's voice boomed. "Tired of being interfered with. Tired of playing by the rules. Tired of playing these stupid games."

She clicked her fingers, and they were elsewhere.

SUNLIGHT DAZZLED HIM. A cold wind tugged at his jacket.

"What the fuck?" Ack-Ack Macaque put up a hand to shade his eye and squinted into the early morning light. He was back on Earth, on top of a building. A city stretched beneath him, all glass and stone. Vapour steamed from rooftop vents. The sound of traffic drifted up from street level.

"Where are we?"

"New York." Célestine stood ten metres away, beside a telescope mounted on a metal pole. "At the top of the Empire State Building."

He blinked, eye still adjusting. The Founder was here too, standing away to the side like a referee in a boxing match.

"How?"

"I told you." Célestine's voice was loud and dangerous. "I'm sick of playing by the rules. We built this world. If we have to, we can change whatever we want."

"Then why have you waited this long?"

She glared at him. "Because I was trying to do it properly. I was trying to build an empire that would last a hundred thousand years."

"But you've fucked it up now, yeah?"

"Because of you, you loathsome fleabag."

His Colts were gone. He had nothing except the knife in his boot, and he didn't think that would do much good against her titanium skeleton—especially if she could change the laws of physics at a whim. He looked desperately around the viewing gallery.

"But why bring me here?" he said, playing for time, hunting for a weapon.

Célestine laughed, and it wasn't a pleasant sound.

"Have you ever seen *King Kong*?"

Ack-Ack Macaque shrugged. "I've never been to China."

"She means," the Founder said, interjecting at last, voice sour with exasperation, "that she's going to kill you."

Ack-Ack huffed. He didn't like the look of this at all. In the space of an hour, he'd gone from glorying in the power of the alien weapon to standing helpless and unarmed in front of his greatest enemy. The turnaround seemed far too fast, and tipped in favour of the wrong party.

"She can try." He took up a fighting stance. He knew he was outgunned and outclassed, but that wouldn't stop him. If the metal bitch wanted to end him, she'd have a fight on her hands. He wasn't about to go gently into any goodnight, no sir, and he'd rather go down fighting than give her the satisfaction of admitting defeat.

In fact, screw her. Screw the lot of them.

With a yell, he flung himself forward. Célestine didn't even try to dodge. She stood her ground as his fingers clawed for her, and slapped him away at the last minute with a backhand that felt like a blow from an aluminium baseball bat.

He tumbled over and over, fetching up against the wall at the foot of the rail.

"Ouch, fuck." Stunned, he shook his head, trying to clear the red mist that interfered with his vision. Dimly, he saw the cyborg striding towards him. He grabbed a railing and pulled himself unsteadily to his feet.

"Had enough?" he asked her, and hawked a wedge of bloody phlegm into the dust. "Because I can do this all day."

Her lip curled. With a gesture, she parted the railings behind him. Off-balance, he teetered on the edge of a drop that seemed to fall away beneath his heels forever. The cars four hundred metres below looked like ants; the people like bacteria.

Hey, that's cheating!

He windmilled his arms to keep his balance, and had a sudden flash of another time and place, of a metal bridge over a deep canyon, and an airship passing beneath.

Célestine stepped forward. She had her hand pulled back, ready to shove him over the edge. As she lunged towards him, he grabbed her wrist and heaved backwards. If he was going over, he was going to take her with him. He heard the Founder yell, "No!" But it was too late. He was already falling, and Célestine's body toppled after him. He kept a death grip on her arm. If she tried to teleport, he'd go with her. If not, well…

Let's see how her metal head survives when it hits the pavement from this height.

The observation deck fell away behind them. The wind roared in his ears.

Oh crap, this is it…

He stared at death, in the form of an onrushing sidewalk.

Then the view blurred. A mirage shimmered beneath him. He felt himself buffeted up, banging his head against Célestine's metal chest. With a bang of displaced air and a flash of white light, the *Ameline* levered itself into existence, hanging in the sky metres from the wall of the skyscraper, jet thrusters whining.

Ack-Ack Macaque and Célestine hit its upper surface and rolled apart.

> HELLO!

Ack-Ack lay gasping for breath.

"What?" The voice had been speaking to him in his mind.

> I'M THE SHIP. I'M CONNECTED TO YOUR GELWARE BRAIN.

He shook his head. Close to the vessel's nose, Célestine clambered awkwardly to her feet and looked around, seemingly dazed.

"Shut up." He glanced around for a weapon, but found none. The alien pod lay beneath the bows, and he couldn't get to it from here.

> I'M THE *AMELINE*, MONKEY. I'M TRYING TO HELP YOU.

"Then kill this metal bitch."

> CAN DO. BUT YOU'RE GOING TO HAVE TO HELP.

Célestine fixed on him and started walking forward, hands grasping like claws. Ack-Ack Macaque danced backwards, staying out of reach.

"How?"

> MY WEAPONS ARE UNDERNEATH. I NEED YOU TO THROW HER OFF SO I CAN GET A CLEAR SHOT.

"I can't, she's too strong."

> THEN FIND SOMETHING TO HANG ON TO.

Without further warning, the old ship rolled. Ack-Ack Macaque lunged for one of the handholds he'd used earlier. He wrapped his fingers around it and clung. Less nimble, Célestine toppled. She lost her footing and fell, over and over, towards the ground. Ack-Ack Macaque felt his arm being torn from its socket. He snaked his tail through the next handhold along, using it to help support his weight.

The *Ameline* was still at ninety degrees to the ground when the weapon at its tip fired. A burning shaft of starfire speared the falling cyborg and, as she tumbled, diced her into glowing chunks. Still dangling precariously, Ack-Ack Macaque watched the burning debris rain onto Fifth Avenue.

"Yeah!" he yelled into the wind. "Take that! You see what you get when you mess with my friends?" He sent a gob of spit sailing earthwards. "Try teleporting your way out of *that*!"

EPILOGUE

GONE

Farewell dear mate, dear love!
I'm going away, I know not where,
Or to what fortune, or whether I may ever see you again.

Walt Whitman, *Good-Bye My Fancy!*

Ack-Ack Macaque clawed his way around to the airlock. When he got there, he found Victoria and K8 waiting for him. They pulled him inside and helped him to a chair, then let him catch his breath as the old ship powered up, away from the city.

"Thanks," he gasped when he could finally speak.

"Don't thank us," Victoria said. "We had nothing to do with it. One moment we were standing on the *Sun Wukong*, the next we were here, on the ship."

"But I thought—"

> AND DON'T LOOK AT ME, EITHER. I WAS MINDING MY OWN BUSINESS BEFORE SOMETHING ZAPPED ME INTO THAT HORRORSHOW.

Ack-Ack Macaque frowned. He scratched his eye patch.

"The Founder," he said quietly. She must have used her powers—her knowledge of the simulation—to teleport the ship and his friends here, the same way Célestine had brought him. "I guess she wasn't as bad as everybody said, huh?"

K8 gave him a sceptical look, one eyebrow raised.

"You really have lousy taste in women," she said.

Ack-Ack Macaque gave a snort. "You're talking about the mother of my babies."

"That's as may be, but I'll bet you that's the last we'll ever see of her."

The ship gave a couple of final bumps, and then steadied. Katherine Abdulov appeared from the hatch leading to the bridge.

"Célestine's dead," she said. "We scanned the wreckage. There wasn't a piece of her left that was bigger than an orange."

"So it's over?" K8 asked.

Victoria shook her head. "There are still the cyborgs on Mars. If we don't deal with them now, who knows what they'll throw our way next time."

The young Scot pouted. "And how long's it going to take us to get *there*?"

"Six months."

From the ladder that led from the ship's bridge, Katherine Abdulov cleared her throat. "Perhaps I can help?"

They all looked at her.

"I've been doing some calculations with the ship," she said. "We think we can tow you."

"Would that be faster?" Ack-Ack Macaque asked.

Kat grinned. "I reckon we could get you there in six weeks."

Ack-Ack Macaque sat bolt upright. "Hot damn! That's more like it. I'd go nuts rattling around that airship for half a year."

"And then, after that," Kat continued, "maybe you could help us?"

"In what way?" Victoria's eyes narrowed suspiciously.

Kat's smile turned serious. "Napoleon and I go back a long way," she said. "And it's good to have him back, even if he is a monkey now. Besides, there are other builders out there. What say we go and throw a wrench in their plans?"

K8 laughed. "A monkey wrench?"

Ack-Ack Macaque fixed her with his most withering scowl.

"Not funny."

He turned his stare on Katherine. "Do you think we can track down the Founder?"

"Possibly." Abdulov stuck out her bottom lip. "I mean, we've done it before. She'll know we're looking but, in theory, yes."

"Good." He shifted himself on the seat, getting comfortable. "Because I want my babies back."

His arms and legs felt as if they were made of wood. The accumulated aches and pains of the last few days—the barks, bruises and grazed knees; the multiple punches, kicks and bites—had taken their toll. As Victoria and Kat continued to plan their next move, he let his solitary eye fall closed.

With the *Ameline*'s help, they could be on Mars in a matter of weeks. And then the real fighting would start: monkey versus machine in a battle to the death, on the red sands of a dying world, with all the other worlds of creation at stake and an infinite playground stretching out all around them.

All they had to do was seize it.

Six miles above New York City, the *Ameline* readied her engines. Her course was set: first, a jump to rendezvous with the *Sun Wukong*, and then onwards, ever onwards, through all the billions of possible worlds.

Her fusion reactor came online, generating power for the jump engines. Deep in her belly, the engines began to spin up until the old ship felt she could leap the length of the universe in a single orgasmic bound.

> HOLD ONTO YOUR HATS, she warned her passengers. Her scanners took a final, almost lingering sweep over the blue and green marble that was the Earth. Then all the readouts on her bridge spiked at once. The *Ameline*'s engines tore a hole in the walls of the multiverse. There was a blinding flash of pure white light, and then they were all gone and elsewhere—humans, monkeys and spaceship alike.

CODA
THE LAST MACAQUE

EVENTUALLY, ACK-ACK MACAQUE found himself standing at the gates of the final citadel. He had his flying goggles down, protecting his good eye from the dry desert sand that swirled around him, catching in his fur and working its way into the seams of his clothes. His white silk scarf straggled out like a banner in the wind. The tip of his cigar flared.

"It's about fucking time," he said.

In his wake, worlds had burned; armies had been vanquished and whole populations liberated. Companions had been lost—some into happy retirement, others into irretrievable destruction—but much also had been gained. He had acquired new scars, new aches, and he had reclaimed memories from his previous lives: as Napoleon Jones the daredevil space pilot and sometime card sharp, and later, as Napoleon Jones the viral prankster in the source code of The Recollection.

Jones' knowledge—all the tricks that had allowed the man to infiltrate the system and hack the artificial multiverse in which they now all lived—had served Ack-Ack Macaque as he fought to throw off the yoke of the Architects, and bring down those who had set these pocket universes up as personal fiefdoms.

But through it all, he'd remained who he was. He could have changed himself. With his recovered mastery of the virtual world, he could have taken any form he desired. He could have become human, but he elected to stay a monkey.

He was stubborn like that.

He was Ack-Ack Macaque. It suited him, and he reveled in it. Napoleon Jones was a memory from another life. This time around, he had been born a monkey, and a monkey he would stay.

He stepped forward and kicked the citadel's wooden gate.

It was unlocked.

Drawing one of his Colts, he stepped through, into the relative shade and shelter of the inner courtyard.

No water played in the central fountain. No goats or chickens fussed in the dirt.

Once, this place had housed an army. Discarded spears lay scattered on the flagstones; haphazard fragments of body armour had been piled against the inner walls; loose, upturned helmets had become little bowlfuls of windblown dust and sand. The soldiers who'd once worn them had died centuries ago, carried away by a mediaeval plague that had unwittingly been carried east by crusaders, and which had then gone on to depopulate this entire timeline.

Ack-Ack Macaque knew that's why she was hiding here, on this empty, barren world, this dead planet. The woman he'd come to see. She thought nobody would look for her here, among the ruins of civilisations that had choked and died during the so-called Age of Chivalry.

She'd thought she would be safe here, find a refuge in the stillness of an empty world, but she had been wrong. He had found her. After all these years, all his efforts, he had tracked her here.

And now it was time to end their little game.

On the far side of the courtyard, beyond the sand-choked fountain, stood a simple sandstone chapel with a flat timber roof and coloured glass in its windows. Gun at the ready and tail swishing, he stalked towards it.

"Honey," he called around the cigar, "I'm ho-ome."

Behind him, the wind moaned against the citadel's walls. The large wooden gates creaked on their hinges.

"Hello?"

Still there was no reply. For a moment he wondered if he had been wrong, and she had already fled—or had simply never been here in the first place.

Then the chapel door opened. He turned sideways and straightened his right arm, bringing his pistol to bear on the figure standing in the candlelit gloom within.

The Founder drew back her lace veil and blinked into the sand-strewn brightness.

"Hello, Napoleon." She was wearing a black, Victorian-style dress. Her eyes glanced past his shoulder. "Are you alone?"

"It sure looks that way."

"No Victoria?"

"Nope."

The older monkey shrugged her thin shoulders.

"That's a shame; I always liked her."

"And the kids?" Ack-Ack stepped forward menacingly.

"Your boys?" The Founder raised her face to the sky. "They're out there somewhere, among the worlds, carving their own trails of chaos. They might even be fathers themselves by now."

Ack-Ack's fingers curled against the handle of the Colt.

"You lost them?"

"I didn't stop them from leaving."

"Same thing."

"No, there's a difference." She lowered her chin. "Now, why don't you put your gun down and come in? I've got some tea on the boil."

She held the door for him, but he stayed where he was.

"I've come a long way," he said.

The Founder cocked her head to one side.

"To kill me?"

Ack-Ack tightened his grip on the pistol.

"You're the last of the Architects."

She looked at him and scratched her grey-haired muzzle.

"You're far too late."

"What do you mean?"

A gust from the main gates whirled sand around their feet. The Founder raised a hand to shield her eyes from the sun.

"I'm already dying," she said.

"Bullshit." Ack-Ack Macaque lowered the weapon. "You're immortal. You're programmed that way."

"I changed the programme." She smiled, and her yellow fangs shone in the desert glare. "Now it's slowly deleting me, cutting away chunks of personality and memory."

Ack-Ack struggled to understand. With his free hand, he pushed his goggles up onto the top of his head.

"You're *dying*?"

"A piece at a time. Like a kind of self-imposed dementia."

"But why?"

"Because it's harder than dying all at once." She laughed bitterly. "And I don't deserve to go easily. Not after what I've done, and the people I've killed."

"So, we're not going to fight?"

She shook her head.

"You really are a simple soul, aren't you?"

"Then, *what*?"

"I have a gift for you." The Founder bustled into the depths of the chapel and, still wary, he followed.

*   *   *

INSIDE, THE PLACE smelled of incense and old, sick primates. There was no furniture to speak of, simply a mound of straw in the centre of the floor, and a simple stone altar at the far end, on which a single candle burned. A wood-burning stove crackled at the other end of the room, heating a pan of water.

The Founder was rummaging in an old leather saddlebag that lay on the flagstones beside the straw bed.

"Here," she said. She straightened up with difficulty. In her palm, she held a pair of small, shiny objects. He took one and turned it over in his hand, frowning.

"What the fuck is this? A bullet?"

"It's the way out."

"Suicide?"

Her hand flicked out and cuffed him across the head, knocking his goggles askew.

"No, idiot." Ignoring his indignant growl, she raised her arm to the timber ceiling in a sweeping gesture that took in the world on which they stood, and all the other worlds beyond. "It's the way out of the programme, the exit door to the multiverse. The escape button for the whole game."

Ack-Ack held the bullet between finger and thumb. It was small, but surprisingly heavy.

"How does it work?"

"It's a piece of code. You swallow it and it translates your code—the description of your physical and mental form—into a format the printers on the Ark can understand."

"The Ark?"

"It's the control room for the multiverse. Once we take these, we'll be deleted from this timeline and recreated on the Ark, in flesh and blood bodies, in the remains of the real world."

Ack-Ack frowned. He had Napoleon's memories of a twilit universe, its energy almost expended, its light all but burned away—its inhabitants scoured to digital code by The Recollection.

"Didn't you guys build this place to hide from the real world?"

"We did."

"Then why would you take one of these?"

She raised her chin, looking directly into his eyes in the candle's flickering light.

"Sometimes one of us had to go back, to keep the machinery running, or make a change."

"And now?"

Her gaze dropped to the flagstone floor.

"I want to see the sky again before I die." Her voice was a hoarse whisper. "The real sky, or at least whatever's left of it."

THE FOUNDER SWALLOWED her pill first. She took it dry, and it went down with difficulty. She choked it down and then reached for him, beseeching him to follow her. Before their hands could touch, she broke apart in a cloud of pixels that swirled like blown sand for a moment, before evaporating into the chapel's gloom.

Ack-Ack Macaque looked at the place where she had been standing, and then down at the bullet-shaped thing in his palm.

He seemed to have spent his life moving from one false reality to another. First there had been the game. Then he'd been yanked out of that and told he was in the real world. Only it hadn't been the real world, just one of a billion timelines in an artificial multiverse. Everything he'd considered real had always turned out to be a fiction. Time and again, the rug had been pulled from beneath him. And now he had the opportunity to leave this existence for another, more authentic version of reality?

"Different day, same shit."

He touched the bullet with the leathery index finger of his other hand.

Napoleon Jones had once existed in the real world, back before The Recollection and the creation of the multiverse. His early memories were filled with stars and cities and women illuminated in the pale lights of distant ports; his later, post-Recollection memories with a universe gone to wrack and ruin.

Ack-Ack sniffed.

What the hell, he thought. The universe outside might be fucked, but at least it was real. At least if he had to die—and he knew he was getting old, certainly approaching the upper limit of a natural monkey's lifespan—he'd rather do it out there, in the real world. He'd spent the last few years crashing around the multiverse righting wrongs and wreaking vengeances. He'd had enough virtual reality to last him several lifetimes. If he had to go, he'd prefer to get a final glance at the sky before he went. Like the Founder, he wanted to get a glimpse of reality before he disappeared off to wherever dead monkeys went. He didn't want to spend the rest of his mortal existence cowering in a simulated prison, no matter how large.

Besides, who knew what mischief she might be capable of? Out there, unsupervised, she could reboot the entire multiverse, causing it to revert to factory settings. If he wasn't out there to keep an eye on her, she could delete him, and set herself up as a god.

With a curse, he clapped his hand to his mouth. The bullet was hard and sourly metallic, but it wasn't the worst thing he'd ever ingested. He tipped his head back and swallowed hard...

AND WOKE ON a bed, beneath a blue light. The Founder was standing beside the bed, dressed in the same black dress and veil.

"How do you feel?" she asked.

Ack-Ack Macaque sat up. The room they were in looked like an infirmary: all shiny white plastic.

"I feel strange."

"You're on the Ark, in a freshly-printed body. It'll take a while for your sense of balance to settle down."

"My stomach..."

"Artificial gravity. Give it a few minutes."

Keeping one hand on the bed, Ack-Ack Macaque got to his feet. He appeared to be wearing the same clothes he had in the chapel, even down to the familiar creases and scuffs on the elbows of his jacket. He looked at his hands, turning them over and back again, noting the scars and lines.

"I'm the same."

"What did you expect? To come out as Napoleon Jones? I told you, the device you swallowed copied your appearance and fed it to the printers. They simply assembled you as you were."

"So I'm still old?"

"And I'm still dying."

Ack-Ack rubbed the patch covering his left eye socket. He had phantom eyeball itch, and it was driving him crazy.

"Do you think those printers could manage a good cigar?"

"I don't see why not."

"And a bottle of rum?"

"I'm sure. But first, I want to see the sky."

She led him out of the room and into a wide corridor, at the end of which he could see a large, circular window.

The sky beyond the glass was dark. As he got closer to the window, his sight began to adjust, and he made out a few sickly lanterns in depths of the blackness. Nothing else. No clouds of dust or spinning black holes; nothing but emptiness receding in all directions, forever.

"That's it?" He'd expected something grander, more apocalyptic. The Founder sniffed.

"Welcome," she said, "to the end of the universe."

WHEN ACK-ACK MACAQUE felt stronger, the Founder took him across to another window. Only, instead of looking out at the withered sky, this one looked inwards, into the interior of the Ark.

"What the *fuck*?" Ack-Ack pressed his hands and face against the glass. Somehow, the view of the interior seemed larger and more vertiginous that the view of empty space had been.

"It's called a Dyson Shell," the Founder said. She was looking weaker by the moment. Whatever she'd done to herself, the effects seemed to have accelerated since her emergence into the real world. "It's an artificial shell the size of the Earth's orbit, with an inner surface area equivalent to five hundred million Earths."

"And that thing at the centre?"

"That's a naked singularity. The remains of The Recollection."

"What the fucking hell is a singularity?"

She patted his arm, her touch like the brush of a bird's wing. "You don't need to know. Suffice to say, it powers the whole structure."

He gave a shrug.

"If you say so."

The Founder was silent for a moment, gazing out at the curving landscape. "This is where the last humans came, before the end. Before the multiverse."

"And now we're the only ones here?"

"Nobody else knows how to get out of the simulation." She coughed into her hand.

Ack-Ack looked at the view for a moment longer, then turned away. The scale was wrong: too big for the mind to comfortably grasp. He could feel his sense of reality wavering, and knew there would be only one sure cure. Cosmological wonders were one thing; alcohol was another.

"Let's get a drink," he suggested.

He took the Founder back to the room where he'd awoken, and she showed him how to tell the printer what to make. It contained patterns for all sorts of unlikely things, from hot dogs to bulldozers. He instructed it to spit out a bottle of its finest Caribbean rum, and two glasses.

They sat on the bed and raised a toast.

"You know," he said, "you were the only…"

She put a gnarled and frail finger to his lips.

"Shush," she said. "Don't spoil the moment."

"What moment?"

"This…"

Her glass crashed to the floor and she fell back onto the bed. Ack-Ack leapt up and took her by the shoulders.

"Holy shit," he said. "What are you doing? Are you all right?"

The Founder laughed weakly.

"Oh, Napoleon. Of course I'm not all right. I'm dying, you ass."

"And what am I supposed to do?"

"Save them?"

"Save who?"

"Everybody." The Founder coughed wetly. Something in her chest sounded as if it had come loose.

"This structure can't last much longer," she said. "A few thousand years, maybe. Maybe a little longer." She coughed again. Ack-Ack tried not to flinch from the droplets that hit his face. "But when the universe finally falls, this place falls with it, and everybody in the multiverse will die."

Ack-Ack looked around the room.

"Yeah, big whoop. Right now, I'm trying to think of a way to save *you*."

"Don't bother." She smiled, and he glimpsed blood on her teeth. "Just rest assured that this is the way I want it. Out here, like this, with you."

He sat back on his haunches.

"You're stubborn as a goat."

"And you smell like one."

Ack-Ack laughed, and lay down beside her. After a moment, he took her hand.

"So, what do I do?" he said. "Can I go back?"

"There wouldn't be much point." The Founder was finding speaking laborious. Her breath wheezed between words. "Time in the multiverse simulation runs much faster than it does out here. When we built it, we speeded it up, to give each world as much time as possible before the end." She broke into a long series of coughs. When they finally subsided, she said, "Decades have passed in there since we left. Our boys will have grown and had families and died. New generations will be rising. There won't be anybody you know left in there."

"So, I just stay here?"

"You can save them. We didn't make the speed of the simulation fast enough. They only have a few tens of thousands of years. You need to increase it for them, give them more time to come up with a solution of their own. Overclock the system as far as it will go."

"And how do I do that?"

"Ask the computers. They'll show you."

"And what will that achieve?"

The Founder tensed, and he could see the pain writ large on her face. She tried to say something but the breath wouldn't come. Her eyes went wide with panic and her hand gripped his. For a moment, all he could hear were the noises she made as she tried to inhale. Then she looked at him as if she hadn't a clue who he was. Her hand went limp in his. Her head fell back against the blanket, and she was dead.

ACK-ACK MACAQUE WALKED the interior of the Dyson Shell. Its builders had sculpted the inner surface to resemble meadows and moorlands, mountains, lakes and deserts. At the moment, he was passing through a region of high Alpine meadows, all green grass and bright yellow flowers. Bees buzzed and birds trilled. Whenever he was hungry, one of the Shell's drones would manufacture food and water. Whenever his boots wore out, they'd make him a new pair. Everything he needed was there for his convenience.

All he carried were his memories.

In the weeks since the Founder's death, he'd worked with the Shell's computers to retune the multiverse. As she'd suggested, he'd overclocked each timeline, vastly increasing the amount of simulated time each of them would experience before the universe containing the Dyson Shell finally wound down. Each simulated timeline now had a billion, billion subjective years ahead, in which to grow and develop.

He'd given the countless millions living in the simulation—including any descendants he might have—their chance to make something of themselves; an opportunity to expand and grow across geological vistas of deep time. And who knows, perhaps they'd figure out a way to transcend the death of the universe.

A billion, billion years was time enough for almost anything.

He paused at the top of a slope and looked out across the valley below, watched the grass shiver as the wind moved over it, and filled his nose with the scent of the flowers. Far below, a river lay like a vein of silver.

Having achieved all that, he reckoned an old monkey could retire satisfied.

With so much of the Shell to explore, he could walk for the rest of his life and never cover the same territory twice. And whenever he got sick of walking, he'd build a campfire and drink rum and sing old songs until he passed out. And when he woke, he'd start walking again.

He'd done all he could. He'd saved everyone. And now he'd decided to stay out here in the twilight of the real universe, wandering the surface of the Dyson Shell in an otherwise empty cosmos, orbiting a naked singularity in the darkness at the end of time.

ACK-ACKNOWLEDGEMENTS

THANKS TO MY wife, Becky and my daughters, Edith and Rosie; to my parents and siblings; to Jon Oliver and the team at Solaris; to Jake Murray for his excellent cover paintings; to my beta readers, Rebecca Powell, Su Haddrell, and Neil Beynon; and to everyone else who encouraged and supported me during the writing of these three books.

Gareth L. Powell
Bristol, October 2017

BONUS STORY

ACK-ACK MACAQUE

ACK-ACK MACAQUE FIRST lumbered his way into my consciousness some time in 2006, and I still have no idea where he came from. One day, I simply found myself repeating his name, over and over and over again, like a tune I couldn't get out of my head.

Ack-Ack Macaque. Everything else came from those four syllables. Catchy and deceptively simple, unpacking them demanded I come up with a world in which a monkey could credibly pilot a fighter plane.

About a year later, the following short story appeared in the September 2007 issue of *Interzone*, the long-running UK fiction magazine. Writing of it on his website, the novelist and comics writer Warren Ellis memorably described it as: "The commercialisation of a web animation into some diseased Max Headroom as metaphor for the wreckage of a fucked-up relationship."

I like that description.

This was his first public appearance; these were his first baby steps into the world; and I hope you enjoy them.

Gareth L. Powell
Bristol, July 2012

ACK-ACK MACAQUE
Gareth L. Powell

I SPENT THE first three months of last year living with a half-Japanese girl called Tori in a split-level flat above a butcher's shop on Gloucester Road. The flat was more mine than hers. We didn't have much furniture. We slept on a mattress in the attic, beneath four skylights. There were movie posters on the walls, spider plants and glass jars of dried pasta by the kitchen window. I kept a portable typewriter on the table and there were takeaway menus and yellowing taxi cards pinned to a corkboard by the front door. On a still night, music came from the Internet café across the street.

Tori had her laptop set up by the front window. She wrote and drew a web-based anime about a radioactive short-tailed monkey called Ack-Ack Macaque. He had an anti-aircraft gun and a patch over one eye. He had a cult online following. She spent hours hunched over each frame, fingers tapping on the mouse pad.

I used to sit there, watching her. I kept the kettle hot, kept the sweet tea coming. She used to wear my brushed cotton shirts and mutter under her breath.

We had sex all the time. One night, after we rolled apart, I told her I loved her. She just kind of shrugged; she was restless, eager to get back to her animation.

"Thanks," she said.

She had shiny brown eyes and a thick black ponytail. She was shorter than me and wore combat trousers and skater t-shirts. Her left arm bore the twisted pink scar of a teenage motor scooter accident.

We used to laugh. We shared a sense of humour. I thought that we got each other, on so many levels. We were both into red wine and tapas. We liked the same films, listened to the same music. We stayed up late into the night, talking and drinking.

And then, one day in March, she walked out on me.

And I decided to slash my wrists.

*　*　*

I'VE NO IDEA why I took it so hard. I don't even know if I meant to succeed. I drank half a bottle of cheap vodka from the corner shop, and then I took a kitchen knife from the drawer and made three cuts across each wrist. The first was easy, but by the second my hands had started to shake. The welling blood made the plastic knife handle slippery and my eyes were watering from the stinging pain. Nevertheless, within minutes, I was bleeding heavily. I dropped the knife in the bathroom sink and staggered downstairs.

Her note was still on the kitchen table, where she'd left it. It was full of clichés: she felt I'd been stifling her; she'd met someone else; she hadn't meant to, but she hoped I'd understand.

She hoped we could still be friends.

I picked up the phone. She answered on the fifth ring.

"I've cut my wrists," I said.

She didn't believe me; she hung up.

It was four-thirty on a damp and overcast Saturday afternoon. I felt restless; the flat was too quiet and I needed cigarettes. I picked up my coat and went downstairs. Outside, it was blisteringly cold; a bitter wind blew, and the sky looked bruised.

"TWENTY SILK CUT, please."

The middle-aged woman in the corner shop looked at me over her thick glasses. She wore a yellow sari and lots of mascara.

"Are you all right, love?"

She pushed the cigarettes across the counter. I forced a smile and handed her a stained tenner. She held it between finger and thumb.

She said, "Is this blood?"

I shrugged. I felt faint. Something cold and prickly seemed to be crawling up my legs. My wrists were still bleeding; my sleeves were soaked and sticky. Bright red splatters adorned the toes of my grubby white trainers.

She looked me up and down, and curled her lip. She shuffled to the rear of the shop and pulled back a bead curtain, revealing a flight of dingy wooden stairs that led up into the apartment above.

"Sanjit!" she screeched. "Call an ambulance!"

*　*　*

ACK-ACK MACAQUE rides through the red wartime sky in the Akron, a gold-plated airship towed by twelve hundred skeletal oxen. With his motley crew, he's the scourge of the Luftwaffe, a defender of all things right and decent.

Between them, they've notched up more confirmed kills than anyone else in the European theatre. They've pretty much cleared the Kaiser's planes from the sky; all except those of the squadron belonging to the diabolical Baron Von Richter-Scale.

They've tracked each other from the Baltic Sea to the Mediterranean and back. Countless times, they've crossed swords in the skies above the battlefields and trenches of Northern Europe, but to no avail.

"You'll never stop me, monkey boy!" cackles the Baron.

THEY KEPT ME in hospital for three days. When I got out, I tried to stay indoors. I took a leave of absence from work. My bandaged wrists began to scab over. The cuts were black and flaky. The stitches itched. I became self-conscious. I began to regret what I'd done. When I ventured out for food, I tried to hide the bandages. I felt no one understood; no one saw the red, raw mess that I'd become.

Not even Tori.

"I did it for you," I said.

She hung up, as always. But before she did, in the background, I heard Josh, her new boyfriend, rattling pans in the kitchen.

I'd heard that he was the marketing director of an up-and-coming software company based in a converted warehouse by the docks. He liked to cook Thai food. He wore a lot of denim and drove an Audi.

I went to see him at his office.

"You don't understand her work," I said.

He took a deep breath. He scratched his forehead. He wouldn't look at my hands; the sight of my bandages embarrassed him.

"The Manga monkey thing?" he said. "I think that's great but, you know, there's so much more potential there."

I raised my eyebrows.

"Ack-Ack Macaque's a fucking classic," I replied.

He shook his head slowly. He looked tired, almost disappointed by my lack of vision.

"It's a one joke thing," he said. He offered me a seat, but I shook my head.

"We're developing the whole concept," he continued. "We're going to flesh it out, make it the basis for a whole product range. It's going to be huge."

He tapped a web address into his desktop, and turned the screen my way. An animated picture of the monkey's face appeared, eye patch and all.

"See this? It's a virtual online simulation that kids can interact with."

I stared at it in horror. It wasn't the character I knew and loved. They'd lost the edginess, made it cute, given it a large, puppy dog eye and a goofy grin. All the sharp edges were gone.

Josh rattled a few keys. "If you type in a question, it responds; it's great. We've given it the ability to learn from its mistakes, to make its answers more convincing. It's just like talking to a real person."

I closed my eyes. I could hear the self-assurance in his voice, his unshakable self-belief. I knew right then that nothing I could say would sway him. I had no way to get through to him. He was messing up everything I loved— my relationship with Tori, and my favourite anime character—and I was powerless in the face of his confidence. My throat began to close up. Breathing became a ragged effort. The walls of the office seemed to crowd in on me. I fell into a chair and burst into embarrassed sobs.

When I looked up, angrily wiping my eyes on my sleeve, he was watching me.

"You need to get some counselling," he said.

I TOOK TO wearing sunglasses when I went out. I had a paperback copy of *The Invisible Man* on my bookshelves and I spent a lot of time looking at the bandaged face on the cover.

April came and went. Ashamed and restless, I left the city and went back to the dismal Welsh market town where I'd grown up. I hid for a couple of months in a terraced bed and breakfast near the railway station. At night, the passing trains made the sash windows shake. By day, rain pattered off the roof and dripped from the gutters. Grey mist streaked the hills above the town, where gorse bushes huddled in the bracken like a sleeping army.

I'd come seeking comfort and familiarity but discovered instead the kind of notoriety you only find in a small community. I'd become an outsider, a novelty. The tiniest details of my daily activities were a constant source of fascination to my elderly neighbours. They were desperate to know why I wore bandages on my arms; they were like sharks circling, scenting something in the water. They'd contrive to meet me by the front door so they could ask how I was. They'd skirt around a hundred unspoken questions, hoping to glean a scrap of scandal. Even in a town where half the adult population seemed to exhibit one kind of debilitating medical condition or another, I stood out.

The truth was, I didn't really need the bandages any more. But they were comforting, somehow. And I wasn't ready to give them up.

Every Friday night, I called Tori from the payphone at the end of the street, by the river.

"I miss you," I said.

I pressed the receiver against my ear, listening to her breathe. And then I went back to my empty little room and drank myself to sleep.

MEANWHILE, ACK-ACK Macaque went from strength to strength. He got his own animated Saturday morning TV series. Pundits were even talking about a movie. By August, the wisecracking monkey was everywhere. And the public still couldn't get enough of him. They bought his obnoxious image on t-shirts and calendars. There were breakfast cereals, screensavers, ring tones and lunchboxes. His inane catchphrases entered the language. You could hardly go anywhere without hearing some joker squeak out: "Everybody loves the monkey."

My blood ran cold every time I heard it.

It was my phrase; she'd picked it up from me. It was something I used to say all the time, back when we lived together, when we were happy. It was one of our private jokes, one of the ways I used to make her laugh. I couldn't believe she'd recycled it. I couldn't believe she was using it to make money.

And it hurt to hear it shouted in the street by kids who only knew the cute cartoon version. They had no idea how good the original anime series had been, how important. They didn't care about its irony or satire—they just revelled in the sanitised slapstick of the new episodes.

I caught the early train back to Bristol. I wanted to confront her. I wanted to let her know how betrayed I felt. But then, as I watched the full moon set over the flooded Severn Estuary, I caught my reflection in the carriage window.

I'd already tried to kill myself. What else could I do?

WHEN WE PULLED in at Bristol Parkway, I stumbled out onto the station forecourt in the orange-lit dawn chill. The sky in the east was dirty grey.

The pavements were wet; the taxis sat with their heaters running.

After a few moments of indecision, I started walking. I walked all the way to Tori's new bed-sit. It was September and there was rain in the air. I saw a fox investigating some black rubbish sacks outside a kebab shop. It moved more like a cat than a dog, and it watched me warily as I passed.

THE AKRON CARRIES half a dozen propeller-driven biplanes. They're launched and recovered using a trapeze that can be raised and lowered from a hangar in the floor of the airship. Ack-Ack uses them to fly solo scouting missions, deep into enemy territory, searching for the Baron's lair.

Today, he's got a passenger.

"He's gotta be here somewhere," shouts Lola Lush over the roar of the Rolls Royce engine. Her pink silk scarf flaps in the wind. She's a plucky American reporter with red lips and dark, wavy hair. But Ack-Ack doesn't reply. He's flying the plane with his feet while he peels a banana. He's wearing a thick flight jacket and a leather cap.

Below them, the moonlight glints off a thousand steam-driven Allied tanks. Like huge tracked battleships, they forge relentlessly forward, through the mud, toward the German lines. Black clouds shot with sparks belch from their gothic smoke stacks. In the morning, they'll fall on Paris, driving the enemy hordes from the city.

THE STREETLIGHTS ON her road were out. She opened the door as if she'd been expecting me. She looked pale and dishevelled in an old silk dressing gown. She'd been crying; her eyes were bloodshot and puffy.

"Oh, Andy." She threw her arms around my neck and rubbed her face into my chest. Her fingers were like talons.

I took her in and sat her down. I made her a cup of tea and waited patiently as she tried to talk.

Each time, she got as far as my name, and then broke down again.

"He's left me," she sobbed.

I held her as her shoulders shook. She cried like a child, with no restraint or dignity.

I went to her room and filled a carrier bag with clothes. Then I took her back to my flat, the one we used to share, and put her to bed in the attic, beneath the skylights. The room smelled stale because I'd been away so long.

Lying on her side beneath the duvet, she curled her arms around her drawn-up knees. She looked small and vulnerable, skinnier than I remembered.

"Andy?" she whispered.

"Yes, love?"

She licked her lips. "What do your arms look like, under the bandages?"

I flinched away, embarrassed. She pushed her cheek into the pillow and started to cry again.

"I'm so sorry," she sniffed. "I'm so sorry for making you feel like this."

I left her there and went down to the kitchen. I made coffee and sat at the kitchen table, in front of the dusty typewriter. Outside, another wet morning dawned.

I lit a cigarette and turned on the television, with the volume low. There wasn't much on. Several channels were running test cards and the rest were given over to confused news reports. After a couple of minutes, I turned it off.

At a quarter past six, her mobile rang. I picked it up. It was Josh and he sounded rough.

"I've got to talk to her," he said. He sounded surprised to hear my voice.

"No way."

I was standing by the window; rain fell from an angry sky.

"It's about the monkey," he said. "There's a problem with it."

I snorted. He'd screwed Tori out of her rights to the character. As soon as it started bringing in serious money, he'd dumped her.

I said, "Go to hell, Josh."

I turned the phone off and left it by the kettle. Out on the street, a police siren tore by, blue lights flashing.

I mashed out my cigarette and went for a shower.

Tori came downstairs as I took my bandages off. I think the phone must've woken her. I tried to turn away, but she put a hand on my arm. She saw the raised, red scars. She reached up and brushed my cheek. Her eyes were sad and her chest seemed hollow. She'd been crying again.

"You're beautiful," she said. "You've suffered, and it's made you beautiful."

THERE WASN'T ANY food in the house. I went down to the shop on the corner but it was closed. The Internet café over the road was open, but empty. All the monitors displayed error messages.

The girl at the counter sold me tea and sandwiches to take out.

"I think the main server's down," she said.

*   *   *

WHEN I GOT back to the flat, I found Tori curled on the sofa, watching an episode of the animated *Ack-Ack Macaque* series on DVD. She wore a towel and struggled with a comb. I took it from her and ran it gently through her wet hair, teasing out the knots. The skin on her shoulders smelled of soap.

"I don't like the guy they got in to do Baron Von Richter-Scale's voice," she said.

"Too American?"

"Too whiny."

I finished untangling her and handed the comb back.

"Why are you watching it?" I asked. She shrugged, her attention fixed on the screen.

"There's nothing else on."

"I bought sandwiches."

"I'm not hungry."

I handed her a plastic cup of tea. "Drink this, at least."

She took it and levered up the lid. She sniffed the steam. I went out into the kitchen and lit another cigarette. My hands were shaking.

When I got off the train last night, I'd been expecting a confrontation. I'd been preparing myself for a fight. And now all that unused anger was sloshing around, looking for an outlet.

I stared at the film posters on the walls. I sorted through the pile of mail that had accumulated during my absence. I stood at the window and watched the rain.

"This isn't fair," I said, at last.

I scratched irritably at my bandages. When I looked up, Tori stood in the doorway, still wrapped in the towel. She held out her arm. The old scar from the scooter accident looked like a twisted claw mark in her olive skin.

"We're both damaged," she said.

ABOUT AN HOUR later, the intercom buzzed. It was Josh.

"Please, you've got to let me in," he said. His voice was hoarse; he sounded scared.

I hung up.

He pressed the buzzer again. He started pounding on the door. I looked across at Tori and said, "It's your decision."

She bit her lip. Then she closed her eyes and nodded.

"Let him in."

HE LOOKED A mess. He wore a denim shirt and white Nike jogging bottoms under a flapping khaki trench coat. His hair was wild, spiky with yesterday's gel, and he kept clenching and unclenching his fists.

"It's the fucking monkey," he said.

Tori sucked her teeth. "What about it?" She was dressed now, in blue cargo pants and a black vest.

"Haven't you been watching the news?" He lunged forward and snatched the remote from the coffee table. Many of the cable channels were messy with interference. Some of the smaller ones were off the air altogether. The BBC was still broadcasting, but the sound was patchy. We saw footage of burning buildings, riots, and looting. Troops were on the streets of Berlin, Munich and Paris.

I asked: "What's this?"

He looked at me with bloodshot eyes. "It's the monkey," he replied.

WE SAT TOGETHER on the sofa, watching the disaster unfold. And as each station sputtered and died, we flicked on to the next. When the last picture faded, I passed around the cigarettes. Josh took one, Tori declined. Out in the street, we heard more sirens.

"You remember the online simulation? When we designed it, we didn't anticipate the level of response," he said.

I leaned forward, offering him a light.

"So, what happened?"

He puffed his Silk Cut into life and sat back in a swirl of smoke. He looked desperately tired.

"There were literally thousands of people on the site at any one time. They played games with it, tried to catch it out with trick questions. It was learning at a fantastic rate."

"Go on," I said.

"Well, it wasn't designed for that kind of intensity. It was developing faster than we'd anticipated. It started trawling other websites for information, raiding databases. It got everywhere."

Tori walked over to the TV. She stood in front of it, shifting her weight from one foot to the other. "So, why hasn't this happened before? They've had similar programs in the States for months. Why's this one gone wrong?"

He shook his head. "Those were mostly on academic sites. None of them had to contend with the kind of hit rates we were seeing."

"So, what happened?" I asked.

He looked miserable. "I guess it eventually reached some critical level of complexity. Two days ago, it vanished into cyberspace, and it's been causing trouble ever since."

I thought about the error messages on the monitors in the café, and the disrupted TV stations. I sucked in a lungful of smoke.

"Everybody loves the monkey," I said.

A HANDFUL OF local and national radio stations were still broadcasting. Over the next hour, we listened as the entity formerly known as Ack-Ack Macaque took down the Deutsche Bank. It wiped billions off the German stock exchange and sent the international currency markets into freefall.

"It's asserting itself," Josh said. "It's flexing its muscles."

Tori sat on the bottom of the stairs that led up to the attic. Her head rested against the banister.

"How could you let this happen?" she asked.

Josh surged to his feet, coat flapping. He bent over her, fists squeezed tight. She leaned back, nervous. He seemed to be struggling to say something.

He gave up. He let out a frustrated cry, turned his back and stalked over to the window. Tori closed her eyes. I went over and knelt before her. I put a hand on her shoulder; she reached up and gripped it.

I said, "Are you okay?"

She glanced past me, at Josh. "I don't know," she said.

THEY ENGAGE THE Baron's planes in the skies over France. There's no mistaking the Baron's blue Fokker D.VII with its skull and crossed-bones motif.

The Akron launches its fighters and, within seconds, the sky's a confusing tangle of weaving aircraft.

In the lead plane, Ack-Ack Macaque stands up in his cockpit, blasting away with his handheld cannon. His yellow teeth are bared, clamped around the angry red glow of his cigar.

In the front seat, Lola Lush uses her camera's tripod to swipe at the black-clad ninjas that leap at them from the enemy planes. Showers of spinning shurikens clatter against the wings and tail.

The Baron's blue Fokker dives toward them out of the sun, on a collision course. His machine guns punch holes through their engine cowling. Hot oil squirts back over the fuselage. Lola curses.

Ack-Ack drops back into his seat and wipes his goggles. He seizes the joystick. If this is a game of chicken, he's not going to be the first to flinch. He spits his oily cigar over the side of the plane and wipes his mouth on his hairy arm. He snarls: "Okay, you bastard. This time we finish it."

THE FIRST TWO planes to crash were Lufthansa airliners, and they went down almost simultaneously, one over the Atlantic and the other on approach to Heathrow. The third was a German military transport that flew into the ground near Kiev.

Most of the radio reports were vague, or contradictory. The only confirmed details came from the Heathrow crash, which they were blaming on a computer glitch at air traffic control. We listened in silence, stunned at the number of casualties.

"There's a pattern here," I said.

Josh turned to face us. He seemed calmer but his eyes glistened.

"Where?"

"Lufthansa. The Deutsche Bank. The Berlin stock exchange..." I counted them off on my fingers.

Tori stood up and started pacing. She said, "It must think it really is Ack-Ack Macaque."

Josh looked blank. "Okay. But why's it causing planes to crash?"

Tori stopped pacing. "Have you ever actually *watched* the original series?"

He shrugged. "I looked at it, but I still don't get the connection."

I reached for a cigarette. "He's looking for someone," I said.

"Who?"

"His arch-enemy, the German air ace Baron Von Richter-Scale."

Tori stopped pacing. She said, "That's why all those planes were German. He's trying to shoot down the Baron. It's what he does in every episode."

Josh went pale.

"But we based his behaviour on those shows."

I said, "I hope you've got a good lawyer."

He looked indignant. "This isn't my fault."

"But you own him, you launched the software. You're the one they're going to come after."

I blew smoke in his direction. "It serves you right for stealing the copyright." Tori shushed us.

"It's too late for that," she said.

The TV had come back on. Someone, somewhere had managed to lash together a news report. There was no sound, only jerky, amateur footage shot on mobile phones. It showed two airliners colliding over Strasbourg, a cargo plane ditching in the Med, near Crete. Several airports were burning.

And then it shifted to pictures of computer screens in offices, schools, and control towers around the world. All of them showed the same grinning monkey's face.

I pushed past Josh and opened the window. Even from here, I could see the same face on the monitors in the café across the road. A thick pall of black smoke came from the city centre. Sirens howled. People were out in the street, looking frightened.

I turned back slowly and looked Tori in the eye. I started unwinding my bandages, letting them fall to the floor in dirty white loops.

I said, "I don't care about any of this. I just want you back."

She bit her lip. Her hand went to her own scar. She opened and closed her mouth several times. She looked at the TV, and then dropped her eyes.

"I want you too," she said.

THE BARON'S BURNING plane hits the hillside and explodes. Lola Lush cheers and waves a fist over her head, but Ack-Ack Macaque says nothing. He circles back over the burning wreck and waggles his wings in salute to his fallen foe. And then he pulls back hard on the joystick and his rattling old plane leaps skyward, high over the rolling hills and fields of the French countryside.

Ahead, the Akron stands against the sunset like a long, black cigar. Its skeletal oxen paw the air, anxious to get underway.

Lola's lips are red and full; her cheeks are flushed. She shouts: "What are you gonna do now?"

He pushes up his goggles and gives her a toothy grin. The air war may be over, but he knows he'll never be out of work. The top brass will always want something shot out of the sky.

"When we get back, I'm going to give you the night of your young life," he says, "and then in the morning, I'm going to go out and find myself another war."